THE BLOOD ANGELS
OMNIBUS

ON THE REMOTE planet of Cybele, the superhuman warriors of the Blood Angels Chapter fight a losing battle
against their most bitter enemies, the forces of Chaos.
After Battle-Brother Arkio leads a glorious counter-attack
that has the enemy reeling, there is talk that this is a holy
sign. Is Arkio blessed?

When Brother Arkio claims to be a reincarnation of Sanguinius, the Blood Angels' spiritual father, the message is
clear: follow me or die. Rafen kneels before Arkio and
swears an oath of devotion – but the words are ashes in
his mouth, and in his heart, he knows that he and his
brother will have a reckoning that only one of them will
survive…

The scene is set for what could be the destruction and
damnation of the entire Blood Angels Chapter.

By the same author

FAITH & FIRE
HORUS HERESY: THE FLIGHT OF THE
EISENSTEIN

*More action-packed omnibus editions from the war-torn
Warhammer 40,000 universe*

GAUNT'S GHOSTS: THE FOUNDING
by Dan Abnett

GAUNT'S GHOSTS: THE SAINT
by Dan Abnett

THE ULTRAMARINES OMNIBUS
by Graham McNeill

CIAPHAS CAIN: HERO OF THE IMPERIUM
by Sandy Mitchell

THE SPACE WOLF OMNIBUS
by William King

THE SOULDRINKERS OMNIBUS
by Ben Counter

BLOOD RAVENS: THE DAWN OF WAR OMNIBUS
by CS Goto

THE EISENHORN OMNIBUS
by Dan Abnett

LET THE GALAXY BURN
Edited by Marc Gascoigne & Christian Dunn

THE BLOOD ANGELS
OMNIBUS

JAMES SWALLOW

BLACK LIBRARY

A Black Library Publication

Deus Encarmine copyright © 2004, Games Workshop Ltd.
Deus Sanguinius copyright © 2005, Games Workshop Ltd.
All rights reserved.

This omnibus edition published in Great Britain in 2008 by
BL Publishing,
Games Workshop Ltd.,
Willow Road,
Nottingham, NG7 2WS, UK.

10 9 8

Cover illustration by Clint Langley

A CIP record for this book is available from the British Library.

UK ISBN 13: 978 1 84416 559 9
US ISBN 13: 978 1 8470 220 1

See the Black Library on the Internet at
www.blacklibrary.com

Find out more about Games Workshop
and the world of Warhammer 40,000 at
www.games-workshop.com

Printed and bound by CPI Group (UK) Ltd, Croydon, CR0 4YY

IT IS THE 41st millennium. For more than a hundred centuries the Emperor has sat immobile on the Golden Throne of Earth. He is the master of mankind by the will of the gods, and master of a million worlds by the might of his inexhaustible armies. He is a rotting carcass writhing invisibly with power from the Dark Age of Technology. He is the Carrion Lord of the Imperium for whom a thousand souls are sacrificed every day, so that he may never truly die.

YET EVEN IN his deathless state, the Emperor continues his eternal vigilance. Mighty battlefleets cross the daemon-infested miasma of the warp, the only route between distant stars, their way lit by the Astronomican, the psychic manifestation of the Emperor's will. Vast armies give battle in his name on uncounted worlds. Greatest amongst His soldiers are the Adeptus Astartes, the Space Marines, bio-engineered super-warriors. Their comrades in arms are legion: the Imperial Guard and countless planetary defence forces, the ever-vigilant Inquisition and the tech-priests of the Adeptus Mechanicus to name only a few. But for all their multitudes, they are barely enough to hold off the ever-present threat from aliens, heretics, mutants – and worse.

TO BE A man in such times is to be one amongst untold billions. It is to live in the cruellest and most bloody regime imaginable. These are the tales of those times. Forget the power of technology and science, for so much has been forgotten, never to be re-learned. Forget the promise of progress and understanding, for in the grim dark future there is only war. There is no peace amongst the stars, only an eternity of carnage and slaughter, and the laughter of thirsting gods.

CONTENTS

Author's Introduction   9

Deus Encarmine   13

Blood Debt   289

Deus Sanguinius   327

Appendix Angelus   599

Acknowledgments   639

DEUS VITAE

AUTHOR'S INTRODUCTION

I REMEMBER THE first time I ever saw a Space Marine.

He was a small chap, not more than a couple of inches tall, there in a glass case at Games Workshop's original store in Hammersmith. Pointy-faced helmet, shoulder pads all studded, bolter down and at the ready. He had an air of gothic cool about him; hints of a dark purpose and power that could dominate a battlefield. As a poor young gamer, I didn't spend my hard-earned cash on just any old piece of lead – I had to be motivated; and so I was when I studied that miniature and wondered – *'What's his story?'*

The year was 1984, and the grim future of the 41st Millennium was on the horizon, a gathering storm about to break across the world of gaming. Back then, I never dreamed that one day I would be telling stories about that Space Marine's kinsmen and the battles they fought in the name of the God-Emperor of Mankind, but two decades later I found myself invited to write epic tales of the Adeptus Astartes, and their adventures; and then, just as back in 1984, I found myself drawn to the noble and terrible charisma of the

9

Space Marines, and one Chapter in particular – the Blood Angels.

Then, as before, I found myself asking the same sort of question – *'What's their story?'*

What you hold in your hands is a collected edition of *Deus Encarmine* and *Deus Sanguinius*, my first two novels for the Black Library. As well as the duology, there's also some additional content between these covers, in the form of a short story and an appendix; the story is *Blood Debt*, an 'origin' tale about the character of Inquisitor Ramius Stele, and the appendix is a 'minipedia' covering elements from the books and the Blood Angels mythos. I like to think of *The Blood Angels Omnibus* as the book equivalent of a movie 'Director's Cut', so I guess that would make this introduction my 'director's commentary' and *Blood Debt* the 'deleted scenes'…

With that in mind, I'll tell you how I got here. *Deus Encarmine* was my first 'feature length' piece of fiction writing for Black Library, after having done my novice training writing Space Marine short stories for the late, lamented *Inferno!* magazine. My stories about the Doom Eagles Chapter caught the interest of editor and cat-lover Lindsey Priestley, and she approached me to talk about writing a novel. The mighty Adeptus Astartes are the iconic figures of the Warhammer 40,000 universe and I was fascinated by their core themes, of unswerving dedication to duty and – as someone without siblings himself – of brotherhood and what it meant to share that bond of blood and duty. I knew I wanted to tell Space Marine stories, but any story I told would flow directly from the character of the noble Chapters I chose to write about. It was William King, creator of the *Space Wolf* series of novels, who gave me a piece of useful sage advice; take a Chapter whose stories have never been told and make them your own. I went back to my rulebooks and studied the Astartes, looking for the one band of brothers that cried out to me – and I knew at once it had to be the Blood Angels.

I'd previously written about a Blood Angel successor Chapter – the Flesh Tearers – in a short story called *Crimson Night*, where they featured alongside the Doom Eagles; and the more I thought about the Sons of Sanguinius, the more I was convinced they were ideal for storytelling. Every writer looks for dramatic conflict in their protagonists, and these guys have it in spades. The core of the Blood Angel temperament is their dual nature; on the one hand they are imperious and handsome warriors of the highest nobility; but at the same time they hide a dark and bloodthirsty side that constantly threatens to overwhelm them. Their greatest gift is also their greatest curse.

Such men, with their struggles within and their battles without, are the kind of characters that adventure writers like me live for.

When I told Lindsey I wanted to write a Blood Angels book – at that time, the only Space Marine Chapter from the First Founding that had not appeared in novel form – the response was strong, and I was on my way. At the beginning, I pitched two Blood Angels tales. The first was a straightforward action adventure involving a small group of battle-brothers trapped behind enemy lines on the surface of a world in the throes of a Chaos invasion, but the other (which at the time had the working title of *Sacred Blood*) was a big, epic tale that would push the Chapter to the very brink of civil war. I'll be honest, I didn't think it would get past the Black Library team. It was too contentious, too ambitious for my first Warhammer 40,000 novel; but I was pleasantly surprised to be proven wrong. Lindsey returned and gave me the go-ahead to write it… but with one condition.

'This story is too big to be told in just one book,' she told me, 'make it two.'

And so *Sacred Blood* became the *Deus* duology.

Two novels. One story. All epic.

Any tale about the Space Marines is, in some manner, a tale about brothers, and the *Deus* books are no different. In these novels, Rafen and Arkio, two Blood Angels who are brothers by their birth, find themselves on either side of a rising schism that threatens to tear apart their Chapter from within. As the story unfolds, these men are set on a path that can only lead to one shattering confrontation – a confrontation that could destroy the Blood Angels and turn the Sons of Sanguinius to the dark path of the Chaos gods.

And Space Marine stories are also tales about faith – in your beliefs, in your friends, and in your future. In these novels, Rafen finds his faith tested almost to breaking point, and emerges all the stronger for it.

I write this introduction after the release of my fourth and most successful Warhammer 40,000 novel to date, *Horus Heresy: The Flight of the Eisenstein*, but in the years since the release of the first Blood Angels novel, these stories have been the ones that I am always asked about. Every Games Day or Conflict event brings the same question – 'When is the next Blood Angels book coming out?' I can safely say that I haven't left Rafen or his Chapter out in the cold, and I'm planning to return to the 41st Millennium very soon; what happens in these books is just the opening act, and the challenges that will face Brother Rafen are only just beginning...

For Sanguinius and the Emperor!

James Swallow
London, September 2007

DEUS ENCARMINE

CHAPTER ONE

AMID THE GRAVES, it was difficult for Rafen to tell exactly where the sky ended and the land began. He became still for a moment, halting in the shadow of a large tombstone in the shape of a chalice, the muzzle of his bolter calm and silent at his side. The wind never ceased on Cybele; on it came over the low hills and shallow mountains that characterised the planet, moaning mournfully through the thin stands of trees, rippling the grey-blue grass into waves. The gently rolling landscape flowed away from him toward an endless, unreachable vanishing point, an invisible horizon where grey land met grey sky. The distance was lost in the low clouds of stone dust that hovered overhead, stained like a great shroud of oil-soaked wool. The haze was made up of tiny particles of rock, churned into the sky by the torrent of artillery fire that had etched itself across the planet hours earlier.

Cybele wailed quietly around Rafen. The wind sang through the uncountable numbers of headstones that ranged away in every direction as far as his visor's optics could see. He stood atop the graves of a billion-fold war dead and listened to the

breeze as it wept for them, the famil... ...on self-
caged frenzy boiling away beneath ...ght have mistaken
control.

Steady and unmoving, an ...e were places on Cybele
Rafen for a tomb marker ...f Space Marines topped great
where stone-carved li... hallowed grounds, men bred from
towers of granite. A bloodline were buried as a measure of
Brother Rafen's respect for th planet and the great memorial that it represented to the Imperium. The moon of a vast gas giant, Cybele was a war grave world, one of hundreds of planets declared Mausoleum Valorum throughout the Ultima Segmentum. Rafen kept his statue-like aspect as a flicker of movement danced on the edge of his auspex's sensors.

Presently, a figure emerged from behind an oval sepulchre carved in pink vestan stone, and it nodded toward Rafen before making a series of sign-gestures with a gauntleted hand. The two of them were almost identical: their man-shapes broad and hulking in red ceramite sheaths, the colour glistening from the soft, reverent rain.

Rafen returned the nod and emerged from his cover, low to the ground and swift. He did not pause to check if Brother Alactus was following him; there was no need. As Alactus followed Rafen, so Brother Turcio followed Alactus, and Brother Bennek followed him. The team of Space Marines had drilled and fought alongside each other for so many decades that they functioned as pieces of the same machine, each a finely-tooled cog linked to the other, operating in perfect unison. To move now in silence, without a single spoken word between them, was child's play for soldiers who had trained to fight under the most testing conditions. He could sense their eagerness to meet the foe; it was like a palpable scent in the air, thick and coppery on his tongue.

Rafen slipped around a smashed obelisk that rose like a broken bone from the cemetery grass, an accusing finger pointing upward and decrying the foul clouds. He dropped down into a shallow valley. A day earlier, this sheltered place had been a devotional garden dedicated to naval pilots lost in the war for Rocene, but now it was a ruined bowl of broken earth. A stray round from the enemy's opening sub-orbital bombardment had landed here and carved out a hemisphere of ground, fusing the dirt into patches of glassy fulgurites. Brown puddles gathered where ornate caskets were torn open and their contents scattered around Rafen's metal-shod feet: bones and decayed, aged medals crunched into the dirt where he walked. The Space Marine picked his way through the skeletons and traversed the opposite lip of the crater, pausing to check his bearings.

He glanced up to see the shape of an angelic statue curving away above him, arms and wings spread as if about to take flight. The statue's face was unblemished and perfect; its eyes were raised to stare at some exquisite heaven that was an infinity away from the crude reality of this earthly realm. For one serene moment, Rafen was convinced that the stone seraph was about to turn its countenance to him, to display the face of Lord Sanguinius, the hallowed founder and primogenitor of his Chapter. But the instant fled, and Rafen was alone with the dead once more, stone angel and Blood Angel alike both wreathed in the mist and rain. He looked away and allowed himself to listen to the wind once more.

Rafen felt a churn of revulsion in the pit of his gut. A fresh sound was being carried to his helmet's auto-sense array, buoyed along with the ceaseless moans of the breeze: screaming, thin and horrific. It was a noise torn from the very darkest places in a man's heart, an utterance that could only have issued from the lips of one truly damned. The Space

Marine surmised the Traitors were preparing to make an augury from the entrails of one of their slaves before they began another sortie.

Rafen considered this for a moment. If the archenemy were getting ready for another attack, then it made his mission all the more urgent. He moved off, a frown forming behind the formidable mask of his breather grille. A troop of lightly armoured, fast-moving scouts would have been able to accomplish the same task in half the time. But every single one of the pathfinder squad in Rafen's detachment had been killed in the first assault, when a fusillade of krak shells had torn through their ranks. He had been standing in the lee of a Rhino's hull when the shriek of superheated air signalled the incoming salvo, and in his mind's eye Rafen recalled the moment when a scout bike had spun up and over his head, as if it were nothing but a plaything discarded by a bored, petulant child. All that remained of the young Space Marines were some torn rags and flecks of burnt ceramite.

He buried the dark ember of his anger deep and pressed on, shuttering away his recriminations. It mattered little now what they had been told before arriving on Cybele, that the posting here was purely a ceremonial one, that it was a matter of honour rather than a battle to be fought. Perhaps he and his battle-brothers had been lax to believe that the corrupted would have no interest in a cemetery world; now they would repay that mistake with the blood of their foes.

Rafen slowed to a steady walk as they closed in on the grove the enemy had chosen for their staging area. The pristine, manicured lawns of the graveyards elsewhere were no longer evident here – around the perimeter of the Traitor camp, great dark tendrils of decay were trailing out through the grasses, emerging through an expanding ring of soiled plants and toxic slurry. In some places, the ground had broken open like an old wound and disgorged the dead from beneath it. Grave markers lay slumped and disfigured next to black twists of bone vomited from the newly putrid earth. Rafen's finger twitched near the trigger of his bolter, his knuckles whitening inside his gauntlet. The rush of righteous fury was tingling at bay within him, the longing for combat singing in his veins. He gestured for the other Blood Angels to stand back and hold their positions. He found a vantage point at the corner of a ruined vault and for the first time that day Rafen laid eyes on the enemy. It was all he could do to resist the urge to riddle them with gunfire.

Word Bearers. Once they had been an Adeptus Astartes Chapter of the most pious nature, but those days had long since turned to dust. Rafen's lips drew back from his teeth in a sneer of disgust as he watched the Traitor Marines move to and fro, marching arrogantly between tents of flayed ork-hide and the still steaming orbs of grounded dreadclaw landers. He closed his ears to the pestilent shouts of the enemy demagogues as they wandered about the edges of the encampment, spitting their vile prayers and chants over the cries of the slave-servitors, and the incessant cracks of neuro-whips against the backs of the helots.

The Word Bearers were a dark mirror of Rafen and his brethren. Their battle gear was doused in a livid scar-red the shade of fresh gore, their armour dominated by a single sigil – the face of a screaming horned demon against an eight-pointed star. Many of the Chaos Space Marines sported horned helms with filigree and fine workings cored from children's bones, or pages of blasphemous text drawn on skin-parchment and fastened into the ceramite with obsidian screws. Others went about bareheaded, and these ones displayed faces rippled with ritual wheals, tusks or hooks of warped cartilage.

It was one such Traitor Marine who was carefully ministering to the torture of the slave whose screams had carried so far on the wind. One of his arms ended in a writhing cluster of metallic tentacles that flicked and whipped at the air as if they had a mind of their own. In his other hand, the torturer held a vibra-stave that he used like a sculptor, lopping off slips of flesh with infinite care. The victim's cries wavered up and down the octaves and Rafen abruptly realised that the enemy soldier was playing the man like an instrument, amusing himself by composing a symphony of pain. Rafen looked away, concentrating on the mission at hand. His squad leader, Brother-Sergeant Koris, had made the orders quite clear – Rafen and his team were to merely locate the enemy camp and determine the strength and disposition of the foe. They were not to engage.

Training his auspex on the assembled force, he picked out assault units and the massive bulks of Terminators, but only a handful of vehicles. He considered the options: this might be a testing force, perhaps, maybe a blunt brigade of heavily armed troops sent in to probe the defences of the planet before a larger attack could begin. For a moment, Rafen wondered about the fate of the ship his company had left in orbit; it was a forgone conclusion that if so large a Traitor force had made planetfall, the skies already belonged to the enemy. He did not dwell on the prospects of what that would mean for them. With a full half of their force dead or crippled in the initial surprise bombardment, the Space Marines were reeling and on the defensive; the momentum of battle was on the side of the foe.

But in the next instant, Rafen's grim train of thought was abruptly stalled. From out of the open hatch of a deformed Razorback transport strode a figure that came a full two heads higher than every other man in the Traitor camp. His armour was chased around its edges with sullen gold plating and traceries of infernal runes that smudged and merged as Rafen's auspex struggled to read them. Wrappings of steel chain ending in flaming, skull-shaped braziers dangled from his arms and waist, while his shoulder plates mounted a fan of necrotic spines that appeared to be venting thin streams of venom into the air. Rafen had seen the champions of the archenemy before and so he was in no doubt that the being he looked upon was the master of the war force at Cybele.

A fragment of memory drifted to the front of Rafen's mind as he watched the tall Word Bearer approach and converse with the torturer. He recalled a snatch of description from the indoctrination lectures of his training, the words of old Koris back when the grizzled veteran was serving as a mentor. The Word Bearers, who forever bore the aberrant mark of Chaos Undivided, practised their foul religions under the steward-ship of the highest ranked Traitors among their number – and Rafen was sure that the tall one was just such a being. A Dark Apostle, and here, in his sights! The hand around the bolter twitched again and he allowed himself to entertain the idea of killing this bestial adversary, despite the sergeant's orders ring-ing in his head. Bloodlust rumbled distantly in his ears, the familiar tension of pre-battle humming in his very marrow. With a single shot, he might be able to send the enemy into instant disarray; but were he to fail, their survey would be compromised and his brethren back at the Necropolita would be lost. Reluctantly, he relaxed his grip a little.

In that moment of choice, Rafen's life was almost forfeit. A fierce rune blinked into being on the Space Marine's visor, warning him too late of movement to his flank. With speed that belied the huge weight of his battle armour, Rafen spun on his heel, reversing his grip on the bolter as he did. He came face to face with a Word Bearer, the Chaos Space Marine's hideous countenance a series of ruined holes and jagged teeth.

'Blood Angel!' it spat, declaring the name like a venomous malediction.

Rafen answered by slamming the butt of his bolter into the Word Bearer's face with savage ferocity, forcing the enemy warrior to stagger back on his heels and into the cover of the vault. He dare not fire the weapon, for the report of a bolt shell would surely bring every Traitor in the camp running, and he knew that none of his other battle-brothers could come to his aid lest they expose themselves. It was of little import, however, Rafen had killed enough warp-spawned filth to be sure that he could murder this heretic with tooth and nail alone if need be. Caught by surprise, he had only heartbeats in which to press his advantage and terminate this abomination – this thing that had polluted the universe since before he was born.

The Word Bearer's hand snapped toward the gun on its waist. Fingers with far too many joints skittered across the scarlet armour. Rafen brought the bolter down again and smashed the hand flat like a pinned spider. The Traitor recovered and swung a mailed, spike-laden fist at Rafen's head; the blow connected with a hollow ring and Rafen heard his ceramite helm crack as fractures appeared on his visor. Letting the gun drop into the oily mud at his feet, the Blood Angel surged forward and locked his gloved hands around the Word Bearer's throat. Had his enemy been helmeted too, Rafen would never have been able to strike back at him this way, but the corrupted fool had thought this place secure enough to show his face to the air. Rafen pressed his fingers into the tough, leathery hide of the Word Bearer's neck, intent on showing him the cost of his folly. Gouts of thick, greasy fluid began to stream from the Traitor's wounds, and it tried in vain to suck air through its windpipe, desperate to scream for help from its brethren.

The spiked glove returned, crashing into his head again and again. Warm blood filled Rafen's mouth as his teeth rattled in his jaw. The Traitor butted him, but the Blood Angel stood firm, the joyous lust of his hate-rage flattening the pain. Rafen's vision fogged with the sweet anticipatory surge of a hand-to-hand kill, as the Traitor's black snake-tongue twitched madly, lapping at breaths it could not draw in. He was dimly aware of the Word Bearer punching and striking at his torso, flailing to inflict some sort of damage on him before he ended its repellent life.

Rafen registered a flashing bone dagger at the edges of his vision, then the sudden bloom of pain on his left thigh; he ignored it and squeezed tighter, compacting the Word Bearer's throat into a ruined tube of bloody meat and broken cartilage. Voiceless and empty, the Traitor Marine died and slipped from his ichor-stained fingers to the ground. Rafen staggered back a step, the thunder of adrenaline making him giddy. As his foot came down, fresh streams of agony surged out of his leg and he saw where the Traitor's tusk blade had cleanly pierced his armour. Shock gel and coagulants bubbled up around the wound, and turned dark as they struggled to combat the after-effects of the cut. Rafen grimaced; the daemon knives of the adversary always carried venom and he did not wish to be cut down by the dying blow of such an unworthy foe.

The Blood Angel gripped the haft of the Chaos blade and he felt it writhe and flex in his grip, quivering like a creature seeking escape. He could feel the movement of bladders inside it, fleshy organs pulsing as they sucked in his blood like a parasite. With a snarl, Rafen tore the serrated weapon from his thigh and held it up before his eyes. The blade was a living thing, each ridge of its saw-tooth edge a yellowed chevron of enamel crested by a tiny black eye spot. It hissed and chattered at Rafen with impotent hate, contorting in on itself. Before the Space Marine could react, the blade puffed up its air sacs and spat out a cloud of his siphoned blood, scattering it in a fine pink vapour.

Rafen broken the thing in two but it was too late: in the enemy encampment, the Word Bearers had stopped what they were doing and were glancing upward, nostrils and tongues taking in the thin stream of scent-taste.

He swore a blistering curse and tossed the dead creature aside, breaking vox silence for the first time in hours. 'Fall back!'

The four Blood Angels erupted from cover, moving as fast as their augmented limbs and power armour would let them; ten times that number of Word Bearers crested the lip of the grove and gave chase, bolters crashing wildly and voices raised in debased exaltation.

In the encampment below, Tancred hesitated, the vibra-stave wavering in his hand as he shifted forward to join the pursuit; but then he realised that his master had not moved an inch, and with careful deliberation he relaxed and cocked his head.

Iskavan the Hated, Dark Apostle of the Ninth Host of Garand, let his bloodless lips split in a smile wider than any human orifice was capable of. One of his tube-tongues flickered in and out, sampling the damp air. 'A mewling whelp,' he pronounced at last, rolling the faint flavour of Rafen's spilt blood around his mouth. 'A little over a hundred years, by the taste of him.' He eyed Tancred. 'Perhaps I should be insulted that these mongrels saw fit to send children to spy on us.'

The torturer glanced back at the twisted ruin of flesh that was his handiwork. 'A handful of scouts are hardly worth the effort, magnificence.'

Tancred saw Iskavan nod in agreement from the corner of his eye, and he suppressed a smile. The Word Bearer had risen to the rank of second to the Dark Apostle through a mixture of guile and outright ruthlessness, but much of his skill stemmed from his ability to predict Iskavan's moods and to know exactly what his commander wanted to hear. In four and a half centuries of service, Tancred had only earned his master's displeasure on three occasions, and the most severe of those was marked forever on him where his organic arm had been severed by Iskavan's dagger-toothed bite. The torturer gave his tentacle replacement an absent flex.

'Let the hungry ones hound them back to their verminous hiding place,' said Iskavan, as much to Tancred as it was to the rest of the Word Bearer camp. 'We will join them momentarily.' The Dark Apostle turned the full force of his baleful gaze on the torturer and toyed casually with a barbed horn on his chin. 'I shall not be interrupted before I have completed my sacrament.'

Tancred took this as a cue to continue and beckoned a pair of machine-bound helots forward. Each of the once-men picked up an end of the rack on which Tancred's victim lay. The homunculae moved into the centre of the camp on legs of burping gas pistons, their arms raw iron girders ending in rusty blocks and tackle, rather than flesh and bone. Their burden was moaning weakly but still clinging to the ragged edge of life, thanks to the consummate skill of Tancred's art.

The Word Bearer bent close to the dying slave's head and whispered to him. 'Give,' he husked. 'Give up your love.'

'I do,' the helot managed, between blood-laden gurgles, 'I give my heart and flesh and soul to you, great one.' His teeth appeared in a broken grin, the beatific glaze in his eyes locked on the heavy, dolorous clouds overhead. 'Please, I crave the agony of the boon. Please!' The slave began to weep, and Tancred ran his clawed hand over the man's scarred forehead. The poor wretch was afraid that he would be allowed to die without the exquisite pain of Iskavan's blessing.

'Do not fear,' Tancred cooed. 'You will know torment such as that which Lorgar himself endured.'

'Thank you! Oh, thank you!' The helot coughed and a fat globule of heavy, arterial crimson rolled from his mouth. Tancred resisted the urge to lick at it and turned to bow before his master.

'With your permission, lord Apostle?'

Iskavan wet his lips. 'Bring me my crozius.'

THE BLOOD ANGELS had reinforced the edifice of the Necropolita even as the dust was still settling from the bombardment, toppling stone needles and broad obelisks to serve as makeshift cover. The building had been an ornate combination of Imperial chapel and outpost facility, but now it was in ruins. Its sole occupants, the priest-governor of the planet and his small cohort of caretakers, were among the first to perish when the building's central minaret had been struck. Now for good or ill Cybele was under the complete command of Brother-Captain Simeon, the ranking Space Marine officer. Crouching atop the corner of the Necropolita that still stood, Simeon was the first to see the enemy approach through the tombstones, and he drew his chainsword with a flourish.

'Sons of Sanguinius!' His voice cut the air like the peal of a cloister bell. 'To arms!'

Below him, where the marble plaza ended and the graveyards began, Brother-Sergeant Koris dug one armoured hand into the fallen stone pillar and pushed himself up to sight toward the foe. He saw Rafen's unit charging and firing, sending controlled bursts of bolter-fire over their shoulders as they closed; behind them was a seething wall of Chaos Space Marines, a cackling, screaming horde that moved like a swarm of red locusts.

'Brothers on the field! Pick your targets!' he ordered, and to illustrate his point, the seasoned soldier shot the head from a Word Bearer just hand-spans away from Turcio's back.

Bennek was less fortunate, and Koris growled in anger as the Space Marine lost his leg from the near miss of a plasma gun. Bennek's armoured form tumbled and dropped, and the Word Bearers rolled over him without stopping.

With a yell of effort, the crimson flash of a Space Marine leapt over Koris's head and twisted in mid-air, landing perfectly behind the stone barricade. The sergeant turned as Rafen, panting hard, brought up his bolter and laced the air above him with shot; a Traitor who had been snapping at his heels made it halfway over the obelisk before Rafen's shells sent him screaming backward. The air sang with energy and explosion around them as the two sides clashed.

'Damn them, these fiends are on us like desert ticks!'

Koris gave Rafen a brief, sharp grin. 'You brought some company back with you then, eh lad?'

Rafen hesitated. 'I...' Salvos of Traitor gunfire chopped at the dirt near their feet.

'Brother Rafen!' Simeon loped over the pockmarked ground toward them, weaving around the flashes of new impact craters and the keening of lethal ricochets. 'When I told you we needed to study the enemy closely, I did not expect you to take me so literally.' The captain let off a ripping discharge from his bolt pistol, right into the enemy line. 'No matter.'

Koris drew back from the skirmish and let Turcio take his place. 'Speak, lad. What do these warp-spawn have for us out there?' His voice was urgent, carrying over the constant fire.

Rafen gestured to the south. 'An assault group, most likely a reconnaissance in force,' he replied, calmly relaying his report with the same dispassion he would have showed in a training exercise. 'A squad of Terminators and armour, at least three Razorbacks.'

Simeon grimaced. His few Space Marines with little or no heavy weapons would be hard pressed to hold the line against such a detachment. 'There's more,' he added – a statement, not a question.

Rafen ignored the low hum of a bolt that lanced past his head. 'Indeed. Terra protect me, but I looked upon one of their foul ceremonies, a sacrificial augury. There was a Dark Apostle in the camp to observe it.'

'You're sure?' Koris pressed, the crack of rounds flicking off the tiles around them.

'As the God-Emperor is my witness,' Rafen replied.

Simeon and Koris exchanged glances; this made matters more complicated. 'If one of those arch-traitors has befouled the graves here, then his plans for Cybele are clear.' Simeon loaded a fresh clip into his gun, eyeing the torrid battle line as blood-red and gore-red armour clashed and fought. 'He will seek to erect one of their own blasphemous monuments here and salt the earth with their profane benedictions.'

'It shall not be,' Rafen grated. A heat of fury flooded into him.

'No, it shall not,' Simeon agreed, bearing his fangs. With a roar, he dived into the fray, his chainsword braying as it cored a Word Bearer sending it skittering over the marble. Rafen and Koris waded through the fight with him, weapons flaring.

'Hear me, Blood Angels!' Simeon's voice called. 'In the name of the red grail, turn back this tide–'

The captain's words were cut short as a tiny supernova engulfed him, and wreaths of hot plasma turned the stone to slag around his feet. Rafen had a single, momentary vision of brilliant white, then Simeon's ammunition packs detonated all at once and threw him aside in the shock wave.

ISKAVAN GATHERED UP his most impious symbol of office and cradled it as a parent would a beloved child. The crozius in his hand gave off an actinic glow that surged as his fingers wrapped around it. The weapon sighed, pleased that its master was near, excited by the prospect of what was to come next. Murmuring a litany of un-blessing beneath his breath, the Dark Apostle dipped the disk of blades at the staff's head into the catch-bucket beneath Tancred's torture rack. He stirred the thick, fresh blood. The liquid flashed into steam, boiling around the accursed weapon.

'From the fires of betrayal,' Iskavan droned. 'Unto the blood of revenge.'

Tancred raised the vibra-stave over the helot's body, so he could see that death was upon him. 'By the bearer of the word, the favoured son of Chaos.' The torturer plunged the stave into the slave's stomach and tore it open, savouring the screams.

The Word Bearers standing watch around them spoke as one voice. 'All praise be given unto him.'

Iskavan held up his soaked crozius to the grey sky, the ritual of desecration repeated once again as it had been on countless worlds, before countless victories. He glanced at Tancred, who hunched over the spilt innards of the sacrifice. 'What do you see?'

It took the most supreme effort of Tancred's life to lie to his master. 'Death comes. Lorgar's sight is upon us.' The words were almost choking him. 'We shall feed the hunger of the gods.'

His black heart shrinking in his chest, Tancred stared at the entrails before him in fear and dismay. The loops of fallen intestine, the spatters of blood, the placing of the organs – the configuration was terrible and ominous. There, he saw the signs of something impossibly powerful rising into life, a coming force so strong that it dwarfed Tancred and his master. The play of light and shadow was confused, and so the torturer could not be sure from where this energy would emerge, but he could see clearly that it would bring ruin and destruction in its wake. At last, he managed to tear himself away from the sight, his final reading bringing a disturbing prediction to bear. Both he and Iskavan would not live to see the end of the events they would set in motion on this day.

The Dark Apostle met his gaze and something like suspicion danced there. 'Is that *all* you see, Tancred?'

The words pushed at the torturer's decaying lips, fighting to be heard, but he knew with blind certainty that such a fatalist divination would enrage Iskavan, to the degree that Tancred would be first to taste the freshly-blooded crozius's power. He looked down in what he hoped would seem like reverence, praying to the gods that he be spared his master's displeasure. 'I see death, lord.'

'Good.' Iskavan chained his twitching, eager weapon to his wrist. 'Let us take the word to our adversary, and see them heed it… Or perish.'

The Chaos Space Marines whooped and yelled black hymnals and mantras as the battle force rolled forward and amid them all, Tancred picked at his newborn fears like a scabbed wound.

SIMEON'S VIOLENT END tolled around the perimeter like a death knell; it was felt almost as a physical shock by the Blood Angels ranged about the Necropolita's edge. The hero of Virgon VII, victor at the Thaxted Insurrection and decorated warrior of the Alchonis Campaign, was gone, swept away. The brother-captain was honoured and respected by every Space Marine in the Chapter, and in the centuries they had fought alongside him, each one of them could trace a debt of life to the bold officer. Rafen himself had almost been killed on Ixion by a mole-mine that Simeon had spotted a moment before it emerged. And now, as the Blood Angel considered the patch of scorched ground that marked the spot where the captain had died, he found the memory of that moment slipping away from him, as if it too had been lost in the plasma burst.

Koris was the ranking officer now, and the craggy old warhound seemed determined to cut a blood cost for the captain's death from each and every Word Bearer. But Rafen knew the veteran better than most of the Space Marines there, and he saw the signs of distress on his former teacher that others did not.

For all of Koris's encouragement and rousing, Simeon's sudden killing had dealt their morale a fatal blow, and the will of the remaining men lay wounded, bleeding out into the grass.

Rafen saw the surge in the enemy line as the rest of the Word Bearers' force joined the fight, and in that moment, he was certain they would die here. Unhallowed lighting flashed in the distance from a blazing force weapon, and the Traitors roared with approval. They drew back, a ruby tide retreating from the land's edge before returning as a flood. And then on they came, killing and ripping Rafen's comrades into fleshy shreds. His gun clattered, the barrel spitting hot as rounds big as fists tore into the foe – but then a sound, a heart-stopping shriek of sundered air, fell across the battlefield.

Rafen instinctively looked up, and felt ice in the pit of his stomachs. Swooping in through the low cloud by the dozen were bright red Thunderhawk drop-ships, each one bristling with missile and cannon, each one heavy with more Space Marines to feed the fray. Half-glimpsed in the contrails and gunsmoke, the flyers looped over the enemy and turned.

'We are lost,' said Turcio, as if the words were his dying breath. 'With such reinforcements, we will be drowned in a sea of corrupted ones.'

'Then we'll litter this place with their dead before we do...'
Rafen's voice tailed off as the Thunderhawks opened fire as
one, and bright spears of light lanced from their lascannon.
But the shots never reached them. The beams fell short of the
Space Marines and struck the middle of the Word Bearers'
force with devastating effect, killing a unit of Chaos Terminators in one blaze of fire. Now the other flyers released packs
of hellstreak warheads, which tore into the Traitors with furious abandon.

Rafen's eyes widened as the leading drop-ship cut the sky
above him, and in a blink of crimson he saw the sigils
painted on the aircraft: a pair of silver angel's wings, adorned
with a shimmering teardrop of blood. As the Emperor willed
it, so the Blood Angels had been delivered from the jaws of
oblivion by their battle-brothers.

CHAPTER TWO

IN THEIR UNFETTERED arrogance, Iskavan's Word Bearers had expected only token resistance at the Necropolita. With the unerring accuracy of their artillery strikes from the murder-class cruiser *Dirge Eterna* in low orbit and the lightning speed of their ground assault, not one of the Traitor Marines had doubted that the day would be theirs. The de-consecration of Cybele in the name of Chaos Undivided would come to pass, or so they had believed. Those certainties were now ashes in the mouth of Tancred, who watched as his soldiers became screaming torches of flame under the punishing beam salvoes from the Blood Angel's Thunderhawks.

The torturer had paused as the entire forward phalanx of his most celebrated warriors vanished in a plume of blazing hell-gun fire. The Space Marines on the ground, the tiny band of men who just seconds before had counted their lives on the ticks of a failing clock, surged forward with renewed vigour and scrambled over the dead Word Bearers to break the Chaos line. And with his enemy dropping from the grey sky on wings of fire and his soldiers falling about him, Iskavan turned a stony countenance on Tancred. Then he gave the order that disgusted the torturer to his very core. The Dark Apostle told his troops to fall back, and, cursing the corpse god of men with every step they took, the Word Bearers broke apart and drew away, fading into the endless graveyards.

Tancred studied the face of his commander and he saw the anger of his men reflected there; and yet still he had given the demand. It was almost as if – dare he even *think* such a thing? – Iskavan had been given orders to let the Blood Angels live. It was the sacred war doctrine of the Word Bearers to advance, advance and never give quarter, yet Iskavan called out for them to retreat and led them into the shadows without comment or explanation. Tancred considered this as they broke away by ranks, firing as they went. There would have to be some plan that his master had concealed from him, some greater scheme at work that would later redeem this indignity. The torturer prayed that this was the reason. The only other alternative was that Iskavan had realised that Tancred's prognostication had been false. If that were true, Tancred would never see his death coming.

RAFEN STAYED CLOSE to Koris as they tore chunks out of the Word Bearers' division. Eventually it fragmented, until at last there was no enemy to follow. The brother-sergeant halted his men at the ridge where Rafen had hidden in the shade of the angel statue. The young Blood Angel glanced up to see the graceful stone figure still there, untouched by the passing of the archenemy.

Koris approached him, the old warrior's bearded face grim. 'They've gone to ground. Without a force big enough to seek them out, we'll not be able to destroy them all.'

'We live still,' said Rafen, hardly believing the turn of events himself.

Koris gave him a brusque nod. 'Aye, but this matter is not concluded, lad. Not by a long way.' A drop-ship turned overhead, the roar of its engines halting the conversation until it passed downwind. 'Those horned bastards never break unless they have to. I'll warrant they'll be digging in to make ready for a counter-strike before sunset.'

Rafen watched the Thunderhawk drop into a hover to let a couple of men descend to the ground. 'But with reinforcements, they'll be no match for us.'

'Do not be so sure,' Koris spat. 'They caught us unawares once, Rafen. By the Throne, they'll have more surprises in store.' He made a cutting gesture with the blade of his hand. 'The Word Bearers are tenacious.'

One of the Blood Angels from the drop-ship approached at a run. 'Hail!' he called. 'I am Corvus. Who commands here?'

'Brother-Sergeant Koris of the Fifth Company,' the veteran Space Marine replied, tapping his heart and his head in a gesture of gratitude. 'You have our thanks.'

The warrior threw a glance over his shoulder, in the direction of the ruined Necropolita. 'The governor is dead, then?'

Koris nodded. 'Along with every member of his retinue, and our captain. I am what passes for authority on this planet now.'

'No longer. You will find that burden has been lifted from you, brother-sergeant,' the Blood Angel said smoothly. 'By his decree, the Inquisitor Ramius Stele has declared the planet Cybele under his stewardship from this moment onward. He expects you at the star port immediately.'

'Stele?' Rafen repeated. 'The leader of the *Bellus* Expedition?'

'The very same. The ship stands at high anchor above as we speak,' said Corvus, then added, 'The inquisitor is not known for his patience, brother-sergeant.'

Koris made a sour face and headed for the Thunderhawk, the rest of the squad filing into the ship alongside him. 'Rafen, you'll accompany me.'

He nodded. 'I confess I am curious to see the faces of our saviours.'

Koris said nothing as they scrambled after Corvus into the drop-ship's cramped interior.

FROM THE AIR, the true scale of the Word Bearers' attack was made manifest. The Thunderhawk's pilot kept the aircraft just below the lower edge of the cloud deck, rumbling over the thermals that coiled up from smoking bomb craters bored into the blue-green turf. Endless rows of identical grave markers stretched to the horizon from every direction. Blackened darts of poison were strewn where the warheads had fallen, and the toxins and manufactured taints had been worked into the metal of the shells so that they spread corruption on everything they touched. The landmarks of giant crypts dotted the landscape like bunkers in a war zone.

'What is that?' Turcio asked, pointing at a livid purple stain around the base of a memorial ziggurat.

'Binder fungus,' said one of the other Space Marines, without looking. 'The enemy lace their engine fuel with it, so it is cast adrift in the air from their exhaust fumes.'

'What does it do?'

'Whatever they want it to,' snapped Koris. 'The Chaos biologians impose patterns on the spores with their rituals. When the fungus takes root and grows, it forms the shapes of their vile symbols.'

Turcio's nose wrinkled, as if he smelled something foul. He could see where the mould was already taking on the shape of an eight-armed star.

The myriad rings of weapon strike points drew overlapping ovals around the landscape, many of which were centred on the site of the Necropolita. Rafen's only memory of the ornate marble keep was when they had first approached it, as they drove in from the east on the Great Penitent Bridge that spanned the Ghona Canyon. The Blood Angel had chanced to look through the firing slot of his Rhino's door and saw the magnificent white shape thrusting into the air, circled by thin towers in organ-pipe clusters. Gone now, all rubble and shattered ivory splinters. The flyer banked as they passed the ruins; the direct hit that had killed the priest-governor had blown the building down like a house of tarot cards. Rafen noticed a pair of grounded drop-ships nearby, survivors loading themselves aboard in skirmish lines. His augmented vision counted few men on the ground, however; it seemed that a retreat was in progress, not a reinforcement.

'We have been ordered to draw all forces back to the star port,' Corvus spoke, as if he saw the question forming in Rafen's mind. 'We noted from orbit that the Necropolita was lost. The port makes a better location for a strong-point.'

Rafen agreed; it was a tactically sound choice. After the Word Bearers' bombardment, Captain Simeon had said the very same thing, but the enemy strikes had been carefully targeted to down the bridge behind the keep, and with only one or two remaining ground vehicles in their possession there had been no way for Rafen's detachment to cross back over. The handful of Chapter serfs and men they had left behind at the port had no doubt been killed in the same shell deluge that struck the outpost.

The canyon flashed past beneath them, the torn edges of the suspension bridge blunted and bent. The great statues of Cybele's first pilgrims that held up the trestles were gone, dashed to pieces on the ravine's floor kilometres below.

Rafen glanced at his battle-brother. 'There was a naval warship that brought us here, the *Celaeno*. What was its fate?'

Corvus shook his head. 'I do not know the specifics, but it is my understanding that the frigate's remains were detected when we emerged from the warp. The Word Bearers' vessel we engaged in orbit must have caught them unawares.'

'Unfortunate,' Rafen said. Koris stood nearby, silent, his face steady and unreadable. The younger Blood Angel considered the men aboard the *Celaeno*, imagining them unprepared and alone before the ferocity of a Chaos strike vessel more than twice their tonnage. He hoped for their sake that the Emperor had taken their souls quickly.

The flat ferrocrete expanse of the star port appeared beyond a strip of woodland, clusters of hangars and fuel tanks visible in the distance. The landing field was practically unmarked by enemy fire, which instantly made the plans of the Word Bearers clear: they intended to keep the port intact so that they might use it themselves. Without ceremony the Thunderhawk's nose dipped sharply into a landing pattern.

THE BATTALION LAID out at the port seemed a world away from the tattered remains of the late Captain Simeon's company, who trickled out from the returning drop-ships with their armour scorched and pitted by near-misses and shrapnel. The wounded Space Marines were guided by Apothecaries to a makeshift staging area, while the others stood warily in a loose group as the Blood Angels from the *Bellus* ranged around them, their battle gear parade-ground pristine and untouched.

The survivors of the Word Bearers' attack were stern-faced and muted; each of them had been convinced, as Rafen was, that they were due to meet their end this day. Simeon's death and the sudden reversal of their fortunes had left them in sombre mood. Brother Alactus was leading them in a prayer of thanks to Terra, but none of them could shake the pervasive sense of doom they felt in the endless field of tombstones. Nearby, servitors were assembling the remains of the Guardsmen that had been garrisoned at the port's orbital defence guns; each of the men had died in horrific pain from the nerve toxins dropped by the Word Bearers. Their bodies were twisted and gnarled by the muscle spasms that killed them. The faint bouquet of the poison, far too weak to give a Space Marine anything more than a mild headache, still lingered in the air.

Koris and Rafen left Turcio to assemble the troops into some semblance of order and moved deeper into the port, past pairs of Baal-pattern Predator tanks and land speeders. Some of the vehicles showed battle honours on their sponsons that Rafen did not recognise.

'You have seen many engagements, Brother Corvus?' he asked the Space Marine who walked with them.

'The greenskins may be dull-witted beasts, but they fight hard,' he replied. 'You know the mission of the *Bellus*?'

'Who could not?' Koris was blunt and clipped. 'A most sacred endeavour indeed.'

Rafen answered with a nod. To great fanfare and good omens among the Chapter faithful, the battle barge *Bellus* had been sent on its way a decade earlier by Commander Dante himself, high lord of the Blood Angels. Crewed with a hand-picked force of men on an assignment to trace an artefact that dated back to the Horus Heresy, the *Bellus*'s quest was to recover the archeotech device known as the Spear of Telesto, an object thought lost in the confusion of those dark times. It was only the chance discovery of a storehouse of documents on Evangelion that had led to the founding of the ship's mission, and under the command of Ramius Stele – an inquisitor of most rigid nature trusted by both the Chapter and the highest levels of the ecclesiarchy – Dante had sent the *Bellus* to the ork-held worlds on the borders of the Segmentum Obscurus. Word of the expedition's imminent return had been spoken of among the Blood Angels for many months now.

Corvus was speaking. 'It has been a challenging campaign, but we were blessed. Sanguinius was watching over us.'

'And the spear?'

Pride swelled the Space Marine's words. 'Secure in the deep holds aboard *Bellus*.' He glanced at Rafen. 'Truly, brother, it is a sight to behold.'

'You laid eyes upon it?' said Koris, in a low voice.

'We all did,' Corvus noted. 'Stele himself brought it out of the ork warren on the morning we killed the last of them. He held it up for every man to see.' His eyes glazed over for a brief instant, as the moment replayed in his mind. 'I felt the radiance of the Lord Primogenitor upon my face that day.'

'Hard to imagine a servant of the Ordo Hereticus would be allowed to place his hands on something so sacred,' Koris said, his voice carefully colourless. 'Some Blood Angels would decry such a thing.'

Corvus gave the veteran a hard glance. 'Only those who do not know Stele would say the like. He is a true comrade to our Chapter.'

'Of course,' Koris allowed. 'I do not mean to infer otherwise. The honour debt between the Blood Angels and Inquisitor Stele is well documented.'

Rafen watched the interplay between the two men and said nothing. Throughout all his years of service, Koris had never been one to take anything at face value, and he would often probe and press at the thoughts of the men he served with. Sometimes he challenged them to the point of near-heresy. It was, he had often said, the only way to see the truth behind the prayers and catechism that formed so much of their daily lives. *To believe, one must first be the greatest sceptic.*

Rafen had seen the tapestries of Riga that hung in the silent cloister of the fortress-monastery on Baal, they depicted the ancient depictions of Sanguinius and the Spear of Telesto in action against the Slaughter-Lord Morroga. The great battle was rendered in threads dyed a million shades of red, every strand coloured in the blood of a fallen brother. And across the vast, heavy landscapes of dull ruby, the golden archangel who was their Chapter's founder was shown – his beautiful face in its most terrible aspect, driving back the tide of Chaos. In every panel, the holy spear blazed like a shard of the sun, and Rafen found himself wondering what it would be like to hold the haft of a weapon that once belonged to his eternal liege.

The trio came to a halt outside an ornate pavilion of dark material that sported arcane wards and had silvery threads that chased through it. Dangling across the threshold was a pair of braziers forged from steel-plated skulls. Each grinning visage was crested with a stylised letter 'I': the unmistakable mark of the Inquisition. The tent was protected by a pair of Blood Angels honour guards, their golden helmets glinting in the watery sunlight.

'Brother-Sergeant Koris, if you will attend? Lord Stele awaits your report.' Corvus gestured for the veteran to follow him inside.

Rafen made to accompany them, but the closest honour guard came off his mark and blocked his path. 'Just Brother Koris,' said Corvus.

Koris threw Rafen a look. 'Stand to, lad. I'll not be long.'

Reluctantly, Rafen did as he was ordered. The Inquisition's penchant for secrecy and obfuscation grated on the Blood Angel, as it did on most members of the Adeptus Astartes. Space Marines believed in the strength of direct action, of decisive deeds set forth without the petty minutiae of politics and endless discussion. Although he would never give it voice, Rafen disliked the fact that someone like Stele could sit here in the midst of a Chapter encampment as if he were the Chapter's master in all things. Rafen turned away, dismissing the thought – and found himself staring at a familiar face.

White flashes from the winged crests on the armour of a tall Blood Angel drew his gaze. The figure strode purposefully across the star port runway from the mouth of a freshly landed Thunderhawk, with a pair of Space Marines trailing at his flanks as a personal guard.

'Sachiel?' he called. 'Brother Sachiel?' Although it was a breach of protocol to address a priest in such an informal manner, Rafen spoke without thought and approached him.

The man gave Rafen a quizzical look. Then abruptly, a thin smile of recognition emerged on his face. Sachiel threw a glance at one of his guards, then back to Rafen. 'Can it be?' he asked. 'Rafen the Ready, as I live and breathe?'

Despite himself, Rafen frowned at the nickname from his days as a novice on Baal Secundus. 'You are well, Apothecary?'

Sachiel tapped an armoured finger on his shoulder pauldron. 'Time has passed, Brother Rafen. For the glory of Sanguinius and by the grace of our comrade inquisitor, my rank is now that of high priest.'

Rafen gave him a reverent nod. 'Forgive me, lord. It pleases me to see you alive after all these years.'

'Indeed,' Sachiel replied, with the very smallest hint of pride. Like his brethren, Sachiel's powered armour was blood red, but as an honoured Sanguinary High Priest, his battle gear was trimmed with lines of white detailing. A number of purity seals were fixed about his waist, beneath a bone-coloured crest of two spread angel wings. Rafen noted the shape of a velvet drawstring bag on his hip; inside, Sachiel would be carrying the traditional symbol of his rank among the Blood Angels, a sacred chalice modelled on the great red grail of Sanguinius.

Rafen did not dwell on the question of how Sachiel had advanced in rank so quickly during the *Bellus*'s mission; he was certain that if the verbose priest's personality had not changed in ten years, he would soon be regaled with the whole tale.

Sachiel's smile grew. 'This is certainly an omen of good fortune. It is not enough that we paused in our journey through the Empyrean at just the right moment to hear the cries from the *Celaeno*, but to arrive here and discover our own battle-brothers in need of deliverance...' His hand strayed to the bag on his belt. 'The God-Emperor guides us in all things.'

'As he wills,' Rafen agreed.

'And yet...' Sachiel seemed not to notice that he had spoken. He studied him carefully. 'I sense that your faith has been sorely tested this day, Rafen. I see it in the poise of your stride, the lilt in your voice.'

Unbidden, a flare of irritation sparked inside the Blood Angel. What could he know of Rafen's thoughts? 'I faced the archenemy, as is my eternal duty, and you say I was *tested*? You know this within moments of meeting me, despite the fact that we have not laid eyes on one another for a decade?' Rafen found himself falling back into the same patterns of rivalry he and Sachiel had shared as trainees; the two men had never overcome their mutual dislike.

Sachiel gave a languid nod, his expression laced with a faint air of superiority. Rafen remembered why it was he had never enjoyed the priest's company. 'I do. But I could not expect you to understand the things I have seen during the voyages of the *Bellus*, Rafen. While you have served Sanguinius in your own way, I have ventured into the very heart of the xenos and faced the absolute inhuman. Such things change a man, Rafen. They grant you insight.'

You have not changed at all, Rafen thought, *except you may have grown more vainglorious.* But instead of voicing these thoughts, he nodded to the priest. 'I imagine it must be so.'

Sachiel's smile remained fixed, and Rafen was certain that the Sanguinary Priest knew exactly what question was pressing at the Space Marine's mind; the thought that had been clamouring to be voiced from the very moment he had heard the name of the *Bellus*. After a long silence, he spoke again. 'I must ask, Sachiel. Rumours have spread throughout the Chapter since the astropaths received word that the *Bellus* was to return. There is the talk of deaths among the brethren sent to recover the spear.' He paused, the next words heavy and sharp in his chest like rough-hewn lumps of lead. 'What became of my brother? Does he still live?'

Sachiel cocked his head. 'Your brother? But are we not all brothers under the wings of Sanguinius, Rafen?'

'If it pleases you, high priest,' Rafen's temper flared again, 'I would have you tell me what happened to my sibling Arkio.'

The Apothecary gestured to one of his guards, and the Space Marine holstered his weapon, reaching up to remove his combat helmet. 'The bonds of blood transcend all others,' Sachiel said, quoting a line of scripture from the book of Lemartes, 'but no blood runs stronger than that of Sanguinius.'

Rafen said nothing. Even when they had fought alongside each other as novice brothers, Sachiel had always tried to turn each conversation into a lesson, as if he felt the need to constantly prove his knowledge of Imperial dogma at every opportunity. Rafen preferred to keep his faith a personal issue and illustrate it with deeds, rather than trumpet the words incessantly. At that moment the Space Marine guard at Sachiel's side revealed his face.

His younger brother's youthful and yet serious countenance stared back at him, and Rafen broke into a broad grin. 'Arkio! By the Throne, you're alive! I had feared the worst.'

Arkio gave a rueful smile. 'Well met, my brother. I—'

Rafen didn't let his sibling get any further, crushing him into a bear hug with a bark of laughter. Their armour clanked together; and for the first time since he had set foot on Cybele, Rafen's black mood was forgotten.

CORVUS STEPPED TO one side and came to attention as Koris halted. With his helmet cradled under one arm, the veteran Blood Angel's vision was only as good as the augmented occulobe grafted to the back of his retinas. Under normal circumstances he would have been able to penetrate the darkness, but here inside the inquisitor's tent the shadows that fell around him were as deep as the void of space itself. The sergeant wondered if some sort of witchery was at work; he did not know enough of Ramius Stele to glean what powers the inquisitor had at his command. He knew only of the tale of Stele's honour debt, and the unbreakable ties that made the man a trusted comrade of the Blood Angels – but as with anything that was declared a matter of faith, it was in Koris's troublesome nature to question it.

The true story of the debt was known to a select few, and even a seasoned warrior like the sergeant understood it only in the broadest strokes; there had been an incident when the inquisitor was travelling aboard a navy ship with the great Brother-Captain Erasmus Tycho of the Third Company.

Allegedly, a daemon had manifested inside the ship's engine core and Stele had killed it single-handedly when the beast had battered Tycho into unconsciousness. The hereticus agent's actions had earned him a personal commendation from Commander Dante and the respect of the Legion Astartes.

Part of the darkness before him shifted – a cloth drew open from another chamber inside the tent's voluminous folds – and he caught the scent of parchment and oil before a figure stepped into the light. Koris had seen the inquisitor only once before, at a conclave of Blood Angels following the great victory at Thaxted Duchy; then, the sergeant had been one of hundreds of men who heard him speak from a podium. Here and now, he had the immediate sense that Stele remembered him, even though his had been a single face among many.

'Honoured sergeant,' Stele's voice was rich and resonant. His bald scalp glittered in the thin yellow light of the glow-globes, making the aquila electoo on his forehead seem bright in comparison. 'I am distressed to hear we arrived too late to preserve Captain Simeon and the Governor Virolu.'

'As am I, honoured inquisitor. The Word Bearers' attack came without warning. Several brothers lost their lives under their guns, and others now flounder with severe wounds.'

Stele approached an ornate chair but did not sit. 'I have learned that the *Celaeno* was obliterated by a warship called the *Dirge Eterna*. I led the *Bellus* against the foul vessel, but it retreated behind the gas giant and may hide there still.' He absently touched his ear, where a silver purity stud glinted. 'I chose to save your lives rather than pursue it.'

'My men thank you.'

The inquisitor made a dismissive gesture. 'As the Emperor wills. It was a calculated risk, sending empty Thunderhawks from the port to harry the enemy line from the air. Had the Word Bearers not broken, it would have been for nought.'

Koris's expression hardened. 'They have not broken. They will regroup and attack again.'

Stele looked directly at him for the first time. 'You are correct, sergeant. The sons of Lorgar do not retreat without good cause, and even now my auxiliaries in orbit are reporting signs of their formations.' He paused, considering something. 'I am about to take my leave and return to *Bellus*, so that I may direct the search for the *Dirge Eterna*. But I wanted to look into the eyes of the man who held the line at the keep before I departed.' Stele gave a thin, humourless smile. 'I see I have little cause for concern.'

The veteran flashed a glance at Corvus, who stood silently by. 'What will be the disposition of my men?'

Stele turned and walked back toward the other part of the tent, pausing only to recover a pict-plate. He gave Koris a sideways look. 'I am placing the Sanguinary Priest Sachiel in command on the surface. You will obey his orders as you would mine.'

'And those orders are?'

'Hold,' Stele said as he walked away, his back to the Blood Angel.

THE SHUTTLE CUT the air with a crackling roar as it blazed into the clouds on a white spear of flame. Arkio watched it go with a reverent cast on his face. 'Lord Stele returns to our barge,' he noted. 'I think the enemy counter-attack shall not be long in coming.'

The pair of them stood alone on the ferrocrete apron. Rafen studied his younger brother without answering. His mind picked over the memories of the last time they had spoken; it had not gone well on that day. Arkio had told him of his acceptance into the *Bellus* expeditionary force and Rafen had disagreed with his choice. Such a mission was for seasoned Space Marines, he argued, and Arkio was anything but that. Although Arkio was Rafen's junior by a few years, they had become Blood Angels at the same time. Nevertheless the elder brother Rafen could not shake the duty that he had sworn to his father as a child: that he would protect Arkio for as long as he lived. They parted with cross words between them, but on the morning of the *Bellus*'s launch, Rafen had swallowed his pride and made peace with Arkio's choice. If they served in the same company, Arkio would forever be seen as a youth in comparison with Rafen, so until he stepped from his elder's shadow, Arkio felt he would never achieve the fullness of his potential. And so they parted with a salute, each man proud of the other, but secretly afraid that they would never meet again.

'You've changed,' Rafen said at length, 'and yet, you have not.' He chuckled. 'My brother has matured while he was away from my stewardship.'

'True enough,' Arkio noted, not without a touch of challenge in his voice. 'I've shed blood on countless worlds and faced more foes than I thought possible. This and more, brother.'

Rafen accepted that. 'You make me proud, Arkio. Proud that we share a bloodline as much as we are warriors in the name of the Golden Throne.' He hesitated, his voice thickening. 'I hoped… I hoped that I would not see my end until I learned of yours, brother. This very day I feared that I was moments away from the Emperor's peace, and nothing vexed me more than the thought I would not know the fate of my kinsman.'

'You know it now, brother,' Arkio said carefully. 'So does this mean you will seek out death?'

Rafen gave him a sharp look. Arkio's words were curiously barbed, his manner outwardly calm, but with a cold glitter dancing in his eyes. He truly has changed, Rafen thought, and perhaps in ways that hide themselves from a first glance.

The Blood Angel pushed his musings away. How could he have expected the callow youth of ten years gone by not to mature and grow hardened by the ordeal? He had no doubt that Arkio was probably looking at him in the same fashion, wary of a man who at once was his blood relative and a stranger.

'My fate will come to me without me having to look for it,' Rafen said with mock lightness. 'Perhaps it already has.'

'Perhaps–' Arkio began, but then his words died in his throat. Both he and his brother froze as the wind brought a faint clatter to their ears.

'Bolter fire,' Rafen snapped, and grabbed his weapon. Arkio mirrored his actions, and the two brothers broke into a run, toward the port proper.

BRASS LEAVES FORMING the bridge's iris hatch sighed open to admit the inquisitor and his retinue. The two honour guards immediately stepped into alcoves either side of the door, and Stele's lexmechanic and trio of servo-skulls hovered close by.

'Captain Ideon,' the inquisitor addressed the Blood Angel's officer wired into *Bellus*'s command throne. 'Status?'

'Under way, lord.' The Space Marine's voice was a guttural snarl that issued not from his lips, but from a bulbous vox-coder implanted in his neck. 'We will reach the orbit of the gas giant in moments.'

Stele examined the view ahead in the vast holosphere that dominated the wide control deck. The Cybele moon was depicted as a small, featureless ball to one side, dwarfed by the mass of the supergiant planet that forever held it locked in a tidal embrace.

'Contact,' said a servitor to his right. 'Capital ship, deceleration curve evident.'

Inside the sphere, the image remained static. 'Where?' Stele demanded, gesturing at the space ahead. 'Where is it?'

'Astern.' The display flickered before resolving into a larger-scale view, which showed the planet far behind them. A blinking glyph formed in close orbit.

'It's the *Ogre Lord*,' Ideon noted. 'A grand cruiser, repulsive-class. They must have been hiding out above the pole, waiting for us to break orbit.'

'Then where is the *Dirge Eterna*?' Stele snapped, even as new detections bloomed into life on the holosphere. The cruiser they had been pursuing was now emerging from behind the gas giant with two more ships in line formation.

'Confirm, *Dirge Eterna* and unidentified idolator-class raiders on intercept course,' droned the sense-servitor. 'Advise condition on battle stations.'

'Rot them, they planned this!' Ideon spat static. 'Shall we engage, my lord?'

Stele gave a brisk nod. 'Weapons free, captain. They'll burn for their temerity.' About the bridge, gun-helots began a litany of prayers as they sought firing solutions for the battle barge's missile batteries.

The finger-thick cables feeding into Ideon's skull brought with them vox traffic from the surface of Cybele and sensor readings of innumerable landers falling from the central hull of the *Ogre Lord*. 'Sir, I read a massive drop assault in progress on planet... Without orbital cover, the men on the ground–'

'They will fight and they will die,' Stele said. 'For the glory of the God-Emperor and Sanguinius.'

ON CYBELE THE Word Bearers boiled out from behind the marble tombstones and low sepulchres in a tide of screaming, chanting ruby. Man-forms in pitted, ancient armour turned the manicured lawns black in every place where their clawed boots fell. The toothed tracks of their Rhinos ground the grave markers of brave men into powder behind them.

Rafen found Koris at the spearhead. The veteran's gun was hot with constant fire; his crimson greaves were dashed with licks of polluted blood. From the corner of his eye, Rafen watched Arkio move and shoot, pause and reload, without a single gesture or movement wasted. He grinned; he would look forward to hearing his sibling's tales of battle when this was over.

'How did they cross the bridge?' he said aloud, discharging a burst into a pack of turbulent enemy hymnal-servitors.

'The point is moot,' Koris retorted. 'It matters little where we kill them–'

'Just as long as we kill them,' said Rafen, switching his bolter over to single-shot mode. He paced rounds into the face and chest of a Chaos Space Marine emerging from a sluggish Chimera transport.

'Listen!' Nearby, Brother Alactus was calling out. 'Do you hear it?'

Rafen strained his senses to pick out the noise from amongst the crash of bolters and the foul cacophony of the Word Bearer's exaltations. 'Thrusters!' Alactus shouted. 'Listen! Our deliverance falls from the skies for the second time today!'

Arkio paused, replacing a spent sickle magazine. 'I think not,' he said grimly.

Something in the tone of Arkio's voice made Rafen pause and look skyward. From the thin grey morass of Cybele's clouds came a myriad of iron teardrops, each one glowing cherry-red with the displaced heat of re-entry. Rafen heard Koris curse under his breath, as the skies above turned black with enemy landers.

CHAPTER THREE

THE OGRE LORD spat murder and flame across the surface of Cybele, raining destruction over the grasslands and shallow mountain ranges. To the far north-west, where the great Valkyrie towers climbed skyward, it sent atomic warheads and fuel-air explosives laced with poison. The minarets were the glory of generations of memorial artisans, commissioned by the Adepta Sororitas to venerate those lost in the savage Phaedra Campaign; each one was hollow, their innards a network of acoustic channels cut from raw marble. In the high season, the wind would sing through them in perfect tones of mourning. But no pilgrims stood before the towers as the archenemy's nuclear retribution bloomed overhead, and no human ears heard the final, awful screams that were forced from within them, in the seconds before the shock wave of super-heated air scoured them from the face of the planetoid.

Closer to the starport, low-yield munitions and finely targeted lance strikes fell on the Imperium forces. Rafen was dazzled as a discharge ate into the ferrocrete apron. In an instant, the rock flashed to toxic vapour and air molecules crashed as heat split them into atoms. A skirmish line of Blood Angels' tanks caught in the weapon's footprint became blackened humps of slag, featureless and smouldering. Overhead, precise discs of sky shone through the wide holes the beam weapons punched in the clouds.

As fallout ash began to settle, all about him the air was cut and slashed by the profane hoots of the enemy. Garbled litanies and exhortations of violence assailed his ears, blasphemous descants warring with repellent pulpit speeches broadcast from speaker horns. Without conscious thought, Rafen's lips began to move, forming the words of the Barbarossa Hymnal, and as he gave it voice, he heard the song spread to his battle-brothers on the firing line. He drew strength from the sacred lyrics, and advanced.

Turcio was at his right hand now, a heavy bolter in his grip. Rafen did not ask where he had acquired the weapon, rather he marvelled at his brother's use of it, as shells cascaded from the muzzle and shredded the enemy advance. The hymn's words became a dull rumble in Rafen's ears, as a hot flood of adrenaline charged through his muscles. The eager twitching of his gun-hand's fingers returned, so he gave it freedom, his bolter joining the chorus of chain-fed death laid down upon the Word Bearers. At the edges of his vision, crimson spectres danced just out of sight – the ever-present ghost of the rage. Rafen kept the dark impulses firmly in check – control was the key to staying alive in a battle like this one.

Waves of spiny dreadclaw drop capsules landed around them, the earth shaking with each hammer-blow impact. Like vile seedpods, they broke open to spit out fresh Chaos Space Marines or the warped forms of dreadnoughts. Every one of them added to the bloody discord of the battle, tearing Cybele's quiet landscape of pious contemplation into shreds. Rafen removed his combat blade from the eye socket of a

Word Bearer who had strayed too close, and wiped gore from the serrated edge. Turcio's gun bawled and cut another Traitor down, splitting him asunder as surely as if he had been gutted by a chainsword.

'Still they come,' the Space Marine said through gritted teeth, 'How many more?'

'Too many,' Rafen retorted. 'Blood for blood's sake!' He bellowed, firing to underline his words with lead. More landers came to rest in the distance, the closest collapsing a crypt with a gust of decayed air. Rafen paused, readying a brace of krak grenades to feed its passengers the moment one of them dared to emerge. He waited until the broken slabs of the tomb roof began to move and lobbed them in. He dropped to one knee as the explosion coughed, the muffled report lost in the clamour of the Word Bearers' advance. Rafen sighted at the ruined crypt, taking a moment to kill any stragglers that might have survived. But instead of a seeing a stunned Traitor emerging from the rock, a thick pincer-like limb extended itself from the stones. The heavy iron armature wavered and then came down hard, biting into the turf. Rafen and Turcio stumbled backward as more legs grew out of the rubble, pushing up a box-shaped body with a toothy fan of blades.

'Defiler!' Turcio cried out the machine's name, and rang bolt shells heedlessly against its gore-streaked hull. Rafen was more careful. He placed single rounds into the clusters of weapons along the war engine's flanks, hopeful that a lucky hit might crack a flamer line or sever power cabling. The red metal of the walker rippled under the strain of sudden movement, as the skin of a vast beast would show the flexion of its muscles. It let out an ear-splitting honk from a war trumpet as it pulled itself up on six fat legs. It was met by an atonal choir of replies. Rafen's gaze flicked to the other landers that had come down with this one and saw that each had the same cargo: a dozen more Word Bearer defilers were stepping from their pods, swivelling their guns to bear. As the first jets of burning liquid promethium gushed across the Blood Angels' forces, Rafen yanked on Turcio's arm to pull him out of the firing zone.

Somewhere in the melee, he had lost sight of Arkio. He had been distracted by the crack-snap of lasgun shots. Rafen returned fire and ejected a spent magazine, while Turcio covered him.

'Those grotesques will overrun us!' Turcio snapped angrily, 'Where is our armour?'

Rafen remembered the boiled pools of metal that had once been tanks and said nothing. He ignored Turcio's words and watched the defilers shifting into position: the walkers were preparing to break the Blood Angels' line. If they had still had armour, the Space Marines might have stood a chance at blunting it, but with these light arms... The endless rain of Word Bearer troops was tipping the odds ever further against the Blood Angels, even with the men left behind by the *Bellus*.

Wherever he was, Brother-Sergeant Koris had come to the same conclusion. The veteran's gruff voice issued out of the Space Marine's ear-bead. 'Fall back to the inner fence by squads!' came the order. 'Let these warp-spawn come at your heels, but don't get caught up!'

'Let's move,' Rafen shot a glance at Turcio. 'Come now, we'll give them their push and then shove it back down their throats.'

Turcio glanced over his shoulder as they ran, fighting down his disquiet.

A CHAIN-REACTION of short-circuits sent sparks ripping across the portside gun console, and frying the synapses of the cannon-servitor connected there. Stele wafted a hand in front of his face to dispel the burnt meat stink that assailed his nostrils. The other gripped the brass rail that bordered the warship's giant glasteel porthole. They were close enough to one of the idolator raiders to actually see it with the naked eye, the tumbling dart of metal stark against the emerald hue of the gas giant. The quick application of a tactic refined by Ideon's anti-ork sorties had granted *Bellus* first blood against the Chaos flotilla. A high-gravity turn, more akin to the manoeuvres of Thunderbolt fighters than capital ships, had allowed the battle barge to rake *Dirge Eterna* with her bow guns, although the nearest of the small raiders had surged forward to protect the large ship, as if its crew would receive some cryptic honour for accepting the hell storm intended for the cruiser.

The wounded raider was bleeding gases into the void and Stele's servo-skulls relayed scans of a cracked fusion bottle. He pressed one finger on the glass, blotting out the shape of the vessel. The ship was a cripple, and so the inquisitor had already dismissed it from the complex game board arrayed in his mind.

Captain Ideon was conversing with one of his subordinates. 'Set to work on repairing the torpedo tubes first,' he ordered. 'The warp drives can wait.'

Stele took a quick step forward. 'So our damage is worse than you first stated, captain?'

Ideon's face remained fixed but his voxcoder's tones w terse. 'I have revised estimates.'

As they pulled away from their first strike, the sec had come about to flank the *Bellus*, taking adva weakened void shields to the aft. Hard impa quarter had sent tocsins wailing on every Ideon had said nothing, Stele knew th abled – at least, temporarily.

In reply, a blue-helmed Devastator Space Marine sent a pair of missiles into the defiler's prow. The rockets leapt eagerly to meet their target, and a dozen troopers poured fire into the same place, forcing the machine to stagger backward.

'Rafen!' The Blood Angel turned to see Koris, his gun smoking. 'Report!' The veteran absently brushed rock chips off his armour as a stray round shattered a decapitated statue close by.

He jerked a thumb at the sky to indicate the Chaos command ship. 'They must be spawning up there like maggots, brother-sergeant. There are four of them to every one of us...' His words trailed off. 'Tycho's blood, this isn't the kind of hit-and-fade we've handled before. They mean to raze the planet and make trophies of us!'

'Aye,' Koris said with a dour nod. 'This world has no tactical value, but they choose it because their very presence here is an affront to the Emperor.' He shook his head. 'A world full of graves and just a handful of men to guard it? Bah! We're standing on the lip of a corpse-grinder!'

Shapes moved in the smoke, white and red flickering amid the grey. 'Take care, Koris,' Sachiel's voice was clear belittles us all.' The Sanguinary ith a unit of men at his heels. oncern that none of them was

iel, his voice low. 'Pragmatism od Angel, priest. I taught you ll a whelp.'

had other teachers since you, s learned.' He gestured with men who survived the bom- hem to come forward and reinforce the line.' Sachiel threw a nod to the Space Marines with him and they rushed forward to take up firing positions at the barricade.

'To what end?' Koris demanded. 'We are assailed on all sides – those blighted scum are tightening the noose around us as we speak! Surely you see that?'

'Lord Stele's orders were to hold,' the priest shot back, 'and hold we will.'

The sergeant showed his teeth at Sachiel's tone. 'Hold what, priest? Tell me that. What patch of ground? A metre? A kilometre?' He shook his head. 'We stand and we die, and Stele – if he is even still alive – returns to find the Word Bearers chewing on the bones of my men.' He flashed a glance at Rafen. 'I will not allow it.'

'The port must not fall–'

'It has already fallen!' The words bubbled up out of Rafen before he was even aware of it. Sachiel gave him a barbed look. 'We're just slowing them, not halting them.' As if to lend its agreement to the words, one of the defilers spat out a deafening hoot of sound as it speared the husk of a smouldering speeder. 'We need to regroup, before it's too late.'

Despite himself, Sachiel hesitated. The priest's many battles over the decades had been in conflict with xenos scum of every stripe, but this was the first time many of the warriors of the *Bellus* had met their traitorous brethren at close hand. As much as he loathed admitting inferiority in anything, he had to admit that Rafen and Koris had the greater benefit of experience against this foe. Sachiel's fingers strayed to the bone wings on his breastplate and the ruby blood droplet depicted there. There would be no glory in dying in a graveyard after surviving so much to recover the spear.

'Give the order,' he told Koris, after a long pause. 'But watch your tone in future.'

The sergeant turned away and relayed the command, leaving Sachiel and Rafen together. 'You dislike me, don't you?' The priest said suddenly. 'You have never given me any more than what is expected of you.'

Rafen covered his surprise at Sachiel's words. 'It is my duty to respect the holders of the grail–'

Sachiel waved him into silence. 'You respect the office, but not the man, brother. Even after all these years, you slight me.' The priest turned as the rest of the Blood Angels began to draw back. 'But I will have your respect, Rafen,' he said gently. 'You will give it to me.'

Rafen tried to form an answer, but none came to him. Koris's voice in his ear-bead pulled his attention away.

'There is a gap in the Word Bearer line to the north. Take the lead and secure a regroup point at the reservoir dome'

'Acknowledged,' he said. 'I'll need some men.'

'You can have one. Go with your brother.'

The Blood Angel came about as a throaty roar signalled the arrival of a fast attack bike from across the landing field. The low-slung motorcycle growled to a halt and idled. Arkio beckoned to his elder brother. Rafen gave him a nod and bounded up to the rear spoiler, gripping the back of the seat with one hand. Arkio gunned the engine, and the bike threw itself into the wavering lines of mist. Behind it, a crimson stream of Space Marines disengaged from the fierce fighting, and with weapons running dry, they reluctantly gave their backs to the enemy.

ARKIO TORE ACROSS the flat apron, veering the bike around the remains of drop-ships, skirting the places where beam fire had cut the ground. With his bolter clasped in his free hand, Rafen picked targets as they moved and strafed them. Arkio arrowed the vehicle toward a pack of Word Bearers pushing forward from the western side of the port and triggered the twin guns atop the front wheel. Orange tracer lanced through their warp-changed bodies even as the sound of the bike's approach reached their ears.

'There!' Arkio shouted over the engine's roar. 'I see the breach!'

Rafen followed his brother's outstretched arm. Ahead of them, the Word Bearer line had become strung out where the Traitors had allowed their fire discipline to become lax. To Rafen's trained eye, the weak point stood out like obsidian against ivory. 'Sergeant Koris,' he spoke into his helmet communicator pickup, 'rally to us. We're breaking through.'

'Firing!' called Arkio, as he unleashed the twin bolters again. Rafen hesitated as something caught his eye back in the smoke haze.

'What is it?' asked his brother.

'I thought I saw…' Rafen replied, dispatching a Chaos Space Marine fumbling with a tube-launcher. 'People.'

Then they were off the level ground of the ferrocrete and into the mud and grass of the graveyards, and all of Rafen's attention was spent on the enemy troopers, who popped up from behind the headstones like targets in some carnival shooting gallery.

WHILE SACHIEL LED Koris and the troops from the barricade in an orderly retreat, there were other Blood Angels' units following the same orders. From the hangars came the few walking wounded that had not been killed when the makeshift hospital had been bombed, and with them the support units whose Predators had been razed in a single shot from the *Ogre Lord*'s cannons. Injured and bleeding, they fought hard all the same, daring the Word Bearers to try and stop them.

These were the Space Marines who came across the eight skinny men standing in a ragged group in the middle of the landing field. A novice scout found them first, all of them stumbling around in little circles, humming and mumbling to themselves. Their mouths and eyelids were sewn shut, and some sort of blade-edged chain tied them together in a loose knot.

'What are these?' The scout asked his commander, a craggy-faced sergeant. The humming voices were rising in volume.

The sergeant glanced over his shoulder at the wave of approaching Blood Angels and the fire they laid down behind them. He had no time to halt the retreat because of some addled civilians. He stepped closer and studied them. When he was at arm's length, he realised that their skins – which he had thought were dark in tone – were actually covered in tiny writing. The sergeant saw the representations of a many-angled star drawn there in millions of configurations, and he spat in disgust.

'Heretics,' he growled, and every gun around him came up to firing position. 'Execution detail! Kill–'

His Space Marines didn't hear the command. The humming chants of the eight men was so loud now, it blotted out his voice.

The scout, who hadn't taken his eyes off the figures since he first saw them, watched it happen: a sparkle of unleashed psychic energy licking between the men, fanning out into a coruscating globe of sickening light. Linked together since birth and imprinted by Iskavan's psyche-mages, the eight channelled all their mental energy into the one unstoppable release that was the sole purpose of their lives. They were a psionic munition with a war-shot of pure, violent intensity. Their power arced through every one of the injured Space Marines, and then they died, turning to ash; but none of this mattered to the men their discharge had touched.

The minds of the surrounding Blood Angels – more than three-quarters of the survivors of the two Word Bearer attacks – were shredded instantly; their higher reasoning and intelligence wiped clean. All that remained was naked, primal aggression, and the very darkest core of unchained bloodlust. Brothers who had known each other for centuries, allies and comrades, fell upon one another with monstrous abandon. Sachiel and Koris watched helplessly from outside the radius of the psi-weapon, as Blood Angel killed Blood Angel amid the lusty cheers of their enemies.

OUT IN THE Word Bearer lines, Iskavan the Hated bellowed with laughter and shouted his delight to the sky. 'Forward!' He called to his host. 'Take the port!'

'There are more out there, my lord. You're letting them go?' said Tancred, realising too late that his words might be interpreted as disrespectful.

'I intend no such thing.' The Dark Apostle gestured with his crozius. 'No victory is so complete as the one that comes over an enemy that is broken. We winnow these wretches until only the very strongest of them remain.' In anticipation, Iskavan's tongues emerged from the forest of teeth behind his lips. 'And they will be the ones we will leave begging for the beautiful tortures that please the gods.'

Tancred pushed all thoughts of his dark prediction away and presented his master with an agreeable aspect. 'By your command.'

The Traitors moved forward over the bodies of the dead.

BY NIGHTFALL, THE last of the Space Marines that had escaped the psi-blast had stumbled back to the rally point. Rafen's heart turned cold and heavy in his chest as the weak warmth of the day faded. As light drew out of the landscape around him, so hope seemed to follow it. In the dank shadows cast by the reservoir's dome, injured men and battle-weary survivors sat in sombre silence. Rafen walked among them, sparing a nod or a gesture of solidarity to those he knew personally. Outwardly his manner was neutral, but within it was burdened with grim malaise. There were hardly a handful of them now, not a single man above sergeant's rank or armed with more than a bolter. He passed Koris as the veteran spoke in low, angry tones to Sachiel; his first order had been to tally up the ammunition and weapons held by the survivors and Rafen could tell just by his expression that the numbers were poor.

Rafen sat by Turcio as he worked to patch his armour with glutinous sealant. Nearby, a watchful Arkio cleaned his bolter. Rafen's brother had returned from a patrol with Alactus to report the terrible sights of the Traitors' victory revels only an hour earlier. The wind brought the sounds of distant shrieks for all of them to hear. Some of them belonged to voices that Rafen recognised.

'Once again we wait for death,' Turcio's voice was a hollow echo.

'Not for the first time,' Rafen agreed, forcing the doubts from his words, 'but we will prevail. We are Blood Angels.'

Perhaps on another occasion, the sentiment might have been enough, but here and now Turcio met Rafen's gaze and he saw the spectre of dread there. 'I pray that is enough, brother, or else we will join the men on whose graves we trampled today.'

'We will not die here,' Rafen said without heat.

Turcio saw the lie and looked away. 'You know that we will. And it shames us all that these animals will dance upon the bones blessed by the Throne.'

Arkio came to his feet in a rush, startling Rafen. 'No,' he said, exasperated. His voice carried iron with it. 'What shames us is that any Blood Angel would countenance defeat at the hands of the corrupted!' He advanced on Turcio and pressed a fist into the other Space Marine's chest.

'The blood of Sanguinius courses through us all. It is the very stuff of defiance and honour, but you speak as if your heart pumps water in its place!'

The low murmur of speech in the camp was suddenly gone; every man was listening to Arkio's words. They were caught by the abrupt passion that surged from them.

'I face my fate with clear eyes,' Turcio managed. 'That makes me no less a battle-brother!'

Arkio's expression was a mix of concern and sadness. 'My poor friend, you have lost your faith and yet you do not see it. Here,' he handed Turcio his knife. 'If you are so sure of death, take this now and slit your throat.'

'Arkio–' Rafen began, but his sibling held him at bay with a hand. Something in the younger Space Marine's manner made him stop and fall silent.

'Take it,' he repeated.

'You mock me!' Turcio snapped, his colour rising. Without warning, the Space Marine's dispirited mien broke and in its place was a hot rage. 'I will take a thousand Word Bearers with me before I go to the Emperor's side! I will not end my own life like some mewling, broken imbecile!' The words flowed out of him in an angry rush.

'*There!*' Arkio's face split in a savage grin. Inexplicably Turcio did the same, baring his fangs. 'You see, my brother? *There* is the fire of our Lord Primogenitor! Look within, see it! It still burns in your breast! I merely had to remind you of it...' The younger Space Marine turned to face the rest of them, the knife glistening in his hand. 'Look at us, brothers! Have we escaped the enemy only to let them win without a shot? Did our comrades die today just so we might wallow in despair?'

'No!' A dozen men shouted out in answer, and Rafen was one of them, speaking without thinking. Something bright and powerful flashed in his brother's eyes, and he was roused by it. Arkio's every word was crystal clear, each sentence resonating with righteous energy.

'The Traitors think we are broken, beaten, defeated!' he growled. 'By Lemartes, I say this is not so! I say we will yet bleed them white and send them running!'

Rafen's gaze locked with his younger brother's for a second. Arkio looked about him, taking in the faces of all the assembled Blood Angels. In the dimness, the Space Marine's sharp-angled face and his cut of golden hair made him seem like one of the renditions of the honoured warriors of antiquity, in portraits at the fortress-monastery. In a moment of strange disconnection, Rafen saw Arkio as if he were a Blood Angel from the time of the Heresy, an ancient face of the Chapter's most glorious past; then the image passed, and Arkio was speaking again. 'The Traitors do not have the honour to meet us in open battle. They nip and strike at our numbers, wear us down. The Word Bearers do not just wish us dead… They desire the destruction of our souls as much as our flesh! But to the last man we can defy them!'

A chorus of assent greeted his words; but then one voice sounded above them all. 'Your ardour does you credit, lad,' said Koris carefully. 'But rhetoric is never a substitute for gun and blade.'

Sachiel's face set in pious indignation, but before he could censure Koris for his interruption, Arkio nodded respectfully to the veteran. 'The honoured brother-sergeant is right, of course – but I have more than just words to offer.'

'Explain yourself.' Rafen demanded. He fixed his eyes on his sibling, part of him marvelling at a facet of his brother he had never seen before.

The young Space Marine stooped and pulled at something concealed in the long grass. With a grinding of hinges, a hidden maintenance hatch came open in his hands. 'If it pleases my brothers to hear it, I dare to have a strategy. A way we can take the fight to the foe, even with numbers as small as this, and still cut their hearts from them.'

CHAPTER FOUR

ALACTUS SHOOK HIS head and smiled coldly. 'Have you been so long from true battle that your brain has softened, whelp?' He stood up and approached Arkio, the rhythm of his gait suggesting he might strike the Space Marine. 'While you were playing games with greenskins, the rest of us have been fighting the real foes of the Imperium! You presume much to speak so boldly of an untried plan in such a facile tone!'

Arkio stood his ground and let the insult roll off him. 'I would respectfully hear your thoughts, brother.' Alactus was barely a few decades older than Arkio and he had little cause to cast the other Space Marine as his junior. Arkio ignored this fact and let him speak.

'You spout a few words of holy writ and think that you can turn the tide of battle? You have much to learn.' Now the tension in the camp came to a knife-edge, every strain and unease among the survivors rushing to the surface.

'Then teach me, Alactus,' Arkio said mildly. 'You say you doubt my prowess and that of my comrades from the *Bellus*, but I know you do not. I see a different reason behind your outburst. You are afraid, and you turn it on me instead of the enemy.'

The other Space Marine's face flushed crimson with barely restrained anger. 'You ask me if I know fear? You dare?' he roared. Alactus stabbed a finger in the direction of the starport. 'You were not there to see the weapon those unholy fiends unleashed upon our brethren! I was in the last of the ranks to retreat, I stood with Koris and watched the witch-fire engulf every Blood Angel who followed behind us!'

'I, too,' said Corvus, from the shadows. 'I saw it. Men with their dignity stripped away by the touch of Chaos, rendered into blood-hungry beasts. They conjured the red thirst from every one of them.'

The phantom of their Chapter's gene-curse forced a sullen silence over the assembled men. The anger fell from Alactus's face and he became ashen. 'I *am* afraid, Arkio. Though we face the darkness without until we die, there is no Blood Angel who does not fear the beast within. Any man who says he does not lies to himself. It is what makes us sons of Sanguinius. Our strength... Our bane.' He shook his head. 'That these Traitors might seek to use it against us chills me to my marrow.'

Corvus nodded his agreement. 'By the Emperor's grace, we few have survived this day, but to have seen such a sight and still live...' He shuddered.

Sachiel's voice was a low growl. 'This morbid prattle spreads like a virus! Your brothers died for the Throne! You should be honoured to join them!'

'No, priest,' Arkio broke in, his subdued words reinforced with quiet humility. He hung his head. There was pain in his eyes. 'Forgive my disagreement, but there is no shame in what has been said here. What kind of men would we be if we could watch our kinsmen die and feel nothing? Are we more than mindless killing machines in the garb of flesh?' He looked up again, and Rafen felt a physical shock as their eyes locked. Tears coursed down Arkio's face. 'I weep for my brothers.'

Arkio took Alactus's hand and grasped it firmly. 'I weep for them and I know your fear, brother – but if this is true, you too must know my fury as well, my wish to punish those who transgress against us!'

A change passed over the face of Alactus. 'I do,' he agreed. 'I know it in my heart and my blood.'

Arkio looked to the Sanguinary Priest, and to Rafen's surprise Sachiel too nodded his agreement. 'We are Blood Angels,' said Arkio, his voice thick with emotion, 'and we carry the flaw, but as Argastes said in the litany vermilion, we are not weak because of it!'

'The black rage makes us strong,' said Sachiel, quoting the passage from memory, 'because we must resist its temptations every day of our lives–'

'Or be forever lost.' Koris finished. 'Arkio is right. We have no choice but to fight.'

Rafen felt the words resonate in his chest. A renewed sense of purpose bloomed among the men, and suddenly the wounds and privations of the battle seemed cursory things. The will had been in them all along, he realised, and it merely took the spark of his brother's words to rekindle it. Rafen spoke quietly to his brother. 'You are full of surprises, kindred.'

Arkio gave him a brittle smile. 'No, Rafen. I am as you are, a Space Marine and servant of the Emperor and Lord Sanguinius. No more.'

'And how will we serve them now? You spoke of a strategy…'

The young Blood Angel stooped. 'Look here, brothers.' He gestured towards the hatch he had opened in the ground. 'During the battle I became separated by the shelling. A mortar round took me from my feet and I found myself thrown against a grille on the surface of the landing field…'

'A drainage channel,' said Turcio. 'There are many of them throughout the starport.'

'Indeed. The rainy season on Cybele is fierce, is it not? And the waters are diverted here, to the catchment reservoirs.'

Koris gave a quiet grunt of laughter. 'By the oath, this bold young pup has found us a route back to the port. The flood channels can take us right under the Word Bearers.'

Sachiel studied the open hatchway. 'A clever tactic, Arkio. But what are we to do with this course? If we emerge in the midst of the Traitor scum, we will be no better off than if we had stayed at the barricade.' He gave Koris a hard stare. 'And as I was told, that would be certain death.'

'It would,' Arkio noted, 'which is why we would send only a few men. Brother-Sergeant Koris will correct me if I err, but I believe that only one is required to operate the port's defence batteries, yes?'

'The anti-ship guns?' Koris nodded, and looked to a surviving Techmarine from his company. 'If you took Lucion here, it could be accomplished.'

The Techmarine tapped the cog-and-skull symbol on his chest-plate in a gesture of agreement. 'I can turn my hand to that. It would be simple.'

'But once you have the guns, what then?' asked Sachiel. 'They cannot depress low enough to strike at the Word Bearers.'

Rafen felt a rush of excitement as he saw the plan unfold in his mind. 'We will not use the guns on the ground troops. We target the *Ogre Lord* overhead.'

'The command ship?' said Lucion. 'It orbits directly above us… If it fell from the skies, it would be like a storm of meteors…'

'Aye, this borders on madness,' said Koris. 'But for Sanguinius, it will be done!'

Sachiel reached for the velvet bag on his belt. 'So ordered. I will take command of the strike team personally. Arkio, for your eloquence you will join me with Corvus and Lucion.' He turned to Koris. 'Brother-sergeant, choose a squad of men to accompany us. You will lead the remaining troops to stage a diversionary raid on the perimeter once we are within the port's confines.'

Koris masked his ill humour at the orders with a salute; the veteran had clearly hoped to lead the team himself. 'As you command.'

As Sachiel stepped away, Rafen laid a hand on his commander's shoulder. 'Sergeant, I would have you choose me to go too.'

Koris raised an eyebrow. 'You want to keep a watch on the lad, eh? In case he has any other flashes of tactical brilliance or sudden urges for oratory?' The elder warrior gave a terse nod. 'Very well. Take Alactus too, and draw full stocks of ammunition from what assets we have.'

'Lord, that will leave the rest of you with next to nothing–'

'Bah,' Koris waved him away. 'We'll beat them with stones and harsh language if need be. You take your brother's plan and make it work, Rafen.'

Rafen said no more, as a silence fell across the survivors. Sachiel held up a brass chalice and murmured a benediction. Each of the Blood Angels was drawn to the glittering replica of the red grail. The priest drew his combat blade across his bared forearm and let a thin stream of blood trickle into the cup. Then he handed it to Koris, who did the same. The chalice went from man to man until each of them had added a run of their own vital fluid to the mixture. The container had the same shape and form as the most sacred and ancient of the Chapter's artefacts, the red grail that contained the blood of every Sanguinary High Priest. So the Chapter's scripture said, these men – of which Sachiel was one – shared an iota of the primarch's blood; it was injected into their veins in a sacred ritual. Now the priest took a draught from the cup. 'By blood we are bonded,' he intoned, 'and by blood we serve.'

He passed the chalice back along the line of men, and each of them sipped from the dark, coppery liquid. 'We drink deep of victory, and remember the fallen.' The cup, empty now, returned to Sachiel's grasp. 'For the Emperor and Sanguinius!'

With one voice, the last warriors of the Imperium on Cybele took up the cry. 'For the Emperor and Sanguinius!'

THE FLOOD CHANNEL was a tight fit for the Space Marines, and it was a credit to their battle discipline that they moved quietly through the waist-deep water, never once brushing against the worn brickwork that closed in around them. The water-course was not the product of a single construction: over the centuries, the pipes had been extended and built over one another as more and more of Cybele's surface had become a resting place for war dead. In some parts, the Space Marines were able to stand line abreast instead of single file, passing through the stone foundations of huge crypts and mausoleums. Alactus led the way with a faint biolume in his hand. The dull green glow from the lamp shifted and danced off the walls and the sluggish water.

Rafen picked out the shapes of small vermin and carrion insects as they scattered from the light. Now and then, Alactus would pause and study the path ahead, the faint glow illuminating aged text in High Gothic on the subsided memorial stones. The Space Marine studied one such monument, canted at a wild angle, half buried in the earth. The names of hundreds of men were carved there in an endless train of letters; victims of some long-forgotten atrocity on a world that likely no longer existed. Since he was a child, there had always been something about tombstones that at once attracted and repelled Rafen; it was as if he sensed that one day he would discover a stone that bore *his* name. The moment of reverie broke as he became aware of Lucion behind him. Alactus had started forward again, and Rafen followed on.

As they moved closer to the starport, the occasional breaths of night air along the tunnels became more frequent, and with them they brought disturbing sounds that were ghostly and incoherent. Rafen noticed that the water had changed consistency; it ran more sluggishly now, and it had a dark, oily sheen. Alactus paused again and made a quick set of gestures with his hand. Rafen showed him a slow nod to indicate he understood and relayed the signs to Lucion behind him. The Space Marine on point had found a place where the walls had partly fallen in, and they would need to drop to a crawl to pass it. Alactus slid into the thick waters and the light from the biolume vanished with him.

Rafen let his helmet visor adjust to the darkness, rendering the channel in a monochrome grey. He felt a pat on his back and he went down to his knees, then his chest, and into the liquid embrace. Submerged, the Space Marine moved forward by touch, letting his fingers lead him through the heaps of rubble and thick slides of disturbed earth. Once, his hand traced over the shape of something that felt suspiciously like a human femur, but then he was past it and rising up from the viscous grip of the run-off. Alactus pulled him to his feet and Rafen reflexively drew his hand across his faceplate to wipe off the oily matter. The red ceramite glove came away with purple-black clots of coagulated fluid glistening on it. Rafen realised that he had been holding his breath, even though the sealed Adeptus Astartes power armour had its own internal oxygen supply. Toggling a vent in his gear, he allowed himself to sip at the air in the flood channel, and a million scent-tones raced through his sense memory.

The channel was knee-deep in blood, and he did not need to look at the other Space Marine to see that he knew it too. As the other members of the squad emerged, Rafen looked up to take in the place where they had risen.

They were inside the perimeter of the starport now. By Rafen's reckoning they were quite close to the place where the first Thunderhawks from the *Bellus* had touched down. The narrow pipe had given way to a tall, vaulted run-off chamber where other, smaller effluent channels converged. Some six metres above his head, set in the landing field's surface, was a long slot that showed dark sky beyond, barred by thick rods of steel grille.

In the rainy season, water would sluice off the ferrocrete pads and through those grids, but what fell from them now was something quite different. Irregular shapes were heaped over the drains above, piled in discarded heaps. They were bodies and there were countless dozens of them, some still clad in broken pieces of Blood Angel armour. A continuous rain of blood was falling, the vital fluid of their dead brethren greeting them like some arcane shower of anointment.

Beyond the mournful patter of the dead men's blessing, there were other noises that merged into one rolling thunder of sound. Demagogues and mechanised loquitur-drones led the massed ranks of Word Bearers above them in thanksgiving for their victory. Rafen resisted the urge to spit and turned away. Arkio stood close by, his helmet turned to the sky, his expression hidden behind the fearsome mask.

'Brother?' Rafen's voice was a whisper. 'Do you see something?'

With a near-physical effort, Arkio broke away from the sight. 'Only the dead.'

THE WORD BEARERS had made camp amid the port's broken structures. Tancred found his liege-lord picking at a heap of soft, fish-belly white meat. He appeared deceptively languid in his auto-throne with one hand cupped under a Space Marine helmet. Iskavan eyed the torturer as he approached and held the helm to his lips, licking cold blood from it.

'Speak.' Iskavan grunted. Tancred knew instantly from the tone in his voice that the Dark Apostle was annoyed, even though they had won the day against the Blood Angels.

'News from orbit, master. The *Dirge Eterna* has located the human ship in the atmosphere of the gas giant world and commenced bombardment from low orbit. Guided by the ruinous powers, we will force them from their hiding place or destroy them.'

Iskavan spat harshly. 'A fine victory indeed,' he said with leaden sarcasm. 'But no amount of holy murder will lessen my disgust!'

Tancred's tentacle-hand shivered, as it always did when he was concerned. 'Lord, what ails you? You have taken this world in the name of the blight but yet you stand aside from our victory revels. I would know why.'

In answer, Iskavan drained the last draught of blood from the Astartes helmet, then pitched it away into the chanting crowds of his own soldiers. 'You were there, Tancred. You saw it as well as I did.' He shook his head. 'By the order of our warmaster, we fell back. We *retreated*.' Saying the word made the Apostle twitch with anger. 'What orders are these that a Word Bearer must step back from an enemy?' With that he was on his feet, kicking over the food tray. 'Ever forward, never back! That is our creed, by Lorgar's eyes!'

Tancred stood his ground. 'Above all others, we are bound to serve the word of Lord Garand…'

Invoking Garand's name had the desired effect: the Apostle's mood softened – but only a little. 'There is more at work here than we know, Tancred,' he hissed. 'Garand moves us about like regicide pieces on a hooded board and grants us the merest slips of information, but Iskavan the Hated is the pawn of no one!'

'But what choice do we have, dark one?'

'What choice?' Iskavan snorted. 'What–' Without warning, the Chaos warlord's voice choked off in mid-sentence and he licked at the air. When he spoke again, all trace of his previous mood was gone. 'Do you taste that, Tancred?'

'My lord?'

The Apostle jumped down from the makeshift dais where his throne sat and beckoned a warrior to him. 'You! Give me your name.'

The Word Bearer bowed to his master. 'I am Xanger FellEye, if it pleases great Iskavan.'

'I scent men hereabouts. Gather your most zealous and search the perimeter.'

Without another word, the Chaos Space Marine turned and ran to his task. Tancred watched him go. 'Lord, surely no more than an insignificant few of the man-beasts remain alive? Our puppeteers saw to that.'

Iskavan's hideous mouth split in a too-wide smile as he recalled the injured Blood Angels murdering one another in frenzy. 'Yes. If Garand had granted us more of those precious psyker-helots, then this world would have been subdued in an hour, not a day.' He dismissed the thought with a blink of his yellow eyes. 'How many are left does not matter. It only matters that they are left.' Iskavan drew himself up to his full height. 'Tancred, when the dawn rises on Cybele I will erect the first great obelisk to the glory of Chaos Undivided, and mark me, I shall have it made from the fresh-hewn bones of the Adeptus Astartes.'

THE EDGE OF the sprawling Chaos encampment seemed close enough to touch through the optics of the gun's target scope. 'I have a target, sergeant,' Turcio sub-vocalised, the sensor pickups in his throat relaying the words as clearly as a shout. The Space Marine held his aim steady on the Word Bearer guard post; he was still carrying the laser that Rafen had pressed into his grip in what seemed like an age ago.

'Hold your fire, lad,' the veteran replied. 'We'll go just as soon as the priest says so.' The remnants of his unit lay in wait, spread out behind him and hidden in the lee of a hill. All of them were burning for revenge.

Turcio watched the Traitor Marine pause at the door of the ruined hut. One squeeze of the trigger plate and its head would pop like an overripe fruit.

'Wait for the word,' Koris repeated, as if he read his mind. 'It'll come soon enough.'

FELLEYE FOUND HIS thoughts wandering as he approached the edge of the landing fields. Under other circumstances, he might have called it a blessing that he had been selected for a mission by the Dark Apostle himself – but the events of the day on this blighted corpse-world had left him, like many of his comrades, disturbed. Of course they had routed the hated Blood Angels – and Xanger had never doubted that would take place – but Iskavan's confused orders during the initial assault had left the Word Bearers under his command wary. And now there was this, the sudden demand to search for survivors. FellEye was torn between his desire for the raucous cacophony of the victory carousal and his duty to his lord. Hushed whispers that Iskavan's mind was unsettled had long been spoken of in the Legions of the ninth host, and many of the men blamed the Apostle for their poor victories of late – but until today the veteran Word Bearer had never given them any credence.

He sniffed the air. The Dark Apostle said he smelled man-flesh out here, but then so could Xanger. The whole moon was a repository for rotting human carcasses, after all, and the earth was churned to mud where bright rivers of enemy blood had pooled. FellEye shook off the thought. It was not his place to question the orders of an exalted one. Not yet, anyway.

One of his men grunted through his tusks. 'I saw movement.' The other Word Bearer pointed at a metal grate in the ferrocrete.

'Open it,' Xanger commanded, gesturing to the rest of his patrol with the flat of his hand.

The tusked Chaos Space Marine bobbed his head in a bow and tugged the covering off with a squeak of complaining hinges. He dropped into a crouch so he could see clearly into the flood channel.

Sachiel's chainsword entered the Word Bearer's flesh just above his sternum and sank into the meat of him, before ripping back out in a wound that opened his skull from the inside. The Traitor fell away as the Blood Angels erupted from their concealment, boiling out of the vent in a burst of red.

Xanger fired wildly. Bolter rounds from his skull-mouthed weapon skipped across the runway as he walked his fire into the mass of emerging enemy bodies. The other Word Bearers in the patrol reacted a spilt-second slower than he; they were surprised by the sudden appearance of the foe in their midst. These men paid for their laxity with their lives. FellEye's shots clipped a figure and one of the Blood Angels tumbled back the way he had come. Just as suddenly the guns of every Space Marine converged on him and Xanger's millennia of service to Chaos ended in a screeching whirlwind of agony. The warrior's corrupted form came apart in chunks of decayed flesh and ceramite.

'The word is given,' Sachiel hissed into his throat mike as the other men dispatched the rest of the patrol. 'Commence attack!'

'LORD, PLEASE,' TANCRED said, a lilt of concern in his voice, 'I fear you may be allowing your mind to play tricks–'

'Silence!' Iskavan cuffed him to the ground with a cursory flick of his wrist. 'Rally the men! Don't you hear it? Gunfire!'

Tancred struggled to recover his dignity, fuming inwardly. 'Perhaps you are mistaken, dark one. All I hear is the popping of human bones on our pyres, the spree of our warriors.' But just as he spoke, the torturer caught the distinctive snap-crack of a laser discharge on the wind. Rising to his feet, he looked to the western edge of the starport and saw beams flaring there and the hot globes of grenade detonations. 'Forgive me, lord! You are correct!' He bellowed commands to the soldiers around him and wrapped his tentacles around his plasma pistol. He was not aware that Iskavan was looking in the opposite direction.

'Where are they?' the Dark Apostle asked, turning to study the distant flares of Sergeant Koris's attack. Iskavan's eyes narrowed. 'An echo, then,' he told himself, dismissing his suspicions.

Cowering in case he might be struck again, Tancred held up his master's crozius. 'Your weapon, lord...'

Without another word, Iskavan took up the device and strode westward, eager for battle.

'THEY'RE TAKING HEAVY fire,' Lucion said, his face implacable as he listened to the signals from Koris and the Space Marines at the diversionary front.

'Then let us make use of every second they give us,' Sachiel snapped. The priest looked up. Just as they had planned, Alactus had led them to the shadow of the four great defence cannons that loomed over the starport in stubby, sharp-edged ziggurats. Thick tubes emerged from the capstones of each construction, tilted at steep angles toward the sky. Inside those imposing structures were mechanisms and conveyers that fed shells as big as Thunderhawks into gaping, hungry breeches.

'We'll need to pass the gate...' said Rafen, considering the doors that blocked the firing bunker from the outside world.

Arkio smiled. 'I have an idea.' A vehicle, far enough away to miss them as it raced toward the attack on the perimeter, rumbled by in the mists. Arkio filled his lungs and shouted, his voice carrying. '*Hail!*'

Alactus grabbed his arm, a second too late. 'You fool, what are you doing?'

The running lights on the vehicle twitched and grew as it turned and approached them. The shape of a Word Bearer tactical Space Marine was visible, half out of the roof hatch. He threw a chest-beating salute at them as the tracked machine slowed in jerks and fits.

'A Rhino,' whispered Rafen. 'One of ours...'

The transport was indeed of Blood Angels' issue, but as it came closer it was clear that a glancing melta-blast had ripped most of the port armour away. The old Imperial or Blood Angel sigils had been painted over with crude Chaos symbols.

Rafen could see three more Word Bearers through the hole in the hull.

'Hail!' the Traitor called, as the Rhino skidded to a halt. 'Host-brothers! Will you come join our hunt for the men-prey?' In the darkness, with their wargear coated by blood and detritus, the armour of the Blood Angels appeared the same shade as the gore-red the Word Bearers wore themselves; it was enough for the enemy to lower their guard.

'I think not,' said Arkio, and opened fire. Rafen and the other Blood Angels did the same, killing everything inside the Rhino before they could even draw a weapon.

'Good thinking,' Sachiel commented, striding over to the idling vehicle. 'Get these unblessed monstrosities out of this machine. Lucion!' He addressed the Techmarine. 'Take the wheel.'

'IDIOTS!' SAID NORO, his one organic eye squinting through the fire-slot. 'The Rhino is returning.' The Chaos Space Marine gave his comrade a quick look of confusion. 'What now?'

The other Word Bearer shrugged, the gesture magnified ten-fold by the bulk of his armour. 'Be wary,' he hissed through blunted snake's teeth. 'I will meet them at the gate.'

Noro watched him turn the crank that released the iron doors to the firing bunker. Typically, it was he who had been left behind when the humans started shooting and the other Word Bearers in his squad wanted to go and join the battle. Noro shook his head in disgust. Dropped from the *Ogre Lord* in the very last wave, Noro's unit had missed every moment of the fury, and then they'd been ordered to guard the defence battery instead of taking part in the communion. He hadn't even *seen* a single live Blood Angel all day. Noro cursed his luck and spat hissing acidic phlegm on the stone deck.

'Something is amiss.' said the other Word Bearer, studying the approaching Rhino. 'The vehicle is gaining speed.'

And then, the bionic optic in his other eye socket provided him with a close-up image of the transport. Noro saw the distinctive winged blood drop on the armour of someone inside the vehicle, and he knew precisely what was going on. 'Warp take them!' he screamed. 'Secure the gate!'

To his credit, his comrade didn't ask for an explanation. Instead he turned the crank the other way and forced the iron doors to reverse back into the closed position, but the effort he'd used trying to open them made the task twice as hard and twice as long. So the gates to the bunker had three feet of clearance between each edge when the prow of the Rhino struck them at full throttle.

Lucion handled the tracked transport like a guided missile and rammed the gate at precisely the point where their resistance was least. The impact stunned the Techmarine into giddying moments of semi-consciousness, but the rest of the team had jumped free just seconds before the collision. Now they poured in behind the broken form of the Rhino, forced like a crimson wedge between the doors.

Noro's comrade was gutted by a lucky collateral kill when splintering segments of the Rhino's tracks took his head from his shoulders. There were other Word Bearers in the bunker, but they had not even understood that anything was amiss until the transport's explosive arrival. Now all of them were taking up guns, shooting and dying as the Blood Angels brought them death.

Arkio was at the head of the pack, his bolter a murderous roar of devout vengeance. 'Imperator excommunicatus!' he cried, sending the Chaos Space Marines and their chattering servitors screaming into hell.

Noro thought about his warp-forsaken luck and crossed gazes with the young Blood Angel. The Word Bearer fired his bolt pistol, but the rounds never seemed to even get close, skipping away as if the human had some charm about him. Noro cried out in Lorgar's name and rushed forward to bury his knife in the furious face of the whelp, if nothing else, but he was met by a horrific storm of metal-shattering bullets.

Noro was the last of the Word Bearers in the bunker to fall, and Arkio pitched back his head to cry out in anger. 'More!' he spat. 'More to slake the thirst!'

'Aye! *More!*' Alactus was with him, eyes wide with need.

Rafen shot his brother a glance as he helped Lucion to extract himself from the crumpled Rhino. 'Which way now?'

'Down.' Lucion indicated a wire-cage lift. 'The firing control is below us.'

Sachiel ran his hand over the white and red of his armour. 'By the grail, Sanguinius graces us this day! We turn the tide!'

As they rode down into the lower level, Rafen chanced another look at Arkio. For a moment, the orange hue of the emergency lamps made his armour seem bronze in colour, and Rafen was reminded of the Riga tapestry again; then the moment passed, and they had arrived.

A few single-shot kills made short work of the helots cowering amid the consoles, and while the Space Marines cleaned up, Lucion began the ritual of activation. Above, inside the stone ziggurats, the four gun tubes groaned and shifted, as if the weapons themselves sensed what was about to happen.

BELLUS BURST FROM the gas giant on the shock wave of a nuclear firestorm, volatile elements in the planet's air combusting around her. Although he had no firing solutions, Captain Ideon ordered every gun to fire blindly, sending up a wall of destruction. The battle barge raced away, and the Cybele moon grew rapidly in its forward screens.

'This was an error,' Ideon grated, 'We will be caught between the ships.'

Inquisitor Stele shook his head. 'Study the aft monitors and tell me, captain, would we have not been destroyed if we had remained?' View-plates aimed astern showed the flaming patch spreading to ignite pockets of gas all across the massive planet. 'Those corrupted scum would see the entire world put to the torch just to end us.'

Ideon's impassive face twitched slightly. 'You may have only delayed our fate, my lord, and not for long.'

'Contact,' droned one of the servitors. 'The *Ogre Lord* has seen us. She is bringing all weapons to bear. *Dirge Eterna* is also turning for broadside.'

'Not for long,' Ideon repeated.

FINES OF RUST flickered through the shafts of their biolumes as the massive gun carriages turned to track the Chaos cruiser in orbit. Nerves jerked in Lucion's cheek as a trio of mechadendrites extended from his skull and into waiting slots in the targeting pulpit.

Three of the four loading glyphs had now turned green, and Sachiel was becoming impatient. 'What is the delay?'

Arkio answered for Lucion. 'We must fire the guns as one, high priest. We may not get a second chance, and the rounds will do the most damage if they strike together.'

Deep, bass thunder rolled around the chamber and the last glyph changed colour. 'Ready.' Lucion's voice was breathy and distant. 'The Emperor's eye sees the enemy. His wrath is at your command.'

Sachiel nodded at the young Space Marine. 'Let the honour be yours then, Arkio.'

'Thank you, lord.' A fierce smile danced over the lips of Rafen's sibling, and he placed a hand on Lucion's shoulder. 'By the blood of every brother dead this day, let their vengeance be fulfilled!'

'So shall it be,' intoned the Techmarine.

THE GUNS DISCHARGED so close together that the report from the muzzles came as a single thunderous howl of noise. The shockwave compacted rings of air into dense hoops of vapour around the barrels, and an earth tremor took ill-prepared Word Bearers and Blood Angels alike off their feet.

Four huge rocket-assisted proteus-class anti-starship munitions screamed skyward with a sound like tearing flesh. The *Ogre Lord* did not see them coming until it was too late. The enemy warship, still turning to face *Bellus*, had put all power to her lances and dorsal void shields, leaving the belly she bared to the moon below utterly unprotected.

Each of the shells found purchase in the hull metal of *Ogre Lord*, the staged fusing in their adamantium-sheathed warheads pushing them through the plates of ablative armour and into the soft meat of the ship's interior. There, the main fusion cores that were the poison hearts of the proteus missiles went critical and detonated.

Ogre Lord rippled from within, and shattered.

CHAPTER FIVE

'VANDIRE'S OATH!'

The curse slipped from Brother-Captain Ideon's voxcoder in a spit of static. Wired as he was into every sensor output from the detectors that lined the *Bellus*, the ship's commander viewed the death of the *Ogre Lord* with a thousand eyes. He was witnessing the killing of the Chaos cruiser in ranges of vision beyond ordinary sight. In the higher frequencies of infra-red, Ideon saw plumes of hot atmosphere gush out into the black void; under warp-scan, he saw the twinkles of aberrant daemon-life as they tore asunder in explosive decompression and through the lenses of the rho-field trackers he watched the bright flood of liberated mesons and neutrinos as the enemy vessel's fusion bottle cracked. Even at this distance, waves of hot energy from the blast licked at the *Bellus*'s void shields.

Ogre Lord came apart like rotten wormwood struck by a hammer. Great chunks of the craft span away propelled by the monstrous detonations of the proteus missiles. Chainfire licked across the upper quarter of the ship as it distended and broke, and munitions blocks of shells all exploded at once.

'Glorious,' said Stele, the angles of his face lit by the backwash of light from the ruined craft. 'Do you see, Ideon? The Emperor delivers us.'

Under his breath, the officer whispered a prayer of thanksgiving and continued to monitor the fragments of *Ogre Lord*'s hull, which were now flickering embers as they dropped into Cybele's upper atmosphere. 'I wonder who fired those shots from the surface?'

'A bold soul, I would warrant,' Stele fingered the purity stud in his ear. 'Such a fearless gambit will turn the skies to fire down there, and set the archenemy on their heels.'

Ideon hoped he would live to meet the man who had pulled off so risky a gambit. But perhaps the poor fool would perish along with the Word Bearers on the ground when the *Ogre Lord*'s remains began to rain down. In the periphery of his normal vision, he noted the way that his astropaths were twitching and cowering as the enemy cruiser succumbed. The psychic death-screams of untold numbers of the corrupted in close proximity disturbed their mental equilibrium. Ideon idly wondered what consequences that effect would have on the enemy psi-sensitives on the planet.

Stele spoke as if he had read the captain's mind. 'There were a great many slave-psykers on board that ship. I imagine their deaths would have been a mercy for them.'

With effort, the captain pulled his attention away from the dying ship. 'We must act swiftly to enjoy this bounty.' He flicked a glance at his adjutant. 'Where is the *Dirge Eterna*?'

'Still turning,' the Blood Angel snapped, without looking up from the pict-slate in his hand. 'The loss of the other vessel has confused them – they are in danger of extending too far from their attack pattern.'

'Perfect.' Ideon's eyes narrowed as he willed the hololithic screen before him to display a fresh series of firing solutions. 'Bow guns to ready condition. Bring us to bear.'

'Complying,' answered the servant at the helm. 'Number three gun does not answer.'

The inquisitor raised an eyebrow and made a *tsk* noise. Ideon ignored him, a feral heat building in his chest as the screen drew about to show the other Chaos vessel. 'We'll shoot with what we have. Fire at will.'

A sensor-servitor let out a chirp of warning. 'New target entering the firing line!' As the sightless bondsman bound into his scanner pulpit registered the incoming Idolator-class ship, Ideon saw it too in his mind's eye. Raw jags of data streamed into him down the lines of his mechaden-drites. The dagger-form of the raider copied the same manoeuvre that had crippled its twin in the earlier engage-ment, physically placing itself in front of the *Bellus*'s war shots to protect the *Dirge Eterna*. Some higher element of Captain Ideon's tactical intellect turned this over, wonder-ing just what it was about *Dirge* that made it so worthy of protection, but that was a matter for consideration after the second raider had been punished for its audacity.

His synthetic voice spat and hissed. 'If they are so eager to court oblivion then they'll find we have it to spare. The order is revised: strike that idolator from my sky.'

'Your will,' nodded his adjutant, and the junior officer repeated the command to the cannon-servitors.

The raider rotated to present its prow to the *Bellus*. The idolator ship was distinctive: the broken red tooth of the bowsprit was dominated by a huge brass-plated dome in the shape of a human skull. The eyeless shape was tipped backward, as if it was screaming, and from the open jaws a blunt gun muzzle emerged. Ideon had once been told that the figurehead skulls of these vessels were made from metals recovered from the bodies of the dead. They were forged with the iron recovered from the blood furnaces of slaughterhouse worlds in the Eye of Terror. He did not care if the rumour was true; the archenemy's ships could be made from the bones of the Chaos gods themselves, for all that it mattered to him. They would die like all the other traitors that ever dared to cross the Blood Angels.

'He means to ram us,' said the adjutant, half-statement, half-questioning.

'Then show him the error of his ways,' rumbled Stele.

Bellus obeyed.

THE BATTLE BARGE'S hammer-shaped bow sported four massive gun tubes each the length of a Cobra-class Imperial destroyer, and in a glare of violent discharge, all but one of them spat their death-loads at the idolator. Each cannon was powerful enough to deal a shattering blow to void shields or hull armour, and to use them against a lighter capital ship like the Chaos raider was complete overkill. Shots from the first, second and fourth guns – the third was still inoperative – savaged the vessel and opened it to the vacuum. Unlike the *Ogre Lord*, whose crew had moments of screaming fear to understand what was happening to them, the raider simply ceased to exist.

In one murderous detonation of energy, steel and twisted bone-metals flashed to atoms and became gas; it was as if the ship had been flung into the heart of a star. Under Ideon's command, *Bellus* pushed on through the expanding wave front of the ship's vaporous remains and bore down on *Dirge Eterna*. With the balance of power tipped back towards the Blood Angels, the enemy ship fell away from the gas giant and made speed for Cybele's orbit, raked by the barge's sub-cannons as she passed. With her engines still below full capability, *Bellus* could only begin a slow turn to follow it.

THE VERY AIR itself was aflame on Cybele as Rafen and the rest of the strike team stumbled from the defence battery bunker. The night sky was no longer dark: wide trails of hot orange fire criss-crossed it in a web of glittering colour. Wreckage screamed through the ragged remains of clouds overhead. Vast slabs of metal as big as islands threw themselves from horizon to horizon, scattering rains of dirty, molten droplets behind them.

Arkio's face was lit with savage fury, and he stooped to drag a leg's-length of iron bar from a shallow impact crater. It was a fragment from the Chaos cruiser after the fall. The rod went slack, the heat of re-entry making it distend. 'What worthless things these creatures are,' he grimaced, 'Curse them for forcing us to sully our hands with their blood.'

Lucion held up his hand. 'Listen... Do you hear that?'

Rafen's brow furrowed. The ceaseless screeching of the Word Bearer demagogues and the noise of weapons fire had been such a constant companion over the past day that changes to the cacophony were not immediately apparent to him. But then he caught it too, and strained the sensitive lyman organs in his ears to separate the sound from the hypersonic shrieks of falling debris.

'The Traitors... What are they doing?' Gone now were the spitting blasphemes of the Word Bearer war-priests, and in their place were anguished yelps and utterances of wretchedness and woe.

Sachiel spared Rafen a grim smile. 'We have dealt them a terrible blow, kinsmen. They feel keenly the deaths of their foul brethren and it vexes them. Listen to them, they nurse the pain like it is a physical wound!'

The priest was correct. The Word Bearers' chants were no longer monotonous litanies and corrupt hymnals, but keening wails and funereal chants.

Alactus laughed. 'Then we'll give them something to weep for, eh?' He hefted his bolter and made a show of cocking it.

To the west, the fighting between Koris's unit and the main force of the Word Bearers was still going on, but now the exchanges of fire were desultory and sporadic, as both sides reeled from the eruption of death-flame from the heavens.

'Your orders, then, high priest?' Arkio asked. Strangely, it seemed that none of the Blood Angels had thought to move until the young firebrand had brought it up.

'Yes, of course,' Sachiel said, distracted from the burning sky. 'We should regroup with Sergeant Koris before the enemy gather their wits.'

'I'll take the lead,' Arkio snapped, and with that he was away, racing across the starport fields, dodging from cover to cover. Rafen kept pace with him, pausing to conceal himself in the lee of a wrecked Thunderhawk as once more the sky tore open with the passage of another piece of ship. The dense fragment of hull struck the hills a few kilometres distant with a white flash that underlit the smoke clouds. The shock of the impact reverberated through the ground as the sound of the landing snapped past them. Bits of the *Ogre Lord* would be raining down on Cybele for days to come.

Rafen considered the ashen landscape. 'Blood and martyrs, brother. We may have done more damage to this world with one shot than the Traitors did all day...'

'What does it matter as long as we kill them in kind?' Arkio's voice was cool and distant. 'I am the Emperor's servant, and by my hand his enemies perish.' The younger Space Marine leapt from cover as a loose knot of firing Word Bearers approached. Rafen joined him.

Iskavan the Hated gave one of his flamer-troops a savage kick, pushing the wounded Chaos Space Marine face-first into a mouldering pile of dead men. The injured Word Bearer was one of the lucky ones; the Dark Apostle's accursed crozius had already fed on the life of a dozen more Space Marines who had been too slow to follow their master's commands.

The lord of the ninth host was literally incandescent with rage. Discs of turbulent electro-telepathic force encircled his head in coronets of lightning. They glowed about his bony horns like Saint Elmo's Fire. In the near distance, cracks of bolter rounds signalled the places where Word Bearers and Blood Angels fought, but around the main mass of the Chaos Legions were disordered lines of hand-to-hand fighting. Every member of the host had felt the death-throes of the war-psykers on the *Ogre Lord*, the black shroud of their screaming minds reaching out to hammer all the warp-touched who walked on Cybele. The Word Bearers stood fast and weathered the shrieking. Their disciplined mentalities were rigid and resistant, but the cackling minor daemons and countless legions of helots they had brought with them went mad from the sound in their heads, and they turned on one another.

The unexpected side-effect from the Blood Angels' sneak attack now changed the Word Bearers' forces from precise, mechanical formations into a raging, uncontrollable rabble. Iskavan roared with inchoate anger as a dozen gun-servitors dared – *they dared!* – to attack him in their maddened fury. Slug-throwers burped fat discs of serrated metal at him and blunderbuss horns vomited rains of lead shot, every pitiful round rebounding off his ruby armour. He replied with the most terrible blades of his crozius, sweeping the slave creatures away in a screeching arc of gore and entrails. The Dark Apostle could not reach the enemy Space Marines for hundreds of his own helots were now attacking the Word Bearers and each other alike, tearing at the sallow skin of their faces in vain efforts to quell the insanity boiling through them. Iskavan's crozius jumped and sang in his mailed fist, rattling the chains that bound it to him. The weapon was spooked by the thick taint of mind-death in the air, and it craved blood to drown out the sensation. The Word Bearers' leader gave it what it desired by the gut-load: he buried the seething blade head into the bellies of the men-forms around him.

'Rip them apart!' he bellowed, as much to himself as an order to his warriors. 'Kill for us or be killed by us, you maggot-blood wretches!'

Tancred was suddenly at his side. Perhaps the torturer has been there all along but it was only now that Iskavan noticed him. It mattered little, and it took a moment of effort to pull the crozius away from the neck of his second. The weapon moaned at the blood denied it. 'Magnificence, the bound daemon-forms are tearing themselves apart!'

He gestured with his tentacle hand and the Dark Apostle saw the rank of wheeled black bone cages, marooned now in the midst of the infighting helots who were supposed to be dragging them toward the enemy. Inside each enclosure a minor daemon beast was held. They were throwing themselves against the bars in bloody madness, and beating their skulls and limbs against the confinement. These were not the towering princes of the warp that the followers of the eight-blade star lived in fear of; they were smaller, bestial life forms, the empyrean's equivalent of animal predators. They possessed a savagery that nothing from the mortal realm could match, and in conflict they would sow fear and disruption in enemy ranks, provided they were directed properly. Now they were spoiled and crazed, worthless in battle for anything other than cannon fodder. Iskavan cast a disgusted look around and watched the keepers of the beasts fighting one another while others were being chewed apart by their very charges.

'Wasted! Wasted!' he spat, lamenting the finely wrought battle plans he had laboured on in the days prior to their arrival on Cybele. The Dark Apostle drew up his crozius with its red blades shining like a beacon, and bellowed out his commands. 'Clear a path through these chattering dastards! Cut the daemons free!'

'My lord, the creatures are broken minded – they will tear apart everything in their path!'

'Of course, you fool!' Iskavan spat, waving his weapon, 'but all that will be there will be the corpse-god's men and those fit for death! Now by my decree, release them!'

The Word Bearers parted like a falling wave and drew back from the skirmish lines. At Tancred's direction, sharpshooters blasted the fat phase-iron padlocks off the bone cages from a safe distance. As one the inhuman ravagers threw themselves into the melee, fighting and eating and gorging on fresh meat.

SERGEANT KORIS AND his men met the largest of the things as it stumbled toward them, licking gore from its mouthparts. For a moment, the veteran thought the daemon had two heads, as it appeared that one of them was attached to the end of its arm. But then it popped the skull into its mouth and crunched it down, flicking the blood of one of its unholy brethren aside in an almost human gesture. It threw back its head and hooted wetly.

The daemon had too many legs, some of them arched upward in spindly arcs of bone, others low to the ground with fat ropes of muscle. A nest of barbed forelimbs snapped at the air as it came toward them, on its sinuous neck bobbed a broad oval head that seemed to be a random collection of eyes and teeth. It spat out a thin line of black drool before surging forward, to come at the Blood Angels in a stumbling run.

Koris had no need to remind his men to maintain fire discipline. All of them knew just how low on ammunition they were, and not a single Space Marine would waste even one bolt round on a chanced miss. When the warp-beast was close enough that its fetor engulfed them, they shot it. Rounds clacked off the bony claws and egg sacs in its torso with hollow sounds, leaving no mark of their passing. Other more precise shots blinded eyes or gouged divots of hairy flesh from its hide. It was heedless, however, and the Blood Angels scattered as it dived into them. Koris saw Alactus sweep away under the thing, but by the luck of Sanguinius he dodged each crushing footfall as it passed over him. Corvus was not blessed by the same fortune: he spun out as the beast ripped at him with a sickle barb. Another Space Marine, one of the *Bellus* contingent whose name Koris had not learned, died as his bolter choked on an empty magazine. The daemon opened him up with mad fury, shaking its head so that the razor teeth in its mouth could crack his ceramite cladding. As it swallowed him, Koris gave the command to fix bayonets, snapping his combat knife into the magnetic mount on the bolter's foregrip.

And then, through the mass of screaming, dying helots came a dozen more Blood Angels, their guns fat with ammunition and spitting fire.

'Koris!' Sachiel's voice hummed over the communicator. 'Cover fire!'

'With what–?' The sergeant demanded, but his words were ignored. He saw the Sanguinary High Priest come forward. He was brandishing his chainsword and pistol and laying rounds into the mottled hide of the warp-beast. *The eager fool! He'll be killed!*

The creature sensed the white and red shape in its peripheral vision and spun in a tight circle. As it did so, it whipped out its barbed tail to knock down a dozen more Blood Angels with callous relish. The shock of the strike pushed Koris reeling against a tilted headstone, so that his fire was directed away from the creature's head.

Rafen saw the beast's move coming a split-second before Arkio and he dropped, snapping out a kick at his brother's ankle. His sibling fell just as the spiny club of meat at the end of the creature's tail thrummed over their heads. 'Watch it!' he added.

Arkio's eyes were elsewhere. 'Sachiel! Guard yourself!'

The priest went off-balance. The beast was far faster than he had thought; its huge legs belied the thing's nimble movement. He slashed the chattering chainsword at one of the meaty limbs, but his cut was shallow and did nothing but anger the daemon-beast more. With its hindmost claw, it tore into the Space Marine who stood to Sachiel's right, then threw his corpse into the priest. The impact tossed Sachiel into a shallow crater and the lanyard connecting his sword to his gauntlet snapped. The blade buried itself upright in the mud, teeth growling.

Dark malice glittered in the creature's myriad eyes and it flicked at the dirt. It resembled a housecat with a rodent, unwilling to bring the kill too quickly for all the sport it would lose. It ignored the bolt rounds that bit into it from the other Space Marines. It wanted to *play*.

Rafen squinted into the target sight of his gun and saw Sachiel's face behind his half-mask. The priest's skin was pale and drawn with exertion. With unfocussed eyes he was winding up his flank where the beast had casually cut him. Rafen's finger froze on the trigger. If he had to he would grant the priest the Emperor's peace rather than let him be a meal for this monster.

Then, like a rising rocket, Arkio burst from his cover and crossed the distance to the beast in a dozen loping steps. The daemon gave him a desultory swipe, angry to be interrupted in its game, but the young Blood Angel dodged easily. He swooped to snare Sachiel's fallen chainsword. He brought the buzzing blade around in a flickering arc and cut cleanly through a knee joint. A leg as thick as two men fell away in a gout of thick blood, and the creature let out a thunderous shriek. With one splayed claw it pinned Sachiel to the dirt, and snapped at Arkio with the others, probing and shifting in place.

'He's going to kill it,' Rafen heard Turcio's comment over his ear-bead. The Space Marine was unable to keep the awe at Arkio's daring from his voice. Rafen fired into the beast, doing his best to cover his brother's actions. Arkio darted back and forth beneath the animal, slashing at soft parts that lay between iron-hard pads of chitin. Gushes of black fluid spurted from the wounds with ropes of slick, slime-covered intestines drooping from their open mouths.

Sachiel made some sort of strangled yelp – possibly a call for aid, or a warning to Arkio – and his hand flapped feebly at the creature's claw. The Sanguinary Priest attempted to stab the beast with the acus placidus on his wristguard, but the steel needle could not penetrate the hard bony spines. A shiver ran though the daemon, and for a second Rafen saw a shimmer of pain in its eyes. The agony of its wounds was at last making its way to the thing's tiny feral brain, enraging it even further.

Before he could react, the monster coiled all its movement into one lightning-fast spin, lashing out at the irritant beneath it. Arkio did not cry out when one of the creature's blade-quills rammed through his armour. The yellow cartilage emerged from his shoulder with a mist of bright blood about it.

Rafen felt his stomach fill with ice; such a wound would surely be mortal, and his sibling's life was measured now only in seconds. Rafen's vision blurred crimson with a haze of hate and he bounded from cover, heedlessly racing at the creature. From the edge of his rational mind, something hot and black began to uncoil. The dark shadow of the gene-curse boiled up inside him, desperate for release. He bellowed an incoherent war cry, his bolter running red-hot as he emptied it into the beast. Rafen saw Arkio dead, cast aside in the mud, with the whirring chainsword still ticking over in his mailed grip. As lucidity threatened to flee from him, Rafen had a mirror-bright flash of memory of his father, on the day that he and Arkio had set off for Angel's Fall and the place of challenge. *Watch over the boy, Rafen. I ask nothing else of you.* His father's face seemed to flow and merge like mercury, shifting into that of the primarch, and Arkio.

Then the impossible became real before his eyes. Arkio rose in one swift motion from a puddle of rainwater and his own blood, apparently ignorant of the vital fluids that streaked his wargear or the black tear in his chest. With a single stab, he drove the sputtering, buzzing teeth of Sachiel's weapon into the throat of the daemon-predator, and buried the weapon to its hilt. The gnashing blade severed the thing's vocal chords and cut off its cries in mid-scream. Arkio rolled the weapon back through the beast's gut and it came apart with a noise like ripping cloth. Organs and undigested pieces of men emptied on to the grass in wet heaps. The beast wheezed and died.

As quickly as it had appeared, Rafen's rage abated, and he was at his brother's side, holding him up. Arkio gave him a wan smile and wiped black gore from his face.

'How could you…?' Rafen began, words failing him. 'The wound…'

Arkio face was pale with blood loss but his eyes were as hard as diamond. 'Faith is my armour, brother. Sanguinius protects.'

'By the grail, he speaks the truth!' Sachiel approached them, favouring his injured flank. 'Did you see him, Rafen? The Lord Primogenitor himself would have been proud to witness such bravery!'

Rafen said nothing and nodded. He was unable to draw his eyes away from his brother's injury; the cut was deep and bloody, but where it should have torn open arteries and exposed his gory bones, the gash was wet with life, almost as if it were knitting together as he watched.

'Arkio, you are touched!' Sachiel added with a gleeful spark in his voice. But a seed of uneasiness was being lodged in Rafen's heart.

THE ARTIFICIAL FLATLANDS of the starport, once drab and featureless, were now stained with thousands of gallons of blood in all shades of crimson, from the rust-brown of humans to the bright scarlet that coursed through the veins of the Adeptus Astartes, and the night-black slicks of ichor from the corrupted ones and their minions. Cybele's grasslands, which for so long had consumed the flesh and bone of the Imperium's war dead, were now dyed with the gore of those who fought upon its soil.

Surrounded by the ragged remains of his warband, Iskavan the Hated turned his too-wide mouth to the sky and screamed his rage at the dirty clouds. The sound of his anger cowed his men. It drowned out the constant impact of wreckage plunging from orbit. They were on the verge of losing the engagement to the Imperials, and it drove the Apostle into apoplexy.

At last he recovered enough to speak coherently, instead of hissing and spitting. 'What ill-starred fate is this?' he demanded of the night. 'By the eight, we were promised victory this day!' Almost the instant the words left his corpse-like lips, the Dark Apostle was turning on Tancred, his crozius humming loudly. 'You.' The Word Bearer champion loaded the word with absolute loathing and ire.

The torturer willed himself into stillness, terrified that even the slightest gesture would reveal the duplicity of his earlier prognostication.

'You told me you saw success, Tancred,' Iskavan's voice hovered dangerously low. 'Where is it?' he growled. *'Where is my victory?'*

'Th-the manner of the Empyrean cannot always be–' the torturer fumbled at an excuse, but the Apostle backhanded him across the face.

'Silence, pestilent fool!' He pushed Tancred away and advanced on his men. 'The eye take these subhuman dregs! We are the sons of Lorgar, bearers of the word!' Raw fury blurred his features with an unholy psychic light. 'We have lost our ships, our beasts and helots, but yet we still have our hate!' Iskavan pointed his crozius at them. 'Hate enough to choke the bloody mongrels of the carrion god!'

Iskavan expected the Word Bearers to roar back at him with hungry approval, but only silence greeted him. The Apostle was about to strike the nearest Traitor Marine dead for their intransigence when he suddenly realised why. A hooded form was walking through the unkempt lines, glittering with dark witch-fire.

'Iskavan, my servant. Hear me.' The voice it spoke with was a breath from a rotted tomb.

'Warmaster Garand…' For the briefest of instants, the Chaos champion's face twisted in a sneer, but then he dropped to one knee and made the sign of the eightfold star. Without hesitation, the remainder of the Word Bearers mimicked his actions. The only sound was the thin keening of the accursed crozius. The weapon was nervous and afraid at the outpouring of ebon psi-energy that lapped about the hooded one's body.

'I would know your mind. Your intentions.' Breathy and disordered, the speech seemed to come from the hazed air itself.

Iskavan could barely keep from spitting as he grated out a reply. 'I intend no less than to fall on the man-beasts with the curse of great Lorgar on our lips! Kill and kill and not yield!'

'No.' The shock of the denial was so great that Iskavan actually dared to look up and into the stygian depths of the hood. A null void stared back at him. 'You will leave this place. I command it.'

A vein throbbed in the Dark Apostle's face. 'Lord, I... You cannot! We are Word Bearers! We do not retreat! Not again!'

Malice hung in the air between them. 'I must be mistaken. For a moment, I thought you had dared to question me, Apostle.'

Iskavan forced himself to be calm. 'No, warmaster. The error was mine.'

'Just so.' The hooded figure shimmered, and for a moment it became ghostly and insubstantial. 'Even now, your personal cruiser evades the mongrels to reach transport range of this world.' It pointed a crooked finger toward the horizon. 'Recover your teleport beacon and prepare to evacuate.'

'My lord–' began the Apostle, in one final, imploring entreaty.

'Go now,' the voice added as an afterthought. Then as suddenly as it had appeared, the figure dissolved into the dark, leaving a psyker-helot quivering in its place. The twisted slave had briefly hosted a fragment of the warmaster's essence. But that fleeting contact had been enough to warp it into a mess of singed flesh.

Iskavan exploded with anger and roared, smashing the helot into bloody chunks with the crozius's blades. 'Tancred!' he shouted, eyes afire. 'Gather the men! As the *Warmaster* commands–' he paused, the emphasis on Garand's rank dripping venom, '–we quit this blighted place!'

AND SO AS dawn crept over the forest of broken monuments, Cybele once more was a domain of the Imperium of man; but the blight of the Word Bearers' filthy touch was on everything, from the earth itself to the scars that criss-crossed the orange-purple sky. Rafen returned from a sweep of the port with Alactus to find Sachiel ministering to Arkio. He was blessing the works of Lucion as the Techmarine fixed a ceramite patching solution over the gouges in his armour.

The priest ended his litany with a whisper of the primarch's name and turned, as if noticing Rafen for the first time. 'Brother,' he began. 'What of the enemy?'

For a moment, Rafen was at a loss for words. He spread his hands to indicate the silent battlefield around them. 'Gone,' he managed, at length.

Arkio grinned, his perfect white teeth showing through his dirt-coated face. 'I knew it would be so! In my bones, I felt it!'

'There's nothing left but the dead and the dying... and us.' Alactus noted. 'We found a few helots here about, and they were dispatched without incident. They appear to have done our job for us, killing one another.'

Sachiel nodded. 'I have word from the *Bellus*. Inquisitor Stele will reach orbit in a matter of hours.'

'They live? Emperor be praised.'

'Indeed,' Sachiel continued. 'The comrade inquisitor informed me that their long-range scanners detected the

Dirge Eterna on a departure course. It seems we gave the sons of Lorgar a bloody nose that sent them scurrying back to the maelstrom!'

Rafen shook his head. 'That… cannot be. The Word Bearers do not retreat. It is not their way…' His jaw tightened. 'Perhaps this is a ploy, honoured priest. They may have salted Cybele with munitions or some sort of delayed-action weapon–'

Sachiel's lips twisted. 'Rafen the Ready, always ready to find fault, eh?' He took a step closer. 'Can you not accept that perhaps our strength of arms was enough to drive them back? Must you belittle our victory even as we hold it in our hands?'

'Strength of arms?' He couldn't keep the incredulous tone from his voice. 'Tell me, Sachiel, did you take part in some *other* battle last night, and not the one where we were outnumbered fourfold by the Traitors? They had us on the brink, and then they let us live! Do you not wonder why?'

The Sanguinary Priest shook his head. 'No, I do not, because my faith answers that question for me. Why did we win?' He placed a hand on Arkio's shoulder plate. 'Victory came to us through the spirit of the Lord Sanguinius himself.' He turned away from Rafen, dismissing him without a word, and addressed the rest of the ragged group of men. 'Hear me, warriors of Baal, sons of the blood! This day you may meet the rising sun with pride and honour, as we drink deep and remember the fallen! Know this,' he paused, drawing his grail from the drawstring pouch on his belt, 'By the credo vitae, Sanguinius is watching over us, guiding our hands…'

Arkio came to his feet as Sachiel spoke, sparing his sibling a brief, troubled glance before he joined the other men in genuflection.

'The primarch walks among us,' Sachiel intoned, studying Arkio's face. 'He moves through our actions.'

Rafen considered Arkio for a long, leaden moment; it was subtle and almost invisible, but the Space Marine could see something changed in his younger brother's manner. It was not the confidence, or the strength that he had grown into in maturity, but an unknowable shift in his eyes. There was a distance, a preoccupation with some inner conflict that he could only guess at.

Overhead, more trails of vapour from debris inched across the heavens, their feathered edges blurred into blades of white.

CHAPTER SIX

THE DIRGE ETERNA moaned. Throughout the cruiser's decks, the bondsman crew and the Word Bearers aboard her felt the vessel's lament. The ship's mood was a reflection of the minds she carried. They had been buoyant and bristling with savagery as they had approached Cybele, but now they were mournful and dispirited as they left the world behind them. Their mission had been a failure, and there was not a single Traitor Marine on *Dirge Eterna* that did not burn with impotent anger and shame.

There had been a very real moment when rebellion flashed in the eyes of these once-men. Iskavan had reappeared on the transmat pad, and as he kicked away the twitching form of a Chaos Space Marine who had malformed in the teleporter, he gave out the order to retreat in a baleful voice that brooked no argument. The Word Bearers had been stunned to hear the words fall from his lips, and only the terrible aspect of his face had kept them from rash and hasty recriminations.

Retreat. It made the ship sick to have that order spoken aboad her.

In the lower decks, where the corrupted practised the unholy consecrations of their wargear or prayed for blasphemous guidance from their gods, word spread of events on Cybele. The *Dirge's* crew had seen the death of the *Ogre Lord* first-hand, but none of them had expected it to cost them the fight. Some of the bolder dissenters wondered aloud if Iskavan had lied about the orders from Warmaster Garand; they gave voice to the opinion that the Dark Apostle had become craven and fled the field of battle in disgrace. Those Chaos Space Marines were all dead now; Tancred's trusted agents had ensured that each one had been isolated and killed with the maximum of agony. To placate his master, the torturer had kept two alive and performed some intricate pain works upon them, as a diversion for Iskavan – but even this amusement did not cheer him and the Apostle had wanted nothing more than to remain in his chambers and nurse his anger.

Once or twice in the past few hours, Tancred's thoughts had drifted towards plotting an escape or some other scheme to hold off the end he had glimpsed on the planet, but each feeble idea flickered out against the inexorable certainty of it all. He might delay or avoid his fate, but Tancred knew that spilled blood never lied to him. It was not that the torturer was a fatalist – he had simply come to realise that he had nowhere else to go.

The cruiser was beyond the gravity shadow of Cybele's gas giant world now, in the free space between the inner orbit zone and the system's asteroid belt. Like everyone on board, as well as the ship herself, Tancred felt directionless and empty. He wandered the decks. Now and then he would brush his tentacles over the breathing walls between the bone stanchions and coo softly to the *Dirge*. Like Iskavan, he too had a fondness for the vessel that extended back for decades. Both of the Word Bearers had been foot soldiers aboard it in earlier black crusades, and Iskavan had come to consider the cruiser charmed. When he had ascended to the command rank of Apostle under Garand, he demanded the Murder-class vessel be the one to bear his flag. Other host masters made their commands on bigger, heavier craft like the Executor-class hulks or even the huge Despoiler battleships, but Iskavan preferred the speedy, nimble cruiser. Both he and Tancred understood its moods; they could sense the ship's will leaking out through the deck plates and the baffles. But on this day, even the sightless, deaf and psi-blind servitors labouring in the cesspools would know that *Dirge Eterna* was dispirited.

The torturer walked without a conscious route in mind, and so it was with mild surprise that he found himself in the gallery above the aft-deck arena. It was a diamond-shaped space, open to the stars above through a glassteel window that was etched with runes and long lines of text that moved like a maggot nest. Below him, a single figure was fighting a dozen scopus drones. Two plasma weapons screamed hot against the fleshy target-servitors. He recognised the Apostle's fighting style in an instant: Iskavan liked to press in close to his foes, even when using a mid-range weapon, and his master's feral anger brought his motions a frantic pace that even the most accomplished warrior could not hope to match. The energy coils atop the plasma pistols burned blue-white with radiation backwash, singing through the spaces between Iskavan's blurry form and the hapless drones. When only two were left, the Apostle suddenly threw the guns away – even though they still glowed with charge – and rushed the servitors. Before the bulky men-forms could react, he was on them, one in each spike-fingered hand, grinding the meat of them together. He roared as he twisted their flesh, folding bone and skin and organ into an indistinguishable mass that oozed between his gauntlets.

Iskavan drew back and spat. The sparring match had fuelled his irritation, rather than cooling it. 'Tancred,' he growled. 'I know you are up there. Come down.'

The torturer did as he was told, and with each step his fear increased. If the Apostle was to end his life for failing him on Cybele, it would be here and now.

As he approached, Iskavan was crouching next to one of the drone's bodies, picking at it. The Word Bearers' commander snagged something fat and grey from the body and ate it. He chewed with a faraway look in his dark eyes. The drone sobbed weakly, barely clinging to its pathetic semblance of life.

'My victory is still on that planet,' he said quietly. 'I would have it now if only we had stayed.' Iskavan threw Tancred a glance. 'Is that not right?'

The torturer nodded. 'As you decree it, magnificence.'

Iskavan stood up and indicated the scopus at his feet. 'Indulge me, Tancred. Perform your augury again. Here, now. With this.'

The demand surprised him and put him off-balance for long moments. 'My lord, that would be… inappropriate…' Tancred fumbled for an excuse.

'Inappropriate?' The Apostle's voice was loaded with menace. 'Do not test what little patience I still have, old ally.'

Resigned, the torturer knelt by the servitor and began to make the sacred signs across the flesh, removing his vibrastave from the scabbard on his hip. 'My reading may not be accurate,' he said through dry lips. 'This body is not properly prepared.'

'Do it,' Iskavan snarled.

Tancred mouthed a word of power and cut the drone open, spilling its innards on the scratched metal floor of the arena. Almost instantly, he saw the same patterns emerging that had come to him in the camp on Cybele, but now they were more urgent. The light and shade were screaming a warning to him. Death was close at hand; it might even be in this very room.

'What do you see?' The Apostle's mouth was at his ear, breath hot and foul with corpse meat.

'I see death,' Tancred blew the words out. 'Death and death and death.'

'The Blood Angels, yes?' Iskavan demanded, pressing into him.

No. Yours and mine. 'I cannot be sure–'

A swift kick took Tancred off his feet, landing him in the charred remnants of another corpse. 'Be sure!' Iskavan roared, eyes afire. 'Or else you are useless to me!'

Above, on the fascia of the glass roof, a glittering shape unfolded from amid the snarls of text, and Tancred was momentarily distracted by it.

'Answer me!' said Iskavan.

'Dark one, above you–'

The Apostle turned just as the sense of a heavy, frigid presence entered the arena space. On the glass, the words merged and shifted into a horned visage that was cut from nightmare cloth. *'Iskavan, and your little lie-spinner. Heed me.'*

Tancred's master dropped to one knee. 'Warmaster. I had expected you to contact me via my astropath–'

Garand's sketch-face became a death mask with a crooked grin. *'This manner of address amuses me. It has so much more bearing than a mere proxy manifestation, yes?'*

'By your will,' Iskavan said. 'My flesh and my soul for Chaos, liege. What would you have us do?'

There was laughter, hollowed by the distance it had travelled across the Immaterium. *'Oh, I taste your anger from here, Iskavan. Your rage is barely contained at the indignity I have forced upon you.'*

As if the Chaos lord's words had given him permission, the Apostle's self-control snapped. 'Yes, rot and blood, yes! Every black soul aboard my ship seethes at this abuse of our war doctrine! I ask of you, warmaster, what possible cause could force us against Lorgar's way?'

The sinister humour faded like vapour. *'Insect! You seek to question me, to seek the meaning in my plans? Your mind is fit for direction and orders, not the match of wits with the Chaos-blessed!'* Garand's face loomed down on them. The glassteel distended and warped with the force of each word. *'Do not presume to comprehend the scope of my intentions, Iskavan. A larger plan is at work and you are merely a small part of it. You are a tool, Apostle, you and your host. Be thankful I grant you a mind at all, unless you desire to become a servitor-vessel for my will!'*

For a moment, Tancred thought that Iskavan would explode with an angry tirade against his master; but instead, the leader of the ninth host closed his eyes. 'As you say it is so, and I ask once more. What would you have us do?'

The warmaster's voice began to dwindle, as if he was losing interest in the conversation. *'Take your ship and return to our base on Shenlong. Reinforcements await you. Assume command at the Ikari Fortress in the capital city and hold there.'*

'And the humans we did not kill on Cybele, what of them?'

The ghost of a dark smile glittered on the glass, fading. *'The Blood Angels will come to you, Iskavan. Of that, you can be certain.'*

THE LANDER SETTLED on spears of white fire. Retro-rockets blew a thin nimbus of smoke away from the starport's main landing pad. Sachiel brought the Space Marines to order as the drop ramp yawned open, allowing a trio of servo-skulls to escape into the air, with their null-gravity impellers humming.

The inquisitor was the first to disembark, advancing fearlessly ahead of the gold-helmeted honour guard that accompanied him. Stele was dressed in field battle dress now. He had discarded the formal cloak he had worn on his first landing and chosen something more practical. He made a show of surveying the ruined starport. One hand clasped the sacred symbol of his order where it dangled from a necklace, the other rested on the grip of an ornate, custom-made lasgun. He gave a grim, measuring nod. 'You have done the Emperor's work this day, Blood Angels.'

'As is our duty,' Sachiel added. 'Comrade inquisitor, what state is the *Bellus*? We feared you might have fallen to the foe.'

Stele gestured to a gaggle of serfs aboard the shuttle and they clambered down in awkward steps with cargo pods in their hands. 'Brother-Captain Ideon is a fine officer, but even his rare skills could not protect her from injury. It will be another day before the ship returns to full operational status.' He allowed himself a thin smile. 'We claimed two archenemy ships and drove one from our sight.' Stele patted Sachiel on the shoulder. 'But you, priest, your actions here were nothing short of Herculean. The killing of a grand cruiser from the ground... Magnificent.'

The Blood Angel bowed. 'Your praise is wrongly directed, lord. It was one of my men who conceived of the plan to shoot down the Chaos hulk.' He indicated Arkio. 'Bloody, bold and resolute, as the best of us are.'

Stele accepted this. 'Brother Arkio, isn't it? Yes, I remember you. I have observed your actions for some time. I sense a bright future stretching out before you.' He glanced at Rafen, standing close by. 'Who is this?'

'Brother Rafen, if it pleases the lord inquisitor,' he replied. 'Of the late Captain Simeon's company.'

'Ah, one of Sergeant Koris's troops.' He turned slate-grey eyes on Rafen, examining him as if he were looking for flaws in a gemstone. 'I see something between you and brave Arkio here. You are brothers by birth, yes?'

'We shared the same parents on Baal Secundus, lord.'

Stele nodded. 'A rarity. It is most uncommon that two siblings from a single generation be found suitable for Astartes recruitment. I'll warrant none here would know the bonds of bloodline as well as you two.'

The comment hung in the air for a moment, and Rafen's eyes narrowed, unsure of the inquisitor's meaning. 'We are all brothers under the wings of Sanguinius,' he said after a pause, repeating the words Sachiel had said a day earlier.

Stele seemed to be content with the answer, and returned his attention to the Sanguinary Priest as the serfs continued to unload the transport ship. 'I have brought fresh supplies from *Bellus* and narthecium for your wounded, Sachiel. You have secured the port?'

'If you wish to call it that,' he said, weariness colouring his tone for the first time. 'Our counter-strike sent confusion through their ranks, to such a pitch that they ran from the field of battle. Brother Lucion detected the energy patterns of multiple teleportation signatures just after dawn. If, as you said, the Word Bearers' surviving starship left orbit, I would say that they were soundly defeated.'

A nerve jerked in Rafen's jaw, but he kept his mouth closed. Stele eyed him. 'You have something to add, Brother Rafen?'

Sachiel aimed a pointed glance at the Blood Angel as he answered. 'Such behaviour is uncommon for the Word Bearers, inquisitor. We should be wary of any victory that comes so easily.'

Stele glanced around at the heaps of the dead. 'One would hardly call this skirmish an easy one, Rafen… But yes, I see your point. It would be unwise to…' The inquisitor's words faded into silence. On the ramp, his lexmechanic froze in place.

Sachiel's face creased in concern. 'Comrade inquisitor? What is wrong?'

'Heed Rafen's words,' Stele intoned. 'I sense the archenemy's taint nearby.'

THE LAND RAIDER had come apart in a storm of shrapnel in the first wave of bombardment from the Word Bearers. While Simeon and his men had been caught unawares at the distant Necropolita, other barrages of laser fire and crude warheads had lanced into the Blood Angels' units left to defend the port. The raider crew had been one of them, and as they had churned up the broad treads of the tank to ride it out of harm's way, the ionised air at the lip of the beam blast flattened it like a hammer. The forward half of the vehicle was torn off in a hurricane of volcano-hot gas, while the rest of it spun away to eventually come to rest, cherry-red and steaming, on the scorched ferrocrete. Throughout Cybele's night cycle, the raider wreckage had contracted and cooled, the metal ticking and snapping. Word Bearers and Blood Angels alike had used the machine for cover in the thick of fighting, but now it stood ignored and forgotten in the lee of shadows cast by columns of smoke. It was less than six hundred metres from the spot where the lander had put down.

Inside the raider's torn hull were many dead men, and the pieces of many more. It was a red profusion of warped ceramite and torn plasteel, the mass of corpses so badly disfigured that it would be difficult to distinguish enemy from ally at first glance. But amid this litter of cold flesh there was one single thing that still lived, although its life was ebbing from an orchard of livid wounds across its torso.

Noro's breath rattled in his clotted throat. He tried very hard not to move each time he sucked in and pushed out a breath. Every last muscle flexion sent darts of pain from his bloated gut, where the cold, leaden weight of a dozen bolter rounds lay lodged in him. In the firefight that took place at the defence battery, Noro took a spread of bullets at close range, and by rights he should have died, but his sheer bad luck and the layers of fat on his corrupted hide had prevented death from taking him easily. And so, with sweet agony lighting him up inside, Noro had finally risen from unconsciousness to crawl on his hands and knees from the missile bunker.

No one had noticed him inching his way across the ground. Above him, cannon fire and hot flame gushed back and forth as he dragged his carcass from one piece of broken cover to the next. With slow and ponderous execution, Noro's thoughts had gradually come around to the matter of what he was going to do. The Word Bearer had been unable to find a medicae or even a helot with rudimentary field surgery skills, and with each passing hour he had grown more and more angry, pressing himself back from the edge of coma through sheer force of hate. When his winding blood trail brought him to the debris of the land raider, he discovered a bolter, undamaged and fully loaded, still gripped in the severed hands of a Blood Angel. Noro took the gun and made himself a hide within the wreck. Quietly nursing his pain, he waited.

STELE CLOSED HIS eyes, and the air seemed to turn greasy and cold. In the next second he looked up and the sensation vanished. 'There!' he snapped, dodging to the right.

Rafen saw the discharge of the bolter before he heard it. The shell cut through the air where Stele had been standing and into the chest of an unlucky servitor behind him. He was just about to turn when the crack of another shot reached his ears, bringing his bolter to bear. 'The raider!' The Blood Angel released a salvo of shots to ring against the wreck's hull and received another blast in return. The rounds went high and wide of him.

Stele's hand came out of nowhere and pressed Rafen's gun downward. 'No, no killing. I want this one alive.'

The inquisitor stood up, presenting himself as a target. His arms were outspread in offering.

'Lord, seek cover!' Sachiel cried. Arkio was already scrambling toward the raider with Alactus a step behind him, but Rafen could see the glitter of light on the weapon's scope as the gun bore down.

Stele looked directly into the unblinking lens of the targeter and Rafen felt the peculiar thickness in the air once again. It was like being on the edge of a storm, concentrated along the channel of the inquisitor's sight line. The Blood Angel's gut knotted at the taint of psyker-scent about him.

Noro's eye could not blink. The muscles on it were rigid as stone, the optic jelly of the orb twitching with impotence. And likewise, no matter how hard he tried, he could not will the finger about the gun's trigger to contract. The Word Bearer was locked in place, unable to do anything but stare into the face of the bald human at the other end of his target sight. The man never moved, but he seemed to grow to fill every inch of the Traitor Marine's perception. At no stage did he speak, but he imposed his will to suffocate any thoughts Noro might have had to run or fight. He wanted nothing more than to scream, to cry out and die and let the wounds have his life at long last.

Stele answered him as the thoughts formed in his mind. 'Your prayers will go unanswered, corrupted one.'

Noro tried to curse him, but there were shapes in red armour clustering in all around him, ripping the gun from his grip and carrying him away.

Rafen watched Arkio and Alactus drag the wounded Word Bearer from the wreck, for a moment believing that the Traitor was dead, because he was rigid and unmoving. 'A survivor. There may be others.'

'Perhaps,' Stele mused. 'In any event, this one will serve us well enough.' He nodded to his lexmechanic. 'Locate somewhere secure and construct a makeshift crucifix. Inform Captain Ideon I am going to delay my return to *Bellus*.' The inquisitor glanced at Rafen and Sachiel. 'Your experience with the tactical situation here will prove useful to me. I will have you attend... I may need you to prompt my investigation.'

'Investigation?' Rafen repeated.

Stele nodded. 'We have an unexpected bounty, Brother Rafen. Soon, we will return to *Bellus* and mark our success with ceremony, but for now, come watch me put this monstrosity to the question.' Without another word, he took off after the lexmechanic, the servo-skulls darting to follow.

Sachiel gave Rafen a look. 'Have a serf bring out a chirurgeon's kit,' he said. 'The inquisitor will require tools.'

WHEN IT WAS done, Rafen felt soiled. He had no sympathy for the Word Bearer, not a single iota of sorrow for the perverse beast – after all, the thing had known the implications of its actions from the moment the Traitor Legion had embraced the Horus Heresy – but the overspill from Stele's searing mind-witchery seemed to cling to everything around him. Ignorant of the Inquisition's methods, Rafen had expected Stele to attack the Word Bearer with blades and barbs, but his technique had been more disturbing than direct. The lexmechanic directed a Techmarine to jury-rig a crude extricator from parts of a sentinel power-loader. With the X-shaped crucifix erected in one of the burnt-out hangars, Stele set to work.

Arkio and Alactus stripped the Traitor of his wargear and torched it with a plasma burst. Unlike the hard ceramite armour of the Blood Angels, the Word Bearer's mail was a curious amalgam of metals and tough, rubbery flesh. It bled profusely when they cut it from him, trailing nerve fibres and veins across the stone floor. When they set it alight, it squealed as it crisped into ash.

The naked bulk of the corrupted was a ruin of scars and open wounds. Stele chose a few of them at random as places to stab fine trepanning needles or skin shears. This was only the opening move. The inquisitor made quite sure that the Traitor was not going to die. He began a whispering conversation with it. Once in a while, the enemy soldier would cry out or curse them all, shaking with horrific violence. Rafen listened hard, but he could not make clear the words the inquisitor spoke. He was only a few feet away, but Stele might well have been on the other side of the world.

There came a moment when he gestured to Arkio, pointing him out to the Word Bearer. The ghost of a smile danced on Stele's lips and the Traitor began to weep. Inch by inch, moment by moment, the Chaos Space Marine broke a little more until finally, in the stifling air thick with ozone and organic waste, it sagged and became little more than a pale sack of meat. For long seconds no one spoke. The only sounds were the wounded, husky breaths that sighed from the Word Bearer.

The inquisitor drew away from it and Rafen saw him lick his lips like a man at the end of a particularly tasty meal. 'Shenlong. This is the world from which they struck at us.'

Sachiel's pale face turned to Rafen. 'Your company is more familiar with this sector than the *Bellus* crew. What do you know of this planet?' His voice could not mask the disquiet at what he had witnessed.

Rafen thought for a moment before answering. 'A forge world, honoured priest. Until very recently, one of ours.'

Stele raised an eyebrow. 'Explain.'

'Shenlong is... was one of many munition manufactories for the Ultima Segmentum. The world became isolated by a warp-storm several months ago, and under cover of the turbulence the planet was invaded by the archenemy. Shenlong and every human on it have been declared lost to the Emperor's light, lord.'

'Indeed?' Stele said, absently tapping a finger on his lips. 'Where is this blighted place?'

'Coreward, perhaps a week's travel in the empyrean.'

The inquisitor digested this information with a slow nod, and then turned to Sachiel. 'Priest, gather the men and prepare to lift for *Bellus*. I must review the information I have gleaned from our friend here.'

'Lord,' Rafen pressed, 'if you are considering that we leave Cybele, you should know that our orders were from Commander Dante himself, to hold post here until relieved–'

Stele waved him into silence. 'We shall see what orders are given, Rafen. We shall see.'

The lexmechanic spoke for the first time. His sibilants hissed and ground together like cogwheels. 'Master Stele, your specimen still lives. If you wish, I will cull it.'

'No,' the inquisitor tossed the word over his shoulder as he walked away. 'Sustain the Traitor for the moment; bring it up to the ship. Its dissection may yield more data of interest to us.'

BY NIGHTFALL CYBELE was home only to the dead. Thunderhawks and cargo lighters from *Bellus* ranged back and forth between the surface, and the battle barge brought up the remains of men and material that might later be salvaged. While Techmarines directed hordes of serfs to repair the warship's warp motors, Apothecaries ministered to jars of amniotic fluid in the infirmary. Each canister contained progenoid glands harvested from the Blood Angels killed in the planetside fighting. Shoals of the spheroid organs floated there within the green, life-sustaining liquids, and inside each lay a precious storehouse of genetic material.

These simple egg-shaped sacs of flesh were the most priceless and delicate resource on the ship. They were even valued more than the holy artefact that had been the object of *Bellus*'s mission. Without the gene-seed that nestled within the progenoids, the future of the Chapter would be threatened. Each was thick with the raw matter of the Blood Angels, nascent zygotes that could be taken and implanted in a new generation of initiate recruits in the chamber vitae of the fortress-monastery on Baal. Through these elaborate knots of genetic complexity, the departed would give life to a new generation of Adeptus Astartes, so beginning the cycle of death and rebirth over again.

Rafen studied the work of his Apothecary brethren through the glass walls of the medicae sanctum. He became lost in the precise ballet of their actions. From the very start of his life in the Blood Angels, Rafen had always admired the work of the men who served the Chapter as field surgeons and biologians: such skills with the workings of the flesh were beyond him.

'Rafen,' the voice was roughened with fatigue.

He turned to face his trusted mentor. 'Brother-sergeant.'

'You left the meal early, Rafen. I was surprised,' Koris said mildly. 'Most of us had an appetite to choke a sand-ox.'

'I had my fill,' he said, a little too quickly. The kitchen vassals of the *Bellus* had provided a rich spread of protein-heavy meats and broth for the survivors of the battle for Cybele, but Rafen's appetite had been lost to him. He ate cured steaks cut from dried fire scorpion, but the taste of home brought him no succour.

Koris watched him. 'This has been a strenuous posting,' he said, with characteristic understatement, 'and tricky. I had not thought we would leave the war grave world again.'

'Nor I,' Rafen agreed. 'But perhaps Sachiel was correct. The primarch watches over us.'

The sergeant spat out a chug of gruff, humourless laughter. 'Our liege lord has better things to do than keep an eye on Space Marines, lad. We are the sharp edge of his blade, no more. We serve and we die, and that is our only glory.'

Rafen laid a gloved hand on the glass partition. 'Glory enough for them, I would hope,' he added, inclining his head toward the progenoid jars beyond.

'Aye, if we ever return home…' Koris looked away.

The Space Marine shot the elder soldier a loaded glance. 'Old man, do not cast out cryptic comments to me like some addled seer. Speak plainly, teacher. We know each other well enough for that.'

Koris gave him a sharp nod. 'Aye, that we do.' He lowered his voice. '*Bellus* was on course for Baal to return the spear, as we all know – but now word has come to me that Stele intends to cut that journey short.'

'We have been aboard this ship for less than a day and already you know this?'

'The manner of how information comes to me is not your concern, lad. Live as long as I have and you'll learn the knack of it too.' Koris's face was a grimace. 'Mark me, the inquisitor intends to turn *Bellus* about and make a new heading.'

Rafen shook his head. 'This will not happen. Captain Simeon's orders were to maintain the garrison on Cybele, and if Stele makes any new dictate it will be to take up that posting.' He pointed at the zygote jars. 'The dead here with us proves that the planet has value to the Traitors… He could not simply abandon it.'

A thin sheen of anger coated Koris's words. 'Lad, how can you be blind to what takes place right in front of you? For all Stele's honour debts with our Chapter, what is he? A servant of the Ordo Hereticus, not a Blood Angel! He will seek the path that brings him glory, as every blighted one of his kind will do!'

'Sergeant, there are many who would see the taint of heresy in those words.'

'Then the warp curse them,' hissed the veteran. 'I have no time for the petty edicts of such men. Do you not see, Rafen? This fray on Cybele turns the battle lust of our brothers, and Stele only needs to mould it if he wishes to use it for himself.'

'How could he do such a thing?' Rafen dismissed the older Space Marine and made to walk away, but Koris snared his arm in an iron grip. 'Brother-sergeant…'

'Some of the men have already begun to speak about Arkio,' Koris whispered darkly. 'His bravery on the surface with the daemon, the ploy that ended the *Ogre Lord*… They credit him with the victory.'

'So they should,' he replied hesitantly. 'My brother showed uncommon daring.'

'Uncommon, yes. Such that some think him blessed by Sanguinius.'

'Maybe he is.' The answer tasted flat and dry in Rafen's mouth.

'And who would gain by exploiting such a thing, lad? Consider that.'

Rafen shook off the veteran's grip with an angry jerk. 'You have always been my most resolute mentor, Koris, but you let your distrust of all things blind you.'

The sergeant accepted this with a slow nod. 'Perhaps, but if you ever fail to question what lesser men take on faith, Rafen, then it is you that is truly blind.' The elder Blood Angel stalked away, leaving his former student to weigh his words in silent consideration.

CHAPTER SEVEN

THE GRAND CHAMBER on the *Bellus* could dwarf the cathedrals of some colony worlds. It was a cloister for giants: huge column-towers rose up to an arched roof that webbed together with beams and vaults. At the far end, past the tight ranks of worshipful Space Marines, the wall that faced the bow of the battle barge was dominated by a circular lens of stained glass and worked metals: it was a rendition of the Lord Sanguinius in his most bloody aspect. The sun-bright gold of his sacred armour was streaked with the scarlet blood of his enemies, and his head was thrown back in a roar of victory. As he entered the chamber, Brother Rafen found his attention was instantly drawn to the shining white fangs bared in the primarch's open mouth. He found himself suddenly aware of the same sharp teeth in his own jaw. Like the handsome, noble profile that he shared with his brethren, it was just one aspect of the genetic lineage that connected them to the godlike figure in the glass.

Rafen had never been aboard *Bellus*, and so the majesty of the hall was new to him. As he walked forward among the solemn lines of battle-brothers, he found it hard not to become drawn into the myriad devotional artworks and stone scrolls of script work fashioned overhead. There were whole Chapters from the Book of Lemartes, and pages from the testaments of the lords of Baal, all cut in obsidian that glittered like dark arterial blood.

And still, his eyes were constantly pulled back to the glass. The closer he got to the altar at the head of the chamber, the more detail seemed to rise from the image. Now he could see the shadowy shape of the Emperor above and to the right of Sanguinius. He was looking down on him with cool pride. Arrayed around the edges of the disc were versions of moments from the blessed angel's life – as an infant, falling to the surface of Baal; a boy, killing a fire scorpion with his bare hands; airborne on his angelic wings, flame licking about his gaze; and in single combat with the arch-traitor Horus, just before his own death. For a moment, Rafen felt transported by the sight of it, as if he were home on Baal Secundus once more. All the confusion and emotion of the past few days was gone – but then he spied the shape of the gas giant planet looming beyond the pane and the instant was gone.

They reached the place of honour near the altar and as one, Rafen and the rest of the survivors from the battle on Cybele dropped to one knee. The sharp tang of the sacrament incense drifted down on them from the floating sensors above.

In the silence of the chamber, Sachiel's voice was a breaking wave of noise as his armour's audial pickups broadcast his words to speakers hidden in colonnades about the hall. 'Yea, for the Emperor and Sanguinius, we stand and we serve.'

Every Space Marine in the room repeated the phrase; the walls rumbled with the chorus. From the corner of his eye, Rafen could see Arkio silently mouthing a litany and beyond him

Lucion, Turcio and Corvus. The Techmarine held one hand to the Adeptus Mechanicus cogwheel-and-skull symbol on his chest, while Corvus clasped absently at the healing wound the daemon-beast had inflicted on him. Turcio was immobile, eyes tightly shut.

The Sanguinary High Priest climbed a coil of wooden steps to the broad pulpit, and bowed to a flickering hololith of Brother-Captain Ideon. In millennia past it had been tradition to have the ship's commander present during a mass, but war had evolved to the point where captains were now permanent fixtures on the bridge, so this was no longer possible. Ideon was still present in spirit if not flesh. He was alone on the command deck with his senses hardwired into the machine-ghost of the *Bellus*. He would observe the ceremony through the eyes and ears of the innumerable monitors dotted about the grand chamber's expanse.

Rafen raised his head slowly and for the first time noticed Inquisitor Stele in the shadows of the platform. He was watchful of Sachiel in the same manner that the Emperor of Mankind watched Sanguinius in the glass image above.

Sachiel stood behind the lectern and placed his hands on the winged blood droplet that crested it. 'This day we give thanks to our lord and the master of mankind for the glorious bounty of war. We pledge our lives and our very blood to Sanguinius, our faith and our honour, until death.'

'Until death,' cried the chorus.

The priest gave a pious nod. 'We venerate our brothers who fell on Cybele. Some of them were proud men who had given their oath to the mission of the *Bellus*. Sadly they will now never see it completed.' He opened a large book bound in the dun-coloured hide of a Baalite sand shark and ran a finger along a line of names. Each one was freshly written in blood. 'We speak of them now and charge their lives to the memory of the sepulchre of heroes. Know their sacrifice and honour it.'

From behind him, Rafen heard the faintest of sighs. Koris was kneeling there, and Rafen wondered how many of these ceremonies the veteran had witnessed. Too many, he would warrant.

Sachiel began the roll call of the dead. 'Brother-Captain Simeon. Brother-Sergeant Israfel. Brother Bennek. Brother Hirundus. Apothecary Veho–'

With each name, the Blood Angels gave a gesture of salute, touching their balled fists to the places on their chests beneath which beat their primary and secondary hearts. There were thousands of fingers tapping in unison on their torso plates, signifying that the dead men would live on in the hearts of their brethren.

After the procession of names, deeds and honours, the priest's litany came to a close and Sachiel shut the book with grim finality. As Rafen watched him, the Space Marine remembered his thoughts in the graveyard. He wondered when his name would be read aloud to such a gathering. With a blink, he brushed the distracting thought away, just as a new voice rose to fill the chamber's stillness.

'Comrade Brother Sachiel, I wish to address these brave warriors,' Stele stepped forward from the back of the pulpit and surveyed the assembled men. The lamplight glittered off the intricate working of threads on his cloak. The complex letter-string design was similar to the tent-cloth Rafen had seen down on Cybele. No doubt they were psionic wards or some such arcane magick against the enemy's mind-witches.

Sachiel gave a shallow bow to the inquisitor and allowed Stele to take the stage. 'Blood Angels, hear me,' he said, in rich stentorian tones. 'Know that the Lord of Man has worked through us in this challenging engagement with the archenemy. It was by His will that those of us on board the *Bellus* intercepted the cry for help from the *Celeano* and came to Cybele. It was by His will that we were able to drive back the hordes of the hated Word Bearers, on the surface and here in the void. In His eyes and in those of His most trusted warrior Sanguinius, we are blessed.' Stele grew rueful in his expression. 'Here, so far from their birth world, the brothers who fought and died might have fallen unremembered by those who remained on Baal, but we will never forget them.'

Rafen's eyes narrowed as a ripple of agreement slipped around the chamber. The inquisitor was being careless with his choice of words – such a statement might be thought by some to cast doubt on the Chapter's dedication to distant, less important missions, such as the Cybele garrison.

Stele continued. 'And now the choice faces us, warriors. Do we remain and bury the dead without taking vengeance? Or do we bring the wrath of the Imperium and the Blood Angels to the Chaos filth on Shenlong?' Dark light glinted in his eyes. 'You who have served and fought with me these ten long years will know my heart on this concern!'

Many of the assembled Space Marines growled and spat at the name of the enemy. For a moment the hall was a jumble of voices. Rafen heard Koris give a cynical grunt. The veteran's earlier prediction was coming to pass.

'Lord inquisitor,' Sachiel said quietly, his voice barely audible beyond the confines of the pulpit. 'I would of course endorse you in this action, but the matter is unresolved. If we were to leave Cybele without sanction from Lord Dante–'

Stele smiled thinly. 'The commander will see the merit in my orders, Sachiel. You know that to be true.' Before the priest could answer, the inquisitor raised his hands to call for silence. 'Blood Angels! There is no doubt that your primarch turns his beneficent gaze toward us! We are the soldiers of the *Bellus*, and we bear the very weapon that Sanguinius was granted by the God-Emperor himself!'

There was movement behind the pulpit and a gaggle of shrouded servitors from Stele's retinue came forward. They carried a lengthy case cast from solid titanium, the surface intricately worked with symbols of the Chapter, the Imperium and the Ordo Hereticus. Rafen felt a physical shock as he realised what the container was for. *By the Throne! The spear!*

'Our victory on Cybele was our sacred duty,' the inquisitor glanced down at the assembled Space Marines before him, 'but there is one among you who excelled, who showed the true power of the birthright that sings in your blood, even when defeat was upon us!' Stele's eyes locked on Rafen's sibling. 'Brother Arkio! Come forward.'

Arkio did as he was ordered and stood up, climbing into the pulpit. Stele's servitors halted before the young Blood Angel and presented him with the metal case.

'Open it,' Stele ordered him. 'In recognition of your daring, yours shall be the honour of presenting the Spear of Telesto.'

Arkio reached out and with trembling hands turned the latches that sealed the container closed. Behind him, Sachiel gripped his grail and uttered the words of the litergus integritas.

A joyful warmth infused the metal as Arkio laid his hands upon it. When he slid the clamshell container open he saw inside an object as bright as a shard of the sun.

The radiance from the weapon swept across the length of the grand chamber in a wave of pale golden light. Below the pulpit Rafen stifled a gasp as the glow caressed the bare skin of his face. From the corner of his eye, he saw Turcio avert his gaze; he was overcome by emotion. But Rafen could not look away from it. There, before him was the Spear of Telesto in all its mellifluent glory. The Riga tapestries did not even come close to the majesty of the sacred lance.

The blade itself, an elongated tear cut with a hollow in the centre, represented the single drop of blood that Sanguinius shed when he swore fealty to the Emperor. Glittering with an inner light, it rested atop a sculpted haft that showed the angel of blood, clad in the monastic vestments of a Sanguinary High Priest. His perfect face was lost in a voluminous hood and his mighty angel wings spread against the air; and below that, a single purity seal that bore the personal mark of the Emperor himself. It was the most incredible sight Rafen had ever seen, and his heart ached with it.

Once more the words rang out across the hall, this time from Arkio's lips. 'For the Emperor and Sanguinius!' Rafen's brother felt the nerves in his arms tingling as his blood surged with adrenaline. The gene-template of the spear's ancient technology could sense his closeness and the fragmentary elements of the Sanguinius's stock that sang though his veins. Unbidden, Arkio broke protocol and touched the ageless lance.

'No–!' Sachiel blurted, starting forward to grab the Blood Angel's hand. He advanced barely a half step before Stele snared him and held him back. The inquisitor shook his head once, eyes cold with menace, and the priest was suddenly cowed.

Arkio's limbs seemed to work mechanically, and he removed the weapon from the case, raising it in his left hand in a mirror image of the Riga artwork's last panel: Sanguinius victorious over the corpse of Morroga. The spear vibrated in his grip like a live thing, a streak of amber lightning frozen into physical form. Uncanny energy lit the teardrop blade from within and, like a supernova, a pulse of white light flared.

Rafen saw the colour wash across his brother's body and Arkio's flesh seemed to melt into the features of his liege lord. His crimson battle armour turned gold and white wings flared from his shoulders. Then, just as quickly the spear grew quiescent again and the vision was gone.

The silence that followed was so complete that for a brief instant Rafen feared he might have been struck deaf. But a moment later every Blood Angel in the chamber erupted in full voice, calling out the name of their primarch until the very walls seemed to shudder with the sound of it. *Blood's oath! Did I truly witness this? Could my brother be touched by the angelic sovereign himself?* The questions hammered at the inside of Rafen's mind, rocking him to his core.

In the pulpit, where Sachiel stood transported by the sight and Arkio's face was wet with tears of joy, the Inquisitor Stele watched the young Blood Angel with satisfaction. Despite himself, he was unable to keep a thin, icy smile from his lips.

WORD OF THE 'miracle' in the grand chamber spread like wildfire throughout the decks of the *Bellus*, to every Space Marine and serf in the service of the Blood Angels' Chapter. Arkio's moment in the pulpit was replayed over and over on devotional screens dotted throughout the battle barge, and the effect was electric. Believing their mission ended, the morale of the Space Marines abroad the *Bellus* had dipped once they had set course for home. Each of them had been proud to have completed their task and they were looking forward to seeing Baal again, but a subtle melancholy was stalking the ship all the same. The *Bellus* crew knew their odyssey was nearly at an end, and it saddened them

But no longer. Arkio's presentation of the spear rekindled the bright fury of the Blood Angels and for the survivors on Cybele it became a rallying point. Men who had stood with

Rafen and been ready to welcome death with open arms changed overnight. Suddenly they became fierce and blood-hungry. During firing rites and maintenance duties, even in the midst of daily battle drills, conversations turned towards the battle-brother the men called 'the Blessed', and the burning need for vengeance on the denizens of Shenlong.

Bellus remained in orbit of the mausoleum planet for several days as work on the engine repairs approached completion, and it came as no surprise to Rafen when Sachiel ordered an increase in tactical ground assault drills. He tried to find Sergeant Koris, but the aged veteran was elusive. Change flashed through the air aboard the battle barge, and in its wake a need for war resonated in the hearts of every Space Marine. If blood was not soon shed, he reflected, the men would go wild.

Rafen's mind was a storm of conflicts. He had not laid eyes on his sibling since the end of the ceremony for the fallen, but Arkio had constantly remained at the forefront of his mind. Try as he might, he could not shake the indelible image of his younger brother cast in the guise of Sanguinius. The vision in the grand chamber echoed the brief moment of dislocation he had experienced on Cybele during the Word Bearers' assault. At the time he had thought himself fatigued and distracted by the turn of events, but now the incident had taken on another, more troubling quality.

Rafen was no psyker, nor some mind-witch cursed with aberrant sight, and yet the brief visions had been clear as day. In other circumstances, he might have suspected that the flaw was exerting its insidious influence on him, but the taint of the black rage was a maddening, berserker force and never so subtle. Turcio, Lucion and Corvus all spoke of the pulse of light and the silence that followed it. Their voices were reverent with awe when they mentioned Arkio's name, and Rafen soon grew weary of Blood Angels he did not know pestering him with inconsequential questions about his brother. He kept his own counsel, but in truth, Rafen was not sure what to make of Arkio's so-called 'blessing'. He loved his brother, and he knew him as well as only those bound by family could, but something rang ill in his mind. It lurked, faint and dim in the corners of his thoughts, colouring his every waking moment. With such doubts in his soul, he went searching for Koris.

INQUISITOR STELE HAD made good use of the interrogation chambers on *Bellus* throughout the duration of its mission to find the Spear of Telesto. Many were the victims that had passed through the brass iris hatch to gaze upon the last thing they would ever know in life: the engines of inquest, the tables with fans of sinister blades and the chair bolted to the deck. Over the years as *Bellus* had moved from world to world, Stele had ordered his retinue to alter the basic mechanisms used by the Space Marines to hold prisoners. They had gradually crafted an inquisitorial tool that resembled the great siege perilous in the schola hereticus where he had studied. Stele ranged his gaze around the chamber as he entered, taking in the dark metal stanchions, the wreaths of incense and the shadowed deep beyond the floating glow-globes. It was a fine stage for a player such as he.

Removing his cloak, he brushed a little dust from his fingers before crossing to the torture chair. The Word Bearer, the heretic that called himself Noro, was restrained there. He was bloody and pallid, but he still lived. Stele gave the bullet wounds on his torso a measuring gaze. They had scabbed over with flecks of black matter, but continued to weep pus and thin fluids. It would be a while yet before he would die.

'Eminence,' said the lexmechanic, announcing itself with a grind of leg-irons. 'I have continued to transcribe every utterance of the Traitor. He has done little but bombard me with foul language and unholy curses.'

The inquisitor nodded, his gaze flicking up to the servo-skulls that orbited around him in languid circles. 'Seek penance once your duties here are complete, then,' he ordered. 'Cleanse yourself of exposure to such apostasy.'

'Your will.' The servitor bowed.

Stele approached the Word Bearer and with great effort, the enemy soldier raised his head. He had to smother a flicker of pleasure when he saw the fear ignite in Noro's eyes. Nothing excited Stele more than the certainty that he instilled terror in others. He put on a mocking face. 'Does it hurt, little traitor?'

Remarkably, the Word Bearer summoned some strength and threw him a defiant grimace. 'Death to you and your corpse-god, maggot excrement!'

A smile crept across the inquisitor's face. 'Ah, good. You still have some fight left in you. There is no challenge in draining the mind of one utterly broken, I have found. Such easy tasks dull one's skills.'

'Begone!' snapped Noro, his voice cracking. 'Leave me and take congress with animals, man-filth!'

The lexmechanic twitched as if the insults were a physical blow. 'Lord, what purpose is served by keeping this specimen alive? I intuit that it is an inferior heretic, not privy to any information of value beyond what you have already extracted.'

'No, I beg to differ,' said Stele, glancing at the servitor. Then he looked away and in an utterly different voice he said a single word. '*Somnus.*'

The statement hung in the air like coils of smoke, and it made the lexmechanic twitch. Then without warning, the bondsman's eyes rolled white into his head and he lolled in a nerveless slump. Behind him, the three servo-skull monitors settled gently to the floor and fell silent. The utterance triggered a post-hypnotic suggestion that Stele had long ago planted in the lexmechanic's mind, and in the brains of the centuries-dead servants whose skulls were now his mechanical guardians. Until the inquisitor chose otherwise, he and his victim were alone in this place. Every monitor and sensor that studded the interior of the rest of the Blood Angels' battle barge was diverted from this room. It had been one of the first things that Stele had done after boarding *Bellus* ten years earlier.

Noro was fully aware of what was happening around him, and confusion crossed his face. Stele spared him a look and then stepped very close to the Word Bearer. Noro tried to avoid the inquisitor's touch, but with his body held to the chair by thick iron rods, there was little that he could do to stop him. Stele cupped the Traitor Marine's head in his hands and for one terrifying moment, Noro thought the bald man was going to kiss him. 'What... What are you doing?'

'You will tell me all you know of Shenlong's defences, creature,' he whispered.

'I'll give you no more. You took the planet's name from me, and for that alone I have failed my covenant...' He took a shuddering breath. 'Go to Shenlong, human, go there and meet my brothers! They'll devour you raw!'

The inquisitor pressed his jaw shut. 'Soon enough, but first we must sit a spell and talk, you and I.'

'No–' the Word Bearer forced out a denial. 'I'll die first.'

'In time,' Stele agreed, the aquila electro-tattoo on his forehead glinting, 'but before you do, you will show me all.'

Noro's face went cold as the heat from his feverish skin was sucked away by the inquisitor's icy fingertips. He felt his rough, diseased flesh shift and melt. Stele's digits merged into his epidermis and then through it like soft clay, into the bone and brain matter inside. The Word Bearer tried with all his might to force out a scream, but Stele closed his throat with a slight gesture of pressure.

Just as before on the surface of Cybele, the inquisitor filled the Traitor Marine's vision, but this time he grew and grew, flowing like liquid to fill the empty vessel of Noro's perception. With him came an ink-black shroud of silence that suffocated the heretic; it was an immutable shade, the colour of terror. The Word Bearer had served the lords of Chaos all his life and revelled in the dark ways of the eightfold Undivided, but now what he saw uncoiling from the man-thing's mind struck him as the absolute purity of evil. Noro had never dared, never in his most savage and murderous moments, to believe that something so utterly abhorrent to life could exist. This was no human psyker phantom; it was the undistilled taint of hatred, clinging to the man like a parasite. As Noro's sanity came apart inside him, the Inquisitor Lord Ramius Stele began the slow and deliberate rape of the Traitor's mind.

The lexmechanic had been correct: the Word Bearer was no more than a line soldier, a Chaos Space Marine with nothing other than the will to fight and die for the word of Lorgar. A higher-ranking veteran would have direct knowledge of military dispositions and troop concentrations, but Noro could only offer fleeting memories of the invasion of Shenlong – flashes of atrocities and bloodletting that lodged in the killer's mind.

'Nothing–' Noro managed to shove the word from his lips.

Stele's eyes narrowed, and he marshalled the dark around him, coiling it into razored ribbons of psi-stuff. Then, with abominable precision, he flayed open the heretic's memories. Noro began to shake and twitch as the floodgates of experience opened in him. Suddenly *everything* that had ever happened to him was recalled at once, and his mind shrivelled under the weight of it. Casting through the ocean of recall, Stele trawled for the smallest of incidents, patterning them and weaving them together against the black. He took sideways glances, momentary snatches of conversation overheard, and blinks of remembrance. Stele discovered a myriad of fragmentary sights that not even the Word Bearer was aware he had seen and laced them into a whole. There, in jigsaw-pieces, were the approaches to Shenlong, the paths along the ever-shifting corridors between the minefield blockade that encircled the forge world.

Swiftly he withdrew from the heretic's flesh and mind and stepped away. A thin sheen of sweat coated his brow. 'Ah,' Stele croaked, dry-throated. 'Thank you.'

Noro vomited explosively, throwing up bile and blood. 'What...' The Chaos Space Marine's voice was a hissing shriek. 'For hate's sake, what are you?'

The inquisitor stepped around the inert lexmechanic and recovered a dull metallic object from a secret inner pocket of his cloak. He did not grace the Word Bearer with an answer.

The prisoner had fouled himself in fright. Mad alarm shone bright in his reddened eyes. 'No human could...'

Stele walked back to the torture chair, concealing the thing in his hand. 'What are you babbling about, creature?' he asked idly.

Noro indicated the lexmechanic, the hatchway and the world outside it with spastic jerks of his head. 'They can't see it...' The Word Bearer suddenly broke into hysterical laughter, 'but I can!'

'Be silent.' Stele's hand came around to Noro's throat. In a blur of motion the weapon in his hand cut cleanly across the thick meat of his neck as if it were passing through thin air. Thick blood flooded out in a gush, choking the Word Bearer into stillness. After a moment, the inquisitor began the careful task of cleaning the stiletto molly-knife he had used to dispatch it. The weapon's fractal blade was so sharp that the task of wiping blood from it took slow and careful deliberation.

When he was done, Stele spoke the command word again. The lexmechanic and servo-skulls returned to wakefulness with no perception of missing time. He was halfway to the door when the servitor remarked. 'The specimen... He appears to have taken his own life...'

'Yes,' Stele noted absently. 'You saw it happen, didn't you?'

The lexmechanic gave a slow blink, as if the progress of that thought was particularly sluggish in its mind. 'I saw it happen,' it replied, after a lengthy pause.

'Have it dissected,' said the inquisitor, and then as an afterthought, he added, 'and the heart and the skull – have them sent to my quarters.'

RAFEN FOUND THE veteran in heated debate with Sachiel as he entered the *Bellus*'s tacticarium. Normally, a rank-and-file Space Marine of his standing would have been denied access without the permission of a senior battle- brother, but his connection to Arkio suddenly made such concerns trivial in the eyes of the men-at-arms who guarded the hatchway.

'Why ask my opinion if you do not heed it?' Koris was saying. 'Or do you merely wish me to tell you what you want to hear?'

Sachiel's face hardened. 'Your words are always noteworthy, Brother Koris, but that does not guarantee I must follow them. Do not forget yourself, sergeant!'

Rafen noticed Arkio standing to one side, back-lit by the glow of a hologrammatic display tank. His sibling caught his eye and nodded a greeting. Rafen saw the mirror of his own face there, drawn by fatigue. Perhaps the 'miracle' had been harder on his brother than he suspected.

'I have conferred with the inquisitor and I concur with his recommendations. *Bellus* will withdraw from orbit and set out for Shenlong with all alacrity,' said the priest. 'It is only fitting that we take the Word Bearers the reprisal they are so richly due.'

Koris snorted. 'What does a torture-master and questioner know of Space Marine tactics? Think, Sachiel! Shenlong sits amid an ocean of nuclear void mines that an Imperial grand fleet would have difficulty in destroying! I would never deny that the Chaos rabble deserve to drown in their own blood, but *Bellus* is just one ship – how can we hope to penetrate such defences?'

The priest flicked a glance at Arkio. 'Sanguinius will provide the means,' he snapped.

'Really?' Koris arched an eyebrow, and looked at the young Space Marine. 'Tell me, will he reach out and sweep the mines from the sky for us?' He snorted. 'I have been a son of Sanguinius for twice your life span, Sachiel, and I know that he helps those who help themselves... And without help we cannot crack Shenlong!'

'The inquisitor has secured the secret approaches to the planet,' Arkio said quietly. 'The way through the mines is known to him.'

Sachiel smiled thinly. 'You see, Koris? Your concerns are unfounded.'

'Are they? Suppose we *do* make it to strike range of the surface, what then? With our losses on Cybele, this battered company is well below full strength.'

Rafen spoke for the first time. 'The Word Bearers' forces on Shenlong will be superior in numbers,' he said, announcing his presence.

The priest eyed him. 'A single Blood Angel inspired by the righteous power of the Emperor is worth a dozen Traitors! We do not fear them!' He rounded on Rafen. 'You lack faith in the decisions of your superiors, Rafen, I see it in your eyes! We must strike while we have the element of surprise... Every day we tarry, the corrupted reinforce themselves on a world they stole from the Imperium!'

'If it pleases the high priest, all I suggest is that we seek reinforcements from Baal,' retorted Rafen. 'We should remain at Cybele until Commander Dante can send us more ships, then we can leave a holding force here and sortie to Shenlong in good order–'

Sachiel silenced him with a shout. 'No! We have the blessing of the primogenitor on our side and our victory is assured! Look around you, Rafen!' He cast his arms wide to encompass the other Blood Angels in the room. 'Your brothers are blood-hungry! They do not wish to wait for reinforcements; they want to make the Word Bearers pay! Pay for every soul taken and inch of earth soiled with their worthless lives!'

Rafen felt a light touch on his arm and looked up into Arkio's eyes. 'Trust me, brother, when I promise you we can succeed.'

Sachiel turned his back on Koris, dismissing him, and called to the serf attending him. 'Pass the word to Captain Ideon. Under my orders, the command is given! We weigh anchor and warp for Shenlong!'

Koris stalked from the room without another word, leaving Rafen to watch his old mentor go.

CHAPTER EIGHT

THE WARP BOILED at the edges of Ramius Stele's mind. The hot touch of the raw, inchoate energies licked at his soul in searing, unearthly caresses. And yet these were merely faint ghosts of the true power of the empyrean, refracted through the ever-present barrier of the ship's geller field. The inquisitor delighted in it. He was alone in his private chambers aboard *Bellus*, and he had the freedom to direct himself into the trance-state where his mental vigour had free reign. As the battle barge carried itself through the trackless gulf of the empyrean, Stele willingly relaxed the complex psionic shields that guarded his mind and allowed himself to hear the babbling screams and entreaties of the things that lived in the non-space realm. Giddy with it, he let himself teeter on the edge of the psychic abyss, excited by the danger and the adrenaline rush like a climber atop the highest mountain. Only he had the power of will to hold himself back from the brink of madness where other men would have faltered. Only Ramius Stele was possessed of such mental strength as to resist the siren call.

Life moved out there, not the shapes of organic substantiality that lived in the material domain, but constructs of pure thought and raw, raging emotion. He listened to them as they cut invisibly past *Bellus*, rode their wakes and took the smallest morsels of mental sustenance from their passage. This was Stele's most secret vice, the sin that he hid deep in his soul, far from the casual telepathic probes of the few Blood Angels Librarians that still served aboard the ship – and for that, it was made all the more sweet. Each time it became a little harder to reel himself back into the world of crude matter, each time he dallied a little longer than before. But he revelled in it, even though he knew it might destroy him.

When *Bellus* made the transit from the Immaterium and into the void at the edge of the Shenlong system, Stele gave a wan sigh and gathered himself together. The inquisitor observed a minor engagement from the window of his chamber, as *Bellus* caught a Word Bearer Iconoclast-class destroyer on picket ship duty. The vessel's commander had been hideously inattentive, and barely had half his void shields been raised before the battle barge's main guns had ravaged the knife-blade hull. Burning like an oil-soaked rag, the slaughtered destroyer tumbled away into space. Stele gave a nod of approval. The quick killing of the Chaos starship guarding the warp point would allow *Bellus* to continue its approach to Shenlong undetected. If his schemes fell into place as he had foreseen, the Blood Angels would be well within strike range of the forge world by the time the Word Bearers knew they had intruders.

He mumbled a short prayer of petition to the hololithic display tank in his quarters, and the device obeyed. It projected an image of Shenlong from the ship's long-range sensor pits. Hazy and indistinct, the unremarkable planet drifted with vast bands of tiny spheres girdled about it. Stele extended a finger into the hologram and ran it over the floating dots. Each one was a compact thermonuclear charge, a city-killer warhead riding a thruster nest with a simple logic engine to command it. As the planet turned, so they communicated with one another to form a perfect, impenetrable net about the manufactory world. The inquisitor dragged up a fragment of memory from the stores of hypno-taught facts impressed into him as an initiate of the Ordo Hereticus. Shenlong had been a weapons fabricator since the Dark Age of Technology, here they built shells and bombs for a billion little wars in continent-sized production plants. The secrets of the minefield that shrouded it were, like so much in the Imperial era, lost to terra's tech-magi. Stele gave a slight sneer. The curtain of atomic death had not stopped the archenemy from perverting men in positions of power, to grant them the secret corridors through the ever-shifting field of weapons. And now he had done the same, ripping the way from the memories of the dead beast Noro. Still, it would be a slow and dangerous approach. They would have to avoid other Chaos patrol ships and hold fast to a course that was as reliable as the mind of a maddened killer.

The inquisitor turned as the faint taste of a psyker reached his telepathic senses. Smothering his disdain, he gestured to a machine-bound servitor and it released the seal on the door to the chamber. The hatch dilated to reveal a pair of Blood Angels and a hooded figure trailing a train of mechadendrites behind him.

The aged Master Horin. Stele knew the astropath before he saw him. After all this time, he could mark the mind-scent of every psyker on board *Bellus* with perfect accuracy – and this one he found particularly objectionable. The bony old fool was a stubborn creature, and far less susceptible to subtle coercion.

'Lord inquisitor,' began the telepath, 'as your orders command, I bring you a communication of the utmost urgency. A message arrived after our emergence from the warp.'

Stele studied the stunted man-thing. Vitae tubules and connectors that webbed Horin into his machine pulpit trailed across the floor behind him, drooling out watery nourishment fluids. The astropath had forcibly extracted himself from his console and come to Stele's chambers, rather than dictate the signal to his coterie of quill-servitors. Did he detect some faint irritation in Horin's sibilant voice? A glimmer of resentment at being forced to take the message he carried not to Captain Ideon, but to Stele for first approval? The inquisitor gave a slight smile. It was difficult to read the emotional states of an astropath – if they even had them at all. 'Warriors, you are dismissed,' he said. 'Wait outside.'

The astropath gave the slightest sideways glance at the Space Marines as they left him alone. It was irregular that a command-level communication would not be voiced within earshot of a senior Blood Angel. Stele watched him intently. The inquisitor's mental feelers wove invisible patterns in the air, seeking some sense of the moment.

'You have news from Baal,' Stele said slowly, the smile fading. 'You have told no one else?'

'Your orders demanded nothing less,' said the astropath. 'I have not spoken the signal until now.'

The inquisitor came closer, the action deceptively casual. 'Then speak.'

Harmonics inside the astropath's augmented throat resonated for a moment, and then it uttered a string of numbers. 'Cipher, omnis secunda. Directed to Ideon, brother-captain commanding warship *Bellus*. Telepathic duct, Astropath Horin. Penned by his High Lord Commander Dante of the Blood Angels.'

Stele frowned at the mention of Dante's name and began formulating the steps he would be forced to take.

The timbre of the astropath's voice took on a more husky tone, but the words came in faltering starts. Horin carefully reconstructed the message, careful to speak it in the order that it had been written. His words were Dante's, parroted from across the void. 'Honoured Captain Ideon, and the Lord Stele, my greetings to you... The *Celaeno's* call for succour has reached us and we are gratified that *Bellus* may come to the aid of our brethren.' Horin licked his dry lips. 'It is my decree that *Bellus* remain on station and assist in holding the Cybele outpost. Secure the planet and communicate your status with haste. A relief force will be dispatched on receipt of your reply.' There was a moment's pause, and Stele wondered if the astropath was eyeing him, 'This is my command, for the glory of the Emperor and Sanguinius. Dante, Chapter Master of the Blood Angels.' The psyker twitched, and punctuated the ending of the message with a quiet cough of sound.

Stele was quite close to him now. 'Thank you, Horin,' the bald man said, using the astropath's given name for the first time in ten years.

He nodded. 'By your leave, then, I will inform Captain Ideon that we must return to Cybele.'

'No, that won't do,' Stele said conversationally. 'That won't happen.'

Horin's mechadendrites stiffened. 'The message stated–'

Stele shook his head. 'There was no message. You came here to kill me.'

The astropath's hood jerked, as if the statement had been a slap in the face. 'What is the meaning of this?'

The inquisitor cocked his head to get a look at Horin's hidden face, and from nowhere, hot sparks of colour began to lick around his fingers. Stele's eyes flashed with witch-fire. 'Dance for me,' he whispered.

The astropath froze, he had been granted one terrible moment to understand just what Stele's intentions were. Then his muscles rebelled against all conscious controls and the elderly psyker's mind-barriers shattered. Unable to stop himself, he launched at the inquisitor with clawed fingers and bared teeth. 'Nuuuuhh–'

Stele worked a bore of mental energy into the centre of Horin's mind and twisted it. The astropath spat and hissed like an animal. His eyes revealed the terrified truth that he had no command over his own flesh. 'Guards!' Stele shouted at the top of his lungs. 'Help me!'

The two Blood Angels raced into the room to see the inquisitor wrestling with Horin. 'The astropath is tainted! The warp has poisoned him with madness!' Stele gave the old man a vicious shove and he stumbled back a few steps.

The Space Marines needed no further prompting. They tore Horin apart with snap-fire bursts from their bolters. Shells ripped exotic metals and bionics from age-spotted skin and brittle bone.

Stele slumped to the ornate tiled floor, and one of the Blood Angels came to him. 'Lord, are you injured?'

He made a play of weariness. 'Terra be praised, I am unhurt. If you had not been so quick, the turncoat could have killed me...'

The other Space Marine nudged Horin's corpse with his boot. 'It is dead,' he pronounced, somewhat redundantly. 'Another warp-witch too weak to resist.'

'Yes,' Stele agreed, rising to his feet, 'the siren call of the empyrean is strong enough to exploit even the smallest deficiency in the servants of the Emperor.'

* * *

THE GRAND CHAMBER was dark now, each of the biolumes and braziers that had glowed with light during the remembrance ceremony were now dull and black. The only illumination came from infrequent clusters of candles dotted here and there inside the wrought-iron frames of devotional subshrines. Rafen savoured the smell of the hot wax as he passed them, the scent of the pungent Kolla tallow bringing sense-memory of valleys on Baal Primus to mind.

The thoughts fell away as he approached the head of the chamber, his boots tapping on the stone flooring. A knot of silent Space Marines parted to let him through, and there at the foot of the altar knelt his brother. Arkio completed the last few words of the prayer of the red grail, and then looked up at him. Rafen was struck by a sudden sense of distance in Arkio's eyes.

'Brother,' he said. 'You are still troubled.'

Rafen knelt alongside him and made the sign of the aquila. 'By a great many things.'

'And am I one of them?' When Rafen hesitated, Arkio continued, 'Do not be concerned, kinsman. I do not fear, and neither should you.'

'I... Saw something, a light, when you touched the holy lance...'

Arkio nodded, and turned his eyes up to the glass portrait of Sanguinius. 'That was his blessing, Rafen. On me... On all of us. Do you recall the lessons when Koris told us of the Emperor's divine weapons? Did we ever dare to dream we would one day see such a thing?'

Rafen gave a slow nod. The legendary armaments from the rise of the Imperium were spoken of in hushed reverence. Weapons like the Spear of Telesto and its cousins the Frostblade Mjalnar and the Soul Spear, the great Blade Encarmine and the Black Sword of the Templars, all of them forged in the fires of the Emperor's righteous fury. Any one of the blades would elevate a man to glory, if he had the will to wield it.

Arkio's elder brother struggled to find the right words, but every sentence that came to his lips felt clumsy. Emotion and thought churned inside Rafen. Where was the bright, dauntless young novice Space Marine that he remembered from their days of training on Baal? How had his sibling changed from that to a taciturn and introspective man, heavy with the weight of dogma? 'This miracle,' he said carefully. 'It has altered you...'

A rare smile escaped Arkio. 'How could it not, Rafen? I felt him touch me, brother, I felt the primarch's hand across my brow, and the bequest of his inheritance.' He looked away. 'I am changed, of that there is no doubt. The boy who joined you at Angel's Fall is gone now.'

Rafen suddenly felt alone. 'And yet, I remember that time as if it were yesterday.'

ON THE DAY they arrived, the blood-red sun was at its apex above the stone floor of the amphitheatre at Angel's Fall. The red giant cast a punishing heat across the length of the arena, beating down on the crowd of aspirants gathered there. Like all the other trials they would face, it was one more test to weed out the weak of heart and impure of soul. They were a rough and wiry bunch; muscles honed in the hard way of life that Baal's worlds forced upon its people. None of them were more than fourteen summers old, but to call them immature would have been a grave misnomer. There were no children here.

Outside the natural stadium, they would have sported tribal pennants and colours – and some would have been at each other's throats because of it – but here within the walls of the proving ground they were no longer sons of the tribes

of the Blood: they were postulants clamouring for a chance
to ascend to the near-godhood of the Adeptus Astartes. From
the stone ridges around them, hooded figures kept watch
with slug throwers and long blades. These men were the
unchosen, the warriors who had pledged to guard the place
of the trial until death. They scanned the skies and waited;
the sons of Sanguinius would arrive soon.

In the weeks leading up to the time of challenge, Rafen and
Arkio had set out from the lands of the broken mesa clan
with three more youths. They were the very best that the tribe
had to offer, each of them lethal fighters hardened at an early
age by living in one of the planet's most hostile regions. They
were ideal candidates to be risen, so the clan masters said.
Rafen thought otherwise. He was a firebrand youth then,
undisciplined and wild, quite unlike the man he would one
day become. Some of the tribe said that he was sent to the
trials not because he was capable of winning, but in hopes
that he would die. Rumour had it that they were to rid them
of his recklessness.

Rafen was determined to prove them wrong, even if he was
honour-bound to protect his younger brother Arkio. For his
part, Arkio's heart was strong and open. He was forever willing to see the wonders of the universe in every new
experience, but he was guileless and trusting, too naïve for
the brutal future that awaited them as Space Marines. Along
the way, the other three were killed: one was turned to a dry
husk by thirstwater, another dashed on to rocks when his
angel's wings – the primitive gliders the Blood used to navi-
gate the canyon winds – came apart in a sandstorm. Rafen
was forced to break the neck of the last when he succumbed
to the incurable venom of a shellsnake.

And so the trials began. The sky chariots fell from the air; the
machines that he would later know as Thunderhawks landed

in screaming gusts of flame. From within came men in shining red greaves and vambraces, and helmets adorned with the most holy symbol of the pure one. The Blood Angels walked among them like figures from some fantastic dream, picking out aspirants who sported the taint of mutation for cancellation, or dismissing those they saw as wanting. One Space Marine approached Rafen and Arkio, his helmet clasped under one arm.

'Do you whelps have the temerity to think you could serve my beloved Chapter?' His face was grizzled and iron-hard.

Arkio had been properly reverent in his answer, but not Rafen. 'Test me and we shall see who has the courage, old man.'

The Space Marine did the last thing Rafen expected of him: he smiled. 'Indeed we will. I am Koris, brother-sergeant of the Blood Angels Fifth Company. Impress me, if you can, lad.'

They made them fight with lances and staves, knives and short-swords, staffs and weapons made from chains and weights. Koris pushed them through mazes where the walls sprouted blades and arcs of electricity; he made them run races with heavy pack and gear while other Blood Angels strafed them with gunfire. They drilled and they fought and many of them died. Rafen would see Arkio in passing as the brothers went to and from each gladiatorial combat; they would exchange a nod or a wave with a bloodstained hand. Each time, there were fewer and fewer of them, and as the tournaments extended into days, the numbers of the aspirants dwindled still further. From the survivors would be drawn the fifty who would board the sky chariots for Baal, the mother world of the secundus moon that hung across the night like a baleful eye. Rafen excelled even his own arrogant standards, beating off every challenger until he found himself under the gaze of Koris once more. The veteran sergeant was an arbiter of the challenges, and those chosen by him would join the Space Marines.

With Koris as his audience, Rafen soundly beat his opponent – Toph, a pup from the junkhunter folk of the great sear – never realising that the sergeant saw his insolence as the seed of his undoing.

'Do you believe you can fight all your enemies alone?' Koris asked him.

Rafen sneered. The question was ridiculous. 'Of course.'

'No Blood Angel fights alone,' said the sergeant. 'All Blood Angels fight as one, as a brotherhood in the name of the Emperor. If you cannot understand that, then you have already failed.' Perhaps Koris believed that Rafen could be trained, that he could be broken of his complacent manner. In any event, he allowed the boy to remain in the trials, and for his next test he faced a youth named Sachiel. 'Are you ready to face defeat?' Koris asked him.

'I will never be ready to fail!' he retorted hotly.

Sachiel was the very opposite of Rafen: he talked too much; he appeared soft, almost pretty compared to the hard aspects of the other aspirants. But he was cold and capable in the fighting pit. Sachiel felled Rafen and mocked him for it. 'Ready for that, were you?' he sneered, 'Rafen the Ready, ready to lose?'

Arkio helped him patch his wounds as best he could and in a moment between bouts the younger brother implored the elder to curb his nature. 'Rafen, you and I can survive the challenges if we are strong for one another. Our bond mirrors that of the Blood Angels. Together, we are unbeatable.'

Rafen waved him away. 'You are too credulous, boy. A man fights alone; he dies alone. That is the way of it.' Arkio said nothing more. Rafen's fierce determination to become a Blood Angel initiate consumed him. It was born from the overwhelming desire to prove his worth to Axan, their father and war-chief of the broken mesa clan. If Arkio returned a failure then it would be expected and accepted because he was the second son, but as the elder brother, Rafen would suffer a disgrace that would follow him for the rest of his life.

The next day they ran the shifting maze, carrying an electrified baton in a relay race to the finish and Rafen – arrogant, purposeful Rafen – ran it alone, leaving his team mates behind to beat Sachiel into second place. He lit up the air with his fierce defiance. 'Anyone!' he growled. 'I can beat anyone!'

'Can you?' Koris stepped forward and removed every piece of his armour, until he stood disrobed before the youth. 'The time has come to make an object lesson of your pretension, lad.' He threw Rafen his bolt pistol. 'I have no armour to protect me, nothing to augment my strength. Hit me with the gun, just once, and I'll declare your trials complete... But if I touch you, you fail.'

Ignoring Arkio's pleas, Rafen picked up the pistol and let fly, chattering bullets snapping through the air at the Blood Angel. But Koris was no longer there, he moved like a hawk, impossibly fast. Rafen had barely felt the recoil from his first shots before the sergeant kicked his legs from under him and ground the youth's face into the dust.

'To become a Blood Angel, a man must know the pride of great Sanguinius, but also his humility as well,' Koris told him, 'You wallow in the former and show none of the latter. You are dismissed.'

The sergeant left him there in the sand, and on his knees, he watched the old veteran cast his endorsement of Sachiel and Arkio to become initiates to the Chapter. Unable to meet the gazes of those around him, Rafen drew up what little of his strength remained and left Angel's Fall behind. Broken and dispirited, he wandered out into the desert without direction; a colossal storm descended on him. There, in the razor-winds,

Rafen waited for death, too late at an understanding of what his insolence had cost him.

He had been found wanting and in this harshest lesson Rafen realised that he had squandered his chance at greatness. He took what little, bitter comfort he could from the knowledge that Arkio would walk with the Astartes. But for him his life was over. In the midst of the raging tempest, Rafen became lost in the territory of the fire scorpions, Baal's most fearsome predators. Soon an immature warrior male was stalking him, acidic flame-venom dripping from its barbed tail in anticipation. As big as a full-grown man, the beast fell on the youth, enraged by his violation of its domain. So overcome with despair was he that Rafen was almost willing to let the animal end his life, but then in the thunderclouds he glimpsed a vision of something impossibly bright and powerful. Perhaps it had been a trick of the mind, some hallucination brought on by melancholy and fatigue, but in that moment Rafen saw the face of Sanguinius watching him. The pure one stood in judgement of the boy, and Rafen realised that this was the true test of his mettle: if he died here, lost and alone in the wilderness, then he would truly have failed every tenet that the tribes of the Blood and the Adeptus Astartes lived by.

Fuelled by his revelation, determination flooded back into the lad, and with the fierceness he had shown in the arena, Rafen pierced the creature's carapace with a stone knife and killed it, just as Sanguinius had done in the legends of the angelic sovereign's childhood.

It was only then that Rafen realised the lights he had seen in the sky were those of a stricken Thunderhawk plummeting to the ground. Damaged by a violent blast of lightning as it made for orbit, one of the Blood Angels' ships crash-landed a few kilometres away from him, in the very heart of the scorpion hunting fields. Rafen rushed to the aid of the survivors and found a handful of aspirants there: Arkio, Toph and Sachiel among them. The old warrior Koris lay bloodied and unconscious, and the rest of the senior Blood Angels aboard were dead. Sachiel stepped forward to assume command and demanded Rafen leave them; a failure had no place alongside true sons of Sanguinius.

Such an insult would normally have boiled Rafen's blood, but he had taken the sergeant's lesson to heart and stood firm. He had hunted in these lands since he was old enough to carry a spear and he knew the ways of the fire scorpions. With such an outright invasion of their territory, the pheromone scents of the beasts would go mad and they would attack in massive numbers. Resisting the urge to do battle alone, Rafen rallied the aspirants to fight as a team, holding off the warrior scorpions until the insect's giant queen revealed itself amid the swarm. The youths fought like lions, and even as the brave Toph died in the claws of the queen, Rafen killed the animal and set the scorpion pack in disarray. When the storm broke and a rescue ship arrived, they came to find Koris still alive and a dozen young men surrounded by a sea of dead enemies.

As the veteran was awakened from his healing sleep, Arkio relayed the tale of Rafen's leadership and argued for him, even to the extreme of refusing his own ascension if his brother's victory was not acknowledged. For his part, Rafen bid to take his leave and wished Arkio a fond farewell, believing that he would never see his sibling again. But Koris commanded otherwise. 'The veil lifts from your eyes, boy,' the old warrior said. 'You have at last understood the teaching that eluded you for so long.'

'Yes,' Rafen admitted. 'He who fights alone dies alone, but those who battle as brothers will live forever.'

The veteran smiled again. 'You have redeemed yourself, Rafen of the broken mesa, and with the death of the aspirant Toph I have need of a courageous soul to take his place.' He held out a hand to the youth. 'Will you follow me, Rafen? Will you tread the path of the primarch and embrace the brotherhood of the Blood Angels?'

The words leapt from his lips. 'I will. This day I vow to become a Blood Angel worthy of the Lord Sanguinius himself!'

AND SO FOR the first time, the sons of Axan left the cradle of their birth and crossed the chasm of space between Baal Secundus and the mother world Baal. If they thought they knew hardship, then Rafen and Arkio were proven wrong as they crossed the arid wastes of the massive desert world. Here they glimpsed the crumbling stumps of what had once been magnificent cities. There, amid the pinnacles of mountains that cut at the sky with blade-sharp peaks, stood the fortress-monastery of the Blood Angels. None of the aspirants had ever seen so huge a structure before, not even the mighty carving of Sanguinius cut from the bare rock of Mount Seraph. It thrilled and terrified them in equal measure.

Koris led them into the chambers of the abbey keep where they walked among the number of the Blood Angels' brethren, eyes wide as saucers at the inhuman nobility and beauty of the warriors. Like their primarch, the fully-fledged Blood Angels carried the genetic mark of Sanguinius and the shadow of his exalted countenance in all their aspects. In comparison, the malnourished and weather-beaten youths of the Baal moons were feeble waifs. The Sanguinary Priests in their armour of white and crimson came for the aspirants, and took the fifty to the great chapel where they were locked in for three days and nights. They stood vigil without sleep, without food or water. Alone, Rafen would not have been able to endure the test, and as the hours crawled by, he saw some that dropped from exhaustion. They were removed by the priests, and their fates never spoken of, but with Arkio at his side, the brothers kept each other strong. When at last the fourth day dawned, they were still standing to meet the bearers of the red grail when they sundered the holy seal on the chapel door.

The handful of men who remained drank from the sacred cup, and Rafen's weary mind came alive as the fluid touched his lips. Rich and coppery, the liquid in the chalice flowed from the veins of the most senior of the Sanguinary Priests – and through their bodies flowed an iota of the very blood of the angel lord himself. Energies and thoughts at once alien and familiar to Rafen coursed through his body, the touch of the fluid laying his soul bare to scrutiny by the Chapter's brethren. Rafen embraced it and cast away the last ties to his old life. The warrior boy of the broken mesa clan was gone now, and in his place stood a man whose future stretched away before him in a golden path of glory and adventure. Darkness, warm and calming, enveloped the aspirants, and the sleep of change was upon them.

RAFEN REMEMBERED WITH absolute clarity the moment the sarcophagus was opened and his altered, enhanced eyes took in their first sight. Perhaps fittingly, it had been of Arkio. His brother was standing in mute shock at the changes wrought on him, and studying his fingers and his hands as if they belonged to someone else. Rafen saw the face of the Space Marine before him – for he was no longer a mere man – and knew it to be his kinsman, even though this new Arkio stood twice as tall, was broad with muscle and crowned with a face that by turns mirrored his countenance, his father's, and that of Sanguinius. The gazes of the two siblings met as the blood-servitors removed the probes and channels from their bodies. As one they broke into laughter, amazed and relieved and surprised at what fate had granted them.

Rafen could not be sure how much time had passed. Later he learned that they had been taken from the chapel after the vigil and locked in the hall of sarcophagi under the chants of the credo vitae. There, they had lain for a year in the sleep as a potent cocktail of nutrients, modificational potions and blood from the red grail coursed through their systems. In those months, the servitors had implanted the hallowed gene-seed of the Chapter and watched it remake them.

As Rafen, Arkio and the other aspirants had slumbered in blood-warm dreams kindled from the genetic memory of the primarch, their bodies accepted the potent new organs that made them into Space Marines – the secondary heart, the catalepsean node sleep-killer, multi-lung, occulobe, the omophagea, ossmodula and others. They stepped into the light as the living avatars of the gods they had once worshipped, but this was just the first of many steps. No human would have been able to withstand the training they endured, the impossible hardships and extremes of physicality that the instructors forced upon them. At all times, Koris was there, pushing each of them beyond the limits to achieve more, to go deeper, to fight harder. Through every challenge, Arkio and Rafen supported one another, kinsmen in blood and brothers in battle, drawing strength from their unbreakable bond. And as much as they changed, their hearts remained the same. Rafen's unswerving fortitude and his relentless bravery grew tenfold, while Arkio kept his courage and his unbreakable spirit of adventure.

Until now.

* * *

RAFEN'S REVERIE FADED as quickly as it had come and he returned to the moment. His brother's gaze was steady and cool on him under the dim glow of the grand chamber's candles. He could see it in Arkio's eyes as clearly as if it were inscribed like the scriptures in the stonewalls. The humble soldier his younger sibling once was had vanished, subsumed into the man before him now, just as the wiry clan boy of his youth had been transformed inside the hall of sarcophagi.

With effort, Rafen pushed a question from his mouth. 'I cannot believe that you... that you liken yourself to our primarch? No man could dare to take such a mantle upon himself...' His lips trembled as he spoke.

Arkio smiled, and the gesture made Rafen's heart freeze in his chest. 'But I am not a man, brother. I am a Blood Angel.'

He was unable to speak. Then, a shape in jet-black armour adorned with bone-white skulls and purity seals hove into view. 'Brother Arkio,' said the Chaplain, 'if you would attend me? There are... questions.'

The Space Marine nodded and came to his feet. 'Do not fear, Rafen,' he whispered. 'Trust in me.'

Rafen gave no reply. He was locked in a cycle of dread about what his brother's words could mean. *He is lost.* The thought shocked him. *My brother is lost to me and I am caught between the ties of blood to my family, and my duty to the Chapter...*

CHAPTER NINE

THE SHENLONG MINEFIELD was a death zone. As *Bellus* edged her way into the outer reaches of the belt of warheads, Brother-Captain Ideon registered the shapes of broken hull metal and shattered rock. The mines were complex and intricate devices, so his Techmarines had explained to him; they possessed a logic brain capable of determining the difference between an inert form like an asteroid and an active craft like a manned warship. Scattered about the battle barge were the remains of men who had not possessed such information, who had blindly charged into the zone, casting their fates to chance in hopes of running the forge world's blockade. He detected pieces of an ork rok and other remains that might have been from reavers or perhaps an Imperial ship caught when the Word Bearers took the planet for themselves. Shenlong had become enemy territory, a vast trap for the unwary.

The *Bellus* was solely his responsibility now, and he extended himself into the ship's systems. His mind embraced the warship's machine ghost like a trusted comrade-at-arms. The rudimentary spirit of *Bellus* knew Ideon well and it welcomed him in, letting the Blood Angel move his consciousness from the fleshy form connected to the bridge throne deep into the barge's command pathways. Ideon's psyche sent out impulses that might normally have made fingers or toes flex gently; instead, they made etheric rudders twitch and retro-rockets spit in readiness.

From a great distance, he heard his own synthetic voice issue out from a throat voxcoder. 'Set condition one through-out the ship, special alert status. All exterior running lights are to be doused. All hatches sealed. All zero critical systems are to be quiescent.'

'Confirmed,' Ideon was aware of his aide, the veteran sergeant Solus, as the Space Marine read the ship's status from a pict-plate. 'Silent running.'

Irritation underlined Solus's words, and Ideon felt a swell of sympathy. Like every Blood Angel on board, Ideon's heart raced at the prospect of action, and the stealthy, slow approach they were now forced to make chafed at him. Ingrained in every one of them was the appetite for combat – not the distant, ranged affair of some warfare, but the imme-diate thunder of close quarter fighting. Blood Angels lived for the scent of the foe's open veins, the scream of the dying enemy and the hot rush of power that came from watching them perish, and feeling the blow of their last breath. Ideon knew that some of this brethren pitied him. They saw the crippled old warhorse bolted into his command chair, never to stand again or to rip the unholy apart with his bare hands. But here, in a sacred symbiosis with the *Bellus*, Ideon still knew the delirious, giddy rage of bloodlust – only now, his hands were energy lances and his fangs the fusion torpedoes eager in their launch tubes. When *Bellus* killed an enemy ves-sel, Ideon knew it as if it were *he* that cracked open the hull and sucked the adversary's life into the void.

Sensing itself in his thoughts, the battle barge's machine spirit growled softly at the edges of the captain's mind. It too was impatient at such slow progress. Ideon calmed it as he did his own anger: he forced the need away. With the hundredfold eyes of the *Bellus*'s servitors, he watched the broken fuselage of a frigate drift past, bereft of life where some imprudent officer had let zeal outstrip intellect. Such a fate would befall *Bellus* if Ideon's control slipped, even for a moment.

The mines were never still. As one, the huge flock of spheres rotated with Shenlong's day and night cycle, gradually moving to remain equidistant to one another. An elaborate cognitive engine on the planet below monitored the weapons constantly, so Stele had said, and it randomly generated tubes of open space within the field to allow ships safe passage from orbit to surface, in order that Shenlong's contribution to the Imperial war effort be maintained. But the cargo lighters that carried the tonnage of krak missiles, fusion charges and the giant atlas- and proteus-class warheads were either grounded or destroyed, and the manufactory's mighty engines of creation were silent down there. Perhaps the Traitors intended to ransack Shenlong and steal every bomb and bullet upon it, or perhaps they wished to make the forge world their own; Ideon cared not. For now, his mind was engaged in the singular task of bringing *Bellus* to operational range of the surface. That this world had once been a shining jewel in the Imperium's industrial crown was of no concern; Shenlong belonged to the Word Bearers now, and they had stained it black with their profane presence.

He was dimly aware of someone entering the command sanctum, and the *Bellus* obediently showed him a display of the upper tier. He saw his own body there, at rest in the throne as if in a light doze, Solus to his right. Then Inquisitor

Stele came into view, accompanied by his lexmechanic and the ever-present servo skulls.

'Grave news, brother-captain,' Stele began, his face a grim mask. 'The astropath Horin is no more. He fell from the Emperor's light and forced his death upon me.'

'Horin?' Solus grated. 'He has served this ship for three centuries!'

'How did it occur?' Ideon asked. His face remained immobile, but mentally he frowned. This was not a matter he wished to address while gently directing the helm-servitors on the course ahead. He turned a degree of his attention to the bridge and away from the ship's navigation.

Stele described Horin's falsification of a signal from Baal as an excuse to gain access to the inquisitor. He told of his sudden attack, and the astropath's death at the hands of the Space Marines. 'I took it upon myself to examine his body,' he finished, 'and I found this.' Stele displayed a glass cylinder, within which floated a fat maggot nesting inside a diseased black organ. 'In his heart is the pupae variety of some poisonous daemon. I suspect that it may have formed within him over a long period of time.' He held the jar close to his face. In truth, the corrupted flesh it contained had never been anywhere near Horin; it had been harvested instead from the corpse of the dead Chaos Space Marine Noro. This small piece of theatre would allow Stele to affirm his killing of the astropath.

'Have that pestilent object destroyed at once!' Ideon's voice snapped with static. 'Jettison it into the void, but I will not have such foulness aboard *Bellus*!'

'Your will, brother-captain.' Stele agreed. 'I will attend to it.'

The inquisitor's words had barely left his mouth before one of the servitors droned out a warning. 'Collision alert. Incoming, port quarter, upper deck.'

Ideon resisted the urge to curse his luck and forced a hard turn from the rudder. The *Bellus* showed him the object, a lone mine drifting silently toward the battle barge's prow. The inquisitor's arrival had been enough to divert his attention for a crucial second. Now the warship was within strike range of the weapon.

'Stand aside!' Solus yelled, anticipating the captain's next command, and Stele obeyed. Although the inquisitor held sway over the mission of the *Bellus*, Ideon was still the ship's commanding officer and in matters such as this, the superior voice.

As large as it was, and even with full reverse thrust the battle barge would take long minutes to negate its forward speed and come to a halt – and such an action would register like a flare on the sensor webs of the other mines. His dour face unchanging, Ideon ordered the helm-servitor to alter course and turn *Bellus* toward the approaching mine.

The ship's machine spirit quarrelled and snarled, railing at Ideon for such a suicidal action. Now the device was seconds away from impacting the hull and nothing would stop it. The captain saw Solus's knuckles turn white where he gripped a stanchion. The mindless servitor continued to obey, and *Bellus* presented her hammerhead bow to the bomb. There was a moment when it seemed that Stele was about to say something; then Ideon felt a dull ring from the ship's outermost extremity.

'Impact,' the servitor reported tonelessly. 'No detonation.'

'How did you know?' Stele asked, a half-smile playing on his lips.

Ideon's body did not move, but the ersatz voice from his vox-coder belied his relief. 'I served aboard the strike cruiser *Fidelis* at armageddon. She was a mine-layer, among other things, and in my duties I learnt the limitations of that weapon.' He activated the holosphere, displaying the schematic of a mine. 'It is my understanding that Shenlong-pattern warheads have a delayed fusing mechanism. I closed the distance to ensure that the mine did not have time to arm itself before it struck the ship, so it did not explode.' There was a sound like a sigh. 'Such a tactic will not work twice, though. We were lucky... I estimated our success at only one chance in ten.'

'Sanguinius protects,' said Stele.

Sergeant Solus studied the new data as it scrolled across his pict-plate in thin lines of high gothic. 'Brother-captain, the mine... It did not disintegrate when it struck us. The device remains lodged in the outer hull.'

'Dispatch a tech-adept to ascertain the weapon's status,' Ideon replied. 'Horin and that creature... There have been enough unpleasant surprises this day. I'll not brook another.'

Solus nodded. 'I will send Brother Lucion.'

'He may need assistance,' the inquisitor broke in. 'Perhaps Brother Rafen should accompany him?'

Solus looked to Ideon and the captain's voice hissed from the speaker on his throat. 'So ordered.'

WITH CAREFUL DELIBERATION, Rafen placed his metal-shod feet on the exterior hull of the battle barge, one step after another. He was alert for the hollow thump as the magnetic adhesion pads in his armour held fast. A few feet ahead of him, Tech-marine Lucion ambled easily across the ship's fuselage as if it were second nature to him.

And indeed, it probably was. Rafen's years of fighting experience as a Blood Angel had taken him to dozens of different environments, from ice worlds like Tartarus to the Zaou marshlands, but his company had fought in the vacuum of space on rare occasions. Lucion, by comparison, had been billeted aboard *Bellus* since his passage from initiate status, and he knew the outside of the massive battle barge as well as the corridors within it. Rafen listened to the echo of his own breathing and warily followed the Techmarine. Something about the dead silence of space unnerved him and made him feel vulnerable; he preferred to walk in places where the sound of an enemy's approach could be heard.

The Techmarine's gait was that of an experienced spacer, he reflected. Every one of the machine-adepts that served the Adeptus Astartes seemed a breed apart in many things, not just such small details as this. While his power armour was no more powerful, Lucion seemed to be able to move more easily in it, and Rafen found himself wondering if the Techmarines used their superior skills with such things to enhance and alter their own wargear.

Indeed, Lucion's armour was already heavily modified as that of all his kindred were; from the backpack power unit that supplied energy to the sealed suit, the tech-brother sported the folded metal sculpture of a servo-arm. Collapsed now, the additional limb ended in a deceptively large gripper, which the adept could operate like an extension of his body. Rafen had seen Techmarines use the devices to tear bolts from a stuck land raider hatch or to manipulate eggshell- thin circuit plates. Not for the first time, he considered the rumours that shrouded the way of the tech-adepts. Some said that during their apprenticeship to the Adeptus Mechanicus they were altered in some fashion, their loyalties split from their mother Chapter. Did the quiet, affable Lucion conceal some other agenda? Rafen shook the thought away, dismissing it; recent events were making him see contrivance in everything around him.

'Hail, Brother Rafen,' Lucion called over the vox. 'To the starboard, do you see it?'

Rafen followed Lucion's outstretched hand and saw the distended sphere embedded in the fuselage. 'Is it active?'

'Let us pray not.'

They approached the weapon and Rafen kept a respectful distance from the device. Lucion threw him a look and beckoned him closer. 'It won't bite, brother.'

Rafen was not so sure, but he stepped over all the same. In the silence, the Techmarine's servo arm quivered into life, opening to its full length. With all three of his limbs, Lucion made a complicated sign in the space above the device, and Rafen caught the faint whisper of a secret litany in his ear-bead. With deft, economical movements, the adept set to work removing rune-engraved screws from the mine's outer casing, placing each one in a drawstring bag tethered to his waist so that they would not float away in the zero gravity. 'Maintain a close watch,' said Lucion, his helmet inches away from the blackened exterior of the mine. 'If I am distracted by some enemy, we may both die because of it.'

In actual fact, it was highly unlikely that the Traitors even knew that *Bellus* was here. And it was even less likely that they knew what was transpiring on her hull – but the sacred edicts laid down in the ashes of the Heresy, committed to the Codex Astartes, the Space Marines' war book of tactics and conduct, demanded that no Space Marine ever set foot outside an airlock alone. Rafen wondered why he had been chosen to stand guard over Lucion. It was not a task without risk; if the adept made an error or did something else to displease the mine's machine spirit, their proximity to the resulting detonation would turn them both to wisps of plasma. *A sobering thought,* he reflected.

The Techmarine's actions held Rafen's attentions, but only for a moment. He had never been one to wonder about the intricate working of the machines that powered the might of the Imperium. Beyond his typical training in the maintenance and operation of his weapons, Rafen simply accepted that the

Chapter's technology served him and fulfilled its purpose, just as he did for the Emperor. He had no desire to steep himself in the doctrines of the Machine God, the divergent aspect of the divine regent that the Adeptus Mechanicus paid fealty to. He heard Lucion give a brief prayer of thanks to the Omnissiah as the warhead's access panel slid open on century-old hinges.

Rafen cast a glance over his shoulder, back along the hull of the *Bellus*. Dark and dormant, the massive starship seemed less like a vessel ready for battle than a broken piece of pitted landscape, cast off the surface of a world to float as a cold island in the void. The vessel's angular conning tower rose over the plain of the mid-decks, as broad and threatening as a thunderhead. Not a single sliver of light escaped the shutters sealed over all the windows and vents; nothing betrayed the battle barge's intent to pour red death on Shenlong's cursed overlords.

If the dorsal fuselage of *Bellus* was his point of reference, then Shenlong itself floated like a gargantuan rising moon, slowly advancing up and over the ship. Badelt, the forge world's actual moon, was invisible from this angle. The vessel's orbit had been carefully plotted by Ideon's navigators to ensure that sunlight reflected by the lone natural satellite would not illuminate *Bellus* in any planetside optical telescopes. Rafen watched the lazy progress of the planet; it was turning into night as it rose, the hazy grey of the Terminator crossing the surface as it banished day. The Blood Angel studied the darkening world and saw the glows of cities engulfed in flames, and the curls of cloud lit from within where tactical nuclear bombs had cut radioactive scars in the earth. Even in the hard light of day, little of Shenlong's true face could be determined; millennia of combustion and fumes from factory cathedrals as big as nations had long since cloaked the industrial world in dirty smoke.

Rafen felt the familiar twitch in his fingers again. Down there, uncounted numbers of Word Bearers were casting the

Emperor's likeness down in flames, and erecting their own foul temples and tormenting the populace. Even though the rational, logical part of his mind knew that the enemy forces were vastly superior, the passionate energy in his blood boiled for a chance to kill and destroy the Chaos filth. As he and Lucion had made their way to the airlock, both the Blood Angels had sensed anticipation in the atmosphere. All about them, warriors drilled and prepared for combat, or armed themselves. Some were sitting at the feet of battle Chaplains, their heads bowed in war prayers. It was almost a palpable thing, like a faint musk upon the wind. The tethered might of Sanguinius's bloodlust was straining at the leash to be free, free to unleash a crimson hell on all those who dared oppose the God-Emperor of Mankind. Rafen's lips drew back from his teeth in anticipation, his fangs drawn with predatory desire. It was almost enough to distract him from his deeper, more troubling concerns. Almost.

He looked to the place on Shenlong's dark surface where, by his rough reckoning, the planet's capital city stood – and at its heart, the ferrocrete edifice of the Ikari fortress. Rafen had heard tell that the fortress was a twin to any of the great monastery citadels of the Adeptus Astartes, an enormous strongpoint from which Shenlong could be governed. The history books said the Ikari fortress had been inspected by no less than Rogal Dorn himself, the primarch of the Imperial Fists Chapter. Dorn had apparently declared the fortress to be 'adequate', high praise indeed from the dispassionate lord of the Imperium's greatest siege masters. Rafen's doubts reasserted themselves, as he understood just how hard the Blood Angels would be tested to break such a fortification.

He looked away from the planet, and blocked out the misgivings that rumbled at the back of his mind. These distractions were cancer to a member of the Legion Astartes.

The smallest seed of a doubt could bloom into hesitation that could cost him his life on the battlefield. The fight for Shenlong would be difficult enough without him letting his concentration go elsewhere. These thoughts played on him as Lucion did something to the mine, and the limpid green glow from within the warhead's workings faded out to nothing. The Techmarine's task complete, he stepped back from the inert munition and once more sang a short, quiet litany of thanksgiving. Lucion's speech was soft in Rafen's helmet, but he caught the words of respect paid to Sanguinius, to the Machine God – and to his brother.

He spoke Arkio's name in the same breath as our liege lord and the Emperor. Rafen could hardly believe such a thing. *What insanity is this?*

Lucion turned to face him, and something about the Techmarine's body language told Rafen that he knew he had been overheard. 'The weapon's ghost has been silenced,' he said carefully. 'It sleeps now.'

'We just leave it there, then?' Rafen was surprised at the annoyance in his own voice. 'Lodged in the hull like a tick?'

The Techmarine's head bobbed. 'It cannot explode now, brother. Not even a lightning bolt from the Omnissiah himself could return it to life.'

'Very well, then we go.' Rafen smothered his irritation and began the steady walk back along the hull. Lucion fell in by his side, his gait easy beside Rafen's slow-footed strides.

After a long moment, Lucion spoke again, and this time it was with the air of an expectant child. 'Rafen... I must ask you... What is Brother Arkio like?'

Rafen grimaced behind his breather mask. 'Like? He is a Blood Angel,' he replied tersely. 'He is my sibling.'

'But his manner, his bearing,' Lucion pressed. 'I never knew him... Before. What was he like when he was younger?'

The Techmarine's idolatry fuelled anger in Rafen's chest and he fixed him with a hard look. 'What would you have me say, Lucion? That he cut stones in two with nothing but a word from his lips? That he fell from the sky on wings of fire?' He turned away, pulling open the airlock's outer hatch. 'Arkio is a Space Marine, no more and no less. Ask him yourself and he will tell you the same.' Without looking to see if Lucion was behind him, he advanced into the chamber beyond, his mood darkening like the Shenlong sky.

STELE STALKED THE corridors of the *Bellus* like a shadow, a ghostly presence at the edge of perception. He watched for the slightest hint of any mental essence extending beyond the hull walls, alert for the smallest iota of thought that might be detected by the traitor psykers below. He found nothing, and it gave him cause to smile thinly. The players and the setting were ready for the execution of the next great act in his performance, and Stele toyed with the delicate thrill that the gambit brought him.

Ramius had always been at his most alive in the construction and execution of his schemes, even from the earliest days as an ordo initiate; such things, after all, were the meat and drink of his sect. He considered the development of his plots and counter-plots to be like a perfect clockwork construction, a grand creation of gears and cogs cast from the emotions of men. Stele could never slake the sweet anticipation that dripped from such moments as this one, as he finally set the wheels spinning. It was his intention that there would be war on Shenlong, and it would be bloody and glorious.

Grave-silent and watchful, *Bellus* hung in low orbit and waited. No stray energies or signatures radiated from her, no action on board was taken without careful deliberation and pace. To the machine eyes on the surface, the warship appeared as one of a thousand pieces of space debris, adrift in the night sky on a slow course toward a fiery death in re-entry.

The inquisitor left the ranks of Chapter serfs and men preparing wargear and marshalling weapons to return to his sanctum. It was necessary for Stele to be correctly garbed, and his shipboard robes were ill suited. There was a field-habit of fine grox skin that would better suit the circumstances.

On reflex, Stele's hand snapped toward the blade concealed at his waist as he entered his sanctum. There were intruders here, and the brief moment of smug satisfaction had blinded the inquisitor to their presence. His fingers were almost at the pommel before he halted. Seven Space Marines stood in a loose semi-circle in the middle of his chambers, and as one they had all raised weapons at his brisk activity. Forcing back a grimace, Stele turned the movement of his hand into a brushing motion, as if he were flicking away some particles of dust from his cloak. He hid his annoyance well, through years of practice, aware that the Blood Angels were evaluating everything about him.

At the centre of the group stood Brother-Sergeant Koris. The crimson armour of his form seemed utterly out of place in the dim shades of Stele's sanctum. And out of place he *was*, for it was only by the inquisitor's express summons that a Space Marine was allowed to enter. The presence of Koris and the others here and now was an unsubtle message from the veteran warrior. *You cannot keep us out.*

'My lord inquisitor,' Koris said levelly. 'I would speak with you.'

Stele gave him a gracious nod and moved into the chamber, as if it were he who had ordered them to this meeting. 'Of course, honoured sergeant, how may I assist you?' In the shadows at the edge of the room, one of Stele's helots cowered behind a plinth and he shot the slave-servitor a brief, venomous look. The pathetic creature would pay for failing to alert him to the arrival of the Space Marines.

'The mission on which we are about to embark troubles many of us,' said Koris. 'Although we desire the death of the Traitors, we are concerned that the odds make this a pointless endeavour.'

Stele studied the faces of the Blood Angels. Like Koris, all were seasoned soldiers with centuries of battle experience behind them. Most of the men were survivors from Simeon's company on Cybele, but there were also sergeants from the *Bellus* contingent. None of them were cowards or men shy of battle; they were intelligent, ruthless warriors and they knew the jaws of a meat-grinder were opening before them. The inquisitor let none of this show on his face.

'Yours is not to question the word of the Emperor, Koris. If he orders you to march to your deaths, then march you shall.' Stele's voice was airy, as if he were commenting on the taste of some fine morsel of food.

'So we would,' Koris's eyes narrowed, 'but these are not his commands. The priest Sachiel's skills in the way of the Blood are unquestioned, lord, but he is no tactician. He plans to commit our forces to an all-out assault... And I fear that our brothers will be dashed on the walls of the Ikari fortress while the Word Bearers take only minor casualties. A staged series of small raids would be far more effective.'

'Why do you tell me this?'

'If it pleases the lord inquisitor, you have Sachiel's ear. You could intercede, persuade him to alter his plans.'

Stele gave Koris a bored look. 'Surely you have made your concerns known to him, yes? Yet he chose not to take your advice?'

The sergeant gave a single sharp nod. 'He suggested I was lacking in faith.'

Stele took a step closer to Koris. 'Are you?'

Caged fury illuminated the old soldier's eyes. 'I am a son of Sanguinius,' he hissed, 'and my faith is hard as diamond!'

How easy it is to kindle the warrior's fury. The Space Marine was following the path Stele was setting for him; he was one more piece of the clockwork ticking along its pre-destined route. 'I do not doubt that, but why do you not share his certitude in our victory? Sachiel believes, as I do, that your lord primarch has blessed us. You doubt this insight?'

For the first time, hesitation crossed the sergeant's face. 'We… I… am unsure, lord.' He licked his lips. 'The youth, Arkio… It is difficult to accept…'

Simplicity, Stele told himself, *it is so simple to manipulate men like Koris. They may pretend to question their dogma, but in truth they are the most steadfast and inflexible believers of them all.* 'Koris, did you think it easy for me to accept? I, who have travelled to thousands of worlds and seen sights to chill the marrow and uplift the heart? You will be able to return to your homeworld of Baal after the raid on Shenlong is over to hero's honours, but before that may happen you must release your scepticism!'

'But did Commander Dante himself not say that a Blood Angel who does not strive to question is no better than a mindless servitor? I cannot accept that we will be victorious on Shenlong by faith alone!' Koris looked away, his rush of words a shock to himself.

The inquisitor gave a staged sigh, seamlessly changing tack. As with every plan of his creation, Stele kept it hidden beneath a bodyguard of lies: Horin's murder, the blackened heart cut from the Word Bearer, each was one more distraction from the truth of the inquisitor's plan. Now, he unveiled another falsehood, one sharpened and targeted like a missile directly at the Blood Angel's Achilles heel – his sense of duty. 'Very well, then, you leave me no choice, sergeant. What I am about to tell you must not leave this room.' Stele approached his hololithic projector and called up a display of the Ikari fortress. Like most of the records of the obelisk keep they were sketchy and vague, but these were different from those in the *Bellus's* librarium. A deep passage was shown under the construction. 'I want your oath, Koris,' Stele said with force. 'All of you.'

Each of the Blood Angels looked to the veteran and he nodded. 'You have it.'

Stele pointed at the falsified display, so perfect in its mendacity. 'Sachiel is a fine priest but he is, as you have said, not a soldier as we are. And so, I kept this information from him.' He glanced at the Space Marines, who were all watching him intently and hanging on his every word. Gently, he allowed his mind to probe at them, easing them a little closer to his turn of thinking. 'Only a select few men know that the Ikari fortress conceals an ancient Adeptus Mechanicus laboratory, and inside that lies a device of incredible power.' The image showed the blurry rendition of an eldar webway portal. 'Our goal on Shenlong is not to drive out the Word Bearers, as Sachiel thinks, but to secure or destroy this device on pain of death.' Stele gave Koris a comradely nod. 'Now do you understand the importance of this mission?'

The sergeant examined the scan carefully. Stele kept his face neutral; the forgery was utterly impeccable and certainly good enough to fool a rank-and-file Space Marine. In reality, the lower levels of the Ikari fortress concealed nothing more than a waste recycling system and a network of torture cells. This lie would serve him by silencing Koris with his own duty. In ten years of service on the *Bellus*, the inquisitor had come to realise that all men wanted something to believe in, and it was the very nature of a Space Marine to crave a cause. If Koris and his dissenters would not follow Arkio, then it was merely a matter of fabricating a reason that they *would* die for.

The veteran spoke, and Stele knew then that he had snared the Blood Angel. 'Why did you not reveal this earlier? Why conceal it, inquisitor?'

'You know the ways of the Ordo Hereticus,' Stele said confidentially. 'They would see me executed if they knew what I had just told you. But I have always trusted the word of a Blood Angel.'

Koris was grim-faced. 'Then we will take this mission as Sachiel orders. It will cost us, but we cannot let the Chaos filth hold such a threat against the Imperium.'

Inside, Stele was jeering at them. 'Even if it costs your lives?' The sergeant nodded and the inquisitor turned away, summoning a servitor. 'Then, comrade brothers, before you depart to prepare for the assault I would ask you to grant me a small boon.'

'Name it,' Koris said warily.

The servitor returned with a tray; on it was a replica of the red grail and eight ornate steel cups. 'I would share a benediction with you all.' He poured a measure of the thick crimson liquid into each goblet and they all took one. 'To victory on Shenlong,' Stele toasted. 'For the glory of the Emperor and Sanguinius.'

'For the glory of the Emperor and Sanguinius.' The seven men repeated the words with one voice and sipped from the cups.

Silence held sway for a long moment, then the veteran spoke. 'Perhaps... I may have been hasty in my evaluation of you, lord inquisitor,' said Koris.

'An occupational hazard,' Stele noted.

The sergeant said no more, and with a circumspect salute, the Space Marines left the chamber.

Stele spoke a word of power and sent out a cantrip to seal the iris shut behind them. Then he drained the rest of the fluid in the chalice and let out a bubbling, hateful laugh. The liquid rolled down his chin and dripped to the floor. It was sacred blood, after a fashion, but not the vitae of Sanguinius.

He glanced at the cowering servitor, and then paused briefly before beating it to the floor. Then, with slow deliberation, the inquisitor used his heavy boot to crush the serf's throat.

Satisfied, Stele swung his arm and threw the grail at the wall of the chamber, where it shattered in a wet crash of sound. *The fools will learn too late that my schemes are not to be disrupted*, Stele told himself. *Shenlong's skies will weep blood!*

'I command it!' he shouted, his voice echoing about the empty room.

CHAPTER TEN

RAFEN BOWED HIS head as the Barbarossa hymnal came to a crescendo. A thousand voices carried the sacred lyrics up to the roof of the staging deck. On all sides, Blood Angels made their prayers to the primarch and the God-Emperor. As the song ended, he ran a bare hand over his bolter, to touch the inscriptions that he had painstakingly etched there over the decades of his obligation. No two weapons in the service of the Chapter were alike; every Space Marine turned his own into a combination of gun and prayer icon. Rafen's firearm carried the listing of each battle he had fought, as well as passages from his favoured Chapters in the book of the lords. He knew them all by heart, but the presence of the words was a comfort that strengthened his resolve. Turning the gun to face away from him, he opened the breech in the ritual manner and waited for the war blessing from a Chaplain.

His eyes ranged around the deck. Columns of vehicles were shunting slowly into the mouths of Thunderhawk drop-ships, Baal-pattern Predator tanks rumbling in line with Rhino and Razorback transports. He and the majority of the other Blood Angels would be taking a different route to the surface of Shenlong; the elongated teardrops of dozens of Deathwind drop-pods were laid open before the assembled troops. Rafen fancied they looked like some strange seed from a giant metal plant. Indeed, when they fell on the Word Bearers, they would sow the germ of the Emperor's revenge upon the stolen forge world.

A sudden commotion drew his attention. In the forward ranks, hushed voices spoke in urgent tones, breaking position to cluster around one of their number. Rafen came up from his knees and approached. He saw Turcio, and the battle-brother turned to face him.

'Rafen, perhaps it is best if you stand clear–'

He pushed past and saw Sergeant Koris kneeling in what appeared to be deep, reverent prayer. Then the old warrior's body twitched and a low growl escaped his lips. Rafen went cold; he recognised the signs immediately. 'When…?'

'He was sullen when he arrived,' Turcio whispered, 'and as the hymn continued, he seemed to grow more distracted.' The Blood Angel licked his lips. 'I fear this is a matter for the Chaplain.'

Rafen ignored him and dropped to his haunches so that he might look Koris in the face. 'Brother-sergeant? Do you hear me?'

Koris raised his head and the breath caught in Rafen's throat. The veteran's face was flushed with barely suppressed rage, his eyes dark pits of animal hate. He showed his teeth and flecks of spittle left his lips. 'Rafen!' he snapped. 'Ah, lad, the wings, do you hear them? The sound of the foe and the clarion of foul Horus?' Muscles stood out on the sergeant's neck as he strained to contain the boiling passion inside him. 'The Emperor's palace lies breached, you see?' Breath hissed through his teeth. 'Is this real? I see it and yet I do not see... The cup! Is it poison?'

Turcio gave a curt nod. 'It is the black rage.'

The gene-curse. To speak of it was almost a taboo among the Blood Angels, and yet the black rage, the flaw, the red thirst, whatever name it was given, was the very thing that defined the character of the Chapter. Space Marine scholars and the historians on Baal would often speak of the genetic legacy of great Sanguinius in reverent tones. So strong was the potency of the pure one's gene-seed that even ten millennia after his death at the hand of the traitorous Warmaster Horus, the psychic echoes of that last horrific confrontation were indelibly imprinted on the cells of every Blood Angel. At moments of great stress, the power of that trauma rekindled itself in them, as it had in Koris. To a man, each of them knew the delicious might of the rage as it beckoned from the ragged edges of their battle frenzy, but it was the constant test of their character to hold back from the madness of the berserker. This force that lurked in the collective race memory of the Baalite warrior sect would come to the fore – and as it was now, on the eve of battle a Blood Angel would become consumed with the imprinted recollection. They would see the world as Sanguinius saw it, and come to believe that they were the primarch himself, fighting Horus to the death while great Terra burned around them. To men so touched, the gates to madness would swing wide.

Rafen placed his hands on the sergeant's shoulders. 'Koris, listen to me. It is Rafen, your friend and student. You know me,'

'I do...' Koris managed. 'You must beware... The foetid blood! The tainted chalice...'

'These are visions you see. You must not let them over-come you, or the rage will engulf your reason!'

For an all too brief moment, Koris's glazed sight seemed to clear. 'I feel the pain of his death like it was my own! It races through me... But something... Wrong...'

Rafen was aware of a shape in black armour approaching. 'Brother, stand aside,' said Turcio. 'You must not interfere!'

'What transpires here?' The Space Marine looked away from the old warrior and into the monstrous skull-mask of a Chaplain. Rafen recognised the priest as Brother Delos, the same man who had approached Arkio in the grand chamber.

'Your eminence,' Turcio began. 'I fear that our honoured Sergeant Koris teeters on the brink of the flaw.'

Rafen turned on them both, anger building. 'I will not hear of this! He has looked into the face of the rage a thousand times and held his soul from it, this time will be no differ-ent!' Even as the words left his mouth, Rafen knew it would not be so.

Delos slid back his visor and laid a hand on Rafen's arm. 'You cannot win him back with words, brother,' he said softly. 'The thirst takes the greatest of us... Lestrallio, Tycho at Tempestora, even Mephiston–'

'Mephiston did not yield!' Rafen barked.

The Chaplain studied Koris with a skilled eye. 'But only Mephiston. Your mentor will not resist the pull much longer. Would you let him go mad from the pain, brother? Or will you stand aside and let me grant him a chance for peace?'

Rafen felt the fight leave him. Delos was right. 'But why now? The rage does not simply appear like this! I have fought with Koris time and again, and never before have I seen him so stricken!'

'One cannot know the way of the great angel,' Delos said solemnly, helping Koris to his feet. The veteran's eyes were glassy, and each of them knew that what he saw now was a battle ten thousand years past, not the decks of the *Bellus*.

Remorse cut into Rafen like a blade as Delos signalled to another black-armoured figure to guide Koris away. The sergeant tensed and threw a growl over his shoulder. 'Rafen! Beware... traitors!'

Turcio shook his head sadly. 'Already he confuses this moment with the duel against Horus.'

'Are you sure?' Rafen retorted bitterly.

Delos weighed his crozius arcanum in his hand. Light glittered off the red wings of its skeletal escutcheon. 'Koris is not the first to fall to the thirst this day, and I fear he will not be the last. It is another omen, that Sanguinius stands close to us and there are those who become consumed in his radiance.' At a subtle signal from the elder priest, the Blood Angels' Chaplains began the sombre chant of the mass of doom.

'The moripatris,' breathed Turcio. 'The way is opened toward the Death Company.'

'This is not right!' Rafen's voice was a growl. The old warrior had been a mentor to him for as long as he could remember, a successor to his father now long turned to dust in the lands of the broken mesa. It seemed unconscionable to simply let him go without a struggle after so many battles hard-fought. 'You heard him say it, something is wrong!'

Too late, Rafen realised that his outburst had attracted unwanted attention. From a gantry above the deck he saw Inquisitor Stele fix him with a steady gaze. In moments, the ordos agent had descended to approach, with Sachiel following at his heels. 'What did Koris say?' Stele asked without preamble.

'He spoke of traitors,' Rafen replied. 'He talked of a poisoned chalice.'

Stele said nothing as Sachiel nodded thoughtfully. 'That is to be expected. In the rage, many things become confused. Koris no doubt referred to the traitors of Horus.'

'Traitors who served Chaos while pretending to serve the Imperium.' The words were out of Rafen's mouth before he could stop them.

'At first,' Stele's jaw hardened a little. 'But Horus had turned against the God-Emperor long before he fought Sanguinius.' When the Space Marine did not answer, the inquisitor threw Sachiel a glance. 'Priest, it is your authority that shall be affected by the loss of Sergeant Koris.'

'He'll serve the Chapter as well in the throes of the thirst as he would elsewhere,' said Sachiel, ignoring the pained look on Rafen's face. 'He will become one of the Death Company, as all those who succumb shall.' He stepped forward and gestured. 'Brother Rafen, you will assume command of the sergeant's squad for the assault on Shenlong.'

As protocol demanded, Rafen gave a shallow nod of obeisance. 'Your will.'

Sachiel raised his voice and spoke to the air. 'To arms!'

OUTSIDE THE WALLS of the Ikari fortress, the raised sounds of chants and moans turned Shenlong's smoke-choked sky into a hellish hall of discord. Iskavan turned away from the window to survey the fire-damaged chapel interior. His gaze passed over Falkir, the Word Bearer commander in charge of the Chaos occupation force on planet. 'If it pleases the Dark Apostle,' said the Traitor Marine, 'I would ask how I can serve this host.' His coarse voice echoed off the walls.

Iskavan gave the voluptuous form of a Slaaneshi daemonette an appraising look and then turned to face Falkir. 'As well you should, Castellan.' He sneered at the honorific as if it amused him. 'Turn your troops to their posts and have them prepare for war. Open the cages of your warbeasts. Run out your guns.'

Falkir's face twitched and he glanced over at Tancred. The torturer returned a neutral aspect to the Shenlong garrison commander. He was unwilling to commit even the smallest tic of emotion to the debate. 'Eminence, this pathetic world is ground beneath our heel! I admit that some of the human cattle here still resist the path that Lorgar has brought to them, but we will see to that–'

'Idiot!' Iskavan snarled. 'I care nothing for the meat you lord over on this blighted ball of rust! They are no threat! I order you to prepare for an enemy from without!'

Falkir's obsequious manner vanished. 'Do I understand you correctly? You have come to my prize world with an enemy at your backs?'

'You dare?' The Apostle ground his gauntlet into a spiked fist. 'I have commanded you! See to it!'

Falkir spat. 'Shenlong's skies brim with killers. No human could penetrate the minefield.'

'They come.' Iskavan looked away, studying the night sky. 'Garand himself spoke of it. They come and we will crush them against the anvil of our hate.'

'What poor prophecy is this?' Falkir demanded. 'You have come on a fool's errand–'

From the horizon, a flash briefly turned night into day, and rumbles coursed through the stone of the fortress. Iskavan faced Falkir with a cold smile. 'You see?'

Another blast lit the sky again, closer this time. Then another, and the third struck the castle keep like an earthquake.

IT WAS NOT true that Space Marines know no fear. All the warriors understood the stark power of that raw emotion, but unlike common men who served in other armies, the Adeptus Astartes were the masters of their fear. They took it, moulded it, and turned it against their enemies. They assumed its mantle; they became fear incarnate. It was to them an honoured comrade that joined them on every sortie and sharpened their lust for bloody combat. Chaplain Delos drank it in now as the Death Company Thunderhawk punched through Shenlong's cloud cover and turned toward the Ikari fortress.

A dozen crimson gunships followed the black-painted warbird in a loose delta formation, lit by the fires raging across the capital city. Fat balls of hot flak peppered the air about them. The wings of the flyers rocked as they passed sudden updrafts and pockets of turbulence. At the head of the Blood Angels' invasion, at the tip of the spear, the ebony Thunderhawk screamed, her array of cannons and missiles spitting at the fast-approaching fortress walls. The ship was as dark as the night, brilliant crimson saltires the only decoration over her fuselage. The same pattern was repeated inside the craft, on the armour of the men who rattled and snarled at enemies seen and unseen. Each warrior had ritually altered the livery of the Chapter's wargear. The crimson banished beneath a coating of black paint and crested with red crosses. Black as murder and red as ruin, they howled for annihilation.

Delos cast his eyes over the figures before him. He alone maintained a grip on his sanity as the Death Company's Chaplain, every other Space Marine was wracked by the terrible power of the thirst. Some were silent and introspective with it, while others raged in maddened chorus at traitorous foes long since dead. This was Delos's lot, to take those who had fallen from grace and to lead them into the jaws of battle. They would fight with the assurance of men who held no dread of death, their fears washed away by tides of blood. Delos was simply a herdsman, a pastor and guide who served only to direct them and then unleash these poor souls in a dark hurricane.

'The barrier falls!' cried a voice, and Delos saw Koris surge forward against his restraints, hand clutching the hilt of a brazen power sword. 'Horus bears his throat, Dorn! Summon Guilliman and press the attack!'

The Chaplain could not keep a frown from his face. *He is lost in the primarch's memories and sees us all as figures from the past.* 'Of course, brother,' he said. 'It will be done.'

'I'll carve my name into the arch-traitor's heart!' Koris pointed. 'There! The nest of the enemy!'

Delos saw a shape emerging from the smog: it was the Ikari fortress. It was a volcano grown in the middle of a cityscape. The massive conical construction rose into a flat mesa where bristling gun towers clawed at the sky. In rings around the girth of the keep there were missile carriages, between balconies and the ruins of ornate carvings.

Weapons turned to track the Thunderhawks and the passage became violent. The Chaplain spied the points in the outer walls where lance fire from orbit had made lucky strikes – yes, there to the west, a lengthy crack in the fascia that cried out to be opened still further.

Koris recoiled and released a moan of pain. 'The blood!' he said through gritted teeth. 'The cup of blood was poison! Damn his eyes!' Delos reached out a hand to reassure him, watchful of the veteran's countenance. The Chaplain had shepherded many Blood Angels to their last in the Death Company, and each took a different path into the abyss. 'Curse him! He means to destroy us all!'

Delos gave a slow nod. 'Horus will perish brother, we shall see to it.'

'Horus lies dead!' Koris shouted, and his sight seemed to clear for a moment, 'The traitor... *Stele*!' Pain rose in the warrior's body and he went rigid.

The Chaplain nodded again, the words misconstrued. 'Fear not, Koris. Lord Stele will know of your bravery–' Delos's sentence was lost as a laser struck a chunk off the Thunderhawk's undercarriage. He bellowed a command to the pilot. 'Report!'

'We are undone!' came the reply. 'We cannot land!'

'Then we shall not land!' Delos retorted. 'Power to the thrusters. Take us into the breach. Unlock all weapons and munitions, release the seals on the engine-soul!' Without waiting to see if his orders were followed, the Chaplain pulled at a lever on the wall and a series of explosive bolts ignited along the length of the hull. Planes of steel plate fell away from the Thunderhawk as hatches were ejected into the air, and the restraints holding the black-armoured warriors snapped open. The hot Shenlong wind roared into the open cabin, and the Death Company answered it. 'Brothers, take to your wings!' Delos held fast his crozius, its blue light illuminating him.

Koris let out a wordless cry of vengeance and bared his sword; the thirst had consumed him once again, and without pause he leapt into the air. Delos followed, along with the rest of the men. The yellow jetpack flame buoyed them up and away from the plunging drop-ship.

Anti-aircraft fire converged on the Thunderhawk and set it aflame, but still it fell like a blazing arrow toward the breach in the citadel. Delos saw the aircraft strike with perfect accuracy then the dark metal form vanished in a sphere of white release, and the Ikari fortress trembled. The Death Company fell into the flames, weapons erupting, and the Traitor Marines died with barbarous laments on their lips.

* * *

THE THUNDERHAWKS HAD come on the heels of the orbital bombardment from *Bellus*; so now in the wake of the gunships came the fall of drop-pods bristling with battle-ready Space Marines. Rafen's mouth formed the words of the litergius sanguinius as the hold of Shenlong's gravity pulled his pod down toward the surface. Above his head in the array of thruster jets, a simplistic logic engine shifted the descent of the capsule and aimed it squarely at the heart of the enemy stronghold. He felt the aspect change as the pod altered course and he gripped his bolter in anticipation.

Rafen looked around the men crammed in alongside him – Alactus, Turcio, Lucion and others – and saw how they looked to him with unquestioning loyalty. He was in command of their squad now, Sachiel had decreed it. He had ordered the other Space Marines to show him their deference as they had to Koris. Rafen looked away. He felt unworthy of such an honour so wrongly earned. Rafen fully expected to rise to leadership rank in due time, but to have it thrust upon him in the same moment as his trusted mentor was snatched away by the flaw... His mind was a whirl, and once more he murmured the words of the litergius, hoping that he would draw guidance from them.

A glyph illuminated on the lander's inner wall. 'Prepare for deployment!' he ordered. The squad secured their weapons and chanted the prayer of engagement. Rafen made the sign of the aquila as the capsule's descent rockets flared. Rich chemical foam gushed in to fill the interior, forming a glutinous cushion about them. It was to be a hard landing.

Shedding waves of re-entry heat, Rafen's pod joined a hundred others as they crashed into the barrage-ravaged walls of the fortress. Some of the craft touched down in the plaza below, settling amid chattering defilers and legions of tanks. Others used the velocity of their passage to pierce the castle bulwarks, slamming through rock like the fists of an enraged god.

Rafen blacked out for a moment as they hit. The shock-gel around him had absorbed most of the g-forces, but still the impact rang the drop-pod like a cloister bell. Then the foam was sinking away, and the spitting hiss of displaced air signalled the opening of the hatches. He was on his feet, the awesome energy of his Astartes physiology shrugging off the effects of the concussion.

'For the Emperor and Sanguinius!' The call leapt from his lips, and although he had uttered it a thousand times, the exultant cry did not diminish in force. Rafen threw himself from the pod. The capsule had blown through a gunport and spent its kinetic energy forcing a channel down through two levels of the fortress. It had come to rest in a chapel once used by Imperial weapon crews. Rafen's first sight was of a statue of the God-Emperor, decapitated and fouled with plasma burns. A hot knife of hatred surged through him and he cast around for something to kill in revenge for this besmirching.

There were perhaps a dozen Word Bearers scattered about; it was difficult to tell exactly how many, because the pod's explosive arrival had smashed them into a mess of limbs and torsos. Still, something wailed in the wash of red gore, and a body rose to aim a bolter. Rafen moved as if he were liquid mercury, fast, untouchable. Dodging clumsy fire from the injured Traitor Marine, he sent a burst of rounds into the warrior, ending him.

At the chapel entrance, a bent, hooded figure moaned an entreaty to Rafen, his scarred hands begging him for help. He assumed it was a man, perhaps some servitor that had survived this long amid the occupying army. Rafen stepped to him and took off the head, hood and all, with a single swipe from his combat knife. They had no time for liberating prisoners, and the figure might just as well have been a turncoat. He regarded the headless body as it fell, fountaining crimson. If he had been a loyal subject, then he was beside the Golden Throne now.

Lucion approached, the arcane display of his signum raised. 'Our position is confirmed,' said the Techmarine, reading a datum. 'We are but a short distance away from the breach.' He pointed away along a corridor. The pod's calculating machines had worked well: they had been deposited close to the main thrust of the attack. Under Sachiel's orders, all the Blood Angel forces were to converge and seize the fortress's central access shaft. Once this had been taken, every level of the keep would be open to them.

Rafen allowed himself a moment to consider Koris. He would have been there now, fighting and killing in the Emperor's name, each sword-blow a step closer to his own ending. 'Take the pace!' he called, setting off at a run. 'Swift and deadly, Blood Angels!'

THE IKARI FORTRESS mimicked the cone of a volcano from the exterior, but the pattern of the natural formation extended within as well, like a real cinder mountain. The stronghold was webbed on every level with a network of horizontal channels, along which ran trams that could carry men and hardware to all points of the building. Each of these fed from a central well that fell from the crest of the tower to the deep sub-levels. Instead of boiling magma, the lifeblood of the fortress was manpower, and under Imperial rule it had flourished. The Word Bearers had taken the building in a day, thanks to the perfidy of a cadre of Nurgle cultists that had infiltrated the tower. These death-worshippers had spread a fast-acting plague that indiscriminately killed the defenders, opening the way for the invasion.

Falkir, spying his point of entry as the most logical target for a counter-strike, reinforced the roof with guns and men. He had never expected the Blood Angels to hammer their way through solid rock instead. Rafen's squad converged on the aperture made by the ship guns, and when they reached it, they found carnage of a like that gloried their Chapter's name.

It was all Delos could do to keep up with the Death Company as they ran like screaming banshees into the thick of the Word Bearers' forces. The Chaplain buried the fizzing head of his crozius in the chest of a Traitor Marine and gutted him. Hot blood exploded from his victim. He flicked the gore away with his free hand and spotted Koris at the lip of the central chamber. The veteran's sword was a blur of motion, carving apart Word Bearers while the twin-barrelled bolter in his other hand thundered into a mass of furies. A breed of primitive, predatory daemon beasts, they resembled mutant gargoyles with heads full of eyes and teeth, claws sprouting from every limb and a mad lust for killing. The screeching lizard-daemons snapped at him, and in return he tore them limb from limb, forcing the gun barrel into the mouth of one before opening the beast up with fire.

Reinforcements poured in from the side channels – the enemy was not ready to give way so easily – and they met Rafen's men and a dozen other Blood Angels' squads like two crashing waves. Gunfire and wrath blazed across the complaining metal floors, once again blood-red and gore-red armour clashing as they had on Cybele.

The furies came in a flood of green scales and yellowed teeth, rolling up over the walls from the lower levels. They threw themselves into the mass of Space Marines with abandon, and Rafen was dashed to the floor. For a moment, he was facing straight down, and through the iron grid decking he could see the shape of the central lift dais on its way up from the sub-level. His optics focused; the oval platform was a writhing mass of horned things baring head-splitter axes.

'Bloodletters!' he shouted, rising to his feet. 'Below!' There were moments before the lift reached their level, and when it did, the odds would tip in favour of Chaos. Sachiel's brutal plan of attack would be blunted here in the mouth of the wounded tower. Rafen punched the heart out of a screaming fury, and threw the corpse aside, forcing himself toward the edge. Caught in the throng of the battle, he would never reach it before the elevator arrived.

Beyond, he saw Koris, black and red in his rage, step up to the guardrail of the chasm. With a single swipe he decapitated three Traitors and then called out. 'I see him! Guard the redoubt, Guilliman! I go to face Horus!'

'Koris, no!' The words left Rafen's lips as the sergeant leapt over the rail and fell into the mass of Khornate creatures. Hot rage engulfed Rafen and he cried out, murdering and killing to feed his anger.

THE BLOODLETTERS TORE at Koris's dark armour with their hell-blades, ripping shreds of ceramite from his torso and shoulders. He did not need to aim his blows; everywhere his power sword fell there was a shrieking daemon-beast to die by it. His target lay at the middle of the massing throng, and he cut his way forward.

'Horus!' he bellowed. 'Face me! Face Sanguinius!'

It turned. Koris, maddened by the rage, saw the face and form of the arch-traitor there, the fiend that had butchered his liege lord. What the delusion hid from him was a dread-nought, a clanking hulk of warped metal baring clusters of autocannon and a buzzing chainfist. The awful mechanism fired at him, burning into the crowd of daemons, killing more of them as it swept up to find him. Koris leapt, the strength of his primarch racing through him. He discarded the spent bolter, and two-handed, he took off the infernal device's right arm with the sword like an arc of blazing steel. Hooting with the neuro-shock, it slammed him to the deck with a steaming cannon muzzle and stomped on Koris, hard. A clawed foot splayed over his chest and ground him into the platform.

Bones cracked and organs burst inside the veteran. Yes, now he was at one with Sanguinius, in the blessed grip of agony, the ghostly sensation of broken wings at his back. All things seemed to be in double vision for Koris. One was the face of events here on Shenlong, and the other a return to the ancient conflict aboard the battle barge of Warmaster Horus. He was Koris, veteran sergeant of the Blood Angels, chosen of Dante, warrior of the Death Company – but he was also Sanguinius, lord of Baal, the angelic sovereign and the master of the red grail. 'Chaos filth!' he spat, coughing out tissue and clotted blood. 'I name you traitor! Face me and die!'

The dreadnought loomed over him and laughed, just as the elevator drew level with the breached floor. The veteran heard Blood Angels fighting and dying there. Koris pulled his muscles into line one last time and screamed with the pain of it. He forced himself up and out from under the steel foot. Fists mailed about the hilt, he rammed the power sword into the machine's groin, then up and into the chest, to the rotten core where a crippled Word Bearer lay coiled like some aborted foetus.

It struck him back by reflex, throwing the Space Marine clear across the gantry, before sinking to its rusted knees. With only a brace of autocannons in place of a hand, it could not remove the blade that pierced the power core at its heart. Scattered around the machine-form in disarray, the horned bloodletters milled and chattered in anger and frustration.

The Word Bearer dreadnought had served his Legion for uncountable ages. As a flesh and blood warrior, he had stood in the service of the Emperor in the years before the great awakening, as his kith knew the Heresy. He marched at the purging of Fortrea Quintus, and had willingly followed his Primarch Lorgar into the Maelstrom. He did not know his own name, it had been lost to him in a war with the Ultramarines at Calth, and there too his body had been surrendered to this ambulatory coffin, where he could better serve the Dark Apostles against the corpse god. Thus, without name and without epitaph, the dreadnought died flailing as the reactor in his heart overloaded.

The blast threw everyone to the ground, enemy and ally alike. Seeking the path of least resistance, the shock blew along the central shaft, immolating a handful of loitering furies and making ash of the bloodletters. And then, with a lowing moan of tortured metal, the elevator came apart in molten leaves. Aflame, great axe-heads of decking cut away and tumbled down toward the lower levels, sending up storms of sparks where they collided with the stone walls.

Rafen regained his footing and threw aside the ragged hunks of flesh that had recently been a daemon-form. He caught a Word Bearer who moved a fraction too slowly and granted it the last bolt in his weapon's magazine. The Traitor did not die instantly, so Rafen beat it to death with the burning muzzle of his gun, striking the thing's ugly face over and over again until it became a mess of indistinct matter. The explosion had turned the Blood Angel's hearing into a cascade of sharp ringing, and without voice from any of his brethren, Rafen reloaded and tore into whatever living things he could find that bore the mark of Chaos Undivided. He gave them all an invocation cut from hateful curses. He damned them to the Emperor's cold mercies as he severed them from their lives. The floor became slippery with mixed blood and other fluids, which drained and fell into the darkness of the lower levels. Silence fell there as the Blood Angels asserted their superiority. Now and then, a blast of gunfire signalled that Alactus or one of the other men was executing someone who was still alive.

Rafen killed for the red thirst; he felt it gather around him. He longed to let it in and engulf him, or to feel something of the same madness that had taken his mentor. But it ebbed and receded from him wherever he tried to find it. If a time were to come when he sank into the grasp of the blessed angel, it would not be now. He came across Delos, his Chaplain's armour was glistening. His grinning death mask helmet was streaked with gore. The horrific aspect was at odds with the delicacy he showed as he spoke the words of the Emperor's peace over a fallen member of the Death Company. Rafen knew the dead man – he was a veteran Space Marine, an associate of Koris's from Captain Simeon's command.

'Too many elders took the scarlet path this day,' said Delos, as if reading his mind. 'Noble, senior brothers, all drawn by the flaw as if from nowhere.' He shook his head. 'This omen may be good or ill, Rafen.'

'We… We have taken the well.' he replied in a dead voice. 'Sachiel's plan unfolds.'

'Rafen!' Turcio's yell hung in the blood-wet air. 'Here, quickly!'

'What is it?'

'Koris! He lives, but not for long! He asks for you!'

RAFEN SPRINTED ACROSS the heat-warped decking to a darkened corner of the chamber. Turcio backed away, a look of trepidation on his face. 'You… You should speak to him.'

He said carefully, avoiding looking directly at the veteran's broken body. Some among the Blood Angels thought of the black rage as a virus, and kept their distance from those who exhibited it. Rafen angrily waved him away and knelt next to his old mentor.

Koris's wounds were horrific, and his voice was thin and distant. 'Rafen. Lad, I see you.'

'I am here, old friend.' Rafen's throat tightened. In his agony, the veteran had regained some small measure of lucidity.

'The pure one calls me, but first I must... Warn...'

'Warn me? Of what?'

'Stele!' he spat. 'Do not trust the ordos whoreson! He brought me to this, all of it!' Koris's hand gripped his wrist, the strength ebbing from him. 'Arkio... Be wary of your sibling, lad. He has been cursed with the power to destroy the Blood Angels! I see it! I see—'

Then the light faded from the old man's eyes, and Koris was finally lost to them.

CHAPTER ELEVEN

Bellus awoke from her slumber with terrible violence. The shutters covering her bow peeled back to open the angry mouths of lance batteries and torpedo tubes. The battle barge disgorged shells laden with explosive charges and other warshots that carried men instead of combustibles. Captain Ideon planned each launch down to the split second, and in a perfect ballet, dropships and bombs rained down on Shenlong. Ideon did not trouble himself with concerns about civilians or loyalists down there; the Word Bearers had taken the forge world only recently, and it was likely that Imperial patriots, perhaps planetary defence force troopers or even Guardsmen, were still resisting the Chaos invaders. Those men and women would die tonight. They would be erased from existence in the same crushing fists of fire that tore apart the Traitor Marine divisions. But such collateral damage was the manner of orbital bombardment and those who went to the Emperor tonight would be counted as heroes.

Immobile on his command throne, the captain's mind looked in every direction at once. He was waiting for the sign that would begin the next phase in his battle plan, and as if on cue, a shape emerged over the curve of Shenlong, rising up from an extremely low orbit.

'New contact,' sang one of the sense-servitors. 'Murder-class cruiser on intercept vector, closing at high speed.'

Ideon's pale face moved rarely, and the musculature in his skin was flaccid and ill-used these days. Nevertheless, he managed to peel back his lips in a faint, predatory smile. 'Well met, *Dirge Eterna*,' the captain said to the Chaos warship. 'You'll not flee the field this time.'

Ranged at the observation cupola at the head of the bridge, Sachiel glanced at Arkio and grinned. 'The skills of our brother-captain are uncanny, yes? He predicted that the Traitor ship would take such an orbit and leave us a brief window of attack on the capital.'

Stele stood behind them, and answered first. 'Ideon understands the behaviour of these Chaos filth. Their paranoia would never let them hold in geostationary position – they fear attack from all sides at all times, and so they circle the world like a jackal guarding a carcass.'

Arkio's mind was elsewhere, his hands gripping the brass guide rail. 'Forgive me, high priest, but how long must I remain aboard ship? Even now, the last of our invasion force departs for the surface and I hunger to join them.'

Sachiel smiled, aware that Stele's eyes were upon them both. 'Soon, Arkio. Very soon. The inquisitor has something special planned for the Traitors, and it will be your glory to take it to them.'

The young Blood Angel's eyes glittered with anticipation as he met Sachiel's gaze. The Sanguinary Priest was struck by the play of reflected laser-light off the youth's aquiline face, the gaunt and noble cut of his chin and cheekbones. *By the grail, the boy could be Sanguinius himself.*

'Entering firing range,' said the scanner servitor.

Stele turned in place to watch Ideon. 'Captain, at your discretion?'

Ideon did not need the inquisitor's permission, and the comment irked him slightly. Then the *Dirge Eterna* rose in his weapon sights and he felt a swell of anticipation. 'Bow guns stand down, power to void shields.'

'It is done,' Solus replied, glancing up from the console pit beneath the captain's bronze throne. 'The engineseers report that the sub-light drives are content and prepared for full thrust.'

'All ahead full,' Ideon's reply came without pause. 'Bring us to the bastard.'

The *Bellus*'s executive officer relayed the command into a mouthpiece at his neck, spreading the word throughout the battle barge. Instantly, the warship's thruster grid crashed into life, and forced the vessel forward with a gut-wrenching lurch of motion.

At his vantage point, Arkio saw the inner edge of the minefield receding. The three-dimensional warfare of starships was not his area of expertise, but he understood the pattern to which Ideon was working. Although there were hundreds of kilometres of vacuum between them, *Bellus* and *Dirge Eterna* had little room to manoeuvre. They were sandwiched between the wall of mines in high orbit over Shenlong and the planet's atmospheric envelope below. The orbital corridor they fought in had barely enough room for a ship the size of *Bellus* to turn about at maximum thrust, and Ideon's plan to engage the Chaos cruiser was dangerous. The smallest delay or a mistake in orders would send the battle barge into the ionosphere and burn her to the keel. It was like two men conducting a knife-fight in a coffin.

'Incoming fire from the Traitor,' said Solus. 'He's trying to push us back into the mines.'

'Ignore it. Have the bow crews reload with the special warshots. Give me the status of the port and starboard batteries.'

Brother Solus relayed the data, and as the information flowed directly into Ideon's mechadendrites, the first licks of laser flame struck *Bellus* hard. The aged warship took the blow in her stride and turned into it, bringing as little of her aspect as possible to face the *Dirge Eterna*. 'All parallel guns answer ready.'

'Then, by the Throne, fire at will.'

Arkio watched. On one level, he hated the idea of being nothing more than an observer, but on another he found himself fascinated by the steady, deliberate pace of the combat. He absently ran a hand over his face. Strangely, the engagement felt familiar to him, as if he had watched other battles like this from similarly lofty heights. For a moment, he blinked and saw not Shenlong and the *Dirge*, but a different, blue-green planet and a massive Chaos barge, hideously beweaponed and blasphemous in its arcane geometry, then the image was gone.

The Murder-class ship presented its port side to *Bellus* as the two vessels came alongside one another in a deadly jousting pass. In a tactic dating back to the birth of mankind's naval wars, both starships unleashed a punishing broadside, and for a second the space between them was threaded with hot lances of light and the thin trails of missile salvoes. *Bellus* rocked with the impact and lost pressure on a dozen decks. Huge petals of hull metal shredded from her flank along with fountains of breathing gas and water ice. Vacuum-bloated corpses followed them.

Ideon did not ask for a damage report. He felt each one of *Bellus*'s wounds as keenly as if it had been cut into his own hide. As the two ships moved out of the merge, he barked out his next orders. 'On the word, emergency turn, maximum displacement!'

Solus blinked. 'Engineseers report that optimal power is not available, lord. The machine spirit is reluctant–'

'Damn the thing!' Ideon grated. 'The word is given! Turn the ship!'

Ideon's aide nodded again and sent the command, gripping the closest stanchion for dear life. Arkio felt a shift in gravity in the pit of his gut and the deck threw him into the guardrail.

Bellus moaned like a wounded animal as she suddenly bled out the acceleration force of a dozen gravities. Massive thrust jets fired along her port flank as one to bodily ram the ship around. The barge bowed under the massive stresses, losing more air and men. On the bridge, a hololithic screen spat sparks and exploded, killing a servitor instantly and maiming a Blood Angel's officer.

'Turning!' called Solus, 'Aspect change on target!'

Ideon ignored the pain and his voxcoder crackled with venom. 'Too slow, *Dirge Eterna*! I have you!'

The Word Bearer ship was also coming about, but with none of the wild daring that Ideon had demanded of his vessel. Slowly, inexorably, *Bellus* brought her bow to aim at the cruiser. Now the positions were reversed, and it was the *Dirge* trapped between the minefield and their enemy.

'Bow guns!' Ideon snapped.

'They… Do not answer,' Solus admitted, 'Perhaps the crews were injured–'

Ideon cared not. 'All tubes, fire for effect.'

Once more, Solus relayed the order. If the men in the forward weapons channels had been slowed in their duties by the force of the fierce turn, the firing command would see them vented into space as the gigantic torpedo tubes yawned open.

From the crimson maw of the *Bellus*, a fusillade of dark shapes emerged and raced toward the enemy ship. Arkio watched them go. His throat tightened as he suddenly realised they were flying wide of the mark. Incredulous, he could do nothing but stare as they passed the *Dirge* and blew apart in puffballs of flame and glittering metal. 'A miss!' he cried.

'No,' said Ideon. 'Watch.'

Where standard warheads had just an explosive charge, the torpedoes that *Bellus* had fired carried jury-rigged cases of metallic chaff and heat flares – and on the artificial sensors of the silent mines behind the cruiser, the colour of their blasts registered like the eruption of a dozen suns. Techmarine Lucion's examination of the mine that hit *Bellus* had revealed exactly how the devices had worked, and Ideon's tech-adepts exploited this new knowledge. As if they were a swarm of wasps brought to sudden anger, the docile mines nearest *Dirge Eterna* fired their thrusters and dived into the craft. Each detonation attracted another, and then another, until the enemy ship was smothered in bursts of nuclear fire.

'Bring us to a stable altitude,' the captain's voice betrayed a veil of smug satisfaction. 'Damage control details to their stations.'

Sachiel blew out a breath. 'And now the Word Bearers are stranded on Shenlong.'

Arkio turned away from the burning ship, eyes keen with anticipation. 'We shall make it their grave marker.'

THE WORD BEARERS were waiting for them on the ground level of the fortress. The broadest part of the entire tower, the vast circular floor spread out around the central shaft like a desert of metal decking. The atrium was so high and wide that entire city blocks could have fitted in the gaps between the ranks of handling gear and machinery. Open doors that led into a spray of manufactory hangars yawned open, through gates as big as the *Bellus*. Overhead, mechanical gantries and hanging monorail trams stood mute witness to the maelstrom of carnage below. There was no moment of peace to be found anywhere here, only the constant disorder of unfettered warfare.

Methodical and inexorable, the Chaos Space Marines came forward in ranks, flowing around the obstacles in their path. The incessant braying of the demagogues rebounded from the metal walls, a ceaseless cacophony of monstrous and profane screaming. The Blood Angels met them with equal ferocity, flooding out from the open shaft in a storm of brazen red. Rafen and Alactus fought side-by-side, thrown together by chance, bolter and plasma gun shouting death back at the enemy.

No man among the Space Marines would have voiced it from his position deep in the killing frenzy, but the Word Bearers were forcing them back inch-by-inch. For all the reversals of their fortunes, for all the time that Koris's mad sacrifice had bought them on the upper floors, there were simply more of the Traitors than there were of them. Bloody attrition would tell the day, and with each surge of men who dived gleefully into close-quarter combat with the magenta-hued enemy, less and less of the Astartes warriors remained to hold the line. Eventually, the press of corrupted flesh and steel would force them into the walls. There was nowhere else to go: if they could not break through the enemy the only other route was pure suicide, down into the sub-levels where the Ikari fortress's prison cells lay. In those dark warrens crammed with wretched and broken civilians the Word Bearers would be able to bottle them up and slaughter them at will. At least on the open deck, they had a chance to fight and die with glory. With their rage ignited, retreat was not an option.

Rafen was a furious engine of destruction, a whirlwind of razors as he cut into a pack of Chaos Space Marines. As Alactus felled targets by plasma immolation, Rafen ran the monsters through with his combat knife and the shells from his trusted bolter. In the brilliant crimson heat of his fury, he sheared heads and limbs in clean strikes, and when the opportunity presented itself, the Blood Angel let his fangs rip into those who were fool enough to bare their flesh. The perfect sheen of his battle armour was streaked with gore, and he paused to spit out a glutinous flush of bile. His face soured. The blood of these mutant blackguards was of a poor vintage, thick with taint and worthy only for spilling.

'Do you see him?' Alactus shouted over the crackling hiss of steam rising from his gun muzzle. 'There, the great horned pestilent from Cybele!'

Rafen looked, and in the middle distance saw the hulking shape of the Dark Apostle Iskavan, bellowing some foul cry with his dripping crozius raised high overhead. 'Curse the warpspawn!' he retorted. 'We could not be so lucky to find him dead, eh?'

Alactus fired a few shots in Iskavan's direction in reply. 'No matter, we'll gut him as we have the rest of his breed!'

Rafen answered with fresh gunfire, but the rational, tactical part of his mind knew that the odds were thinning. Beyond Iskavan's personal guard, Rafen could see fresh numbers of Word Bearers walking at steady parade ground pace, up from the mouths of the shell factories beyond the fortress proper. For a fanciful moment, he wondered if the fabricator plants were stamping new Word Bearers out of plate steel, just as they did stubbers, grenades and warheads. Just then a lick of burning promethium from a Chaos flamer almost cut him down, and he fired blindly. The Emperor gave him his eye for that moment and a lucky round penetrated the Traitor Marine's fuel canister. With a cough of displaced air, the flamer bearer turned into a torch and wailed, dying.

ISKAVAN WAS DROWNED out by the roar of his men as he came to the last words of Lorgar's great invocation. He felt their excitement ripple through him like a delicious wave. At his flank, Falkir spat harsh, clipped commands to his subordinates and turned to face the Apostle, an ugly grin on his shark-toothed features. He crowded out the torturer Tancred, who hung back and watched the unfolding melee with a grim countenance.

'Master, I bring you my finest and most puissant warriors!' Falkir made a theatrical gesture with his clawed hand. 'Behold, the vox baiulus obliterati!'

Iskavan raised a pallid eyebrow. He was amused by the Castellan's melodramatic presentation and favoured him with a flicker of his tongues. From the midst of the rank and file Word Bearers came a Legion of Chaos Space Marines unlike any that stood on Shenlong. These were no longer beings that could be called man or daemon, but some otherworldly union of the two. They came in a slow and purposeful march; the thick stocks of their limbs were as wide as tree trunks. It was difficult to see where the lustreless corpse flesh of their heads and arms ended and the bruise-coloured metals of their power armour began. Great pipes of horn or hollow cartilage undulated up from their spines and knotty ropes of sinew fat as telegraph cables webbed their arms. Perhaps at one point they might have had hands and fingers as Iskavan knew them, but now the great clubs of meat that were their forearms sprouted hooked blades and an organ-pipe profusion of gun barrels.

'Obliterators!' Tancred breathed. 'By the eye, they are magnificent!'

Iskavan gave the torturer an arch look. 'You think so? Then you may lead them.'

Tancred hid his surprise. It was ever his way to remain within his master's reach and it had been so for centuries of service together. The Apostle bore down on him and showed him a mouth of wicked fangs. 'Do not tarry, Tancred,' he growled. 'Go to the enemy and show your mettle. It has been too long since you tasted blood at the front.'

The torturer was aware of Falkir watching him. He was ready to strike him down if he dared to disobey. Tancred's tentacle hand betrayed him and twitched as he tried to formulate an excuse. 'Dark one, I–'

'You are favoured by me,' finished Iskavan. 'Have you not foreseen victory for us, Tancred?' He pointed at the main body of the Blood Angels with his crozius. 'Go now, and fetch it to me.'

The Word Bearer priest's death-vision glimmered at the back of his mind and he forced it away. To admit such a thing now, after he had concealed it for so long, would mean execution. He nodded and stepped into the horde of obliterators. 'It is my honour to serve,' he said, unable to mask the bitterness in his tone.

'Yes,' agreed Iskavan. 'It is.'

The grotesque hulks of meat and metal lumbered onward, the line troopers falling aside as they continued their ponderous advance. Around Tancred, their arms merged and reformed into lascannon maws, the tines of radiating power mauls and meltagun muzzles. At his order, they began a constant stream of fire into the Blood Angels, and in their dozens Imperial Space Marines were cut apart by bolt and beam.

* * *

RAFEN POURED ROUNDS into the torso of the nearest obliterator and growled with frustration. The thing's head retreated into the muddy pool of flesh-metal between its shoulders and howled back at him. He spat out an order and Turcio answered it with return fire from a missile launcher. Rockets looped and struck the Chaos puppet with bright orange impacts. The Word Bearer fell, and was ground underfoot by its inexorable brethren.

'Is there no end to the blasphemies of the foe?' Alactus demanded. 'What unholy fiends are these?'

'Hybrids,' said Rafen. 'A godless amalgam of human flesh, daemon and armour. Every breath they draw is an offence to life!'

Alactus poured plasma flame at Tancred's force. 'We'll end them, then!'

'Aye!' Rafen joined him, and another obliterator sank to its knees.

There came a pronunciation from every communicator in the Blood Angels' line, strident and high, broadcast from the *Bellus* high above them. 'Sons of Sanguinius! Stand to and hold the line!'

Rafen recognised Sachiel's voice and he grimaced. 'What does he think we are doing?' he said aloud, low and angry.

'The rout of the archenemy begins now!' said the Sanguinary Priest, his words bubbling over with ecstatic power. 'As our liege lord did, so our vengeance falls from the sky on burning wings!'

Deep in the mass of the Word Bearers' advance, beyond the ranks of the advancing obliterator cult and the frothing waves of Chaos Space Marines, an actinic glitter of light unfolded out of the air. Hard jags of artificial lightning leapt from it to strike Traitors dead where they met its path, and the air went hot with ozone and the screams of tortured energy.

Rafen instinctively knew what it was; the crawl of his skin and the sudden sympathetic lurch of his gut warned him of an imminent teleport arrival. The pinprick of light expanded and shuddered as the laws of matter and space were briefly circumvented in the halls of the Ikari fortress. A flat crash of displaced atmosphere echoed and sent a bow wave of spent energy across the decking. It scattered the Word Bearers in a perfect circle, and there, stood atop the bodies of a dozen Traitors twisted into warped slag, were ten figures.

Seven of them were Blood Angels, and all but one of those wore the jump packs and polished gold helmets of the honour guard. Rafen saw Stele there among them, he held a vicious force axe in his right hand and his ornate lasgun in the left. Two gun-servitors, their forms not unlike the Chaos obliterators, flanked him and began to fire at anything wearing magenta. Sachiel's voice rose in a screaming hymnal, the bronze grail in his hand raining hot blood about him. Each Space Marine was shocked by the sight of the warrior standing with the Spear of Telesto in his grip. Its shimmering colour wreathed its blade in an illustrious, ephemeral banner.

'Arkio!' Perhaps Rafen said the name, or perhaps it was Alactus, it mattered not. The sight of the spear and the youth in the gold helmet was like the ignition of a flash-fire amid the Blood Angels, and as one they tore fire into the Word Bearers' assault.

Rafen was on his feet and surging up over broken fragments of cover before he was even aware of his own actions. Alactus was steps ahead of him, the blue-white generator rings of his gun bright with discharge. Battered and injured, the Space Marines found their second wind and tore into the Traitors with hellish ferocity. Turcio rammed the mouth of his missile gun into the chest of a towering obliterator and blew it apart in a flaming discharge, spattering Rafen and Alactus with hot globules of daemon-flesh. Everywhere Rafen looked, he could see the divine radiance of the holy lance falling across the gore-streaked wargear of his battle-brothers, lighting them up with a righteous fury the likes of which even the Emperor himself would have applauded. Some part of the Space Marine wanted to rein his excesses in and exert control, but too much of him gloried in the bloodletting. It was not the black rage that consumed him now, but the desire for revenge: for Simeon, for Koris, for every Throne-fearing man, woman and child that had died at the hands of Chaos. Rafen longed to have the spear and see it cut the enemy to ribbons.

Stele was lost in the tumult; he was surrounded somewhere by packs of snarling furies and the helldog forms of flesh hounds. He let his servitors make short work of them, as he channelled his mind-essence through the force axe. Nothing stood to fight where the inquisitor walked, and even as he killed and killed, his psyche ranged above the battlefield, prowling like a hawk. Sachiel, his guardsmen tight about him, led the new arrivals into the thick, shredding Word Bearers.

Without reason or conscious choice, Rafen found himself leading the charge across the metallic decks. In that moment of ellipsis something chose to push him to the head. Without pause he took the chattering bolter in his hand and struck an obliterator where its lascannon arms were bleeding coolant and oily fluid. The thing spun and gave out a thin scream, disturbingly childlike for something so huge. He sprinted and leapt over the corpse with a war cry on his lips – and there he saw the face of the torturer from Cybele.

Tancred had his vibra-stave gripped in his nest of tentacles and a lasgun in the near-human talons of his other limb. A panicked beam shot scored a finger-wide gouge in Rafen's vambrace but it did not stop the Blood Angel. His combat knife flashed and Rafen cut the torturer's hand off at the wrist, gun and all falling away in jets of adulterated blood. Tancred rammed the stave into Rafen's side and the sparking tip skittered off his inviolate armour. The Space Marine's mind possessed the strange clarity of pure fury, as if seeing everything through some perfect lens of hate. He caught Tancred's stave in his free hand, and instinctively forced it back at the torturer's face. The Word Bearer saw then the instrument of his own death: the ghost-shape from the blood augury resolving into his weapon, and it was gripped in the hand of a crimson assassin. Rafen drove the vibra-stave up through Tancred's jaw and out through the top of his distorted skull.

ISKAVAN FELT TANCRED's ending and cursed. On some level he sensed regret, but only for a brief moment. He roared at Falkir and the rest of his troops, pointing at Sachiel's honour guard. 'This is their reinforcement? Ten men? By Skaros, we'll make flutes of their bones!' His accursed crozius hummed in mad rage. 'Destroy them!'

THE SPEAR OF Telesto worked and Arkio felt as if he were merely a vessel for the weapon, like the igniter for an explosive power so far beyond him as to be unimaginable. And yet, every second the weapon sang in his grip, and the teardrop blade brought ruin to hundreds of Traitor Marines, he felt himself *changing*. Power the likes of which he had never dared imagine coursed through Arkio, and his mind struggled to grasp it. The closest thing he could approximate it with was his rebirth when he left the sarcophagus on Baal for the first time, but even that was a pale shadow compared to the majestic force running through him now. He was a hundred feet tall. He could see the passage of bolts and laser blasts as if they were suspended in the air. He was invincible. By the lords, he was *godlike*.

Arkio counted the Word Bearers in an eye-blink. There were too many, the spear told him. Their numbers must be thinned, and not at the sluggish pace of gun and chainsword. The Blood Angel saw it clearly: action and reaction surfaced in his mind as if he had always known precisely how to wield this weapon. Arkio swung the spear about him and drew in energies untouched since the heresy. He gathered them effortlessly at the tip of the teardrop blade. In the golden backwash of light, he felt the bones of his face altering, becoming the mask of someone else, someone unaccountably older and wiser.

Now! Mellifluent flame spilled forth from the holy lance in a wide fan and washed over the battle like a flood. Every Word Bearer it touched caught fire and burned alive, and ahead of the wave rode a psychic storm of absolute terror. Those Chaos Space Marines not kindled into powder ran screaming in fear. Iskavan himself pitched his own men into the fire's path and broke, all sign of his unstoppable resolve shattered before the might of the spear.

The firestorm lapped over the corpses of the dead and engulfed the Blood Angels. Rafen saw it coming. His body froze at the sight of it; he was unable even to throw up his hands and cover his face. He saw himself dying along with the rest of his brethren as his sibling's uncontrolled release of the lance's power killed enemy and ally alike. But the gold flames crashed over them leaving nothing but a surge of adrenaline as their primarch's legacy brushed past. The uncanny sophistication of the Telesto weapon saw the markers of Sanguinius's own bloodline in all the Blood Angels and turned its power from them.

Silence fell across the Ikari fortress as the last flickers of light died out around the spear. Slowly Arkio removed his golden helmet to drink in the destruction he had wrought. Across the carnage, his gaze met Rafen's and the smile on the younger man's face was a warped mirror of the sanguine angel himself. But instead of nobility and purity dancing there, Rafen saw an aspect as cruel as a razor's edge and his heart froze in his chest.

WINDS OF ASH blew across the plaza before the fortress, billowing in great, silent wreathes. The atomised remnants of Word Bearers, the cinder gathered in drifts of grey snow, pooling in the lee of revetments and towers. Rafen left boot-prints in the matter of the dead as he crossed the broken square, to wind a course around the wrecks of burnt-out Blood Angels' Razorbacks and Chaos defilers; the latter were surrounded by wards made from tapes of parchment shot through with holy text, in order that the unhallowed influence be held at bay, even in death. At the edge of the plaza, Rafen found Brother Delos supervising the Chapter's serfs in the collection of the deceased.

The Chaplain gave him a solemn nod. His face was streaked with soot. He did not need to ask what Rafen wanted. 'Over there.' He gestured toward a line of canvas bags, each dotted with purity seals and generic prayers in High Gothic. Delos turned his back and gave Rafen the privacy he needed. Although the bodies of the honoured dead would be properly venerated in ceremonies aboard *Bellus* in the days to come, he knew from personal experience that some men needed a moment of solitude to bid their comrades farewell.

When he was sure he was unobserved, Rafen gently opened the canvas to reveal the face of Koris's corpse. The pain the veteran's face had displayed in the moment of death was mercifully absent, and the Blood Angel found himself heartened that his old mentor was at peace now, sitting at the Emperor's right hand.

'Rest now, my friend,' he whispered. But as he spoke Rafen's heart felt hollow. Koris's last words were burnt into his mind like a livid brand. The sergeant's gaunt face implored him: *Be wary of your sibling, lad. He has been cursed with the power to destroy the Blood Angels!* What was he to make of such an avowal? What glimpse of truth had Koris been granted as his soul briefly merged with that of Sanguinius?

That Koris had not trusted the Inquisitor Stele was a matter of course, but in his dying breath he had cursed the ordos agent, and blamed him for his fall to the black rage. Perhaps it had been some final spite of the bloodlust madness that had consumed the veteran, striking out even as he died. Yet Rafen could not shake the sense of utter *wrongness* that surrounded him. Sergeant Koris fell to the flaw too quickly, too easily. How convenient it was that one of the most respected – and outspoken – elders in their warband had died, leaving Stele's influences unopposed.

Rafen was shocked at his own defiance, and the thoughts that came to mind – thoughts that some would name as heresy of the highest order. He shook his head. These matters, of Arkio's changed ways, of Sachiel's ruthless commands and Stele's manipulations, they ranged beyond Rafen's experience as a warrior and a servant to the Throne.

He placed a hand on Koris's chest, in a spot where a laser had burnt off the black paint of his Death Company colours to reveal the crimson teardrop beneath. 'Help me, teacher. For the last time, show me the path.' In that moment, Rafen saw the head of the sergeant's vox transmitter, sheared away from his neck ring. The youth bent down and carefully pulled the wire-thin apparatus free. It was a command-level contact rig, capable of sending messages directly to upper echelon units and to ships in orbit. Unlike the unit in Rafen's armour, Koris's gear was encrypted with codes and machine keys that gave him access to all facets of the Blood Angels' command structure – and in an emergency, even to the homeworld itself.

Cold clarity descended on Rafen as he understood what he was honour bound to do. *These matters can only be settled by one man*, he told himself. The Space Marine spoke into the transmitter.

'*Bellus*, respond. Telepathic duct protocol required, expedite immediate.' The device tingled in his fingers as it sampled his genetic imprint, attempting to verify his identity as a Blood Angel. It would be a gamble, but it was likely that the *Bellus* crew did not yet have a full accounting of those killed in battle and so the dead man's cipher clearances would not have been cancelled.

He heard the dull rattle of a servitor voice in the veteran's helmet. 'Confirm, Sergeant Koris. Your orders?'

'Encryption protocol omnis maximus. Direction, to the high office of the Lord Commander Dante, Fortress Baal.'

There was a pause, and for a brief instant Rafen thought he would be discovered. What he was doing now would be grounds for extreme sanction, at the very least. 'Ready to transmit, Sergeant Koris,' came the voice. 'Begin.'

Rafen took one last moment to ensure that no one could see or hear him, and then he took a deep breath, tasting the ashen remains of the dead on his lips. 'My Lord Dante, I must inform you of recent circumstances on the worlds of Cybele and Shenlong, and aboard your servant starship the *Bellus*.' Crouched over the corpse of his mentor, Rafen began to recount the turn of events that had brought him to doubt his faith itself, in urgent and hushed tones.

Perhaps the astropath who carried his message was truly ignorant of Rafen's deception, or perhaps he chose to send it anyway in some small act of defiance for the killing of Horin. Whatever the motive, the Space Marine's imperative issued forth unchallenged into the void and raced away along invisible lines of telepathic force, leaping from beacon-mind to relay-psyker, and crossing the galaxy toward the Blood Angels' monastery holdfast on Baal.

CHAPTER TWELVE

THEY CAME FROM everywhere: from hideaways in the warehouses, from inside inert furnaces and the basements of a thousand tenements. The people of Shenlong emerged into the light of the dawn blinking away tears and raising their hands in supplication. They had been delivered from the defiance of the Chaos demagogues that had stalked their streets promising them only death. The Emperor's gaze had seen their predicament. He had answered the prayers they had whispered in the ruins of blasted churches. He had sent the Blood Angels to end the Word Bearers' invasion with devout fire.

Others did not rejoice. There were those who had been quick to accept the word of Lorgar, the ones who had torn down the icons of the Imperium and swiftly built Word Bearer temples in their place. These Shenlongi found themselves ripped from their beds and hung from the monorails, or thrown into the foundry flame-pits to choke on sheaves of infernal propaganda. Blood continued to flow in the ashen, rust-marked city zones, and old rivalries blossomed under cover of the liberation.

Stele observed much of this from his vantage point on the plaza's edge. The segment of the planet visible to him was a writhing microcosm of all of Shenlong. Word had spread quickly of Arkio's deeds and since first light civilians had been arriving in ragged packs to see the Blood Angels with their own eyes. And the warrior who held the golden Spear. The inquisitor turned as the Space Marine approached him; even before he heard Arkio's footfalls he could sense the humming power of the holy lance draw near. Stele's gaze, like everyone else's, was drawn first to the weapon, and then to the man who gripped it in his fist. The inquisitor had been the first human to touch the Spear of Telesto in centuries; he had torn it out of the claws of the ork warlord that stole it. The decerebrate beast had not even the slightest inkling of what the blade could do, only that it had value. Perhaps, if it had possessed a smidgeon of true intellect, the barbaric animal would never have dared to take it. But it had, and with the action, Stele's intricate, clockwork plans had been set in motion.

Still, the archeotech device had never revealed itself to him as it had to the Space Marine. Stele smothered a surge of jealousy. The spear might have kept its secrets, but it would still serve him. In fact, it would be a far better tool in Arkio's hands than in his.

The people who had made their pilgrimage to see the blessed one parted before Arkio like scythed corn. They were dazzled by the weapon's radiance even in quietude. *How typical of the Imperial citizenry*, Stele reflected, *so desperate in their bleak little lives that they accept any ray of divinity that shines upon them.* He would make good use of that when the time came.

'Lord,' said Arkio and nodded. He did not avert his gaze from the inquisitor's eyes. Already, the potency of the weapon was manifesting through him in subtle, arrogant ways. *I chose well*, Stele told himself.

'Comrade Brother Arkio. You performed flawlessly. Truly, you are the vessel for the power of Sanguinius.'

Arkio seemed weary. 'In his name and in the Emperor's. I only hope it was enough…' He glanced at the pilgrims, who shied away under such scrutiny. As an Adeptus Astartes, Arkio was conditioned to expect lesser men to fear him as one of the Emperor's chosen, but the veneration these people showed was something else. It was something deeper and more primal. 'Why do they watch me so?'

Stele glanced at Sachiel as he approached. 'It is my estimation that nothing as magnificent as the spear has ever been seen on Shenlong. These commoners see the radiance of the Golden Throne caught in the blade's light. Is it any wonder they grovel before it?'

Arkio studied the spear. It was dormant, but still it cast a directionless, honeyed glow. Gently, he returned it to the case brought forth by Stele's servitors and closed the lid. As the container closed over it, a sense of uncanny warmth faded from the air and Arkio's brow furrowed.

Sachiel was animated. The Sanguinary Priest was wound tight with energy. His face was florid with delight. 'I had never dreamed, in all my life that I would be witness to something such as this! Arkio, you prove the blessing for all to see!'

'Aye.' The Blood Angel was introspective and sullen.

Sachiel did not appear to notice. 'The golden helm of the honour guard fits you well, Arkio! You seem born to it.'

Arkio removed the headgear and studied it, as if seeing it for the first time. 'Perhaps.' His voice grew distant. 'I find it unsuitable.'

'In what way?' Stele prodded gently.

Watching the distorted vision of his own face in the amber mirror of the helmet, Arkio shook his head. 'I have... grown beyond the crimson armour of my servitude. I fee I should greet the world clad in gold, yes?' He looked to Stele for some sort of confirmation, as if the thought had come to him from elsewhere.

'You would wish to wear armour as our Lord Dante does?' Hesitation crept into Sachiel's voice. 'But...'

'But what, Sachiel?' said Stele. 'You yourself spoke of Arkio's blessing. Should he not look the part if he is touched by grace?'

The moment of doubt fled the priest's face. The thought that such deeds might be sacrilegious lasted for less than a heartbeat. Sachiel smiled and addressed the other Blood Angels and any civilians in earshot. 'You will be able to say you were here on Shenlong when Arkio the Blessed liberated the Ikari fortress! Today we walk on the pages of history!'

'History?' Arkio's voice was a sneer. 'Today we walk on the ashes of the dead, the corpses of fallen heretics.' He looked across at Stele. 'I have liberated nothing!'

'You won a victory, lad,' said the inquisitor. 'You, and your brothers.'

A sudden, livid flare of anger broke over Arkio's face. 'There is no victory over the Word Bearers without extinction! Their Dark Apostle fled the field. I saw it with my own eyes! How can we lay claim to this world if that viper slithers in its streets? Answer me that!'

Stele toyed with the purity stud in his ear. 'Iskavan the Hated still lives and Arkio is correct. Shenlong will know no peace until we unite it under the banner of Sanguinius and kill every last Traitor.'

'It is their way,' the Blood Angel added. 'They turn worlds to their black cause and poison their peoples. If we do not

drive them out now, we may never have the chance again...
Less we raze this planet and be done with it.'

Sachiel gasped at such a suggestion. 'We came to return
Shenlong to the bosom of the Imperium, not destroy it!'

'Then what do you propose, high priest?' Arkio asked, and
all trace of the Space Marine's hesitance was gone. 'That we
wait and allow them to regroup for a counter-attack? We
must not forget what we learned on Cybele.'

The Blood Angel absently stroked at a panel of his white
and red armour, the bone-coloured sections were daubed
with splashes of enemy gore. 'Yes... Yes, you are correct.'

'We must follow the path laid for us,' said Stele. The
inquisitor was about to say more, but a cold breeze stiffened the air about him. From orbit, his personal astropath
Ulan sent an impression of urgency and concern, a psychic
summons. He forced a flat smile. 'Brothers, I'm afraid I
must return to the *Bellus* immediately. A matter of some
importance requires my attention.' He signalled to the
servitors to accompany him with the spear.

'No,' said Arkio, without looking to see if his command
was obeyed. 'The holy lance should remain close to me.'

Stele's flicker of annoyance went unseen. 'Quite so. How
foolish of me to suggest otherwise.' The inquisitor revised
his estimation of Arkio again; he had expected such defiance to manifest, but not so soon. But it would not suit his
plans to countermand the Space Marine in front of his battle-brothers. Better to let them believe that Arkio held
authority over the weapon. Stele strode past Sachiel and
threw a compelling glare at the priest. 'I will return as
quickly as I can.'

One of the veteran sergeants approached Sachiel and
bowed as the inquisitor vanished into the ashen mists.
'Eminence, what are your orders?'

Sachiel gave him a brief nod and the priest indicated the fortress. 'Sweep the tower and locate a suitable base for an operations centre–'

'Perhaps we will require a chapel as well,' said Arkio, offhandedly.

'–and a chapel as well.' finished Sachiel.

IN THE WEB of sewer tunnels and decrepit flood chambers beneath the manufactory, the Word Bearers walked in silence. They moved in tight lines through pools of tainted, cadmium-laced water and trickles of thin oil that leaked from machines above. Here and there among the groups were packs of feral daemon predators, furies and flesh hounds that lowed, their animal intellects too dull to comprehend what had happened. Falkir followed in the footsteps of Iskavan, with only the Dark Apostle's back for company, as he led them deeper into the network of tunnels. The warlord was heedless of direction; he seemed to take turns at random. The only sounds were the constant footfalls of their boots across the flowing effluent and the faint hum of Iskavan's unquiet crozius.

Falkir wanted to question the Apostle, to seek some sense of his plan, but the first Word Bearer that had dared to speak to Iskavan had found eightfold blades buried in his neck, sucking the black blood from him. The Castellan nursed his anger. He had made a good show of his capture of Shenlong, and the forge world was well on the way to becoming a stronghold for Chaos before the *Dirge Eterna* had arrived. Temples and cursed monuments had sprouted across the planet, forced indoctrinations were taking place everywhere, and Falkir had dared to allow himself a moment of pride. But barely a day had passed since Iskavan the Hated had set foot on the world that Falkir had claimed, and now the Word

Bearers were routed, driven into the tunnels by the Blood Angels and *that* weapon. His hand closed on his chain axe and the Castellan considered burying it in the Apostle's skull.

Iskavan came to a halt and turned. Falkir was startled. Had the warlord sensed his disloyal thoughts?

'This will suffice,' The Apostle gestured ahead with the crozius toward a large open flood chamber, pitted with rust and slurry. It was large enough to hold a thousand men, but Falkir found himself wondering whether there was even a fraction of that number of Word Bearers still alive. 'We hold here. Send scouts to locate any other survivors and regroup.'

'Your will,' Falkir replied tersely.

Iskavan eyed him. 'You have something to say to me?'

Falkir teetered on the edge of open rebellion, and it was only with a supreme effort of will that he kept himself from decrying the Apostle as a fool. 'No, Great One. I am merely... fatigued.'

The Word Bearer warlord snorted. 'You are a poor liar.' He hefted the crozius. 'Search for nine humans. Gather them and bring them here, unharmed.'

'What purpose will that serve?'

Iskavan replied, but he seemed to be speaking to himself more than Falkir. 'My laxity toward Tancred has cost me dearly, and now I pay the price. His vision was a lie...' The Apostle stroked the weapon. 'I shall cast for my own. I will summon judgement for these Astartes filth. I will bring forth a bloodthirster and pay them back in kind.'

ULAN WAS WAITING for him when he docked at *Bellus's* secure airlock. The discreet hatch was a fixture on all Imperial ships above a certain tonnage, regardless of their shipyard or force of origin. Uniquely coded to protein-chain code strings implanted in the skin of inquisitors and their agents, the so-called secret gates could only be opened by those sanctioned by the ordos – or those with a plasma torch and several days to waste. The secure hatch allowed men like Stele to come and go at will, without clearance from a vessel's main docking pulpit. The inquisitor had barely used the gate on *Bellus*, however. He made it a point to mingle with the Blood Angels to earn their trust and respect. An inquisitor who skulked forever in hidden chambers aboard ship would soon arouse suspicion in even the slowest of minds.

But now expediency overrode his carefully constructed appearance of congeniality. His astropath rose to her feet and the hood about her head slipped back a way to reveal a scalp as hairless as his, ringed with an intricate brass circlet. Ulan was a failed experiment that Stele had rescued from an ordos laboratory. She was a psyker tool with a strong, if erratic, ability. The ornate device about her head held her power at bay until he had need of it.

'Speak,' he demanded. The jumble of emotional cues the astropath had sent him earlier made it clear that it would have to be relayed in clumsy words, not the strident colours of her mind-speech.

She kept pace with him as they walked along the isolated tunnel that led directly to his sanctum. 'Honoured lord, in the ninth hour I sensed a taint, a backwash, a touch in the empyrean. The echo of a message.'

His eyes narrowed. 'Another signal from Baal, so soon?'

'Not from Baal, lord. *To* Baal. Sent from this ship.'

'What?' Stele's face tightened with sudden anger. 'Who broadcast it? What was the message?'

'I know not. The ship's telepathic choir detests me, eminence, and they do not allow me to commune with them in the mindscape of the warp. It was only my chance sense of the echo that alerted me to this occurrence.'

The inquisitor's nose wrinkled as if he had smelt something foul. 'Bring them to me, every one of Ideon's astropaths!'

Reaching the iris hatch, Ulan's dead face contorted in the rictus that was her version of a smile. 'If it pleases the lord inquisitor, I anticipated your demand.' The woman's spidery hand worked the hatch control and Stele entered his chambers. There before him were the three surviving astropath adepts who until recently had served *Bellus* under the guidance of the late Master Horin.

Stele did not need to tell Ulan to lock the hatch behind them. He reached out a hand and pulled down her hood, revealing dead eyes cut from black crystal. The inquisitor touched a sequence of jewelled controls on the mechanical crown about her skull, releasing her to unleash her null gift. She closed her eyes and opened the place inside her psyche that held the mind-cloak. Ulan fell to the floor in a heap, twitching and weeping, dying by inches as her aberrant power flooded the room. She would perish if Stele used her in this fashion for too long, but he had brought her close to the brink before and she had always survived it.

The astropaths all reacted in the same way – with utter shock. Ulan's ability cast a bubble of void about the chamber, suffocating the application of any metapsychic phenomenon. The duration of the effect would only last as long as poor Ulan could stand it, but in Stele's experience most psykers folded like decks of tarot cards within moments of being struck psi-blind by her.

Drawing his lasgun, he wasted no time and spoke to the first astropath. 'The signal to Baal. Did it come from the ship? Who sent it?' The psyker pressed at his face, as if that would somehow summon back his powers. 'You all know I killed Horin. Do you wish to join him?'

The astropath licked corpse-grey lips. 'I was in a dormant cycle. I know nothing of–'

Stele frowned, and fired a point-blank shot. The corpse fell, joining the whimpering Ulan on the floor. Stele shrugged off his battle-coat and with it, any pretence at civility.

'Talk, witch!' He forced the hot pistol barrel into the fleshy wattles of the next telepath's neck, relishing the scent of cooking meat.

The astropath tried and failed to summon help with a mental yelp. And when it was clear that none was forthcoming, it began to whimper. The psyker gave a nod of its jowls to the last of the adepts. 'He was the duct. I overheard him.'

'Good,' said Stele, and pulled the trigger again.

The last adept was Horin's protégé, and he tried to cover his terror with a façade of cold indifference. Stele rested the gun on his forehead. 'Who sent the message?' He leaned closer and played a guess. 'Someone on the surface, yes?' A tiny twitch of the eye answered him as well as any confession. 'What was said?'

One of Ulan's moans punctured the air and it emboldened the astropath. 'Whatever you plan, inquisitor, Lord Dante knows what has transpired. Your machinations will be brought to light.'

The imperious look on the astropath's face was enough; Stele shot him. He let the body fall then in a sudden fit of fury he tore a dozen more blasts into the corpse, spitting and cursing the psykers.

After a while he calmed himself and brought Ulan out of her trance, reactivating the circlet. She was weak and blood issued out of the orifices in her face. Removing a vial of a xenos medicine from a concealed chest, Stele injected it into one of her skull sockets. After a while, she began to recover.

Ulan showed the death's-head grin again as she saw the dead psykers. 'I live to serve,' she hissed.

'Yes, you do,' the inquisitor agreed. 'You will present yourself to Captain Ideon and inform him that you alone will fulfil the role of the choir from now on.'

Ulan replied with a sluggish nod.

'You are more than capable,' Stele added. 'First, though, you will speak for me.' He dragged her to her feet and held her tightly, his muscular fingers finding ghost-metal contacts beneath flaps of plasti-flesh on her face. 'Open the way, girl. I have a message of my own.'

The hunched woman stiffened as her mind expanded beyond the bone cage of her skull, out through the hull of *Bellus*, beyond the veil of the space outside and into the torrents of the Immaterium. Stele guided her like a rider, aiming Ulan's telepathy into a core of black null-space lurking above them.

A dark and inhuman form lurking there saw Stele come closer, and it was happy to welcome him.

THE STINK OF spent flamer fuel still hung in the air where the Blood Angels had torched the pennants and cursed banners of the Word Bearers, but aside from some ashen heaps in the corners of the room, the tabernacle was much as it had been when Falkir took it for his throne room. Arkio stalked the perimeter of the chamber and peered into the anterooms that split off from it, as if he expected to find some lurking Chaos lackey cowering in the shadows. He seemed disappointed that he did not, Sachiel noted.

'The spear should remain here, I think.' said Arkio. 'This room is suited for defence. It will be safe.'

'Well chosen, blessed one,' the priest replied.

Arkio's face twisted. 'Why do you call me that, Sachiel? It does not sit well with me.'

'I cannot deny the truth of my own eyes, Brother Arkio. No one could look upon you after what you did today and not think you honoured by the primarch.'

'No?' Arkio studied him. 'I have eyes and ears, Sachiel. I saw how my brothers changed their ways toward me after I touched the holy lance during the remembrance. Some looked upon me with bewilderment, and others...'

Sachiel's smile froze. 'There are no dissenters here, Arkio.'

He gave a humourless laugh. 'I would guarantee that Koris would say otherwise.'

'The honoured sergeant will say nothing.' Sachiel frowned. 'In his infinite wisdom, Sanguinius chose to take Koris to his heart and grant him power of the black rage. He and others.' Arkio said nothing and the priest continued. 'Certainly, this is an omen. Those who welcome your sanctification are strengthened by the pure one and those who do not... The scarlet path beckons them.'

Arkio looked squarely at Sachiel, and suddenly he was the young Space Marine again, callow and untested. 'What if I do not want such an honour, priest? What if I long to join my brothers once more, to stand with my sibling Rafen and fight the foe with blade and bolter?'

The Sanguinary High Priest placed a hand on Arkio's back and gently guided him toward the glass window and the balcony beyond. 'You have left those days behind you, my friend. Sanguinius has chosen a new direction for you, and we cannot doubt the insight of his choice.'

The two of them stepped out into the weak Shenlong daylight, into the sight of legions of people. Blood Angels stood side by side with tattered PDF troopers and haggard civilians, and with one voice they roared their approval.

RAFEN SHRUGGED OFF the hands of a child who stroked at his greaves with all the reverence of a holy icon. Beside him, Alactus and Turcio shook their bolters to the sky and joined in the battle cry of their Chapter. 'For the Emperor and Sanguinius!'

'Sons of the Blood! Loyal servants of the Imperium!' Gripping his simulacrum of the red grail, Sachiel's voice carried from the balcony above the plaza. 'Hear me! This world sees the light of the Golden Throne once more, and the Lord of Baal casts his beneficent gaze upon it! Behold, the hero of the forge world, the liberator of Shenlong – Arkio the Blessed!'

Before, on other planets, Rafen had seen the masses of the Imperial people enraptured by the God-Emperor, but always from a distance. Now, among them, he was buffeted in the whirlwind of emotion that claimed his battle-brothers as easily as it did the commoners.

'Arkio held the Spear of Telesto!' continued Sachiel. 'By his hand, the Word Bearers were destroyed! Your victory is his!'

The crowd began to chant his brother's name and Rafen frowned. Sachiel spoke as if it were Arkio alone that had taken the fight to the Traitors, but what of the hundreds of other Blood Angels that had died this day? What of Koris and the Death Company?

'It is written in the book of the lords that those alone blessed by the Emperor may touch the holy lance and live; but it is only one whose living blood carries the essence of the great angel himself that may command its power!' Sachiel raised the grail high and turned it so that the crimson fluid inside anointed Arkio's head. 'We are all sons of the Blood, my brothers, but today the pure one walks among us once more! Here stands Arkio the Blessed, Sanguinius reborn!'

The force of the priest's words was so strong that the congregation – for that was what it had become – came to their knees in supplication. Rafen found himself bowing without conscious effort, dropping in with Alactus and Turcio.

'Glorious,' breathed the other Blood Angel. 'We are sanctified…'

Some part of Rafen's mind shouted at the discord of the moment. *This is madness! My sibling, the reincarnation of our primarch?* Impossible! And yet, he was still captured by the divine power of the moment.

Then Arkio spoke, and the plaza fell silent. 'People of Shenlong. Our battle is not yet ended. The corrupted still conceal themselves in your cities and we shall not be free until every last Chaos proselyte is found. I ask of you; where are the Word Bearers?'

A ripple of confusion flowed through the crowd, and slowly voices were raised, men hesitantly admitting that the whereabouts of the Traitors was unknown. Rafen saw Sachiel whisper something in his brother's ear and Arkio gave a reluctant nod. 'If you will not answer, then measures will be taken.' The crackle of a vox command sounded in Rafen's ear, and as one a handful of honour guard Blood Angels came to their feet. 'Those who hide the impure will be punished,' said Arkio.

Without warning, a dozen Shenlongi surged to their feet. Random figures raced forward as a strange madness seemed to sweep through the crowd. 'Yes, yes!' cried voices. 'Show us the way!'

'We are faithless!'

'Punish us! We are the lesson!'

On pure reflex, the Space Marines opened fire into the crowds, gunning down the people who rushed at them. To Rafen's horror, the Shenlongi welcomed the bolter rounds with beauteous smiles and open arms.

IN THE UTTER silence of his reclusium, Commander Dante rose slowly to his feet as he formally ended his meditation with the last words of the vermillion catechism. Genuflecting to the two icons before him, he made the sign of the aquila to the largest of the pair, representing the God-Emperor on his Throne, and then the hand-to-hearts gesture of fealty to the statue of Sanguinius. The primarch of the Blood Angels stood before him rendered in the rust-red stone cut from Baal's desert landscapes. The likeness showed him in hooded contemplation, his mighty wings at rest and the holy crimson cup grasped in his hand. Dante mirrored the aspect of his liege lord and bowed one final time. 'On this day, as on every other, I ask you grant me wisdom and strength, great Sanguinius, so I may guide our Chapter to ever greater glory.'

Satisfied with his completion of the ceremony, Dante backed away from the altar and donned the long white robes of his office. His chamber stood at the apex of the fortress-monastery's highest rooftop, set between a pair of towering steeples. One of the walls was given over to a window of invulnerable glassteel. Dante approached it and surveyed the environs of the abbey far below him. There in the parade grounds, legions of men in crimson armour drilled endlessly, not a single one of them out of step or inefficient in his movements.

In the depths of his memory, the commander recalled a time when it had been he that marched there, daring to steal a look up at the distant towers and wondering what it would be like to walk their halls. But that had been more than ten centuries ago, and all the men he had called comrade then were dust now, their names cut into the obsidian glass of the sepulchre of heroes. Dante saw the shape of his own reflection in the window, his hawkish countenance marred by this small moment of introspection. The aquiline jaw and nose were the frame for eyes that missed nothing. He had the aspect of a predator at rest – but not at rest for long. He frowned. A sullen mood was upon him, and he could not pinpoint its source. Dante was no psyker, but millennia of living among the Blood Angels and commanding their path through history had given him a sense for the pitch and moment of the Chapter. He heard the approach of boots from the echoing hall beyond his chambers and instinctively knew something ill was at hand.

Hidden servitors opened the reclusium doors and Dante turned to see the man who served as his strong right arm stride forward. The chief Librarian bowed low, the filigree of skulls on the edges of his red robes pooling around his feet. 'My lord, forgive this intrusion.'

Dante beckoned him to his feet. 'Mephiston, old friend, no doors are ever closed to you.' The commander spoke truthfully, the Librarian's psionic powers were formidable and if he so chose, there would be little that could bar his way within the fortress's walls. Mephiston met his gaze easily. Dante did not demand, as some Chapter commanders did, that his men treat him as some avatar of the primarch's divinity and avert their eyes. The master of the Blood Angels studied the warrior-psychic that the Astartes knew as the lord of death. Where Dante's face was the mirror of Sanguinius's patrician wisdom, Mephiston reflected the controlled malevolence that seethed beneath the thin veneer of their civility. Scholars spoke of the Librarian's ability to transfix an enemy with the potency of his glance, and even Dante could sense the pressure of those burning eyes.

'A matter of delicacy and utmost concern has arisen, and we must address it with haste, commander.'

Dante bid Mephiston to sit with him on a bench before the altar, but the Librarian refused. Whatever had transpired had wound him tight with tension. The commander's ill mood washed forward in a surge and Mephiston nodded, sensing the unformed thoughts in Dante's mind.

'A signal came to us, relayed across the segementum from the Shenlong star system. Our astropaths confirm that the message originated aboard the battle barge *Bellus*.'

'Brother-Captain Ideon's command,' said Dante. 'Was he not ordered to remain at the war graves on Cybele?'

Mephiston nodded. 'But this is no simple disobedience, lord. The wording was confused, and I suspect it was sent in a hurry, but it speaks of incidents on the battlefields at Cybele and again during an attack on Shenlong.' The Librarian took a breath. 'It speaks of a brother wielding the Spear of Telesto as Sanguinius himself did, and of a growing belief that our angelic sovereign's blessing is manifesting upon him.'

For a long moment Dante found himself robbed of words. He raised his eyes to the statue of Sanguinius for a moment, searching out guidance in the hooded face. 'Repeat it to me,' he ordered, and with a nod, Mephiston drew the words of Rafen's urgent entreaty from his eidetic memory and spoke them aloud.

Dante's brows knit in concentration as he heard the Space Marine's account of the Word Bearers' assault on Cybele, the arrival of *Bellus* and the subsequent commands of the priest Sachiel and Inquisitor Stele. When the Librarian finished, the commander sat silently for a while.

'This Sachiel sees the touch of the pure one on the warrior Arkio.' Dante turned the thought over. 'Such a conviction is fraught with portent and exigency, and much of it ill starred. What confirmation do we have that this fable is true?'

'The message bears the code-ident of a trusted veteran, Sergeant Koris of Captain Simeon's company. I took the liberty of reviewing his chronicle. He is a man of exemplary courage, lord, yet he is given to occasional displays of scepticism. I would not doubt the veracity of his statement... Although there were some troubling anomalies in the voice-print trace.'

Dante nodded. 'How many times has it been, Mephiston? How many Blood Angels have believed themselves impressed by the spirit of our lord and claimed to be the vessels of his power?'

'Too many, commander. And yet, are we not all recipients of Sanguinius's eminence to some degree?'

'Indeed,' Dante agreed, 'but we honour the primarch among all things and do not pretend to usurp him.' His eyes narrowed. 'This business of the spear, that the relic should be used so blatantly and without my sanction... It is troubling. We placed our trust in Stele and honoured our blood debt to him, but if we were mistaken...'

'Such supposition wastes our energies, lord,' Mephiston said crisply. 'The way forward is clear – we must isolate this Arkio, and bring him and the holy lance back to Baal without delay.'

'I order it so. You will charge Captain Gallio with this task. He has served me well among the honour guard and his loyalty to the primogenitor is unyielding. Grant him command of the cruiser *Amareo* and give him leave to select a force of men.'

Mephiston nodded. 'If it pleases the commander, I will send Brother Vode also. He is one of my best acolytes and his second sight is unparalleled in seeking out the taint of corruption.'

Dante looked at him. 'Is that what you suspect to find, brother?'

The Librarian's hard face did not betray any emotion.' We cannot afford to step blindly into this matter.'

'Just so,' agreed the commander. 'This message... It would not go well if the contents of Koris's signal were to reach the rest of the Chapter. There would be confusion, at best. At worst, the seeds of a schism.'

'I have seen to this, lord. The astropath duct that accepted the transmission has been sequestered on my order. I will personally supervise the erasure of his memory engrams.'

Dante rose to his feet and walked back to the window. 'Then send the ship, and we shall see the truth behind this "blessing" for ourselves.'

Mephiston paused at the reclusium's threshold, the doors yawning open before him. 'My lord...'

Dante heard something in the Librarian's voice that he had seldom encountered before: a hesitation alien to the lord of death's awesome reserve. 'What concerns you so, old friend?'

'We stand and speak of this Arkio as if he is already proven false... But what if the lad truly *has* been touched by the Deus Encarmine?'

To his dismay, the commander of the Blood Angels had no answer for his trusted comrade's question.

CHAPTER THIRTEEN

THE CORRIDORS OF the fortress were choked with repentants, shabby in torn clothing and bloodied bandages. These pathetic souls were the survivors of the occupation, the ones who still had strength to walk, to petition the Blood Angels for succour. On the lower levels, Rafen had passed gangs of Chapter serfs under the supervision of a Sanguinary Priest as they divided the spoils from storehouses from beneath the tower. The cases of medicines and food were divided among the starving, sickened civilians. There was little to go around, as much of the perishables had been put to the torch by Falkir's battalions. Like those swarming the plaza, the people who blocked Rafen's way as he walked the building seemed to be subsisting solely on faith.

The Blood Angel was troubled. Over and over, the sight of the honour guard picking out and cold-bloodedly murdering civilians replayed in his mind, disgusting him to his core. Rafen did not shun hard deeds when they were needed, but that casual display of callousness made his gut tighten. The Shenlongi people had been liberated, and to squander their lives in order to make a point went against every moral fibre of the Space Marine's being. But worse than the act itself was the doe-eyed acceptance of the non-combatants, the way they were almost joyful to embrace the burning bolter rounds, as if their willing sacrifice was worthwhile.

Someone jostled Rafen and his temper flared. 'Get out of my way!' he snapped, turning a stern face on the man who had touched him.

'Forgive me, lord, but I wanted to thank you...' He was thick with dirt and a patina of brick dust, but through it Rafen could still clearly make out the pattern of a tattered planetary defence force uniform. An officer, by the look of the sigils on his sleeve.

'For what? I do not know you.'

'Oh, no, it is not for myself, lord, but for my sister. Not only did your Chapter release us from the grip of Chaos, but your kinsmen granted her the murdergift.' He bowed his head as he spoke.

'Murdergift?' The strange word left a foul taste in Rafen's mouth. 'You thank me because your sister was shot dead by the honour guard? No, no–'

'Please!' The PDF soldier pressed closer to him. 'You must understand, we were so close to cracking! If another day had passed without an answer to our prayers, many of us would have been sure that the Emperor had turned from Shenlong...' His voice dropped to a confessional hiss. 'Some of us... We were almost ready to submit to the word of Lorgar...' Then he beamed at Rafen. 'But you saved us from that! My sister gladly gave herself in payment.'

'Madness!' Rafen tore his arm away from the man and drew his combat knife in a bright arc of fractal-edged steel. 'Tell me, if I told you to plunge this into your heart, would you do it?'

The officer tore open his tunic without hesitation and exposed his pale chest. 'My life has value only by your command, lord!' He seemed ecstatic at the possibility that Rafen might kill him, then and there.

The Blood Angel's face twisted in disdain, and he backhanded the man with the pommel of the blade. 'Begone, craven fool!' Rafen stalked down the corridor, furious. Was this the state of the people he took an oath to protect? Were the men and women of the Imperium so weak of mind that they would spring on any edict, no matter how loathsome, and claim it as the divine word of the God-Emperor?

He reached the towering copper doors that opened into the chapel from which Arkio had made his address. Senior battle-brothers entered one by one, under the expressionless eyes of two honour guardsmen. They carried slung power axes and hand flamers, the ignition torches dancing at the end of the funnel-shaped muzzles. One of them blocked Rafen's path.

'You will remain outside.' It was a voice that expected no argument.

'On what authority?' Rafen demanded. 'I am Brother Rafen, sibling to Arkio–'

'We know who you are,' said the other guard. 'This conclave is for the veterans of our Chapter, and you are not one of them.'

Rafen pressed against the first guard's chest, daring him to push back. 'I will speak to my brother, and no man, golden-helmed or otherwise, will prevent it!'

From the corner of his eye, Rafen saw the second Space Marine's gauntlet drop toward his axe and he tensed. But then a strong hand pulled him back. 'We'll have no trouble here!' said Delos, and Rafen turned to face the Chaplain's skull-mask.

'Rafen, speak to me.' Delos led him to a quiet alcove. 'What is wrong?'

He looked away. 'Cleric, I cannot hold my tongue any longer. The events of recent days, the changes that have been wrought... My mind is awhirl with contradictions and I fear I may drive myself mad with them!'

Delos nodded slowly. 'I understand, brother. This has been a trying time for all of us, and our faith has been challenged.'

'Yes! Yes!' Rafen retorted. 'You understand, Delos. This... miasma that has swept through our ranks, it is unconscionable. I cannot explain what has happened to my brother Arkio... And what took place in the plaza, never before have I seen the like–'

The Chaplain nodded again and there was a smile in his voice, incongruous as it issued from the mouth of the steel skull. 'You are confused, Rafen, and that is natural. Much has happened since *Bellus* arrived at Cybele and we all feel the strain of it. Too many brothers have passed, your mentor among them, and it gnaws at you.' He pressed a black-gloved hand on Rafen's chest. 'You would not be a son of Sanguinius if you did not feel each death as keenly as we do our lord progenitor's, but he has extended a hand to us from the past, my friend, and Arkio is his vessel.'

Rafen's expression froze. He could not see Delos's face, but he knew that the Chaplain had been drawn into the same influence that spread wide among his battle-brothers. 'Yes, of course,' he said in a neutral voice. 'Thank you for your wisdom.'

Delos beckoned him. 'Come, Rafen,' he said, 'it is only fair that you be present to hear the words of your sibling as well. Accompany me.' The Chaplain waved away the two honour guards and Rafen followed him in, ice forming in the pit of his primary stomach.

There were dozens of Blood Angels arranged in a loose pair of semi-circles at one end of the chamber. At the opposite side of the chapel, where the glass window and the balcony lay, Rafen glimpsed more men with golden helmets, weapons slung but nonetheless watchful. Beyond them, he saw the tell-tale blink of white and red. Sachiel was there, conversing with another Space Marine. Arkio had his back to the group, and were it not for his posture, one might have thought him to be a normal Space Marine. All soldiers of the Legion Astartes were genetically engineered for superiority in both mind and body, and the legacy of that alteration extended into the most basic of things, including stature and carriage. Every Space Marine carried himself like a stormwalker, well over two metres of pure-bred warrior striding among the lesser races of common men like some figure of legend made manifest. Yet Arkio seemed to stand even taller than the rest of them. It was undeniable. Some aura, intangible and commanding, bled into the air around his sibling from his sheer force of presence.

'What has my brother become?' Rafen whispered to himself.

'This is a proud moment for all Blood Angels,' said Delos, and Rafen could not be sure if the Chaplain had heard his comment, 'I would submit that even Dante himself would sit a while to see what will transpire here.'

Rafen's gaze swept the room, surveying the faces of the Space Marines who went bareheaded and the body language of those who did not. Each of them was tense with anticipation, earnest with questions for the blessed one. The cold in his chest gripped Rafen's hearts with icy fingers. *They all look upon him with reverence. By the grail, what if I am the only one who doubts? With Koris dead, could it be that I alone question this?* And then a more insidious thought pushed its way to the front of his mind: what would Rafen do if he were wrong? If Arkio were truly touched by the hand of the great angel, then to voice any mistrust of his divinity would be tantamount to the highest of heresies. *And yet... I cannot shake this sense that something is very, very wrong...*

With this vicious cycle turning through his mind, Rafen saw Inquisitor Stele emerge from an antechamber, his lexmechanic shuffling along behind him. The ordos agent spoke quickly to Sachiel and then stepped up to the chapel's lectern.

'Comrade brothers,' Stele's voice was firm. 'Matters have come to a point where we must chose a path forward, and so I set before you this design.' He paused, scanning the room and taking a moment to gauge the mood of the Astartes veterans. Stele's eye lingered on Rafen where he stood at Delos's side, and a frown threatened to form on his bald pate. The inquisitor leaned forward, his aquila electoo catching the light of the photon candles. 'The archenemy on Shenlong is bloodied but not defeated, and he has exchanged his strengths for new ones. Where we were the fluid force striking at a stationary target, now the Word Bearers are scattered and mobile, and it is the Blood Angels who are pressed into defending the Ikari fortress. We all know the battle doctrine of the Word Bearers. They fight until death, and although the blessed Arkio may have broken them, they will regroup and return to plague us.'

'We shall garrison here, then?' said a seasoned sergeant from the assault company. 'Seek out these scum and kill them before they can hit and fade?'

There was approval from Stele. 'This forge world owes its life to the Blood Angels, and we shall not soon release it.' He glanced to where Arkio sat, as if seeking permission to continue. 'Shenlong's planetary governor was murdered on the first morning of the Chaos occupation, and none of his staff have been found alive.' The inquisitor knew this for a fact. He had made personally sure of it by quietly executing three ministorum functionaries in a cell deep below the chapel. 'I am therefore assuming the duties and position of interim governor, and I choose this building as my stronghold. In this role, my first edict will be to petition the Blood Angels to eradicate the stain of Chaos from this world.'

'It will be done!' said Sachiel, his voice tight with eagerness.

'Of that I have no doubt,' the inquisitor replied smoothly. 'Now I yield the floor to Brother Arkio.'

Rafen sensed the flood of scrutiny that raced through the other Blood Angels as his younger brother took the lectern. Arkio gave the assembled men a cool smile. It hung strangely on his sibling's face. It was not an expression that Rafen could ever remember seeing on him before; it was an aspect that was at once imperious and commonplace, infinitely old and undeniably youthful. He wondered that if their father were here in the room, would the grizzled old clansman have even recognised his second born son? Almost as the days passed, Arkio's face bore less and less resemblance to his former self and more and more the idealised, noble contours of the high angel of blood.

Delos mumbled a prayer beneath his breath and Rafen heard him speak of 'Arkio the Blessed' – the same litany that Lucion had uttered on the *Bellus*. Arkio's legendary exploits were already accreting their own mythology, his faithful feeding their own beliefs. Rafen found he could not meet his brother's gaze, for fear that the youth would see the doubt in him. On some level, he wished that he could embrace Sachiel's declaration of divinity. In a small way he envied the other men for their unquestioning devotion, but Rafen's hearts and soul were tied irrevocably to the edicts of his Chapter and the word of the God-Emperor, and there was no provision there for the coming of a new Sanguinius.

'Brothers, your support gladdens me and I am honoured to accept it.' Arkio indicated the chapel window. 'We will purge

the taint from Shenlong together and make this world a beacon of righteousness.' There was a scattering of agreement
throughout the group. 'I… *We* have been tested, kinsmen.
Tested and found ready for the greater challenges ahead.
Shenlong is but the first world we will liberate. In the years to
come, we will look back and say here–' He slammed the
lectern with a hand, a fierce grin on his face. 'Here was where
our Blood Crusade began! I have accepted the counsel of
Lord Stele and his eminence Sachiel and now I put to you a
plan that will begin a new era in the chronicle of the sons of
Sanguinius.' He paused, and the air was thick with tension.

Rafen watched, awe-struck. With just a few simple words,
Arkio was holding men with ten times his experience and age
as enthralled as the newest initiates.

'We will take the Word Bearers and break them as they tried
to break this world, and as we do, I will call upon the people
of Shenlong to join us in our struggle. In the name of Sanguinius, we will raise a force from these blighted souls and in
his glory return to Baal in triumph, with Iskavan's head atop
our standard! And there, we will rally our Chapter for a campaign the likes of which even the God-Emperor himself has
never seen!'

'Assemble an army?' said the assault sergeant. 'Blessed, we
are Adeptus Astartes, each man an army of one. It is not our
way to recruit common soldiers.'

Sachiel answered him a nod. 'You are correct. Not the old
way – but the path we travel now will take us beyond the
unwavering creeds laid down in the Codex Astartes.' He
smiled. 'Our fealty to Guilliman's ancient treatise has never
been the strongest, as we all can agree. We are Blood Angels
and what suits us is anathema to the stolid Ultramarines and
their kindred…' Several of the seasoned troopers murmured
an accord. The Space Marine warbook of sacred battle

doctrines had been crafted by the authoritarian primarch of the Ultramarines Chapter, Robute Guilliman, but his suspicion of the Blood Angels had been well documented and, even ten millennia past his death, the warriors from Macragge were still antagonistic toward them. 'We'll write our own principles, a vermilion codex better suited to men who know blood and who have been blooded!' This time the ripple of agreement was more forceful and aggressive.

'And what will we do with these conscripts?' Delos dared to venture a question.

'We will take a thousand of the best that this war-beaten world can offer us and turn them into a legion of aggressors sworn to the banner of the blessed! They will be the first warriors of the reborn, for the greater glory of Sanguinius!'

Stele had been silent but now he took the priest's words as his cue to interpose himself. 'The way ahead is clear, but it is also dangerous for us.' He spread his hands. 'We witnessed the power of the great angel unleashed, aboard *Bellus* and again in his divine fury within this very tower. We cannot question what we have seen with our own eyes, and yet... Distrust still festers among us.' The inquisitor did not look in Rafen's direction; he did not have to. 'I have learned that a person – *a sceptic* – saw fit to communicate with his fellow doubters on your homeworld of Baal. The contents of this communication are lost to me but I have inferred the essence of them.'

A grim silence descended on the room, and Rafen forced himself to remain unmoved by the inquisitor's veiled probing. If there were any other men here who were not wholly convinced of Arkio's sanctification, then their hesitancy would be withering now beneath Stele's baleful glare.

'There are those who do not accept change,' he continued, stalking along the edge of the room. 'They cannot release their adherence to ancient, decrepit dogma even when the proof of its inadequacy is put before them. These men keep our beloved Imperium locked in a state of ignorance and stagnation. They will not accept anything that challenges the status quo, and they are willing to kill whole worlds to preserve it.' He hung his head. 'I have seen it, among my own fraternity in the Ordo Hereticus, and now this message concerns me that such conspiracies may touch the brotherhood of the Blood Angels as well.'

Delos shook his head. 'With all due respect, Lord Stele, you must be mistaken. No Baalite son would ever embrace such duplicity!'

The inquisitor tapped his chin. 'I can only hope that you are correct, Chaplain. But as Arkio accepted my counsel, I would ask you all to do the same. Be watchful, comrade brothers, for the Word Bearers may not be the only enemy we face here.'

With this dire caution hanging over them, Sachiel distributed data-slates with single use code strings so that orders could be read before self-deleting. He dismissed the veterans and watched them file from the chapel mulling over the commands they had been given. As Chaplain Delos exited, Sachiel saw a single Space Marine remaining. 'Rafen.'

'High priest. I would speak with my brother.'

'Indeed?' Sachiel arched an eyebrow. 'Perhaps your time would be better spent preparing your squad for combat. I'll overlook your clandestine entry into a meeting that you were not cleared to join, but I strongly suggest you leave now. What little good favour you have is running thin, Rafen.'

'Are you afraid I might talk some sense into him? He scoffed. 'Stand aside, Sachiel.'

The Blood Angel's face flushed red, matching the crimson of his wargear. 'You will address me as Sanguinary High Priest!'

'What is this?' Arkio asked, detaching himself from conversation with Stele. The inquisitor gave the room a deceptively vague look and left, the chattering lexmechanic at his heels. 'A disagreement?' said the young Blood Angel, the potent clarity of his voice silencing the argument before it could progress.

'There is a point of doctrine that we do not see eye to eye on,' said Rafen.

Sachiel's colour was high but he forced his voice to remain level. 'Your sibling wishes to speak to you, blessed.'

'Alone,' Rafen added.

The priest gave a rigid half-bow to Arkio. 'By your leave?'

Arkio nodded, and Sachiel strode away after Stele. Rafen's brother cocked his head. 'I have asked you this before, and now I say it again. You are troubled.'

Rafen watched Sachiel's back recede until he was sure he was out of the room, and beyond earshot. 'You dismiss a high priest without a word, Arkio. You, a battle-brother with only one service stud on his brow. How has this come to pass?'

Arkio looked away. 'I did not seek this gift, brother. It came to me of its own accord.'

'A gift, is that what it is?' Rafen said with disquiet. 'From where I stand I wonder if it is a curse. What else could drive men to murder the innocents they swore an oath to protect?'

'I regret those deaths, but perhaps those repudiations were necessary.'

'You have a name for these executions? So do the Shenlongi! They call them the "murdergift", like it is some benediction! What insanity is this?'

'I take no pleasure in it.' Arkio fixed him with a hard gaze, and for the briefest of instants Rafen felt his resolve weaken. 'But we cannot hold to the old codes, kinsman. We cannot continue to cling to the ways of the past. We must be brutal if we are to forge a path to the new future...'

Rafen's fists balled of their own accord. 'You talk but you say nothing. All I hear are empty phrases and rhetoric better suited to politicians than Space Marines! Brother, I don't pretend to understand what has happened to you but I know this – your new path veers away from our sacred pledge to holy Terra! Can you not see, if you go on you will damn us all as heretics!'

Arkio's mood altered in a heartbeat. His face darkened. 'You dare speak of heresy? You, who look upon me with doubt as plain as day? How can I win the hearts of my battle-brothers when my very blood himself thinks I am false?'

'I have never said–'

'I thought I would be able to confide in you, that you would understand, but I was mistaken! Perhaps Sachiel was right when he said that you would be jealous I was chosen.'

'It is not jealousy!' Rafen growled, his voice drawing the attention of the honour guards. 'I am concerned for you.'

'Ah, yes,' Arkio said, 'the oath to father. Even after all this time, you still see me as the skinny boy in need of protection, yes?' He summoned the guards with a nod. 'I told you before, that Arkio is gone. I am changed.'

Rafen felt defeated; his words were clumsy and harsh, and now he had done nothing more than drive his brother further away. 'Arkio, I have a duty…'

His sibling's face softened, forgiveness in his eyes. 'So do I, Rafen, and I hope you will realise that they are one and the same.' Arkio looked at the gold-helmeted Space Marines. 'My brother is leaving. Secure the chapel after him. I must meditate.'

Rafen saw Arkio reaching for the case that held the Spear of Telesto as the copper doors slammed shut.

FALKIR'S MEN USED chains stolen from the factory zones above to hold the nine offerings in place. They tied loops of the heavy metal rings around their ankles. The Chaos Space Marine examined them with the same regard he would have given the sewer effluent that fouled his boots – these humans were such fragile, mewling little things, so far removed from his monstrous form that the Castellan found it hard to accept that he had ever had even the remotest kinship to their race. He drew up ancient recollections of the Word Bearers' birthworld of Colchis and the humans that had scurried there. These Shenlong people were the same, puny and without value. Despite Iskavan's orders to keep them alive, Falkir toyed with the idea of gutting one, just to amuse himself.

As if he was summoned by the thought of him, the rumble of the cursed crozius announced the Dark Apostle's presence. Iskavan scowled at the scraps of his army where they stood in sullen groups around the perimeter of the flood chamber. His displeasure flowed off him in waves, more potent than the stinking fetor of the drain ducts.

'Shall we proceed?' Falkir asked.

Iskavan spat and pushed him away. 'Stand aside.' The Apostle reached under a ruddy skin-cloak that dangled near his bolter holster and removed a fat tome from within its folds. There were chains around the book that glittered with threads of rare orihalcium. Each link was worth the price of a man's life. The Word Bearer commander looped them around his wrist and the sorcerous codex obediently snapped open at pages filled with spidery text in iridescent inks. 'That one,' he said, pointing at the closest offering – a swarthy-skinned man in the garb of a balladeer. Falkir grudgingly clasped the man by the scruff of his neck and bent him down. The bard had soiled himself in fright.

Iskavan began to read aloud from the book. The words were sounds that did not fit in the material world. They resembled inhuman ululations and strange cadences that made the air shiver with their passage. As he spoke, the Apostle reversed the grip on the crozius and used the sickle-sharp blade on the lower end to slit the offering's throat. A fan of blood tore out of him, but instead of falling to the floor, it whirled into the air, each droplet hardening into a ruby bullet. The eight other humans screamed and wailed, sensing their deaths would be next. They pulled fruitlessly at the chains, only to stumble and fall as the bloodstorm ripped into them and cut them to ribbons. The globules spun about in a swarm of red.

Flesh and crimson fluid began to coalesce in the middle of the remains of the sacrificial victims, organs and meat tearing out of the corpses to come together in a purplish mass of matter. Iskavan waited patiently for the shape of a Khornate bloodthirster to form, but no daemon emerged. Gradually a formless blob of protoplasm congealed into something barely recognisable as a face. The wet orb of gore spun in the scarlet rain.

'Not enough!' it screamed. 'Need more! More more more!' Iskavan studied it with a frown. This was not supposed to happen. The summoning should have been sated and allowed the chosen of the skull throne to manifest, not beg for more.

'It's still hungry,' said Falkir. 'What else can we feed it?'

'You.' The Apostle didn't hesitate, and kicked Falkir's legs out from under him. The Word Bearer swore as he fell face-first into the bloodstorm.

With a gust of coppery vapour, the rain of liquid engulfed Falkir and filled him up like a vessel. Iskavan watched intently, waiting for the telltale horns, tail and batwings of a bloodthirster to burst from the seams of his armour. The Khornate creature would corrupt Falkir's body still further and it would emerge from his mortal form armed with a hellfire whip, a heartseeker axe and a desperate desire to kill.

But to his slow dismay, that did not occur.

Whatever possessed Falkir slowly got to its feet and confronted him. Where the Word Bearer's ruined face had been there was now an ever-shifting mass of warped flesh. It was never static, it constantly morphed from form to form. It seemed to smile at him.

'What are you?' the Apostle demanded. 'By Lorgar, I summoned the child of Khorne, not some pathetic changeling!'

'Show respect to the servant of Tzeentch, beastling!' it cackled. 'No bloodthirster for you! The Warmaster Garand has forbidden it!'

Iskavan's tongues twitched. 'How dare you presume–'

'A messenger instead for the master of the ninth host. Hear this! I am the conduit for your lord's most black and hurtful displeasure!'

Before the eyes of the Word Bearers, the daemon's chimera face took on the terrible aspect of the High Warmaster Garand, battle commander of a thousand hosts and the Dread Witch-prince of Helica. Many of the Chaos Space Marines knelt in demonstration of their allegiance, but Iskavan remained standing. The dark realisation that was building at the back of his mind kept him on his feet.

'Iskavan, you blind, stumbling fool!' Garand's voice spat from the changeling's mouth. 'In the maelstrom's name, you cannot even be trusted to fail!'

'Why have you interfered with my summoning?' growled the Apostle, ignoring the insult. Iskavan's black heart hammered in his malformed ribcage. The Warmaster's powers were potent indeed to have reached across the Immaterium and turned aside the daemonic invocation.

'You shall have no reinforcements from the warp, worthless dolt! You should be corpseflesh now! I sent you to Shenlong to perish on Blood Angels' blades, and perish you shall!'

'No!' Iskavan snorted, waving his crozius, fighting away a sudden confusion. 'You could not... It is not–'

Garand's psychic presence was like a lead weight pressing down on the warriors in the chamber. 'Weakling! You are the least of my army, Iskavan! The victories you brought me have never been sufficient, your conquests irrelevant, your temples to our gods found wanting! Now I rid myself of your dead, useless band!'

The Apostle tried to deny the charges, but a voice inside him saw the truth in the Warmaster's words. The ninth host were the poorest of the Word Bearers; they were constantly one step behind the glories and honours of their corrupted brethren. 'My warriors have served the greater cause of Lorgar's word for centuries!' he retorted hotly.

Garand's voice roared with cruel laughter. 'As cannon fodder, perhaps. You are fit for nothing else. Even now you are too dense to comprehend! You are a throwaway, Iskavan! The ninth host is nought but a grand sacrifice!'

'The retreats you ordered on Cybele?' said the Apostle. 'The orders changed without reason or purpose? What have you done?'

The Falkir-thing stepped closer. 'Know this. I have willingly renounced your forces in order to bring the Blood Angels to Shenlong, wretch!'

Garand's words aboard the *Dirge Eterna* flooded back to Iskavan. *A larger plan.* The daemon nodded as realisation dawned on the Word Bearer's face. 'Yes, you see it now? The design that I oversee is no less than the corruption of the entire Blood Angels' Chapter!'

'Impossible! Their sickening loyalty to the corpse god is unquestioned! It cannot be done!'

I have allies,' Garand was dismissive. 'In the despoiler's name, I will rival Horus in his grand turning with this deed – and you, Iskavan, your blood will oil the wheels of its consummation!'

'No, I will not allow you to throw away our lives–' he began, fighting the waves of controlled agony that radiated from the Warmaster's psi-surrogate.

'Allow?' Garand jeered, 'You cannot prevent it! The lie-spinner Tancred knew it to be true, he saw your doom in the entrails of the dead!'

'Tancred? But he said he saw nothing…'

Again, the laughter pealed off the stonewalls. 'Look how useless you are! Even your minions hide the truth from you!' Falkir's possessed body launched itself at the Dark Apostle. 'You are a disgrace to the eightfold star! Iskavan the Hated? You are Iskavan the Mocked! You could not live like a warrior of Chaos, but perhaps you will be able to die like one!'

'*No!*' The Apostle's bellow shattered the spell Garand's voice had cast, and with a strike of his crozius, Iskavan batted the messenger daemon across the chamber. The flesh-form cracked against the far wall and shivered. The Warmaster's face began to melt away as the psychic link faltered. The Word Bearer commander stormed across to the creature and roared into its face, his rage manifesting in coils of searing lightning. 'Hear this, Garand! We are sons of Lorgar and not mere pawns for you to play and discard in your games! I'll raze this world to ash before I surrender!'

He dropped the daemon to the floor and turned to face his men, the full force of his dark soul boiling to a murderous intensity. 'Gather all weapons! Muster the furies and the hounds!' The Apostle's venom made his crozius wail in sympathetic anger. 'For hate's sake,' he cried. 'We will put this world to death!'

The effect of Iskavan's passion was instantaneous. With one voice, the Word Bearers cried out, 'Unto the blood of revenge, we bring the word of Lorgar!'

Without the stifling edicts of the Warmaster's orders to shackle him any longer, a hundred horrors scratched at the edges of Iskavan's mind, a hundred terrible revenges to inflict upon the Blood Angels and the Shenlongi cattle. He smiled. He would begin with the wounded, the women and the children.

Something nudged his leg and he glanced down. There, coiled at his feet, the warped flesh that had once been Falkir blinked back at him in hopeful entreaty.

'The messenger daemon still lives,' remarked a grizzled Havoc Space Marine, drawing a bead with a man-portable lascannon. 'What is to be done?'

'Bring it,' Iskavan said after a moment. 'I'll find someone for it to kill.'

THE WIND WAS the colour of old blood. It carried flecks of rusted metal in whirls of razored fines. And it carried something else to the plaza, where Rafen stood alone in contemplation. The wind bore shrieks of the like that only the worst of fears can conjure, sounds that death itself would recoil from. Rafen's enhanced hearing read them as clearly as if they were broadcast over his vox-link, and he remembered the winds of another world's screams.

Another Blood Angel beside an idling Rhino pointed south-wards. 'Do you hear that? I think it's coming from the valetudinarium.'

'The wounded,' Rafen gasped, and then in a flurry of motion he grabbed at the transport's roll bar. 'You can drive this thing?' he asked.

'Like the wind,' said the Space Marine.

'Then we go,' snapped Rafen. With a thunderous roar, the Rhino's tracks bit into the stone road and it leapt forward, into the screams.

CHAPTER FOURTEEN

THE RAPACIOUS PACE of conflict in the 41st millennium was fed by myriad worlds, each churning out megatons of military hardware by the freighter-load. Shenlong's speciality was its shells: from tiny, low-calibre bullets suitable for an assassin's kissgun to the colossal ship-cracking torpedoes fired from battleships. Munitions rolled out of the forge world's manu-factoriums to stoke the unending inferno of the Emperor's wars. Every centimetre of the rusty planet's surface was thick with factory complexes, worker-towns and warehouses. There was nothing that did not orbit around the needs of the mills: schools and cathedrals, agri-domes and heat sinks, water plants and sewerage works were all squeezed into the gaps between the looming walls of the weapons shops.

In such a place was the valetudinarium of Saint Mandé the Amber, a hospital founded by the order of the eternal candle in the wake of the Hoek Insurgence. Built atop a cav-ernous factory, the clinic dealt mostly with the outbreaks of military-grade viruses that regularly affected the workers. These men and women fell foul of the toxins they were forced to load into planetary-denial bombs and other scorched earth munitions. In the careworn halls of tile and stained glass, priests ministered to wounded civilians crowded into the overflowing wards. Few of the Adepta Sororitas hospitallers posted there had survived the initial Word Bearers' attack. Those that had lived made their prayers to the Throne and paid thanks for their liberation, only to discover they had been premature.

Buoyed by rage at Garand's deception, Iskavan's Word Bearers emerged from the watercourses under the valetudinarium in a tide of murder and hate. The lowest levels of the hospital were the most fortified, and it was there that the sisters had hidden the sickly children, the pregnant women and the old. The Traitors rose among them, their nightmares given horrific, blade-sharp form. Iskavan personally murdered the last Sororitas on Shenlong as his brethren hung innards from every wall, painting the corridors with innocent blood.

They met weak resistance from a handful of hobbled PDF soldiers as they rose into the main levels of the clinic. The blinded and crippled took up guns and fought to the death. Iskavan let his men have their butchery without sanction, while he slipped away to find a tool that would enable him to unleash his hatred on the entire planet. The screaming horrors wrought inside the valetudinarium leaked into the air.

BLACK JETS OF smoke shot past Rafen's face from the Rhino's exhausts, popping as the vehicle's over-charged engine roared like a caged animal. The driver cut sparks from the roadway as he forced the transport around a corner without losing momentum. The Rhino's tracks bit into the ground and clawed through debris. A makeshift roadblock built of pieces of furniture and oil drums exploded as the Rhino's spiked dozer blade swept it away.

Rafen's torso protruded from the vehicle's rooftop hatch, and he held fast to the pintle-mounted storm bolter. A coil of belt-fed shells fed from under his feet, clattering over his armour as he turned in place, lancing tracer where enemy troopers appeared to snap-fire at him.

'There it is!' The driver's voice yelled.

The road terminated in the forecourt of the hospital. The arching gates that had once blocked the way were long gone, destroyed by whatever had blown down the walls. Beyond, Rafen spied the flares of gunfire inside the building. The Rhino rumbled over the entrance. 'Full throttle!' Rafen shouted, 'Shock deployment!'

'Aye!' came the hearty reply, and the transport's motor revved louder.

Rafen let fly with the bolter, cutting into the hospital's portico, and at the last moment he dropped down into the Rhino's hull. The driver reversed traction on the starboard track and the transport came about, the portside face turning into the ruined entranceway. The Rhino broadsided the building and took down a length of wall as it did so, sliding to a screeching halt in the main atrium.

Rafen knocked out the pintle's anchoring pin and tore the storm bolter free. Then he was out of the hatch and firing. Glass as old as the Blood Angel himself crunched beneath Rafen's boots as he ran. Ruined urns spilled plant matter in drifts where stray rounds had cut them open, and everywhere there were corpses. Figures in white, clinic functionaries and medicae; others in rags, the sick and injured.

The Space Marine saw the shape of a Word Bearer warped to slag by a melta blast and grinned. At least the enemy was not advancing without cost.

Something moved at the edge of his vision and he twisted. A soldier loped toward him, a pistol in one hand. The man's face was hidden behind bandages, and below his left knee there was only a ragged stump.

'Lord,' he said. 'We were afraid no one would come...'

'We heard the screams,' Rafen said grimly. 'Report?'

'Swarmed on us like ticks.' The trooper halted. His breathing was laboured, and Rafen could see where his fatigues were coloured with blood. 'Got in through the lower levels and cut us to pieces.' He gestured with the gun. 'It's madness in there... Traitors gunning down anything that moves, no rhyme or reason, just killing for the love of it...'

'How many other troopers?'

The man reloaded as he spoke. 'Too few to make a difference.'

Explosive charges grunted on the upper levels, and a fresh shower of broken glass rained down on them. Rafen followed the sound and saw shapes in magenta ceramite moving along a raised balcony. 'There!' As one, they opened fire, storm bolter and pistol bellowing a murderous harmony.

A hapless Word Bearer took the brunt of the salvo and danced a frenzied jig as he was torn apart. Lascannon bolts seared the air in return and Rafen made for cover. The trooper stumbled after him. He fired again, the ammunition belt whipping and snapping at the air as it fed into the weapon. Rafen's fire ate chunks from the pillars and statuary as the enemy tried to use them as cover. The wounded trooper was careful and slow with his weapon, firing at Word Bearers as they popped up or unwittingly exposed a limb in their haste.

The storm bolter fell silent and Rafen discarded it without hesitation, unlimbering his trusted bolter from the strap on his back. He glimpsed movement on the upper level, and for a second he saw the hulking form of the Dark Apostle between two gnarled columns; then the loathsome figure was gone.

'If he is here, then hell will be two steps behind him.' Rafen said aloud.

THE NOISE OF the explosion reached Arkio's ears. 'There!' He stabbed at the air with the spear, and the holy lance hummed. 'Do you see it, the smoke rising from the hospital?'

Sachiel gave a curt nod. 'Blessed, there's nothing in that quadrant but sickly natives. It's a diversionary raid.'

Arkio turned on him with such swiftness that the priest actually recoiled. 'No! There will be no diversions, no feints – The Word Bearers have nothing to lose, and we must meet them before they can use that against us!'

'What can they do?' Sachiel scoffed. 'After your victory there can be no more than a handful left. We could garrison here and let them batter themselves to death on the walls of the fortress if you wished–'

Arkio's face was hard with fury. 'I do not! They have presented themselves and we must destroy them! No other outcome will suffice!' He stepped away from the priest and vaulted up on to the parapet. 'Remain here if you will, Sachiel. I go to take the fight to the foe!' Without warning, Arkio projected himself off the balcony and dropped, plummeting downwards.

Sachiel reached for him, too late to stop the young Blood Angel. The priest saw Arkio's fall, convinced that he would witness the blessed broken apart by the impact of his landing. The blazing rod of the spear glinted as he descended.

Men in the plaza saw him coming and parted like a breaking wave. Arkio struck the stone with a concussion that cut a shallow bowl in the square. Without a scratch or an injury upon him, Arkio rose from the crouch where he landed and crossed to the ranks of a bike squadron. Awed silence followed him, and no one, not Blood Angel or Shenlongi, dared to speak.

Arkio selected a bike and mounted it, kicking the starter into life. He swung the humming spear across the handlebars, like the lance of a jousting knight. 'Men who would follow Sanguinius,' he called, gunning the motor, 'Follow me.'

The cycle ranged away along the road like a guided missile. In its wake, Space Marines and civilians alike followed with Arkio's name on their lips.

THE IRONWOOD DOOR narrowly missed Adept Pellis as it blew off its hinges and slammed into the wall. Splinters from the frame clipped his face and made him yelp. He scrambled desperately for the small window in the cramped fasciculus, sending cascades of parchment scattering behind him. The window was bolted into the stone walls, but any rationality Pellis once had was now washed away in a tide of fear. He clawed pointlessly at it, tearing the skin on his fingers and weeping.

Pellis chanced a look over his shoulder and regretted it. A man-shaped thing bent its head to enter the room, and it snarled as it tried to stand up. The low ceiling of the file store forced the monster to bend its warped neck. 'You,' it said, in a voice like snapping bones. 'Adept Biologis?'

In spite of everything, Pellis's bloody hand grabbed at the insignia on his robes that signified his ranking among the magis biologia. The adept had never known that fear could be as strong as this, and the approach of the man-thing made his body rebel, his bladder loosening.

The Chaos Space Marine looked away to address one of its fellows. 'Are there no others?'

'One, great Apostle, but very injured. The human attempted to take its own life with an ornamental dagger. It's bleeding to death.'

Pellis nodded robotically. That would have been Thelio. The aged Adeptus Mechanicus priest had always been overly proud of his gaudy decorative knife. The Word Bearer accepted this and hauled Pellis to his feet. 'You understand the germs and infections used beneath?' The huge monster pointed his spiked crozius at the floor, indicating the factory far below.

Again, Pellis nodded with mechanical precision. That seemed to satisfy the beast, although the angry sketch of a face did not alter in aspect. 'Then come. I have a task for you.'

RAFEN LEFT THE trooper – he never stopped to ask his name – in the atrium and followed the sounds of sporadic gunfire out into a courtyard between the hospital and the slums surrounding it. Great oval vents protruded from the floor, as tall as a man, venting streams of thin, warm smoke. Corners of buildings were collapsed into one another, and a wide crack in the decking allowed sounds from the manufactory to fill the air. The scene could have easily been the surface of any inhabited city after a firefight, but the rent in the ground showed that the footing beneath Rafen's boots was only the roof of a far larger complex below. The actual surface of Shenlong was perhaps twenty levels below him.

He hesitated in the shadow of one of the vents as a string of bolter fire echoed behind him. Rafen heard rough laughter and then a death-cry that could only have come from the injured soldier. He cursed and sank into the shade as a column of Traitor Marines emerged. At the forefront strode the Dark Apostle Iskavan, and he held a struggling man in one hand, dragging him by his robes.

The moment of hesitation on Cybele returned to Rafen. He had placed the Word Bearer in his sights and had not fired on him that day, in deference to orders from a brother now cold and dead. By the Emperor's grace, here he was again, and this time there was nothing to stop him. With infinite care, Rafen gently raised his bolter and laid aim on the Apostle's horned scalp. He would get one shot; it would have to count.

Rafen braced himself, took half a breath. He fired.

By some irony of fate, the bolt round in the breech was one that had been forged on Shenlong more than two hundred years earlier. It crossed the distance to Iskavan's skull and impacted with a shriek of savaged air, knocking the Word Bearer to his knees.

Rafen charged out of cover, turning the gun to fully automatic fire, cutting into Iskavan's honour guard. The Word Bearers split, some firing back, some taking cover. Rafen performed a swift shoulder roll and rose where the Apostle had fallen. He would take no chances; one bolt would not be enough to end the Traitor's filthy life.

Part of a broken statue by his legs blurred, distracting the Blood Angel. A bifurcated stone cherub suddenly turned from stone white to blue-green-gore-red and came at him. It moved so fast that Rafen's eyes could not catch it, forms shifting and changing. The thing morphed into a mass of teeth and bowled him over, snapping and biting. He shot at it in searing point-blank blasts, but each round seemed to flow through a new hole in its mass.

It distracted the Space Marine long enough so that powerful hands could grasp the hilt of a fallen weapon and strike at his back. The impact of Iskavan's crozius threw Rafen at one of the vent tubes and he bounced off it. Bones fractured inside his armour. Before he could even stop his fall, Rafen's injured legs lost purchase and he slipped into the rent in the ground, the breach in the stone flooring swallowed him up, bolter and all.

Iskavan took a step forward and strained, the muscles on his face bunching. The black disc of the bolt's entry wound steamed as the flattened bullet head slowly eased itself out of the bloody hole. The Apostle dug his nails into the skin and tore the round out of his skull, flicking it away with a growl.

The daemon giggling inside Falkir's warped host-body keened, blinking too many eyes at the fissure that had taken the Blood Angel from him. Iskavan gestured with his weapon. 'Make yourself useful. Kill that wastrel.'

The messenger-creature whooped with joy and flowed across the stonework like a maggot. Its skin flickered in and out of colour synch with the red rock.

The Dark Apostle gathered up Pellis from where he had fallen. 'There is a funicular tram to the lower levels. Show it to me.'

Pellis nodded, head jerking and unable to stop.

FOR A MOMENT it seemed like Rafen was hovering there in the hot smoke that billowed up from the mills below. Then he was falling, dropping past strings of cables and rusted girders, plunging toward the foundries where pots of molten steel yawned like orange mouths. Something clipped his leg and he spun: a hanging wire. He had an instant to glimpse a web of metallic lines then he landed with a bounce in a net of filaments. Rafen rolled over, bobbing up and down like a cork afloat on the ocean. The wires around him clicked and sang. He was suspended in a cargo net, high above the factory floor, and as he scanned the air around him with his enhanced eyes, the Blood Angel could pick out crossbars, knots of cable and hanging gantries.

James Swallow

Over the loops of greasy wire came the hooting Tzeentch-thing, sloughing off bits of the decayed Word Bearer and sprouting limbs wherever it needed them. Rafen still had his bolter, held tight in a rigid grip.

The daemon sprang at him. It was so close he didn't bother to shoot it, instead batting the thing aside with the gun. The Falkir-thing chittered and growled, one spider-leg producing the dead Word Bearer's chain axe. It struck out, and missed Rafen but cut through a dozen steel cables. The net complained and tilted, dropping Rafen another five metres onto a train of cargo containers. He scrambled to move as the daemon flung itself down after him.

The Blood Angel ran, leaping the gaps between the containers, advancing along the train as the line of pods drew toward an automated loading crane, which loomed large over the monorail like the raised tail of some vast scorpion made of black steel. A broad sunflower of metal petals fanned out above the train as the cargo pods passed beneath it, and Rafen saw his chance. Ignoring the agony lancing through him from the wounds on his legs, he turned every effort of his might into an upward leap and snatched at the claw-grab. His free arm found purchase, and Rafen flipped himself up and over. He landed badly, and almost slipped off the greasy metal of the derrick. Below him, at the far end of the train, the messenger-thing coiled and spat at him, ready to jump.

Rafen fired again. He was rewarded with a shriek from the creature as hot rounds tore off a chitinous limb. It skipped over the train of containers, springing from one to another, dodging his fire. Rafen caught a glimpse of a cargo module just ahead of him. It was marked with the livid warning runes for liquid promethium. He angled his gun down. As the daemon's clawed feet landed on the module roof, the

Blood Angel sent a cascade of shells into the tanker wagon, punching into the volatile fluid within. The resulting detonation turned the train into a snake of fire, and in an eye-blink the creature was immolated. Fatty globules of warped flesh, broken shards of bone and other twisted pieces of organic debris blew into the air accompanied by the thing's unnatural death-scream. The backwash battered Rafen with a fist of woolly heat and the Blood Angel looked away.

Below, a glitter of unholy light illuminated the eightfold blade of a corrupted crozius. Rafen let his helmet optics bring the sight closer. There was the Apostle, advancing from a rail carriage with his men and the captive adept. He followed the direction they were heading in and saw it just beyond the glow of the foundries: a tank farm of pressurised cylinders tall as obelisks, nested in ferrocrete and adorned with symbols of skulls and interlocking circles. The bioweapon crèche.

MANY OF THE Word Bearers had been left to indulge their base desires while Iskavan escorted Pellis below. They were a ragged approximation of what they once had been. They were no longer the precise, drilled squads with their inexorable martial might but raging hurricanes of weapons fire and uncontrolled violence. Hordes of them congregated on the quadrant outside the hospital, roaring profane exaltations and fashioning obscene altars from the bodies of the dead.

From the rust-laden mist that ghosted Shenlong's streets came the building thunder of engines, a wall of sound that advanced across the Traitor ranks and gave them pause in their ministrations. The gore-spattered warriors presented their weapons to the haze and shot into it; fierce returns of bolter fire lanced back at them. Twin guns mounted on the prows of a legion of attack bikes screeched as Arkio led the Blood Angels' charge.

Red machines threw themselves out of the rust storm and rode down the Word Bearers, and at their head was the Blessed. Arkio stood in his saddle and rolled the Spear of Telesto over his head, cutting hot glyphs of gold lightning though the bodies of the enemy. Chaos Space Marines, havoc troopers and a handful of obliterators, all were penned in and gunned down by the Blood Angels. Bright fountains of arterial fluid issued into the sky and the sons of Sanguinius opened their mouths to it, drinking in the gifts of their enemy's death. Warriors leapt from bikes at full throttle, tearing their foe's throats from them and biting deep into exposed flesh. Blood, dark and clotted, flowed in rivers.

Men on foot followed behind the bikes. These were not Adeptus Astartes, these were commoners, some with looted guns but most with tools and blades. Many of them wore hastily made sashes with crude symbols – a version of the Blood Angels' winged droplet crossed by a golden spear. These people had been the ones who had never dared to even look upon a Traitor's face. Now they poured over them, dying in their hundreds as they hammered the Word Bearers with spanners and rocks. They offered the blood of the fallen as boons to the men in crimson armour.

Arkio rallied them with a clarion call. 'No survivors!' The holy lance sang in his grip, leaving trails of red in the air as it gutted the unworthy.

ISKAVAN THREW PELLIS down in front of the control pulpit and let the crozius hover near his face. The adept felt like he was standing too close to a naked flame, his skin steaming.

'These are the germ weapons?' The vile apostate indicated the tanks.

The little man kept nodding. The monster had demanded he lead them to the storage facility. He had obliged, desperate to do anything that would keep him alive for a few more minutes. Pellis retched in fear. The vent levers before him were the emergency shunts that would open the bio-toxin tanks to the air. They were protected by hundreds of wards and purity seals glued to their faces. These immense containers held the gaseous forms of a hundred different poisons. NeoZyklona. Rot-bane. Agent Magenta. The Fell Breath. Their names were a litany of the death-dealer's art; weapons kept for those whose crimes had been particularly offensive to the Emperor.

The Dark Apostle nodded at the banks of gauges and valves. 'Open it.'

'Which one?' the adept whimpered.

Iskavan did something horrible: he smiled. 'All of them.'

'We'll be killed!' Pellis shrieked.

'Chaos never dies,' said the Word Bearer, and with one stroke his weapon turned the seals into flaming confetti. 'But this world will.'

TOO FAR AWAY, Rafen told himself. *Too many of them*. Dangling on the crane, the Blood Angel felt useless as the mechanism moved on its slow circuit of the manufactory. Hundreds of worker-helots and servitors huddled around the shadows of the noisy fabricators, looking up at him with masks of utter fear. These were the lowest of the Shenlongi, the broken and the mind-wiped, and he would get no support from them. Rafen suspected that these pitiful wretches had been slaving away down here since before the Word Bearers' arrival on the planet, turning out shell after shell, and never knowing if the master they served reigned from the Golden Throne or the Eye of Terror.

Even Rafen's powerful hearing could not bring Iskavan's words to the adept to his ears, so loud were the machines about him. But he could intuit the Apostle's plan. It was the ultimate act of spite, a final brutal sting of revenge. Iskavan would condemn himself and his host to agonising deaths, but knowing that this city and then eventually all of Shenlong would perish as well.

'This shall not be,' Rafen declared, and stabbed at the crane's control pulley with his combat blade. The grab was passing over a large ceramic cup, filled with molten steel bound for the casting forge. The Blood Angel punctured the workings, and was rewarded by a shuddering groan from the crane's cable brakes. The heavy grab twitched, and then it fell, reeling out the pulley behind it as the claw head dropped toward the factory floor, with Rafen clinging on. As he descended, the Space Marine ignored the fat sparks that fountained from the brakes and drew a bead on the huge pot. His old mentor's training returned to him and saw the target through Koris's eyes. *Yes. There!*

Rafen's weapon rattled as he let the rounds spark off the sides of the cup, licking at the bolts that held it upright. He ignored the approach of the ground, seeing only the void between his weapon and his mark. The bullets demolished the couplings, and the cup fell, tumbling to the floor like a goblet falling from the fingers of some drunken giant. The canister threw a tidal wave of molten metal at the Word Bearers, and they broke apart like a flock of startled birds.

Rafen never saw the liquefied steel engulf them, the crane grab struck the ground and threw him into a mess of pipes – but he heard it. Rough screaming. The sickening crackles as incredible heat embrittled their ceramite armour and flash-burned their flesh. The unprotected adept would have been cooked instantly under the seething breaker, and workers had probably died too – but that was a small price to pay. The scent of burnt meat reached his nostrils and Rafen felt a sudden surge of hunger in return. The Blood Angel struggled to his feet, his muscles alive with pain. A drool of backwash hissed and lapped at his boots.

Then a huge and wrathful shadow surfaced in the tide of glowing fluid and tore itself out of the thick, searing embrace. Iskavan the Hated leapt out of the shimmering river and came at Rafen, gobs of cooling steel streaming out behind him in a silver halo.

TWENTY LEVELS ABOVE, Arkio froze as a shudder of sympathetic pain lanced through him. The flash of a mind-image: a massive shape made from steaming metals and boiling flesh, suffocating him in darkness. The Blood Angel reeled from the sensation, the spear humming in pity.

A voice came to him. 'Brother?' Alactus reached out to help steady him, but hesitated, afraid to lay a hand on the bearer of the holy lance. 'Blessed?' he asked. 'What is it?'

Arkio shook off the sensation and cleared his head with a shout. 'Below!' he cried, whirling the spear about and slamming the teardrop blade into the ground beneath his feet. 'The true battle lies below!'

Alactus backed away as a white sphere of energy collected at the tip of the spear. Arkio threw back his head and bellowed, his fangs bared to the russet skies above. The sacred weapon punched a void in the grounds of the valetudinarium and a hot wind gushed out. The manufactorium was now revealed; it ranged away into the depths and the thrashing metal shapes of the mills were in constant motion. There, beneath Arkio's feet, he could see the light of weapons' fire and the distinctive blue aura of potent psychic discharges.

AT ANGEL'S FALL, when Rafen had been an aspirant and his arrogance had forced Brother Koris to best him in single combat, the Blood Angel had known what it felt like to be overmatched. That day under the hot rays of Baal's star was here again, replayed in the iron pit of the weapon shops of Shenlong. But now the foe that stood before him was a Dark Apostle bristling with the black power of Chaos. This time, the lesson Rafen would learn would cost him his life.

Iskavan's dousing in liquid steel had scarred him beyond recognition. He had lost one of his tongues. The pain of the burning metal was so strong that he had bitten it off in agony. His deconsecrated armour was no longer the dull, magenta hue of the Word Bearers' Legion, but a sooty-black, the tone of torched flesh. The spines that sprouted from his back were bent or broken, leaking clear pus. He had lost at least two of the bony horns from his face. Yet still he came on, a rage that towered like mountains animating him through a painstorm that would have killed a hundred men. Such was his anger and agony that the licks of psionic energy discharging from him arced across the decking and murdered workers too slow to avoid them. This was the foe that Rafen faced.

Bolts thudded into Iskavan to no effect, and the Apostle laid into Rafen with his crozius. Snatching his knife from its sheath, Rafen buried the blade to the hilt in the Word Bearer's exposed neck. Iskavan did not appear to notice, and kicked the Blood Angel away from him. Rafen rolled with the impact and shot again.

Iskavan shouted wordlessly, perhaps in pain, perhaps not. He was batting bolt rounds out of the air with the vibrating force weapon. He swept the eightfold blades down and the Space Marine barely dodged, the serrated edges scoring his armour. The Apostle drew back for a killing blow and Rafen emptied the gun into the Traitor's free hand. At so close a range, the blaze of bullets ripped away everything from the middle of his forearm, shredding bone, muscle and blood into a mess of gelatinous fragments.

'Bastard!' The Apostle poured centuries of hate into the curse and slammed his crozius into Rafen. The blow was imperfect, borne from fury and without any semblance of control, otherwise it would have killed him instantly. Instead, the Space Marine was thrown thirty metres to slam into the side of a cargo unit. Most of Rafen's torso armour was gone, the ceramite ripped away. Bunches of artificial muscle twitched beneath. He felt the full weight of his wargear as the thermal dissipaters in his backpack clogged and shut down. The Blood Angel's head lolled. He had lost his helmet somewhere, and a wound over his brow gummed his right eye closed. Rafen tried to move, and felt broken ribs spearing his lungs from within.

Licking the gore spattered on his face, Iskavan approached, the chain linking the crozius to his arm rattling. 'Ah,' he growled, savouring the taste, 'I know this blood. I know you. From Cybele...' He raised the weapon again, this time for the final blow. 'I gift you with the boon of pain,' he spat, 'to feed the hunger of the gods.'

'No–' Rafen managed and then a bright red dart fell from the dark roof and landed amid the cooling steel.

Iskavan whirled to see a ring of liquid metal surge away from the point of impact. He hissed as he recognised the whelp that had borne the archeotech weapon inside the fortress. And beyond he saw more Blood Angels swarming down walkways and elevators, engaging in firefights with the few Word Bearers he had left to guard the approaches.

'You will injure no more of my brothers,' said Arkio, his voice carrying.

Iskavan roared a battle cry and sent rods of lightning at the youth. Arkio knocked them away with the Spear of Telesto and in a flash he was at the Word Bearer's throat, the lance slamming into the crozius with shrieks of tortured metal. Iskavan's weapon warped the air around it with redolent malevolence and the two warriors went back and forth across the slick decking, blood jetting from wounds where blades made brief contact.

Arkio struck Iskavan's bleeding stump with the blunt end of the spear and he let out a sound that chilled the marrow. The Apostle savagely returned the attack and found a tiny gap in Arkio's defence. A solid hit spun the Space Marine in place and he stumbled. Iskavan, infinitely older and more heartless than the young Blood Angel, did not hesitate to follow the blow and struck once more. The fan of blades locked into the cables and fastenings that held Arkio's back-pack in place and severed them. The compact fusion reactor and the back plate of his armour, all went away in a flood of hurt. Arkio fell in a heap, barely able to hold on to the spear. Unable to move, Rafen watched in horror as the Apostle drew the last reserves of psionic energy from within himself and channelled them into the humming crozius.

The crackling disc of knives fell on Arkio like the will of a vengeful deity – and it met the teardrop blade with a blinding amber flash. The Chaos weapon shattered with the impact and Iskavan staggered back. Rafen's brother slumped as if the effort had drained him of any more fight. But the Apostle was still standing. Iskavan looped the broken chains that had tethered his weapon in one hand and threw it over Arkio's neck.

Rafen tried to drag himself toward his brother, his chest burning. The Traitor pulled the chain tight and choked the life from the Blood Angel.

Arkio's body buckled and shivered. A sound like crackling thunder issued out of him, and he flexed suddenly, the motion throwing Iskavan off him, snapping the chain. The Apostle tumbled away and landed atop the inverted claw grab, the metal fingers cutting into him.

But Rafen saw none of that. His eyes were locked on the brilliant white wings that had emerged from his brother's back. Arkio turned; he was radiant. Golden haloes lensed the air around him, and his face glowed. The expression there was hawkish and noble – but as baleful as hell itself.

Arkio's seraph wings threw him into the air with a single stirring, and he rose to hover over Iskavan's form. With an uncanny economy of motion, he summoned the spear and it flew to his fingers. The Apostle saw his fate coming and tried to pull himself to his feet. Arkio nodded to him, a benediction of sorts, and then his fangs were bared in a terrible cry. He threw the spear like a thunderbolt and it pierced Iskavan's black heart. Rafen watched a flash of gold light envelop the Word Bearer lord. When it faded there was nothing but the lance and ashes.

Time blurred, and then Arkio was at Rafen's side, a gentle warm hand on his neck, feeling for a pulse. 'Brother?' he said. 'You will live. Trust me.'

Rafen's heart hammered. The being before him, the face and the wings, the spear... It was no longer his sibling but the ancient artworks of Sanguinius given human form. Arkio knelt next to him, the very aspect of the great primarch reborn.

'What... are you?' He forced out the words, tears clouding his vision.

Arkio smiled, the beneficent expression of a million chapel windows there on his lips. 'I am the Blood Angel, brother. I am the Deus Encarmine.'

Rafen tried desperately to shake his head, to deny it; but then the merciful void of unconsciousness swept up to take him, and he willingly submitted.

EPILOGUE

A MESSIAH WAS created that day amid the people of Shenlong. In the depths of the factory, the low born joined the Blood Angels and the people of the upper cities, killing every last Word Bearer that dared to defile the planet with their existence. The lesser daemons that Iskavan had released were culled and their bodies were burnt in the huge fusion smelters that made the biggest of the Empire's bombs. Across the city the voices of Astartes and civilian alike praised Arkio's name. He walked among them, the ragged remains of his armour clinging to his chest and the great angelic wings unfurled behind him like magnificent white sails. The rise of the new crimson angel began on the ashes of traitors, as it was meant to be.

RAFEN AWOKE TO find Alactus standing over him. 'Gently,' he said. 'Your healing trance is not long ended...'

'Arkio...' Rafen began, coming to his feet. His head swam and there were darts of agony all over him, but his flesh felt whole. He knew this uncomfortable, vulnerable sensation from battles past. His bones were still knitting, and his altered skin and organs were working him back to full strength. By the colour of his new scars, he knew that little time had passed since the battle with Iskavan.

'The Blessed speaks today.' Alactus said. 'He personally charged me with the task of standing sentinel here.' The Space Marine practically beamed as he said it. Rafen frowned; where was the man who had disputed Arkio on Cybele?

Rafen cast around for his equipment. 'My wargear?'

'Ruined,' Alactus replied. 'The tech-adepts have salvaged some elements, but it will not serve you again. Sachiel has ordered a fresh suit of armour be consecrated for your use.' He paused. 'Your bolter survived intact. It is at the armoury.'

Rafen donned a set of robes, noticing the altered Blood Angel's symbol on them, with the gold halo and spear. 'What's this?'

'The people have created it. They wear it to honour him.'

Anger crossed Rafen's face and he tore the sigil off. 'I'll carry the mark of our Chapter and no other,' he growled. 'Take me to Arkio.'

'That may not be possible. The Blessed is preparing to address the warriors of the reborn–'

'Then take me to the chapel!' Rafen broke in. 'Or else get out of my way!'

STELE GLANCED OVER the balcony at the plaza. There was barely an inch of room out there, with the red shapes of the Blood Angels massing in silent, reverent ranks and the crimson sashes of the zealot army. Already, the warriors of the reborn were swelling with new conscripts every day, more even than could fit aboard *Bellus*. He tapped a finger on his lips as he studied them. Soon, he would have Sachiel select a thousand of the most ardent to accompany Arkio on his return to Baal. A smile threatened to emerge as he wondered what the great Dante would say when confronted with such a sight.

He sensed Ulan's approach and turned to her. She bowed low. 'Lord inquisitor, I bring news.'

He raised an eyebrow. It would be something important if the astropath was unwilling to transmit it from orbit. 'Tell me.'

'In the telepathic ducts I spied a remnant of the unauthorised signal that was sent from our vessel to Baal. It required several days of meditation to unfurl it, but I had some success.'

'What was said?' he asked in a low voice.

Ulan faltered. 'That... datum was lost to me, lord. But I did intuit the code key of the brother who sent it. Veteran Sergeant Koris.'

'Impossible.' Stele snapped. 'Koris was deep in the hold of the black rage, I saw to that.'

'There is no doubt,' she insisted. 'The code was his.'

'Who would dare use the vox of a dead man?' the inquisitor asked. 'These Astartes would not desecrate the armour of the fallen, it is one of their most sacred tenets.' He fell silent as he saw a two figures making their way through the soldiery below, one in armour, the other hooded in robes. Stele knew instantly who he was looking at. 'Rafen.' He glanced at Ulan. 'Return to *Bellus*. I will have need of you later.'

The astropath departed and Stele returned to the chapel where Sachiel stood over Arkio, at once commanding and servile. Chapter serfs crowded around the Blessed, dressing him in a suit of hallowed artificer armour, anointing it with oils.

'Magnificent,' Sachiel breathed, a spellbound look in his eyes.

Arkio did not look up. His ice-blue eyes were fixed on the floor of the chapel, unfocussed as the symphonies of battles fought untold centuries past whispered in his ears. Instead of the flat shapes of the Blood Angels' armour that he had worn before, Arkio was now adorned in sheaths that glistened like bright summer sunlight. The arms and legs were moulded to suggest broad skeletal bones or powerful muscles straining beneath the ceramite, while the chest was broad and chis-elled. Wings cast in white gold that matched those rising from his back adorned the breastplate, framing a single tear cut from a giant ruby. The design repeated on his left shoul-der, while his right bore the image of the holy lance. Every inch of the armour was layered with new engravings, the words of freshly created prayers to the reborn angel. The wargear fitted him as if he had been born to wear it.

'Vandire's Oath!' The curse brought all eyes to bear on Rafen as he entered the chapel. 'You wear the gold?'

Sachiel stepped down to block his path. 'He does, Rafen.'

'But–'

'But *nothing*.' the priest growled. 'You saw the emergence. You were there. Do you doubt your own sight?'

Rafen tried to find the words but they fled from him. He felt Stele's iron gaze boring into him and his knees went weak.

'Rafen, you have brought this moment upon yourself,' Sachiel said, and he drew his reductor with one hand and the red grail with the other. 'It is only by virtue of your blood kin-ship to him that I have tolerated your questioning of the Blessed's divine nature, but now you have come to a moment of choice.' He held the pistol before Rafen's face. 'Choose now, brother. You must swear your loyalty or stand against him. Kneel.'

He hesitated and Sachiel shouted, loud as a gunshot. '*Kneel!*'

Before he was even aware of it, Rafen dropped to one knee and saw the grail near his lips. Dark fluid swirled within.

'By this oath, you pledge your life and your blood to Arkio the Blessed, Sanguinius Reborn, Lord of the Spear,' intoned the priest. 'Your faith and your honour, until death.'

Rafen looked up, and he met his sibling's gaze. There was nothing but lordly hauteur there, and the subtle menace of coiled violence beneath. *If I die here, then the last dissention is silenced*, he thought, *but to take this oath…*

Sachiel's face twisted in a cruel smile and his finger tightened on the trigger. But then Rafen denied him, reached out and took a drink from the cup.

'By this oath,' Rafen began, 'I pledge my life to Arkio the Blessed.' The blood was cold in his mouth, and sour like the ashen words he spoke aloud. He had denied it for too long, but now Rafen saw the truth of his path unfolding before him.

His brother was something strange and terrible, no longer a child of Baal, no longer sworn to their code. With the burning clarity of the rage racing in his veins, Rafen knew that soon a reckoning would come between Arkio and he that only one of them would survive.

Arkio smiled then, and it was awesome to behold. 'Welcome, brother,' he said. 'Welcome to the New Blood.'

BLOOD DEBT

Author's note: This story takes place several years before the events of Deus Encarmine *and the Third Armageddon War.*

THEY ABANDONED THE groundcar at the port gate when blood began to drool from the ventilator grilles. The machine grunted and sighed, the glass in the windows popping as it shifted and changed shape. The two of them ran, boots hammering across the road, shouldering their way through the swarming throng of terrified people.

The woman surveyed the crowds with care. It was not the first time she had been in the thick of a frightened mass, and she knew the capricious nature of a mob's animal mentality. With the right demonstration of force they could be cowed, but just as quickly they might turn murderous. These screaming, weeping, scrambling hordes were heavy with fear. They wanted so desperately to live, and yet she knew that to a man they would be dead or dying before sunset.

She threw a glance over her shoulder and her companion gave her a frown. He had never once looked back at the city they were leaving behind, not from the moment that they had embarked on their headlong flight. In the distance, she could see where some of the taller hive towers had collapsed, parts of their structure altering on the molecular level, steel skeletons running like melted butter as the changes touched them. Building that had stood proud and defiant in the most Imperial of manners were now shambolic, tattered things, flayed of stone and bearing their iron ribs to the sky.

Dots ducked and wove in the air overhead – perhaps carrion birds, or maybe men and women like the ones she had killed to get the car, humans with newly sprouted wings still wet with amniotic fluid.

Hot exhaust fumes threw a sudden curtain of spent-fuel stink over them as a transport thundered upward, the spitting engines vibrating and complaining. She watched it struggling to gain height, the cargo pods clustered beneath dangerously overloaded with refugees. Something inside broke with a cough of grey vapour, and the craft dipped sharply toward the ground. She grabbed her companion's cloak and pulled him into the lee of a blockhouse just seconds before the ship crashed. The concussion blew down the crowd like falling timbers, and for long moments her hearing was replaced by a low, hissing whistle.

He stood first, his mouth moving even though his voice was lost to her.

'This way. Keep going'.

She nodded. Acrid chemical smoke pooled around their ankles as they ran, the rough winds across the landing fields catching the hems of their cloaks and flapping them back like sails. They wore the simple robes of pilgrims, the clothing common to the endless migrations of penitents that came to Orilan to visit the tombs of the Faded Lords; but no pilgrims carried the combat webbing or weapons holsters that they wore underneath. Other ships passed over them, climbing on spears of white fire toward the high clouds. The horizon was full of fleeing silver darts, desperate to escape the horror engulfing the planet.

In the first few hours of the outbreak, the vox-casts had described the effect as a virus, warning people to stay in their homes and avoid large congregations; but it quickly became clear that the changes were not the creation of some malignant micro-organism, nor were they limited to humans. Animals, insects, even plants began to shift and mutate. New forms arose on every corner, disgusting and loathsome things that sprouted horns or festoons of lapping tentacles. And then the inert and inorganic fell prey to the creeping aberration, as iron, stone and plastic warped beneath its touch. Some of the hysterical bulletins spoke about night-dark shadows wafting through the canyons of the city, leaving surreal and unnatural malformations in their wake. Sanity itself seemed to have fled Orilan, allowing things that were once corralled in nightmares to run wild in the cold light of reality.

She shook her head to clear it and blinked. Her companion stabbed a finger at a shifting cluster of people clinging to the edges of a boarding ramp. 'That one,' he said, 'yes?'

'Yes,' she replied. Atop the ramp was a planetary lighter, an orbital shuttle of a crude but quite speedy type. Similar ships were employed across the Imperium and she knew that if circumstances required, she would be able to pilot the craft herself. The lighter wore the logo of a freight haulage agency that carried cargo and passengers from platforms in the orbital rings, to the surface of the planet and back again. She estimated that with enough reaction mass and a good course, the ship might get them to Orilan's outermost moon.

Where the ramp ended, a large servitor drone was blocking the open loading hatch, picking figures from the swarming throng with rough metal grippers. Valuables and items of all sorts, from coin bags to barrels of amasec and musical instruments, lay in a pile near its clawed feet. There were perhaps a hundred and fifty people between the two of them and the servitor. Her face set in a grim mask, the woman's hand dipped into the slit in the folds of her cloak, fingers touching the careworn butt of an old but steadfast stubber pistol. She scanned the people, looking for a target that would make the most disruption when she hit it.

'Wait.' His left hand touched her elbow, and she saw that his right was also swallowed by the mass of his robes. He had that look in his eyes, the misty, slightly vacant glitter that came on him when he was reading people. 'Be ready.'

The words had barely left his lips when a commotion began in the heart of the crowd. A peculiar ululating scream flew from the mouth of a gangly dockworker in a coverall. The unfortunate threw himself about, crashing into other people, screeching as he collided with them. Those around him struggled to get away, sending ripples of motion through the crowd. Figures at the ramp's edges were pushed off and into the sheer well of the exhaust pit below. Ripping sounds came from inside the man's clothing, and dark fans of blood discoloured his torso. From places on his chest and face, forests of needle-like spines erupted, tearing out of him. He jerked wildly, a puppet pulled by pain. The mob cried out in shock.

She watched the change take the dockworker with grotesque fascination. Since the morning, she had seen it occur more than a dozen times, but each riotous mutation was different from the last, horribly watchable in its repugnant display.

'Now!' said her companion, and her fascination snapped like a thread. He was springing forward, the ornate shape of a master-crafted lasgun filling his fist. She fell into the confusion behind him, drawing her own weapon. It was less fancy than his, but just as elegant in its lethality. They reeled from him as he moved. He laid hands on them, brushed them with his fingers, and people recoiled as if they had been burned. Sweat beaded his brow despite the cold air, the effort of it straining him.

Amid the screams and howls, they forced their way through the crowd as ocean predators would knife through a shoal of fish. She felt her gut tighten as the ramp shuddered; the cargo hatch was beginning to descend, preparing to seal the shuttle. 'Two more. Two more,' grated the servitor, taking the coat hems of a merchant gentleman and his mistress, dragging them forward. 'Last ones. No more.'

Had it been necessary, her companion could have communicated his intent to her with a brief thought; but they had been together for so long, faced so many situations such as this one that neither of them needed to consider their next move. The two of them raised their guns and shot the gentleman and lady through the backs of their skulls, blowing brain matter and bone across the servitor's carapace. The machine-slave obeyed its programming automatically and dropped the dead bodies. 'Two more,' it said. 'Last ones.'

Some people understood what was transpiring and tried to push forward, but by then it was too late, and the woman and the man were ducking to get under the hatch, followed by the stooped servitor, it's manipulators full of swag. Fresh blood still dripped from it as the helot worked the locks. Fists rang on the hull, dull thuds resonating into the cargo bay.

The bay's interior was a web of netting and spars, to which dozens of Orilani had attached themselves, terrified that they would be torn out of their escape vessel before it made lift-off. She saw the servitor lock itself into an acceleration couch and grabbed at a loose curl of webbing.

Below their feet, the rocket motor spat out flame, burning alive the people they left behind as it rose into the air.

THE LIGHTER PRESENTED its blunt prow to the sky as it lifted away from the chaos of the starport, sweeping across the edge of the city. The engines laboured to hold the vessel on course, but by the Emperor's grace there was fuel enough in the tanks to burn the boosters hot. The ship clawed into the air, threading through thin streaks of cloud and the sooty plumes of burning buildings.

Something in the haze of corruption moved in a way that windborne smoke never would have. By turns and heartbeats, a black glitter of movement came falling towards the sweating, groaning ship. It was ephemeral and gauzy, a shimmer on spoiled waters, a glow from the wings of an insect swarm. It touched the vessel's fuselage and coated the hull like wet paint, rolling in coils across the metal fuselage, down and about.

Searching. Feeling. Seeking a way inside.

As the vessel rose into Orilan's upper atmosphere, the inky shroud at last found a microscopic flaw in the hull. And with a controlled, fierce will, it poured itself in through the gap.

VONOROF FELT EMPTY and sick, as if the g-forces pushing him into the pilot's couch were leaching his very life essence away. As the blackness of space unfolded across the cockpit window, the pestilent sights he left behind still dogged him, replaying over and over in his mind's eye. The tree outside the chapel as it turned about its length to present a maw of teeth. The roadway that melted under his feet. His daughter wailing as her eyes fell from her head, her face sprouting tendrils and cilia. As hard as he tried, Vonorof could not shake the images away. He blinked.

He was still crying. He had been for quite some time now. The hatch behind him irised open and he gave a start. Panic rolled around inside him and he steeled himself, at last daring to turn and face the figure that had entered.

A pilgrim, his face haunted and drawn. About his neck pooled a rough-hewn hood, framing a bald head dominated by an electro-tattoo of the Imperial aquila. In one ear glittered a single purity stud of old pewter.

Vonorof suddenly found his voice. 'You shouldn't be up here! This is a restricted area–'

'Not to me,' the man's voice was flat with fatigue, but it brooked no argument. He pushed into the cockpit and the pilot glimpsed another figure behind him in the gangway, another pilgrim hanging back. 'Change course,' said the bald man.

Vonorof felt a peculiar tension around the thick brass sockets in the base of his neck, where the sinuous mechadendrites of the lighter's command chair connected directly to his brain. A subtle pressure, pushing on his will. He tasted a greasy sensation in the stale recycled air of the cabin. In all honesty, he had not given a lot of consideration to where he would go when he lifted the ship; he had half-expected not even to get this far. The vague, animal need to escape the insanity on the planet had been driving him with its directionless energy. 'Where to?' he asked, slipping into a position of inferiority before he was even aware of it.

The man pointed; in the distance, starlight glittered off the hull of a vessel in high orbit. Direct machine code feeds from the lighter's cogitators told Vonorof that it was a Gladius-class frigate, a warship of a kind only employed by the Emperor's Space Marine legions, the Adeptus Astartes. 'Approach that craft.'

A flood of panic seized the pilot. The frigate was the colour of old blood, a red scar in the sky, and even from this distance he could see the clouds of debris that were all that remained of craft that had strayed too close to it. 'A blockade ship,' the words spilled from his lips in a rush, 'they'll destroy us, even if there are no infected on board!'

'There is no disease,' said the pilgrim, the weariness hollowing his voice. 'Do as I say.'

Vonorof glanced from the viewport and made eye contact with the man. Instantly, any arguments died in his throat and the pilot found his head bobbing in a wooden nod. The pilgrim's will overpowered him easily, and he turned the transport with quick motions, bringing it on a direct intercept course with the frigate. On some level, a small part of Vonorof's mind rebelled at the sudden compulsion that had come over him, but it was a weak and feeble voice that railed against the man's dominating presence.

HE WIPED A sheen of sweat from his head and licked dry lips. Retreating from the cockpit, he found his companion waiting in the anteroom, watching him with a level gaze. He saw accusation there, a telltale so subtle that only someone who knew her as well as he did could notice. He ignored the flicker of irritation that coiled inside him and sealed the hatch, leaving Vonorof to fulfil his orders.

'You are putting us at risk,' she told him. 'The Astartes will surely obliterate this shuttle.' The woman threw a nod in the direction of the frigate. 'You saw the hull livery. The Blood Angels. They're not known for their mercy.'

'Fortunate for me then that I do not seek it.'

She shook her head. 'We should attempt a stealthy approach to the outer lunar colony and then–'

He held up a hand to silence her. 'Marain, I know what I am doing. Trust me.'

Her eyes narrowed and an unspoken emotional charge passed between them. The issue of trust was a raw wound, a chasm yawning wide between them. After a long moment, he pushed past her, a new kind of weariness in his bones.

MARAIN WATCHED THE man pick his way through a mass of hastily stowed possessions, rooting in the depths of an equipment locker.

'You are so sure of yourself, Ramius.' She studied him with different eyes; curious that he could have that effect on her, not once or twice, but over and over. The first time Marain had laid eyes upon him, she had been afraid of Ramius, although her training forbade her to show even the slightest inkling of it. The man she had feared that day differed from the person she had learnt to respect; in turn, that man was different from the Ramius who had bedded her and shown her love of a sort, for a while; and again, that man was not the man she saw now, drinking from a water pack, pressing at his face as if the skin on it were a poorly-hung mask.

'Your soldier's eyes,' he said quietly, the ghost of a smile on his lips. 'Watchful.'

'It's what I am,' she retorted. 'What I do.'

Ramius turned away. 'There's no war here.'

'You're wrong,' Marain told him, 'There's always war. If there were not, you would have no need for someone like me.'

He peered through a porthole. 'You are more than just a protector...'

The unspoken remainder of the statement made her lip curl. 'Once, perhaps, but not now. That road is closed to us.'

Ramius turned swiftly to face her. Was that hurt in his eyes, some flash of betrayal? Had he expected Marain to take his side in all of this? She held away any reaction, keeping her aspect utterly neutral.

* * *

He read her thoughts in her eyes; he could have laid them bare and known her mind inside out if he was prepared to expend the psychic effort, but Ramius was spent from tension and, although he hated to admit it, guilt. Marain's accusing face, her tawny skin framing a hard line of lips and dark eyes, arranged in judgement of him. In reproach of his mistakes, his folly.

She blamed him for it all, for the madness on Orilan. He could not dispute her. The truth of it was, his curiosity and arrogance would cost a world its life.

Marain came close to him, and he felt a surge of adrenaline as her lips spoke at his ear in a hushed murmur, too low to carry beyond the intimacy of the anteroom. 'You must atone, Ramius. Admit your errors and ask for forgiveness.' For all the quiet of the whisper, it was as loud a demand as a shout. He pulled away, unable to cover the sudden, naked fear on his face.

'I... I cannot.' Ramius husked.

Marain's disappointment coloured her words. 'You will die at the hands of the Blood Angels, along with everyone else on this scow. You have until then to consider your repentance.' She left him there to muse on her words, dropping back into the tunnel to the lighter's cargo decks.

The ship had one compartment that could be considered to be 'luxury' accommodation, at least by the standards of comparison to the rest of the craft. The addition of some threadbare acceleration couches retrofitted from a fire-damaged starliner and a broken entertainment holosphere were all the lighter offered. The cabin was full of people, every seat taken, every inch of tattered carpeted floor filled with human traffic. The air was thick with body odour as the ventilators laboured to handle the miasma generated by the refugees. Under other circumstances, fights might have broken out as people jockeyed for more room; but not this time. The passengers who had bribed or cajoled their way on to Vonorof's shuttle were too afraid to do anything other than watch one another for signs of the change. A dead woman lay in one of the aisles, her skull crushed by the boots of her neighbours. Just prior to lift-off she had begun to writhe, and as one they had piled upon her and murdered her where she sat, terrified that the mutations would burst from her body and turn upon them. Fear drove them, none of them caring if her palsy was caused by something else. No one dared to cough or to speak. None of them wanted to be next.

The compartment adjoined an engineering space. Running the length of the ship, it was filled with pipes for breathing gas and conduits labelled with arcane symbols that only Mechanicus adepts understood. Through this cluttered artery the darkness moved like liquid, flowing across every surface. When it passed the cabin wall it paused. It sensed life in there, very close. Very *afraid*.

The black form drew the gossamer edges of itself together into a ball of diamond hardness, fashioning a blade-point. A flicker of motion forced it into the metal and a finger-thick hole popped open, directly behind the shoulders of a corpulent, sweaty man. Held in place by the press of flesh, he could only flap his hands and wail as the shape punched through his spine and bored through his torso. His dying act was to tear the shirt from his chest; and then the darkness erupted in streams from every pore of his skin, turning him inside out.

People either side of the fat man warped like flowing candle wax, growing fans of teeth or eyes that popped open from boils. Everyone reacted at once, screaming, scrambling, a mass of humans all trying to force themselves through a narrow hatch and away from the tide of changes. The blackness swooped, kissing them with corruption and shredding their bodies. It formed a rudimentary maw from thin streams of matter and contorted, pressing air out of its makeshift mouth. The squeal of noise distorted until it became a recognisable word.

'Ramius.'

MARAIN HEARD THE horrible voice and her blood ran cold. The name tolled like a bell, the ghostly moan resonating down the tunnel. Where the bare skin of her hands clasped the rungs of the access ladder, she felt the metal under her fingers grow warm and pliant, turning fleshy. The air in the conduit became damp and breathy with the bouquet of rotting meat. The tunnel began to undulate and move, growing ribs and coils of cartilage. The sound of bone cracking spurred her into action and she let her weight carry her down to the cargo deck level. Wet trickles of stringy spittle followed, pooling at her feet in frothy puddles. She threw a quick glance up; the tunnel was turning into an open throat, some giant mutant oesophagus. Marain's gun was in her hand as she sprinted forward, shoving blank-faced refugees out of her way.

RAMIUS DETECTED THE psychic spoor of the dark-thing moments before his physical senses registered the stink of rended flesh. Inwardly he cursed; he had tired to the point that his well-honed warning senses had let him down. Tendrils like aerial roots crawled up the walls of the antechamber, probing and tasting. In the places where they touched objects, the tentacle-things split to reveal toothed lips, enveloping each new discovery like a snake eating a rodent. Ramius's gun shrieked, ozone searing the air as laser bolts shrivelled the invading probes. The shots beat them back, but it was only a temporary respite. With cold honesty, he understood that his mistakes had come to gather him to their breast, understanding that his hopes of escape and denial were childish and unrealistic. From below, the mutation hooted its terrible rendition of his name once again.

The clinical aspect of his nature assumed control. Based on his experiments, he had a rough approximation of the time it would take the change to sweep the shuttle. He imagined that outside now, the sleek metal lines of the lighter were slowly turning into swathes of skin and scale. Ramius forced open the hatch to the cockpit, holstering the gun and discarding the pilgrim robes as he did.

The pilot's face was florid; he would be the worst off, Ramius mused, wired into the vessel, feeling each moment of warping as the ship was transmuted. It would not be long before the man would become subsumed into his console, meat and pseudo-flesh merging together; and so time was of the essence. 'Hail the frigate,'

'Wh-what is happening–?'

Ramius slapped him hard across the face. 'Hail them!'

Vonorof worked a set of glyphs and the tinny hiss of a short-range vox issued from a transceiver. 'They won't answer. They'll kill us!'

The cloak fell about his ankles, revealing the ceramite-plate battle jacket beneath, the vest of fine Phaedran silks. He drew an icon from inside the folds where it hung on a thick chain and gripped it. The object responded with an inner fire, lighting the black eye sockets of the skull carved upon it. Vonorof knew the shape of the thing instantly; a thick gothic letter 'I' adorned with runes and chasings.

'Astartes, hear me,' intoned the bald man, 'know my name and purpose. I am the Inquisitor Ramius Stele of the Ordo

Hereticus. My agent and I are trapped aboard this vessel and we require rescue. I carry the Emperor's divine sigil. I must have passage!'

The pilot's lips trembled. Inquisitors were things spoke of in hushed whispers on Orilan; in the streets of the unremarkable outworld. Vonorof had heard stories of men who had actually seen them, but they were more myth than fact, spun with lies and mad truths. He gaped at Stele as the man ignored him, all his attention on the growing shape of the frigate. It was too much for his simple, parochial mind to accept.

'BROTHER-CAPTAIN,' SAID Simeon, 'A development.'

Tycho glanced up, the glow of the pict-plate map beneath him casting a sinister light across the half-mask covering the right side of his face. In the sullen glow of the warship's tacticarium, the haze of hololithic light from the consoles ranged around them gave everything a baleful aspect.

'Speak,' he demanded, the ever-present edge of irritation in his tone, 'I tire of culling these infected wretches, brother. I hope you have something more challenging for me.'

Simeon nodded. 'A signal from this ship,' he tapped at a moving dot on the map. 'The codes are present and correct. It would appear that an Inquisitor of the Imperial Church is aboard. A man of some import and rank among the Ordo Hereticus, so it would seem.'

'Indeed?' said Tycho. 'Unfortunate. Be certain to have a servitor take his name so that his death will be duly noted.'

Simeon shifted slightly. 'You misunderstand me, captain. The man demands assistance. He calls for a rescue.'

Tycho raised an eyebrow at the temerity of the statement. 'Nothing is to leave Orilan alive, Simeon. Those were our orders. The gunners have the ship in their sights, so bid them to fire.'

'With respect, lord, those orders are open to your interpretation.' The other Blood Angel frowned. 'Captain, this is a direct command from a member of the Ecclesiarchy. We cannot simply ignore it.'

Simeon's commander ran a hand over his chin, his eyes narrowing. 'We risk contamination if we enter the craft,' he said, thinking aloud. 'A great hazard.'

'There will be mutants on board,' Simeon added. He knew Tycho well, having served under him for many decades. He could almost see the turn in the captain's mood as it rolled forth like a storm cloud across the sky. Moments earlier, Tycho had admitted to his distaste at a mission better suited to a picket ship of the Imperial Navy; Simeon did not for a moment believe that the rescue would be a hard sell to his commander. They were Blood Angels, after all. They craved the cut and thrust of close-in action, not this paltry stand-off battle. He pressed the issue a little more. 'If the vox-casts from the planet are anything to go by, organics and inorganics will be changing into predatory forms. I would measure the inquisitor's life span in minutes, lord.'

A thin line of amusement pulled at Tycho's lips, and his hand twitched. There; that was the choice made, then. 'Perhaps we should respond. It is only right.' He stood up and strode away from his command dais, Simeon turning to watch him go. 'Have a skirmish force of men meet me in the teleportarium. Tell them to arm for a close quarter engagement.'

Brother Simeon took a half step after Tycho. 'Captain, there is no need for you to go in person. I would gladly take the–'

Tycho silenced him with a look. 'There is *every* reason for me to go.' The eagerness to taste battle, even something as brief as this, danced in the captain's single human eye. 'Tell this Inquisitor that his salvation is on its way.' A slight smile flickered on his lips, and was gone. 'You have the bridge, Simeon.'

MARAIN.

She could tell by the weakness of his mind-touch that Ramius was at the limits of his mental reserves. The telepathic message was a ghostly caress, and she almost missed it in the melee. She broke off the neck of a howling, eyeless mutant child with the butt of her gun as she fumbled out a fresh ammunition pack for the weapon. Marain ignored Stele's entreaty as she reloaded, allowing him to see through her eyes. She gave him freedom to touch her surface thoughts; it was far easier than framing a verbal answer.

Attend me, quickly. The Astartes are coming. Leave these people, they are already dead.

Her face twisted in a grimace. 'Get to the saviour pods!' she yelled at the untainted ones, 'Leave everything and go!' Marain bracketed the shambling, warped things with gunfire, but the more she killed, the more they recruited from the ranks of the panicked Orilani. It was a losing fight.

She forced an elderly man into the nearest pod with an angry shout, trying not to dwell on the logic of her actions. Marain's conviction was fuelled by guilt and responsibility, even as part of her tried to forget that the passengers were just as likely to mutate in the saviour pods as anywhere else. Even if the pods actually launched, what good would it do? Drifting in space, the escapees would suffocate or be shot down, and if by some miracle they made it down to the surface, what would be waiting for them but more new kinds of death?

Ramius was still in her head, leafing through her thoughts as if he were thumbing the pages of a book. She showed him her intent to stay, at least until these poor wretches had escaped this death ship. Ramius tugged on her memories, on the threads of loyalty that she had for him; with a savage mental swipe, she cut them off, heat building in her cheeks, hot tears prickling her eyes. Marain tasted his shocked understanding as he realised she had rejected her unswerving fealty to him. The guardian's sense of duty had been outstripped by Stele's perfidy.

He saw things he had never dared to search for, as she showed him her hidden self, the doubts and fears she had concealed from him. Her training had acquitted itself well, and never once had the Inquisitor suspected that Marain would harbour such ill will toward him. The woman had known all along about the nature of his research, the arcane prohibited experiments that he had been conducting. She had known and said nothing, such was her allegiance, her dogged dedication to him.

But now that had changed; Stele had gone too far, and Marain would be silent no longer. He saw her intentions, to reveal him to the Ordo Hereticus, to disclose the whole sorry story of his transgressions. If she lived, she would expose him.

Marain felt him leave her mind in a gust of psychic cold, a melancholy, sad wind fading away.

RAMIUS STAGGERED WITH the impact of what he had sensed and bumped into the cabin wall. He felt hollow. Marain, the one unchanging rock in the seas of his doubt, and she had elected to betray him. He shook his head. *Could she not understand? He had never intended things to get out of control!* He had only wanted to learn, to understand. Was that so hard for her to comprehend? Did the quest for knowledge make him a traitor? He felt sick inside as he realised that for Marain, the answer was yes.

The pilot slumped forward, dying along with his ship. Stele ignored him, ignored the growing wetness in the atmosphere as the shuttle's metallic slowly turned into fleshy stomachs and stinking gut-chambers. He felt an overwhelming sense of despair that blocked out everything else. Everything was going wrong, and now she rejected him. As quickly as it appeared, the emotion in him became hot anger. *How dare she? How dare a mere soldier sit in judgement of Ramius Stele?*

That she has been his lover gave her no right to castigate him or his methods. So be it, then. She had deserted him, and he would do the same to her. Let her stay on this ruined barge and die with the rest of these unfortunates.

Distracted by his own thoughts, Stele's attention wandered and he did not see it until it was too late.

Vonorof's twitchy body did something unspeakable and lighting-fast, bones snap-cracking as they reversed in their sockets, new lines of mouths opening in fanged maws. The pilot-mutant sprang at him, and Ramius drew back, but there was nowhere to go. The creature's attack knocked the lasgun from his fingers, and before he could muster a spark of psyker force, it was on him, battering his skull against the decking. It screamed and gibbered, words turning into a mush of slurred sound.

Spirals of colour lit behind Ramius's eyes and the breath left his lungs, blood trickling into his vision. He was dimly aware of something else entering the cramped chamber, something larger and deadly. His mind briefly touched the edge of a cool, killer's intellect.

The chattering mutant reared up, ready to tear out his throat; and just as quickly it exploded in a wet gout of purpled matter.

Ears ringing, his vision tunnelling, Stele barely managed to slide free of the mutant's steaming torso as a huge figure hove into sight. He wiped contaminated blood from his eyes to see shimmering greaves of brass and crimson filling his vision. Atop the tower of armour was a face that was half pale flesh, half gold mirror. A sneer coiled on the lips of the lofty figure. 'Bring him,' it rumbled.

'There are others still alive on the lower decks of the lighter.' The second voice came from a red giant standing at the hatchway. 'What is to be done, lord?'

'Save what you can,' said the half-face, the words following Ramius into the darkness of unconsciousness. 'Cull the rest.'

His MIND FLOATED in an ocean of crystal voids, sharp jags of memory and sensation ripping into him, needles of recollection tearing across the inquisitor's psyche. On some level, he understood that his corporeal body was teetering on the edge of coma and within, his psionic essence was undirected and broken, wandering the caverns of his soul. He sensed the boil and churn of the empyrean out there, just beyond the real, the realm of warp space where unknowable things lived. Even as he feared them, there was much of Ramius Stele that coveted the knowledge of these creatures, of how and what they were.

He knew that emotion all too well. It was this drive in him that had brought ruin to Orilan.

There was laughter.

Cruel and mocking, amused at his plight. Stele tried to shy away from it, but it found him wherever he hid.

'*Look what you have wrought,*' The words were the breath of corpses. '*Do not hide from it, Inquisitor. See it. Know it and own your deeds.*'

Against his will, Stele's mind reeled back to the library once more, forced down through the years to the point where it had all begun.

Always the library, the place where he had first glimpsed the great potential for himself. It had been on Ariyo, after the burning of the Simbasa Heretics; there, as the guardsmen put the torch to the storehouse of unhallowed texts, Ramius had dared to read from a volume that fell open at his feet. It had been an accident, just a small thing. He had looked, just dared to look. And what he read, glimpsed even...

What he saw there planted seeds of fervent interest, nurtured by the radicalism already seated in his heart. As the years passed, as he grew more disenchanted with the decrepitude of the Ecclesiarchy and the lackwits among his superiors, Ramius concealed his disgust while he sought out more forbidden knowledge and plumbed the greater depths of psyker witchery.

'*Do you remember the day I spoke to you?*' The voice was enthralling, just as it had been the first time. '*You thought I was a dream. But I was the wind of change upon your limited mind. I opened you, Ramius. You welcomed me.*'

Perhaps this was an illusion, he wondered, some product of his injuries.

'*You know better than that.*'

And then he tasted the name of the creature in his mind. Malfallax.

'*Yes.*' A hot pressure shoved Stele's memories to the secret chamber beneath the old temple on Orilan. To the place where the death of the world had begun, hours ago now, days past.

'*You were unready. Too eager. Look what it brought you.*'

The inquisitor watched the events unfold as if he were a passive observer, merely an audience member at some gaudy theatre play; he struggled fruitlessly, as if he could somehow throw a warning back in time to himself not to begin the Rite of Binding. He had made a mistake. It was so clear to him now in retrospect; one single ritual syllable spoken incorrectly, the emphasis on the rising glottal stop instead of the falling fricative...

A small thing. But enough to uncage the Tzeentch-thing he had called to the chamber.

Stele watched it happen again, sensing his tormentor taking amusement from his squirming. He saw himself walk through the drawing of the circle and the eightfold star within. Then, the lengthy and brutal murder of the vagrant to grant the blood sacrament. At last, the coming of the funnel of swarming shadow shaping into form in the middle of the stone basement. His rapt expression of delight – and then the sudden turn to terror as it struck out, metamorphosing the rock and metal into gnashing teeth, ripping out past the feeble wards he had been sure would hold it. Into the city, hungry for sustenance.

Screaming. Fading.

Free.

Weak denials formed in Ramius's mind. *How could I have known? It was an accident!* He had never intended to unleash the thing, only to capture and study the monstrosity so he might gain insight into the nature of the Change Lord.

Malfallax smiled. 'You delude yourself, Stele. Deep in your heart, you wanted to let it go. There is a part of you that hates the old order, the staid and the static. You lust for change and metamorphosis.'

When he tried to find a way to frame a retort, Ramius discovered his thoughts frozen by the damning truth in the warp creature's words.

'If this is not what you wanted, you could have stepped back from the brink. You chose not to. The willingness to sacrifice the woman is all the proof I require. You want this. You desire to know the the way in which Malfallax overpowers you.'

Stele's psyche recoiled beneath the awful, unstoppable reality. *'And with your own longing you make yourself my willing cohort.'*

The laughter faded and he let the blood-warm darkness swallow him.

THE BLOOD ANGELS marched the survivors into the frigate's launch bay, forcing them into a huddled group in the middle of the deck. Medicae servitors probed and examined them while Space Marines with loaded bolters walked in steady, watchful orbits around the poor wretches. They had all expected to die on the shuttle, but to be rescued by these crimson-sheathed giants was like the hand of the God-Emperor himself reaching down to scoop them from the jaws of death. Panic and terror had been replaced with a different breed of fear, one borne of reverence and a lifetime of awe.

A hatch in the wall irised open to admit one of Simeon's officers, a taciturn codicer in blue armour, his grizzled face lined with age. The Space Marine took a few steps and stumbled to a sudden halt, his jaw dropping open.

One of the Blood Angels guarding the refugees caught sight of his reaction and approached him. 'Brother Varon? Is something wrong?'

'*Daemon*!' Varon suddenly shouted the word, his finger stabbing out at a nondescript woman in a tattered evening dress, rocking gently side-to-side amid the rescued. Corded muscles stood out on the psyker's neck as his preternatural senses tasted the psychic stench of something monstrous hidden inside the cowl of her flesh.

The other survivors threw themselves aside as the woman sighed, each of them all too familiar by now with the ways of the change.

Her body twitched and deflated, crumbling in on itself. A swarm of black motes issued from her eyes, her nostrils, ears and mouth. The Blood Angels opened fire on reflex, cutting down those too slow to get out of the way, laying a spread of bolt shells into the host-corpse. The dead woman flew apart in wet hanks of fast-decaying flesh, but the dark-thing was already free. It looped around like a streamer of liquid shadow and threw itself at the psyker Space Marine, becoming a glistening spear.

Varon marshalled all his ability at once and channelled his Quickening into a mental shield; for an instant he thought it might have been enough.

The force of the daemon's murderous attack shattered his ephemeral defence like brittle glass, melting into the ceramite armour protecting his chest and tearing him inside out like a long and bloody streamer of meat. The shade came around, trailing Varon's blood and viscera, and beheaded a screaming Chapter serf with callous abandon, playing with the disorder it was creating.

IN THE FRIGATE's chirurgery, Stele bolted awake. He reeled up from the examination table where he lay, scattering trays of instruments and knocking aside the medicae servitors tending to him.

'It's here,' he spat, 'aboard the ship!'

THE SHADOW-CREATURE warped the flesh of human and Astartes alike, murdering them by forcing unholy new shapes from their bodies. Some perished as their bones and organs were forcibly altered into eight-pointed stars and hate glyphs. The daemon enjoyed this recreation, but it was secondary to the real reason it had come this far.

With a breathy sigh, it left its toys behind and the creature gathered up enough sustenance from the shrivelled dead. It surged down the corridors of the frigate, painting taint and corruption where it passed. It left a few survivors here and there to speak of what it had wrought; there was no sense in creating such great art if no one lived to witness it.

Down through the deck, shunting and flickering, dodging through barricades and the hastily-erected psyker wards of Tycho's Librarians, it fell through microscopic cracks in the metal and ceramite, tasting power in the air, moving toward it.

In the beating heart of the ship, past the locks made of heavy, poisonous phase-iron and the pitiful spirit deflectors, the shadow at last entered the holy chamber of the frigate's stardrives.

Tech-priests who had never ventured beyond the confines of the drive core scattered, babbling prayers to the Omnissiah or weeping blood. Enginseers brandished tools as weapons and died screeching where they stood.

The daemon made itself into a vague man-shape and drifted to the huge cylinders of the warp engines, stalking forward on pointed, glassine legs.

Beneath the casings of the mighty drives, technologies almost akin to magic seethed and roiled, great powers capable of remaking the laws of the universe barely held in check by weakling organic men with little comprehension of their true potential. The creature smiled and spread itself thin, touching the matter of the engines and changing them by degrees. Slowly it gathered in flesh and metal, and began to build itself a nest.

CAPTAIN TYCHO CAME to him eventually, as Stele knew he would. He watched the sullen light of the floating glow-globes caress the finely-tooled mask across Tycho's cheek and he wondered about what the Astartes hid beneath it. He had picked rumour and hearsay from the minds of the Chapter helots in the medicae chamber – something vague about a disfigurement caused in combat with an ork psyker. If it were true, then little wonder that the brother-captain hid his mutilation. The aesthetic sensibilities of any Blood Angel would be offended by such a sight. On another day, if Stele were not so fatigued from all that had transpired, he might have been able to pluck the whole story from Tycho's mind itself; but Ramius was unwilling to risk such an intrusion, not when his life depended on the goodwill of the Sons of Sanguinius.

The captain wasted no time with preamble and fixed him with a hard eye. 'What is this monstrosity that has come aboard my ship, inquisitor? Tell me what madness unfolded on Orilan that it could spawn something so aberrant?' His face – what Stele could see of it – was locked in a hard grimace.

Ramius measured his every gesture with the skill and care that had been drilled into him since his days as an interrogator-apprentice. One hint of a lie and he knew he would be vented to space. Tycho would be able to do it and claim Stele was consumed by Chaos; he doubted any of the captain's men would leap to the defence of a servant of the Ordo Hereticus. *They respect only brute strength*, he reminded himself. *I will have to display some measure of that in order to sway them.*

He gave a sigh of remorse, calculated to be long enough and deep enough to seem real. 'Captain Tycho, if only you had seen what I have seen…' He shook his head sadly. 'A nest of cultists infesting every level of the hive city. I regret… my own caution led me to them too late. By the time I arrived in their concealed lair, they had already summoned the creature.' In reality, Stele had fabricated evidence to cover his own tracks weeks before he had arrived on the planet, inventing a dozen false identities and faked verification that 'proved' the presence of a cult of Tzeentch in Orilan's capital hive. 'I killed them all, but it was a hollow victory. The damage had already been wrought.'

Tycho watched him, the stony cast of the Space Marine's flesh as immobile as the brassy mask on the other. 'You brought it here.' It was a statement, not an accusation. The Blood Angel seemed to sense the inquisitor was lying about something. It was the nature of the ordos, after all; falsehood was to Stele's kind as armour was to Tycho's Chapter. 'A number of my men, some of my serfs, an untold number of servitors... All lie dead and defiled by the hand of this...*thing*. Those that were not killed outright I have been forced to put down.' He advanced a step and Stele thought he could smell stale blood. 'Now it chews on the heart of this ship like a dog with a shank of meat.' With a sudden shock, the Inquisitor sensed Tycho's surface thoughts as the captain made his demand of him. 'I want this fiend ejected from my vessel, lord inquisitor. *You* will assist me in achieving this end.'

Stele clamped down on his reaction immediately. The last thing he wanted was to find himself in a room with the daemon once again; but to refuse outright would seem like cowardice and lose him the small measure of reverence his high office granted him. 'Captain, with respect, this creature is one of the most powerful daemons I have come across. It is a most deadly enemy, the very essence of change and mutation. It thrives on disorder and–'

'*Chaos?*' Tycho snapped, his tone cracking like brittle ice. 'I want it dead, Stele, and you will help with that desire.' He could sense it clearly now, the blood-need in Tycho's mind. The unchained fury desperate for the battle to come. 'Or should I assume that men of your ilk are as spineless in the face of the archenemy as I have been led to believe?'

Stele's eyes narrowed. *I must play the warrior's game, then.* 'I warn you, captain, keep a civil tongue in your head. I am as staunch in the Emperor's light as you!' The lie glided from him like smooth glass, and inwardly Ramius felt ice form in his stomach. The pull of his oath to the Golden Throne waned with every passing day, conflicting him with the sweet nectar of the warp's promise. A nerve jumped beneath his eye; despite his fears, he still wanted to face the daemon, to *know* it.

'Good,' said the Space Marine, glancing over his shoulder at his second-in-command. 'Simeon, return the Inquisitor's lasgun, and prepare a squad.'

'Your will,' said the other officer.

The ghost of a smile returned to Tycho's face. 'And be sure you lock the hatches behind us.'

THEY BEGAN A decent into a freakish hell, into a passageway of nightmares.

The things lurking inside the corridors of the drive decks dwarfed the stomach-turning mutants Stele had seen on Orilan. Shapes made of skin and bone coated the walls, stretched to impossible heights, pulled thin and taut. Horribly, many of the fleshy forms were still alive, some moaning, others weeping.

Ramius moved amid the towering armoured forms of the Blood Angels as they walked forward with lockstep, stoic caution. As well as returning the lasgun, Simeon had also has Stele's body armour cleaned and patched. It felt heavy and warm on his shoulders, and he fingered the edge of the ceramite plate where it sat beneath his silken vest, knowing that it would not save him from any sort of direct attack.

His gaze moved over the remains of the enginseers, fascinated by the strange inventiveness of the display. The daemon was getting better at what it did, like an artist learning the strengths of a new medium, able now to uncoil better horrors from the sculpted flesh of its victims. Stele wanted to know how that was done. He wanted to understand how a man might take living flesh and mould it so, or sift it through his fingers like dry sand.

Some of the remnants – Ramius found himself thinking of them as such – were still ambulatory, and they crowded toward the Space Marine squad. Tycho led the way through them, rending their warped forms with flares of killing fire from his combi-weapon, the melta gun flashing, catching the ones that got too close with ruby threads cast by lasers in his gauntlets. They screamed and died, boiling to death as they cried out for mercy. The Blood Angel captain's face was grim. Stele sensed his surface thoughts as Tycho forced away any recall of the men these things had once been.

The moist, blood-warm halls were red like raw flesh, and around them steel had turned into arcs of wet bone. Weak orange light spilled in radiant pools. Tycho's metallic armour made him seem like a bronze statue, one that had grown bored with standing atop its plinth and stepped down, away to seek foes to kill.

Deeper they went, and the freak show grew more nauseating. The mutants attacked in small groups, then in waves that came back and forth. Perhaps they craved pain or just the nothingness of release; Stele folded closed his mind to them, searching instead for the pulse-beat of the daemon itself. Searching and finding.

All about him the Blood Angels fought with ruthless, passionate fury, gunning down creatures who had been their Chapter serfs only hours earlier. The inquisitor kept his lasgun close, pressing it to his chest like a talisman of protection, now and then daring to venture a shot at something that caught his eye.

They passed through flaps of rubber that resembled the valves of a heart, and then they were inside the core. Obscene geometry and ranges of bony spars spread out above them, glistening with new change. The shapes of the drive chamber were subsumed under undulating sheets of skin, the remains of a dozen enginseers flayed and merged together; it was impossible to see where the frigate ended and the monster began.

Concentrating, he let his preternatural senses sweep the chamber. And there, there it was, resting inside a nest of bones. Stele found the heart of the creature with his second sight, inherently sensing the collection of clouded, alien thoughts inside a rough bole of flesh atop the primary reactor dolmen.

Tycho watched his reaction and read what he needed from it. 'There!' he shouted, pointing upward. 'Fire for effect!' The Blood Angels unleashed shot and shell against the daemon, and in return it extruded sinuous arms with teeth and barbs, slashing in scythes at the Space Marines.

Stele broke from the group and sought cover as Tycho's men died, cut into pieces or beheaded; others were quicker, ripping at the claws with power fists, blasting them with bolters. Black, oily blood jetted across the undulating deck and the Tzeentch-thing screamed.

Ramius aimed his gun but hesitated, his finger frozen on the trigger. He found himself enraptured by the unbearable shapes of the monster above. That such things could be done – and this was only a *servant* of the Malfallax, which in turn was only a princeling daemon. Stele did not see chaos or order; he saw only incredible power, enough to remake the galaxy if one could only master it. He lost himself in it, the fight ranging around him unnoticed.

A helmet with a Space Marine's head still within it bounced to a halt at his feet, and Tycho's bronzed form blurred toward him, shoving the Inquisitor aside as a spidery thing on nerve tendon tethers clawed and snarled. The Blood Angel killed it with a crash of bolter shells and Stele blinked, returning to the moment.

'What are you dithering for?' Tycho snarled, 'My men are dead, only we still stand! Work your witchery, psyker, or you are useless to me.'

Distracted for only an instant, the brother-captain missed the approach of a blunt hammer of fatty meat. The flesh-club struck him in the head, and Stele, rooted to the spot, saw Tycho spin away like a discarded rag. The Blood Angel warrior careened off a piece of steel plate and fell to the deck with a massive crash of stressed metal.

Stele ran to his side, panic rising in him. Tycho was the only thing that could protect him from what he had unleashed on Orilan; without the Blood Angel, he had nothing, no armour, no defender... 'Captain!' Ramius shook the Astartes, but Tycho did not respond. The warrior was insensate, but his chest still rose and fell in shallow breaths. Unconscious then, but still alive.

He saw Tycho's combi-weapon lying on the floor and took a half-step toward it. The idea of taking it up himself died in this mind; the gun was so massive he would never have been able to lift it.

Icy fear and tingling adrenaline flooded Stele's body. He looked up, searching for a means of escape, and instead found a nest of eyes blinking at him from the topmost tiers of the warp towers. It sent claw arms down toward him, slow and steady. The sinuous limbs wandered around him, tapping disinterestedly on Tycho's armour, scraping at the floor. Ramius saw that they were made of human flesh; he saw a bondsman's tattoo visible on one elongated stabbing arm.

'Human,' said the daemon, the voice echoing with the resonance of its distant master. 'What will you do now?' Across some great vastness, the Malfallax was working the shade-thing like a marionette, talking through it to him. 'If fear is all you have, then your life ends here. If not...'

Ramius had the sudden impression that he was being offered something. 'I am afraid,' Stele said aloud, 'but I am more hungry than fearful. Hungry for knowledge.'

Dark laughter boomed off the shivering walls. 'Such greed. Your species has an almost infinite capacity for it.' Part of the eye cluster detached from the large mass, transforming into a wispy shadow as it drifted down to approach him. 'The path branches before you, Stele. Defy me and perish, or take my blessing and walk the Way of Change.' When Ramius hesitated, the shade congealed before him, becoming vaguely human in shape. 'You want to *know*, don't you?' The question made his mouth fill with saliva. 'There is no better way than the one I offer. Take it, and your mind will be opened to sights you never dreamed of.'

Stele closed his eyes and felt himself nodding. Had there ever really been any doubt? Now that the offer was there before him, had he ever really considered refusing it? *No.*

Ramius felt the frigid, exhilarating rush as a tiny fraction of the essence of the Malfallax entered him, and made itself a nest inside his mind. A hard seed of blackness formed in the core of his psyche, and in a strange way, he felt free.

Marain. He banished her as his last regret, the last connection that held him to humanity. She had been the voice of his conscience for so long... but now he understood that such a thing only held him back from greatness.

And then there was the voice. 'Ramius!'

He spun on his heel, suddenly dizzy, dislocated from the world around him. A voice from the grave? Even as he banished her from his mind, he heard Marain's words.

He stared, incredulous, as she crossed the chamber toward him, her gun in her hand, tears streaming down her tan cheeks. For a moment he thought she was some apparition, perhaps a mind-ghost conjured by the daemon to taunt him; but in the next instant, the raw energy of the seed the Malfallax planted inside him shot power through his psyche and he read her like a book.

Ramius understood instantly; she had survived – *how like her to do that* – and come aboard Tycho's ship with those from the shuttle. But the joy that might have once touched him at the sight of her was gone, swallowed by his new master's touch. His affection for her was absorbed, dissipated. Gone. A surge of resentment rose and then fell under the weight of his new insight.

She aimed her weapon at him. Yes, he understood. She had followed the Space Marines down through the ship, stalking him. 'Heretic!' spat the soldier. 'It sickens me to think I laid with you! You have discarded everything you swore an oath for!'

Harsh and bitter laughter bubbled up from deep inside Stele's chest. There was no humour in it, only a dark and terrible knowing of his own soul. 'Marain, you do not understand. You are so limited in your sight, you cannot see–'

'I see enough!' she cried. 'You are a traitor!'

The sinuous, rustling whispers of the daemon knitted in a blasphemous chorus over their heads. The inquisitor was aware of the Malfallax watching them both, enjoying the bitter hate radiating off the woman as if it were some rare and delicate wine. The creature was doing nothing to intervene, content to let the moment play out as it might.

He spoke Marain's name again and took a step toward her. 'There are none that know me as you do. There is no living soul that has shown me the loyalty you gave. Do not end that now.' He extended a hand to her, and beneath the surface of the skin black clots of fluid swarmed and moved. 'Cast off your doubts. Join me. We can discard the petty dictates of the Emperor and forge our own path. Together.' Stele meant every word; he was standing on the brink of something incredible, and to have her follow along with him... to share it would be glorious.

There was a moment – he saw it there, as bright as daybreak in her mind – when Marain allowed herself to consider accepting his offer, just for the briefest of instants. She teetered on the edge of agreeing to it, just to be with him again, just to fulfil the edict that had been drilled into her since birth; but then the colour of the thought faded into nothing and white-hot hatred unfolded in its place. The crude maw of her gun danced in front of him, and he had no doubt that she aimed it at a place where it would kill him with the first shot. Marain swore a gutter oath that curled his lip in kind. He had his answer, then.

'Fallen whore of the Ruinous Powers,' she shouted, 'you dare to try to tear me from my God-Emperor! I will kill you!'

'Then do it,' echoed the daemon voice, finally venturing to speak. 'But she can't, can she? A man she has sworn her life to protect, a corpse god she has sworn to obey, and now she must destroy you to appease the other.' Every mouth of the Malfallax smiled. 'What delicious pain.'

'Marain–' Stele began, but her only reply was a face of rage and a storm of gunfire.

'End you!' she spat, throwing herself at him, stitching a line of incendiary bullets across his torso. Stele howled and tore his silken vest from him as it burst into flame. Shots that would have ripped him open before warped and deflected about him, the black power of the mutation inside him charging his psyche with monstrous force.

The inquisitor opened himself to the dark and embraced the rage. 'You faithless bitch!' he thundered at her. 'You are nothing to me!'

Tears of anger and pain streamed down Marain's face as she emptied her gun into him. She drew her fractal knife and made to plunge it in his heart.

'*No!*' Stele shouted the word; perhaps it was a cry against her, or perhaps against himself, but the result was the same. Conjured from the warp itself, a haze of pure purple-white fire blazed from Ramius's fingers and enveloped the woman's shrieking body.

It was over in a split second. Marain twisted, became a charcoal sketch against the glare, then ashes.

Then nothing.

The daemon began to laugh, the voice growing louder and louder until it beat at Stele's mind, mocking him for his towering folly.

'Silence!' he spat out a scream that rended air and matter, the hellbolt that killed Marain magnified a thousandfold; for one brief instant the inquisitor became a tornado of psychic force, and with it he ripped the shade-daemon from existence.

As the power abated, he dropped to his knees amid the decaying meat and wept.

IN THE AFTERMATH, Simeon came to the chambers they had assigned to him and gave a shallow bow. The Blood Angels treated him differently now; despite his commander's orders, Simeon had followed Tycho into the drive decks rather than seal them shut behind him. It was he who found Stele crouched by the brother-captain's body, while all around him was dead and disintegrating, the binding power of the shade-creature gone.

Tycho's wounds had been grave, and even now, days later, he still lay in a healing trance, but Simeon informed him that the Blood Angel would live to fight again, in no small part thanks to the Inquisitor's help.

He nodded, holding back a hollow smile. Ramius wondered; did the Malfallax foresee this turn of events? When the Blood Angels entered to find the daemonic presence banished and only he and Tycho still alive, it was Simeon who assumed that Stele had marshalled his abilities to save their vessel. Had the Malfallax goaded him into obliterating its avatar, in order to cement a respect for him among these Astartes? He had no way of knowing; but Ramius had always been a man with an eye for circumstance and the knowledge of how to turn it to his advantage.

With Tycho in the depths of unconsciousness while Stele made his pact with the warp, no other soul that drew breath knew what had happened in the engine room, and they never would. Only Marain had been witness, and she... she was cut from his life.

His heart hardened. It was all he could do not to mock them when the earnest and serious Blood Angels praised him for his heroic act in saving the frigate. He listened intently, nodding in all the right places, as they told him that he would accompany them to their fortress-monastery on Baal. There the honour of a 'blood debt' would be granted to him. Such gestures of respect and trust were rare. He said the right words and accepted graciously, while inside the privacy of his own thoughts he considered how he might use that misplaced confidence to greater advantage. Not now, perhaps, but one day.

From the bridge he watched storms of cyclonic torpedoes obliterate Orilan, erasing the last traces of his apostasy. In the fires he thought he saw Marain's face, her dying image dragging away with it the last human part of his soul.

Eventually he left the Blood Angels behind, and retreated to his sanctum, peeling back the layers of his mind to touch the immaterium beyond space as the ship ventured into the warp. A malleable, ever-changing voice was waiting for him with plans and ideas and subtle whispers.

Willingly, Ramius Stele followed it into the darkness, turning his face from the Emperor and opening a path toward the Ways of Change.

DEUS SANGUINIUS

CHAPTER ONE

IN THE MIDST of all the madness, the warrior found himself a small corner of darkness where he could shut himself off, a tiny sanctuary of silence. It was his shelter, after a fashion, a bolthole in which he could shutter away the churn of doubts and fears and concentrate instead on finding answers to the questions that plagued him. The room had once been a basement store for volatiles and dangerous chemicals, and it still carried the tang of free hydrocarbons in the thick air, the very stink of them embedded into the dull iron walls.

He peered out of the doorway to ensure that he was not being followed, and then shouldered shut the heavy hatch. It met the frame with a low booming, and he closed the latches. The biolume in the ceiling was cracked and dull, a thin trickle of greenish glow-fluid staining the cage around it. The chamber's only real light source was the grille near the top of the wall, which peered out at ground level to the streets beyond. Now and then, the faint snap-crack of a lasgun discharge passed through the vent, and the wave-like rush of a distant cheering crowd.

He removed the heavy hessian sack from the cord across his shoulder and dropped the bag to the floor. The delicacy he displayed seemed at odds with the huge, muscled figure he presented. Even out of the characteristic power armour of the Adeptus Astartes, the warrior manifested an impressive sight in his tunic and robes; he would tower over normal men even when barefoot, and the Space Marine filled the room with his presence. Gently and with reverence, he drew the sackcloth from the object he had so painstakingly recovered from the rubble of the street chapel. It had been buried there, forgotten by the people who had once paid fealty to it in favour of a new subject of devotion. That thought brought the beginnings of a glower to his hard, blunt features, and he forced it away.

The hessian bag fell away and in his cupped hands the Space Marine held an icon of the One True Master. It was a representation of the God-Emperor of Mankind, there in his infinite sagacity at rest atop the Golden Throne of Terra. He ran his fingers over the old, careworn idol; it had been made from brass off-cuts, from a factory that forged shells for the Leman Russ tanks of the Imperial Guard. He placed it on an upturned wooden box so that it rested in the shaft of light falling from the vent grille, the rays of the tepid orange sun casting it with a faint halo. He folded his arms over his chest, hands like flat blades, wrists crossed; the fingers and thumb taking on the shape of the double-headed Imperial aquila, one eye looking to the past, the other staring into the future, unblinking.

The Blood Angel bowed his head and sank to his knees before the Emperor, then spread his arms wide to show his wrists to the air. A mesh of faint scars caught the light on his forearms, the silent trophies of a hundred battles. Across one limb there was the red ink of a tattoo, showing a single drop of blood framed by two wings.

'In the name of Holy Terra,' he said, his voice low, 'in the name of Sanguinius, Lord of the Blood and the Red Angel, hear me, Master of Man. Grant me a fraction of your most perfect insight and guide me.' He closed his eyes. 'Hear these words, the contrition of your errant son Rafen, of Baal Secundus. I beseech you, Lord Emperor, hear me and my confession.'

THE INQUISITOR RAMIUS Stele rose to his feet, his meditation at an end, and gathered himself together. He rubbed a hand over his brow, touching the aquila electoo on his bald pate, and frowned. The closer he came toward the fruition of his plans, the more it seemed to fatigue him. He sniffed and his fingers wandered to his nostrils; they came away with a trickle of blood on them, and the inquisitor grimaced at the dark, purple-black fluid. Cautiously, he dabbed away the liquid with a kerchief and watched the stain spread across the cloth, moving like a cancer over the cotton threads.

Stele balled the kerchief and stuffed it into an inner pocket of his robes, dragging the heavy coat of his office about his shoulders. The symbol of the High Inquisition, the stylised capital 'I' in brass adorned with a white gold skull, hung from a chain about his neck, and Stele fingered it absently. There were times when it felt as if the medallion was a noose upon him, weighing him down, tying him to the petty world of men. He glanced at the emblem, rubbing away a faint bloodstain from its surface. Soon enough, he would be rid of it, rid off all the trappings that bound him to the corpse-god.

Stele took a moment to look about him, at the walls where dull brown handprints and splashes of old gore still marred the walls. In the battle for Shenlong, this place had been the site of one of the Word Bearers Chaos Space Marines' most brutal atrocities, where civilians had been gutted alive as a penitent sacrifice to the Ruinous Powers. While many of the chambers in the Ikari fortress had been cleaned and reconsecrated, Stele had quietly ensured that the death room had remained as it was. Here, where the screaming souls of the brutalised dead had etched their pain into the stone and mortar, the inquisitor found the membrane between the world and the warp to be thinner. Resting here, letting his psyche drift free of its organic shell, Stele could taste the faint, seductive texture of the empyrean just tantalisingly beyond his reach. It was for him a far more divine experience than kneeling in false piety to the Emperor of Man.

Stele left the dank room behind and exited, to find his honour guards waiting outside. Towering above him in their crimson sheaths of ceramite armour, bolters at arms, they seemed less like men and more like animated statues cut from red rock. Only the brilliant polished gold of their helmets set them aside from the rank and file of the Blood Angels Space Marines. Stele paid them no heed. He had no idea of who these men were, their names, hopes and dreams, anything; in truth, he cared less for them than he did his automaton servo-skulls, which rose from the floor on gravity impellers as he strode away. The silver orbs hummed after him, watchful as hawks, with the Space Marines two steps behind.

At the junction of the corridor, Stele's lexmechanic stood waiting, lurch-a-backed. Its head bobbed by way of a greeting. 'Your meditation is concluded?' The servitor became nervous in the confines of the room and it had elected to remain outside for the duration. 'Matters present themselves for your attention.'

'Indeed,' he replied. The last traces of the dark miasma clouding Stele's mind faded away, the seductive vestiges of the warp's caress retreating. He missed it.

'Your servant Ulan has descended from the *Bellus* with news,' the lexmechanic continued. 'A concern which she was unwilling to confide to me.'

Was there wounded pride in the servitor's voice? Stele doubted it; his helot's mentality had been so thoroughly expunged in its service that there was little vestige in it that could be considered to be a personality. 'She waits in the chapel for your indulgence, inquisitor,' it added.

'Good, I will attend to her before I–'

An anxious, wordless shout broke through the air and Stele whirled in surprise. His hand drifted toward the butt of the elegant lasgun in his belt, but his action was slow and leisurely compared the whip-fast movements of the honour guards. The Blood Angels had their bolters to bear in an instant, training their weapons on a trio of figures framed in a side corridor.

At the head of the group was a man, florid-faced with watery eyes. His clothes, and those of the two women with him, were worn and slightly unkempt but in a rich, opulent style. Stele decided that they were most likely from Shenlong's mercantile class, dispossessed land-owners still clinging to the courtly ways of life from before the Word Bearers invasion. 'My-my lord inquisitor!' said the man, lips trembling. 'Forgive me, but–'

He took half a step closer to Stele and suddenly one of the Space Marines was there, blocking his path like a crimson wall. 'Stay back,' grated the Blood Angel.

The lexmechanic turned on the other Space Marine. 'How did these civilians get in here? These levels of the Ikari fortress are prohibited to all but the servants of Arkio the Blessed and the God-Emperor.'

A pair of gasps fled from the lips of the two women at the mention of Arkio's name. The man made the sign of the aquila and bowed his head. 'Please, forgive me, lords, but it was in devotion to his name that we dared to venture past the wards below...'

Stele raised a quizzical eyebrow and stepped forward, gently pushing the Space Marine's bolter away. 'Really? And what devotion do you have to share?'

The man licked his lips. 'I… We… Hoped to lay eyes upon the Blessed himself. To ask for his benediction.' He wiped a tear from his eye. 'All that we have was taken in the invasion. We have nothing now.'

Inwardly, Stele sneered. This pompous oaf was weeping over the loss of his money and chattels while others on Shenlong could barely feed themselves. The man's words did nothing but reinforce the inquisitor's hatred for the corruption of the Imperium, the maggot-ridden carcass of a society that served only to glorify the empowered and the rich. Stele betrayed none of these thoughts outwardly. 'Those of us who show our devotion to the Blessed will be rewarded,' said the inquisitor. 'Will you do so?'

A flurry of nods came from the merchant. 'Oh yes, yes! For the one who liberated us, I would gladly give all that I can, and ask only for his beneficence in return.'

'You would give all that you can,' Stele repeated, allowing the hint of a smile to cross his lips as he studied the women. The resemblance between them was clear. The younger of the two, perhaps no more than sixteen summers, watched him with wide eyes. She was attractive, in a virginal, parochial sort of way. The other, closer to his age, had the docile look of enforced pliancy about her. Stele considered them both; perhaps he could grant himself a distraction. 'This is your wife and daughter?' he asked, the question trailing away into the air.

'Uh…' The man fumbled at a response and found none.

Stele nodded. 'Take them to my chambers,' he told the honour guard, and the Space Marine obeyed, ushering the women away under the eye of a bolter. 'I'll call upon them at my leisure,' The inquisitor threw the man a nod. 'Your devotion is great. The Blessed has a worthy servant in you.'

As he continued on his way to the chapel, Stele heard the man mumble out ragged, broken words of thanks.

RAFEN HAD NOT dared to enter any of the tabernacles inside the Ikari fortress, all too aware of what he would see inside. Troops of Shenlongi had taken hammers and chisels to the intricate mosaics and the friezes that the Chaos invasion force hadn't already destroyed, and pulled them up. The enemy was gone now, routed and killed, but the people they had briefly subjugated completed the deconsecrations the Word Bearers had begun. Only the object of their veneration differed. In place of sanctioned Imperial idolatry they had daubed crude renditions of the Blood Angels sigil and the newly-created icon of their Blessed Arkio, the golden halo crossed by a shining spear. The sight of it burned in Rafen's heart like a torch, but he could not dare to speak openly of the doubts that thundered about him, much less even consider giving a confession in such a place. There was no doubt in his mind that any words he spoke would be spirited away to the ears of High Priest Sachiel, and to have him listening to Rafen's heartfelt thoughts would be a grave mistake.

Neither could Rafen visit one of the churches that the commoners and citizens used, down in the city-sprawls crammed into the gaps between Shenlong's kilometres-high factory cathedrals. The sight of a Space Marine, even one without his hallowed armour, would never pass unnoticed among the populace – and just as the people had taken Arkio to their hearts in the fortress, so the man they called the New Blood Lord had also supplanted the Emperor in chapels all across the forge-world.

So here, in a dim and ill-lit chamber, in a street ruined by shell fire and abandoned by life, Rafen had created his own place of worship, some small and safe conduit to his messiah where no prying ears would spy upon his prayers.

'I must confess,' he told the brass idol of the God-Emperor, 'I was forced to forsake my oath to the liege lord of my Chapter, to turn from Sanguinius to my sibling... the man they call Arkio the Blessed.' Rafen bit back the tremors in his voice. 'I know not what my brother has become, but only that my heart cannot accept what Sachiel and Stele claim to be self-evident. I cannot accede that Arkio is Sanguinius Reborn, and yet knowing this I took an oath of fealty to him.' He shook his head in answer to an unspoken question. 'This is not cowardice on my part, I swear. The Sanguinary High Priest Sachiel would surely have executed me had I not knelt before Arkio, but with my death there would be no voice to speak out against this insanity. Forgive me, lord, for this duplicity.'

Rafen drew a shuddering breath. 'Grant me insight,' he said, entreaty in his voice, 'show me a path. I ask of you, what do you wish of me? On Cybele, against the assaults of the foul Word Bearers I was ready to give my life and come to your right hand at the Throne, but in your wisdom the warship *Bellus* came to our aid and with it my young brother. I thought I was blessed to see my sibling after so long apart... Our ties of blood are as strong as the fellowship of my battle-brothers.'

The Blood Angel recalled the instant on the war grave world when Arkio rose in their moment of blackest despair, with a plan to turn the fight against the Traitor Marines; Arkio's uncanny flash of brilliance led them to bring down a Word Bearers warship and beat back the Corrupted from Cybele. At first, it seemed no more than a chance insight from Rafen's sibling, but then the young Space Marine had single-handedly saved Sachiel's life from a daemon creature, rallied the men and become the figurehead which turned the tide against the Chaos forces. By the time they had left Cybele aboard the *Bellus*, there were men wondering aloud if Arkio was not touched by Sanguinius himself, and then came the moment when the Spear of Telesto seemed to prove the truth behind the whispered rumours.

STELE LEFT HIS guard at the tall copper doors to the chapel and strode inside, the lexmechanic's clawed iron feet clattering after him. The astropath Ulan stood in the centre of the chamber, arms folded. Her sightless eyes glanced up from the hood of her dark robes and she gave a half-bow. 'My lord inquisitor,' she began, her quiet tones a whisper of wind through gravestones.

He approached her, for one brief moment letting his gaze stray to the titanium canister that lay atop the altar. The thought of the coiled power inside the long container made him thirst in a way that nothing else could slake. With a near physical effort, Stele turned his whole attention to the thin psyker girl. 'Speak to me.'

Ulan glanced at the lexmechanic, and Stele nodded, turning. 'Servitor, wait outside.'

The machine-slave turned on its heel and left them to their privacy. As the chapel door thudded shut, Ulan began to talk. 'Matters aboard the *Bellus* proceed, Lord Stele,' she said carefully. 'Questions as to the fate of the astropath Horin and his chorus have been suppressed. There is no other conduit to the galaxy at large now, save me.'

Stele made a dismissive gesture. 'You came to tell me that which I already know?' Without his notice, the inquisitor's trigger finger twitched, unconsciously repeating the action it had performed when Stele executed the *Bellus*'s cadre of telepaths. 'I installed you aboard the battle barge to be my eyes and ears.'

'And so I am,' she replied. 'I have news. The warning that was sent from Shenlong to Baal, the message to the Blood Angels Commander Dante... It has been heeded.'

'Dante has replied?'

She shook her head. 'The master of the monastery on Baal favours a more direct approach, Lord. A ship is on its way. I have intercepted the shadows of signals from the depths of the immaterium. It will arrive soon.'

Stele accepted this with a nod. 'Do you know what kind of vessel? Something more powerful than the *Bellus*?'

'Unlikely,' she noted. 'There is but one Blood Angels ship matching the tonnage of the *Bellus* within operational range of Shenlong, and that is the *Europae*, the Lord Mephiston's personal command.'

'Dante would not send his lieutenant Mephiston without good cause,' Stele spoke his thoughts aloud. 'Not yet, at any rate. No, it will be a smaller craft.'

'The advent of any Adeptus Astartes reinforcements will jeopardise the strategy,' Ulan said flatly. 'They will be outside our sphere of influence, an incalculable variable. The matter must be addressed.'

'Yes, and so it will be,' said the inquisitor, considering the situation. 'Return to orbit and maintain your post. You are to contact me the instant Dante's envoy reaches contact range.' Stele toyed with the silver purity seal stud in his ear. 'I must prepare.'

'New arrivals will not be turned so easily to loyalty to the Blessed,' the psyker warned. 'Termination presents the better option.'

'You are too narrow-minded, Ulan. Commander Dante is about to deliver me a valuable object lesson.' Stele dismissed her with a wave of his hand. 'Go now.'

When he was alone, the inquisitor let his control slip away and he crossed to the altar and the metal box upon it. The grey cylinder bore sigils and purity seals showing the oaths of the Ordo Hereticus and the Blood Angels, some engraved in the titanium itself, others on strips of sanctified parchment, fixed by fat discs of sealing wax embossed with devotional symbology. He laid his hands on the surface of the container and felt the warmth radiating out from the object inside. The Spear of Telesto, one of a handful of battle weapons and hallowed objects forged – so the myths would have it – by the very hand of the God-Emperor himself. The inquisitor felt himself drawn magnetically to the umbra of the device, even now as it lay in quietus.

Stele smothered a surge of jealousy; the reaction was the same each time he considered the Space Marine Arkio and his affinity with the artefact. On the mission of the *Bellus* into ork space to recover the archeotech weapon, it had been Stele who wrested it from the grip of a greenskin warlord, Stele who held it high in victory, but only in Arkio's hands had the Holy Lance awakened. On some basic, animalistic level, he could not excise the constant core of resentment he felt for the young Astartes.

He shook the thoughts away. The higher part of Stele's mind, the ice-cold engine that calculated the intricate clockwork of his schemes, knew better. Arkio was the ideal candidate to wield the spear, the perfect subject for veneration by his battle-brothers – and in the end, Stele's guidance of his path would lead the inquisitor to such power that would make the spear seem like a child's toy in comparison.

'MY BROTHER LAID his hands on the Spear of Telesto,' Rafen's words echoed off the iron walls of his makeshift meditation cell. 'The Holy Lance that Sanguinius himself once commanded, and then...' His voice trailed off, the memory as fresh now weeks later as it had been the moment it happened. For a brief instant, Rafen felt the divine radiance of the spear on his face again, the golden light shining off the teardrop blade as Arkio held the haft high in the Great Chapel of the *Bellus*. Try as he might, Rafen could not explain what he had seen that day. The sudden vision of his sibling's face melting and merging into a brief incarnation of the long-perished primarch of the Blood Angels, the winged Lord Sanguinius.

'It was his example that lit the way to this blighted world.' The Blood Angel's head bobbed as he considered the desolation of Shenlong. 'Fired by the oratory of Inquisitor Stele, my brethren clamoured for a chance to visit retribution on the Word Bearers who had desecrated Cybele. It was only Brother-Sergeant Koris and his fellow veterans who spoke of caution, and they were censured for it.' The words were suddenly flowing from Rafen's lips in a torrent; it was as if speaking them aloud lifted a great weight from his shoulders. The icon of the God-Emperor watched him with calm and unmoving eyes, silently listening to the Space Marine as he unfolded the tale.

He opened his mouth to speak again and a knife of emotion cut into him. Rafen saw Koris's face there before him, the craggy old warhound, eyes hard but never without honour. It had been one of the greatest privileges of Rafen's service to count the veteran as a mentor and a friend, but all the strength the Space Marine could muster did not stop his former teacher from falling into the dark grip of the Blood Angels gene-curse, the warped berzerker battle lust known as the black rage. Inducted into the Death Company, as all men who succumbed to the red thirst were, Rafen had watched Koris as the old warrior relived the great battle of Sanguinius against the arch-traitor Horus, played out in the depths of the Ikari fortress. 'He died there,' Rafen told his god, 'and you took him to the peace he deserved... But he did not release his grip on life easily. His words... He left me with a warning.'

The moment replayed in the Space Marine's mind.

'Rafen. Lad, I see you.'

'I am here, old friend.'

'The Pure One calls me, but first I must... Warn...'

'Warn me? Of what?'

'Stele! Do not trust the ordos whoreson! He brought me to this, all of it! Arkio... Be wary of your sibling, lad. He has been cursed with the power to destroy the Blood Angels! I see it! I see–'

'Gone now,' Rafen admitted, 'and without him I felt cut adrift and alone, while my brothers took up Arkio's cause as their own. I saw no other path to take... I broke the disciplines we swore to and damned protocol...' He shook his head, calculating the enormity of his transgressions. 'Under cover of lies I sent word to the monastery on Baal and the Lord Commander Dante, in hopes that he might come to end this madness... But in your wisdom, you have yet to guide him here.'

Rafen opened his eyes and looked into the unmoving face of the God-Emperor. 'I beg of you, lord, I must know. Am I the heretic, the dissenter, the apostate deserving only of death? If Arkio truly is the Great Sanguinius reborn, then why do I doubt it so? Which of us is the one fallen from the path, he or I?'

'LORD INQUISITOR?'

Stele turned to see Sachiel approach, a questioning look on his face. The Sanguinary High Priest's battle armour caught the light through the chapel windows, glinting off the white detailing that marked his wargear. Stele stepped down from the altar and fixed him with a sullen eye. 'Sachiel. Where is Arkio?'

'The Blessed observes the trials in the plaza below, Lord Stele. He bade me to find you.' Sachiel paused, frowning. 'He has questions...'

Stele crossed to a set of stained-glass doors and waved his hand over a discreet wall sensor. On ancient mechanics, the glass gates parted to reveal a broad stone balcony jutting from the equator of the fortress. The instant the doors opened, a wall of sound thundered into the chapel; all at once, there were chants and cheers of victory, the screaming of the dying, the discharges of multiple weapons. The inquisitor walked out into the noise, to the lip of the balcony, and Sachiel followed.

Below them, the vast open plaza fronting the Ikari fortress was a ring of shanty-built grandstands and huts ringing a makeshift arena. The floor of the stadium was littered with the dead and a few pieces of broken cover. Gunfire flashed and snapped back and forth as figures swarmed over one another, some armed only with blunt clubs and crude knives, others clinging to lasrifles or ballistic stubber guns. In the stands, the faithful roared in approval as kills were made and the numbers of the fighters gradually diminished.

Stele glanced at Sachiel. The Blood Angel observed the unfolding battle with an arch look, clearly unimpressed by the crudity of the fighting. 'How many so far?' he demanded of the priest.

'Three hundred and nine chosen at last count,' he replied. 'The Blessed himself is making the selections.'

Stele saw the sunlight glinting as it touched a huge figure in golden armour, drifting over the battle on angelic wings. As he watched, the messianic shape singled out a wiry man wielding two swords and nodded to him. He dropped his weapons and wept with joy, the crowd chanting its accord once again. 'One more,' said Stele. 'We'll have the thousand soon enough.'

'As the Blessed chooses,' said the priest. 'He will have his army.'

The inquisitor looked away. 'You don't approve?'

Sachiel's face flushed red. 'How can you ask such a thing? It is as Arkio commands, and he is the Reborn. I would not question his wisdom.'

Stele smiled. 'The Warriors of the Reborn,' he said, gesturing to the men penned into a holding area at the edge of the arena. 'A thousand of the most zealous and devoted to the name of Arkio... And yet, there are Blood Angels who hesitate at his decision to raise this helot army.'

Sachiel blinked. 'We do not doubt,' he snapped, 'It is only... new to us. Understand, inquisitor, we have lived our lives to the tenets of the *Book of the Lords* and the *Codex Astartes*, and the recruiting of these commoners goes against those convictions.'

'We are past the time for ancient dogma,' Stele replied, 'Arkio the Blessed ushers in a new age for the Blood Angels, and the Warriors of the Reborn are merely an aspect of that.' He pointed into the crowd of tired, bloody fighters. 'Look at them, Sachiel. They have fought all day and still they would cut out their own hearts if Arkio demanded it of them. When he embarks on his glorious homecoming to Baal, the chosen thousand will accompany him. They will be the vanguard of a new breed of initiates to the Blood Angels, a new generation of the Adeptus Astartes.'

When the priest did not answer him, Stele turned to press him for a reply; but instead he saw the look of surprise on Sachiel's face.

'The Blessed...' began the priest.

From nowhere a sudden rumble of wind beat at Stele and he staggered back a step, forcing down the urge to shield himself with his hands. A shape, swift and brilliant, rushed up before the edge of the balcony and hung before him, blotting out the glow of the Shenlong sun. Sachiel fell into a deep bow and tapped his fist to the symbol of a winged blood droplet on his chest plate. The inquisitor looked up into a face of striking nobility, a countenance that combined a most patrician aspect with the promise of a darker heart beneath. A face that mirrored that of Sanguinius himself.

'Stele,' said Arkio, hovering there on wings spread like wide white sails. 'I would speak with you.'

'I saw him turn death upon innocents,' Rafen's voice was heavy with anguish. 'By my blood, I watched my own brother cull men and women all too willing to accept murder, as if it were some horrific benediction. This is not the promise to which I granted my life as an aspirant. This is not the Emperor's will, I hope and pray that it is not. Arkio rules this world now by force of temper, with Sachiel as his instrument and the Inquisitor Stele as advisor forever at his side. It is not *right*. By the Red Grail, the marrow in my bones sings it is not so!' Anger boiled up inside Rafen and he came to his feet, fists balling, his words bouncing off the chamber walls. 'I pray that Lord Dante will have the grace and wisdom to end this matter before our Chapter is split asunder beneath its weight, but until that moment comes I must answer the call of my blood.' He took a breath, his burst of fury subsiding. 'Until a sign comes to me, bright and undeniable, my heart will set the compass of my deeds from this moment forth.'

Rafen laid a hand on the icon of the Emperor and bowed his head once again. 'Hear me, hear the pledge of Rafen, son of Axan, child of the Broken Mesa clan, Blood Angel and Adeptus Astartes. I recant the false oath I have taken to Arkio the Blessed and in its stead I restore my allegiance to Sanguinius and the God-Emperor of Mankind. This I swear, my blood, my body, my soul as the price.' The declaration seemed to take all the energy from him, and Rafen staggered back a step. 'This I swear,' he repeated.

After a long moment, he gathered himself together and opened the hatch, pausing to throw the holy icon a last glance. Here, in this forgotten place, the symbol would lie safe from the hands of those who sought to revise their beliefs in the face of Arkio's new Blood Crusade. 'There is one thing of which I have absolutely no doubt,' he told the statue. 'A single act for which I know I and I alone will be responsible. By what means and when are unclear to me, but my brother Arkio will perish and I shall be the one to end him. I know it in my blood, and it damns me.'

Rafen left the room behind, the leaden burden of his dilemma pressing down upon him as he stepped back into the Shenlong sunlight. He picked his way through the ruined streets and did not look back.

Before him, the vast cone of the Ikari fortress rose to fill the horizon like a monstrous volcanic mountain.

CHAPTER TWO

ARKIO DROPPED TO his feet on the balcony with a whisper of air through the wings at his back, and cocked his head. Sachiel fell to one knee and averted his gaze, while Stele gave a shallow bow. The gestures seemed to satisfy the Blood Angel. 'Lord inquisitor, I have questions.' His voice was cool, assured and direct, with none of the hesitation that had plagued him in the past as a youth.

Stele resisted the urge to smile. 'Blessed, I will answer them if I can.'

'Your counsel has meant much to me in these past few weeks,' Arkio began, 'and your guidance has helped me to understand the path Sanguinius has laid before me.'

'I am merely the lamp to light the way, Great One,' Stele allowed. 'I took on the governorship of this blighted world only because I saw it wanting. No honest servant of the Imperium would have done any less. That I could help you into the bargain…'

Arkio accepted this with a cursory nod. 'And we have done well here, have we not? The taint of Chaos has been burnt from the streets of Shenlong.'

Sachiel cleared his throat self-consciously. 'All the Word Bearers that intruded on this planet lie dead, lord, that is true... But our search still continues to find and purge any sympathisers.'

Stele watched Arkio assimilate the priest's words; only a short time ago, it had been Arkio who had suggested they annihilate this world completely rather than chance the survival of any cohorts of the Chaos Gods. But that was before his transformation, before Arkio's brutal duel with the Dark Apostle Iskavan the Hated in the manufactorium below the city. With his physical changes, Arkio had also altered within. He had become, to all intents and purposes, the living reincarnation of the Blood Angels primogenitor, and the former Space Marine revelled in his newly found divinity. He wore the sacred golden artificer armour of his Chapter with the arrogance and hauteur of one whom had been born to it. Yes, Stele told himself, I chose him well.

'The men speak in whispers and keep their fears from me,' Arkio turned his back on them and wandered to the edge of the balcony, watching the continual pit-fight. 'But yet I hear them.'

Sachiel's face twisted. 'What dissent is this? Lord Arkio, if there are weaklings and craven among our forces, I would know it. The honour guard will see them repudiated for such failings!'

Stele arched an eyebrow. With little prompting, Sachiel had stepped into the role the inquisitor had laid for him with gusto. So focussed was the priest on adhering to the word of his new master that he hardly noticed he was sanctioning the censure of his own battle-brothers.

Arkio shook his head slowly. 'No, Brother Sachiel, no. These men are not to be chastised for their fears. What leader would I be if turned away every Space Marine who dared to wonder? A fool myself.' The warrior's wings had folded back on themselves now, and they lay flat against Arkio's sun-bright armour.

'If it pleases the Blessed,' said Stele, 'what have you heard?'

'My brothers are conflicted, inquisitor,' said Arkio. 'They look upon me and see the truth of my change, of the Great Angel's hand on my soul, and they believe. But word spreads now among the ranks of the Blood Angels here on the planet and above on the *Bellus.*' He gestured toward the sky. 'I have heard men speaking of Dante and Mephiston, and questions of our Chapter brethren on Baal.'

'They fear you will not be accepted by the Lord Commander,' Stele said gently, providing the words to the rumour that he himself had quietly seeded. It had been a simple matter to fan the flames of righteousness in the Space Marines who had laid their fealty at Arkio's feet; it was the nature of the devout to seek enemies in all those who did not share their beliefs.

Sachiel made a negative noise. 'Lord, this matter trivialises your Ascension. I grant that yes, perhaps our battle-brothers at the Baal monastery may have their doubts about you, but when they lay eyes on you, they will know as I do – that you are the Deus Encarmine, the Reborn Angel.'

Arkio hung his head for a moment. 'Can you be sure, my friend? I still look to my own face and wonder at the changes wrought on me by fate. Mortal men could do no less.'

Stele took a calculated pause before answering. 'Blessed, as you speak of this now I must admit that I too have heard these misgivings among my comrade brethren. I chose to keep it from you as I believed it to be beneath your concern.' He shook his head, adopting a look of contrition. 'I am sorry.'

'Then tell me now, Stele. What is said?'

'As you say, Great Arkio. The men see themselves set apart from their brothers elsewhere, blessed by your arrival in their midst – but they fear Dante's reaction to your Emergence.'

The Blood Angel fixed him with a questioning look. 'But why, Stele? Why should they be afraid of that? Dante is a good and honourable commander. He has led our Chapter through adversity and strife for more than one thousand years, his character is impeccable.' Arkio gave a quick, bright smile. 'I welcome the moment when I will be able to face him with this miracle.'

And there it was, the opening Stele had been waiting for. With care, he marshalled his lies and pressed them home. 'But will Dante welcome you, Blessed? When you enter the grand annexe of the fortress-monastery, will Dante kneel and give you his fealty as we have? Will his Librarian Mephiston bow to you? What of Brothers Lemartes, Corbulo or Argastes? Will they see the truth of it?'

'Why would they do otherwise?' Arkio said darkly. 'Why would they doubt me?'

'Dante did not witness your miracle,' broke in Sachiel, 'He would ask for proof...'

'Proof?' Arkio snapped, and his wings unfurled in a flash of white, his eyes shining with sudden intensity. 'Proof denies faith, and faith is all that we are!'

'You yourself said that Lord Dante has commanded the Blood Angels for over a millennium,' Stele took a step closer to Arkio, 'and some might argue, too long. Such a man would not step aside easily, Blessed, even in the face of such divinity as yours. And Mephiston...' He shook his head. 'The psyker they call the Lord of Death has always held himself to be the heir apparent to the mastery of the Chapter. These men... I would not vouch for their magnanimity in this matter.'

Arkio shook his head again. 'No. I will not hear this. What has happened to me is a blessing from the Emperor for every Blood Angel, for our entire Chapter, not just the Space Marines here on Shenlong and the crew of *Bellus*. I have been chosen, Stele. Chosen by fate to be the vessel for a power far greater than myself! Sanguinius makes himself known through me, returns to us after so long departed. I will not conceive that this marvel...' He paused, his fangs bearing in a snarl as he fought down his anger. 'That *I* will be the cause of a schism among my brothers. No! It shall not be so.' In one single bound, Arkio stepped up on to the lip of the stone balcony and swept off it, a crash of air filling his wings. The golden figure dropped back into the arena, into the thunderous adulation of his warriors and his subjects.

Stele watched him go, aware of Sachiel as the priest came closer. 'Would that his wishes become reality,' said the inquisitor gravely, 'but it may not go as the Blessed would hope.'

Sachiel had a faraway look in his eyes, as if the Apothecary's mind was focussed on some distant vanishing point, on events yet to come. 'You... could be right, lord inquisitor. If Dante denies the Ascension of Arkio, it will split the Blood Angels asunder.' The sombre thoughts were hard for the priest to articulate. 'There could be a... a civil war. A severing greater than anything our Chapter has ever known before.'

'Indeed,' Stele intoned, 'and such a break would not be as congruous as those that created the Successor Chapters, the Blood Drinkers and the Flesh Tearers, the Angels Vermilion, Encarmine and Sanguine...'

'We will find adherents in those bands,' Sachiel said quickly, 'once word spreads of the Blessed. If what you suspect comes to pass, Dante will be unable to deny the Rebirth when all our battle-brothers give credence to it.'

The inquisitor gave a sigh. 'Perhaps, Sachiel, perhaps. I hope that these dark possibilities we consider now remain just that – but if not, we must be prepared.'

The priest watched Arkio as he swooped and dove over the great arena. 'To do what, lord? To go to war with our kinsmen? I hardly dare to speak such a thing.'

'If the Blood Angels on Baal are unwilling to accept Arkio for what he is, as the avatar of the Sanguine Messiah, they may need to be *encouraged* to believe.' Stele met Sachiel's gaze and held it with his cold, glittering eyes. 'If they do not, then those who resist the divine design must be purged.'

The High Priest replied with a slow, serious nod, and Stele drew away a smile.

RAFEN KEPT OFF the more heavily trafficked streets as much as he could, but eventually he was forced to walk out in the open, amid the endless confusion of markets, portable shrines and thronging Shenlongi citizens. He was on the far side of the Ikari fortress to the combat arena, but still the sounds of the chanting crowds were filling the air, humming up and down the octaves like distant surf breaking on a shore. The Space Marine spied several knots of excited natives clustered around jury-rigged speakers in shop doorways and windows, the sound boxes hastily tapped into the webs of lines from the factory-city's vox-net. Tinny commentaries issued out of the speakers, encouraging hoots of excitement from some and groans from others. The fruits of wagers, dog-eared handfuls of Imperial scrip, changed hands as candidates for the Warriors of the Reborn died off or were chosen for the thousand.

Rafen did his best to keep to the edges of the highway, head bowed and hood up; but there was little he could do to avoid towering over the civilians, the tallest of whom could barely reach the Space Marine's shoulder. With awed whispers they parted in front of him like water flowing around a rock. Some of them, the more daring, would reach out and run a finger over the hem of his garment. He considered giving them a flash of his teeth and a snarl to keep them at bay; but what good would it do to instil an even greater fear of his kind in these people?

Something crunched beneath the sole of his sandal and Rafen paused. With the tip of his foot he nudged a broken tin object out of the dirt. It had been cut from an old recaf can and bent into shape as... what? The Space Marine became aware of a skinny child watching him with an open, gap-toothed mouth. The street urchin was smeared with rusty dirt and bore a scarred cheek. In front of the child was a box filled with more tin shapes. Rafen looked closer. Some of the crafted things were crude copies of the Blood Angels crest, others a model of the Spear of Telesto, even a miniature figure of a winged Space Marine. He indicated the object at his feet. 'You made this?'

The child nodded once, with no change in expression. Rafen picked up the ruined effigy and deposited it back in the box. Closer, he could see that the juvenile was a girl. On the blemished side of her face she was missing a patch of hair. He nodded to himself; the child had been caught in the nimbus of a plasma shot. 'You are lucky to be alive,' he told her.

She nodded again, and closed her mouth. On her dirty tunic, Rafen saw a rendition of the spear-and-halo badge that Arkio's supporters were popularising and frowned. He surveyed the contents of her box, then looked up and met her gaze. 'There are no icons of the Emperor here,' he said quietly. 'You will make no more of these others from now on, understand? Only symbols of the God-Emperor.'

'Yes, lord.' At last she spoke, and it was with a piping, tremulous voice.

Rafen turned and walked away, resuming his path toward the fortress. Behind him, the people on the street scrambled to press money into the girl's hands, suddenly desperate to buy an icon that a Blood Angel had touched.

CHAPLAIN DELOS WAS waiting for him at the foot of the fortress tower. 'Rafen,' the black-armoured priest beckoned him closer. 'I did not see you at prayers–'

'Forgive me, but I took my devotion alone today, Chaplain,' he replied. 'I required... solitude.'

'Just so,' said Delos. 'The arming ritual demands your most serious mind. It is good that you have prepared.' The priest walked him into the massive inner atrium of the fortress, past the metre-high piles of devotional objects and invocation plaques left by the citizens. 'I know these times have been difficult for you.'

Rafen said nothing and walked on.

The Chaplain took his silence for assent. 'The deaths of your Captain Simeon on Cybele, the fall of Koris to the red thirst...' He shook his head. 'And your sibling... None of us have been through the maelstrom of things as you have. But it pleases me that you have come to understand the glory of Arkio's blessing.'

'Yes,' Rafen kept his voice neutral. Delos did not seem to notice.

'That you took his oath, that gladdens me, Brother Rafen. I was afraid you might also succumb to the red thirst as Koris did.'

'Were there any men who refused?' Rafen said suddenly. 'Did any battle-brother refuse to bend his knee to Arkio?'

Delos looked at Rafen with a confused smirk. 'Of course not. Not a single Blood Angel could deny his Ascension.'

'No,' said Rafen, 'of course not.'

The Chaplain stepped forward and opened the doors to the consecration chamber and beckoned him inside. It was gloomy in the room, the light of hovering biolumes casting a viridian haze over everything. A spider of metallic arms moved in the shadows and a Techmarine emerged.

'Brother Lucion,' said Rafen.

Lucion gave him a nod of acknowledgement and gestured to a low iron bench. Across the surface were the parts of a suit of Adeptus Astartes power armour, and around the table a trio of hunched servitors twitched, awaiting the Techmarine's command.

'We shall commence,' intoned Delos.

Without ceremony, Rafen disrobed, discarding his common cloth and sandals, revealing the glistening ebony sheath of his black carapace. A living compound of plastics and alloys, the dark material had been implanted under the skin of his upper torso in his seventeenth year, as the final part of his initiation and transformation from Baalite tribesman into Blood Angels Space Marine. The neural sensors and transfusion shunts that bloomed from the surface of the carapace opened like the yawning mouths of tiny birds, ready to accept the interface jacks of his new armour.

As Delos began the Litany of Armament, he set a grail-shaped censer swinging from his hands. Lucion gave a burst-command in chattering machine code, and as one the servitors went to work, fitting the components of the Mark VII codex power armour to Rafen's body. The Space Marine joined in the chant where his answers were needed to complete the rite. Thermonic garments slid across him; flexible myomer muscle encircled the meat of his limbs, arranging itself to enhance and augment his physical strength; over this came the outer layer of bonded ceramite and plasteel weave, tough enough to turn a glancing bolt shell at twenty paces. Rafen slid his bare feet into the hollows of his greaves, the gyroscopic stabilisers in the broad boots humming into life.

As the armour wrapped itself around him, the Blood Angel felt a measure of comfort from the familiar touch and scent of the wargear. The power armour he had worn since his initiation had been destroyed in combat with the Chaos champion Iskavan, the centuries-old hardware ruined by the claws and blades of the Word Bearer. Perhaps some elements of his old gear might remain among the components he now donned, but for the most part he was clothing himself in the armour of dead men. On the inner surfaces of the boots, the wrist sheaths, the chest plates, there were lines and lines of tiny scripture, etched there by blade-point over hundreds of years. Each piece of the codex armour carried the history of its wearers, a roll of honour naming the men that had borne it into countless battles. The gear that Rafen would now call his own had been in service to the Chapter for half a millennium or more.

One of the servitors handed him a gauntlet, and Rafen paused. Etched in the ceramite about the wrist guard was a name that he knew. 'Bennek,' he said softly.

'Brother?' Lucion gave him a questioning look. 'Is something amiss?'

Rafen shook his head, remembering Bennek's death on Cybele. His comrade had been struck by enemy plasma fire and crushed beneath a horde of Word Bearers. Rafen thrust his hand into the gauntlet and made a fist with it, silently vowing to avenge his battle-brother's death.

Lucion leaned in and attached Rafen's left shoulder guard, running his claw-hand over the winged tear of blood embossed on the surface. The Techmarine gripped the opposing piece and moved to place it over the right arm, but Rafen's eyes narrowed and he blocked Lucion with the flat of his hand. He pointed at the other shoulder guard. 'What is this?' Along with the traditional white teardrop design that symbolised the Third Company of the Blood Angels, the armour bore a new sigil – a golden spear surrounded by a halo.

The Chaplain and Techmarine exchanged glances. 'In honour of Arkio, brother,' said Delos. 'To signify our presence here as witnesses to his Emergence.'

Rafen hesitated, thinking of his oath, then looked away with a nod. Lucion attached the pad without comment. Finally, the litany concluded with the Chaplain's benediction over Rafen's helmet. The Space Marine allowed the servitors to place it over his head, and he heard the hiss and click of the neck ring sealing him into the wargear. Inside the accustomed confines of the armour he felt alive again, the second skin of metal and plastic as natural to him as breathing. Rafen dropped to one knee and made the sign of the aquila.

'I am armoured by the Emperor himself,' he said, recalling the words of Dante from the eve of the Alchonis Campaign. 'Righteousness is my shield. Faith is my armour and hatred my weapon. I fear not and I am proud, for I am a Son of Sanguinius, a protector of mankind. Aye, I am indeed an Angel of Death.'

'Blood for Sanguinius,' Lucion and Delos spoke together. 'Blood for the Emperor. Blood for Arkio, the Angel Reborn.'

Beneath the blank mask of his helmet's breather grille, Rafen's face soured at the last words, and he came to his feet. Lucion presented him with an object wrapped in red velvet. The Space Marine unfurled the cloth from his bolter and ran his fingers over the gun's surface. This was the only piece of his equipment that had survived the clash with Iskavan intact, and Rafen felt a curious sadness as he read the engravings he had placed on it during his years of service. The bolter was a remnant of the old Rafen, he realised, the Blood Angel who had been content in his service to Chapter and God-Emperor, never daring to question his place in the scheme of things; not so now. He worked the slide on the weapon and loaded it, the last action in the ritual completed. Rafen brought the bolter to a battle-ready stance with a snap of boots on stone.

A voice came from the doorway. 'Ah, my brother is whole once more.' Delos and Lucion bowed as Arkio strode into the chamber. Even in the poor light of the room, the Blood Angel's golden armour seemed to glow with an inner luminescence.

'Blessed,' began the Chaplain, but Arkio waved him into silence.

'Delos, if you would permit me, I would speak with my sibling alone.'

'Of course.' The priest gestured to Lucion and the two Space Marines took their leave, the tech-servitors waddling out after them.

Arkio placed a hand on Rafen's shoulder and smiled. 'I promised you that you would live, did I not?'

Rafen recalled his brother's words in the wake of the duel with Iskavan. 'Yes. I thank you for my life.'

The smile broadened, and once again Rafen was struck by the uncanny similarities between Arkio's new aspect and the renditions of Sanguinius that hung in the chapels. 'Formality is not needed between us, Rafen. You are my blood kin as well as my battle-brother.' He tapped the sculpted breastplate of his armour. 'I want you close by my side. We have great works ahead of us, kinsman, high deeds that will be spoken of throughout the galaxy.'

The display inside Rafen's helmet told him the comparative positions of the nearest Blood Angels. There were four honour guards outside the chamber, along with Delos and Lucion; even the swiftest of them was a full ten seconds away. Arkio stood within arm's length of Rafen, his mood relaxed and his guard apparently lowered. His brother was without headgear, the bare skin of his throat visible. Rafen was aware of the weight of his bolter in his mailed fist, a full magazine of shells there in the clip. It would not take much; just a jerk of the wrist to bring the muzzle of the gun to press against Arkio's chest, one squeeze of the trigger to discharge a point-blank burst of fire. Even the hallowed gold artificer armour would not be able to withstand such a strike. In that moment, Rafen imagined the look of shock and pain on Arkio's face as the bolt shells tore into his torso, punching his organs through his back in a riot of fluid and matter. He could almost smell the hot blood, the taste of it on his tongue flaring as the red thirst caressed the edges of his mind. The opportunity was here, now. All Rafen need do was raise his weapon and murder his brother, and he would put an end to all question of this Emergence. The thought of it repelled and agitated him in equal measure.

'What... what deeds?' The words came out of his mouth of their own accord.

'A Blood Crusade,' Arkio said firmly. 'Once I have united the Chapter under our banner, we will draw together all the successors, all the Sons of Sanguinius. By the grail, we shall cut the cancerous heart of Chaos from our space.' He gave his sibling a clear-eyed look, the pure power of his disposition overwhelming at such close quarters. It was little wonder that lesser men would die for one such as he.

Rafen's bolter felt like it was as dense as neutronium, too heavy to move. 'How?'

'We'll begin with the Maelstrom, brother. Fitting that our first target will be the nest of the Word Bearers, yes? I will personally see to it that their foul cadre is purged to a man.' Like the monstrous Eye of Terror, the horrific realm of warped space known as the Maelstrom was a gateway into the chaotic realm of the Ruinous Powers, and it was in this twisted zone that the Sons of Lorgar had made their throneworld. Arkio nodded to himself. 'Commander Dante has allowed them the privilege of life too long, I think. As Sachiel said, it is not enough that we drove them from Cybele and Shenlong. We must drive them from existence.'

'The priest,' Rafen said in a chill voice. 'You value his words more than those of our Chapter's lord?'

Arkio's eyes narrowed. 'Dante is not here, Rafen. Dante did not see, as we did, the merciless intent of Iskavan's hordes. Had we not intervened, a world would have been put to death.' He looked away. 'I have always honoured Commander Dante in word and deed, but now I find my perspective changing, brother. During my time on the mission of the *Bellus*, away from Baal, perhaps it was then that I first began to wonder if his stewardship of our Legion was all it could be...'

Rafen stifled a gasp. 'Some would call that dissidence.'

'Who?' snapped Arkio, 'Who would dare say that to me? Was it not our old mentor Koris who said that men must question all that they believe, or else they are fools?'

'And what did it bring him?' Rafen said bitterly. 'Lord Dante is a fine commander.'

'Yes, perhaps. Perhaps he was, five hundred years ago at the peak of his powers, but what of now? It was the inquisitor who drew me to this fact, Rafen – among all their victories, have the Blood Angels truly assumed their place as the first among equals before the Emperor? Look back to the death of our Brother Tycho at Hive Tempestora. One of our greatest falls and nothing is done? We should have led a reprisal force to wipe out a dozen ork tribeworlds as payment in kind. And Dante did not!' He turned away, presenting his folded wings to his brother. 'In eleven hundred years at the head of the greatest Chapter of the Legion Astartes, what progress has he made toward the mastery of our gene-curse? None!'

Rafen could not believe what he was hearing, the open scorn in Arkio's voice. 'Brother, what has driven you to this?'

Arkio fixed him with a level gaze. 'I have had my eyes opened, Rafen.'

'By Stele? By *Sachiel*?' He tried and failed to keep a mocking tone from his voice.

The Blood Angel gave a snort of derision. 'Rafen, you are transparent to me. Now I see why you falter at these ideals – it is not your will that prevents you, it is your pride. Your… rivalry with the priest runs deep, yes? Neither of us will forget that it was he that almost cost you your chance to become a Chapter initiate.'

'You are right,' Rafen admitted. 'But it is not just my dislike of Sachiel that colours my words. I implore you, brother, do not follow the counsel of the priest and the inquisitor blindly–'

'Blind?' Arkio repeated, his mood turning stormy. 'Oh no, Rafen, it is you who refuses to see.' He paused, moderating his annoyance. 'But still we have time. I keep you close, brother, because you remind me that no path is the easy one. I question and you question me. You are the devil's advocate.' Arkio gave him another brilliant smile and patted him on the shoulder. 'Thank you.'

Rafen watched him leave, the hand around his bolter's pistol grip as rigid and immobile as cast iron.

IN THE SILENCE of the Sanctum Astropathica aboard the *Bellus*, Ulan drifted in zero gravity, a weave of mechadendrites and brassy cables snaking from slots on her skull to banks of murmuring cognitive engines. The psyker's mind was spread as thinly as she dared, the energy of it dispersed into a wide net. Her concentration was paramount; if she were to let her thoughts drift further for even an eye-blink, what little there was to call her personality would be picked apart on the winds of the empyrean. She was a spider now, settled at the nexus of a web she wove from her own psy-stuff. Ulan lurked there, sensitive to any perturbation in the rolling non-matter of the warp, looking and watching for patterns.

There were things out there. She was careful not to let her attention turn directly upon them, cautiously watching them only by the wakes they left in passing, the shimmers as the anti-space stretched under their weight. Ulan kept her terror for these things under the tightest control of all; they liked the taste of fear. Even the tiniest speck of it could call them across the void like sea predators scenting drops of blood in the water.

Then they were gone as quickly as they had arrived. Ulan was listening again, watching, waiting.

And there was her target. Very distant but approaching quickly now, cutting through the immaterium like a sword blade. A man-made object, swift and deadly in aspect.

Ulan smiled and gathered herself back together. When she had recovered enough of her potency, she focused on her master and sent him a single word.

Soon.

IT WAS LATE for Firing Rites, and so the range was deserted. Rafen was inwardly pleased; he did not feel like company for the moment, and the questions and comments of his brethren would have not been welcomed. He loaded a fresh sickle magazine into the bolter and took aim with the naked eye, releasing a series of three-round bursts into the rotating target stands.

He frowned at the results. His weapon had been knocked off true when it fell from his hands in the manufactory. With care, Rafen adjusted the pitch of the foresight. The simple, disciplined action gave him focus away from the churning concerns in the back of his mind. Intent on the work, he realised too late that someone else had entered the chamber.

Rafen looked up and scowled.

'Here you are,' said Sachiel, with false lightness. 'Your new armour fits you well, brother.'

He returned to his bolter, unwilling to waste breath on pretended pleasantries with the Sanguinary High Priest. 'I will strive to be worthy of it.'

'I am pleased to hear you say that. The Blessed was quite concerned that you be returned to duty status. Arkio... It appears he has a greater degree of lenity for a blood relative, than for other men.'

Rafen reloaded the bolter and slammed the magazine home with force. 'Do not play word games with me, Sachiel,' he said sharply. All at once, his tolerance for the conceited priest vanished. 'You have come here to say something to me? Speak and be on your way.'

Sachiel's face reddened but he kept the annoyance from his voice. 'Your bluntness could be construed by some as insubordination, Rafen. I would pay it mind if I were you.' He leaned in to speak in a low, loaded whisper. 'The Blessed may have reason to endure your dispute of his divinity for now, but I would not test him further, brother. A wise man would do well to heed a warning and keep his silence.'

'Your words could be construed by some as a threat, Apothecary,' said Rafen, mimicking his tone.

'They might at that,' Sachiel agreed. 'If you continue to challenge Arkio, there will come a time when his favour will wane. And when that moment comes, it will be my pleasure to see you branded a heretic.'

Rafen angrily rose to his feet in a rush from his firing stance, the bolter still hot in his hands. Sachiel was caught by surprise and backed away a step. 'Your counsel is appreciated,' Rafen said coldly, shouldering his weapon. 'But if you forgive me, I have duties to attend to aboard the *Bellus*.'

'What duties?' demanded the priest.

'The memory of the dead, Sachiel. I must pay my respects to the fallen in the ship's great chapel.' He pushed past the Apothecary and walked away.

'Take care, Rafen,' Sachiel called out after him, 'lest you wish to join them too soon.'

CHAPTER THREE

RAFEN FELT THE pull of Shenlong's gravity lessen as the Thunderhawk rose out of the forge-world's atmospheric envelope. He glanced through the viewport – the dun-coloured sky beyond had faded to a dirty purple and now it was the black of space. Craning his neck, he could see the curvature of the planet, a blanket of rusty pollution over the industrial landscape.

The transport rocked as it changed course. Rafen knew the interiors of these craft as well as he did the words of the Chapter hymnals, many was the occasion that he had been crammed into the heavily armoured cargo deck of such a vessel, shoulder to shoulder with other Blood Angels. The vibration of the floor beneath his feet never failed to kindle a faint anticipatory thrill in his chest. It was so often the precursor to battle, but not today. The Thunderhawk carried only munitions on this journey. Rafen had half-expected not to find a flight back to *Bellus*'s anchor at high orbit, but by luck one of the barge's auxiliaries had been preparing for lift-off. The transport was taking advantage of the forge-world's full stocks of shells to rearm the warship, ferrying case after case of missiles where it might normally have loaded

Rhinos and Space Marines for ground assault. The warheads filled the hull spaces, leaving scant room for anything else.

Rafen was not the only passenger. Personally supervising the cargo was the battle barge's second-in-command, Brother Solus. Rafen could not recall ever having seen the man outside the bridge of the *Bellus* before. Solus seemed more like an extension of the will of the ship's commander, Captain Ideon, than a person in his own right.

Solus threw him a cursory nod as he passed through the cabin. 'We'll dock soon,' he noted. The Space Marine paused and gave Rafen a questioning look. 'I was not aware you had been ordered to return to the ship.'

Much of the *Bellus's* crew had been granted planetfall leave in a gesture of magnanimity by Inquisitor Stele, following his assumption of the brevet governorship of Shenlong. In the wake of the Word Bearers invasion, the forge-world had declared a celebratory holiday and Chapter serfs and commoner crewmen had been only too happy to join the festivities. The carnival mood Rafen had glimpsed in the Ikari district was everywhere, all of it alive with the worship of Arkio. The pressure of that and the knowledge that Sachiel was surely watching Rafen's every move had driven him to look for solace somewhere – anywhere – away from Arkio. A spell aboard the quiet corridors of *Bellus* would give Rafen time to think, he hoped. None of this, however, he confided in Solus.

'My mentor, Brother-Sergeant Koris,' said Rafen. 'He lies in the grand chamber aboard the barge. I wish to pay my respects to him, and enter his name in the *Book of the Fallen.*'

Solus nodded. The ritual was typically performed by a Sanguinary Priest, but often men who had served closely with those who died would carry out the rite as a personal farewell, writing the dead man's name in their own blood as a lasting salute. 'I did not know him. From what I saw of him, he seemed an… outspoken warrior.'

'Indeed,' Rafen agreed, 'he was that.'

'A pity he did not live to see the Emergence,' Solus continued. 'A great many of our brothers fell for that piece of dirt.' He indicated Shenlong with the jerk of his chin. Even though he was Astartes to the core, Solus still had a spacer's dislike for planets.

A hatch hissed open to admit a bondman in flight crew gear. He bowed quickly to Solus. 'Lord, we are receiving an alert from *Bellus.*'

'To what end?' the Space Marine demanded.

'A starship is approaching the planet. Our cogitators believe it to be the strike cruiser *Amareo.*'

Rafen straightened. 'One of ours.' He felt his pulse quicken. The arrival of another Blood Angels vessel could mean only one thing: the clandestine message he had sent using Sergeant Koris's vox-net transmitter had got through to Baal. 'Is it known who is in command of the cruiser?'

The serf nodded. 'Yes, lord. The pennant of Brother-Captain Gallio flies from the *Amareo*'s bridge.'

'Gallio…' repeated Rafen.

'You know him?' said Solus.

'Only by reputation. He was a contemporary of my late commander, Captain Simeon.'

Solus considered this for a moment, then turned to the crewman. 'Contact *Bellus*. Inform Captain Ideon that we are diverting to intercept *Amareo*. Protocol requires that a ranking officer welcome Gallio to the system.'

The serf saluted and returned to the bridge. Rafen watched him go. 'Lord, should not the *Amareo* be received by a quorum of senior Space Marines?'

Solus nodded. 'Correct, Rafen, but with much of the crew planetside for the celebrations of the Ascension, I doubt Ideon could find others to be spared.' He beckoned him to his feet. 'You and I will have to suffice.'

The Thunderhawk's engines throbbed and the light through the window shifted as the ship changed course. Rafen looked out and saw a splinter of silver and red hanging in the dark like a thrown knife; his search for respite would have to be postponed.

ULAN'S WARNING BROUGHT a thin smile to Stele's bloodless lips. Seated cross-legged in the centre of the bloodstained death room, the inquisitor's dark grox-hide coat pooled out around him like spilled ink. In the dim half-light, he appeared to be some sort of strange extrusion growing out of the patches of dried crimson. Stele gave a quick look at the door; if he were disturbed, if his concentration was broken, then all of this would be for nothing. There was a shock-ward attached to the inside of the hatch, primed and ready to deliver a massive electric charge into anyone foolish enough to try to open it from the outside.

He reached into one of dozens of secret pockets in the coat and retrieved two vials of bright, fresh blood. Stele had drawn the fluid himself, from the necks of the merchant's wife and daughter as they had lain spent at his feet, compelling them into death so that the liquid might teem with the vital essence of their brutal, potent murder. Uncapping the vials, he licked his lips as the smell of the liquid reached him. Gently now, it was important not to waste even the smallest drop.

Stele closed his eyes and jerked his wrists; the contents of the vials flickered into the air in a wet arc, tracing precise lines that bisected one another. In that moment, the gloomy, meat-wet room quivered with the psychic fingerprints of agony, and Stele slipped his mind into the non-space at the edge of the warp. To the layman and the untrained, Ramius Stele appeared to possess formidable pskyer talents, but in truth he was a man of only middling mental power in comparison to many of the Imperium's telepathic agents. Stele's talents lay not in the brute force application of his psychic ability, like those of his servant Ulan, but in his subtle use of them. Stele's mind was less a sword, more a scalpel, but still utterly lethal when used correctly.

The inquisitor ignored the thrilling warmth of the energies around him, resisting the urge to dip into them like a welcoming ocean. His resolve firm, Stele let his abhuman senses map the space around Shenlong in shades of psionic force. Up above, where *Bellus* lay, was the faint ember glow of the latent minds aboard her. Flickering and wavering among them was Ulan's bright and dangerous psychic imprint. She was a firefly in a bottle, her power bouncing off the walls of the inhibitor coronet he forced her to wear. Had Stele chosen to channel his mind through hers, what he did now would have been far easier, but her erratic character was too unpredictable for something that required so delicate a touch.

He passed further out, ignoring the dots of light on a small craft suspended mid-way between *Bellus* and the new arrival, letting his spirit-self approach the *Amareo*. A dart of indistinct fear rose and fell in him as he sensed the clear, steady glow of a psyker mind on board the starship; on some level, he had been concerned that the arch-telepath Mephiston would be the first to come and confront Arkio. For all his arrogance, Stele was not so foolish as to think he could match wits with the Lord of Death – at least, not at the moment. But as he predicted, the Chief Librarian of the Blood Angels had sent a proxy in his place, and it was this trained psyche that glittered before him. It had none of the random, freakish coloration of

Ulan's mentality. This was a keen, acute mind born of the psykana librarius.

All the more reason to tread carefully, Stele reminded himself. The inquisitor raised his hands so that his ghost-fingers barely touched the corona of the psyker's aura and let the surface details of the Librarian's mind reveal themselves. The Blood Angel was without his psychic hood for the moment, a piece of good fortune that would make his task easier. The inquisitor's subtlety was his greatest skill, his target would never suspect that Stele's dark touch was spreading over his mind like some dark sheen of oil.

'Your name...' Stele said aloud to the dank air, 'You are Brother Vode, Epistolary to Mephiston. He has sent you... Sent you to taste Arkio's mind...' And there it was, drifting inside Vode's thoughts, perhaps even too faint for the Space Marine to know himself, the cold splinter of doubt and suspicion. Stele made a low chuckle in the depths of his throat. Mephiston had dispatched the best of his Librarians on this mission, but in doing so opened Vode to the thought that he would be venturing into the souls of heretics. Stele laid his hands upon Vode's nascent misgivings and began to massage them, working them deeper. Even at such a distance, the taint of the Blood Angels psyker's loathing for apostates leaked into the mind-space like black ichor.

With ghostly pressure, Stele nurtured Vode's doubts, sweat beading his bald brow with effort and concentration.

BROTHER-CAPTAIN GALLIO entered the cruiser's training gallery and found Vode immediately. The Librarian was in the midst of a series of regimented *kata*, a complex dance of advances, parries, and blocks. In his hand, the psyker held a formidable-looking force axe, a full half of Gallio's height and forged from bright steel made in the foundries of Luna.

The axe head quivered in the light, the crystalline blade flickering with the witch-fire of psionic energy.

The captain's eyes seemed to slide off the metallic curve, as if his vision could not hold the shape of the weapon in his gaze. Gallio, like most Adeptus Astartes, held a powerful distrust of anything that bore the mark of the psyker. To him, those who had this aberrant curse were to be considered a danger, or at the very best, to be pitied. It was through the lens of such minds that the first gateways to the warp had been opened, and with them the lurking powers of Chaos that made the immaterium their home. This was the fear that lay at the heart of the psychic 'gift'; those who were weak in spirit would find themselves seduced by the raw energy of the warp space. Such souls could become conduits for daemonic intelligences, flesh vessels for creatures that were hate incarnate.

Gallio approached Vode carefully, watching the precise ballet of the psyker's fighting style. There was no wasted movement there: each simulated blow of the axe was economical and clear-cut. Every iota of Gallio's battle instinct was keyed to the war against Chaos, and on some level he believed that such witch-minds deserved only death. And yet, here was a psyker who bore the mark of the Blood Angels. Before him stood a man that embodied both the magnificence of a Space Marine and the dark potential of a monstrous psychic. The duality of the matter perturbed him.

Vode came about and halted, the humming force axe hovering between the two men. Vode had eyes that were so pale as to be almost grey. Gallio resisted the automatic surge of revulsion in his gut as the faint glow from the weapon drew all the moisture from the air.

'Honoured captain,' said Vode quietly, showing no concern at Gallio's expression. 'I am prepared. What is your bidding?'

The Librarian was nothing like his master, the notorious Mephiston, Gallio noted. The Lord of Death was a gaunt, imposing figure in red-gold ceramite, where Vode was a rugged fireplug of a man with skin the colour of dark wood. 'A transport approaches from the *Bellus*. We must be prepared to receive them.' Unlike the rank and file of the Blood Angels, Librarians wore armour that was blue in coloration, with only a single crimson shoulder pad. It was another factor that set them apart from the rest of their brethren, thought Gallio.

Vode nodded. 'As you order.' With care, the psyker drew his axe back to a sling across his armour, the tiny licks of cerulean lightning fading from its surface. Vode's face twitched slightly and something moved inside the neck ring of his battle armour. From thick bulges about his head, panels made of fine circuitry and crystal matrices extended in a tripartite cowl. Gallio watched with slight distaste as the pieces of Vode's psychic hood connected themselves to brass sockets in the Space Marine's skull.

'Do you… sense anything?' said the captain.

Vode gave a slight smile. 'All the myriad ways of the traitor are subtle and complex, brother. I will root them out, if they conceal themselves here. But for now, there is no–' The expression on the psyker's face changed in a flash; his eyes narrowed and his lips thinned to a line.

Instinctively, Gallio's hand dropped to the bolt pistol in his belt holster. 'Brother Vode?'

Then the moment was gone, and the Librarian shook his head. 'A passing shadow,' he said. 'The taint of the Word Bearers lingers still in this star system, brother-captain. Faint, like fading smoke…'

The answer did little to satisfy Gallio. 'This way,' he indicated.

Vode strode after the officer, a frown threatening to form on his face. For an instant, just the smallest of moments, the psyker had felt the touch of something corrupt. He ran his fingers over the trio of purity seals on the breast of his armour, turning the sensation over in his mind, the weight of a new doubt preying on him.

THE DROP RAMP of the Thunderhawk opened like a yawning mouth and Rafen followed Solus down it. Glancing around the hangar bay of the *Amareo*, he saw a dozen more ships of the same class in launch cradles, armed and set for attack. A troop of Space Marines stood waiting for them in two tight lines, ostensibly an honour guard but just as easily a combat unit. There were other Blood Angels nearby in twos and threes, observing with cold, keen eyes. Rafen's impression was one of preparation; the men aboard *Amareo* were unsure what to expect on Shenlong, and they had taken to book and bolter in readiness. He felt a curious foreboding; these battle-brothers were here only because of a secret message that *he* had sent, and Rafen felt some measure of responsibility for them.

He caught sight of the dark hue of a Librarian's wargear as they set foot on the strike cruiser's deck. The psyker hovered at the shoulder of a senior Blood Angel who studied them with a hawkish manner.

Solus tapped his fist to the blood-drop symbol on his chest. 'Brother Solus and Brother Rafen, requesting permission to come aboard.'

The Space Marine returned the salute. 'Granted. I am Captain Gallio.' He nodded at the Librarian. 'Epistolary Vode, my adjutant.'

'Your arrival is unexpected,' said Solus.

Gallio gave Solus a penetrating stare. 'I think you know why we are here, brother. I have come on the express orders of Lord Commander Dante himself, to see with my own eyes what has transpired on Shenlong.'

'You come to venerate the Blessed Arkio, yes?' Solus replied. 'I suspected as much.'

'We shall see who will and will not be venerated,' Vode broke in, his voice thickening. He studied Solus and Rafen with open scrutiny, and both men felt the pressure of his mind upon them.

'Why did you depart Cybele when orders were sent that *Bellus* should remain there?' Gallio demanded. The captain wasted no time in cutting to the core of the matter.

Solus shook his head. 'I know of no such orders, Captain Gallio. My commander, Brother-Captain Ideon, followed the directives of Inquisitor Stele to weigh anchor and make best speed to this system. Our orders after the rout at Cybele were to contain and destroy the Word Bearers warband here.'

Gallio frowned. 'Those commands were not sanctioned by Baal.'

'If that is so,' Solus retorted, 'then how did you know to locate *Bellus* here?'

'A message was sent to the fortress-monastery,' said Vode. 'The contents of that message raised some questions of integrity.'

'There are only loyal Sons of Sanguinius here.' Solus said hotly. 'Who sent this signal? Tell me his name!'

'Brother-Sergeant Koris.'

'Koris is dead,' said Rafen, unable to keep an edge of pain from his words. 'He was killed in the attack on the Ikari fortress. I witnessed him pass from this life.'

Gallio and Vode exchanged glances. 'It is the content of the message that is of gravest concern to Lord Dante. Koris, if it were he, spoke of a "transformation". By Dante's order, I am to evaluate this occurrence in the commander's stead.'

Rafen felt his throat tighten. The Librarian's eyes had not strayed from him, and Vode's powerful gaze made the Space

Marine feel like a tiny speck swarming under the lens of a microscope. *He knows.* The Blood Angel could sense Vode's inner sight picking at his mind.

Solus gestured at the Thunderhawk, his face taut with concern. 'Perhaps you should accompany me back to the *Bellus*, captain. We could provide you with a complete tactical report on the Cybele battle and–'

'If this "blessing" of which you speak is true, I will not tarry to debate the matters surrounding it,' Gallio interrupted sharply. 'Answer me, Solus. Where will I find Inquisitor Ramius Stele and Brother Arkio?'

The Space Marine's face darkened with anger. Gallio's bluntness rankled. 'Lord Stele has taken stewardship of Shenlong from the Ikari fortress in the capital district. Arkio the Blessed resides in the chapel there.'

Vode broke eye contact and nodded to the *Amareo*'s commander. 'Then that is where we will go.'

Solus took a step forward. 'He is the Angel Reborn. You cannot simply bid him to your beck and call.'

'Until we make our determination, he is nothing of the kind,' Vode replied with icy certainty.

Rafen saw an opportunity and spoke again. 'Brother Solus, this matter will be resolved with alacrity if we proceed as Captain Gallio demands. With your permission, I will accompany the captain back to the surface to assist him.'

Solus gave Gallio a hard look, then glanced at Rafen. 'Perhaps you are correct, brother.' He turned back to the Thunderhawk. 'Once these men see the Blessed, any disagreeable hesitancy will become redundant.' He threw them a last look as he reached the hatchway. 'I will return to *Bellus* and inform the inquisitor of your impending arrival.'

Rafen turned away as the ramp slammed shut to find Vode watching him once again. 'I am at your command,' he said.

Gallio indicated a shuttlecraft parked nearby. 'This way. You will use the journey to tell me all you can about this Arkio.'

'Yes, Rafen,' added Vode. 'We would know more of your younger sibling.'

THE STATUE HAD been moved from the grand chamber of the *Bellus* and brought down to the chapel, there to stand in pride of place before the altar. With appropriate ceremony, the icon of the Emperor of Man had been shifted behind the statue, towering over it like a watchful father at the shoulder of a dutiful son. Arkio ran his bare fingers over the ancient stone. The pinkish marble came from a mountain range on Baal Primus.

He touched the face of the statue. The likeness was baring its throat in supplication, eyes closed and mouth slightly open, neck muscles taut. A crown of sculpted jags about the tousled hair of the head signified the solar glow of a halo. Arkio followed the line of the nose, the jaw, down the neck and to the sternum. Of its own accord, his hand came to his own face and traced the same course. The shapes of both were so close as to be almost identical.

He backed away a step, taking in the whole statue of the Blood Angel Sanguinius. His seraph wings arched over his shoulders, the Pure One wore the robes of an initiate priest – a sign of his humility – and his arms were outstretched. In the right, he grasped the skull-shape of the Red Grail, from which fell the four drops of blood that Sanguinius had shed for his Chapter; his left arm was upturned, and from the wrist fell a torrent of his blessed vitae.

With perfect grace, Arkio balanced on the uppermost step of the altar and raised the wings that folded from his own shoulders. The mighty pinions were no longer new and strange to him, now Arkio took his angelic limbs to be as much a part of him as any other. He extended his arms and mimicked the pose of the statue, tipping back his head and showing his throat.

'Magnificent.' Sachiel's voice was thick with barely contained emotion. Arkio opened his eyes and relaxed as the Sanguinary High Priest approached him. Sachiel dropped into a bow. 'Blessed, it is confirmed. A warship from Baal has taken up station alongside *Bellus* and a party from the vessel is on the way as we speak.'

Arkio bid Sachiel to his feet and listened intently as the priest relayed the message from Solus. 'Captain Gallio is joined by Librarian Vode and your brother,' he concluded, a slight annoyance colouring his tone at the mention of Rafen.

The Blood Angel paid it no concern. 'So soon,' he murmured. 'Dante has moved quicker than I had expected... But this shall not be an issue. Give the order to provide Gallio's shuttle a priority flight corridor.' Arkio indicated the ceiling above them. 'Have his ship vectored to the landing pad on the roof of the fortress.'

Sachiel swallowed hard. 'My lord, is that wise? Perhaps it might be more prudent to land him at the starport and bring the captain's party here in a convoy. We could... control them more easily if the circumstances required it.'

Arkio shook his head. 'What will come to pass, will come. I will look Gallio in the eye and offer him nothing but the truth. Where he goes from there will be his choice alone.'

The priest hesitated. 'Blessed, as ever you exhibit the wisdom of the Great Angel, but I must confess I fear the reaction of these new arrivals.'

The chapel doors opened as Sachiel spoke to admit Inquisitor Stele and the drifting shapes of his servo-skulls. 'I will add my voice to my comrade's,' said Stele as he approached. 'He speaks with concern for you and our enterprises, Arkio.'

'Thank you for attending me,' said Arkio. 'I would not wish to proceed without your counsel, Stele.'

The inquisitor gave a gracious nod. 'Forgive my delay, but I was meditating...' He patted his brow with a kerchief; there was a thin sheen of perspiration coating his bullet-like head from his mental exertions in the death room.

Arkio studied both men. 'Your considerations are noted, but I stand by my order. Gallio and Vode will come here to me, and I will answer all questions.' He straightened, glancing back at the statue of Sanguinius. 'It is my duty to the Chapter.'

'Of course,' Stele demurred, 'and to that end, might I suggest we proceed as ceremony demands? I have assembled the honour guard to attend you.'

Arkio gave him a cursory nod and stepped away, walking to the balcony where the battle trials still raged below.

Sachiel leant close to Stele's ear. 'The moment is upon us, lord inquisitor,' he said quietly. 'We will know where the loyalties of Dante's men lie.'

'Indeed,' Stele purred. 'Arkio hopes for the best, but we... we must prepare for the worst.'

'Of that, there is no question,' replied the priest, his eyes bright with righteous fervour.

'I sent the message.' Rafen watched the play of emotions over Gallio's face as the captain considered his words. 'As Koris lay in death, I used his vox to transmit a signal to the *Bellus* and beyond.'

'Subterfuge,' said Vode grimly. 'What you have done violates protocols of discipline and rituals of the fallen.'

Rafen gave a rueful nod as the shuttle rumbled through the atmosphere. 'I am only too aware of that.'

'The strictures are clear, only a Techmarine may handle the wargear of the deceased in anything other than the most desperate of circumstances,' Gallio replied.

'The future of our Chapter is in the balance,' Rafen snapped, a little more fiercely than he would have liked. 'What could be more desperate?'

Gallio considered the Space Marine's words. 'The issue of your actions is secondary to the issue at hand, Rafen. Any decision that you may or may not have behaved improperly is deferred, for the moment.' He looked away. 'What you have told us of this change in Arkio... it is remarkable.'

Vode nodded. 'Aye. And terrifying as well. I sense forces at work here that reach beyond my ability to define. Great powers, moving into conjunction.' The Librarian's hands had strayed to his force axe, unconsciously kneading the grip.

Gallio noted the psyker's small sign of agitation but let it pass unremarked. 'Rafen, you would know Arkio better than any man. These physical changes of which you speak are shocking enough, but his soul... I ask you, when you look into your brother's eyes, what do you see?'

An involuntary shudder passed through the Space Marine's massive frame. 'When we were youths, it was I that was the reckless one, captain. Arkio was open and guileless, he was pure of spirit... It was his influence that helped me to turn my ways, the younger helping the elder.' For a moment, Rafen lost himself in reverie. 'Now... now that youth is gone. It is still Arkio's soul that lives behind those eyes, brother, if that it what you truly wish to know... But for all the changes wrought upon him in these passing weeks, it is his manner that is most altered.'

'Explain,' demanded Vode, tension in his voice.

'Arkio is arrogant now, where before he was humble. Whatever the hand that guides his new path may be, Arkio himself *believes* in it. Within the halls of his heart, he has no doubt that he is the Deus Encarmine.'

'And if we must disabuse him of that belief,' Gallio said, 'what then?'

Rafen found he could not look the captain in the eye any longer. 'I dread to think,' he said. 'I dread to think.'

In the long silence that followed, the shuttle's deck canted as the craft dropped through thick cloudbanks and down over the factory sprawls.

'We are close,' Vode said abruptly.

Gallio gave Rafen a last, measuring look, and then signalled the other men in his personal guard. 'Prepare for landing.'

A BLACK-ARMOURED figure stood waiting for them as they strode off the shuttle pad, Gallio's four men in a line behind the captain, Vode and Rafen. The Chaplain saluted the officer and the Librarian, throwing Rafen a wary nod.

'I am Brother Delos. Welcome to Shenlong, Captain Gallio. It is an honour to receive a warrior of such noted standing within the Chapter.'

Gallio ignored the greeting, and held out a metallic scroll case. 'I carry the letter of Lord Commander Dante. In this place, I speak for him. Chaplain, I would see the warrior Arkio.'

Delos faltered for a moment, eyes flicking to the scroll case, then to Rafen and finally back to Gallio. 'As you wish, captain. The Blessed will receive you in the fortress chapel.' He turned. 'Follow me.'

Rafen remained silent as they ventured down through the Ikari fortress, boarding the recently repaired elevator platform to descend to the core levels. For the second time that day, he felt the pressure of scrutiny from eyes all around him. As they passed groups of Space Marines, helots and scattered packs of pilgrims, conversations fell silent and barely concealed suspicion greeted them at every turn.

'They know we have come to judge him,' Vode hissed. 'They resent us for even considering the fact.'

The copper doors of the chapel opened to admit them, and Gallio strode boldly past Delos to enter first. Arkio came to his feet from the dais where he sat and the shock of the sight of him almost staggered the captain to a halt.

'Emperor's blood!' Gallio breathed. It was a living, breathing rendering of Sanguinius that stood there, wings bright as sunfire, the golden armour aglow with honeyed radiance. Arkio inclined his head in greeting and Gallio found himself physically resisting the urge to kneel. A palpable energy of personality crackled in the air, drawing all things to Arkio.

'By the Throne, it is the Pure One.' It was one of Gallio's men that had spoken, his voice hushed and reverent.

Vode smothered his words with a venomous rejoinder. 'That remains to be seen.' The Librarian still gripped his force axe; it was not quite in a battle-ready stance, but close enough to make any seasoned warrior wary of him.

Rafen felt a hand on his shoulder. Delos drew him back to halt at the doorway of the chapel. 'Stand down, lad. This is for the Blessed to decide.' He hesitated as Arkio approached the men from the *Amareo*. Beyond his brother, Sachiel looked on with obvious impatience, while Stele stood in the shadows. The inquisitor seemed muted, eyes distant and unfocussed.

'I am Arkio,' he began. 'I greet you as a brother, and honour you as Lord Dante's proxy.' The figure in gold gave a shallow bow, the tips of his wings touching the mosaic floor. 'What would you ask of me?'

'The truth,' Gallio replied. 'To know what force has brought you to...' He hesitated, searching for the right words, 'to this transformation.'

Sachiel bolted forward from the altar, an intense expression colouring his face. 'What *force*?' he repeated. 'Even the blind know the answer to that question. Do you not see him before you? He is the Blessed Angel Reborn.' Sachiel's eyes shone. 'Sanguinius has returned.'

'All of us carry the vitae of the Great Angel within us,' Vode snapped angrily at Arkio, 'but we do not claim to usurp his place. Our primarch lies millennia dead, yet you presume to take his name!'

Arkio gave a gentle shake of the head. 'I presume nothing. As you asked, so I offer only truth.'

'*Your* truth,' said Gallio. 'If you are what you say you are, then you will accompany us back to Baal, where the veracity of your claim will be put to the question. You will release this world and Inquisitor Stele will return governorship of Shenlong to the Imperium.' He paused. 'Commander Dante gives this order, and you are to heed it.'

Rafen's gaze happened on Stele; the Hereticus agent rubbed his brow, his gaze fixed on the Librarian Vode. The Blood Angel looked to the psyker and saw him tense with fury.

Then Arkio said the words that Rafen feared the most. 'I am beyond Dante's authority now.'

'*Heretic!*' The curse exploded from Vode's lips, his dark skin shading with rage. 'The hand of Chaos hides here. You are *impure!*' The Librarian's words sent a shock through the chapel, and white lightning crashed across the floor. It happened so fast that Rafen saw only a blur of blue and yellow. Vode sprang at Arkio, his force axe flaring with psy-flame. The curved blade met the gauntlet of the gold artificer armour and deafening thunder assailed his ears.

CHAPTER FOUR

VODE'S MIND WAS drowning in thick streams of glutinous hatred and black, oily darkness. At first, in that moment aboard the strike cruiser, he had thought nothing of the brief contact that had wafted over his psychic senses, passing like a diaphanous veil. There one breath, vanished the next. The mind-space about Shenlong was still dirty with the passage of the Word Bearers, their disgusting mental footprints like profane scars only visible to a psyker such as he. The bright purity of his force axe was a comfort to him. It was a talisman, a badge of the Space Marine's charmed life in the Emperor's service.

Vode listened to Rafen's words as they approached the Ikari fortress, outwardly fixed on the Blood Angel's face, but inside, his preternatural intuition buzzed like a warning siren, louder and louder in his ears as they came ever closer to the chapel. The Librarian tried to hold on to the sensations, to cup them in his hands and make some sort of sense to them – but it was like trying to pick out the perfume of a single black orchid through a sea of charnel house stench. And then in the chapel, he laid eyes on the golden armour and knew instinctively that he had found his way to the epicentre of this great skein of corruption. The Blood Angels psyker had faced this breed of witch-kind before: outwardly flawless, perfect and beautiful. Within they were rotted corpse-flesh, maggoty hearts pumping spoiled blood through bone voids.

He struggled to banish the image, blinking it away. For a second, everything seemed to shift and waver, and part of him cried out, *No!* Deceit laced the air. He glimpsed the man from the Ordo Hereticus across the stone floor, half-clad by shadows. For an instant, it seemed as if he, not the winged one, was the source of all the darkness here. Confusion creased Vode's brow; he had to be sure.

Then, as quickly as it was there, the impression fled and the hissing pressure behind his eyes returned in tenfold force. Vode looked at Arkio as the armoured figure spoke in silky tones to Captain Gallio. The psyker saw two visions of him, one over the other, each warring for prominence in his mind's eye. There was the Reborn Angel, a new Sanguinius glorious and unblemished in his holy perfection, radiant as the Throne of Terra itself, and there was the other.

It turned his stomach to see it. The gold armour was scarred and dull, black with shed blood. There were no eyes in the face of cracked, white porcelain, only pits of empty space; and the wings, foul things flensed of skin and barbed with hooks and broken razors. It spoke and the noise made Vode's bile rise to his throat. 'I am beyond Dante's authority now,' it jeered.

If the others in the chapel saw Arkio as he did, then they were either struck dumb by his awfulness or else bewitched by the apostate's illusory beauty. From the corner of his eye he saw Stele twitch, but the surge in hate that flowed through him at the same moment made the inquisitor seem immaterial. If no man here could or would act, then it was only Vode that could end this parody of the primarch's majesty. The thunderous heat of the black rage came upon him and the Librarian sent it crackling into the haft of his force axe. He shouted his malediction at the top of his lungs. 'Heretic. The hand of Chaos hides here. You are *impure!*'

Vode's weapon moved as if it were guided by the hand of the God-Emperor himself, cutting a flashing arc toward the skull of the pretender. Every ounce of mind-power from his Quickening channelled into the force axe. 'Hell spawn!' he spat. The crystal blade struck Arkio's wrist-guard with a roar of rended air. Like water pouring off a glass dome, the blue-white psy-fire fell away from the axe head, streaking around Arkio in harmless rivulets. An invulnerable sphere of crimson and gold danced around him at the edge of perception, the halo blunting Vode's attack into nothing.

SACHIEL'S REDUCTOR WAS in his hand as the Librarian struck, dancing, searching for a target. All about him, Arkio's golden-helmed honour guard brought up their weapons on reflex, and he glimpsed Gallio's retinue doing the same. The *Amareo*'s captain was crying out, reaching with one hand, his other skimming toward the butt of his holstered bolt pistol. A voice was shouting from the chapel doors, an indistinct red man-shape turning in the grip of a black figure; all this in a heartbeat.

Arkio's other hand came up and punched Vode away. The epistolary flew backwards, boots scraping across the stone as he struggled to keep his balance. With an eyebrow arched, Arkio reached for the force axe where it rested, lodged between plates of gold. The Blessed removed the weapon and, with a tightening of his fist, broke the axe handle in two.

Vode screamed and threw a curtain of lightning at him, racing back to leap at Arkio's bare throat, fangs flashing. Again, the Quickening parted around his golden form and he shot out a hand. Arkio's dart-sharp fingers impaled the ceramite chest plate of Vode's power armour and buried themselves to the knuckle. The Librarian's bolter was in his grip, and, even as blood bubbled from his mouth, Vode let shell fire crash out and flare across the room.

Unaimed, heedless bolts skipped close to Sachiel and the shock brought him to action. He lunged at Gallio with the reductor, clipping the Blood Angels captain's scalp. No word of command was uttered, but with the priest's gesture a tiny hell was unleashed in the chapel. The Blood Angels of Arkio's honour guard and Gallio's detachment alike opened fire on one another, burning rounds lancing back and forth across the room in a screaming web of death.

'*No!*' The cry was Rafen's, but it sank unheard under a tidal wave of gunfire, and with strength that belied his age, the Chaplain Delos shoved him back from the fray.

Arkio flicked Vode's corpse from his hand like a discarded piece of meat, aloof as bullets keened and hummed off his golden ceramite chest. Gallio's troop, outnumbered two to one by the honour guards, danced and spun as multiple bolter shells tore through their battlegear and cut them apart. Gallio was the last to fall, thick arterial blood running in rivers from every joint in his armour. His pistol dropped from nerveless fingers and the captain sank to his knees, eyes glazing.

Arkio came to him and cupped Gallio's chin in his hand. 'You have brought my worst fear to life,' he told the dying man. 'You will not be the last to perish.'

The captain gasped out a final breath, and with that it was ended; the entire exchange had lasted hardly a tick of the clock.

Rage filled Rafen and he punched Delos, turning the black-armoured Chaplain with the blow. He forced his way through the ranks of gold-helmed men and down to the blood-slick mosaic floor. Suddenly among the dead, he felt like weeping.

'What…' He could barely speak. *'What have you done?'*

Arkio looked him squarely in the eye and Rafen's veins filled with ice. 'These men,' said his sibling, casting an offhand wave at the steaming corpses, 'they were here to destroy us, kindred. I knew it from the moment they entered the room.' He glanced up, addressing every Blood Angel in the chapel. 'Hear me, brothers. We have been forsaken. These men came to condemn, not to know me.'

'There was to be no question of truth.' said Sachiel, taking up the call. 'Gallio's psyker was an assassin. Dante fears the Blessed Angel, he fears the threat that Arkio represents.'

'You have killed our battle-brothers,' Rafen said in a dead voice.

Arkio shook his head, a flicker of hurt in his eyes. 'No, Rafen. None of these men were brothers to me, or to any of us. In their blood I see the real truth of it. Dante denies me.'

From the altar came a strangled choke, and Stele stumbled forward, his face drawn and wet with perspiration. His eyes bulging with effort, the inquisitor gasped for air. Rafen felt the same actinic tang of psyker-taint in the air, just as he had when Stele tortured the Word Bearers prisoner they had captured on Cybele.

'Lord.' Sachiel said. 'What is wrong?'

'The ship…' Stele choked. 'May be more of Vode's kind… More aboard the ship… don't let them…'

Sachiel met Arkio's gaze and the figure in gold gave him a sharp nod. 'I will not put any more of my brethren at risk.' Arkio cocked his head and spoke into a hidden vox pick-up at his neck. *'Bellus*, heed me.'

The shock of his brother's intent startled Rafen. 'Arkio, you cannot–' Sachiel interposed himself between the two siblings, blocking Rafen's outstretched hand.

Arkio glanced at him. The weight of ages glittered in his eyes. '*Bellus*,' he said, his voice instantly carried to Captain Ideon aboard the battle barge, 'Captain Gallio and his men have revealed themselves as traitors to the way of Sanguinius. We shall not suffer the *Amareo* to live.'

Rafen's breath caught in his throat, and for one moment of hope he believed that Ideon would refuse such a command; the brother-captain was a veteran warrior, not a zealot so easily swayed as Sachiel.

Then that hope guttered out and died. 'Your will, Blessed,' said Ideon, his voice distant and mechanical through the vox.

HIGH ABOVE THEM, the battle barge's starboard side rippled with activity as cannon hatches irised open and guns ran out on firing cradles. Missile batteries, lances and lascannon twisted in cupolas and turrets, finding the blade-like profile of the rapid strike cruiser *Amareo* in their sights. In allied space, with no threat to be determined, the cruiser's commanding officer had placed no power to the ship's void shields and so *Amareo* was naked to the unleashed fire of a ship that dwarfed her by fifty magnitudes of tonnage. Ideon did not flinch from the order; the concept of such a thought never once entered his mind. He had seen Arkio with what remained of his own eyes, tasted the coruscating power of his aura through the sensor web of the *Bellus*. The brother-captain had no doubts, and he fired.

It was a small mercy, perhaps, that the men aboard the other ship never saw the attack coming. They died without knowing where the blow had come from, lives snuffed out in an instant. *Amareo* exploded beneath a hellstorm of energy, and once again the battle barge was alone in the skies over Shenlong.

RAFEN SAT AT the edge of the chapel chamber, on the shallow steps leading down to the mosaic floor, and he found he could not move. A distant flash of memory returned to him as he sat there, eyes unfocussed and shoulders hunched. As a boy, when his journey to Angel's Fall was still a dozen cycles away, Rafen had become separated from the tribe during a migration. As a sandstorm had descended on him, the child had become disoriented and lost, wandering through the stinging dust clouds until at last he beached himself on a rocky outcropping and waited for the end to come. Hours passed as he stared out into the roiling storm, and the lad had known then what it was like to be dwarfed by the force of things larger than he was. Against the storm, his flesh and bone were ineffectual; the realisation of his own powerlessness had sobered him. Rescue had come, eventually. His father Axan emerged from the clouds and carried him to safety – but Rafen had never forgotten the hollow knowing that the storm had forced upon him.

Here and now, with the stink of spent cordite and spilled blood still lingering in the air, he felt that sensation all over again. For all his prowess, all the strength and fortitude granted to him as a Space Marine, Rafen felt powerless and weak as events rumbled on over him, crushing him beneath their passage. He looked but did not see the bodies of Gallio, Vode and the others. The Blood Angel felt empty inside, like the tin icons he had seen in the street urchin's box. It was his audacity that had summoned the *Amareo* to Shenlong, his daring to send the secret message to Commander Dante, and now his own warrior-kin were dead. *If I had kept my silence, these men would still be alive*, his inner voice tormented, *their blood is on my hands.*

Sachiel summoned a gaggle of servitors. 'Take these traitors and put them to the torch,' he ordered. 'They shall not soil the presence of the Blessed one moment longer.'

Arkio knelt on one knee close to Gallio's remains, studying the shattered face of the dead man. 'Wait,' he said quietly. His words were almost a whisper, but they carried like a thunderclap. 'Priest, you will harvest the progenoid glands of these men and see them preserved with our fallen aboard the *Bellus*.'

'My lord?' Sachiel blinked. 'But these recreants have proven themselves unworthy of your beneficence – they opposed you.'

Arkio's face was downturned. 'In life, yes. But perhaps in death they can be born anew to the will of Sanguinius.'

Stele mopped his brow with a delicate kerchief. 'You truly are the Angel's Son, Arkio. Even in the face of a turncoat, you show forgiveness...'

The figure in gold armour raised his head; tears glittered on his face. 'I weep for the destiny lost, Lord Stele,' he told him. 'These men might have stood beside us if they had been granted the choice. Instead, Dante has indoctrinated them with his fear. Fear of *me*.'

The inquisitor spied the silent Rafen from the corner of his eye, but he continued on to Arkio. 'Blessed, it is as I had expected it to be. While the will of the God-Emperor would make our species masters of the galaxy, there are those who turn his words to their own selfish ends...' He hesitated, breathing hard. The effort Stele had expended influencing Vode's mind had left him weakened. 'The noble purpose of the Imperium is smothered under the prejudice of men with limited vision... and you, you are the embodiment of a threat to that.' He gestured to the dead. 'Here is proof of it.'

'What does this mean?' Delos voiced the question on the minds of all the Space Marines in the room. Each of them having seen the miracle of Arkio's Emergence themselves, they had no doubts about rallying to his side, but the bloody line they had crossed this day gave each and every one pause. Like the Chaplain, they looked to Arkio for guidance.

Sachiel spoke for him. 'It means there is a schism in our Chapter, brothers. Commander Dante sought not to learn from the Blessed, but to judge him as wanting and put him to the sword. Dante denies the Ascension, and he must be forced to see the error of his ways.'

'I have met the commander,' said Delos, 'and in his eyes I saw a man not easily swayed. If he will not recant and join the banner of Great Arkio, what then?'

Sachiel scanned the room, meeting the eyes of every man there – all except Rafen. 'All those who oppose the dominion of the Reborn Angel are faithless, and they do not deserve to bear the hallowed legacy of Sanguinius. The only reward for those men is to share in the fate of Gallio and his assassins.'

Another Space Marine spoke up. 'What you suggest...' he was hesitant and afraid, 'it is tantamount to civil war. We would be forced to turn against those of our own Chapter.'

'Look around you, comrade brothers,' Stele broke in. 'Your hand has been forced. You have already done that!' The inquisitor stabbed a finger at the broken remains of Vode's force axe. 'They came to kill. They came to murder Arkio in order to preserve Dante's command of the Blood Angels.'

'But Vode was a decorated warrior,' said Delos. 'He would not simply–'

'Brother,' said Arkio, and the Chaplain instantly fell silent. 'The psyker looked upon me and saw nothing but murder.'

Delos gave a slow nod. 'Forgive me, Blessed. As you say, so it is.'

With an abrupt flash of movement, Rafen came to his feet. 'So what now, my brothers? Do we declare a holy war against our own kind? Shall we take up arms and lead an invasion to Baal, or perhaps even to Terra itself?'

'Be careful, Rafen–' Sachiel began, but Arkio silenced him with a look.

'No, no, priest. Rafen's questions deserve answers.'

'We must not follow this path, Arkio.' Rafen's voice was desperate. 'Turn back and reject it. We cannot have war among the Blood Angels – if we fight amongst ourselves, we will be destroyed as surely as if our enemies wiped us from existence.'

Stele took a shuddering breath, watching the two men carefully. The future came to a balance point here in this moment; the inquisitor's delicate plans were caught like a fly in amber. Arkio's response to his blood brother would either release them or shatter Stele's careful machinations utterly.

'As ever, my elder kinsman cuts to the heart of the matter, and for that I am grateful.' He shook his head. 'No, Rafen, I do not wish to sow insurrection among our Chapter. This matter must be resolved before more blood is shed. You are right, we must strive against war.' Arkio turned to Sachiel. 'Dante's proxy wished to bring me in chains to Baal where I could be prodded and toyed with like some addled mutant. I will not submit to that.'

'What do you suggest, Blessed?' the priest replied.

'Select a location in neutral territory,' he ordered. 'Find a world where we can meet face-to-face, on equal terms. Send Dante a message that I wish to resolve this division between us.' He glanced at Rafen, eyes afire. 'I would not have embraced the glory of the Deus Encarmine only to see it spent turning Blood Angel against Blood Angel.'

'Your will be done,' Sachiel bowed. 'And what of our followers among the commoners?'

Arkio came up to his full height and strode toward the ornate glassteel doors that led to the chapel's balcony. 'I will address the people and my Warriors of the Reborn. They deserve to understand what has transpired here today, and to where it may take them.' Honour guards opened the doors as he approached. 'I shall take my thousand with me,' he declared, 'and then on to Baal.' Arkio stepped out into the wan sunlight of Shenlong's day and the adulation of the crowds blotted out all other sound.

Rafen watched his sibling bask in the glow of their reverence. 'Do you seek death?' said a voice close to his ear, and he turned to face Sachiel. The Sanguinary High Priest was standing at his shoulder, his face red with restrained anger. 'It would be my pleasure to provide it to you, if that is what you wish.'

He ignored Sachiel's loaded reductor, there in his grip. All other eyes were on Arkio as he began his speech to the factory city. 'What are you afraid of, priest?' he said in a low voice. 'Is your faith in Arkio so fragile that the breath of my voice could send it tumbling?'

Sachiel's face clouded. 'It is you who is without conviction!' he hissed. 'Even in the face of fact, you refuse to give yourself fully to Arkio's fealty.'

'I took his oath–'

'Did you?' The priest prodded him in the chest. 'Did you take it *in here*?' Rafen hesitated for a split-second, and Sachiel gave a twisted smile. 'I thought not.'

Movement caught the Space Marine's eye; unseen by Arkio and the others, the inquisitor was silently making his way through the shady cloisters of the chapel, toward the copper doors. 'I am a loyal Blood Angel and a Son of Sanguinius,' Rafen said to the priest, in tones filled with absolute conviction. 'That has never been in doubt.'

Now it was Sachiel's turn to hesitate. 'I... I have been the Pure One's most pious servant for as many years as you, Rafen.'

'Yes,' Rafen agreed, 'but piety alone may blind you.' He pushed Sachiel's pistol away and stepped past him, following Stele out of the chamber. 'Remember that, the next time you are drawn to shed another brother's blood.'

Rafen left the priest standing alone. Sachiel's brow furrowed and he cradled the reductor, losing himself in the fine tooling and curves of the sanctified device. In the depths of the Sanguinary High Priest's mind, the smallest splinters of doubt lay waiting.

THE EFFORT OF each step was weighing heavily on Stele as he moved through the shadowed corridors of the fortress, a casual observer would have seen nothing amiss, perhaps a slight hurry in his walk, a deepness in his breathing. He was a credit to his Ordo Hereticus training. The inquisitor was fatigued, far more so than he dared to show to Arkio and the Blood Angels. Their kind were animal predators. They could smell weakness like the scent of an open wound. His performance had reached a critical phase and he could not afford to be seen as wanting.

Stele paused for a moment and patted at his brow once more with his kerchief, rubbing at the aquila electoo. The knots of tension in his muscles were waning, but he still ached from the sheer physical effort of expending his psychic reserves on Vode. He took a deep breath. There had been a flash there in the chapel when Stele's keen psychic focus had slipped, just for a second. The epistolary instantly knew it, and turned his inner eye on the inquisitor, for one brief moment seeing him for what he was – the manipulator behind the unfolding events. Stele's whole plan had almost unravelled right there; if Vode had realised that it was he, not Arkio, that was the source of the dark energies in the room, the inquisitor would have died on the end of Vode's axe. *Thank the warp, it was not so*, he told himself. Stele managed to recover, pressing Vode to turn his ire on Arkio once more, and things had unfolded as they were meant to. While he conjured sheets of invisible force to protect the young Space Marine, Sachiel and the others had followed the patterns laid out for them and taken things to their conclusion. The actors were playing their parts, just as he had foreseen it.

The chambers Stele had taken as his living quarters were nearby, and as he approached he could already feel his strength starting to return; still, he would need to take a resting trance in order to be ready for the next progression. He allowed himself a smile. That was the beauty of his plan, the inquisitor considered, the perfection of all the best schemes. It was not that Stele forced these men to veer from their chosen path by sheer brute coercion. Such a performance lacked subtlety and elan. No, Stele's skills came in the gentle push, the honeyed word in the doubting ear. His expertise was in gently guiding the righteous and honourable into places where it became easy for them to make questionable choices. Men like Arkio and Sachiel. The inquisitor would lead them over one moral line, then another and another, until they were set on a path to damnation.

He had done it many times; he was good at it. But this would be his greatest work. Before it had been men, sometimes nations, that he led astray. Arkio, Sachiel, the Blood Angels... to turn a Chapter of the Emperor's most loyal Space Marines would be his crowning glory.

The door to his chambers opened under his hand, but Stele hesitated. He felt a presence close by. Inwardly he frowned.

Someone was shadowing him, following him through the dim halls of the fortress. Had he been recovered, at his full capacity, he would have sensed the watcher automatically, but his wearied mind still buzzed with fatigue. Careful to ensure he gave no sign of awareness to his observer, he entered the room and allowed the door to remain open behind him.

THE HAND OF *Chaos hides here.* The words turned over and over in Rafen's mind as he kept pace with Stele, careful to keep out of the inquisitor's line of sight. He had seen the way that Vode had stared at Stele in the chapel, the momentary look of pure revulsion on his face. What had the Librarian seen? Rafen's gut crawled at the thought of the mind-witchery that passed between the two men. As much as he disliked the arrogant Sachiel, Rafen could not bring himself to believe that the Sanguinary Priest would ally himself with the Ruinous Powers, and for all the changes that had been wrought on Arkio, his sibling refused to consider him a traitor.

Stele. He lurked in the background, concealed and yet visible, always there with a word or deed when a choice presented itself. Sergeant Koris had died cursing him, and once again Rafen found himself wondering what insight his old mentor had gained in the throes of the deadly red thirst.

The Blood Angel saw the open door and slipped through it. Inside, the room was muted. The last fading streaks of thin, watery daylight managed to push through thick brocade curtains to illuminate a suite of rooms, dissipating as the sun dropped below the industrial horizon. This had once been the domain of Shenlong's governor, and Stele had claimed it as his planetside residence in the days after the death of the Dark Apostle Iskavan. Rafen hovered close to an array of tall tapestries that depicted the history of the forge-world, from its discovery in the distant past to the consecration of the planet as a weapons manufactory.

'Don't stand on ceremony, Rafen.' Stele's voice seemed to come from everywhere at once. 'Come in.'

The Space Marine's face twisted in a scowl, but he did as he was bid. Stele emerged from a pool of shadows on the far side of the wide room. The light from the window rendered him in shades of grey, like a charcoal sketch on dull paper.

'Have you come to kill me, Rafen?' he asked conversationally. 'Do you wish my death?'

Rafen scanned the room for any signs of the inquisitor's hovering servo-skulls and found them humming quietly in the eaves, crystal eyes intent. The needles of small-bore lasguns tracked him as he moved. 'Would your murder end this madness, inquisitor?' he replied.

'Madness?' Stele repeated, taking a seat in a large chair. 'Is that what you see in the plans of the Blessed?' He covered his exhaustion well as he sat.

'Not since the Horus Heresy has Astartes turned upon Astartes, yet I saw the same crime unfold in the chapel.' Rafen's jaw hardened with anger. 'You did nothing to stop it.'

Stele cocked his head and gave a shallow nod without speaking. Slowly, carefully, he began to gather in what remained of his mental fortitude.

Rafen did not notice. 'Is it not the code of the Ordo Hereticus to seek out and purge that which falls from the Emperor's Light?'

'Are you suggesting that Arkio is a heretic, Rafen?'

'I...' The Space Marine faltered at the question, unwilling to voice such a thing. 'His path... It will lead only to darkness and death.'

The inquisitor made a noise of dismissal. 'Consider this, Rafen. Perhaps it is not Arkio who is the apostate, but Dante.'

Rafen's eyes flared with bright fury. 'You dare to profane the lord commander's name?' His hands bunched into fists. 'Perhaps it is *you* who is the agent of disorder here.'

He expected the inquisitor to become enraged, but instead Stele fixed him with a strong, unwavering gaze. There was a look in his eyes that might almost have been pity. 'Comrade brother,' he began, in a fatherly voice, 'we are at a juncture of history, you and I. It is no dishonour to be awed by events such as those that have taken place in recent weeks. Your brother's rise to ascendancy on Cybele, the Emergence that you were witness to in the manufactorium... Lesser men would be broken under the weight of such things.'

Rafen felt his words of reply dying in his throat, his anger fading.

'But you, Rafen, you are at a different crossroads. Your choice is one that no other Blood Angel faces. You cannot go forward without first resolving it.' Stele's voice never rose in volume, but seemed to grow to fill the room, pressing in on the young Blood Angel from all sides. 'You are filled with questions and confusion,' the inquisitor continued.

Unbidden, Rafen nodded to himself. The doubts, the unending distrust that he had carried since the battle for Cybele returned to him all at once. Like a black, suffocating coil, the dark thoughts unfolded from the deeps of his soul. Rafen staggered back a step; suddenly, he felt the consequence of them like a physical force.

'Why do you continue to question your brother?' Stele urged. 'Is it because you truly doubt what he has become, or is it because you are jealous of your younger sibling?'

'No...' Rafen forced the words out of his mouth. 'Father... He...'

Stele's presence seemed to permeate Rafen's perception. 'You look upon him and you feel rejected, yes?' He pointed a sharp finger at the Space Marine, his voice rising. 'You see him resplendent in the golden armour of the Great Angel and cry out *it should have been me*!'

'Yes.' The reply came from nowhere, startling Rafen even as he said it. 'No. I do not... Arkio is not ready!' He staggered backward, his hands coming up to press against his face. Every single doubt and misgiving that had ever plagued Rafen was welling up inside him like a foul surge tide. Clinging wreaths of despair enshrouded him. *I am Adeptus Astartes*, his mind cried out, *I will not submit!*

'But you must,' Stele answered, the inquisitor's voice humming in his very bones. 'You must give up your life for Arkio – don't you understand? It is you that holds him back from true greatness, your influence that ties him down! You always treated him as the lesser, the unready youth, but in truth it was you that feared him.' Rafen was on his knees now, and Stele's tall form arched over him, towering and monstrous. 'You could never admit that his success would be your failure.'

In the canyons of Rafen's mind, he relived the moment when he was rejected at Angel's Fall, when he walked out into the deserts to die an ignoble death rather than face his tribe with his inadequacy.

Stele saw the memory and honed it into a blade, cutting into Rafen's will with all the psychic force he could muster. 'You should have died that day. You should have let him go alone on to achieve his destiny...'

'Yes.' Rafen choked on the word, staggering to his feet under the weight of the suicidal gloom enveloping him. 'Father, I failed you...'

Stele could barely contain the cold smile that threatened to break across his thin lips. With one final effort, he rammed home a black psy-knife of pure misery into Rafen's troubled soul. 'You can still save him, Rafen.'

Save him save him save him save him save him save him save him. The words echoed through his sensorium. 'How?' he wailed.

'Die.' Stele's voice cracked like thunder. 'Die for your brother, Rafen. End your life and free him.'

Free him free him free him free him free him free him free him free him. 'No… no… no!' Suddenly Rafen was running, the corridors flashing past him, the city beyond, crashing through the streets, heedless and broken. *You must die,* said the voice in his head, *betrayer of blood, you must die.*

'I must die,' he wept, falling to his knees.

STELE'S VISION TUNNELLED and he gasped for breath. The rush of his blood and the thumping of his heart sounded in his ears as he struggled to the chair. The effort of pushing Rafen had left him dry, his psionic will draining the very life force from him to maintain the pressure. He fell to the floor in a heap, a guttural, harsh laugh escaping from his lips. 'Rafen must die,' he said aloud, and then sank into unconsciousness.

CHAPTER FIVE

RAFEN RAN.

The streets of the city, most of them still without power after the Chaos invasion, opened up before him. Warrens of twisting stone canyons deep with shadows drew the Blood Angel in. He crossed rooftops in shuddering leaps, blundering through bombed-out pits where workshops had once stood. He stumbled through voids cut in the city by lance fire and sites where Word Bearers had been put to death.

He ran to escape the pain, the black miasma of despair that snapped at his heels, tentacles of darkness always at his back, hungry for him. He was a heedless engine of motion, mind swept clean of nothing but misery.

He could not stop. If he stopped, the melancholy would engulf him and he would be lost, destroyed by the flood of guilt unleashed from his own psyche. What he had witnessed tore at him like a storm of razors. The transformation of his brother, the deaths of his battle-brothers on Cybele and again on Shenlong, all these things weighed and beat him down. The sheer anguish suffocated him. Rafen watched his comrades die around him, unable to stop it. His mind reeled as he remembered every soul he had known extinguished. He wished that it had been him instead of them.

Mother, perished in childbirth. Omeg, his childhood friend dead from shellsnakes. Toph the aspirant, torn open by fire scorpions. Crucius, shot on Ixion. Simeon, boiled alive by plasma. Koris, lost to the thirst. Gallio, gunned down...

Faces, voices, screams, a torrent of them whirled around him. There was some distant part of him calling, some last inviolate corner of Rafen's soul still begging him to have strength and resist, but moment by moment the voice became fainter and fainter. The touch of Inquisitor Stele's psychic force had broken open the place inside the Space Marine where he kept his blackest regrets, and now they were free, boiling through Rafen, drowning him in his own remorse.

Uncontrolled, the Blood Angel found himself falling, tumbling into a steel door. The hatch parted under his weight and Rafen crashed through in a tangle of armour and limbs. Hands clasping his head, he rolled to his knees. Through misted eyes he saw the place where he had come to rest, and a dart of surprise took him for a moment. Around him was a metal-walled chamber, dim and thick with chemical scent. Against one wall, a brass idol of the God-Emperor lay watching him.

'How?' he asked the cloying air. Perhaps it was the hand of the Emperor that had guided him here, perhaps blind chance or some animalistic muscle-memory, but Rafen's headlong flight from the Ikari fortress had returned him to the makeshift meditation cell he had created for himself in the ruins.

Rafen reached out a trembling hand and ran his fingers over the icon; the yellowed metal felt blood-warm to his touch. Under the unblinking eyes of the Emperor, the crushing weight of his guilt came all at once and he let out a moan of anguish, an echoing, feral cry.

'Holy Master, I have failed you. My life... means nothing. I am broken and defeated, my sorrow unbound...'

The Space Marine's hand closed around the hilt of his combat knife, drawing the bright steel of the fractal-edged blade from its sheath. His limbs seemed to be working on their own, unwillingly following the suicidal compulsion laid into Rafen's mind by Stele's dark influence. The tip of the weapon touched the belly of his torso armour as it dipped downward, the blade inexorably drawn to his flesh.

It was someone else working him now; Rafen was a hollow puppet, woodenly moving through actions that the black power of suggestion forced on him. The knife kissed the red ceramite of his chest plate and scratched a course across the armour as his hand drew it upward.

'I am ended...' Rafen's blade was at his neck, the serrated edge dipping into the meat of his throat. Blood pooled in the lee of the knife as the wound opened, running down the gutter of the weapon, across his bare knuckles and wrist.

Pain came then, pain, and the smell of his own vital fluid. The sensations pierced the shroud of despair gathered about Rafen's soul, punching through the fog of his mind. He gasped – and in that moment everything changed.

A trembling sensation came upon the Blood Angel, every muscle in his body throbbing like a struck chord. The dual pulse-beat of his twin hearts rumbled in Rafen's ears, the racing thunder of blood through his arteries suddenly a roaring torrent. Adrenaline heat surged out from his chest to fill his hollow core. He was an empty vessel abruptly filled with molten energy. Saliva flooded the Space Marine's mouth at the thought of rich vitae on his lips. His vision, clouded moments before with morose shadows, was darkened by a red mist of passion.

Rafen shook with the raw power that welled up inside him, letting it wash away the insidious venom of melancholy. He knew this sensation well: it was the precursor to the black rage. The Blood Angel threw back his head, the brilliant white darts of his fangs baring. The red thirst was upon him, warring with the psychic toxins left behind by Stele's potent mind-witchery.

And still his knife was at his throat, the metal cleaving flesh and threatening to sever arteries. One small jerk of the wrist would be enough. A war was being fought inside the Space Marine: rage facing despair, fury versus misery, white-hot wrath crashing against cold, soul-numbing anguish.

'I... will... not... *die.*' Rafen screamed. He had come too far, fought too hard to be felled by his own inner fears. 'I am Adeptus Astartes,' he roared. 'I am the Emperor's Chosen.' Rich blood tricked down his torso armour, staining the white metal wings surrounding the ruby droplet sigil. '*Sanguinius, hear me! I am a Blood Angel!*'

His sight grew hazy as prickles of gold-white light unfolded out of the air around him. Rafen's words choked off in a gasp as a pressure rose inside his skull, pushing at the edges of his perception. He glimpsed a halo of honeyed illumination glitter about the brass icon in the seconds before the light overwhelmed him. Radiance touched his bare skin with delicate warmth, like the kiss of a perfect summer day. Rafen's heart swelled, the pain, the blood, the misery all swept away from him.

His vision collapsed to a single point: a face, a figure, a shape opening there in the void before him, coalescing from the fines of dust in the air itself. It towered over him, made him childlike in comparison; it filled the room even though the chamber could never have contained it. The golden form accreted and took on features – eyes, nose, mouth. Rafen gasped, the thought of it thrilling at his lips.

'Sanguinius…'

This was no pretender, no Reborn Angel, no mere changed man before him. The mellifluent, achingly perfect face of the Blood Angels primarch bore down on Rafen, a vision of the Great Progenitor of his Chapter invoked from the very matter of the blood surging in his veins. Every battle-brother carried an iota of the Pure One inside him. Since the foundation of the Blood Angels, the conclaves of the Chapter's Sanguinary Priests had kept the living vitae of their long-dead master in the sacred Red Grail, and on their induction into the Chapter initiates would drink from a holy cup that held a philtre of this hallowed fluid. Rafen felt that blood within his blood sing out as like touched like. The Crimson Angel ran a hand over Rafen's face and, with infinite tenderness, drew away the bloody knife. Suddenly the blade seemed his again, his body responding to his commands once more and not the suggestions of another.

Rafen lowered his face to the flat of the knife and licked his own blood; the rich coppery taste was strong and heady. The violence within, the clawing feral might of the red thirst ebbed as he drank, receding – and with it went the vision, the gold aura about him disintegrating. Rafen's hand stabbed outward, fingers reaching for his primarch. 'Lord, help me!' he cried. 'What must I do?'

The crystal blue eyes of Sanguinius took on a sad distance, glancing down at the stained weapon in Rafen's hand, then back to meet the gaze of the Blood Angel. Rafen mimicked his master's action, studying the weapon in his grip.

When he glanced up, he was alone. Rafen sat there until sunrise, weighing his knife in his hand and wondering.

* * *

THERE CAME A heavy pounding on the sturdy nyawood doors and it insinuated itself into the mind of Ramius Stele, dragging him unwillingly from a deep, healing slumber. The noise had been going on for quite some time, so it seemed.

Stele turned where he lay on the floor, a dried patch of dark blood from his mouth and nose sticky on his cheek where it pressed to the careworn stone tiles. Swearing a curse beneath his breath, he pulled himself from the ground to a semblance of standing, the sickly weakness in his stomach making him wince. Energy had returned to him, but he still felt lethargic with the effort of his psionic exertions. He gave a slow shake of the head, forcing away such thoughts. It was time for a communion once again, and it would not do for him to show fragility.

Stele strode to the door, wiping away the caked matter from his face, and opened it. A Blood Angels serf reacted with shock as he did so; the servant had been about to knock again and his hand was raised as if to strike the inquisitor. The serf backed off a step, bowing contritely. 'Forgive me, Lord Stele, but I was afraid you did not hear me...'

Stele held up a hand to silence him. 'I was detained with another matter.' If the helot saw any indication of fatigue in his face, then he gave no sign. 'Where is it?'

The Chapter serf tugged at something behind him in the shadows of the corridor, and, with atonal footsteps, a crooked woman came forward, led into the wan light by a rope about her neck. Stele pulled a ragged cloth sack from her head to reveal her face and the serf recoiled at the sight, nauseated. The woman had no eyes; the Word Bearers had taken them. Her ears and nostrils had also been sewn shut, and there on her forehead in a parody of Stele's Imperial aquila electro-tattoo was an eight-pointed star.

The inquisitor nodded. This would be an acceptable vessel. He snatched the rope from the serf and dismissed him. 'Go now. I will send for you later to dispose of the remains.'

The poor unfortunate had not been asked to take the mark of Chaos Undivided willingly. More than likely, she had probably expected to die in the Word Bearers attack. Instead, some subordinate cohort of the Castellan Falkir, the corrupted invader who had taken Shenlong before the Blood Angels arrived, had picked her to serve as a messenger-slave. There were many of these poor wretches still alive in the warrens of the manufactories. Most had been put to death as a mercy soon after their Chaos masters had been routed, but some had escaped into the industrial zones. Locals had taken to hunting the remainder and bringing them to the fortress as some sort of offering, in the way a feline pet might present its master with half-dead prey. When they brought ones that were relatively intact, Stele arranged for them to be quietly kept in the dungeons below the stronghold. Innocents spoiled by the touch of Chaos; their profaned bodies offered much in the way of arcane potential, if correctly harnessed.

Stele released the rope and let the woman wander blindly across the vast room. It amused him to see panic grow on her face, her hands stabbing out in anxious motions, desperately searching for walls that were nowhere nearby. He watched the slave reach the centre of the room and blunder into the ornate table he had placed there. The jar of ichor sitting atop it upended and spilt on her fingers. A quizzical look on her ruined face, she held up a hand dirty with the matter and touched it to her lips – the only sense she still possessed.

Stele smiled; the concoction brewed from dead Word Bearers hearts stung her throat and she choked off a strangulated scream. The slave dropped to the floor and began to melt like hot wax. Bones and organs, bunches of nerves, raw muscle, all of it shifted and changed, shimmering wetly in the light of photon candles as a whispering metamorphosis took place. Presently, the slave stood, and in the dead sockets it grew new eyes with which to look at the inquisitor.

Stele made a theatrical bow. He had seen this parlour trick too many times to be affected by it. An ephemeral, potent splinter of monstrous psionic will was now inhabiting the helot, turning it into a mouthpiece for his hellish cohort full light years distant from Shenlong. 'Warmaster Garand. So nice to see you again.'

The tiny piece of the Chaos warlord's essence examined itself, the molten skin and mealy matter of the messenger. 'A poor frame for such a force as I. It will not last for long.' Even as Garand spoke through a broken throat, the Witch Prince's energy was burning up the life of the slave woman. 'Perhaps for the better.'

'How so?' Stele asked, approaching the possessed form.

'It means we can forgo your usual tedious prattle.' Garand bubbled blood. 'You have been on this blighted sphere for over a solar month, and yet you seem to have made little progress.'

A nerve in Stele's jaw jumped. 'What do you know of it?' he snapped, his fatigue briefly allowing his annoyance to surface. 'Your blunt intellect has little comprehension of the subtlety of my enterprises.' He made a dismissive motion at the helot. 'These communions I am forced to take with you do nothing but divert my attention from the tasks ahead.'

Garand's fleshy avatar gave him a sideways look. 'Indeed?' it mocked. 'And yet it was my, what did you call it, "blunt intellect" that allowed you to cement your position of authority with these boneless human cattle.' The proxy padded over to him, the psionic stink of Garand's mind-spoor clouding Stele's telepathic senses. 'I broke the sacred compact of the Word Bearers codex in order to lay the path for your scheme, man-filth! I sacrificed an entire host for this endeavour. Never forget that!'

Stele's face soured. 'Don't make it sound like such a hardship, Warmaster. You yourself would have taken the head of Iskavan the Hated if he had not died here. He and his ninth host were of no value to the Ruinous Powers.'

Garand made a negative noise. 'But still… I have fulfilled my part of the bargain. You are tardy with yours.' It spat a globule of necrotic flesh on to the floor. 'There are larger plans at work, Stele. Larger than the turning of these mewling Blood Whelps… If you cannot fulfil your responsibilities–'

'I need more time,' Stele snapped. 'Already, events gather their own momentum. Arkio's powers are still unfolding, the faith of his followers grows stronger by the day–'

'You waste your breath explaining it to me,' Garand said, and nodded to the shadows. 'It is not I you must justify your dilatory manner to–'

Stele's breath caught in his throat as something dark and cold fell across the room like a psychic eclipse. A foetor that could only exist in the unreality of the warp entered the chamber; for miles around, plates of food suddenly spoiled, wine turned to vinegar in corked bottles, births came stillborn. In high orbit aboard the *Bellus*, Ulan's blind eyes wept tears of thin blood.

'No,' said Stele, the denial puny, minuscule. The word fell against a black curtain of shapes that hissed and whirred about him.

From every dark corner came insects, not in mad swarms or crazed armies, but in careful, quiet and orderly ranks. There were flies of every size and colour, spiders and beetles by their hundreds of thousands. They came together into a formless mass, and in moments they became an unholy daemon-shape, united by a single hideous intent.

'Malfallax,' Stele spoke the warp-lord's name and bowed his head. 'I had not expected to greet your magnificence.'

'Better this way,' it said, in breathy tones that were chitin wings rubbing against each other. 'Unexpected.' It bent down and licked absently at the dry patch of blood.

Garand's avatar dropped to the floor in genuflection. 'Great Malfallax, Changer and Monarch of Spite. Your presence honours us.'

The daemon did not acknowledge the Word Bearer. 'Ssssssstele.' It savoured the name. 'Our long-held bargain comes to its fruition, but you tarry. Why?'

The sheer psychic presence of the daemon beat at Stele. 'They... cannot be forced, lord. To guide these Astartes from the corpse-god's will to the way of eight requires time and guileful purpose.'

'A luxury you no longer possess,' the creature replied. 'In the Eye, time changes and shifts as all things do. You must accelerate your plans.'

Stele frowned. 'Lord, if we move too quickly, all I have done may become unravelled. Garand's offering will be forfeit...'

On the mention of his name, the Warmaster's avatar interposed itself. Parts of the flesh-form were alight now, crisping and burning. 'He has spoken. You proceed too slowly. You will move forward at once or I will have this world ended and you along with it.'

BAAL. THE PLANET had been green once, hundreds of thousands of years ago, back before the Imperium had existed. Once, lush forests and oceans rich with life had covered the world, but those were forgotten myths now. Their legacy remained in fossil records as the planet moved on, catastrophic forces scouring the surface until it was a fierce sphere of blood-red rock and sand. The name of the world came from the depths of human history, a cognomen that men had once given to a daemonic beast king. Like its namesake, Baal was an unforgiving master, a place that would destroy the unwary and the faithless.

Fitting, then, that the Blood Angels had come here and turned it to their own purpose. Commander Dante crossed the battlements of the fortress-monastery, the constant desert wind tugging lightly at the hems of his robes. Above the horizon he could see the shapes of Baal's moons in the evening sky, their surfaces glittering.

The constant storms of rusty fines in Baal's upper atmosphere made the skies shimmer with a faint pink glow. Dante's eyes ranged down over the landscape, tracing the lines of the Great Chasm Rift to the north and the towing caps of the Chalice Mountains. After millennia, the warrior was still touched by the sight. Baal lived in his heart, as it did in all of his battle-brothers. In the *Book of the Lords*, there was a passage that talked of the planet's birth, as a place created by the God-Emperor to test the faithful. If that were truly the purpose of Baal, then the Blood Angels had succeeded here. They had taken a world that threw death at anything which dared to stride across its surface, and made it their home. Baal would never be tamed – that was a thing for gods to do, not for men – but it had been taught to respect its masters. The harsh environment lived in harmony with its people. It was only here, in the inner sanctums of the fortress, that the ancient and long-passed character of the planet could still be found.

Dante passed through an ornate airlock made of brass and synthetic diamond plates, and into the arboretum. The air was warm and moist, quite unlike the rasping dryness outside; the slightly sweet smell of rich loam reached his nostrils. From soft soil of dun-coloured earth, trees and plants grew toward a domed ceiling made of oval lenses. Each pane was as large as a leviathan's eye, forged by some process lost to the depths of history. Perhaps, in the beginning, the diamond windows had been clear, but now they were scarred white by untold centuries of scouring sand, shedding only a milky, indistinct light across the vast garden.

The Blood Angel walked with care through the riot of foliage, picking his way around the boles of tawny trees. Some of his brethren questioned the value of this place; they asked why it was that valuable servitors be maintained in order to keep the arboretum alive. Dante suspected that they saw the place as some eccentricity of his, a personal diversion for the master of the Blood Angels. Perhaps it was all of those things, but it was also a vital link to Baal's past. Every plant that grew and thrived here was extinct in the wilderness outside. The garden was a portal into deep time, a reminder of how things could thrive, only to become dust as the future encroached upon them. It was a living reminder of life's struggle against the weight of history.

'Calistarius,' Dante said gently as he approached a clearing. Before him, a man in simple prayer robes knelt on one knee, tracing his fingers across the petals of a bed of white flowers.

'My lord,' said Mephiston, glancing up at him. 'I have not heard that name spoken in many years.' The Chief Librarian of the Blood Angels gazed at Dante with hooded eyes, the burning gaze that so transfixed the minds of his enemies at rest. 'I have not been Brother Calistarius for an age.'

The commander studied the face of his friend and comrade. Dante had been there on planet Armageddon on the night that he had emerged from the rubble of Hades Hive, reborn as Mephiston, Lord of Death. Calistarius had been lost to the red thirst and buried alive, thought dead until a vision of their primarch had guided him back to life. 'Forgive me,' said Dante. 'For a moment, my mind took me back to days past. To simpler times.'

'In this place it is easy to lose one's self in ancient history. Others may doubt the merit of this garden, but not I.'

Dante gave a slight nod; the psyker had picked up on his thoughts. 'You sent word you wished to speak with me.'

'Yes, lord. I thought it best we talk alone, less incautious ears or minds catch wind of what I must tell you.' He gestured around. 'I often come here to meditate, commander. The tranquillity of Baal's past smoothes the path into the empyrean.'

Dante's face became grave. He could tell from his old cohort's tone that Mephiston's news would not be good. 'What have you to tell me?'

'Vode's mind was silenced, Great One. Even as I rested here and projected my thoughts into the void, I felt the edge of a ripple from his psychic shriek.'

'Killed?'

'Aye,' Mephiston said grimly, 'and Gallio along with him. Every man we sent to Shenlong, ended in a blink of fire.'

'You are certain of this?' Dante asked.

'The ways of the warp are never fixed,' replied Mephiston. 'Like desert sand, the real slips through my fingers. But on my sword, I tell you. Those men are dead.'

A cold, sickening familiarity touched Dante, one he had known a million times over since his first command as a Blood Angel warrior. He felt the death of each battle-brother as keenly as he had the very first to die under his stewardship. 'How?'

'I can only guess,' the psyker added, 'but if this Arkio is touched by the ways of Chaos–'

'There must be another explanation,' snapped the commander. 'An accident perhaps, an attack by enemy forces...'

Dante's old comrade gave a slow shake of his head. 'No, lord,' he said, with grim finality.

'You would suggest our own kind have drawn blood against us?' Dante growled. 'I pray you are mistaken.'

'As do I,' Mephiston agreed. He was silent for a moment before he spoke again. 'The *Amareo*'s mission will not remain concealed from our brothers forever, commander. Despite my best efforts, word of it spreads among the men. Soon, questions will be asked.'

Dante shook his head. 'I will not reveal news of this "transformation" until we know the truth behind it. If talk of a second coming of the Great Angel grows, dissension in the ranks will follow.'

'And a schism is something we cannot risk.' He met Dante's gaze. 'My doubts are gone, lord. I believe this boy Arkio is a false messiah. Only out of fear would he have killed Gallio's party.'

'But you said that you cannot be sure that is what took place.'

Mephiston frowned. 'Dark threads gather out there. They knit together in a web of deceit and we are caught in them. Shrouded forces, hatreds incarnate are at work manipulating events. This Arkio is at the hub of them, commander.'

'We can only be sure by facing him in person,' said Dante. 'Until then, he remains an unknown, a tarot card unturned.'

The psyker fell silent again, studying the delicate plants at his feet. 'You know this flower, commander?'

'Redkin,' Dante replied. 'It has not existed on this planet in the wild since the thirty-eighth millennium.'

Mephiston ran a bare finger over the tough, rubbery petals of the white flower, the serrated edge of it drawing blood. Instantly, capillaries in the petiole began to absorb the fluid, turning the plant scarlet. 'The flower's roots mesh with those of the others that surround it,' the Librarian said, 'it shares the bounty it gathers.' In a bloom of crimson, the coloration spread across each of the plants in the cluster. Mephiston's fingers closed around the flower in his hand and crushed it, spilling a trickle of his own vitae on the rusty soil. 'Like us, one gives strength to all. But if that unity is broken…' He paused, cocking his head. 'We have company.'

Dante turned at the sound of the airlock opening. A spindly messenger servitor ambled over on clanking mechanical feet. Once it had been a human being; now it was a device in service to the Imperium, mind wiped of any personality, a featureless automaton made of flesh and implanted steel. Its blank face swung left and right, finally locating the Blood Angels commander. 'With your permission, Lord Dante. A message from Shenlong arrives. Your attention only.'

'Speak,' he demanded.

'Via the astropathic duct Ulan aboard the battle barge *Bellus*, Brother-Captain Ideon commanding, protocol omnis octo,' it recited, relaying the trance-speech from the monastery's own psychic communicators. 'The Sanguinary High Priest Brother Sachiel, chosen of the Blessed Arkio, requests an audience with the Lord Commander Dante on the shrine world of Sabien in nine solar days, on behalf of the Reborn Angel.'

'The Reborn Angel,' Mephiston repeated the title with a sneer on his lips. 'This whelp has no need for modesty, it seems.'

Dante was lost in thought for a moment. 'Sabien. I know it well. There was a Blood Angels garrison there, in the worst days of the Phaedra Campaign.' He frowned. 'Many of our kindred shed blood for every metre of that blighted planet.'

'An abandoned monument world,' said the psyker. 'An ideal location for an ambush.' He got to his feet, fire dancing in his eyes. 'Lord, this is so transparent a trap.'

'Of that, we may be certain,' Dante agreed. 'But this priest Sachiel, if he truly speaks for Arkio, knows only too well that I am forced to agree to the meeting.'

Mephiston's eyes narrowed. 'Commander, you cannot think to accept this so-called "request"? If Arkio wishes to meet, he should come here to Baal.'

'He will not,' Dante retorted, 'and I will not risk more lives to bring him under force of arms. No, we must seek the truth about Arkio and determine if he truly is Sanguinius reborn or an impostor.'

'To do that, I would need to turn my gaze upon him, lord.'

Dante nodded. 'And so you will. You will attend me at Sabien and I will have this Arkio answer for his deeds.'

Mephiston shook his head. 'I cannot allow that.'

The Blood Angel gave the Librarian a sharp look. 'Do you defy me now as well?'

'Forgive me, great Dante, but you are the sworn commander of this Chapter. Your place is here, at the throne of Baal. I shall meet with this Arkio, alone. As your second, I cannot allow you to place yourself in such danger.'

Dante went red with annoyance. 'In eleven hundred years I have led my men from the front! Now some child presumes to the godhead over my Chapter and you demand I stay behind?'

Mephiston's iron-hard gaze never wavered. 'If it pleases the lord commander, I am best suited for this endeavour. For all your greatness, you do not possess the warp-sight as I do. My vision will see the heart of this pretender as plainly as day, and I will not flinch from his execution when the moment comes.' He placed a hand on Dante's shoulder, a gesture of familiarity that no other Blood Angel alive would ever have dared to make. 'My lord, when the men learn of this Arkio there will be questions. They will look to you for guidance.'

'And so I must be here to answer those questions.' Dante frowned. After a long moment, he spoke again. 'Very well. Your counsel has never failed me yet, Mephiston, and I will accept it now. On my orders, assemble a force of your most senior brothers and take command of the battle barge *Europae*. I grant you full power to speak on my behalf and that of the Blood Angels.'

The Lord of Death tapped his balled fist to his chest and bowed his head in salute. 'For Sanguinius and the Emperor,' he said.

'For Sanguinius and the Emperor,' repeated Dante.

RAFEN ENTERED THE chapel unseen and moved from the shadows to the altar. He had barely taken a step when Arkio's crystal-clear voice called to him. 'Rafen. I see you.' His sibling stood up from prayer and beckoned him forward. 'Come now. We are alone.'

The Space Marine walked into the dimly lit transept. 'They say that tomorrow Sachiel will choose the thousand and consecrate the Blood Crusade.' His voice was tight with emotion.

Arkio nodded. 'It shall be thus.'

'And how many will die?' Rafen demanded. 'How many more Blood Angels and innocents will perish?'

'Only those who stand against the will of Sanguinius.'

Rafen faltered for a moment. 'Brother, I beg of you. Go no further. I implore you, in our father's name, do not do this! You will lead the Blood Angels into self-destruction.'

At any moment, he expected Arkio to turn on him in anger, to strike him down for his presumption, but instead the golden figure gave him a sorrowful, pitying gaze. 'No, my kinsman. I will free them. With your help, and Sachiel, Stele, all of us, we will begin a new era for our battle-brothers.'

'Arkio,' Rafen felt his voice catch. 'Can you not see the bloodshed that lies ahead?'

His brother turned away, returning to his prayer stance, dismissing him like some irrelevant vassal. 'I am the eye of the infinite, the Deus Sanguinius. If there is blood to spill, then it shall be spilt in my name.'

Rafen found no more words and fell silent. He turned his back on Arkio and walked away.

CHAPTER SIX

IN THE CONFINES of the makeshift arena, their war had raged for days and nights without respite. Some of them had been soldiers in the Shenlong Planetary Defence Force, desperate to regain a little honour after failing so miserably against the Chaos invaders, others were just citizens, dispossessed by the Word Bearers, lost and purposeless in the ashes of their city. All of them had spirits that were wanting, great voids in their hearts that could only be filled by one who could offer them hope.

This Blessed Arkio did; the Shenlongi had believed themselves abandoned by the might of the Imperium. Their prayers for salvation had gone unanswered, and as the Traitor Marines subjugated them, the vile demagogues of the Word Bearers cult mocked them for their loyalty to an Emperor that had turned his back on them. Those were the darkest days. Some had broken under the yoke of oppression and taken their own lives, others casting off their fealty to Terra and embracing the bloody way of the archenemy. The people had faced their fate with gloom, convinced that rescue would never come.

Arkio changed all that. On wings of sacred fire, he fell from the skies and smote the Word Bearers with his Holy Lance. In less than a day, the Reborn Angel and his cohorts swept Shenlong clean of the enemy and liberated her people. They were all too willing to cast aside whatever devotion they had given to a distant ghost atop a throne a million light-years away; all too willing to bend their knee for a god that walked like a man, passing among them in a vision of golden light. Arkio was their rescuer, and they loved him for it.

When the Blessed's priest Sachiel gave word that Arkio was to draw an army from the people, untold numbers of men and women rose to the call. They would be proud to lay down their lives for their new saviour, taking any chance to stand a little closer to his magnificence. There would be a choosing, Sachiel said, the conscription of a thousand souls to join Arkio on his Blood Crusade. Those so ordained would become the Warriors of the Reborn, and for their hearts and souls the reward of life anew was theirs. The penitents spoke in whispers of the far-off world of Baal, the birthplace of the Blessed, where legends said normal men could be transformed into avatars almost as great as he – the Adeptus Astartes. There was no shortage of volunteers.

In the great plaza on the steps of the Ikari fortress they fashioned an arena from fallen buildings, and inside those who dared to aspire to warriorhood took up arms against one another. Only the strongest, the most ruthless would be selected for the thousand. They began their little war, corralled there beneath the mountainous tower, and they fought and fought. Life by life, hour by hour, their numbers dwindled, the survivors nearing the thousandfold as day followed night followed day.

ALACTUS AND TURCIO opened the gate as the Sanguinary High Priest approached, the dawn light gleaming off the white gold on his armour. Within the arena, the melee had grown quieter and more infrequent as the massed battles of the early days had given way to attrition. Hundreds of commoners had perished in those first confused free-for-alls, gallons of shed blood turning the flagstones brown beneath them. Some of the weapons were crude – clubs, axes, huge steel spanners stolen from the factory cathedrals – while others were more deadly. A few of the applicants had projectile weapons, flamers, even lasers, the guns looted from the corpses of war dead and brought here to turn against one another.

As Turcio watched, the Blood Angel could see a firefight in progress between two men, one barely able to carry the heavy stubber in his hand, the other snapping shots back with some sort of small-bore lasgun. The figure with the stubber gave out a war cry and tried to rush his enemy, but the weapon was too bulky, too heavy for an unarmoured human to manage. He stumbled, and the figure with the laser stitched him with hot fire. He sank to the ground, his corpse catching alight.

Sachiel paused at the arena gate and spoke a whispered command into his vox. In reply an air raid warning siren keened from a high balcony somewhere on the side of the fortress tower. The lowing shriek settled over the plaza and silence fell after it. This was the pre-arranged signal; the trial was over. All across the arena fights staggered to a halt and weapons were lowered. Those who could still move emerged from cover, into the open space in the centre of the battlefield. In the makeshift grandstands erected along the walls of buildings bordering the arena, people boiled forward in unrestrained eagerness to see who would be selected.

The siren shut off and Sachiel basked in the quiet. It seemed as if every eye on Shenlong was set on him. The Blessed had charged the priest with the task of making the final choices, and it was a duty he was only too eager to perform. He entered the arena, with Turcio and Alactus at his sides. Sachiel's gaze ranged over the faces he saw around him, all of them bloody and dirty with the effort of fighting. In their eyes was an unquestioning readiness to do anything that he ordered, and the realisation of that made him swell with power. These men would follow Arkio into the jaws of hell and never question.

To think he had harboured doubts about the raising of this army; now it seemed ridiculous to him. Of course, these were only mere men, no match for the might of a Space Marine like him, but still this helot battalion would have its purpose on the field of conflict. The fact alone that commoners were willing to sacrifice their futures for Arkio spoke volumes for the power of the Blessed. When the Blood Crusade began in earnest, the ranks of the Warriors of the Reborn would swell to ten, twenty times this size. His shook off all thought of his previous hesitancy. Who was he to question the wisdom of the Blessed?

A movement caught his eye and looked down to see a straggle-haired female as she tried to rise to her feet. She could not do it; livid, weeping wounds along her side had opened her to the air. Sachiel studied the injury with a practiced eye. A Space Marine might have been able to survive such a cut, but a normal human would have no chance at all. The woman met his gaze, and there in her eyes was an entreaty so pure and heartfelt it gave the priest pause. He stooped over her.

'Who are you?' he asked.

'Muh-M-Mirris,' she coughed. 'Mirris Adryn.'

Sachiel noted the remains of a small pennant badge on her shoulder. The Shenlongi had a tradition whereby the cadre and rank of a citizen would be displayed through a set of knotted ribbons on their clothing. The woman wore the colours of a mother of three, a teacher. 'Mirris,' he said gently. 'Your children are proud of you.'

'Yes.' She forced a smile, tears streaming down her face. She knew death was coming, and that she would never fulfil the dream of joining Arkio's cohort.

'Let me give you a gift,' began Sachiel, and he drew his reductor from his belt. 'Do you desire the Blessed's Peace, Mirris Adryn?'

'Lord, the offering of the reductor is only for Astartes–' said Alactus, his face a grimace.

Sachiel silenced him with a look. 'All those who serve the Reborn Angel shall share in this.'

Mirris's eyes shone, accepting the benediction. 'Yes, lord. I wish it.'

He gave her a gracious nod and shot her in the heart. The blunt-headed titanium bolt was designed to punch through the hardened ceramite and plasteel of a Space Marine's power armour and pierce the bone cage projecting the organs within, it was the final, honourable solution for a battle-brother too close to death for recovery. Against normal, unenhanced flesh it blew a cavity in the teacher's chest as big as Sachiel's fist. With care, he closed Mirris's eyes and stood, wiping away the backwash of her blood from the device. 'Even in death, the thousand will serve the Blessed as a monument to his righteousness,' he said, his voice clear and hard as it carried across the arena.

Turcio stared at the dead woman, the faint smell of her cooling blood reaching his nostrils through the grille of his armoured helmet. The tang of the scent-taste touched a deep and primal chord inside him. Battle would be coming soon.

Sachiel stepped forward boldly, holstering the reductor and spreading his hands wide. He moved through the crowd of bedraggled and worn fighters, touching some on the shoulders, nodding to others. Each one that he indicated bowed in return, and those around them shrank back to see the greatness in their midst. Man by man, Sachiel chose the thousand. Those that fell short of the benediction watched in mute silence, others breaking into tears. Alactus saw two men place guns in their mouths and end their own lives rather than accept the failure.

In the middle of the arena was the gutted hulk of a Word Bearers Land Raider, a burnt box of warped metal and bony protrusions killed in the opening salvoes from the *Bellus*. He climbed atop the ruined vehicle to address the people before him.

'Your lives are over,' he told them. 'Whatever you were before this moment, whatever your words and deeds before this day, now they are nought but vapour. You are dead and you are reborn. You are the thousand.'

A ragged cheer erupted from the men in the arena, quickly picked up by the watchers in the stands and the streets beyond. The sound carried like a wave, and Sachiel fancied that he could hear the whole of the planet crying out. 'You are the first to bear the honour of the Warriors of the Reborn, the chosen of Arkio the Blessed, the servants of the New Blood Angel. Your names will be carved into history alongside the legions of Sanguinius, alongside the name of Arkio himself!'

The thousand rattled their weapons and sent shots into the sky, a clattering clarion of thanksgiving. 'Mark this day well,' he told them, 'for it shall never come again. In the ages, men will look back to Shenlong and see you all as a beacon of principle and loyalty. They will know you as I do – as heroes of the wars to come.'

The roar came again, and this time it split the air like rolling thunder.

A WRY SNEER formed on the inquisitor's lips as the noise penetrated the stained glass windows of the chapel. The shouting had such force that the ancient panels vibrated under each exultation, and the priest's rhetoric made the sound rise and fall like a conductor directing an orchestra. He considered Sachiel with cold amusement; all men bore weaknesses, even such preternatural superhumans as the Space Marines, and the key to manipulating them was to isolate and exploit those defects. For men such as the late Sergeant Koris, it had taken more application than others, and with Rafen the effort had almost killed him – but he fully expected to hear of Arkio's brother soon, perhaps to be found dead in some dingy corner of the city after taking his own life.

Stele had been forced to drive Rafen into the depths of his own despair to control him, but Sachiel was a different story. A supremely arrogant man among an arrogant breed, the priest's touchstone was his self-superiority. Stele discovered that in his youth, Sachiel had been born into the closest thing that Baal Primus had to aristocratic nobility. A highly-placed warrior tribe with many dominions on the First Moon, he viewed his ascension to the hallowed ranks of the Blood Angels as a matter of course, and Stele had no doubt that Sachiel imagined a future with his hand on the command of the Chapter in the centuries to come. Stele had worked carefully to cultivate Sachiel, over the years of the *Bellus*'s mission into ork space to recover the Spear of Telesto, teasing out the thread of vanity that lurked inside him, feeding it and nurturing his pretension. He had allowed Sachiel to advance quickly in rank and in turn gained a trusting ally. Combined with the priest's fanatical devotion to the cult of Sanguinius, Stele had an agent who would willingly further his plans without ever considering the true motives behind them. As long as Stele kept his purpose cloaked in the mantle of the primarch's rebirth, Sachiel would follow him unflinchingly.

He looked away from the window. Arkio was not present, and to his irritation, the honour guard stationed at the gate to the inner crypt refused to let the inquisitor enter. The young man was in there once again, communing with the Holy Lance. In truth, Arkio's affinity with the archeotech weapon was a source of some concern to Stele. He found himself wondering what secrets the device held, secrets that only someone with Astartes blood would ever be able to unlock. The Blood Angel was meditating in the sanctum, hoping to catch some fragment of his primogenitor's soul from the weapon Sanguinius had once called his own. Stele gave a silent entreaty to the Ruinous Powers that he would find no such thing. If Arkio began to exhibit signs of dangerous independence, all Stele's carefully-wrought plans would be for nothing.

Another lusty roar brought his attention back to the crowds below. Sachiel was building to a crescendo now, unleashing a blazing tirade.

IN HIS HAND the priest held the copper chalice that was the symbol of his high office. He thrust it aloft, and the dawn sun glittered off the replica of the great Red Grail. It held Sachiel's gaze for a moment. One day, he told himself, I will carry the true Red Grail itself, even if I have to wrestle it from Corbulo's dead fingers. The naked avarice in his thoughts sent a thrill through the priest. It was a hidden desire, something he would never have dared to speak of openly – and yet suddenly he felt empowered by it, the daring of such dissension making him bold. The thousand bowed their heads under the shape of the chalice.

'The Blood of ages flows through us all,' he said, phrases from the *Book of the Lords* bubbling up inside him without conscious thought. 'The Sons of Sanguinius will rise to take the galaxy from all those who oppose order and light.' They cheered him on, frenzied and wild. 'The Blessed lights the path, we must lead the way along it and welcome those who praise his name!'

'Arkio!'

'*Arkio!*'

'Praise him!'

Voices all around were raised in adulation. 'We bring light to those who see the truth, and all-consuming fire to those who deny.' Sachiel slammed the grail to his breastplate, tapping it to his hearts. He was shaking with raw emotion. 'Heed me. I am the right hand of the Reborn Angel. I give you all his call to glory. Take up arms, Warriors of the Reborn, take up your weapons and make ready for war.' Sachiel threw back his head and bellowed to the sky. 'This day the old order dies. This day we are *all* reborn anew. This day we begin the Blood Crusade!'

'Arkio! Arkio! Arkio! Arkio!' The chant went on and on until it filled the air.

DESPITE THE BRIGHTNESS of the morning, Rafen could see only shadows. From the roof of the fortress he watched the priest continue his bombast, a tiny figure in red and white he could blot from his sight with the thick of his thumb. There was no silencing his voice, though, every word Sachiel said was being broadcast through the vox network of the Blood Angels and the telegraphs of Shenlong's city-sprawls.

'Those men who seek to control us, we disavow them!' came the priest's cry in his ear-bead, the sound of his voice on the wind reaching him a split-second later. 'The Imperium is choked with petty bureaucrats and debased fools, weaklings who corral the destiny of mankind laid down by the Emperor. Sanguinius knew this. He died in the war with the arch-traitor Horus so the Emperor might live!'

Rafen's lip curled in a sour sneer; Sachiel was warping the truth to suit his sermonising. The priest continued, working himself and his audience into a frenzy. 'But now the Pure One has returned to us, and his sight is unfailing. He came to us because this plague of deficiency has stretched across the stars, even to poison the very highest office of the Blood Angels themselves. We cannot stand by any longer and allow the will of our Chapter, our species to be dictated by impotent men. Now is the day for action, in Arkio's name!'

The crowd roared his brother's name, sending a shudder through the rock. Rafen glanced down at the knife in his hand, still stained with his own dried blood. Hours ago he had been within a heartbeat of taking his own life, and now he was again, but this time it was by his own choice.

'We abandon the rule of these so-called Adeptus Terra!' Sachiel bellowed. 'We deny the dominion of Dante. We find him wanting. From now on, we answer only to the command of the Blessed!' The crowd boiled around the priest and the thousand, demanded answers, begging him for a mandate. They wanted to be told what to do, they would not be complete without an edict to follow. 'Warriors, I charge you. You will stand as cohorts to the Blood Angels aboard the *Bellus*, the sacred flagship of the Blood Crusade. Together we will face Dante and excise him so that Arkio may take his rightful place as master of the Chapter!'

'Vandire's oath...' Rafen felt the impact of the words like a physical blow. He had never doubted that sooner or later he would hear such heresy uttered, but still when it came it made him feel like vomiting. Sachiel stood there advocating murder and sedition, and to Rafen's eternal shame there were battle-brothers who took up the call. All at once he felt tarnished and humiliated, ashamed to admit that he shared blood with these addled turncoats.

'Baal shall come to our fold,' Sachiel roared, reaching a climax. 'All Blood Angels and successors will bend the knee to Great Arkio, or face oblivion.' The answering cry blotted out everything, and Rafen's hot shame cooled into an icy anger. *Could none of these blind fools see it?* As clear as the day, it was there before them, masquerading in comrade's clothes, appealing to their baser natures, their fears and secret hopes.

'Chaos.' Rafen spat the word from his mouth. The hand of the eightfold star moved Sachiel and the others like mindless pawns across a vast game board, marshalling them for ill deeds so huge they were beyond the reckoning of these blinkered, misguided fools. 'Curse me, but I will *not* let this go any further.'

'Brother?' said a voice behind him, and Rafen spun about abruptly. He was caught unawares, his own dark thoughts and the rage of the crowds distracting him. Lucion approached him, a questioning look on the upper half of his face where it protruded over the half-mask of his breather plate. The Blood Angels Techmarine paused, his arms at his sides but the mechanical servo-limb on his back still twitching with concern. 'What did you say?'

Rafen glanced from the knife in his hand, back to Lucion in his armour of red ceramite and cog-tooth gunmetal trim. 'Arkio is no messiah,' he told the Blood Angels Tech-priest. 'My poor brother is an oblivious catspaw.'

Lucion's face went white with shock. 'How can you say such a thing? You, of all men, the sibling of the Blessed.'

'How?' Rafen repeated, advancing on the Techmarine. 'I say it because I am the only one on this desperate world with eyes still clear enough to see.'

Brother Lucion backed away toward the service platform running the height of the Ikari fortress. 'No, no,' he waved all three of his limbs in the air before his face, as if he could banish Rafen's utterance like a nagging insect. 'You are mad.'

Rafen produced his bolter and aimed it squarely at Lucion's forehead. 'On the contrary,' he told him. 'I fear I am the last sane man.' The black tunnel of the weapon's maw never wavered. The Space Marine felt an odd kind of calm sweep over him as the final parts of his plan fell into place. Since the day this madness had begun there on Cybele, a slow-burning certainty had been building in Rafen's soul. In the marrow of his bones he knew the rightness of it, and now it had come to a head. The fear, the constant dark fear that it would be by his hand that Arkio would perish was swept away. As he studied the confused face of the Techmarine, Rafen decided that he would take his own life, and that of every wayward mortal and deceiver that had strayed from the path of light. 'The beating heart of this fortress, the core. You have spoken with its machine-spirit.'

Lucion gave a slow, wary nod. 'Only in the most cursory fashion. I do not fully understand the ways of the reactor-spirit, but–'

He gestured toward the elevator platform with the gun. 'You will take me to it, or I will kill you where you stand.'

THEY DESCENDED THROUGH the interior of the conical tower in the open metal cage of the lift. Lucion whispered a quick litany over the controls and, with a squeak of iron on iron, the platform began a controlled fall past level after level. Rafen kept the Techmarine in his sights, never allowing his bolter to shift from a point targeted at Lucion's skull.

A memory flashed through Rafen's mind, of a similar elevator in the planetary defence bunker on Cybele. He and Lucion had been there as well, Arkio and Sachiel too, dropping into the dark with vengeance on their minds. It seemed like so long ago, as if years and not weeks had passed between then and now. For a moment, the weight of his weariness threatened to come upon him like a heavy cloak, but Rafen shook it away with an angry blink of his eyes.

Lucion was talking to himself. At first Rafen thought he was praying, or worse, using his vox to call for help. 'It's a test,' the Techmarine was saying aloud, giving voice to his thoughts, 'This is a loyalty test. The Blessed is testing my devotion.'

'Would you do anything he asked?' said Rafen.

'Of course,' Lucion replied instantly, as if the answer were as plain as the service stud on his brow. 'He is the Blessed.'

Part of Rafen felt hate and antipathy for his battle-brother as he listened to Lucion's answer. Perhaps, in the weaker minds of ordinary men, it was unsurprising that the commoners took up the cause of Arkio's supposed divinity, but to see it so readily accepted by the rank and file of his own Chapter sickened him. 'Has it ever occurred to you, brother, that you make a grievous error in venerating him?'

'Why would I think such a thing?' Lucion retorted. 'By the grace of the Omnissiah, Sanguinius has been restored to us.'

All the anger that had been building in Rafen for weeks suddenly found an outlet and he snarled at the Techmarine. 'He sprouts wings and suddenly he is a god-prince? Are you so credulous that you cannot see past the glitter of the gold armour?'

They had been travelling down in near darkness for several minutes, and so Rafen could only see glimpses of Lucion's face. Conflicting emotions danced there for a moment before he nodded to himself. 'A test,' he repeated. 'I will not be found lacking, you may carry my word of that to the Reborn Angel himself.'

With a clatter of metal, the elevator halted. 'Fool,' Rafen said under his breath, and motioned to the door. Unconcerned that he still had a gun trained on him, Lucion opened the wire-mesh and walked forward into the sub-level of the fortress. A spotlight mounted on his shoulder snapped on, and Rafen followed the bobbing blob of sodium-white glare.

The Techmarine carefully removed a ring of prayer beads from a rotary lock and powered open a series of thick steel hatches. Inside, there were consoles and panels of such diversity and intricate workings that Rafen was instantly reminded of the *Bellus*'s bridge deck. 'A question,' he said to Lucion. 'Which one of these does the machine-spirit for the power core inhabit?'

Lucion frowned, then pointed at a large, ornate module. 'Here. Although the spirit-programme extends itself out through the entire reactor system, tending to the fusion heart, the cooling factors, the regulatarium...'

Rafen didn't understand most of the tech-priest's terminology, but he grasped enough for his purposes. He drew in a breath. 'The power-spirit. I want you to kill it.'

Lucion blinked. 'Did I mis hear you? Rafen, perhaps you are taking this test too far, but I cannot–'

He shook his head, raising the bolter. 'No test, priest. Do as I say.'

The Techmarine's face drained of colour. 'What you ask is madness, brother. Even if I could, such a deed would enrage the fusion core. It would reach critical potentiality in moments and detonate with enough force to punch a hole in this planet. We would all be destroyed!'

'Arkio, too?'

At last Lucion understood what Rafen's intentions were. 'Oh, Holy Terra, no. Brother, please! I will have no part of this.'

He began to babble and Rafen tuned him out; the tech-priest would not assist him any further. He nodded at the console. 'This one, yes?' Without waiting for confirmation, Rafen raised his gun and unloaded a full clip of bolt-rounds into the device. Lucion screamed, his voice lost in a sudden clarion of whooping sirens.

The Techmarine staggered forward, shaking his head. 'Wha-what have you done? What have you done?'

Rafen reloaded his weapon, slamming a fresh clip home. He was trying to find an answer for the priest when the rush of metal-shod feet signalled the arrival of more men. Figures in red armour appeared at a hatch on the opposite side of the room, visible through the smoke from the console and the strobes of warning lanterns.

'We heard gunfire–' one of them shouted.

'Traitor!' howled Lucion. 'Rafen has turned against us!'

The automatic reaction of the Space Marines was to raise their weapons and fire. Rafen wheeled away, letting off a trio of wild shots as he went through a tuck-and-roll out of the access hatch to the lift shaft. Stabbing streaks of tracer cut through the control chamber and Lucion was hit in the crossfire. He spun in place and stumbled against the wrecked console.

Rafen made it to the metal cage as the other Space Marines dived out of the hatch after him, bolters chattering. Pushing away all thoughts that his targets were fellow Blood Angels, he fired back. Return fire blazed over his head and struck part of the lift's cabling, severing it in a blare of noise. Rafen expected the cage to drop suddenly into the stygian dark at the bottom of the shaft, but the opposite happened, the bolts cut into the counterweight control, and suddenly the lift platform shot upward, trailing streamers of sparks. The acceleration threw Rafen to the deck and pinned him there as the lift raced head-long toward the circle of light above him.

Inside the chamber, Lucion inched himself forward, using one hand to keep his intestines and preomnor organ from spilling out of his belly wound. Here, surrounded by the lights and sounds of the Omnissiah's most holy creations, the Tech-marine felt alive even as his blood leaked from him in brilliant red runnels. He took his other hand and tossed away his gauntlet, so that his last sensation would be the touch of his flesh against the sacred technology. Lucion gripped the thick switch rod beneath the rune that read: 'Emerg. Scram.' in the old tongue and turned it. With a sullen flicker, the lights inside the fortress winked out as Lucion cut off the fusion reaction before it could become critical.

'No victory for you, turncoat,' he gasped, 'no victory...'

THE TECH-PRIESTS insisted on re-consecrating the room before they would set to work in it, and that took the better part of the day, but as Shenlong's feeble sun began to dip beneath the horizon, the Ikari fortress and the district around it erupted with light and power once again, and the people cheered for Arkio's beneficence in saving them from the darkness and cold.

Their idol did not hear their thanksgiving through the veil of rage that shrouded him. 'Answers!' he thundered at Sachiel, the sheer momentum of his anger rocking the priest back on his heels. 'I demand answers. What warpspawn filth could it be that would dare to enter my fortress and render it impotent? Tell me.'

Stele smoothed his formal robes as he entered, giving a cursory bow. 'I shall do so, Great Arkio, but I must warn you. The news is hard.'

'Hard?' he spat, turning from Sachiel to stalk across to the inquisitor. 'You think me some child you must keep insulated from the ills of the world? Tell me, Stele, or I'll rip it from you.'

The force of the youth's words actually made Stele stumble for a brief moment. The awful light of the black rage danced in Arkio's eyes, turning the patrician, handsome face into that of a fanged, angered god. Arkio's aspect mirrored the sacred tapestry of Sanguinius in his blood-thirst that hung in the cloisters on Baal. 'Lord, I have prepared a shuttle to take us both to *Bellus*. It is not safe here on Shenlong for you any more,' Stele began, recovering his poise. 'You will understand my reluctance when I explain myself.' He gestured at the photon candles around the room. 'The cowardly saboteur in our midst, the viper at our breast attempted to smother the will of the machines that empower this edifice. Had he succeeded, he might have caused a catastrophe.'

'Explain, lord inquisitor,' Sachiel ventured, earning himself a leaden look from Arkio.

Stele continued, finding the meter of his performance. 'Were it not for the selfless courage and sacrifice of Brother Lucion, the machine-spirit would have become turbulent, perhaps to unleash the fire of the atom from its heart.' He took a calculated pause. 'The Ikari fortress and all living things for six kilometres in every direction would have been immolated in a nuclear firestorm.'

'Who did this?' Arkio hissed. 'A rogue Word Bearer? One of Iskavan's host that escaped the net of our execution squads?'

The inquisitor bowed his head sadly. 'No, Blessed. It sickens me to say that a Blood Angel was the culprit.'

Arkio froze like a statue, his wings snapping rigid. Behind him, Sachiel took a cautious step closer. 'And his name, Lord Stele?' asked the priest.

'I suspected there was an apostate in our midst when the mind-witch Vode arrived with Gallio and his other assassins,' Stele sneered. 'I have since learned that the vox of the late Brother-Sergeant Koris was used to send a message to Baal to summon them. They came only because the betrayer in our midst called out to that fool Dante, and bid him send killers to end you, Great Arkio.'

'A man still loyal to Dante, to the old order, here?' Arkio's voice wavered, incredulous, so sure of his own majesty. 'After all the miracles I have enacted?'

Stele nodded. 'But graver still is his identity, Blessed.'

'Name him.' Sachiel snapped. 'Name this treacherous bastard and I will have my personal honour guard hunt him down and tear him apart like a prey beast.'

The inquisitor wanted so badly to smile; but that would have spoiled the act. 'My lord, the traitor is your brother. The traitor is Rafen.'

The roar of inchoate anger that erupted from Arkio's throat struck like an elemental force, echoing across the city zones in baleful thunder.

CHAPTER SEVEN

THE STREET WAS alive with gunfire, shots clipping at Rafen's heels, whining off the cobbles to punch craters in the walls. The Blood Angel made a daring move, leaping off a low wall to launch himself behind the cover of a cargo pod. He snap-fired a burst at his pursuers, not expecting to do any more than make them keep their heads down.

Rafen glimpsed them as fleeting images, the red of their armour matching his, the brilliant gold of their helmets catching the light. Sachiel's honour guard had caught him in the alleys and he had led them on a merry dance through the warehouse district. Each time they tried to box him in, he found a route out of their closing net, but each escape was becoming more difficult than the last.

He checked the sickle magazine on his bolter, half-empty. Rafen frowned. The gold-helmeted troopers were wearing him down, making him waste precious ammunition. There were simply more of them than there were of him, and sooner or later Rafen would become too fatigued or too dis-tracted to fight them all. There would have been a time when would have relished the chance to fight against the elite of the Blood Angels, testing his skills against them in a wargame – but this was no exercise, and the battle-brothers who dogged him did not bear harmless marker shells in their guns. The honour guard had been given one order – to capture him, dead or alive.

Rafen chanced a quick look around. In this part of the factory city ponderous monorail hauliers carried crates of shells and warheads back and forth between store yards and assembly lines. Tall construction towers climbed into the dirty sky, dwarfing the blunt wedges of the fabrication barns. He considered his options – unless he could find a way to escape Sachiel's men, they would run him into the ground. It was taking all his effort just to stay one step ahead of them, and a single error on his part would turn everything against Rafen's escape. Shots rang off the exterior of the cargo module as the honour guards found his range. A surge of heat pressed at his back as a plasma blast burnt a wide hole in the metal. He had seconds to make a decision.

Rafen's eyes fell on an enclosure surrounded by racks of missile tubes. The building was dark and silent, probably serving as a temporary storehouse for the munitions. It would do. The Blood Angel took his last smoke grenade and flicked off the pin with his thumb. Dropping the metal egg, he launched himself from cover and into a full-tilt run. He heard shots cracking after him, and then the hollow crump of displaced air as the grenade exploded. A thick veil of metallic haze full of complex chemical strings emerged and filled the canyon of the street. The honour guard came on, moving slowly through the smoke, the visibility of their helmet optics curtailed sharply by the discharge. Their heads bobbed in silent conversation, messages flickering between them on an encoded frequency that Rafen's vox could not read.

Beyond them, Rafen threw his shoulder into a wooden doorway and it splintered under his weight. He dashed inside to be greeted by a forest of warheads ranging back through the building. Hellstrikes built for the wing roots of Lightning fighters and Marauder bombers were bound like cordwood. There were the fat cigars of Manticore missiles, mounted on wooden stays ready to be loaded on firing platforms. The shells of incomplete Atlas-class megaton bombs stood vertically on their aerofoil fins, the unfinished warheads almost scraping the supports holding up the corrugated iron roof. Rafen shouldered his bolter and wove through the inert steel trunks, slipping deeper inside.

Sachiel would never stop hunting him, that much was certain. Rafen had taken his chance to end this madness once and for all in the reactor core, but his spur-of-the-moment plan had collapsed. He had stood for long seconds on the roof of the Ikari fortress, waiting for the eruption of fusion fire to consume him, but it never came. Once again, he found himself running, and this time there was an entire planet of zealots at his heels. Rafen needed to gather his wits, to plan his next move, but as long as the golden-helmed troopers chased him he would be forced to stay on the defensive. Sachiel would only rest when Rafen was dead – and so he would have to find a way to die... for the moment.

There was a rattle of metal above, and the Blood Angel froze, for a moment believing that the honour guard were coming across the roof for him; but then the sound grew into a rushing, chattering roar and he realised it was the rains. Shenlong's rust-brown skies opened, releasing a downpour of polluted water that clattered off the metal roof of the manufactorum. Runnels of thin, russet liquid penetrated through breaches in the corrugated iron, pooling on the stone floor. Rafen caught the noise of heavy boots splashing through shallow puddles.

Sachiel's men followed him into the warehouse, holstering their guns as they entered. A gesture from the veteran sergeant commanding them was the only order they required, and as one they drew their close combat weapons and spread out to search the building. None of the Blood Angels would dare to discharge a bolt or beam in here. A single stray round could end all their lives in a heartbeat if it struck a live warhead.

Rafen moved. On a raised catwalk he located a set of unfinished and skeletal Manticores on a cradle. With a rough jerk, he ripped free the metal petals protecting the inner detonator unit, exposing it to the air. Like most of the other missiles in the store yard, the half-built Manticore munitions were empty of their volatile promethium fuel and still lacked the dense explosive matrix that would give them their murderous power – but the detonator rods were in place, and those alone were the equal of a dozen krak shells. Rafen tore fibrous wires from the missile's innards and used them to tie a quartet of frag grenades in place. His makeshift bomb was almost complete when the drumming of the rain was joined by a new sound – the ripping snarl of a chainsword.

Rafen reacted instantly, barely dodging the blow from the melee weapon. The honour guard's strike flashed past him with a blare of tungsten-alloy teeth, cleaving the wood of the cradle into a whirlwind of spitting splinters. He rolled back as the Space Marine struck out again, rebounding off a stanchion. In the confines of the catwalk gantry, Rafen had little room to manoeuvre and the tip of the chainsword blade cut into his armour, skittering off the chest plate and away. The blow left a finger-wide channel in his wargear.

'Filthy apostate.' snarled a voice from inside the gold helmet, 'You'll bleed for your perfidy against the Blessed!' Rafen parried a third lunge with an ironwood rod he snatched from the cradle, but the shimmering chain-blade bisected his substitute weapon. The Blood Angel pressed his free hand to his helmet, initiating a vox link to the other hunters in the warehouse. 'I have him. Form on me–'

Rafen sprang forward before he could finish the sentence, hands clawing into the shoulder pads of his opponent. With a sudden downward motion, Rafen butted the honour guard across the bridge of his helmet's nose, cracking the optic lenses. The shock of the blow staggered the Space Marine; Rafen was too close for the attacker to turn the sword on him, and he stumbled backwards. The honour guard's right foot slipped back along the decking and into space where the gantry ended. His balance fled and the Blood Angel fell away from Rafen with an angry howl, the chainsword tumbling from his fingers.

The other Space Marine collided with a nest of tool racks and slammed into the stone floor with a flat crash of sound. Winded, he still had enough impetus to draw and fire his bolt pistol, sending a spray of shots back up at the catwalk, in his fury ignoring the risk of a ricochet. Rafen recoiled and grabbed at a knife-switch set on the gantry, yanking it downwards without conscious thought. The release opened a set of clamps holding a drum of Hellstrikes above them, and the canister fell the height of the warehouse, flattening the honour guard beneath it like the blow of a steam hammer.

Rafen shook off a dizzy, sick sensation as he watched the Space Marine twitch and die under the tonnage. It had all happened so fast. 'Primarch forgive me,' he whispered, his blood running cold. 'I have killed a battle-brother...' He had always known this moment would come, from the very instant that he had heard Sachiel decry Dante and exhort the Blood Angels to turn on their heritage, but nothing had prepared him for the physical shock it brought with it. The blood of a Blood Angel was on his hands. *And he will not be the last,* Rafen admitted to himself.

A voice cried out from below him, and Rafen glimpsed red armour and gold masks flashing between the featureless greys of the rocket fuselages. 'There!' came the shout, 'Above. Close in on the traitor and take him.'

Traitor. Rafen felt dislocated from reality to have that hated brand turned on him, but in his beating heart he knew the reverse was true. He stooped, dialling the fuse setting on his grenades, and yanked the firing pin. Bolt-rounds hissed past his shoulders; the honour guards had clearly thrown caution to the wind after he killed one of their number.

Rafen ducked behind one of the inert Atlas bombs and pressed his shoulder into it, rocking the tubular fuselage on its pallet. The tall metal pipe wallowed and shifted danger-ously. He threw himself at it again and the weight of the Atlas shifted suddenly, tilting away from him. Rafen staggered back along the gantry as the hollow tube fell against another of its kind, in turn knocking another off its base. The Atlas hulls rang like bells as they impacted each other, and they tottered like giant ninepins, ripping through stanchions and scattering Sachiel's men beneath them.

In the confusion, Rafen grabbed a chain dangling from the support beams and swarmed down it, swinging to land in a ready stance on the stone floor. He threw a last look at the gantry where his jury-rigged time bomb lay counting down the seconds and sank to his knees. There was a circular grate in the floor, surrounded by small rivers of rainwater pooling from every part of the building. Digging his fingers in the metal grid, Rafen let out a cry of effort and pulled at it. Aged bolts gave way in snaps like breaking bone.

Any moment now. Tossing the grate aside, Rafen pitched for-ward into the murk of the drainage channel, where fast-flowing floods the colour of tilled earth raced by, swelled by the sudden downpour. He fell into the grip of the sewer water and let it drag him away, scraping his armour across muck-encrusted walls.

The honour guards were reaching for him even as the igniters in the frag grenades burnt down to nothing. The explosives blew apart in a ball of orange thunder, catching the detonators inside the Manticores in sympathetic annihilation. In a tenth of a second, the missiles detonated, rippling fire into cases of battle-ready rockets. Flame set flame, fire birthed explosion, and the entire manufactorum ripped itself to pieces in a blood-red hellstorm.

Kilometres away in the Ikari fortress, a wall of noise cracked the ancient glass of the chapel window in a dozen places.

SACHIEL PRESSED ON through the corridors of the *Bellus*, his stride never slowing as Chapter serfs scrambled amongst themselves to get out of his way. The news boiled inside him; the Sanguinary High Priest was wound so tight with the message he carried that he thought he would blurt it out at any second. Space Marines came to parade ground attention as he passed, mailed fists tapping their chest plates in salute, while servitors and serfs bowed low.

There had been a time when Sachiel would have chastised himself for enjoying the veneration of the faithful. In the *Credo Vitae* there were edicts and oaths the Sanguinary Priests were required to avow, dedicating themselves to the sacred Blood of the Chapter, foreswearing any glory for themselves, but those old, weak words seemed so distant and removed now. Sachiel's heart swelled at the notion.

Since Arkio's Ascendance a moment had not passed where the priest did not think himself blessed to bear witness to such a miracle – and more, to be called by the Reborn Angel to serve as his adjutant and loyal commander. A smile crept across Sachiel's face as he entered the cavernous cathedral deck, making his way through the cloisters toward the inner sanctums. Since his youth, he had never doubted that he was touched by greatness. Many of his contemporaries had called him arrogant for daring to voice such notions. Let them have their petty jealousies, he thought, because he had been proven right. Great Sanguinius, to whom Sachiel had dedicated his life, had rewarded the priest beyond his wildest dreams. To be present at an event of such magnitude showed the lie of all those who had upbraided him. Sachiel was no mere priest now; he was the hand of the Blessed, and it was glorious!

His fingers fell to the velvet bag at his belt, and the replica of the Blood Angels chalice he carried there. Not for the first time, Sachiel imagined the moment when he would take the true Red Grail in his hands and accept the role of High Priest over the entire Chapter. The thought of it made his blood rush. Power, naked and beautiful, was within his reach.

The priest walked on alone into the sanctum sanctorum, where only the chosen of Arkio were allowed to tread. Normally there would have been Space Marines on guard here but the devastation wrought by the traitorous Rafen had required the recall of all available troops to the planet. A brief flicker of displeasure crossed his thoughts, but he banished it. Sachiel had hoped that he would be able to present his news to the Blessed in person, but Captain Ideon had informed him their high lord was at rest in his chambers. Sachiel accepted this with a nod, even a god-prince rich with a primarch's potency would need repose on some occasions. Instead, Sachiel would attend Inquisitor Stele and reveal what had taken place on Shenlong. The explosion of the missile store yard had obliterated six square blocks around it. Some of the priest's most loyal men had been turned to ashes in the conflagration, but their sacrifice had been worth it to end the life of the thorn in his side, the faithless and deceitful Rafen. He would swear upon it; nothing could have survived the catastrophic blast.

'You are dead, Rafen,' Sachiel said to the cool, still air of the cloister. Just uttering the words lifted a huge weight from the priest's heart. Ever since they had first laid eyes upon one another, Sachiel and Rafen had brought the worst traits in each other's character to the fore. Now the Blessed's brother was dead, the last tie holding Arkio and his loyalists to the old codes of the Blood Angels was gone, and with it Sachiel's hated antagonist. He could admit it now and release the feeling that had built up inside him. Sachiel loathed Rafen's quiet strength, the manner in which he would sneer at every utterance from the priest's mouth as if *he* were the holder of ordained office, not the priest. He hated the easy way that Rafen had earned the respect of men he served with, while Sachiel remained aloof and indifferent to the Space Marines he outranked. The pleasure he would take in announcing Rafen's end would be as sweet as a fine amasec liqueur.

The Sanguinary Priest paused before a stained glass window showing Sanguinius at the Conclave of Blood, and something in the turn of the primogenitor's face suddenly brought Rafen's final words back to him. *Piety alone will blind you.*

'Fool.' Sachiel spat out the insult automatically, but even as he did there came a nagging irritation in his mind. He hated himself for admitting it, but the deserter had stirred up doubts with that damning utterance. Sachiel looked into the eyes of the primarch, searching for clarity, and allowed himself the indulgence of hesitation. Arkio's path had broken with the tradition of his Chapter, shattering old codes of conduct that before had seemed inviolate. As the Reborn Angel had said himself, they were now writing a new chapter in the history of the Sons of Sanguinius, and the laws laid down by aged and passionless warriors like Dante were too confining, too limiting. On some deep level, the indoctrination of decades of Blood Angels dogma and training rebelled at the thought of Arkio's Blood Crusade and his Emergence – but Sachiel had seen Arkio's divinity shine through, he had felt the divine radiance of the Spear of Telesto upon him. This was proof, not the dusty words of long-perished men from millennia past.

His moment of weakness gone, Sachiel resumed his passage to Stele's quarters. Brother Solus had informed him that the inquisitor had left orders that he was not to be disturbed, but Sachiel waved him away. Such commands did not apply to the High Priest of the Reborn, and besides, Sachiel knew that Stele would be as pleased as he was to hear of Rafen's death. That his body had yet to be found was merely a formality; after such a detonation, all that would remain of Arkio's brother would barely be enough to fill a drinking goblet.

Stepping past the empty sentry alcoves, as Sachiel approached the door to Stele's chambers he tasted something strange in the air. A faint, almost undetectable whiff of brimstone and dead skin. Shaking the sensation away, the priest opened the doors and stepped inside. The atmosphere within felt thick and greasy with dark potency. He heard voices; some seemed to be coming from an impossible distance, others made up of rustling and whispering sibilance. Amid all of them he heard the inquisitor murmuring a gruff entreaty. Without waiting to announce himself, the priest pushed through the voluminous folds of black curtains enveloping the doorway and emerged in the chamber.

What he saw there made a wordless cry of shock erupt from his lips, and Sachiel groped for his pistol in self-defence.

Stele's sanctum was an arched chamber big enough to house a Thunderhawk dropship with its wings at full spread.

Stands of photon candles gave weak, yellowish light that died fighting the heavy shadows that wreathed the room. There were a few biolume globes drifting about on anti-grav impellers, but they too were strangled by the arcane, liquid dark that enveloped everything. To one side was a twitching, steaming sculpture cut out of fast-decaying human flesh. Sachiel knew the smell of putrefaction all too well from hundreds of battlegrounds. It was misshapen and ugly as sin, a parody of life warped by the hand of some crazed sculptor. Bones and cartilage in the body had been reordered to present the shape of a hunched, muscular form. It bore the most striking resemblance to the armour of the Word Bearers that they had executed on Shenlong. The flesh-thing opened a wet orifice in its head and let out an angry moan; and with his back to the door, Stele craned his neck around to spy the stunned priest there behind him. The inquisitor was pale and damp with perspiration, the normally hard and unyielding lines of his granite face soft and pallid.

The priest was only aware of them in the most peripheral of ways, however, his gaze was captured by the thing that towered over all of them, writhing and fluttering in an immaterial breeze. It looked like a pict-print of a hurricane, a frozen tower of wind and storm wreckage that had somehow taken on the aspect of a living creature. His mouth agape, Sachiel understood all at once that the shape was made of paper. All about the walls of Stele's chamber, books lay open, spines broken and covers discarded, their pages torn free to make up the matter of the daemonic creature that rustled and crackled like dead leaves.

'What is this?' Irritation bubbled out of the fleshy avatar, steam popping from blisters all across its skin.

Stele gulped air and turned to face Sachiel, shrugging out of the restricting cloak about his neck. 'You conceited imbecile,' he hissed, the effort of anger trying him to the limit. 'I said no interruptions.'

Sachiel tried to make his mouth work, but nothing seemed to come. He could not look away from the intricate folds of parchment across the daemon's heartless, monstrous face. In a crushing blow of realisation, the priest suddenly understood what he had stumbled into – Stele, the trusted servant of Arkio, was in league with the Ruinous Powers. The thought galvanised him into action. He had to escape, to get away and warn the Reborn Angel that a viper far more venomous than his errant brother lay in their midst...

'Kill it,' rippled the daemon, the words hidden in the sound of fanning pages.

'No,' Stele grunted. 'I need him alive... He is useful to me.'

The priest brought his gun to bear and his finger tightened on the trigger, but he made the mistake of meeting Stele's baleful gaze and abruptly all function in his muscles ceased. 'Nnnnnn–' Sachiel's mind flashed to the moment on Cybele, when the inquisitor had held a Word Bearers sniper in a similar mind-lock. With every gramme of his will, the priest pushed against the pressure in his mind.

'Ah,' Stele managed, eyes watering. The effort was hard on him, coming so soon after spending his abilities on the Blood Angels mere days earlier. He wavered, and felt the phantom grip begin to slacken.

Pages of ancient dogma, documents filled with arcane scripture and illuminated proofs, rustled past him, shifting and reforming into shapes that might have been men, might have been beasts. 'You wish to preserve this manling?' asked the creature, breaths of polluted air gusting through its manifested form.

'Yes, great Malfallax,' Stele bit out. 'We need him.'

'Very well,' said the daemon, and the papers spun around Stele in a narrow typhoon, their edges slicing hundreds of tiny cuts in his bare skin. From its beating heart still floating in the depths of the empyrean, Malfallax projected a concentrated portion of itself into the open gate of Stele's corrupted mind. A black pearl of raw warp briefly entered the inquisitor – and suddenly all his weakness and fatigue melted away, replaced by a giddy psychic head-rush. 'A gift,' the creature whispered.

Colour returned to Stele's face and his teeth bared. 'You are most gracious, Spiteful One.' His eyes bored into Sachiel's, flaying his mind open to the psyker's dark will. 'Kneel, priest,' he commanded.

Sachiel found he had no resistance within him, and he did as he was ordered, the reductor in his hand falling to the tiled floor. His head swam with a sickening roil of recall, as his recent memories replayed in flash-frame blinks of pain – Stele spun though the Sanguinary Priest's thoughts as easily as he might the pages of a book.

Stele gave a grunt of laughter, reading his intent. 'You came to tell me Rafen was dead? Such trivia is hardly worth my notice.'

It was as if Sachiel were kneeling on the edge of a bottomless abyss. The priest's mind fluttered like an insect caught in setting amber, teetering on the brink of a horrific realisation. *Stele is tainted by Chaos, and if that is so then everything he has touched has also been sullied by corruption. By the blood of the primarch, what have we done? I am tainted. The Warriors of the Reborn too? The Spear? Even the Blessed Arkio...*

Stele shook his head. 'Cease,' he said, halting Sachiel's thoughts with a gesture. 'No, priest. I cannot have you venture down that road. Your role is yet to be completed.' His eyes glittered, and the inquisitor threw an ephemeral dart into the Blood Angel's mind. Sachiel screamed as Stele unfolded his psyche and deftly excised his memories, painting blackness over them from the moment he had entered the sanctum. A drool of fluid issued out of the corner of Sachiel's mouth.

'Frail little men-beasts,' Garand's latest avatar said with a grimace, flakes of dead flesh falling from it with each word. 'Its mind may break beneath your ministrations.'

'I think not,' retorted Stele, withdrawing the needle of his psychic power from a blank-eyed Sachiel. 'He will remember nothing of what he saw.'

Rough laughter crackled through the singed papers. 'Ah, Stele. You grow ever distant to your human roots and closer to us with every one of your gestures.'

'It pleases me to hear you say that,' Stele said, with a forced smile. In his mind's eye, Malfallax's dark seed of potency was lodged in his soul, glistening with the eightfold star upon its surface. 'And while it gratifies me to accept your mark, Great Changer, perhaps it might be better for you to withdraw it for now–'

The pages gave an angry wasp-swarm vibration. 'Keep it, my friend. It will be important in the days to come.'

'We shall begin, then,' grated Garand. With a shrug of broken bones, the Word Bearers Warmaster withdrew from his mouthpiece and let it die.

Gently, the ripped shreds of paper began to drift apart as Malfallax retreated from the material realm, leaving the inquisitor with only a decaying corpse and the silent priest for company. Stele watched the pages settle, at once refreshed and newly afraid of the boon his monstrous master had given him.

THE DOCK WAS alive with noise and motion, men swarming like ants around the iron wharves and gantries. Dozens of ugly, bullet-shaped orbital tenders waited at rest on vertical rails, plumes of vaporised liquid oxygen hissing white clouds into the air. Cargo pods, normally crammed full of munitions crates and warheads, were being loaded with human freight instead. Hundreds and hundreds of men, a rag-tag army clad in cloaks and scavenged armour, filed solemnly into the modules. Here and there, tall figures in red armour could be seen, calling out orders and directing the erstwhile soldiers to their departure points.

Rafen watched from his vantage point in a burnt-out building, studying the ebb and flow of the crowds, watching the ordered procession with a practiced eye. He kept his vox on the same channel as the Blood Angels on the docks, listening to their terse communications as he rested, tending to his injuries. In the sewers, the explosion of the warehouse had forced a plug of filthy water into a floodhead and carried Rafen along with it, tossing him like a piece of debris. Sealed inside the airtight frame of his power armour, the Space Marine was forced to ride out the shock wave as each impact against the tunnel walls threw him closer to unconsciousness. The headlong surge along the pipes was a blur of rushing noise and blunt pain, but eventually the flood spent itself and deposited him in an overflow chamber on the lower levels of the factory city. Rafen flexed his arm, grimacing. His skin was marred with broad purple-black bruises where he had suffered impact after impact and the limb was slack where it had been dislocated. Carefully, he gripped his wrist and tugged; with a dull click of cartilage, the joint popped back into place. He shrugged off the pain that came with it.

Using an abandoned chimney stack, Rafen had climbed until he found his current hide. He took stock of his situation, examining his weapons and what little he had in the way of supplies. The Blood Angel considered himself behind enemy lines now, and conducted his battle drill accordingly.

He had no idea how long he would be able to go unnoticed; certainly it might be days before the rubble of the store yard was picked through and the bodies of the dead men counted. He had a window of opportunity, but it would close quickly.

A roar of rocket exhaust drew his attention back to the dock. With a clang of steel on steel, a launch gantry fell away and one of the tenders threw itself into the dull sky on a plume of yellow flame. Fins folded out of the craft as it ascended and Rafen watched it go, disappearing into a sickly glow as it vanished through the low cloud cover. Another fifty or more men for Arkio's helot army were on their way to *Bellus*. There was a flurry of orders over the vox. The next launches were almost fuelled and ready to lift off. Legions of zealots, all of them adorned with the crude halo-and-spear symbol of the Warriors of the Reborn, shifted back and forth, eager to board the ships that would take them to be with their messiah.

Arkio was aboard the battle barge; Rafen had caught a cursory mention of 'the Blessed' and pieced together the meaning. With his brother on the *Bellus* and the army Sachiel had raised from the Shenlongi joining him in their droves, the situation was clear. The Blood Crusade was beginning, and soon the massive warship would be departing. Rafen replaced the gauntlet about his arm and re-sealed his wargear's links. Twice now he failed to bring this travesty of the Emperor's will to an end. Alone with Arkio in the fortress, it had been his own weakness that had stopped him from ending his sibling's life; and in the reactor core, blind chance had prevented the destruction of the tower. If *Bellus* left without Rafen, then Stele would be free to manipulate Sachiel and Arkio to whatever ends the inquisitor chose. The Space Marine's mind returned to the vision he had seen in his makeshift retreat, as it had many times in the past few days. He held his combat knife in his hand once more, then slammed it into his boot sheath with grim finality.

BENEATH THE DOCK platform was a web of supports extending into the dry mud of the riverbed. Orange knots of rust clustered at every giant bolt and weld, releasing rains of ruddy fines with each rumbling blast of exhaust from the tenders launching above. Rafen made his way through broken catwalks and bent spars and selected a pad on the southern edge of the dock where spindly Sentinel walkers had just completed the loading of a brace of cargo pods. The Blood Angel emerged directly beneath the gaping maws of the ship's engine bells, which twitched and hissed as the pilot-servitor in the nosecone ran through the final countdown sequence. The modules packed with soldiers were sealed shut – they would only be opened when the tender had safely landed in an airtight bay on *Bellus* – so Rafen could not enter there. The cockpit, high above him at the tip of the rocket, would not suffice either. Too small, too filled with arcane machinery and Adeptus Mechanicus complexity.

There would be only one route for a fugitive to board the battle barge. He could not chance accompanying other Blood Angels aboard a shuttle or Thunderhawk. Even with the dirt smeared across his armour, he could be seen and recognised. Once aboard *Bellus*, it would be a different story, the vast starship had many places for a careful soul to conceal itself. Rafen grabbed a maintenance ladder and hauled himself up it, into the nest of pipes and feed channels that poured promethium fuel to the engines. As the rockets hummed into life about him, he pushed his broad form into the open framework and found a vee-shaped stanchion that would accommodate his armour. The thunder of the engines built into a deafening crescendo, even through the noise-dampening protection of his helmet. Rafen gave a last look at the life-support monitor gauge on his wrist; all the vacuum seals on his armour were intact. With effort, he dug his ceramite-hardened fingers into the girders and wedged himself in place. Rafen closed his eyes and began a prayer to Sanguinius as gravity laid into him.

Clinging to the underside of the tender, Rafen hung on in grim determination, as the dock, the city and then the cloud-shrouded landscape of Shenlong fell away beneath him.

CHAPTER EIGHT

In the darkened corners of the landing bay, where only the blind rat-hunter servitors would dare to venture, Rafen was concealed. With care, he rubbed away the thin patina of ice that had formed on the outer shell of his armour, the rimes of frost tinkling as his gauntlet brushed them away. The beating of the Blood Angel's heart was loud in his ears as the organ worked to supply additional oxygen to his bloodstream, counteracting the lingering side-effects of the trip through hard vacuum. Rafen's armour had protected him well, but still the incredible cold of space had leached the heat from him, and the Space Marine's muscles were tense. Typically, a Space Marine would have luxury of a chemical sacrament before venturing into the void. The philtre granted by the Chapter priests stimulated the Astartes mucranoid gland, turning their sweat into a complex compound to protect the skin against such punishing extremes of temperature. Rafen had no such defence, however, and the kiss of the airless dark had touched him with its full force.

The machines and men in the landing bay moved in synchrony as each new transport arrived. The shuttles paused just long enough to disgorge their loads of helot troopers before overhead gantries lifted the ships into refuelling sockets or directed them back out to be launched on a return course to Shenlong. Each new group of Arkio's zealots was herded away toward the bilge decks by a clattering servitor or a Chapter serf. The serfs held shock-staves to keep the more curious members of the Warriors of the Reborn in check. Rafen used the magnification functions of his helmet optics to watch the motion of the bondsmen; now and then a battle-brother would intervene, overseeing the activity.

Inwardly, Rafen felt uncomfortable and conflicted. He was in every sense past the point of no return. It felt wrong, *alien*, to be in the midst of his brethren yet also in the thick of his adversaries. Every fibre of his being rebelled against the unwelcome, gut-sick sensation. Like all his kind, Rafen had come to know the camaraderie of his fellow Blood Angels as an extended family, a brotherhood in all senses of the world. By rights, *Bellus* was supposed to be a sanctuary, a place where he should have felt safe and content – instead, it was a danger zone as lethal as any field of melta mines or bio-web. As long as Sachiel thought him dead, then surprise was on his side, but he had to be careful not to squander his only advantage. Too many men aboard this ship knew his face, so to go unhooded would be an instant death sentence. Even with his armour sealed, if he freely moved among the other Astartes it would only be a matter of time before someone questioned him. Rafen needed to find somewhere that his presence would not be challenged.

He shook off the chill as another cargo lighter rumbled past him, the bullet-shaped vessel settling into a landing cradle with a heavy bump and a shower of orange sparks. The brass and cast-iron rig folded up around the transport like a gripping hand and turned the vessel to present it to a debarkation ramp. Rafen moved out of his cover and balanced on the balls of his feet. As with many starships in the service of the Empire, the *Bellus*'s tech-priests encouraged the battle barge's machine-spirit to lower the gravity in the docking bays so that cargo could be manipulated more easily. Rafen felt light here, and he prepared himself for the necessary change in his gait. A cloud of white vapour belched from the lighter's dorsal vents, momentarily occluding the ramp and the cradle. Rafen sprang out of his hiding place, using the mist to cover him. In the long, loping steps that he had been taught, the Space Marine crossed beneath the slow-moving ship and emerged at the foot of the ramp, as if he had been meant to be there all along. The cargo transporter touched the ramp edge with a hollow thud, and all across its hull gull-wing hatches opened.

Men boiled out of the ship in a ragged wave, all of them shivering and trembling, some from the cold and others from awe. Rafen saw a couple of them drop to their knees. At first he thought they might have been injured, but then he realised that they were kissing the deck, genuflecting in honour of the ship they saw as Arkio's sacred vessel. All of the conscripts had weapons, after a fashion. Some had guns, others swords, spears and other bladed things that had a makeshift look to them. Many of them wore armour fashioned from metal junk, although a few sported dark ballistic mesh tunics. Planetary Defence Force hardware, Rafen noted; the wearers were either former members of Shenlong's PDF that had survived the Word Bearers invasion, or else they were opportunists who had looted the bodies of the dead. The Space Marine's expression soured. Either way, they were not worthy to set foot on a fighting ship like *Bellus* – even the lowliest of the Chapter serfs were nobler than this rabble.

The warriors came to a stumbling halt as they saw the Blood Angel standing there before them, cowed by his presence as much as by the incredible sight of the cavernous starship interior. Rafen would warrant that hardly any of these men had ever left their birthworld before today. He scanned their faces and found some with the vacant, transported look of a true fanatic, while others were brutal and crude, the most vicious of Shenlong's dregs. Why Sachiel had selected these men was beyond Rafen's understanding; none of them would ever measure up to the standards of the Chapter. All they were good for would be to die on the point of an enemy's weapon and clog the muzzles of guns with their corpses. He suppressed the urge to sneer. Such tactics were base and ignoble, better suited to the traitor-kin of Chaos than to the Sons of Sanguinius.

'Lord?' A serf approached him with a questioning look on his face. 'How may I assist you?'

Rafen glanced at the bondsman. 'You are to escort these men below, correct?'

'Yes, lord. Is there some problem?'

He shook his head. 'No. The priest Sachiel has ordered that I accompany this party… He wishes me to oversee the transfer.'

The serf nodded. 'As you command, lord.' With a wave of his shock-stave, the servant directed the soldiers from the ramp.

The shabby figures filed past him, some of them averting their eyes, others studying him with a bald mix of hate and fear. Among the men, a single face suddenly leapt out at Rafen – a sallow, drawn complexion atop the remains of a PDF officer's uniform. The man bowed his head as he passed and Rafen watched him go. He had last seen the soldier inside the Ikari fortress, after Sachiel's honour guards had gunned down a group of innocents as repudiation. The man had actually thanked him for the 'murdergift' given to his sister who died in the crossfire, as if it were some great blessing. He seemed drained of all spirit now, a hollow shell stained with blood and driven only by belief in Arkio's divinity.

Rafen followed the group along the echoing corridors of the ship and into the open caverns of the dark lower levels. To call them 'decks' would have been a misnomer: the hull spaces resembled a stygian canyon with plates of fungal growth extending from the steep walls. Sections of decking jutted out here and there, never broad enough to meet the vast skeletal ribs of the ship's inner hull. Webs of cable, nets and rope-bridges looped them together. The warriors made themselves places to live and sleep from jury-rigged hammocks and discarded cargo pods. It was like a series of broken bridges arching over a valley so far below that the floor was lost in utter blackness.

The new arrivals were greeted with a welcome of cold-eyed glares and veiled threats. He lost sight of the PDF officer as the men wandered into the junkyard community, the law of the wild taking precedence as figures among the groups tussled for places to bed down. Rafen left the Chapter serf behind and walked through the encampment, picking his way along creaking gangplanks and between sagging trestles cut from salvage. There were loudhailers dotted about the place, each connected to the ship's primary vox network with knots of wires, the hasty work of servitors under the direction of Inquisitor Stele. Spitting with reverb and interference, data-slate recordings of Sachiel's speeches from the victory on Shenlong were playing, interspersed with snatches of Imperial hymnals. Conscripts clustered around some of the speaker rigs, joining in with the broadcasts. Everywhere the symbol of the Reborn Angel was daubed. Rafen paused at one such display and ran a finger over the still-wet marking. He raised his glove to his breather grille and sniffed: it was human blood.

The Space Marine peered over the edge of the gantry he stood on, wondering how many of Arkio's chosen had already met their end in the darkness below. For all Sachiel's high words and oratory, the thousand-strong army seemed to be filled only by the most heartless or the most fervid of Shenlong's populace. To cast them as men in service to the glory of Sanguinius was an insult to the Great Angel.

Rafen moved deeper into the decks, losing himself in the dimly lit spaces. Down here, there would be no man that knew his face and no one to call attention to him. He would hide in plain sight and prepare; when the Warriors of the Reborn were called to arms, he would be there to stop his brother – or to die in the attempt.

'THE LAST GROUP of lighters is docking now,' Solus announced in his sombre, level voice. 'Engineseers report power to drives is optimal. All rites of passage are complete and *Bellus* is free to make sail.'

'Proceed.' The static-choked order issued out of the vocoder implant in Brother-Captain Ideon's neck, his face immobile. 'Make preparation for warp transit the moment we reach the translation point co-ordinates.'

Solus hesitated; another man might not have noticed it, but Ideon had served with the Blood Angel as his aide-de-camp for decades and the man's moods were as clear to the starship captain as the temperaments of his vessel's machine-spirit. 'Was there something else?' Ideon prompted.

As *Bellus* moved away from Shenlong, the planet slipped from the forward viewport, and with it the wreckage of the

Amareo, some of it still burning as it tumbled in a higher orbit. Solus glanced at the fragment and then away. 'Lord, I–'

The brass leaves of the bridge iris retracted into the walls with a well oiled hiss of hydraulics, and Sachiel entered, his ubiquitous honour guards two steps behind him. Ideon watched him approach through his own eyes and those of the bridge's sentry servitors, the data flowing into his brain through the complex forest of mechadendrites connecting him to his command throne. Solus fell silent, his words swallowed.

The Sanguinary High Priest seemed fatigued, there were dark circles beneath his eyes and his face was paler than usual. Through the infrared monitors Ideon registered a slightly higher skin temperature for Sachiel. Still, he seemed no less animated than usual, and the brightness in his eyes was a strong as ever.

The priest threw a nod to the captain. 'Brother Ideon, what is the disposition of the Blessed's battle barge?'

'Fully prepared, Sachiel,' he replied. 'The navigator assures me that the prayer-computations for the course to Sabien have been completed. *Bellus* will enter the empyrean as scheduled.'

'Excellent. Great Arkio demands nothing less than total efficiency.' Sachiel's voice rose at the end of the sentence and he blinked, as if the effort of the words were difficult for him. His eyes ranged around the bridge, over the hunched chorus of servitors ministering to cogitator consoles, until he found Solus at the wide oval observation window. He homed in on the Blood Angel. 'Brother?' Sachiel began innocently. 'You seem distracted. What can it be that vexes you?'

Solus looked up, not at Sachiel, but to Ideon. The captain remained – as ever – an unmoving statue on the raised command dais. Solus turned to the priest after a long moment. 'Sachiel, I would have you answer a question for me.'

'Name it,' the priest snapped back, a little too quickly.

'What enemy do we go to face, brother?'

Sachiel nodded again. 'Ah, I see. The matter of the *Amareo*'s destruction, yes? It troubled you to give the firing command on a Chapter vessel, did it not?' When Solus did not answer, he pressed on. 'Brother, listen to me. The men aboard that ship were assassins, sent to murder the Reborn Angel and purge anyone who gave fealty to him. That truth is self-evident.' He came closer and touched Solus's arm. 'You did the only thing you could – you helped save the Blessed's life.'

Solus would not meet his gaze. 'I... I have taken the oath for Arkio and the Holy Lance, Sachiel, and I would not flinch against its demands but this...' He glanced out the window at the stars. 'Those men were our battle-brothers, we fought alongside some of them. That we were forced to exterminate them like some common heretics turns my gut.'

The priest's voice was low, but it carried across the room. 'Solus, friend Solus. I understand your feelings. At prayer, I too confessed my mis...' He halted, his face colouring. Sachiel ran a finger over his twitching eye, as if he were banishing some inner pain. After a moment he continued as if nothing had happened. 'Misgivings, yes. To Lord... Lord Stele.' He smiled. 'But I realised, those men had ignored the path of the primarch. That they came here with murder in their hearts made them our enemies.'

'We could have talked to them,' Solus blurted out, 'reasoned with them. Perhaps they would have thought differently if they had understood Arkio's great miracle–'

'No, Solus, no.' Sachiel's expression became one of deep sadness. 'They were lost to us before they even reached Shenlong. Like those who fell from the Emperor's grace in the dark years, those men had chosen a path that pitted them against us. It was their choice, brother, not yours. You and I, all of us remain true to the Pure One.' He nodded at the distant wreckage of the strike cruiser. 'They forced our hand. Those deaths are on their own heads.'

'Yes,' Solus said finally. 'Forgive me my outburst, priest. These past days have tested my faith.'

'As they should,' Ideon's voice buzzed and rumbled from his vox-implant. 'Arkio brings us a new lease of life, and *Bellus* will be the chariot that carries it to the ends of the galaxy.'

Sachiel's head bobbed. 'So shall it be.'

BY THE POWER of forces that dwarfed human understanding, the fabric of space began to writhe and shift around the prow of the *Bellus*. From the places where thought and energy became a unified melange, the raw mind-stuff of the warp spilled into the reality of matter, slicing open a raw, bleeding gate in the void. It was a violent miniature supernova in the blackness, a whirlpool into which the battle barge threw itself. Time, elastic and flowing like molten wax, enveloped the ship and projected it across vast distances. *Bellus* vanished from the realm of men and was gone, cast to the wild currents and energy storms of the immaterium.

IN ANOTHER PLACE and time, the same unthinkable inversion of natural laws was occurring. A leviathan ship emerged from the phantasm of the warp in a violent burst of exotic radiation, coruscating colours and sickly hues of lightning trembling across the vast iron hull. Space itself seemed unwilling to let the vessel exist within its body, as if the vast craft were some metallic cancer growing and polluting the void with its presence. Shedding energy in sheaves of arcane power, the battleship fell from the empyrean realm and reverted to steady, obdurate reality. Engine maws, their exhaust bells as big as volcanoes, took on bloody glows as thrust spewed forth from ancient fusion drives, and with

deadly purpose the warship *Misericorde* made speed toward
its destination.

She was a horrific sight, an engine of torture almost a mile
in length, and on *Misericorde*'s guns many mewling human
worlds had been broken just as men had been broken on the
racks of her dungeon decks. In aspect, the battleship was a
broad dagger, a serrated arrowhead forming her prow, a haft
of razors growing backwards to present the dorsal castle of
her bridge, and below the plunging knives of skeletal sta-
biliser vanes. Guns protruded from every shadowed corner of
the craft, punching through the red skin of the hull like broken ribs. The ship was adorned with skulls by the thousand.
The largest were made from bones, ravaged from the bodies
of dead enemies and fused into shape as badges of victory. At
the very bow of the vessel, a design had been shaped out of
broken pieces of hull metal and ceramite; centred on an
eight-pointed star was the screaming face of a toothed,
horned daemon, shouting defiance and black hate at all of
Misericorde's foes. Like the skulls, the sigil was constructed
from war salvage, but instead of bone, the monstrous face was
cut from the ships and armour of Adeptus Astartes unlucky
enough to fall before the vessel.

In the command sanctum atop the bridge citadel, figures
moved in a precise, careful ballet around the presence of the
Warmaster Garand. The flayed shapes of servitors passed to
and fro, clawed metal feet scratching across the decks as they
went about their business. There was no speech except for the
low, bubbling bursts of machine code between the slaves. The
sound reminded Garand of the chattering predator insects on
his Chapter's blighted forge-world, Ghalmek.

Before him, he could see the *Misericorde*'s hololithic display
presenting their destination – the shrine planet Sabien. It
resembled a ball of age-worn iron, like the warshots spat from

cannon on primitive pre-nuclear planets, it made Garand think instantly of Fortrea Quintus. Recall of the planet sent the Chaos warlord's mind back through the veil of memory, thousands of years dropping away in an instant.

The Warmaster's thin tongue slipped out of his lips to lick absently at his chin barbs. Yes, the similarity was quite marked, and the connection brought a glow of anticipation of the commander's dark heart. Although ages had passed since the day Garand had set foot on Quintus, his memory of the glorious campaign there was still as vibrant and sensuous as ever.

The scent of spilt blood came to his nostrils and he closed his eyes, allowing himself to wallow in the luxury of it for a moment. Garand had been the second-in-command to Brother-Captain Jarulck in those days, when outwardly the Word Bearers still paid lip service to the corpse-god of men. He smiled. Even then, the Chapter had already embraced the perfection of the eightfold path, and the blind fools of the other Legion Astartes had been too pathetic to see the touch of Chaos in their midst. Great Lorgar, primarch of the Word Bearers, had personally charged two thousand men to the subjugation of the planet, and they had taken to it with battlelust in their eyes. Garand recalled Jarulck's fiery oratory to the Quintian natives, the words of power that had drawn the commoners to their banner in their droves. When they marched on their enemy's stronghold in the last days of the conflict, their hordes of followers had perished in the thousands while the Word Bearers lost little of their original number, the bodies of the zealots forming the ramps that Garand's troops used to ford the battlements. Fortrea Quintus fell, but not for the Emperor. With Jarulck's blessing, Garand had been charged with the indoctrination of the locals. He ensured that although the world outwardly paid fealty to Terra, its secret face would forever be turned toward Chaos.

When Horus rose on his great jihad against the weak men-filth, Garand had swelled with pride to learn that the Quintians slaughtered every Emperor-fearing lackey on their homeworld within hours. For his part, Garand cemented his place on the path to high command of a Word Bearers Legion with the blessing of Great Lorgar, but Fortrea Quintus had always remained close to his black heart as the site of his first great victory. Now the smile on Garand's horned and twisted face fell away, his aspect becoming crooked with ill temper.

The Quintus Conversion was at once the source of the Warmaster's pride and his enmity – for it had not been soon after the death of Horus, when the Legions of Chaos were in disarray and scattered, that his prized victory was rendered into ashes by the supercilious Blood Angels. Garand and his hosts had been distant, fighting running battles toward their nest-worlds in the Maelstrom. The Word Bearers had been cut off from the planets they had turned; they had not been there to resist the so-called 'cleansing' by the corpse-god's legions.

Garand listened in impotent anger to the screamed transmissions of astropaths as the Blood Angels swept across Fortrea Quintus and left nothing alive in their path. The prized achievement of his youth was burnt to ashes, kindling within him a dense, diamond-hard hate for the Sons of Sanguinius. Centuries had come and gone since then, but the rancour had never dulled. In a world of warriors who nurtured their hate like keen knives, Garand honed his loathing of the Blood Angels into something utterly murderous and unyielding in its purity.

Sabien filled the shimmering holoscreen and beyond it, the real planet was visible as an occluded disc eclipsed by a swollen, red-orange sun. The Warmaster was almost salivating in anticipation of the battle to come. He loved the impotent screams of idiot piety his enemies released whenever a Word Bearers host made planetfall on one of their pathetic 'holy worlds', how they wailed and wept to learn that the legions of Chaos had sullied their ridiculous worship of that dead freak they so revered. As the *Book of Lorgar* commanded, the Word Bearers were unique among the apostate Legions of the Chaos Space Marines. They alone retained the priests and dogma that their Chapters had kept during their fealty to Earth, but once they had bent their knee to the Ruinous Powers, their soothsayers and psykers embraced the mark of Chaos Undivided, the Blasphemous Hex. Now, when worlds fell beneath their might, the Word Bearers would erect massive monuments to the dark gods of the Maelstrom, they would profane the human churches and ritually deconsecrate anything that purported to glory the name of the Imperium. This and much more was precisely what Garand intended for Sabien.

The planet was a shrine world for the Blood Angels; the Warmaster knew little of the reasons that the Astartes whelps had named it thus, and he cared even less. It had been the site of some great conflict and in their asinine, maudlin way, the Blood Angels had isolated the planet and made it a place of pilgrimage. Sabien had absolutely no tactical value. It had no bases, no minerals waiting to be exploited, not even a population to be tormented and killed – but for the Word Bearers to set foot here would be as much a blow to the Astartes Legion's honour as a spit in the eye of their precious Sanguinius.

'Great Witch Prince,' a servitor addressed him from the control pit at his feet. 'We will achieve orbit momentarily. The assault force awaits your blessing for deployment.'

Garand did not grace the slave with eye contact. 'Send them. Have my personal shuttle prepared. I will attend once the troops have begun their concealment.'

As much as he detested the turncoat Stele, he was forced to admit that the human had provided exactly what was needed. With the galactic co-ordinates of Sabien – a world whose location was hidden from all but the most secret Blood Angels star charts – it had been easy for the swift *Misericorde* to reach the planet before the other players in Stele's little drama arrived. He found the inquisitor an unctuous, arrogant sort, far too enamoured with his own intellect. Had circumstances been altered, Garand would have been only too pleased to have torn the psyker's throat from his neck – *and perhaps I may still have that opportunity*, he told himself – but it was the High Beast Malfallax's wish that Stele be the tool they would use against the enemy.

He frowned; the eye of the mighty Abaddon was upon their endeavour here, and it would not go well if it came to nothing. Garand had given much of his Legion to the scheme, allowing that fool Iskavan to be sacrificed for the sake of Stele's complex gambits, but he could not have anything but cold dislike for the inquisitor. After all, a traitor to his own species was still a traitor, and who could know if he would not turncoat again? Of course, there were those in the Imperium that called Garand and his kinsmen traitor too, but like most of the Emperor's sheep, they did not understand. No Chaos Space Marine was a traitor. If anything, they were the most loyal of them all, casting aside everything that made them weak to give fealty to the most ruthless forces in all creation.

Garand's reverie fell away as he studied the thick ring of asteroids girdling Sabien in a wide elliptical belt. He imagined they were all that remained of some moon, no doubt obliterated in the conflict that made Sabien the blighted sphere it was today. Repeaters from the battleship's machine-spirit confirmed that the shaggy cloud of stones was rich in dense, sensor-opaque ores that would adequately mask the *Misericorde*'s presence. He glanced up, and saw the twinkle of lights swarming away from the vessel's hull. The Warmaster's clawed hand tightened around the blackened iron railing before him in rapt expectancy. The grand plan of his daemon lord Malfallax had moved one step closer to its deadly conclusion. This day would end with the Blood Angels throwing off their allegiance to the Emperor and embracing Chaos, or it would end with their bones joining those of their brethren already perished in Sabien's crypt-yards.

THE DREAM.

At first it had been a minor irritation, some piece of his past life impinging on the changes that fate had wrought upon him. It came in those moments when he was at rest, the brief periods of repose now less and less necessary as the wonders of his new body revealed themselves to him. In the beginning, it was only when Arkio slept that the dream came to him – but now, as the Blood Crusade took its first steps, the apparition had begun to infiltrate his waking moments. Whenever his mind began to drift from the matters at hand, it was there.

Arkio knelt before the vast frieze of Sanguinius in the grand chamber, the majestic face looking down upon him, mirroring his own in its lines of jaw and chin, in the nobility of mouth and eye. His silver-white wings moved of their own accord, gently unfolding in a whisper of sound, the tips of them drooping to pool around the golden shoulders of his artificer armour like a cloak of snow. At rest there on the altar of red Baalite sandstone was the sanctified metal cylinder that held the Holy Lance. Arkio opened the case so the honey-coloured light from the ancient weapon could be free to illuminate him. As he laid eyes on the Spear of Telesto, so once again Arkio felt the hum of unchained power in his veins. The preternatural potency of the Blood Angel bloodline ran strong in him.

Arkio bowed his head; none of the Chaplains in their black armour and skull-mask helmets had dared to approach him when he entered, and without any spoken orders from him, they had sealed the chamber closed. He could not see them, but he knew they had gathered at the far end of the cathedral's aisle, watching him in awe-struck silence. Arkio made the sign of the aquila, the reflexive gesture soothing him.

'Pure One, hear me. Grant me guidance. I am your vessel and your messenger. I will know the way of Sanguinius so I will make it my own. Grant me understanding of this vision that haunts me...'

Arkio closed his eyes and let the dream unfold in his mind. For days now as the *Bellus* raced through the warp, he had been holding it back, resisting the pull of it. The touch of the empyrean seemed to nurture it and strengthen its influence.

It begins on Baal, as it ever does. At the head of a throng of men and Space Marines a million souls strong, Arkio marches towards the gates of the fortress-monastery. At his shoulders are Astartes in armour all shades of crimson – not just Blood Angels, but warriors from the Flesh Tearers Chapter, the Blood Drinkers, the Angels Vermilion and more. There are men in the black of the Death Company, their greaves crossed with the red saltires that mark them as fallen to the rage, but they walk with him as tranquil as their battle-brothers at rest. His presence alone is enough to calm them.

The wind-scoured gates open before Arkio and the monastery presents itself to him and his crusaders. Every figure within, Space Marine and Apothecary, tech-priest and Chapter serf alike, all of them drop to one knee and bow their heads as they pass. There is none of the rough clamour and bellowed shouts that the people of Shenlong poured forth for him – here on Baal, only the wind is heard, and the silence of these faithful marks their devotion to him. None shall chance to speak in the presence of the Reborn Angel, such is their reverence.

Through the silent cloister and into the grand hall. He sees the faces of the greatest Blood Angels as they salute him, fist to chest as he strides past. Argastes. Corbulo. Lemartes. Moriar. Vermento. Even the honoured dead are here to greet him, Tycho standing shoulder to shoulder with Lestrallio, and for a moment, he spies Koris among them, his aspect a flicker, then shadows.

At the altar beneath the towering statues of Sanguinius and the Emperor stand Dante and Mephiston. There is a moment when both men meet his gaze and Arkio fears that he will be forced to draw the Spear upon them; but then both the high commander and the Lord of Death bow to him. Then, and only then, are the voices of his warriors raised, and they shake the pillars of heaven as they call his name.

But from the shadowed corners, something dark and foetid approaches.

'LORD INQUISITOR, WHAT are we to make of this?' said Delos, his voice barely concealing an edge of fearful concern. 'See, the light that falls from the Blessed.'

Stele's face soured as he watched the play of yellow-white colours over Arkio's golden form at the other end of the grand chamber. The hot glow of the Spear of Telesto crackled around him like summer lighting. 'Yes, Chaplain, you were correct to summon me. This… This is a manifestation of the Reborn Angel's will. He prays for guidance in our coming battles…' The lie tripped easily off his tongue.

Delos exchanged glances with his fellow priests. 'But his face… It shifts and moves, Lord Stele. I have not seen the like before… And his cries. I would swear that Arkio is in pain–'

'No!' Stele snapped, 'You cannot fathom the ways of the Holy Lance, priest. Arkio communes with the blood within him, no more. He must… He must be given solace to do this alone.'

'But we cannot–'

'You must leave,' the inquisitor thundered. 'I will stand sentinel for the Blessed.' When Delos hesitated, he stabbed a finger at the chapel doors. 'Out!' Stele's voice became a roar. 'By Sanguinius's name, I command it.'

The moment the wooden doors rumbled shut, Stele broke into a run toward the altar. There was a stench in the air, and it was as familiar to the inquisitor as the sound of his own breathing; dead flesh, hot blood, cold iron.

Chaos.

CHAPTER NINE

THE DREAM COLOURS and darkens. It becomes a nightmare.

And now all transforms into ashes.

In the moment of his greatest triumph, as every Blood Angel living and dead pays fealty to Arkio's name, the shadows gathering in the corners of his vision flood into sight. A wash of aged blood sweeps over everything, turning the men around him into rotting corpses, their bodies flayed under the tide, ceramite turning to paper, skin curdling over greying bones. The stone walls crack and crumble, ageing aeons in seconds. Baal itself cries out in agony at the pollution spilling across it. The dead are a tide about him, oceans of clawed skeletal fingers scoring into his golden armour. Dante and Mephiston clutch at him, screaming in pain, shrivelling eyes begging him for the reason that he has forsaken them.

Arkio's mouth will not form the words, and he does not have an answer for them. All he knows is that this great decay is his fault.

The wave of ruin reaches his boots and climbs him like fast-growing fungus. The golden armour turns to tarnished brass, then dull rust, then crumbling dust. Arkio's voice finds him in time for a soul-shattering scream.

* * *

THE SOUND THAT left Arkio's lips made Stele pause as he skidded to a halt at the foot of the altar. The cry hammered at the walls of the grand chamber, vibrating the stands of photon candles and the censers that dangled from chains high above. He threw a nervous glance to the doors – they remained closed. At least the Chaplain had taken his order to heart. It would not go well if Delos and his battle-brothers observed what was about to transpire. Stele grimaced as he stepped into the halo cast by the Spear. The touch of the weapon churned up complex, heady emotions inside the inquisitor, and he forced them to the back of his mind. He would need all his ability to concentrate on the here and now.

Arkio was trembling, his skin white and wet with perspiration. Shapes seemed to be moving beneath the surface of his elegant face, thin, worm-like cilia pushing at the curve of his cheekbones and his jaw. Stele swore a curse; the young fool had brought this on himself. Unwilling to simply leave the Holy Lance alone, Arkio had spent too much time in the radiance of the device, and now the architects of his change were in danger of spoiling. Dark lesions, hard and black like rare pearls, were appearing over his neck and forehead. Some of them had opened like eyes.

'Too soon,' Stele snapped. 'It's too soon. The mutation was stable, I made sure of it.'

He shrugged off his coat and placed his hands about the sides of Arkio's head. Biting back a sudden urge to throw up, the inquisitor marshalled his strength and let his psychic senses extend through the skin contact. Gently, his fingers began to melt into the matter of Arkio's face.

THE WORST OF *the horrors is left for the last.*

Everywhere his battle-brothers have fallen, a new and monstrous shape takes form, rebuilding itself from the debris of bone and armour. Things come. Unhallowed creatures in sick parodies of Blood Angels nobility, their crimson armour stained with the blood of innocents, the white wings of the Chapter sigil now bones and blades, the red teardrop wet with gore. Horns and teeth sprout from them; their abhorrence outpaces even that of the traitorous Word Bearers. Everywhere, his twisted brethren paint eightfold crosses, throwing back their heads to call Chaos to their midst.

Air thickens about Arkio like quicksand. He reaches for the Holy Lance, the last beacon of purity, even as the skin sloughs off his bones. His fingers touch the warm, yielding metal...

ARKIO'S ARM JERKED, a marionette pulled by a careless puppeteer, and his fingertips brushed the Holy Lance.

Hot air sizzled around the two men and Arkio was shoved backward.

The murky infections across his skin bubbled and popped. Out of sight beneath his armoured chest plate, more cancerous growths erupted across Arkio's flawless body and spat yellow pus. Bony juts of distorted matter pressed at the cage of his skin. The flesh of the young Space Marine, so perfect and magnificent, was rotting inside.

'No!' snapped Stele. 'Not yet. I will not permit it.' Moving through his flesh, the inquisitor's fingers buried themselves in Arkio's spine, probing and feeling for the ebony egg of corruption that had been planted there so many months earlier.

...AND THE SPEAR of Telesto rejects him.

Pain, great stabbing swords of agony more powerful than mortals could comprehend surge into Arkio. He recoils and his body shifts; the flash-burned hand knots and writhes. It become a nest of tentacles and claws. He touches his face and finds an orchard of spines and barbs there, black flapping tongues and runny flesh.

The black tide is in him now, rewriting his soul. He sees it there, cutting the mark of Chaos Undivided into him.

And there is a roaring beast within him, the hateful heart of the red thirst, that welcomes it. Arkio teeters and falls.

He has become the Unblessed.

THERE. THERE IT was, clasping the bones of Arkio's spinal column like a nesting spider. Thin lines of liquid darkness issued out of the egg-form, thousands of feelers infiltrating every organ and element of the Blood Angel's body. So delicate, so subtle were they that only by flaying him open or ripping up his mind on a psyker-rack would anyone discover the lurking poison inside Arkio. It was a black heart of raw, undistilled Chaos. The object was glassy and hard, a piece of some decayed thought-form created by the Malfallax. The Monarch of Spite had made it from himself, granting the seed to Stele on the day that this intricate plan had become a reality. There was not a part of Arkio that was not touched by the mutations the egg created. Its cilia had infiltrated all of him, warping the youth's flesh; it had been this that granted him the gift of his wings, his change, his Emergence.

Stele cooed to the egg, stroked it and calmed the malignant parasite. He had to be careful now, while the mutation progressed slowly and subtly, the taint in Arkio's body would lay undetected – but the foolish whelp's obsession with the Spear of Telesto had aroused the seed. Unless he could quiet it, all these carefully laid plans would unravel.

BEFORE, HERE WAS *where the vision ended, but now it went on.*

Something comes. A man in crimson ceramite, untouched by the mutation and corruption about him. The tides of foulness retreat about his footfalls. Arkio's traitor-self spits and loathes.

There is a blink of yellow light; suddenly the Holy Lance crosses the room and settles into the hands of the new arrival. Arkio, lisping through manifold mouths crowded with the buds of crooked new fangs, speaks his name.

'Raaaaaaffffffffennnn.'

His brother does not know him. Rafen turns the Spear of Telesto on Arkio and plunges it into his heart.

Betrayed, mutated, changed and discarded, Arkio dies screaming.

ARKIO SAGGED AND dropped to the stone floor of the grand chamber, his breath coming in ragged gasps. Deftly, Stele withdrew himself from the flesh of the Space Marine's neck, the skin sealing over like the surface of a pond. A few small rivulets of blood clung to the inquisitor's fingers and he wiped them away with a silk kerchief.

The figure in gold moaned. 'Rafen... No...'

Stele grimaced at the mention of Arkio's brother, watching the lesions on the Blessed's face shrink back to nothing, the raw mouths of weeping sores retreating into the folds of his skin. Once again, Arkio was perfect, an alabaster ideal of the Pure One. His eyes fluttered open.

'Stele?' he asked. 'My friend? What happened to me?'

The inquisitor displayed a mask of concern that hid his genuine annoyance. 'Blessed, praise Sanguinius that you are well. I feared the worst...'

Arkio got to his feet, his wings furling behind him. 'I saw... a terrible vision, inquisitor. A victory snatched away by the tide of Chaos.'

Stele's face remained utterly impassive. 'You must be mistaken, Blessed.'

He looked down at his hands, then to the humming form of the Spear. 'The lance...' Arkio began, his voice catching, 'it turned against me.'

'Impossible,' said Stele, his tone soothing. 'Such a thing could never happen.' He approached the Spear on the altar. 'Look here, Great One. The Holy Lance is yours alone. Touch it.'

Hesitantly, Arkio extended a hand to the weapon, fingers tracing the shape of a hooded figure on the haft of the lance. The Spear of Telesto glowed beneath his caress. Relief crossed the Space Marine's face.

'You see?' Stele smiled. 'It was no vision, Arkio. Just the weight of days preying upon you. The Holy Lance is yours,' he repeated. Inwardly, the inquisitor was relieved. His ministrations had been enough, and the mutations had been suppressed so that the Telesto weapon would not react to them – for the moment.

'It was so real,' Arkio was saying. 'I could feel the hand of the warp inside me...'

'Your mind changes as does your body and spirit, Blessed,' said Stele. 'Only you can know what purpose Sanguinius holds for you. Perhaps this... vision was something of a warning...'

'Explain yourself,' Arkio demanded, his hesitance falling away as his lordly manner returned.

'Perhaps... perhaps the Great Angel is showing you what will transpire if we fail him...'

'Yes...' Arkio turned away. 'That shall never happen, Stele. With your counsel, the Blood Crusade will ignite the stars with its righteous fire.'

The inquisitor gave himself a nod of self-approval. The crisis was passed. 'Indeed it will, Blessed. And we will begin with planet Sabien.'

Arkio nodded and walked on into the transept alone. Stele watched the feathers on his wings flicker as he moved. It would only be a matter of time before the taint of mutation made itself visible again – but if all went to plan, by the time that happened Arkio and his Blood Angels would be glorying in the name of Chaos, and they would welcome it like the gift that it was.

JETS OF SPENT thruster discharge vented from the underside of the Thunderhawk as it settled under the gravity of Sabien. From the deployment ramp at the ship's prow there was a scramble of quick, controlled movement. Four Blood Angels, each grasping a bolter in battle-ready postures, fanned out and stepped into a wedge formation. Their eyes and their guns never stopped scanning the landscape for any sign of movement.

Behind them came a figure towering like a dreadnought, striding with cool purpose across the deck. Two more Space Marines, one a grizzled veteran, the other a tech-priest, followed at his heels. 'Deploy scouts,' he said, his voice carrying over the rumble of engines as a second and third Thunderhawk landed nearby. 'I want a secure perimeter established, brother-sergeant. We may appear to be the first arrivals, but appearances can be deceptive.'

'By your command, lord.' The veteran saluted and broke into a run, growling out commands to a cadre of lightly armoured Space Marine outriders.

The other warrior paused, listening to a voice in his vox. 'Message from the *Europae*, lord. The ship has attained a geostationary orbit above this location. Awaiting your orders.'

Mephiston stepped on to the surface of Sabien and took a lungful of air. Hundreds of scents assailed his heightened sense receptors, his brain quickly processing the smells into familiar categories. *Death. This planet smells of death.*

'Lord Mephiston?' asked the Techmarine, hesitant around the Chief Librarian. Even among the members of his own

Chapter, the supreme psyker of the Blood Angels was feared as much as he was respected.

'The *Europae* is to remain at maximum battle readiness,' replied Mephiston, studying the landing zone. 'What of the sporadic sensor contact in the debris belt?' He glanced up. Above, a ghostly white shimmer could be seen bisecting the blue-orange sky – the thick band of rocks and captured asteroids ringing Sabien, the remnants of the planet's largest moon.

'No further detections,' replied the Space Marine. 'Cogitator reports conclude the contact may have been solar refraction from ice crystals or possible thermal outgassing.'

Mephiston curled his lip at that assessment. 'We shall see.' He left the tech-priest behind and walked out, the squad of tactical warriors moving with him. He eschewed the use of the more typical honour guard Space Marines on planetside missions; he preferred the company of line trooper Blood Angels, better to see first hand the disposition of the men that Lord Dante commanded, better to watch for signs of dissent or corruption.

This was not the first time Mephiston had set foot on Sabien. Once before, several lifetimes ago, he had stood in the same place, breathed the same air. He had been a different man then: Brother Calistarius, a mere codicer centuries away from the events at Hades Hive that would remake him as Mephiston, Lord of Death. Yet, as much as he had changed in the intervening years, Sabien had not altered at all. The shrine world remained as it was, as it had been for hundreds of years after the smoke and ashes of the brutal Phaedra Campaign had cleared. At that time, Sabien had seen the largest loss of life to the Blood Angels Chapter since the battles of the Horus Heresy, and when the world had finally been pacified at the cost of untold expended lives, the Imperial Church had awarded custody of the planet to the Sons of Sanguinius. The site of their desperate last stand against the enemies of mankind became a place of pilgrimage, and it had been on such a journey that the psyker had first come to Sabien.

Mephiston's piercing gaze crossed the broken ridges of the skyline. The Thunderhawks had landed in the city square, in the place where the last great engagement of the campaign had taken place. The open space was littered with fallen masonry as far as the eye could see, shattered spars of rusted iron laid down upon the crumbling remains of columns. The remnants of architecture created in the ancient styles of Old Terra were everywhere. Long halls and cloisters mingled with cathedral towers that once had cut the sky with their magnificence. Now, Sabien's streets were filled with drifts of fallen stone and the towers were humbled. Only a single construction still remained in the middle of the echoing square. Canted at an angle by eruptions of some long-silenced shell fire, a statue on a stone plinth kept watch on the dead city. Somehow, the figure of an angel had never once been struck in all the madness of the fight for Sabien. It remained here now, its features worn to vague shapes, as a symbol of human will.

The Librarian rested one hand on the hilt of his sheathed force sword and closed his eyes. Gently, he summoned the energy of the Quickening that coiled inside his mind, moulding it and absorbing it into his senses. The exhilarating rush of potency ran through him in a shiver, and Mephiston allowed his mind to slip free of its sheath of meat and bone. Gentle blue glows hovered around the horned skulls that decorated his psychic hood and the Lord of Death reached out, searching for life. The ghost of his psy-self slipped through the ravaged streets, a breath of mental power shifting and flowing in a gust of wind.

The dead had left their mark on the psychic landscape of Sabien. In the ruined city there was no place where the scars of violent death could not be found. Anguish and raw pain were burnt into the stonework, as clear to Mephiston's senses as the scorched shadows of human figures left by a nuclear flare. The faded screams of Blood Angels hung about the edges of his esper perceptions, the phantoms crowding him. A nerve twitched in the Lord of Death's jaw. Even for a Librarian of his awesome discipline, it was difficult to sift through the white noise of the haunted city and search beyond. He frowned. There seemed to be something out there at the very edge of his mind-sight, but it was ephemeral, hidden in the clutter of the war dead. Perhaps...

Mephiston's head jerked around in a swift motion, and the Techmarine froze, startled by the action. The Blood Angels psyker looked up into the sky. Evening stars were slowly emerging from the darkening blue, and one steady dot of brightness showed the position of the *Europae*. 'They're coming,' he whispered to himself, his voice too low for anyone else to hear. Like a new constellation flaring into life, Mephiston's inner sight could see the cluster of glowing minds approaching the planet at high speed, and among them he could read the strange flickers of a mentality like none he had ever encountered before.

There was a mumbling crackle of communication from the Techmarine's helmet vox, and he glanced up at Mephiston. 'My lord, word from the *Europae*. The battle barge *Bellus* has arrived.'

He nodded. 'I know. I can taste him.'

BELLUS PRESENTED HER hammerhead bow to her sister ship as she slowed. The vessels were almost mirror images of one another, the huge slab-like hulls beweaponed with cannons and missile tubes. Each displayed a huge disk with the Chapter sigil beneath a golden crest of the Imperial aquila, but the similarities ended at the surface. Across the gulf of Sabien's orbit, the crews of both ships eyed one another with suspicion and doubt. It was a rare sight to see two ships of this class in the same place. Such deployments were usually the prelude to war on a huge scale, and there were many Blood Angels aboard *Bellus* and *Europae* that wondered if war was what would soon follow.

On the command deck, Captain Ideon scrutinised the other vessel with all the tactical acumen he would have given an enemy warship. 'Solus,' he crackled. 'Detector pallets on the port forward quarter read what looks like a fluctuation in her drive coils.'

Ideon's aide nodded from his post at the primary cogitator. 'Agreed, captain.'

'Log that information with the gunnery servitors. It may prove useful if we are required to engage.'

At the observation window, Stele turned away from his conversation with Sachiel to face the captain. 'It saddens me that such precautions must be taken, but after the *Amareo* incident…'

'You may rest assured, the crew of the *Europae* are planning the same for us,' Arkio snapped. He was wound tight with tension, and in long strides he pushed his way past the Sanguinary Priest to face the command dais. 'Ideon. Do you detect any other starships in the area?'

The captain blinked as he addressed the eyes and ears of *Bellus*. 'No, Blessed,' he answered after a moment. 'No contacts at this time.'

'It appears that Dante kept his word,' said Sachiel. The priest seemed muted, his usual bluster quieted. 'Perhaps we may yet see a peaceful path out of this cha–' He stumbled over the word. 'This… This disorder.'

Stele threw him an arch glance. 'Indeed. But I respectfully suggest that our watchword should be vigilance. If Commander Dante decides–'

'Dante is not here,' Arkio broke in, steel in his voice. 'I know it in my bones. He has sent his second, the psyker Mephiston.' The golden-armoured Space Marine looked Stele in the eye. 'Do you not sense him, inquisitor?'

Gingerly, Stele extended the smallest of mental feelers toward Sabien's surface, and just as quickly he jerked it back, like a hand too close to a naked flame. 'The Blessed is correct. The Lord of Death awaits us.' For the briefest of instants, a glimmer of concern crossed the Hereticus agent's face.

Arkio approached Ideon and nodded a command to him. 'Set war conditions throughout the ship, captain. These are my orders – the Warriors of the Reborn will attend me on Sabien. Launch transports and Thunderhawks. I will meet Mephiston at the head of my multitude.'

'I have selected a company of Space Marines, Blessed,' added Sachiel. 'Your army will truly be a glorious sight.'

Arkio nodded. 'Attend me, priest – and you as well, inquisitor. We go to make history.'

Stele gave a shallow bow and followed the Reborn Angel from the room. Entering the echoing corridors, he hung back a few steps and spoke urgently into a concealed vox in his collar. 'Ulan, listen to me. Come to the landing bay and prepare for planetfall. I will have need of you on the surface.'

'Mephiston?' came the reply.

'With haste,' he retorted, quickening his pace.

ELSEWHERE ABOARD THE *Bellus*, the cargo lighters were accepting their loads, each of the bullet-shaped ships sealing shut with a warshot of armed, zealous men. Ideon's orders crackled through the air on every deck of the ship, calling the vessel to arms and preparing the troops for a landing. In the days that had passed between their departure from Shenlong and the arrival here, the Warriors of the Reborn had grown restless and impatient for release. Each group was wired with anticipation as they filed into the transports, their eagerness to prove their worth to Arkio far outweighing their fears.

Rafen carefully joined the rear of a trailing group of helots, keeping as far as he could from the other Space Marines herding the rag-tag army into their troopships. Hidden in the lower decks, the journey had passed quickly for the Blood Angel as he dipped in and out of trance-sleep, his brain's catelepsean node keeping one half of his brain awake while the other slumbered. Rafen was thankful for the capability of the implant. He suspected that the dreams true slumber brought would not have pleased him.

The slave-soldiers marched up the boarding ramp in a loose, undisciplined group, the very antithesis of the finely drilled formations of the Adeptus Astartes. As they entered the cargo lighter's interior, a figure pushed through them, giving out terse orders. Another Space Marine.

Rafen licked dry lips; this would be the moment of truth. If his subterfuge failed now, he would never make it down to the planet alive. He gave the other Blood Angel a cursory nod as if nothing were amiss, and strode past him, up the ramp toward the ship.

'Brother,' said the Space Marine. 'You are overseeing this group? I thought that I was to accompany...' His voice drifted off, confusion in his tone. Rafen recognised him as he stepped into the light, the biolume glow illuminating his face. *Alactus.*

Rafen kept walking, and made an off-hand grunt that he hoped would be enough.

'Wait,' Alactus continued. 'I know you, do I not?' His brow furrowed. 'What is your name?'

How could he not know me, Rafen asked himself. We have served the Chapter together for decades.

'Brother!' The shout halted Rafen at the top of the ramp and he half-turned to glance over his shoulder. Alactus had his hand at the grip of his bolt pistol. 'I asked you a question.' The Space Marine stepped closer, suspicion clear on his face. 'Take off your helmet.'

He glanced at the transport; the helots were secure inside now, and none of them could see what was going on outside. Rafen turned to face the wary Alactus. There were no other men around this high on the launch cradles, just the two Blood Angels.

'Take off your helmet,' Alactus repeated, and the bolter was in his hand. 'I will not ask you again.' The warning in his voice was needle-sharp, the Space Marine would shoot Rafen dead if he did not respond.

Rafen nodded and descended the ramp, unlatching the connector ring on his headgear as he did so. He halted in front of Alactus and turned the helmet off his head. When he met his battle-brother's eyes he saw shock there.

'Rafen!' husked Alactus, 'but you're dead...'

'No,' he replied, and in a single sharp movement, Rafen swung his helmet at the other Space Marine, rushing at him. He smothered the sick feeling in his gut that welled up as he assaulted his former comrade; to do such a thing made Rafen feel soiled, but he knew that there was no choice here. If he did not kill Alactus, then he would perish in his stead.

Alactus was caught by the surprise attack, and the ceramite helmet struck him hard, knocking the pistol from his hands. The gun clattered away as Rafen hit out again, knocking the other Space Marine to his haunches.

'Traitor!' spat Alactus, whipping his combat blade from its sheath. 'Sachiel told us what you did, what you tried to do. You murdered Lucion.'

'I didn't want to–'

'Liar! You craven wretch, you turned on your own brethren. You tried to destroy the fortress – you would have killed us all, you would have murdered the Reborn Angel.'

Anger boiled up inside Rafen. 'You fool. It is not I who is the turncoat, it is you. You and everyone who follows Arkio's misguided insanity!'

'No.' Alactus shook his head, 'I will not hear your falsehoods! He is the Pure One returned–'

'He is nothing of the kind,' Rafen retorted. 'Open your eyes, man. Open your eyes and see the truth, Arkio is just a pawn. Stele is behind this, that ordos mind-witch is clouding everything for his own ends.'

'Lies!' Alactus dived at him, the blade glinting. Rafen blocked, but the knife bit down and cut into his armour. 'To think I trusted you,' hissed the other Space Marine. 'To think we fought together in the Emperor's name when all along you were an agent of Chaos.' He forced the blade deeper and Rafen bit off a cry of pain. 'I will kill you as a gift for the Blessed.'

Rafen's hands snapped up and found Alactus's neck. Ceramite-encased fingers bit into his skin and squeezed. 'Forgive me...' he hissed, the two of them locked together in a death-grip. Rafen felt the knife slashing and cutting, but still he would not release. Blood bubbled from his battle-brother's lips and bone in his throat cracked.

'Damn... you...' Alactus choked and died in his arms, his body turning limp.

Rafen dropped him to the deck and tore the knife from his wound, snarling at the pain of it. He stared at his hands; blood coated them with thick, accusing stains. He remembered the Word Bearer he had killed on Cybele in the same manner, his breath catching in his chest. 'Sanguinius,' he asked aloud. 'Where will this madness end?'

But no answer came to him. Carefully, Rafen replaced his helmet, pausing to recover the bolt pistol before he marched aboard the transport ship. The hatch slammed shut behind him, leaving his comrade's corpse to vent to the void as the shuttle shot away toward Sabien.

'THE SCOUTS REPORT no contact along the outer perimeter,' said the sergeant, 'the landing zone is devoid of life.'

The hint of a sneer tugged at the corner of Mephiston's thin lips. 'Just because they have not found anything does not mean that it isn't there. Be watchful, sergeant.'

The Blood Angel gave a grave nod and pointed into the sky. 'Look there, lord. Ships.'

A rain of transports and cargo craft descended, touching down on the clearer part of the square in the north-west corner. 'Prepare yourself,' Mephiston told his men. 'Be ready for anything.'

Figures in shabby, makeshift uniforms emerged from the shuttles along with the red dots of Blood Angels. The sergeant frowned, scrutinising the warriors with his long-range optics. 'What's this?' he said in a low voice. 'The pretender has brought an army of commoners with him?'

Through an ornate set of magnoculars the Librarian watched the figures moving into a poor approximation of a parade line. 'Ah,' he said after a moment. 'Their eyes, sergeant. Look at their eyes. Tell me what you see.'

The Blood Angel did as he was told. 'They seem... manic, perhaps.'

'Yes. Those men have the fire of belief kindled in them. And those of their number who do not have ill-temper enough to compensate.' Mephiston's fingers drummed on the grip of his plasma pistol. 'Watch them. Their kind are unpredictable, given the right circumstances.'

The sergeant pointed again. 'There, lord, do you see him? I can't be sure–'

The Lord of Death did not need to be told where to look; floating like a mellifluent seraph among a throng of vagrants, Arkio approached them. His armour caught the red-orange glow of Sabien's setting sun and it glimmered off the gold ceramite like liquid fire. Broad white wings formed arcs above his shoulders.

'Emperor's blood...' breathed the sergeant. 'He could almost be–'

'He is not,' Mephiston grated harshly. 'Allow yourself to believe that and you are useless to me.'

'Forgive me, lord, it's just that... I have never seen the like.'

The Librarian could sense the same thoughts on the surface of the minds of all the Blood Angels in his guard. He set his jaw hard and lightly touched the psychic reservoir of his Quickening. Gently, Mephiston used the power to reinforce the will of his men, erasing any germ of doubt before it could grow larger.

RAFEN USED ROUGH gestures with the bolter to make the slave-soldiers go where he wanted. Hidden in the mass of the procession, he was far enough apart from Arkio's loyalist Space Marines that he would not be recognised again. He frowned beneath the visor of his helmet. There, a way ahead of him, marched his brother, and at his side the priest Sachiel, Stele and the inquisitor's retinue. He saw the shambling lexmechanic, the floating shapes of Stele's servo-skulls and a hooded female whose features were invisible beneath a voluminous cloak. Rafen elected to bide his time. His plan, such as it was, was taking shape on the fly. Perhaps, if the opportunity presented itself, he could approach Arkio unseen, and then – would he dare to shed the blood of a brother again?

And this time, the blood of his own kinsman? He had been unable to do it back on Shenlong, and as he searched his feelings, Rafen could not be sure if he would do it now.

At the foot of a Thunderhawk, Rafen could see another figure, an unmistakeable form that seemed cut from a history book. He recognised Dante's Chief Librarian immediately, the most powerful psyker in the entire Chapter – and some said, the whole of the Legion Astartes – watching the approach. Rafen recalled his stony aspect from a statue in the cloisters of Angel's Fall: Mephiston, the Lord of Death. His name was well-earned, for it had been he alone that had looked into the unknowable void of the Blood Angels gene-curse and survived. Only through an incredible force of will had Mephiston passed through the punishing trials of the maddening red thirst and lived to tell of it. Men said that to look the Lord of Death in the eye was to see a window to the black rage and the dark places that waited beyond the realm of life. Mephiston's burning gaze had been known to stop enemies in their tracks and leave them broken and weeping.

As befitting a man of such stature, the psyker wore a crimson cloak inlaid with a profusion of bone skulls, the death-head symbol large on his shoulder pads. The twin rails of a powerful psychic hood extended above his head, and the armour across his torso resembled skinned flesh, glistening red bunches of muscle crossed with death marks and jewelled blood droplets. He was the darkest end of the spectrum when compared to Arkio's golden, mirror-bright form.

'LORD MEPHISTON,' ARKIO said, inclining his head in greeting, 'you honour me with your presence here. Thank you for coming.'

The psyker studied the youth. The sergeant had been correct, Arkio's resemblance to the Great Angel was uncanny. It was almost as if a statue of Sanguinius had shaken off its coating of stone and stepped down from a chapel plinth. Yet, as much as the image matched the legends that had shaped his devotion for so many years, Mephiston could already sense the taint of something foul and corrupt in the air, lingering like spent tabac smoke. He was very careful not to give even the slightest hint of obeisance to the man in the gold armour. This was the one who had ordered Mephiston's protégé Vode destroyed and Captain Gallio's crew executed in cold blood, something the Librarian would not soon forget.

But still... There was some small voice inside Mephiston's mind, some last fragment of his old self as Brother Calistarius, that was awed by what Arkio had become, this perfect living avatar of great Sanguinius. He silenced the discord within him and drew his psy-essence into a single place.

'You are the one they call the Blessed Arkio.' It was not a question. 'You claim that you are the vessel for the Angelic Sovereign.'

'I claim nothing,' Arkio said. 'I simply *am*.'

For the first time, their eyes met, and from within the dark pits of Mephiston's soul, he turned his transfixing glare upon the youth; the sheer force of the mental charge between them set other men staggering upon their feet.

'We shall see,' intoned the Lord of Death, turning his baleful sight on Arkio's very soul.

CHAPTER TEN

DARKNESS COILED FROM the evening sky and crossed the horizon with deep, inky shadows. Some of the Warriors of the Reborn shifted nervously and muttered, weapons rattling as they gripped them harder, afraid of what was to come next. Rafen moved forward through the ranks of men, better to observe the confrontation between Arkio's and Mephiston's titanic wills. He tasted the thick, greasy texture on the chill air, the same oily aroma that he had encountered before when Stele had brought his psychic powers to bear – but this time the magnitude was a hundred times greater, and the thickness of the atmosphere about him made Rafen feel like he was wading through a marshy bog. He could see the hellfire glow from beneath the Lord of Death's brow, his eyes twin embers of controlled menace like distant beacons.

The stink of mind-magick was all about him, and Rafen felt bile rise in his gorge. To be so near to such a naked show of psyker force made him feel soiled and unclean.

He was closer now; he could see Stele's bald head, the glint of the silver purity stud in his ear. The inquisitor appeared to be in distress, as if the effort of standing in Mephiston's aura was almost too much for him. At his side, Stele's woman trembled beneath her hood. Rafen swore he could see thin wisps of smoke issuing from her nostrils. The Space Marine kneaded the grip of the bolt pistol and forced himself to move nearer still.

THE GAZE WAS a lens that opened up the hidden world to Mephiston's perception. The power burning inside him shone through the gates of his vision like the beam of a devout searchlight, pinning the weak and the unhallowed as it fell upon them. His sight-beyond-sight stripped away the illusions of reality and bared souls so that the Lord of Death could examine their pale, naked truths. He saw Arkio as if he were an anatomical sketch drawn from some textbook of the magus biologis, layers of skin, bone, muscle and nerve visible to him. The boy was glass, and Mephiston's gaze shone into him, illuminating every corner of his spirit as searing sunlight falling through a prism.

There. It was concealed well, buried beneath levels of wards and mind-baffles, the matter of it worked into the bone and meat of the Space Marine's body, but the taint could not hide from the unblinking eye of Mephiston's powers. The black ellipse floated among the perfection of Arkio's Astartes physiology, ruining the sacred organic design of the Blood Angel. The seed of Chaos glittered and pulsed.

In a faint way, he was slightly disappointed. Perhaps there was a part of him, however tiny, that had hoped Arkio's story might be true; but instead Mephiston found himself confronted by a dupe, a mutant ignorant of his own poisoned nature. Other men might have felt pity then; but not he.

The Lord of Death marvelled at the perfection and ingenuity of the taint – it was truly a work of psionic art, the construct of a maker both genius and madman. It bore the unmistakable fingerprints of the Changer of Ways across every aspect of its form. He traced thin thought-filaments from the infection, tracking the lines of their mutations, the reordering of fleshy matter that had altered the boy from a Marine to the simulacra he was now. Faint glints of contact danced in Arkio's aura, bending like flowers seeking the sun, all of them turning toward one man.

Stele. Mephiston could smell his emotions like spilled blood, a cocktail of arrogance warring with controlled fear, desire and avarice raging beneath the thin veneer of his icy civility. But the inquisitor was not the puppet master here; like a mirror within a mirror, Stele in turn was being directed by some other intelligence. He let his vision slip over the woman. She was like oil on water, repelling it instantly. Mephiston's sight could not hold purchase on her.

'Tell me, lord,' said Arkio. 'Now you have looked into my soul, what do you see?' The tension in the square came to a knife-edge on his words. 'Will you deny the work of the Great Angel upon me? Or will you accept that I am the incarnation of the Deus Sanguinius?'

Mephiston drew back with a grim sneer on his lips. 'If only your divinity matched the scope of your arrogance, lad, you might be what you appear.'

'How dare you!' blurted Sachiel, stepping forward. 'He is the Reborn Angel, the light of–'

'Silence, priest.' The psyker stilled him with a single glance, and Sachiel clasped at his throat, coughing.

The gracious expression on Arkio's face faded into a blank mask of neutrality. 'Mephiston, tread carefully. I offer you the chance to join my Blood Crusade. Do not be so quick to judge me. Come to my side, and I will welcome you as my battle-brother.'

He arched an eyebrow, gauging the moment. 'And if I do not?'

'It would go poorly for you, Lord of Death. The sands of your life have already run thin on borrowed time. If you test them again, you will not be so blessed as you were on Armageddon.'

A soft laugh escaped the psyker's lips; he decided to allow the boy to talk. 'Your presumption amuses me, Arkio. Tell me, this "crusade" of yours, what gives you the right to dictate such a thing? You speak as if it is your voice that leads our Chapter.'

'And so it will be,' Arkio replied. 'Your master Dante has lingered too long in command of the Blood Angels. He will step aside for me.'

The cold humour vanished from Mephiston's face in an instant. 'He will do no such thing for a pretender whelp like you.' The Librarian's voice was iron-hard and full of threat.

Arkio watched him carefully. 'Perhaps not. If he cannot release his petty fear of me then we will absolve him of his office. With all the due effort that may be required to do so.' The golden-armoured figure summoned a trio of Sachiel's honour guards and the men arrived with a titanium cylinder between them. Arkio opened the case and let the radiance of the Holy Lance light the darkening landscape. With a single swift motion, Arkio drew the ancient weapon and swept it up in a brilliant arc of light.

'The... the Spear of Telesto...' The words fell from the lips of the Techmarine in a humbled gasp.

Arkio pointed the spear at Mephiston, sighting down the length of the haft at him. 'I swear this by the blood of the primarch in my veins. Know me, Librarian. I am the Blood Angels incarnate. I am Sanguinius Reborn.' Gold lightning arced around the teardrop blade at the tip of the spear. 'Give me your fealty or perish. The choice is yours.'

For one dizzying, horrible moment, Mephiston felt his world lurch around him as the lance hove into view. *How can this be? He wields the sacred weapon!* A storm of chattering doubts engulfed the Lord of Death; it was impossible to think that some debased impostor would ever be able to lay hands on the spear, and yet Arkio held the Holy Lance like he was born to it. *Have I been mistaken? Could he really be the Reborn Angel? Who else could know the might of the Telesto artefact?* Mephiston shook the churn of thought away with a shake of his head, tiny darts of blue fire crackling along his crystalline psi-hood. 'No,' he growled. There was some magick at work here, a bewitchery so subtle and insidious that even a weapon forged by Holy Terra could be deceived by it. 'I am not cozened, pretender. Your parlour tricks mean nothing against my faith.' The Blood Angel's hand dropped to the hilt of his arcane force sword, the ancient mind-blade Vitarus. 'No true Son of Sanguinius will ever bend his knee to you, charlatan. You are false.'

A surge of anger thundered through the Warriors of the Reborn and cries of violence burst forth from Arkio's loyalists. Rafen let them jostle him forward.

Arkio shook his head in annoyance. 'Poor, old fool. You are infected with Dante's fear, just as Vode and Gallio before you, just as every misguided man who sits under Baal's sun and believes himself a true Blood Angel. I am the way.' He shouted, brandishing the spear, 'I am the truth reborn. Your blindness sickens me, mind-witch. I pity you.'

Mephiston's troops knotted together, breeches clattering on their bolters in a rush of noise. The Librarian drew himself to his full height, towering over Arkio's golden form and brilliant white wings. 'Save it for yourself, fool. You and your ordos accomplice, all of you are black with the stain of Chaos! It reeks from you...' He stabbed a copper-gloved finger at the inquisitor, who met his accusation with a sneer. 'This weakling is a lackey of the Ruinous Powers, and those who heed his words are equally disgraced with the stigma of heresy!' The psyker's words drew a chorus of denials and vicious retorts. 'Ramius Stele, I name you traitor. You conspire with dark powers and revel in corruption. You are the architect of this apostasy!'

'No!' roared the inquisitor, the shout slamming into the distant ruins like a thunderclap. 'The Blessed is right. You decry all that you fear! Your words are lies, Mephiston, lies. *Arkio is Sanguinius.*'

'Then he shall prove it,' the Lord of Death spat back. 'In the *Book of the Lords*, the Pure One was said to be the match of any warrior that lived. If this is so, then perhaps your so-called "Blessed" would be willing to face a true Blood Angel in single combat...' Mephiston bared his fangs. 'If he is the vessel for the will of the Angelic Sovereign, he will be victorious. If he is a mere pretender, he will die.'

He watched the consequence of his dare as it spread out among Arkio's loyalists, sensing the merge of anger and fear it engendered. He nodded to himself; exactly the reaction he had wanted. Playing the young fool into his hands, Mephiston had brought him to this moment, and now he would butcher the impostor like a prey beast. Such a brutal and very visible destruction of this golden figurehead was necessary – when Arkio died on the tip of Mephiston's force sword, his disciples and helots would break. Their confusion would make it easier for the Lord of Death to execute them. This insurrection had to be smashed in the most public and bloody way possible.

Men on both sides began to draw back, granting room for the coming duel, and Sachiel had found his voice once more. 'It's a trick,' he sputtered, the veins on his neck corded and tight with anger bordering on madness. 'You cannot accept, Blessed. The psyker is goading you.'

Arkio gave the priest a brief, beneficent smile. 'Sachiel, my friend. Your concern for my wellbeing is touching, but misplaced. I will not dismiss this challenge. If Mephiston wishes to see the might of the Red Angel enraged, then by the grail, I shall show it to him!' He stepped forward in a grim-faced swagger, the Holy Lance at rest beneath the curl of his wing. 'I will face any man here,' Arkio told the Librarian, 'and I will send him to the Emperor's grace knowing the truth of my divinity!' He made a show of opening his arms wide to the assembled men, Blood Angels, loyalists, slave-soldiers alike. 'Who here would take up arms to fight me? Which of you will shed your blood to prove the rightness of my decree?'

The sword Vitarus whispered as it drew free of its scabbard. 'Arkio,' growled Mephiston. 'It will be my–'

'*I will face him!*' The cry cut through the air and set heads turning, hands frozen on weapons.

'Who?' said the sergeant at Mephiston's flank. 'It came from over there.' The veteran indicated the mob of Arkio's men with the barrel of his bolter.

The psyker's perplexity increased as the crowd of ragged slave-troops parted to allow a single Blood Angel to come forward. His armour was discoloured by bloodstains and there was a gouge in his chest plate. As Mephiston watched, the Space Marine stepped past Arkio's retinue and removed his helmet. For the first time, he saw an expression on the pretender's face that wasn't anger or arrogance, but pure, raw shock.

'RAFEN!' ARKIO CHOKED out the name. 'You survived...'

'Impossible,' Sachiel shrieked, grabbing at his gun. 'The factory was obliterated, he was inside, he could not have–'

'Quiet, you fool,' growled Stele, forcing the priest to lower his weapon. 'It appears that your news of his death was premature.'

Rafen and Arkio held each other's gaze for a long moment. 'Brother,' said the figure in gold, 'I did not think to lay eyes on you again.'

'I am a survivor,' Rafen replied, the weariness of all that had happened before in his voice, 'and now it has come to this.'

'You tried to destroy me, Rafen. You turned your back on me.' Arkio's words were thick with emotion, pain and fury.

He shook his head. 'I have not betrayed you, kindred. You have betrayed yourself. I warned you. I begged you to step back from the abyss.' Rafen looked away. 'You did not heed me.'

'And now it has come to this,' Arkio repeated. 'Very well, brother. If a son of Axan must die today, then die he will.'

The Lord of Death slammed his force weapon back into its sheath and beckoned Rafen closer. 'Come to me, brother. If you wish this, then let me know you.'

Rafen knelt before Mephiston and raised his head. 'Aye, I wish it.' The light behind the psyker's eyes glowed and burnt a path into Rafen's mind. He felt his body tense and Mephiston's hand shot out, cupping his chin so he could not turn away.

The Librarian's powerful inner sight tore apart any defence of will that Rafen might have thought he had, slipping into the corridors of his psyche in a flood of power. His brain felt like hot magma, churning and boiling as storms of long-forgotten memory were dredged up and examined. Nothing that was Rafen escaped the gaze of Mephiston.

For a brief moment, their mentalities were unified as the Lord of Death sifted through the Space Marine's consciousness. Mephiston tasted Rafen's heart, the colours and shades of his soul – he saw pieces of the man that even Rafen himself could not comprehend. Duty and honour marbled his spirit, they were cut into Rafen like the age rings of a nyawood tree. Once, there had been a time when this man was wilful and arrogant, when it was only his own glory that had occupied his mind; that Rafen was gone, a child grown into an adult with all the knowledge of life's hardest lessons. The Space Marine embodied the ideal of the Blood Angels. He was noble but humble, a warrior but not belligerent. *Among all these brothers who have lost their way, this one alone still walks the path of the Blood. There can be no better champion.*

Mephiston sensed something else, remaining only in fragments and splinters throughout Rafen's spirit. The touch of something higher, the marks where a force of being with powers far beyond the Lord of Death's had briefly influenced Rafen.

A vision…

The Librarian released him and withdrew, the fire in his eyes retreating. An unspoken moment of communication passed between the two men, a sadness at what Rafen had foreseen and what he knew had to be done. 'He is your blood kin,' said Mephiston.

'Aye, lord.'

He nodded. 'Rafen, you are true to our code. I stand aside to let you take my place in this challenge.' Mephiston gestured to the veteran nearby. 'Sergeant, give this man your power sword.'

The Space Marine drew the weapon and presented it to Rafen, who accepted it with a shallow bow. He turned the blade over in his hands, his fingers falling easily behind the spiked guard and into the knurled grip. The sword resonated with dormant threat, the polished silver blade catching the colour of the orange sky in its surface. Rafen traced the shape of a half-eagle cut into the hilt. 'A fine weapon,' he noted.

Mephiston stepped back to give him room. 'This matter will be decided,' he intoned. 'Brother against brother, with victory for the faithful.'

PERFECT.

Stele almost laughed out loud when Rafen took up the sword. This was ideal, he could have done no better himself at producing so exquisite a finale. Brother facing brother, with death alone the reward for Rafen's foolhardy presumption. Such a conflict would be a fitting end for that turbulent Space Marine, and at long last Stele would be rid of the irritant that had plagued him since they had first arrived among Cybele's war graves. It was regretful that Arkio's brother had proven so resistant to the cult that Stele had created among the Blood Angels – such a warrior with so defiant and unyielding a soul would have made a fine addition to the Reborn Angel's retinue. If only he had followed the route of his battle-brothers and truly accepted Arkio's new-found divinity, Rafen would be here now as a lord commander among the forces of the Blood Crusade; instead, he would be its first victim, and his vitae would be the wine of its consecration.

But no, Stele told himself, better that he dies. While he lived, Rafen was random chance, a wild card among the inquisitor's games of engineered plot and counterplot. It had been pure fluke that the Space Marine had been on Cybele when Garand sent the Word Bearers to attack it, but his presence had quickly grown from a minor diversion to the most serious nuisance. Rafen would never truly give his heart to his changed sibling – Stele had known that even when Arkio took his oath in the Ikari fortress's chapel – and so he had to be destroyed.

Rafen would die at his brother's own hand, and with that Arkio would be inexorably committed to a path from the

Emperor's light for all time. Once the blood of his closest kinsman spattered that golden armour, once it hissed into steam from the burning blade of the Holy Lance, Arkio would have severed the last connection that still made him human. Once Rafen perished, Arkio would move ever further toward the eightfold way with nothing to hold him back. He would murder his conscience along with his brother.

Stele sensed Mephiston's attention upon him, and saw the Librarian from the corner of his sight, unwilling to meet his gaze directly. Perhaps the psyker sensed some measure of his thoughts, perhaps not. It mattered little, he would wait for the moment when the light died in Rafen's eyes, and then let loose a call for carnage. With Ulan's smothering mind-cloak to protect them, the loyalists would be upon the Lord of Death and his men in numbers so large that none of Dante's Space Marines would survive.

And if not, there was still one more card Stele could deal, one more player he could deliver to the field.

RAFEN BROUGHT THE power sword to arms and held it at his chest, the blade pointing at the sky. He gave his brother a grim salute.

In return, Arkio's eyes drew into narrow slits as he let the Spear of Telesto slide along his fingers to its full length. Sullen flickers of yellow-amber lightning crackled around the blade and the golden icon of Sanguinius carved in the hilt.

Both men stood for a moment; the battle balanced on a breath of silence as they watched for the sudden flood of muscle movement, the smallest telltale that would signify their opponent's actions. Warrior-to-warrior battles like this were commonplace in the wars of the Imperium, where conflicts were often fought with champions on either side engaging in single combat. Like every Adeptus Astartes, Rafen and Arkio were trained to fight alone, as an army of one; in years past, as initiates, the siblings had sparred on many occasions. Then, they had known each other well enough to counter every attack, neutralise every defence – but time had altered both of them.

Rafen surrendered himself to the moment, allowing his mind and spirit to flow together, merging into a single engine of action and movement. Arkio watched him, impassive and unmoving, a gold statue among the colourless debris of the city square. Rafen's focus narrowed until it was only his brother he saw before him, only the shape of a man. An enemy.

And suddenly he was in motion, a snarl ripping from his lips, fangs baring in fight rage. The power sword sizzled around him in a punishing arc of liquid silver. Arkio reacted, sweeping the spear down in a sharp gesture of defence, falling for Rafen's feint. With his other arm, Rafen brought up the blunt, brutish ingot of his bolt pistol and followed through with a three-round burst of shell fire.

Arkio recovered with frightening speed and turned the glowing lance like a propeller, the humming shaft making a gleaming disc in the air. The bolt rounds whined and screamed as they were shredded by the flickering shield. Rafen extended through his initial attack and spun on his boot, slashing down with a low cut of the sword. The blade sliced through air as Arkio slid away over loose-packed dirt. In a blur, he turned the spear back at Rafen.

His brother spied the infinitesimal loss of balance off Arkio's back foot and advanced, cutting a web of figure-eight lines toward him. The spear tip met the power sword and spat violently, bursts of fat, angry sparks hissing like fireworks as the weapons met and parted, met and parted, met again.

Arkio fell back step after step, unhurried and emotionless. The fan of light from the spinning lance was everywhere that

Rafen's sword blade fell, halting its savage attacks, blunting each stab and cut with a flashing parry. To the untrained eye, it seemed as if the figure in the golden armour was on the defensive, fighting off an endless salvo of strikes. Some of the Warriors of the Reborn made harsh catcalls until the loyalist Space Marines commanding them gave out violent censures. Arkio let Rafen spend the energy of his assault in a flurry of blows, at the same time using the minimum amount of effort to counter. He had expected better from his brother.

Rafen was no fool. If he extended the attack a second longer, Arkio would turn it on him and strike back. He lunged forward, an easy move calculated to look like the action of a fighter frustrated and desperate. Arkio took it at face value and blocked the strike, opening a window of opportunity along his left side for an eye-blink. The winged Space Marine was powerful, undoubtedly, but he lacked the experience of his older brother. Rafen would never have fallen for the feint – but Arkio did.

The bolt gun came from nowhere, suddenly there in front of Arkio's face, the barrel still warm and hot with the stink of ozone discharge. Rafen's finger tightened on the trigger.

Arkio reacted with preternatural speed. His folded wings exploded open in a flare of brilliant white and he shot into the air, flashing out of Rafen's line of fire. The golden figure described a swift, graceful arc up and over his brother's head, spinning and turning toward the ground seven metres distant. Rafen rotated in place, tracking Arkio with the gun. He fired a quartet of shots at the swooping shape, leading the target but missing with each bolt by the merest fraction.

The ground rumbled and rippled as Arkio touched down, the impact causing a shock wave in the centuries-old detritus around them. A grimace marred his perfect features as he whirled the spear to present the glowing teardrop blade to Rafen. Golden effulgence and sparkling particles gathered into a humming sphere of energy at the weapon's tip. Unable to dodge, Rafen saw it coming and raised his hands, gun and sword crossed over his face like some desperate invocation of the Imperial aquila.

The jet of unearthly power detached from the Holy Lance and ripped across the distance between the two men, splitting open and turning into a dancing fence of yellow flame. As it engulfed Rafen, he felt his skin searing; he remembered the Word Bearers, their bodies reduced to ash in the depths of the Shenlong manufactory. For one heart-stopping moment, Rafen thought his world was at an end, but then the flames flicked away, leaving him injured but still alive. He pawed at his face, shaking off a fine layer of ash where his epidermis had been flash-burnt.

'Sanguinius be praised,' he heard Mephiston's voice. 'The Spear of Telesto knows the soul of his Sons! He turns his holy fire from Rafen!'

The Space Marine nodded to himself – of course, the weapon was gene-coded. It could only be used by men who carried the genetic template of the primogenitor within them, and it would not harm those who bore the same mark in their blood. Rafen saw a brief glint of annoyance in Arkio's eyes – he would not be able to do away with him in such a showy display of power as he had the cursed Traitor Marines. It was fitting – the fight would be won or lost on martial prowess, not strength of arms. Snarling, Rafen threw himself at Arkio once more, leading into him with the hissing edge of the power sword's blade.

Arkio bit back an angry curse, rebuking himself for forgetting the weapon's gene-code failsafe. Instead, he dropped the haft of the spear into a two-handed grip, holding it like a quarterstaff. He blocked Rafen's attack, the sword blade bouncing as it struck off the unbreakable shaft of the weapon.

He forced Rafen off-balance and shoved him back, reversing the ploy his brother had used only moments earlier.

Broken drifts of ferrocrete fragments and stone shifted beneath Rafen's feet and he dug in, refusing to let Arkio knock him back. Blade and spear came together, each weapon pressing back to the fighter's breastplates, hot flashes of light flickering over them. The brothers were toe-to-toe, pushing into one another with all the force they could muster.

'Yield, Rafen,' snarled Arkio. 'Yield to me and I will end it cleanly.'

'I will not yield to corruption,' he gasped. 'Brother, there must be something of the man I knew still in you, some piece of your soul that still remains pure?'

'I am purity itself.' Arkio's skin was taut across his face with anger, his fangs bared. 'Ignorant fool, you oppose your very lord. I am the Deus Sanguinius–'

'*You are a dupe!*' Rafen bellowed, howling the words, 'You're nothing but a clockwork toy for that ordos whoreson. He did this, warped you into this mutant obscenity.'

Arkio's threw back his head and roared. '*Liar. Traitor. Coward.*' With a massive, vicious surge of motion, the winged Space Marine brought the spear about and slammed the blunt end into the centre of Rafen's torso with a thunderclap of force.

The impact struck the Blood Angel like a cannon shell and Rafen was blown backwards off his feet. He flew through the air, releasing snap-fire shots from his bolter that went wild, deflecting off broken rock and keening away from indirect hits on Arkio's armour. Rafen landed with a crash of rubble, sending a roil of brick dust up into the air. He struggled, his feet slipping below him.

Arkio became aware of his name on the wind, a heartbeat pulse of chanting from the Warriors of the Reborn as they sensed the end was near for his opponent. Blood as hot as molten iron engorged his body with murderous power, the unchained potential of the black rage unfolding to envelop him. Arkio let out a wordless scream of absolute and utter fury, throwing himself into the air on the great curves of his wings. The spear buzzed and hummed in his hands, twitching like a distressed mount, but he forced it to turn toward Rafen. The lance tried to face itself away from his target but in his ire Arkio would not allow it.

At the top of his arc of flight, Arkio spun about and raced back down into the arms of gravity, wings cupping the wind, diving like a hawk upon prey. The teardrop blade flashed in the dimness.

His bones still ringing with the impact, Rafen forced himself off the ground to confront the attack; the glittering gold shape blurred at him, the lance aimed at his heart. Rafen's eyes met Arkio's and the Space Marine leapt into the air to meet him early.

The instant stretched like melting tallow. Turning, spinning, the lance struck poorly and deflected off Rafen's shoulder in a sizzle of sparks. The Space Marine moved, slipping under Arkio's guard, the two of them passing in mid-air less than a hand-span apart. Rafen's sword led the way, and the crackling power blade found brief purchase. The weapon cut a wound in Arkio's wing, red blood exploding in a crimson blossom, stark white feathers raining about him like falling petals.

Both men landed hard, but only one bled. Rafen turned the sword so that he could see the fluid that kissed the blade. It was wine-dark and sluggish like tar, it was polluted.

'First blood!' shouted one of Mephiston's men, but the cry was lost in snarls and roars of Arkio's loyalists.

* * *

'No...' THE WORD was small and plaintive, a childlike denial of something the eye saw but refused to believe. Sachiel's hands came to his face and it was only then that he realised the voice had been his. A great splash of crimson disfigured Arkio's immaculate golden wargear and the sight of this offence burned into the priest's vision like a brand.

The sharp, tearing agony of the wound seemed to be instantly translated to every member of Arkio's retinue – the sheer shock of seeing their liege lord injured by a mere Space Marine hit them with a physical force. For a long second all of them were stuck dumb by the enormity of it.

Sachiel could smell the blood. As a Sanguinary High Priest, the scent of living vitae was as distinct as the bouquet of a fine wine or the aroma of a delicate flower. Sachiel had known blood all through his service as an Apothecary to the Chapter, and he had tasted a thousand strains and touched a thousand more in his duties. On battlefields he had seen great lakes of it shed by enemy and ally alike, he had witnessed it gushing in red fountains from the arteries of men screaming for the Emperor's peace. Sachiel knew the scent of his own blood, and that of Sanguinius himself as it lay captured and preserved in the Red Grail on Baal. The stench of what leaked from Arkio struck his senses like a mailed fist. He sensed corruption, black and ruinous, some foul seed of pollution swarming and writhing inside the Blessed's veins.

Sachiel's stomachs threatened to rebel and throw their contents on the ground. It was impossible. The priest scrambled inside himself for some explanation and found none – his senses had never betrayed him before and they did not betray him now. Sachiel turned away, blocking out the sight even though the smell was wrapped around him in invisible wreathes. His gaze fell on Stele; the inquisitor was growling some order at his hooded psy-witch. Stele caught his sight for a fractional instant and Sachiel saw him start.

'You,' Sachiel managed, the word bubbling up from a deep, hidden place. 'You...' Like glass breaking, the compulsions Stele had placed in Sachiel's psyche aboard the *Bellus* suddenly shattered. Perhaps it was the shock of Arkio's injury, perhaps some last fragment of Sachiel's honourable self rising to the surface, but in that instant the priest was freed of the psyker's hold on his will.

Sachiel's world, so perfect and so rationalised, so carefully assembled to serve his ego, came crashing down about him. Floodgates of denied, forgotten memories disintegrated and the priest was knocked to his knees by the force of them, wailing. Every line he had crossed, every choice he had made in order to aggrandise himself, and Stele had been there to help him do it. Sachiel's gorge rose as the stink of mutation filled every pore of his skin, contaminating him and choking the air. 'Oh lord,' he wept, bitter tears falling from his face. 'What have I done?' He looked up at Stele and saw the inquisitor staring down at him, an expression of utter contempt on his cruel lips. 'What have you done to me?'

Stele knelt and whispered in his ear. 'I gave you the tools to destroy yourself.'

CHAPTER ELEVEN

THE RAINS CAME from the darkening sky, a whisper of falling droplets spattering across the grey landscape of the dead city-shrine. It hissed over the forms of the rag-tag warriors as they surged forward, rushing to Arkio's flanks.

Amid their lines, the priest and the inquisitor faced each other. Sachiel's tears were lost in the rush of the downpour, his fingers clenching clods of mud where he crouched on hands and knees. The chill, dirty rainwater washed over him and with it, it carried away the scales of willing blindness from the priest's eyes. Sachiel's perfidy was revealed to him with sudden, shattering clarity. No denials could assuage it, no words were strong enough to halt the tide of utter self-loathing that engulfed him. 'I... am... corrupted...' he breathed, damning himself with his own words.

Stele looked at him with complete disregard. Any familiarity or comradeship the inquisitor had shown to Sachiel now fell from his expression, and he understood that Stele had never, ever considered the priest as anything more than a tool. He was something to be used and discarded.

'I had intended to retain you for a while longer,' Stele's voice was low and only Sachiel could hear it, 'but it appears you have outlived your usefulness to me.'

The priest struggled to get to his feet, but his body felt like it weighed hundreds of tonnes. The burden of the sins he had committed were pressing him into the rubble. 'Does Arkio know? I would never have followed you…'

Stele laughed. 'How typical, priest. You think of your own reputation before the fate of your Chapter!'

'You did this to me!'

'You allowed me to. You secretly welcomed it, Sachiel, coveting the Red Grail, nurturing your resentments… You were ideal, your obsession with yourself blinding you to all the pacts you made!' He let out a harsh laugh. 'Fallen Angel, look how far you have tumbled from your perch.' Hellish light glinted in Stele's vision and the priest felt the sickening caress of his mind-touch. *You were not the first*, said the voice in his head, the hiss of snakeskin on bone, *and you will not be the last*.

The awful magnitude of the grand scheme of Chaos became clear in Sachiel's mind, and it turned his hearts to ice. 'No…'

'Oh, yes,' replied Stele, and through the open, bleeding wound self-inflicted on the priest's psyche, he sent a quicksilver hammer of mind-force.

Sachiel's scream merged into a howl of thunder and blood gushed from his nostrils, and wept in runnels from his eyes. *Die!* Stele ripped him apart within, breaking his mind like matchwood. *Perish, Sachiel. I compel you, die for me.*

The body in red and white ceramite collapsed in a puddle of thin pink fluids, death tearing away his last breath on the wind.

Stele masked his smile and fixed a disguise of righteous anger in its place. 'Murderer,' he bellowed, stabbing an accusing finger at Mephiston. 'See, the Librarian has killed our brother Sachiel. He burnt the will from him with his witch-sight.'

The fierce mood of the mob army and the loyalist Space Marines took voice and weapons were turned on Mephiston and his Blood Angels. They were on the verge of an adrenaline-fuelled frenzy, and all it would take would be one word from Stele to tip them over the edge.

He gave it. 'Attack. Destroy them all, in Arkio's name!'

THE RABBLE WAS a living, breathing entity, a war engine made from flesh and bone and ceramite and steel. It moved so fast that Rafen was caught off-guard, the figures in their red cloaks emblazoned with the spear and halo flooding around Arkio's imperious form in a headlong rush. There were loyalist Space Marines in the mass as well, bolters spitting hot fire.

Mephiston's men opened up into the Warriors of the Reborn, scything them down in gouts of crimson. Gunfire and screams merged into a symphony of destruction, raised high to the rattling fall of the rain. Rafen swung and parried with his sword as the mob reached him, cutting him off from his target. He lost sight of Arkio as the golden figure leapt into the sky and cut back toward the edge of the square, then he was fighting hard, his attention on the myriad adversaries upon him. His bolter pistol ran dry and he used it like a club, too far into the thick of the melee to spare the time to reload it. The power sword rose and fell, cutting a path through chattering men who died with the name of his sibling on their lips.

For the first time in what seemed like an age, Rafen felt the familiar tingle of battle lust inside him, the shadow of the black rage. He culled the zealots, losing count of the dead, but Arkio's thousand still had the weight of numbers on their side. Nearby, he caught the crackling hum of a force weapon. Blue lightning licked at the low clouds as the Lord of Death joined the fray.

* * *

ALL ABOUT HIM combat seethed and boiled, yet Stele stayed untouched, his lexmechanic whimpering in a cowering heap at Ulan's feet while the mutant psyker draped her nullifying power about them. The inquisitor examined the chalice in his hand; he had ripped it from Sachiel's belt as the light faded from the priest's eyes, flinging away the velvet bag to reveal the replica of the sacred Blood Angels artefact. He smiled. This simple trinket was the seed of Sachiel's undoing. The Apothecary had always dreamed of becoming the Keeper of the Red Grail, ascending to the highest office in the sanguinary clergy. He had nurtured bitterness toward Corbulo, the battle-brother that held the posting on Baal, and that had been Stele's gateway into manipulating him. With a shrug, he tossed the copper cup away. It was worthless litter now, with as little value to the inquisitor as Sachiel's cooling corpse. He nudged the dead priest with his boot-tip. Stele was glad to be rid of the self-important dullard, one less loose end to dispose of.

Ulan grunted in pain. 'Uh... difficult...' she said through gritted teeth. 'Mephiston's sight... stronger...' A line of purplish blood ran from her nostrils.

Stele made a dismissive gesture. 'In a moment. Where is Arkio?'

'Conflicted...' Ulan managed, nerves in her face jerking. 'He seeks... reassurance...'

'We cannot lose the momentum of the attack,' he growled. Already, things had deviated from Stele's carefully engineered plans with the sudden revelation of Rafen and Arkio's wound through a foolish moment of inattention. 'Attend me,' he demanded.

The thin, pale girl stumbled toward him, the lexmechanic mumbling fearfully in dozens of different tongues. 'Lord...' she said thickly. 'I... am at my limits...'

'Yes, yes,' he retorted, ignoring the agony that radiated off her aura. 'Here.' He grasped her face and let his fingers find the ghost-metal contacts under the polyflesh scabs on her skin. Ulan tensed as Stele corralled and used her haphazard power to augment his own warp-sight. At once he detected the hidden clusters of wild minds on the edges of his sensorium, visible only to him because he knew where to seek them. 'Garand,' he intoned, his voice slicing through the warp. 'It is time.' Stele released the woman with a jerk and her head lolled backward. Ulan's blind eyes showed only the bloodshot whites.

The inquisitor turned in place as he heard the first screams of rocket motors. From concealed hides scattered throughout the ruins, spat from beneath rubble and the protective sheathes of camo-cloaks, salvos of missiles looped in over the edges of the debris-choked square and fell on rods of orange smoke.

EVERY BLOOD ANGEL knew the sound, and they took cover – but the pressing knots of Arkio's zealots made rapid movement impossible. The warheads streaked into the square and struck a dozen points at once, throwing up red-black fireballs. Three of Mephiston's Thunderhawks were instantly crippled or destroyed, and a handful of men were blown apart when the rockets fell short and landed in the melee.

The Lord of Death raised his free hand to shield his eyes from the glare. Hot flame crackled as the rain sizzled into steam, the sudden glow underlighting the grey clouds. 'And so they spring their trap at last. I wondered how long we would have to wait.'

'Indirect fire from the south, west and east quadrants!' the Techmarine reported, fending off a zealot with a punch from his servo-arm. 'Weapon signature does not match Blood Angel munitions.'

'Of course,' Mephiston snapped, bringing up the sword Vitarus. 'And what new player has joined this sorry performance?'

The veteran sergeant nodded to the west as he slammed a fresh clip of ammunition into his bolter. 'I can smell them from here, lord. Horned braggarts by the cartload.'

Mephiston saw figures dropping from the upper tiers of ruined buildings or emerging from concealed trapdoors over rubble-filled basements. They wore armour in a stringent shade of ruby, bedecked with chains and smoking lanterns. Horns sprouted in riots from their helms and heads, and as they came on their voices were raised in blasphemous hymns. 'Word Bearers. The design of this infamy becomes clearer…'

'But the scouts,' said the Techmarine. 'The scouts reported no contacts.'

The Librarian threw the sergeant a grave look, and a grim understanding passed between them. 'Our scouts are all dead,' said the veteran.

From the instant he had spoken of traps and double-crosses to Commander Dante in the monastery's arboretum, Mephiston knew this moment would come; yet as it happened, his ire was not lessened. A guttural snarl bared his canines. 'Blood Angels!' he shouted. 'To arms!'

Vitarus sang high and drank deep from the enemy about the psyker.

'CONFIRMED,' DRONED THE servitor. 'Multiple discharges on the planetary surface, evidence of small-arms fire and medium-yield tactical detonations. Vox traffic intercepts concur.'

Captain Ideon released a slow, metallic growl from his mechanical throat. 'More betrayal,' he snarled. 'Great Arkio was right to suspect the Lord of Death. He has eschewed the hand of peace in favour of attack.' Ideon made a grunt that was his immobile form's equivalent of a nod. 'So be it, then.'

Solus frowned. 'We cannot be sure who fired the first shot. It may have been a mistake...' The words seemed weak as they fell from his lips.

'Mistake?' Ideon rattled, his synthetic voice buzzing like hornets in a tin can. 'Mephiston does not make mistakes, Solus. This is a declaration of war!' The captain's stoic face twitched and the mechadendrites protruding from his skull whispered against one another. 'Prepare to engage the *Europae*.'

'*Europae* is turning,' called the sense-servitor, 'adopting battle stance. Detection transients indicate multiple weapon bay activations.'

'You see?' Ideon husked.

Solus found his words dying in his throat and he turned away. At the same moment, his eyes fell on the hololithic chart in the tacticarium. Warning glyphs were streaming through the ghostly green light. 'There's someone else out there,' he said aloud.

SABIEN'S DEBRIS RING was a mixture of broken stones as tall as mountains and great drifting lakes of frozen ice. Dense with heavy ores, to the eyes of a starship's machine-spirit the belt of asteroids was a confused swathe of garbled, reflected sensor returns. On the surface it seemed like the ideal place to hide a vessel, but no captain would ever have been so foolhardy to attempt such a thing. The blanket of confusion that seeded the ring also made navigation inside its confines virtually impossible. Both the *Bellus* and the *Europae* saw the belt as a natural hazard, just another element of the orbital environment. Neither vessel expected the chilling sight of a starship emerging from the shaggy morass of tumbling stones.

Under power from a hard thruster burn, the Desolator-class battleship extended out of the Sabien Belt like a red blade punched through a torso. The jagged prow dipped like the snout of a hunting predator, moving inexorably to bear on the *Europae*. Asteroids battered into the craft as it moved from the debris ring, punching rents in the hull; the captain of the vessel was willing to allow men on his outer decks to die so that the ship could complete its manoeuvre, weathering the damage. The crewmen aboard Mephiston's flagship sounded alerts and charged their torpedo tubes, gangs of Chapter serfs hoisting warheads as big as watchtowers into the open maws of launchers. The monstrous Chaos craft continued to turn, the target scanners of the bow guns briefly crossing the shape of the *Bellus*. Not one of the weapons released its warshot toward Arkio's battle barge; the battleship crew had their orders, on pain of lengthy and horrific torture, to concentrate all their initial attack on the *Europae*.

SOLUS SAW THE lance batteries wink at him like blinded eyes as the ship turned onward, coming to bear on Mephiston's vessel. 'They... they did not fire on us...' he breathed, hardly able to believe what he had seen.

'Aggressor identity confirmed,' the mechanical chatter of the servitor in the detection pit clattered forth. 'Vessel is the battlecruiser *Misericorde*, line warcraft in service to the Word Bearers Legion and the Ruinous Powers.'

'Vandire's oath!' spat Solus. 'What is this madness?' The Blood Angel's mind raced through the possibilities – could the Chaos ship be some sort of ally to the Lord of Death?

Dare he believe that Mephiston, or even Dante himself was consorting with the scum of the Maelstrom?

'Status of *Misericorde*,' Ideon demanded. 'Are we their target?'

'Negative,' came the reply. 'All guns on the ship are coming to bear on the *Europae*.'

'A third force?'

There was a smile in Ideon's artificial voice as his eyes flicked at Solus. 'An unexpected piece of good fortune! The hand of Sanguinius protects us...'

'But we cannot simply ignore a Chaos capital ship!' Solus blurted out. 'It is our duty to–'

'You dare speak to me of duty?' Ideon snapped, his voice cracking about the bridge cloisters like thunder. 'I, who have served our Chapter for two hundred years from this very throne?' The captain's words dropped to a low rumble. 'Know this, my errant battle-brother, when fate's tarot deals a hand of swords, use them. You know the oath we take.'

Solus repeated the litany by automatic rote. 'To the ship, the Chapter, the primarch and the Emperor.'

'Yes, and while the *Misericorde* is the enemy of the Emperor, the *Europae* is the enemy of our primarch and our Chapter. Mephiston's extermination takes precedence.' In response to a mental command, pict-screens at Solus's station flickered to display long range images of the fighting on Sabien. 'You only have to view the battle unfolding below us to know the truth of that.'

'*Misericorde* is firing,' said the sense-servitor. '*Europae*'s void shields are holding.'

'Let's show those corrupted fools how it is done, eh?' said Ideon. 'The order is, target the *Europae* and fire.'

Solus hesitated.

'Did you not understand the command, Solus?' There was a razor-keen warning in the captain's manner.

'Open fire,' said Solus, in a dead, toneless voice.

THE SQUARE WAS a cauldron of inferno as figures in shades of red clashed across the rubble and the stones. Arkio's thousand-strong helot army in their terracotta robes and the loyalist Space Marines who fought with them clashed with Mephiston's Blood Angels, and they drew fire and laid weapons to bear upon the Word Bearers swarming into the broken arena. There was no plan of battle here, no careful tactics to rout and defeat the enemy – instead each side engaged in the grisly attrition of hand-to-hand fighting. The square became a mass of fire and screams as men and traitors came together to kill or be killed.

In the thick of it, Rafen was a whirlwind of destruction, the power sword running hot in his hand as he tore apart zealots and ripped open Chaos Space Marines. In equal measure the dark glamour of the battle repelled and excited him, the burning flood of adrenaline coming upon him like some ghostly caress. The raging fight was already spilling over the cracked and fallen walls of the plaza, into the surrounding streets. Some of Mephiston's men – veteran assault troops with their characteristic helmets of sunburst yellow – bobbed up on jump packs. They carried plasma weapons and heavy flamers, seeking out the missile shooters still hiding in the ruins and dousing them in liquid fire. On the winds came the smell of cooked meat and the bone-snap of superheated ceramite.

Daggers and work implements turned into clubs rang noisily against Rafen's power armour as a cluster of Arkio's warriors tried to surround him and beat the Space Marine to the ground. Rafen let out a cruel laugh at their idiocy; he pitied these fools, willingly blinded by the dogma spouted by Sachiel. In quick and economical moves, he used every part of the sword to dispatch them, breaking skulls with the flat of the blade and the pommel, cleaving torsos with the keen edge, smashing ribcages with the spiked guard about his fingers. If these imbeciles wanted to die in the name of their false messiah, then Rafen would be more than willing to accommodate them.

The fight ebbed and flowed, moving like an ocean swell. Figures were caught up in the morass, the press of flesh and steel sending Rafen staggering. Somewhere along the line he had lost his helmet. Several times he was forced to halt and seek his direction, and more than once he barely pulled a killing blow before a Space Marine from Mephiston's contingent. Rafen had already ensured that he would not suffer a similar error by burning off the spear and halo design on his shoulder pad with a discarded hand flamer. The dirty black scar on the side of his wargear paradoxically made him feel cleaner, as if the kiss of the burning promethium had purged the taint of Stele and his corruption.

Rafen's boot rang against a hollow shape and it caught his attention. There at his feet, where the spilled blood and grey rain had turned drifts of dry brick dust into tar-like slurry, a body in white and red ceramite had been abandoned. The corpse was pressed into the mud, twisted and broken by a stampede of helots, but Rafen knew it instantly.

'Sachiel...' While the fight had drifted back and forth, the dead priest had remained where he fell, the spotless and immaculate armour he once wore now ruined with bloody footprints and smeared with gore. The Apothecary's eyes were open, blankly staring up into the hissing torrents of rain. Rafen had never had anything other than antipathy for his arrogant rival, but now as he looked upon the expression of horror and despondency frozen on the dead man's face, he felt only pity for the priest. However unwittingly, Sachiel had placed his own quest for glory beyond his loyalty to the Chapter, and here in the dark mire he lay fully paid for that mendacity.

Rafen smacked away another attacker with the butt of his bolter and took a moment to reload. He glanced around as he did, finding his bearings by the actinic glow of blue mind-fire that blazed about the Lord of Death. Steam wreathed the Librarian in white streams where the rainwater flashed to vapour around him. As Rafen watched, the ethereal lightning that haloed Mephiston congealed around the upright spars of his psychic hood, coiling into rods of energy that seared his eyes to look at. Twin horned skulls at the tips of the ghost-metal psy-wave conductors flashed with barely controlled power, and the Librarian swelled beneath his blood red armour, drawing the lethal potential into himself.

Colours and shades that had no place on the plane of the living came into being, the air itself shimmering and bending like a phantom lens. Rafen saw Mephiston's target – a squad of Word Bearers Havoc Space Marines, bristling with heavy weapons. The Lord of Death turned his face to them and his eyes flashed. On the battlefield, Rafen had seen other Blood Angels psykers use the skill they called the Quickening, a blanket of power that could turn the user into a tornado of destruction, but Mephiston was the master of another psionic force, one that dwarfed the talents of the Librarians and codicers who served beneath him. The power of the Smite was unleashed, a blaze of insane geometry cut from liquid light fanning out into a teardrop of pure and undiluted annihilation. The witch-fire engulfed the Havocs and set them alight; ammunition packs detonated and armour split. Rafen instinctively joined in on the great cheer of approval that came from Mephiston's Blood Angels.

He waded forward to meet the psyker commander, saluting with the power sword as the Chief Librarian caught sight of him. 'My lord!'

'Rafen,' Mephiston growled, 'You live still, yet so does your errant sibling.'

'The zealots cut me off from him before I could–' Rafen began, but the rest of his words were drowned out by a roar from Arkio's ragged warriors. The slave army, driven on by some shouted command from the back of their lines, rushed forward. Rafen thought he heard Stele's voice on the wind, but then his attention was on the men tearing at him. At point-blank range he unleashed the bolt pistol, popping heads like overripe fruits, punching holes as big as his mailed fist in cloaked bodies. 'They fight like they are possessed!' he grated, the press of the charge forcing him to Mephiston's flank.

'Indeed,' replied the Librarian, his force weapon slashing a wide arc of blood and entrails. 'They rally to their "Blessed One".'

Rafen ran through a Word Bearer as it emerged from the pack, taking him from jowl to bowel, emptying a nest of blackened, stinking organs on the dirt. 'Lord, my task lies undone. Give me permission to disengage and seek out my brother.'

Mephiston eyed him. 'You wounded him and he fled. What kind of messiah is that?'

'He will return, my lord. I know the conflict inside him, but if I do not strike now, Arkio will return and lay waste to this place. I must find him, while his guard is down!'

'You understand what will occur if you fail, Rafen?' The Librarian's voice was low and hard. 'Even as we speak, my battle barge is engaged in a fight for its survival in orbit. I have left orders with the brother-captain commanding her that if Arkio's loyalists tip the balance, then Sabien is to be targeted with cyclonic torpedoes. Better this shrine world become ashes then this schism be allowed to spread further.'

'I can stop him,' Rafen insisted. 'It is what I came here to do.'

Mephiston gave him a nod. 'So be it, then.' He turned aside and called out. 'Techmarine. Bring Brother Rafen a jump pack, quickly.'

'A jump pack, lord?'

'Arkio has wings. We must give you wings of your own, lad.'

'STELE! WHAT ABORTION have you created now?'

The inquisitor whirled, Ulan clinging to his arm, as a knot of Word Bearers punched their way through the helot lines, with Garand at their head. A loyalist Space Marine foolishly turned his gun on the Warmaster, stepping forward to protect Stele and his retinue from the threat. Garand angrily spat acidic venom and decapitated the Blood Angel with a single sweep of his bane-axe.

'Lord Garand,' Stele said, deciding not to bow. 'Welcome.'

'My patience with this ridiculous scheme of yours is at an end, human.' Garand menaced him with the humming axe. 'You know the bargain! Bring these mewling Blood Whelps to the Banner of Change or forfeit your life.'

'Don't push me, Word Bearer,' Stele shouted, emboldened by the heat of the battle raging around them. 'My orders come from Malfallax, not you! It will be done, but by my design, not yours.'

'Your design!' Garand spat again. 'Pathetic weakling, with your schemes and your little performances, none of that matters now. In Lorgar's name, the battle is joined. These men-prey will stand with the eight or they will perish.'

'No!' Stele roared, and Garand blinked in surprise at the vehemence of the human's denial. 'I have come too far, paid too much for this moment. It is mine, and you will not usurp it, creature.'

'You dare.' Garand's eyes narrowed and he marshalled his psyker potency to chastise the ranting inquisitor – but there was a null void surrounding him, a thick weave of poisonous non-space issuing from the mind of the female trailing at the inquisitor's heels. 'Bah,' snorted the Warmaster, recoiling. 'Have your petty game, then.' The Word Bearers lord brandished his axe and called to his men. 'Pick your targets and cull the Blood Angels. Collateral kills…' and he smiled, '…at your discretion.'

Out of Stele's earshot, a tech-priest slunk forward from Garand's unit to bow at the Warmaster's feet. 'Great Witch Prince, a vox from the *Misericorde*. They have engaged Mephiston's warship, but the presence of the *Bellus* vexes the ship's machine-spirit. The crew is discontent to let a second Astartes craft go unpunished. What should I tell them?'

'Tell them…' A slow and hateful smile crossed Garand's pallid lips and he glanced at Stele. He would castigate the conceited braggart for daring to raise his voice to him. 'Tell them the *Bellus* is to be considered expendable.'

THE BATTLE IN the skies of Sabien changed from a delicate joust to a brutal, punishing fight as the three ships closed the distance between one another. In terms of tonnage the combatants were evenly matched: the *Bellus* and the *Europae* were sister ships, their keels laid down in the midst of the Heresy era, both of them cut from steel forged in the furnaces of Enigma VI, both created according to the sacred tenets of a standard template construct programme from the Mechanicus librariums on Mars. *Misericorde* was longer in the beam but slender where the battle barges were blunt axe-heads in form. Once, the battleship had been a human vessel, but that identity had long been subsumed beneath centuries of creeping mutation, the old self lost and forgotten in the warp. Garand's vessel bristled with hateful power. It was predator-fast compared with the slow, heavy hunters of the barges, but speed and firepower cancelled each other out. Had any two of the ships faced off, the battle's end would not have been easy to predict – but in a three-way engagement, all bets were off.

Misericorde powered forward, the screaming mouths of its drive bells vomiting flame. Lance fire connected the ship with *Europae*, green and red threads of coherent particles stringing between them, then gone. Spherical explosions opened like puffballs into the vacuum, spilling iced gases and spent men into the dark. As the Chaos and Blood Angels ships crossed the distance toward one another, Ideon brought Arkio's flagship up in *Misericorde*'s shadow, allowing the powerful bow guns to rip past the ruby-coloured cruiser and strike *Europae*'s glittering void shields. The barge's ephemeral energy screens flickered and deformed under the onslaught, shedding the might of her attackers like rain, but already the enigmatic field generators in the barge's heart were reacting to the pressure, sending waves of sympathetic panic into the tech-priests that ministered to them. *Europae* was strong, to be sure, but she would not resist so barbaric an assault for long.

In the depths of space, such fights took place at ranges that would swallow a star system, ships hitting ships beyond each other's visual ranges. The close-in fighting of near-orbit engagements was an entirely different game. If one was a fencing match, full of elegant moves and pinpoint strikes, then the other was a dirty street brawl, punches being traded with ferocity and killer intent. *Europae* leapt forward without warning, a plume of fusion fire nova-bright and blinding erupting from her stern. She veered to port in a savage turn that stressed the hull beyond its tolerances, popping out thousands of ancient, giant rivets. The brutal manoeuvre bled speed and gravity away, pushing *Europae* on to a different tack and ending the lives of dozens of luckless crew caught in the wrong sections of the hull spaces.

The turn came out of nowhere and it was near suicidal. Ideon's surprise was enough that he hesitated a second too long as Mephiston's ship presented itself in passing. By the time the command to fire the bow guns had been relayed, *Bellus* was carving at empty air like an addled punch-drunk. *Europae*'s crew was prepared, however.

Secondary batteries, laser cannons with great quartz lenses broad as the eye of a kraken, spat a killing glare over *Bellus*'s starboard flank. The battle barge moaned under the impact, and Ideon felt the screech as the machine-spirit's pain analogue ripped into him. The simple, animal mind of *Bellus* hissed and spat; it lacked the intellect to understand why another Blood Angels ship would attack it.

Europae extended her turn, coming about on a course that would allow the ship to enter *Bellus*'s rearward arc. Even with the acres of armour and double-projected void shielding that protected it, a captain would be courting suicide to allow an attacking vessel the freedom to throw shells and las-fire into his drive nozzles. Ideon spat curses and bellowed out orders, his hands twitching into angry claws in a rare moment of physical reaction. The two barges turned into one another, matching speed for speed as they became caught in a deadly waltz. They continued to trade fire as *Misericorde* came about, sighting the bores of her lethal hellguns over *Bellus*. A human captain might have waited; a human captain might have evaluated the consequences and held his fire until *Europae* became the clearer target. But, like his ship, *Misericorde*'s captain had long forgotten his human origins and any form of fealty to weak abstracts like fidelity or compassion.

The red dagger freed its weapons to do their worst, and *Misericorde*'s starboard armaments blazed in one cascade of hot murder. Many of the shots found their true target, striking vitals all across *Europae*'s hull, but just as many punctured *Bellus*, firing through the loyalist ship as if it were some cursory piece of cover to be disintegrated.

Ideon's primary heart stammered with shock as laser fire tore turrets and minarets from the deck of *Bellus*. His head jerked on old, unused muscles in his neck, the tiny motion the first he had made with it in decades. The captain made eye-contact with Solus and saw the mute accusation in his second's gaze, then a plasma conduit burst behind him and Ideon watched Solus become a shrieking human torch.

'Return fire,' he roared above the din, the shout running into distorted crackle through his implanted voxcoder.

'Which target?' asked the gun-servitor, the dull voice at odds with the violent emotions of the battle.

'All of them,' Ideon demanded, and *Bellus* fired every gun at once, growing spines of laser light and missile fire.

RAFEN'S SKILL WITH the jump pack was hardly a match for the trained battle-brothers of the assault squads, but it was enough to guide him over the dense heart of the fighting, skipping him off the ground in steep, loping arcs of orange flame. He twisted nimbly in mid-air, avoiding the bright streaks of missiles and red bolts of laser fire. At the zenith of a leap from a broken battlement, his sight captured a glint of shining gold and brilliant white.

He skipped off the ground, sparing a moment to shoot dead a helot soldier, then powered back into the air. He spun and turned, became a guided missile himself. Rafen let the thruster pack spew flame and aim him at the cored remains of a cathedral. Only the stone walls remained, the places where great arcs of stained glass once stood now open, wailing mouths. The roof was gone, swept away by some long-faded detonation shock wave, and the endless rush of the rain cascaded over broken teeth of stone. Statues headless, bisected and shattered lined the aisles and transepts. In places, the mosaic floor had collapsed into the crypts below.

Rafen landed in a hiss of sparks from his boots and there, half-cloaked in the shadows of a huge granite altar, he saw a white spread of wings.

'Arkio.' His voice carried the length of the ruined hall. 'This must end now.'

With deliberation, his brother turned to face him, the golden armour emerging from the darkness. Where he had been wounded, a creeping purple-black bloodstain flowed like living oil across his torso. There were tiny pearls of dark matter disfiguring Arkio's face and neck. 'Yes,' he intoned. 'It must.'

And suddenly the dark was banished by a violent surge of yellow lightning as the Spear of Telesto shook into life.

CHAPTER TWELVE

BILE ROSE IN Rafen's throat as he laid eyes on his brother. The alabaster skin of his face, the noble patrician lines were distorted in subtle and cruel ways. 'What have you become?' he asked his sibling.

Arkio eyed him coldly. 'Your better, Rafen. The superior to all living things.' The rain spattered around him as he walked out of the shadows and across the church's ruined nave. 'I have banished all doubts.' He threw a cursory gesture at the altar behind him.

Sheet lightning flashed and illuminated the transept. Rafen gasped as he saw the remains of a statue of the Emperor, beheaded by a single stroke of the Holy Lance. 'Does your blasphemy know no bounds?' he said, shaking with anger, 'It is not enough that you go against your kin and your Chapter, but now you turn your back on the God-Emperor himself?'

Arkio made a lazy gesture with the humming spear. 'What need have I for gods when I am one myself?'

'You are deluded.' Rafen stabbed a finger at Arkio's side, where the sword cut he had inflicted still festered. 'If you are a god, then why do you bleed like a man? Or perhaps, not a man… Perhaps a warp-touched thing, a pawn of Chaos.'

Arkio threw back his head and laughed. The bitter humour echoed off the broken walls. 'Chaos?' He threw the word aside. 'A childish label for something you could never understand.'

'I understand enough,' Rafen shouted back at him. 'My brother, my blood kinsman has been poisoned by the warp. Stele led you to this.' He brandished his sword. 'Recant, Arkio. While there is still time.'

The golden figure spread his arms wide and the wings on his back flowed open in a rush of wind. 'This is not heresy, and I will not recant,' he snarled. 'My eyes are open, brother. I know it all now… Men and monsters, order and Chaos…' He pointed the spear at the sky. 'Just words. There is no right and wrong, no black and white. Only the strong… and the weak.'

'And what am I?'

Arkio ignored him. 'I will not bend my knee to the Golden Throne or the Dark Gods. I pay fealty to no one!' He cocked his head, the metallic sun-shaped halo behind his head glittering in the spear's glow. 'This galaxy will fall to me… I will be the master.'

'It will not,' Rafen grated. His fingers tightened around the hilt of his sword.

Arkio's eyes flashed. 'Then I will burn it to ashes, blind every star, cull every life that defies me.'

There was no hesitation in his brother's face, not an iota of doubt within him. The ironclad certainty of Arkio's words took Rafen's breath away. 'You are mad.'

'Am I?' He drew the words out into a sigh. 'We'll see.'

Red flame exploded from Rafen's jump pack, blasting him forward, fire licking at the walls of the shattered chancel.

Arkio moved so fast he faded into a yellow-white blur, both of them closing the distance down the aisle in heartbeats.

They collided with such force that the impact blew down an ornate colonnade, both of them spinning away from the point of impact on headlong trajectories. Arkio's wings unfurled and he skipped off a broken column, thundering back at Rafen. His brother clipped a wall, and used a hissing jet of thrust to mimic his opponent's manoeuvre. They met again in mid-air over the nave and flashed past each other, blades glittering.

Rafen let out a roar of pain as the hot apex of the lance ran a slice through his thigh, drawing a fan of blood. Arkio wobbled and broke through an obelisk as Rafen's power sword severed the linkage cables on his right shoulder pad, but missed his flesh. The gold hemisphere of metal and ceramite armour spun away and clattered into the shadows. Thin processor fluids leaked down his arm and the cut plastiform musculature twitched.

Rafen landed hard and opened fire with his bolt pistol, thumbing the selector to full automatic fire. Shells crashed from the muzzle of the gun, shedding spent casings in a fountain of gleaming brass. The hot casings clattered to the stone floor, buzzing as they struck the gathering puddles of rainwater. Arkio swooped and looped between the remnants of columns and arcing roof supports, Rafen's shots chewing chunks of ancient masonry from the frame of the church. He bracketed his brother with a hail of bullets, a few lucky rounds kissing his armour and keening away in orange gouts of sparks.

Arkio closed the distance, swinging the spear in a figure of eight that left bright after-images on Rafen's retina. The Blood Angel deftly changed tack, dropping back the pistol to present the power sword. He stood his ground as Arkio dove down at him, waiting for the moment of change when the winged figure would telegraph his attack.

Arkio's face opened in a snarl and he rode the lance like a jousting knight, aiming it directly at the centre of his brother's torso. Rafen bit back a grim sneer and faded into the move, turning, spinning, clashing the sword's bright blade against the adamantium tip of the spear. The blow pushed him back, striking grit and sparks from the stones under his feet, darts of bright light blazing where blade kissed blade. Arkio followed through on the strike with a reversal, sweeping the blunt end of the spear around to catch his legs and trip him. Rafen squeezed the thruster pack control in the palm of his glove for a fraction of a second and let a spurt of flame throw him clear. He flipped in a somersault and landed on a ledge, presenting the bolt pistol again. Rafen emptied the rest of the ammunition clip toward his brother, and Arkio skipped to the side, dodging between the low bulks of burial crypts and monuments.

The golden figure let out braying, harsh laughter as the rounds harmlessly spent themselves on stonework and pavement. Arkio turned on his heel and thrust the Holy Lance at Rafen, willing the weapon to release the powerful energies humming inside it. For the briefest second, the spear seemed to obey him, glowing brightly as a ball of honeyed lightning gathered at the end of the teardrop blade. Rafen sprang from his ledge, skipping off a fallen granite eagle to another naked support beam. Arkio followed him and goaded his weapon to unleash its killing force, but once more the Spear of Telesto shifted in his grip, rolling about its length. It jerked through his fingers as if it were trying to escape him.

'No!' Arkio spat, and in his anger he swung the errant weapon around him in an arc of light, slashing through two support columns and a broken statue. The spear moaned and shuddered. 'You cannot deny me,' Arkio thundered. 'I am your master!' Thick, poisoned spittle flew from his lips in his fury, and his regal face contorted. Scars emerged from his cheeks and forehead, weeping thick oil, bringing with them the hard pearls of black mutation. Arkio seemed unaware of them as they wriggled and moved beneath the surface of his skin, shifting like burrowing beetles.

His instant of rage brought distraction with it, and Rafen exploited the error to the fullest. Slamming home a fresh sickle magazine of bolt-rounds, Arkio's brother threw himself off the stone stanchion and dropped, unloading the gun in a roaring blaze of gunfire. The reports of the bolt-shells came so close together they merged into a ripping snarl of noise. Arkio brought up the spear to deflect them a heartbeat too late, and the discharge struck him in the chest. The white-hot impacts staggered him backward in jerks of motion, the thick bolts ripping long shreds of golden armour from him. Ceramite fragmented and plas-teel broke away, crazing the coating of precious yellow metal.

Arkio reacted with a growling shout of annoyance and shook himself, discarding bits of spent armour clinging to his arms and his chest. Through holes cored in the plates, dusky liquids bubbled and flowed. The mark of Stele's taint was no longer concealed within the prison of his flesh. Released by the wanton hate that churned in Arkio's mind, the changed aspect of the Space Marine was revealed.

Rafen felt physically sick at the sight of his brother. The foetor of him strangled the Blood Angel's senses, and the revelation of a body irredeemably tainted by Chaos was an affront to everything he stood for. Rafen willed himself to forget that some last piece of his blood brother's soul might still survive behind that warped face, and attacked again.

Arkio was ready for him. The winged figure spun the lance and met Rafen's sword with a thunderous strike, shattering the blade of the power weapon. Rafen snarled as he felt his wrist dislocate in the impact. The shock threw him back against a fragmented piece of stained glass as Arkio reared up before him.

The flash of lightning reflected Arkio's twisted face in the age-worn glass. 'Look at yourself!' Rafen shouted. 'Look at what you have become!'

Arkio swung the spear and shattered the glass forever. 'Fool.' he bellowed. 'I know what I am! *I AM SANGUINIUS!*'

Rafen tried to dodge the blow he knew was coming, but it hit him like a falling meteor. One cut slashed across his chest, striking his armour; the second came from the blunt pommel and it sent him crashing to the ground. The Blood Angel struck the mosaic floor with a crash of sound and the stonework gave way beneath him.

He tumbled into a black void and landed hard, the breath singing out of his lungs. Air wheezed through his chest accompanied by rips of pain and his vision fogged. Is this death, he wondered, at last? His fingers traced the shapes of something familiar, and in the dimness he glimpsed the forms of skeletons. Hundreds of them – but not human ones. These were larger, stockier. With a start he understood: Arkio's blow had thrown him into a crypt for Sabien's war dead, where the Blood Angels who died defending the planet had been interred. About the walls of the sepulchre were stone carvings of Space Marines. In the shadows they towered over him like a granite honour guard, mute and strong.

Rafen scrambled to his feet, ignoring the pain. All about him were his brethren, dead for centuries in this desolate, lonely place. A single thought burned in his brain: I will not join them! The fury of it raced through him, igniting an inferno in his veins. The broken sword dropped from his fingers and he clenched his fist, feeling hot anger pour into him. From the edges of his vision came something bright and powerful, a glow of infinite perfection. For one moment, he thought Arkio had followed him into the crypt, but the light of it outshone even his brother in his most omnipotent moment. Rafen looked up and saw the true face of his liege lord filling the air before him, the gene-kindred in his blood manifesting itself to him. The vision overwhelmed him, blocking out all pain, all hesitation. *Sanguinius!*

A rage so pure it burnt white-hot swelled in Rafen's heart, and the red thirst overtook him.

A FRESH WAVE of hooting, horned monstrosities joined the mad throng of the ground battle, blades and guns shouting in the clash. The square was a seething ocean of red shades, crimson fighting against ruby, incarnadine versus scarlet, moving and shifting in bloody tides. Mephiston and his troops ranged in a tight crescent about the remains of their Thunderhawks, pressing forward their attacks with grim determination and cold, cold rage. They faced the wild zealots of Arkio's slave army, and although the Shenlongi helots carried weapons that were mere toys in comparison to the arms of the Adeptus Astartes, the sheer weight of their numbers and the mad passion of their fervour were staggering. The warriors would not surrender or retreat. Only attrition would thin their thousand-strong horde into defeat.

The adherents of Arkio's church stood by Space Marines loyal to the Reborn Angel, but in this small number of red-armoured men the seeds of doubt and misgiving grew large. Many of them found themselves hesitant to fire on their own kind, and they became lost in the sea of conflict. Worse still, the men who had bent their knee to take Arkio's oath were shocked by the arrival of a new force of allies upon the battle-field, ruby-coloured figures who seemed to be fighting not against them, but with them. Word Bearers.

Delos saw the dark shapes of the Chaos Space Marines and felt his gut churn with revulsion. The optics of his death's-head helmet streamed with rainwater and spatters of mud as he fought to clear them. For a moment, he thought he had seen Inquisitor Stele actually standing toe to toe with a monstrous Word Bearer, then the raging mob had obscured his view and the Chaplain found himself pressed against a fallen wall. The weight of his ceremonial crozius arcanium was dead in his hand, desultory glimmers of energy fizzing around the device's ornate skeletal carvings. The weapon mirrored his mood sullen and uncertain. The Chaplain grasped it in his mailed fist and spoke a silent prayer to his God-Emperor. If what Delos had seen was correct, then the man who had been the architect of the Reborn Angel's Ascension was consorting with humanity's vilest enemy. He had to be mistaken. He *had* to be. The alternative explanation made him feel dizzy with dread and horror.

PIECES OF GOLD and tatters of blackened purity parchments fell away from Arkio's wargear, leaving scored metal below. The artificer armour, once unsullied and flawless, was now webbed with scratches and scars. Yellow flecks streamed into the wind like a dust storm, and the crazed blemishes seemed to shift and move in the half-light, tricks of the eye making them into vicious maws and screaming faces. New, inhuman muscles bulged beneath Arkio's chest, and his wings beat hard to hold him in a hover. The inky stain of his wound was grey and pallid, lines of toxin threading into the pinions and feathers, mottling them.

The very smallest glimmer of regret formed in Arkio's mind as he stared down at the yawning crater in the crypt, and he stamped on it mercilessly. No, Rafen would not be graced with a moment more of his attention. His troublesome brother was ended, and at last Arkio had the freedom he had coveted in the dark corners of his soul since childhood.

A low moan, a raw and feral sound, issued up from the void in the stone floor. It sent the Spear of Telesto twitching in his hands once more, as the weapon writhed and shuddered. The sky whitened as lightning flashed daybreak-bright around him, and the dazzle picked out a man-shape in glistening crimson below. On wings of jet fire, Rafen punched into the air and struck Arkio with all his might.

He caught his brother by surprise, and the Blood Angel felt his bones ring with the impact as they hit. Arkio spat out a strangled yell of anger as they flew up into the thick grey clouds. Rain and wind lashed at their faces from the oily banks of vapour, buffeting them. They exchanged blows, Arkio struggling to regain the advantage, unable to bring out the spear to strike back at so close an aggressor. Lightning shrieked close to them, the hot ozone of tormented air searing Rafen's lungs. In the flash of illumination, he saw new lines of the black seed-boils emerging along Arkio's cheekbones, arranged there like ritual scarifications. His eyes were shaded with the purest, darkest hate.

Rafen fought to bring his bolt pistol to bear, squeezing off a salvo of shots. Shells sizzled off Arkio in mad ricochets, some cutting out divots of necrotic flesh, others deflecting from the pieces of armour that still clung to his brother's changed torso. Arkio made a wordless sound of raw rage and snatched at the handgun, his fingers forming a fist around the blocky metal shape. He grabbed the weapon and crushed it to powder in a bony grip. Rafen cried out as his fingers snapped.

Arkio batted him away with a languid backhand, sending Rafen on a wild course as the rockets in his jump pack spat and laboured to keep him aloft. The winged figure turned after his target, in the clouded shadows, his aspect like an angel of death. He tried to aim the Holy Lance after Rafen, but the weapon resisted him. It bent and bowed as he pulled on it, as if the spear was frozen in the air. 'Obey me!' he shouted, yanking ferociously at the haft. 'I am your master!'

In his rage, the darkness hidden inside Arkio came flooding to the surface, the sullen beauty of his countenance shifting into an aspect as thunderous as the clouds about him. The change raced through him, down to the molecular level, the cells of the blood hammering in his veins blackening. Cradled in his grip, the potent technologies of the Spear of Telesto tasted Arkio, sampled him through the genome sensors threaded into the weapon's ornate haft. Ancient science awoke in the lance, so far removed from the advancements of the Imperium as to border on magic. It knew Arkio then, as it had known him in the first moment he laid hands on it – and this time the spear found him wanting.

It rebelled. The scent of Chaos was black and thick in the Reborn Angel, and the Telesto weapon went white-hot in his grip, melting the mastercrafted gauntlets to muddy gold slag. The pain was instant and heartstopping, and by sheer animal reaction Arkio released the burning lance, superheated steam hissing from the burning tissues of his hands. Tumbling end over end, the Spear of Telesto fell toward the ground, lightning catching the teardrop blade, wind whipping the purity seals.

The weapon landed like a thrown javelin, the blunt pommel at the shaft's end cracking the stones of the church floor as it struck them. Whirring with power, the spear came to rest upright, a naked standard in defiance of the forces that had tried to abuse it.

Overhead, Arkio swept toward his brother with his ruined hands opening into claws, the madness of kill-lust in his gaze. His rage was titanic now, and with it he would rip his sibling to shreds, spear or no spear.

Rafen shook off the dizziness threatening to wrap him in its coils and brought up his fists in a fighting stance. He bobbed as his thruster pack choked and coughed. The Blood Angel dared not chance a look at the repeater gauge about his wrist cuff for fear it would confirm what he suspected already – the jet pack was starving of fuel and damaged, and he had only moments of flight left before he fell back into the embrace of Sabien's gravity.

He blinked rainwater from his lashes as Arkio fell upon him, and then once more the two siblings were locked in a tumbling embrace, wrestling amid the storm with nothing but footless halls of air surrounding them. Arkio viciously kicked Rafen where the spear had cut a line through the flesh of his thigh, cracking open the wound again where Rafen's Astartes blood had already begun to clot. He howled and butted his brother in the face, gaining the reward of a fan of oily vitae gushing from Arkio's flaring nostrils. A flurry of punches danced across Rafen's ribcage as impacts dented his ceramite chest guard. He tasted the hot copper of his own blood as the blows rattled his teeth in his head.

Rafen clutched at his brother, raking his fingers down the thick skin over his hairless chest. The mailed red fingers of his battle gloves drew scars across the pallid and gaunt tissue; runnels of tainted blood gathered at wounds where hard marbles the shade of space protruded. He flailed as Arkio crushed him to his breast in a crippling bear hug. Rafen heard his bones breaking with the pressure. His Space Marine physiology made him and his kind uniquely aware of their own bodies, so it was with certainty that Rafen sensed the biscopea organ in his chest burst as his ribs pressed in on it. He was bleeding internally in a number of places.

A blink of white sheet lightning turned his world into a washed-out sketch, just lines and impressions dazzling his enhanced vision. Leering out of the blindness came Arkio's twisted face, framed by the halo about his neck and the beating tides of his mottled grey wings. The sound and the fury of the thunderstorm swept away his younger brother's words, but Rafen could still read the declaration of hate on his lips:

You will die.

There was a word that no Blood Angel would ever choose to speak. It was a cognomen that their enemies and detractors had used since the day Sanguinius took up the Emperor's cause. The name was as old as Terra herself, born from times before men strode the stars, forged in the fears of superstitious hearts. It conjured all the deepest terrors of beasts that feasted upon life and bore the fangs of a bloodletter.

Vampire.

Arkio's mouth split into a smile as wide as his face, a forest of needle-sharp canine teeth blooming from his jaws. He became the avatar of the Blood Angels darkest and most horrific aspect, a monstrous parody of the predator legend. Rafen's brother was crushing the life from him, his last breaths of air escaping in choking, wheezing gasps. As the wind and rain lashed about the tumbling pair, Rafen felt his fury rise as Arkio's hot breath tickled his skin. The winged Angel pressed into him, his red maw of a mouth hungry to tear the meat from Rafen's neck and feast on the hot gush of pulsing life within.

'No!' he roared in defiance. Vision fogging, grey tunnels coiling around his sight, Rafen once again teetered on the abyss of death; and once more, he refused to yield to it.

His hands moved though motions drilled into the marrow of his bones by countless turns of muscle-memory, fingers finding and clasping the hilt of his fractal-bladed close combat weapon. The Space Marine knife had not differed appreciably in its design since the earliest days of the Imperium, the monomolecular edges of the Sol-pattern weapon as familiar to Rafen as they would have been to the first Adeptus Astartes ten thousand years earlier. Yet for all its age, the knife was no less lethal.

Rafen struck violently, bringing the weapon about and thrusting upward into the spaces between his brother's ribs. The knife slid on slick, matted skin and fell into the mouldering wound he had given Arkio in the square. He pressed the blade into the writhing, maggot-infested cut, all the way to the steel hilt.

From Arkio's empurpled lips came a scream of inchoate pain that parted the clouds around them with its force. Suddenly, it was no longer Arkio's beating wings that kept the locked pair in the air, but the chattering, dying thrust from Rafen's assault pack. The grey-white sails fluttered and curled as Arkio's fingers dug into Rafen's wargear, slipping over rain-slick ceramite.

Lightning blazed a strobe image on to Rafen's retina, freezing the instant there in shades of white, orange and purple. He saw agony on Arkio's face the like of which he had never encountered upon any battlefield, and a word, a single word, on his sibling's lips.

Brother.

Arkio's hands skidded away from purchase and his weight detached itself from Rafen in a whirl of streaming rain and falling feathers. He snapped out his arm, fingers reaching to scrape the gold sheaths on his shoulders, missing as Arkio drew away, sinking through the low blanket of boiling grey cloud. Rafen's brother, the Blessed, the Reborn Angel, the Deus Sanguinius, tumbled away like a downed prey bird, falling to earth.

Below, amid the shining wet cobbles and glistening mosaics of the ruined church's nave, the Spear of Telesto sensed him coming. The upright weapon twitched and jerked of its own accord, shifting and turning about its axis to bring the teardrop blade to welcome him. Arkio plunged from the thunderheads and his spine found the head of the lance where his shoulder blades met, at the centre of his outstretched wings. His impact sent the fatal spear through the dense altered bones of his skeleton, bisecting his primary heart and exploding out again though his sternum. A perfectly circular hollow formed in the stonework from the force of the fall, and Arkio lay in it, his corrupted blood thinning in the deluge, casting all about him with a rich pool of purple fluids.

The tear-shaped leaf glowed with golden flickers of colour, evaporating every last drop of his vitae from its immaculate, polished surface.

THE SKY TURNED to hell.

Misericorde brought her fanged flanks to bear upon the two Blood Angels warships, unleashing salvo after salvo of heavy rockets, hull-burners and laser fire into the zone of space about them. Mephiston's flagship *Europae* had speed and motion on her side, using generous bursts of vectored thrust from her tertiary drives to turn and move beneath the sister ship *Bellus*. Spinning about its axis, *Europae* weathered the onslaught, distributing the strikes that reached the battle barge across the ship's glittering void shields.

Bellus, damaged and wounded, reacted more slowly. To the untrained eye, the two Blood Angels barges seemed identical, but at close hand the injuries and scars *Bellus* carried were raw and obvious. *Europae* was fresh from Baal's orbital docks, fully crewed, perfectly maintained and at the peak of her performance; by contrast *Bellus* was tired and worn. The engagement over Sabien was just one more battle in a string of conflicts that the old warship had weathered – the wounds from the fight against the cruiser *Dirge Eterna* at Shenlong, the battleship *Ogre Lord* at Cybele and even the lasting lacerations from the mission into ork space, all of them took their toll on the *Bellus*. She was strung out and hobbled in comparison to her adversaries.

From his command throne, Captain Ideon opened up his ship like a shattered hive of hornets, releasing every weapon and warshot at once. About the barge, space became a clogged web of fire and destruction, heat haze and spheres of detonation falling off *Bellus* in radiant waves. 'Report,' he demanded, automatically turning his attention to Brother Solus's station, but Solus was dead, heaped there in a mess of plasma-seared meat and ceramite. The stink of human flesh came to the captain in a dozen different ways through the senses of the ship's machine-spirit.

Over the crashing din of secondary explosions, a sense-servitor babbled out a reply. 'Multiple critical hits along starboard hull. Breaches on fifty-two per cent of decks. Enginseers report imminent collapse of the fusion core's spirit-monitor.'

'Bow guns,' he roared, thrusting his consciousness through the cybernetic links in his skull to touch the powerful ship-killer cannons in *Bellus*'s prow.

The servitor answered even as the question formed in Ideon's thoughts. 'Inoperative. Crew loss due to atmospheric venting.' The mind-wiped slave chattered in a flat monotone, as if it were discussing something no more vexing than a change in weather.

Ideon glimpsed the ragged metal where the bow of *Bellus* used to be, the tide of fragments and vacuum-bloated corpses streaming out into the black. Hate building inside him, the captain drew every last piece of the ship's offensive capability together and held it in his mind. His normally immobile form on the control throne was rocking back and forth, twitching like a palsy victim from the force of his anger. A strange, inhuman noise threaded out of his voxcoder, the peculiar ululation crossing the din of the bridge. Ideon willingly let himself fall into the screaming embrace of the black rage, his mind disintegrating into the madness of race memories from thousands of years past.

'Kill them all!' crackled the metallic voice.

Europae's patience was at an end, and with unrestrained force she opened fire with every weapon at her disposal, crossing the orbital range to punish *Bellus* for the perfidy of its crew and *Misericorde* for the crime of daring to sully the Emperor's space. In turn, the Chaos warship spat hate back at the Blood Angels, pouring it into the darkness until the emptiness was thick with radiation.

Bellus lay between them, striking out at everything and nothing around it, a mad wounded beast alive with pain and the smell of death. Arkio's flagship was caught in the crossfire of the battle and fell into the hellstorm. In the absolute silence of the void, *Bellus* detonated, breaking into huge splinters of steel, her fusion reactor giving birth to an instant new sun.

On the planet below, the light of her death was lost in the thick clouds.

RAFEN'S THRUSTER PACK ran dry when he was still a thirty metres from the ground, and he tumbled and dropped as if he were made of lead. Slamming his balled fist into the release switch on his belt, he felt the dead weight of the pack detach, and freed of the burden he turned into a spin, crashing through age-rotted beams to land with a bone-jarring crack of sound. A ring of water scattered away from him in a ripple. From his kneeling stance, Rafen rose, his eyes narrowed against the biting winds. He scanned the interior of the church, afraid of what he would see.

And there he saw it.

Pinned to the stone as a gigantic collector might exhibit some rare moth or butterfly, Arkio lay with the Spear of Telesto run through him. All about his sibling was a spreading aurora the colour of autumn, a most unearthly golden light. Favouring his injured leg, Rafen jogged across the transept and came to Arkio's side.

'Brother...'

Rafen gasped in amazement; despite so brutal an injury, Arkio still clung to life with fierce tenacity. His sibling's hands were clasped the haft of the spear, the burning glow crisping away the flesh. Arkio seemed not to notice the pain.

'Brother,' Rafen repeated, searching his sibling's face for the shroud of contamination. Arkio seemed as ruined as the shattered landscape of the city-shrine about them, hollow inside. The black trains of poison boils still seethed beneath his marbled skin, but his eyes... his eyes belonged to the Arkio that Rafen remembered from their youth, the naïve and bold soul that had given him strength and loyalty.

There was pain there, of a kind Rafen had only ever seen in the eyes of sinners and turncoats fallen to the law of the Inquisition. Before, he had never questioned it, but now he saw it for what it was. Regret, so powerful and so heartbreaking that the emotion could barely be contained by a human will.

'*What have I done?*' Arkio rasped, holding his brother's gaze. 'I have broken every compact and promise... I have turned my back on what I am and embraced the void...' He shuddered and wailed. 'Oh, Lord Emperor, I have betrayed all I hold dear.'

His hate-rage ebbing, Rafen found only one answer in the echoing chasms of his heart. 'Yes.'

The humming of the spear gently rose and fell in the fading rhythm of Arkio's secondary heart. Each peak and trough grew longer as life ebbed from him into the stones and the rain. 'I was weak...' he managed. 'I thought I could protect myself from this–' he gestured feebly and his wings jerked in response, '–from falling from the path. My arrogance... I... I believed I was... believed it...'

'I am sorry, Arkio,' Rafen said, silent tears falling from his eyes, drawing lines in dark smears of blood and soot on his cheeks. 'I am sorry I was not there to stand with you, turn you from this corruption.'

'No,' Arkio whispered. 'You share no burden with me, kinsman. I will bear this stigma...' He shivered, a drool of blood escaping from his lips. 'My error. I was weak...'

'Arkio, no... You were... human.'

He forced a wan smile. 'Fear not, Rafen. This is our fate. Both of us saw it.'

Rafen gasped. 'You knew this would be by my hand?'

'Yes. And so it was.' His ruined fingers crossed Rafen's chest plate and touched his brother's cheek. 'You weep for me? That is all I ask, kinsman. The Emperor will damn me for my folly, and I accept that without question... But you... I ask *you* to forgive me. I recant, Rafen. Please forgive me, my brother.'

'I forgive you, Arkio. On our father's grave, I swear it.'

Arkio gave a shallow, final nod of thanks. 'That is mercy enough.' His eyes fluttered closed, and the spear fell silent.

Rafen knelt there for an age, no sound in his ears but the rush and thunder of the rainstorm, no feeling inside him except the raw despair of loss. Finally, his heart brimming with its grievous remorse, Rafen came to his feet with his brother's body in his arms, the Holy Lance excised from the dead man and there at Rafen's shoulder. The warm, mellifluent light of the spear illuminated the ruins about him, and he held Arkio high. He seemed to weigh so little now, as if the burden of his tainted change had run away with his shed blood.

In the near distance, Rafen saw the firefly sparkles of bolter discharges, and on the wind came gunshots, screams and the chants of the Word Bearers. The Blood Angel's face set in grim determination and he advanced toward the fighting. He left nothing behind him but his doubts.

CHAPTER THIRTEEN

CURIOUS, THOUGHT MEPHISTON, how the passage of time became elastic in the throes of conflict. He skewered a Word Bearer and the helot soldier behind him with one swift thrust of the mindblade Vitarus, the force sword immolating them both in gusts of blue flame. Flicking the remains away, he frowned. How long had he been fighting? Crashing thunder bellowed overhead, announcing the flashes of sheet lighting that illuminated the writhing fighters in the square. Rain pelted everything, sluicing off the blood of enemy and ally alike, churning the brick dust and dirt on the ground into a muddy brown quagmire. It was difficult for the Librarian to know exactly how long the battle had been raging; every sword blow and bolt shell seemed to pass in its own small bubble of time, one single instant in the huge cacophony of wanton slaughter. Minutes, hours… it could have been days for all the Lord of Death cared. He was in his element here, an engine of destruction fuelled by the holiest of causes.

He caught the sound of a man's scream, suddenly truncated by the ripping of flesh and sinew. Mephiston whirled to see the golden helmet of a Blood Angels honour guard – one of Arkio's loyalists – sent flying by the blow of the veteran sergeant who had accompanied the pskyer from *Europae*. The Space Marine staggered back, shaking gore from the clogged blades of his chainsword. He caught Mephiston's eye and spared him a grim nod.

The Librarian did not need to employ his psychic skills to read the Blood Angel's mind. This was a sorry, dismal business, being forced to take up arms against men who were battle-brothers. The Lord of Death was sickened by what he and the others had been forced into, and he cursed Arkio and Stele for bringing it to pass. It was enough to purge the galaxy of turncoats and traitors, but to face men who had willingly forsaken their oath to Dante and Baal in favour of some pretender child made Mephiston weary and hateful. For each errant Blood Angel he slew, the psyker spoke a short prayer to the Golden Throne. He did not forgive these men their misjudgements, instead he tallied them as crimes to lay at the feet of Ramius Stele, the architect of this madness. However fate unfolded on this day, Mephiston vowed that the accursed Hereticus fool would not leave Sabien alive.

The sergeant fell back a dozen steps as he reloaded his bolter, before firing again into the mass of raging zealots. 'Bah!' he spat, taking three men with pinpoint head shots. 'These fools don't know the meaning of the word "retreat". We cut them down like wheat and still they come.'

Mephiston strode forward, Vitarus ending lives in sweeps of bright power. 'The wheat dares not oppose the scythe.' For every one of the Warriors of the Reborn trampled into the mud and earth, there were two more behind him, desperate for the glory of death in their messiah's name – or just loathsome enough not to care. Here and there he saw Word Bearers in tightly drilled units, and those he could not see he heard, their foul demagogues spouting dirges and songs of unhallowed praise to the Maelstrom. The Chaos Space Marines took their fury to the Blood Angels, attacking Mephiston's men and Arkio's loyalists alike, ignoring the helots unless the humans were foolish enough to block their lines of fire.

'Red foes, red friends,' snapped the veteran. 'Who is the enemy here, lord?'

'Everyone,' the psyker replied, burning down a dozen more wayward souls with his screeching plasma pistol. 'This is not battle, this is chaos.'

Mephiston's Techmarine thrust his way through the morass of dead and dying, stumbling into ankle-deep pools of fluid. He killed a helot armed only with a sharpened spanner, punching through his ribcage, and threw the dead body aside. 'Lord!' he called as he approached. 'Lord Mephiston.'

Bolter fire in careful, targeted ranks ranged down on them from the middle of the enemy throng, where Word Bearers were marshalling a concerted effort. The Librarian threw back the power of the Smite, a psychic tornado ripping across the square to dismember them.

The Techmarine blinked away the after-glare of the blast and gave a jerky bow. 'My lord, we have but two Thunderhawks remaining and neither can make lift-off. The Word Bearers have six squads pinning them down. I spotted Havoc troopers in their number, although they have not attempted to destroy the transports yet.'

'They want the ships for themselves. What news from orbit?'

Gunfire drew their attention and all three of them fired back at a group of helots armed with civilian hunting lasers. 'Communication is intermittent at best,' continued the Blood Angel. 'High levels of radiation in the ionosphere prevent clear vox transmissions.'

'Radiation?' growled the sergeant. 'From what?'

'*Bellus* has been destroyed, lord,' the Techmarine said dispassionately. 'A fragmentary vox from *Europae* appears to confirm that the loyalist's ship was obliterated in the crossfire between our barge and the *Misericorde*.'

Mephiston shook his head angrily. 'Such waste. Such foolish, pointless waste.'

The Space Marine gestured with a signum, complex lines of data glyphs and warning runes marching across the device's rain-slick screen. 'We are outnumbered on the ground. Force disposition of the loyalists is weak but they overmatch us with the reinforcements of the Word Bearers.' To his surprise, the Lord of Death accepted this dire information with a clinical smile; he was unfazed by the sensor's divination. On the contrary, he seemed to expect it.

'With *Bellus* out of the picture, we can forget calling reserves from *Europae*,' grated the sergeant, shaking rain off his visor. 'They'll have their hands full with the Chaos ship, won't even be able to risk 'porting us more men. We're on our own down here.'

'As it ever was,' Mephiston added. 'So be it.' The psyker toggled a control in the collar of his arching hood and spoke into one of the bone-white skulls that decorated the throat of his armour, where a vox-unit was concealed. 'Blood Angels, rally!' he snapped, the command filtering out to the ear-beads of every man from the *Europae*. 'Your previous orders to contain this rabble no longer apply. Join the fray and leave no foe standing.'

'Aye. *Aye!*' came the replies over the channel.

Mephiston threw himself into the throng, leaving behind the hillock of rubble and stone he had defended to wade deep in the gore of his adversaries. He showed sharp fangs and eyes of fire as death rained down around him, red floods of it flashing in the air.

'Terra and God-Emperor,' breathed the veteran, as he watched the Librarian shred the unwary foes. 'He's not a man, he's a storm with a sword.'

ELSEWHERE IN THE morass, the pell-mell melee moved and shifted like a viral organism, swallowing up those that did not go with the army's flow, killing those that defied it. Delos waded through a sea of angry faces and weeping wounded, all of them merging into one pale orchestra of ghosts, eyes upturned to the grey raging sky, crying to their Blessed. The Chaplain moved among them, a black shining shadow with a grinning skull head. They flinched and recoiled from his crozius as he waved it before him, some of them automatically genuflecting toward an icon of Sanguinius, others hissing in pain as if the sight of it hurt their eyes.

A tinny rattle about his head announced the passage of a metallic servo-skull and Delos knew he was close. There, just a few lengths away, Inquisitor Stele stood in on the crest of a subsided stone dais. At his feet, shivering under a wet, matted cloak, his lexmechanic rocked back and forth, constantly babbling a endless string of words in thousands of Imperial dialects. Delos caught something of his speech when the wind changed for a moment, bringing it to his ears.

'–demnos, dannavik, dorius, delenz, dorcon, daemon, dethenex, dynikas–'

The inquisitor's servo-skulls continually described a lazy orbit around him, occasionally pausing to lance a laser bolt into a target they deemed a threat to Stele. The woman was there as well, never more than a hand's length from him, the lines of her face hiding beneath a voluminous hood. The habit she wore was cut like an astropath's, but she was anything but one of those. Delos was not cursed with the warp eye of psykers but he didn't need to be to smell the stink of the empyrean on the girl. He shook the nauseating perfume of it from his head. Odd how he had never noticed that about her before.

Gripping his crozius arcanum firmly, Delos forced himself up to the dais, his skull-helmet's sneer matching Stele's. 'Inquisitor,' he demanded. 'By the Blessed, I demand you account for yourself.'

Stele arched an eyebrow. 'Chaplain... Delos, isn't it?' He wiped a patina of rain from his bald skull. 'Leave me. I must prepare–'

'For what?' Delos shouted, startling himself with his own forcefulness. 'Tell me my eyes deceived me, Stele! Tell me it was but a mind-trick of Mephiston's!'

'What trivia are you chattering about?' Stele retorted, his attention elsewhere. He glanced at Ulan. 'The boy, the boy! Where is he?'

The psy-witch shook her head, her mind full of razors. 'Difficult….'

'I saw you and the Word Bearer.' In a blink of lightning, Delos saw something shadowing Stele's face; not a wraith or a spirit, but a haze of lines crossing and re-crossing. Eight arrows arranged in a ring. 'It is true,' Delos said, 'you consort with the corrupted!'

Stele grimaced and fixed him with a glare. 'First Sachiel and now you? This conflict is taxing me too much. Things are slipping through the gaps–'

'*Traitor!*' Delos roared, bringing up the crozius to strike the inquisitor.

'Better that than a fool.' Stele raised a hand and a column of pressure shoved Delos in the chest, pushing him back, knocking the power weapon from his grip. The air around him became dry and greasy, the rain fizzing away. Invisible tendrils of psychic force coiled about the Chaplain and slipped through molecule-thin gaps in his armour to touch his bare skin.

'The twisting path,' Stele said, leering at the kneeling Blood Angel. 'Take the path, Delos. *Take it.*'

His mind flayed open and Delos screamed, clawing at his helmet, tearing it from his head. The Chaplain saw his world fall apart around him; he watched a mirror of his life to come as he tore off his allegiance to the Emperor (*I would never do such a thing!*) as he slaughtered Dante and burned Baal's cities (*No! No! This is not true!*) as he fell, laughing with cruel abandon, into the embrace of Chaos (*No!*).

Stele broke off the mental assault and spat on his twitching victim. 'Never question me,' he growled. The inquisitor grabbed at Ulan's arm, pulling her to him. 'I won't ask again! Where is Arkio?'

'Dead.' She drew the word out into a howl.

The inquisitor's face went purple with rage. His jaw worked but no words came to him. Anger robbed him of a voice, and instead he struck out with a balled fist, backhanding the psyker-slave. Ulan stumbled and dropped to her knees, the hood about her head falling to her shoulders. Her pale and hairless pate with its tarnished brass sockets glittered dully. Overhead, the silver skull drones popped in tiny explosions.

Stele gave an incoherent roar of annoyance, the muscles in his neck bunching in tense ropes. 'That worthless, stupid fool. It wasn't enough that he could accept the gifts I gave him, he had to bury himself in the part.' He pulled at the skin of his face, barely able to contain the quaking rage inside him. 'All of it ruined by that pathetic whelp. My plans are ashes now, my greatest performance destroyed by his arrogance!'

'But... but that was why you chose him...' Ulan spat out blood and a broken piece of tooth. 'You wanted a man who could *be* Sanguinius–'

'I wanted a figurehead,' snarled Stele, 'A gaudy token messiah, not a corpse.'

Ulan shakily got to her feet. 'Perhaps he gave you a martyr instead...'

'Martyr...' The word whispered through the inquisitor's lips, a benediction, cooling his burning ire. 'I will not fail now, understand me?' he growled. 'Not now, not in the moment of my greatest triumph. I have made it my design to turn these Astartes freaks to the Banner of Change and I *will not be denied!*' Stele stripped the grox-hide battle coat from his shoulders and dashed the garment on the ground, dragging his ornate laspistol from its concealed holster. 'Plans must be accelerated,' he said. 'The turning cannot wait! It must be here and now!'

'But we are not ready...'

He ignored Ulan's warning and pressed the muzzle of his gun to the palm of his other hand. 'Open your mind to the Spite Lord, witch. Bring him. Bring him now!'

Stele jerked the trigger and the pistol blew a burning hole through his flesh, vaporising three of his fingers and setting his cuff aflame. The inquisitor screamed and clutched at his ruined hand, forcing the jetting blood from his severed veins to spatter about him in the sacred pattern he knew by heart. The geometry of the unhallowed circle came together even as he drew it.

Ulan hesitated. Stele had instructed her on the rituals that would open the conduit to the Malfallax's realm, but now the moment came to do it she found herself afraid. The psy-witch had been a slave since birth, a laboratory experiment before that, and disobedience was not part of her makeup, yet still she balked at this most dangerous command. Stele turned on her and saw the indecision in her eyes. The inquisitor snarled and grabbed her robes, dragging her close to him. The bloody meat of his hand clutched at her neck. She felt warm fluids pulsing over her skin.

'Lord, no...' She managed a weak denial.

'Open the way,' Stele shouted, and with a thrust of his arm, the lacerated fingers sank into the flesh at Ulan's collar. The pallid skin rippled like water and Stele merged his barbed digits into her bone and cartilage. The woman resisted, for what would be the first and last time in her life. It made little difference, as the inquisitor brought his undamaged fingers to her cheeks, the tips scraping away the false scars that hid the blemishes of psy-tuned metal contacts. Ulan could not scream; she could not breathe; she could only hold on and try not to die as Stele used her as a lens for his own psyker talent, magnifying his black will to cut a way into the writhing core of the Eye of Terror.

INSIDE THE NO-SPACE of the immaterium, the creature Malfallax had been waiting, floating and circling the man-filth Stele in the manner of a sea predator scenting prey in distress. Unseen by the denizens of the material world, the realm of the warp was constantly surrounding them, a layer of unreality laid across the sordid, crude matter of their wastrel worlds. The forms the live-things called Chaos, in their limited little ways of perceiving the omniverse, swarmed and thrived in this infinite ocean of mind and emotion. The daemon moved with Stele. Waiting, waiting and watching for the moment when the thrashing and chattering of the quarry was at its peak. Only then would it strike, lapping up the absolute perfection of its fear, sinking in rending teeth, tearing it to soul-shreds.

Now the prey called to him, through the conduit of the mutant abortion created by the corpse-god's science. His instrument Stele cried out for the poisoned hand of

Malfallax. The warp daemon teased itself with the anticipation of the shift; it was so infrequent that the beast could find itself a vessel strong enough to contain its essence for more than a few hours. Most flesh-things in the other reality were gossamer constructs of wet, weak meats. They would burn or inflate or explode if the Malfallax issued even an iota of itself into them – but it had worked hard to prepare for this day. Malfallax, Monarch of Spite, Heirophant of Vicissitude, was weary of partial manifestations, of animating the inert or the mindless to hold a ghost of his full and awful potential. It wanted to step freely into the plane of men and run it red with their bloody terror. Malfallax missed the feel of it over there beyond the veil; it was time to return.

THE SCREAM THAT Ulan released was a sound that no human throat had ever made before. It rang from side to side of the city square, souring the deadened sky of Sabien as it passed, hammering a chill spike of terror into every life that caught the echo of it. Stele withdrew from the shaking body of the psy-witch, the oozing blood from his shattered hand wrapped about his forearm like a red glove. Mad laughter bubbled up from inside him. 'He comes!' shouted the inquisitor, the insane mix of elation and utter dread merging in his chest. Stele spread his arms in welcome as the spilt blood and mud inside the ceremonial circle bubbled and churned. 'Come to me, Void-born! Take form and heed me.'

The black-brown sludge at his feet rippled and built up upon itself, assembling the shape of a hulking figure. It grew something resembling a face and pointed it a Stele, hot coppery breath issuing from the steaming orifices. '*Sssssssssservant.*'

Ulan could not see for the blood streaming from the brass plugs in her skull or weeping in tears from ears, nose and eyes, but she knew where the creature was. The blazing power of its nova heart burned into her mind-senses. Ulan struggled to stumble away, what rationality she still had lost in a primitive desire to flee.

'Come, daemon,' Stele cried out to the mud-form. 'Bear witness with me to this victory. Take shape and release the Way of Change. The Blood Angels will turn to the glory of Tzeentch, they will know and revere him as I have always done.' He stabbed his ruined hand at the shaking woman. 'Fill this vessel and come forth!'

Ulan tripped and fell, the mud sucking at her, holding her down. She shook her head in some feeble gesture of refusal.

'*No.*' The voice was slime on cold rock. The slurry of living mire flashed forward in a wet surge, but not toward Ulan. It rose up around Stele's legs and rooted him to the spot, coiling about him like liquid snakes, filling his clothing.

The inquisitor tried to scream, but as he opened his mouth the blood-mass poured in over his lips and drowned him in thick ooze. *Your reward comes now,* said the Malfallax, each word a psionic hammer blow, *not lordship of these men-prey, not riches and powers as you were promised. You will know the glory of me. You shall carry my essence, become my mount and flesh-proxy...*

Ulan felt Stele's terrible, silent screams as the daemon forced itself into the inquisitor, turning the man into the unwilling vessel for its bloated psychic substance. As much as she hated the malignant blackguard, she found a spark of pity for the man as he was subsumed inside his daemon lord's self. Betrayal and anger, fear and terror so sweet that they clogged her throat with the backwash of their taste; the emotions flooded out of the twisting bag of skin. The creature denied his puppet the chance to frame his feelings as he died, tearing understanding from Stele's mind. He was nothing but carrion for it now: his plans were Malfallax's plans, his grand schemes tiny puzzles in the SpiteLord's rounds of parlour amusement.

And so only Ulan truly witnessed the death of Inquisitor Ramius Stele, of his flesh and his sinew, of his mind and his soul. She heard it rip through the ether and catch her in its razored wake. The psy-witch gibbered and wept, ruined by her proximity to it.

The daemon stretched at the meat surrounding it, and with slow and purposeful motion it unleashed the way of mutation upon its new organic shell. Spewing out the dead mud that had briefly contained it, Malfallax adopted the unhallowed aspect that all his kindred wore as the mark of their fealty to the eightfold way. Stele's bones shifted like putty, hollowing and distending. The pallid human flesh glittered and took on a multihued riot of colours, flashing rainbows as sunlight caught through a prism. The face pressed forward against itself, becoming a hooked beak with deep-sunk eye pits burning with ruin. Gossamer feathers burst from the remnants of the Hereticus uniform, and great scarred wings shook loose from the prison of the skin. Hooks and talons dressed the creature and it gave a long, languid yawn.

Staring out at the human world from inside its new sheath of matter, the Lord of Change glanced at the cowering Ulan and decided it was hungry. Black-barbed claws caught the psyker woman in a pincer grip and brought her to the wicked beak, as a warped voice bayed for fresh, new blood.

Malfallax ate this meal and studied the mad war ranged about it, considering where it would begin.

DELOS LOOKED ON, appalled. At first, the cleric had thought it was more of the mind-trick that Stele had turned upon him, but the stink of the shifting, sinuous beast told his senses that this monstrosity was as real as the hammering rain and the cold mud. His crozius was gone, lost and broken, but he still had his bolter and his blade. Delos drew both, running his fingers over the litany inscribed on the frame of his weapon. He came to the last etching where he had transcribed his oath to Arkio. 'All lies now?' he asked the rushing skies above. 'Have I damned myself?'

There would be no more for Delos to inscribe after today. The Chaplain blinked rainwater from his eyes and leapt at the daemon, calling out the name of his primarch.

Malfallax cocked its head in a quizzical gesture and turned to present itself to the figure in black. It stood on something wet and breakable, hot liquid spurting about its clawed feet. The daemon glanced down, shaking off the blood and organ-matter. Stele's lexmechanic had been too slow to get out of the way, and now the speaker-slave was a paste of bones and metals in the mud.

Delos's shots found purchase in the beast's hide and Malfallax swallowed the pain of them like rare sweetmeats. The daemon curled a taloned finger at the Chaplain and spoke a word of blasphemous power. A rift opened like a bloody wound before his hand and a streak of rose-coloured fire jetted forth, engulfing Delos.

The cleric wailed as the pink flames surrounded and clung to him, burning through his sable power armour. The Lord of Change left him screaming and dying there in the mud and strode away, looking for more prey. Malfallax reached into a sucking void in its chest, its hand disappearing to the wrist. It returned with a hilt in its grasp, and with slow and careful motions the daemon withdrew an edged weapon made from dead men's bones and solid delusion.

The humans had a name for such a sword – they called them warp blades, semi-real constructs existing half-in and half-out of the empyrean, raw funnels of mindform woven into killing blades. Malfallax tested the Chaos weapon in its grip, feeling the weight of it, judging the reach. Satisfied, it drew up the sword and plunged it into a mass of fleeing slave troopers, liquefying their bodies with the speed of its passage. The blade rippled and gasped in pleasure.

'EMPEROR PRESERVE US,' hissed the sergeant. 'It makes me retch just to lay eyes upon it...'

'What manner of thing is it?' added the Techmarine.

'Tzeentch-spawn,' Mephiston replied. The psyker felt the edges of the agony-sphere cast by the warp blade, and his eyes could not focus on the blurring shape of the sword, his vision slipping off the unholy geometry of it. 'A Lord of Change.' He tapped the skull medallion at his throat and spat out an order. 'Regroup. Concentrate fire on the creature–'

The Blood Angels commands were silenced by a screaming crash of sound from the mass of the enemy force. The daemon lord drew arcane runes in the air and unleashed a flood of cold fire across the square. Men caught in the white core of the flames were instantly turned to vapour, disappearing into ash. Those on the edges of the blast caught fire and stumbled about, blind and mad with pain; the ones on the periphery became cursed with the fallout of mutation, spontaneously growing new limbs, bursting out of their wargear or imploding. Mephiston saw several men turn their own weapons on themselves rather than accede to the revision of their throbbing flesh.

Space Marines died on the tip of the monster's ten-metre sword, adding their crimson to the ankle-deep blood swamp. The warp blade left brief tears in the fabric of space where it passed, and things emerged from the hole, chattering with hunger. Saucer-shaped and dripping with toxic cilia, the disc-like warp freaks fell on the injured and the dying like vultures.

Emboldened by their new ally, the Word Bearers flooded forward, shoving aside or killing the hesitant loyalist Space Marines. Mephiston met them with Vitarus singing death, beheading and bifurcating, his plasma pistol hissing hot with discharge. The traitors met steel and died, but for the first time since he had arrived on Sabien, the Lord of Death took a step back as the press of the enemy turned tight like a ruby vice.

'THE EYE OF a hurricane,' murmured Turcio, 'we are caught in a storm.' He fired again at the gaggle of Word Bearers that sniped at them from the remains of a smouldering Thunderhawk, firing past helot soldiers who seemed oblivious to the crossfire passing through their numbers. He ducked to reload and Brother Corvus took his place, pacing his shots. 'By my life... The confusion... What are we doing here?'

'Surviving,' Corvus retorted, killing a Word Bearer with a headshot. 'We are worth nothing if we die.'

'But the Blessed... where is he? Has Arkio deserted us?'

'No!' Corvus snapped back at his battle-brother, but in truth the same fear filled his mind as well. 'He... he must be fighting elsewhere...'

'Where?' Turcio demanded, coming up to join the conflict once more. 'This day had turned to madness. Our hated enemies arise from nowhere, daemons take shape from nothing... Arkio is gone and we are fighting everything that moves.' He grabbed Corvus's arm and looked him the face. 'I don't know what I am any more! Blood Angel? Warrior of the Blessed? Traitor or loyalist? There's nothing but death here, no answers–'

Bolt-fire from the Chaos lines chewed off a chunk of their cover and both Space Marines threw themselves aside as lascannon shots followed through. Turcio rolled over in the mud and found himself staring up at the sky, the endless curtain of grey rain pelting them. Misgivings clouded his mind. Suddenly it seemed like everything that had happened since Cybele was being called in question. 'Sanguinius preserve me, what is our fate to be?'

'Look.' Corvus pointed toward the gutted tower of a long-fallen cathedral, one of only a few structures that still stood above ground level. There was a human figure up there on the stone canopy, atop a broken gargoyle. Lighting gave him form and colour – a Blood Angel, and in his arms a mess of golden shapes, pale flesh and white feathers.

RAFEN LOOKED DOWN on the battlefield and filled his lungs with breaths of wet, metallic air. When he spoke, his voice carried on the wind, echoing through the vox channels of every Astartes on the ground.

'Blood Angels!' he cried. 'Sons of Baal, hear me. The lie has been dispelled, our twisted fate undone. Know this, brothers. We have been betrayed!'

The conflict raged on, but Rafen's voice still reached every corner of the fight, even the helots and the enemy turning to cast an ear toward him. 'All of us hold the blood of Sanguinius inside our hearts,' Rafen called. 'Every man of us is the Pure One in some small corner of his soul... But our primogenitor, our lord and founder... He lies *dead*.' The word thundered across the sky. 'Sanguinius is ashes, millennia gone, no bones, no heart, only blood! Sanguinius died at the hands of hated Horus, he perished at the blade of *Chaos*.'

Angry howls bubbled up from the throats of all the Blood Angels, to a man all of them stirred to violence by the stark truth of Rafen's statement.

'And now the archfoe seeks to turn us all, to drag us to their blasphemy by a false idol...' He held up Arkio's body, high above the throng. 'See. Look at what has been done! My blood kinsman, mutated and warped by the hand of a traitor...' Rafen's voice was choked with emotion. 'They made him think he was the Pure One Reborn... They made us believe. But he was corrupted, poisoned by the pawn Stele! The daemon that walks among you did this, so we would follow blindly, blindly into the abyss.'

A chorus of denials came up to Rafen on the wind, anguished refusals from men who now saw the lie they had granted their fealty to.

'See the truth!' Rafen screamed. 'See my brother fall.' He tipped Arkio's corpse over the edge and let gravity take the winged body from him. In a moment of terrible silence, only the rain spoke as the dead man tumbled end over end, ruined wings flapping, to land in a broken heap on the cathedral steps.

TURCIO SCRAMBLED TO the body and turned Arkio's face to his. He recoiled with horror and stumbled away.

'What do you see?' Corvus asked, his hearts tight in his chest.

'Ruin,' Turcio said in a dead voice. 'Ruin and damnation. Our messiah is black with untruth, brother... Rafen does not lie.'

'ARKIO IS DEAD!' came the cry from the tower. *'My brother perished for this mendacity and it dies with him!'* Rafen drew up the Spear of Telesto and let the weapon's golden light haze the sky around him. 'By the Holy Lance, reject your flawed allegiance to Arkio and remember the true lord, Sanguinius.' He pointed the weapon into the melee and felt it turn hot with willing power. 'See the foe among you and destroy them.'

* * *

ON THE STEPS, Turcio stood back and called to the sky. 'Aye. *Aye*. I renounce the Reborn. I am a Blood Angel!' The battle-brother leapt off the cracked stones and threw himself into the helots and traitors. 'For the Emperor and Sanguinius!'

Corvus yelled the same oath and followed him and across the square, Arkio's loyalists threw off their misguided devotion, the burning power of the spear tearing the shroud of Chaos's confusion from their minds.

MALFALLAX'S ANGER PIERCED the Warmaster's mind like a white-hot arrow, the thread of psychic communion between them so strong it killed two lesser Word Bearers beside the Witch Prince.

'Garand! The man-filth's ridiculous catspaw is cold meat! You promised me this elaborate charade would be a success!'

The Word Bearers commander glanced in the direction of the shambling Lord of Change, far across the battle, and bowed. 'The fool Stele, great heirophant. I tried to control his scheming, but his vanity was his undoing.'

'I have consumed his flesh,' said Malfallax. 'I know his goals. This day may still be won by us, and we may still turn the Blood Angels for our master's pleasure.'

'Forgive me, excellence, but how? With the boy dead, these Blood Whelps will not follow us into darkness.'

Psychic laughter battered at his senses. 'You see only the battle to hand, Garand. There is another way.'

Realisation flooded into the Warmaster. 'The Flaw. The gene-curse of the Baalites.'

'Yessss,' murmured the daemon. 'I tasted it on Cybele through my bound psy-slaves. We will conjure it from these fools and let it consume them – and when they are deep within the black rage, I will lead them to a well of blood the likes of which they will never escape, to the very heart of the Maelstrom itself.'

Garand nodded, awed by the daring of it. 'Your glory, Lord Malfallax.'

THEY MADE WAY as Rafen walked from the cathedral's interior to the place where Arkio's body lay. In his mailed fist, the spear glowed as it had that day on the *Bellus*, when the light of the primogenitor had touched every soul aboard. Gently, he curled the broken wings around his sibling's corpse in a death shroud, while Mephiston's men looked on in silence.

Rafen rose to find the Chief Librarian at his side. The Lord of Death proffered a thick glass injector in his hand. 'Your wounds are severe, brother,' said Mephiston. 'Take this. Corbulo himself gave it to me. It will lend you the strength of the lords.'

He gathered up the exsanguinator and turned it in his fingers. Thick, heavy blood glistened inside it, drawn from the highest Sanguinary Priest of the Blood Angels Chapter. Once this blood mixed with Rafen's own, the essence of Sanguinius would flow even stronger in his veins.

Mephiston nodded at the dead man. 'The time has come to avenge him.'

'It has,' agreed Rafen, and with one single sweeping motion, he plunged the needle into his chest and emptied its contents into his heart.

CHAPTER FOURTEEN

FOR HUNDREDS OF years the landscape of the shrine world Sabien had been silent of human voices, the desolate ruins speaking only with the mournful winds that chased dust and rain through the streets and open spaces. In its own way, Sabien was a mournful twin to the planet Cybele, a sister sphere light years distant toward the coreward marches of the galaxy. Both worlds were markers for the dead, and both had run crimson with the life of both Astartes and traitors. Fate, if such a thing existed, had cast a circular path for Rafen and his brethren to follow. Their journey into darkness had begun among tombstones and memorials, and here and now it would end among the same.

Sabien had known the unbridled passion and fury of the Sons of Sanguinius all those centuries ago, when the long-since dead had fought and perished in order to hold this planet against the legion enemies of the God-Emperor. That power had come again to the silent world, raising up against the thunder of the storm clouds in a brilliant tide of virtuous malevolence.

The Blood Angels did not simply attack, they *detonated* across the war zone in a wave of unfettered rage, a red tide of men plunging into the lines of the Word Bearers and the maddened helot soldiers. They rushed to the fight, rejecting the relative safety of a stand-off battle, throwing caution to the wind in shattering chants and war cries. The unholy hymns of the Chaos Space Marines were drowned out by the lusty roars of their opponents, and then by the massive crash of the two forces meeting like a hammer on an anvil. Metal on metal, chainsword against ceramite, bolter striking flesh, the hissing snap of laser fire – and the screaming. The horrible, heart-chilling screaming. All of it came together in an orchestra of unchained war. The earth quaked beneath the awesome release of mayhem and destruction.

The Blood Angels had returned to Sabien, and a crimson hell came striding with them.

ONLY IN THE crucible of close combat could a man truly understand the measure of himself. It was nothing to stand aside, in the cockpit of a fighter or behind the barrel of a ranged cannon, to press a button and watch a distant foe vanish in a puff of smoke. How could a Space Marine ever know the colour of his heart unless he stood toe to toe with his most hated enemy and took their life as they looked him in the eyes? What truth was stronger than the final moment of reckoning, when weapon matched weapon and the pulse of shed blood sang its symphony?

Mephiston knew this; it was the greatest glory of the Lord of Death's existence to cast the aberrant and the reviled into shreds. He was at the very tip of the arrow of red ceramite that marked the Blood Angels advance, slashing through the lines of Word Bearers and the helots who dared to assault the Space Marines that towered over them. The psyker killed a man, a commoner whose mind had been addled by the Chaos demagogues, killed him with a look from his flinty, iron-hard eyes. The over-spill of Mephiston's Quickening brushed the errant fool and stopped his heart, bursting blood vessels all over the slave trooper's rough-hewn robes. The hot fluid spattered the psyker's muscular body armour and droplets found their way to his cheeks. Mephiston wiped them from his pale, sallow face and licked the blood from his fingers. It was the most perfect wine, a lustrous red vintage filled with heady adrenaline. The Blood Angel's fangs drew out over his thin lips. He was suddenly filled with the anticipation of more, more, *more*!

He threw aside the dead man and cut wet streaks through a Word Bearers Havoc trooper, bisecting the barrel of the lascannon he held and cutting into the pallid white meat of the enemy Space Marine's neck. The force sword's downward fall did not end there, blue lightning clashing and spitting into the body, severing it into unequal chunks. Black liquids issued up from the gaping voids he cut in thick, oily fountains. This was an altogether different draught, raw with the pollution of a thousand years, stinking and putrid. To let such a libation touch his lips... The very idea made Mephiston ill.

Across the falling corpse of the ruby-armoured traitor came more of the Warriors of the Reborn. All of them were throwing off their loyalty to Arkio now that the winged golden figure had been shown dead, their weak little minds turning to the eightfold way as their new saviour. So pathetic and desperate, they were.

Mephiston shouted a hate cry at them and struck out with Vitarus. He held a special place in the rage he carried for the feeble of devotion and the cowardly; these wretched mundanes were thrice damned in the eyes of the Lord of Death. They had allowed their world to be soured by a Word Bearers invasion, they had lacked even the strength of character to stay true to the Emperor's light when Stele had brought Arkio forth as an erstwhile messiah, and now they ran gladly into the embrace of Chaos when that lie was shown to them. These Shenlongi rabble were like broken children, beaten so often by vicious parents that they had come to believe that it was a sign of love. Another man might have found pity for them in his heart, but both of Mephiston's were filled to the brim with only vehemence. He killed them all, cutting and slashing with the sword, taking up those that did not run from him with his free hand to rip their throats from their necks. He drank from their veins to feed the predator-self inside him.

In his frenzy, the psyker glimpsed his brother Space Marines doing the same, rending and tearing, burning down the soldiers of Chaos where they stood and taking the hot, frothing blood from their screaming lackeys. A dark and potent miasma enveloped Mephiston, clouding his reason even as it thickened his wrath. He felt the red thirst beckoning him, opening up to flood the battle with its crimson mist. The black rage was welling up within him, boiling and furious, and the Blood Angels warlord tipped back his head and roared with laughter. Mephiston embraced it.

THE REMAINS OF the half-eaten corpse twisted through the air and landed in a heavy heap near the base of the bomb crater where Turcio and Corvus were bogged down. Corvus shrank back, pacing shots from his bolter, barely glancing at the body. Turcio's gut knotted as he examined the dead man. Like the carapace of some exotic shellfish, the Blood Angel's armour had been cracked open and peeled back to reveal the meaty innards it protected. A slurry of molten bone and liquefied organ meat oozed from the holes where arms and a head would have been. There were licks of glutinous spittle and teeth marks from where the body had been turned into a food morsel.

A wet belch of blood turned Turcio's attention up to the lip of the crater and there he saw the bloated shape of the Malfallax. It eyed him, spitting out an intact human femur from the side of its wide mouth with callous disdain. The newly assimilated flesh of the dead Space Marine bubbled to the surface of the creature's body, merging into the panoply of glittering skins. The Lord of Change moved like oil over water, stagnant rainbow hues shimmering hypnotically. Turcio blinked furiously to shake off the mesmeric allure.

Malfallax picked at the grove of sickle teeth in its mutant mouth. 'Stringy,' it said, sniffing at the discarded corpse. 'Old and tasteless.' The beast winked at Turcio. 'You'll be a better catch.'

The Blood Angel refused to grace the hellspawn with even the most insulting of ripostes and shot at it instead, his bolter hammering in his hands. Malfallax growled and spat as a couple of lucky shots hit home. It moved with unnatural grace, flowing through the air rather than simply stepping through it, glittering through the constant rods of rain in a weaving dance.

'Stele!' spat Corvus, suddenly recognising some vague aspect of the inquisitor still apparent in the corpse-skin worn by the daemon. 'You took him.'

'He wanted it,' retorted the creature, slapping aside a fallen metal stanchion. 'The imbecile desired to know the warp… and my kin are the warp made flesh.' It plucked at the stretched skin about its face, flapping like grotesque wattles.

Turcio and Corvus reacted without thinking, laying down corridors of concentrated fire to pin the monstrous beast between them, but the daemon whooped with wry amusement and let the bat wings at its back lift it clear. They bracketed it with shots, but again Malfallax shifted and merged into the rain, always appearing at exactly the point where the bolt-rounds were not. There in its breast glowed a green oval with a yellow disc in its centre; a boon from its god, the Eye of Tzeentch grew like a living electro-tattoo, and through it the creature glimpsed a measure of the skein of time. Malfallax saw enough of fate's complex weave to know where the Space Marines would shoot, veering here and there to avoid the burning bullets. It was like firing at smoke.

Turcio's gun ran dry and he twisted towards cover, but the beast was already there with unfolding talons as big as the claws of a fire scorpion. It batted him with the blunt of the nails, knocking Turcio into his battle-brother and throwing them both down into ankle-deep mire. Malfallax hooted with delight and clapped its hands together, a disturbingly human gesture for something so alien. The daemon could have easily struck with a killing blow, tearing Turcio open and eating him, but that would have been too quick, it would have lacked finesse. Malfallax loved the sensuous feeling of its new flesh husk and it wanted to revel in its play as long as it could. It opened a number of mouths across the scarred face and torso, and all of them spoke with the same arrogant and chilling voice. 'Where is your angel now, man-prey?' it mocked.

'*Here!*' shouted Rafen, lightning framing him in a flood of blue-white at the crater's edge. The Space Marine pointed the Holy Lance with one outstretched hand. From the tip ran thick streams of Word Bearers blood, and the haft was steaming as it burnt out the taint of the dozens of Chaos dead it had already claimed. Malfallax spied the Spear of Telesto and let free an atonal shriek. Even the proximity of the hallowed archeotech device was enough to enrage the daemon.

'You denied me the chance to bring my revenge to your lackey, warp scum,' he hissed, 'so I will grant it to you in kind.' Rafen twirled the spear above his head and leapt into the air, turning himself into an arrow aimed at the archfiend's beating black heart.

Malfallax's clawed talon came up to protect itself with the speed of a striking shellsnake, catching the haft of the lance as it fell toward his chest. The carvings of Sanguinius cut into its fingers, but Rafen's headlong flight ended with an abrupt jerk, shaking his bones. The spear pressed forward against the daemon's grip, ready to penetrate the mutant skin; the creature held on. Rafen twisted the weapon and the tip of the teardrop blade scarred the sacred eye branded on Malfallax's chest.

The Eye of Tzeentch wept pink liquid and popped like a burst blister, drawing a murderous howl from the daemon. Ignoring the burning agony from its own flesh, Malfallax gripped the lance hard and shook the golden rod. Before Rafen could even let go of his grip, the Lord of Change had used it to slam him into the mud. The Spear of Telesto stung him with gold fire for his viciousness and the daemon screeched again, tossing the holy weapon away into the quagmire. Rafen scrambled after it as the beast mewed, licking pitifully at the crisped ruin where its hand had been.

Turcio fumbled his last clip of ammunition into his bolter's gaping slot and turned the muzzle on the monster. Its attention distracted by Rafen, it presented an unprotected flank to the Space Marine, and the blinded brand robbed the creature of its second sight. Hot bolts stitched blossoms of brackish blood where the hits found their marks. Necrotic skin peeled from yellowed bones, embrittled by the rapid mutation forced on them, and loops of grey intestine emerged from what had once been Ramius Stele's abdomen.

Malfallax twitched and flashed forward, instinctively homing in on the source of the new pain. Pink fire looped about its scarred claw, and the other limb brought up the shrieking bone sword, the warp blade falling in an iridescent arc. The prismatic shimmer was a thing of beauty in its own ever-changing way, and it rooted Turcio to the spot with its majesty until the keening weapon slashed through the breech of his gun and his right forearm.

The Blood Angel was thrown back by the shock of the pain, the consecrated and hallowed icon of his bolter instantly destroyed and his severed limb spewing jets of incarnadine fluids. The reflex reaction saved him from being shredded as Malfallax followed the strike with a downward sweep of his claw. The talons tore through the pauldrons of Turcio's armour and opened his wargear to the navel. A strong grip yanked him back. Corvus dragged Turcio by the neck ring of his torso plate, firing over his battle-brother's stumbling form into the advancing daemon. Malfallax chewed on the bolt shells that struck it, picking the flattened humps of tungsten rounds from the holes in its chest.

There was a flurry of wet motion behind it and the beast craned its elongated neck over a crooked shoulder. Rafen rose from the mud with the spear in a two-handed grip and stabbed forward into the meat of the daemon's exposed thigh. The sparking blade buried itself in the flesh and opened it to the air. Maggots and writhing alien parasites spilled from the cut.

Malfallax spat and turned its attention to Rafen once again. 'Still alive?'

'Still,' Rafen grinned and slashed again, cutting at the creature's hide. The daemon parried the lunges with a swipe of its freakish sword and came forward, heavy hooves punching into the churning puddles gathering in the crater. Rafen saw

Corvus dragging the injured Turcio from the pit and threw them a nod.

The beast saw him do it and cackled. 'You are persistent, human, I will grant you that, but then dogged obstinacy is a trait of the corpse-god's kind.' Hot breath coiled in clouds from its mouths. 'You resist the changing way and that is why you perish.'

Rafen replied with a swooping attack, dancing the tip of the spear about the questing warp blade, slamming it in savage stabs at the daemon's legs. It blocked every strike, trying each time to trap the Telesto weapon in the barbs that lined the edges of the sword. The Space Marine channelled his effort into the spear, letting the lance become an extension of his arms, looking beyond the apex of the glittering teardrop blade, seeing only the points where the daemon bled and wept ichor; but still it fanned the warp blade, the mesmerising arc of colour becoming a dome of mad light. He worked the spear just as he had been taught on the courtyards of the fortress-monastery, blocking, parrying, advancing, thrusting, sweeping, but never gaining more than a cursory bite from the monster's flesh. In his mailed grip, the raw energy of the spear hummed and pulsed inside the ornate shaft and golden crossguard, throbbing with power every time it cut into Malfallax – but still it would not respond to him as it had to his brother Arkio.

There had been a moment there on the rooftop of the ruined cathedral, after he threw Arkio's body to the throng below, when Rafen had thought the Holy Lance was about to open its secrets to him. It glowed in his hands, lighting the world around him. For a fleeting instant, Rafen had known the thrill of connection with the Spear of Telesto, just as Arkio must have, just as the lord Sanguinius himself did in the ancient conflict with Morroga. But it fled as quickly as the flashes of lightning in the steel-grey sky overhead. The lance was a superlative weapon, perfectly balanced and keen enough to slice a hair down its centre; but unless he could unlock its inner power, it was only a relic.

How? he demanded of himself. *How can I open the spear to my will?* Arkio had been changed beyond all normality and the Pure One himself... There was no way that Rafen could compare himself to the Angelic Sovereign. He parried another flurry of violent strikes by the daemon, and one too quick to dodge severed a nest of power conduits on his trunk. He felt the icy cold as super-cooled liquid spurted from his damaged backpack. Patches of frost formed on Rafen's backside and thigh, turning the ceramite and plasteel brittle. The daemon slashed through a toppled stone column to snap at the Blood Angel and he avoided the blow with only a hand's span to spare.

Rafen swore angrily, half in frustration at himself, half in adrenaline-fuelled hate for the Malfallax, and took off a strip of skin from the beast's shoulder, forcing it to stagger backward. It released a gush of cerise flame from its hand, the roseate fire turning broken stone to slag, crawling over the tilled earth like a live thing. A spark of hard rage stiffened Rafen's heart as he attacked again – and the spear responded with him, suddenly melting into his assault, flowing with the press of his muscles. Brief, tiny flares of gold sparks chased each other down the length of the haft. Sudden realisation shook him: *the rage! The gene-curse was the key!*

Malfallax's eyes for the future were blinded but the beast still knew how to play the harp of the fates. All things were under the motion of invisible strings that ranged from birth to death, past to present; they pulled all life and matter like wayward marionettes. This man-thing, this Blood Angel, was as much at the mercy of clockwork destiny as were the stars in the sky, the falling rains, the rising and setting of Sabien's sun. With the paingift of its master denied, the Malfallax's sight of the human whelp's fate was cloudy, but it knew there were many outcomes where Rafen lay dead and ruined, far more of those than the ones where he stood in victory or where he turned to worship of Chaos Undivided. The daemon knew how the Space Marine fought, it had toyed with him and watched his motions. It saw the hesitation telegraphed in his moves, the resistance of the lance in his hands. Rafen was ill at ease with the deadly, pestilent, hateful spear – so Malfallax would use that against him.

In Rafen's split-second instant of indecision, the creature caught the weapon in a toothed niche in the warp blade and twisted. The alien sword sang and left nicks in space-time as it drew back and up, dragging the Spear of Telesto from Rafen's shocked grip before he could react to halt it. Malfallax thrust him back with a pulse of pink fire and tossed the Holy Lance away. It spun into the wet ooze and started to sink.

The Blood Angel beat at the writhing hellfire and stumbled, aware of the chorus of noises around him. Sounds coiled over the arena of the bomb crater in waves, the shrieking of dying men mingled with shot and shell, harsh thunder and sacrilegious war prayers.

'A poor adversary,' rumbled the daemon. 'Such limited sport. Perhaps the mind-witch Mephiston will provide a better challenge, or even your wastrel Lord Dante…'

Rafen's anger flooded out of him like a torrent from a broken dam. 'Chaos bastard! I'll choke you on those words.'

'With what?' it demanded. 'Come, little man-prey, attack me with tooth and claw, if you believe that will make your death have more meaning.'

With a rush of speed, the Malfallax shimmered toward him, fast as mercury. The warp blade spun about in its grip and the calcite stone of the heavy pommel whacked him in the face, splitting his skin and lighting fireworks of pain inside his skull. Rafen staggered backwards and fell. The beast-thing advanced. It towered over him, blocking out the light from the myriad battle fires and the sheets of white in the tortured sky. The burnt, meat-stinking claw pressed Rafen into the cold mud, holding him there so the daemon could finish him with one last slash of the bony sword.

'The spear rejects you,' it chuckled, jerking its head at the bubbling mud pool. 'You are a failure to your Chapter, Blood Angel, just like your craven brother.'

The pressure pulled all the air from Rafen's chest and with it a final, heartfelt denial. 'No,' he hissed, pulling together the burning embers of his blood-tinged fury. 'No! *No!*' Throughout his service to the Adeptus Astartes, Rafen had restrained the black rage within him, holding the reins of the red thirst, never once allowing it to overwhelm his rigid, unbending self-control; now he gave it the freedom it wanted so badly, unleashing the bestial frenzy that was the darkest secret of the Blood Angels.

The red thirst unfurled about him in a storm of seething crimson, a fog of bloodlust madness descending on the Space Marine. The raw energy of his primarch set a flash-fire in his veins, the traces of Sanguinius's genetic code engorged with preternatural power. The heady cocktail of Astartes blood and the potent flood of vigour from the Lord of Death's blood-gift merged into Rafen, filling him with a fury that blazed with unbound, inchoate hate.

The ropes of fate unwound before Malfallax, spinning and snapping in his blinded mind's eye. *Impossible!*

Rafen roared and broke free of the beast's grip, shattering claws as big as scimitars and ripping scabbed skin into rags. He moved at the speed of wrath, an unstoppable bullet of red. The Space Marine's spirit plunged into the rage-sea about him, and there he found the glittering beacon of the Holy Lance. From the slime of the mud swamp, the weapon flew to him, crossing the distance to his waiting grip in an eye-blink. Golden fire, shards of lightning dazzling like fragments of suns, ripped from the air and collected at the hollow heart of the teardrop blade. The weapon was awake, the beating pulse of the sacred spear tasting Rafen's holy anger and knowing it as true.

Malfallax launched itself at him, leading with warp blade, opening rents in reality with cerise darts of fire; it threw the veil of the Twisting Path at the Blood Angel, but every attack fluttered and died against the glory of the Telesto lance. The daemon saw its fate-path curl into black formlessness and cried out in despair.

A wash of mellifluent light flared, and for a brief moment Rafen's battle-ravaged crimson wargear was replaced with golden armour, crested with wings made of white steel. The righteous vengeance of his primogenitor stared out from Rafen's ice-blue eyes and carried retribution into the Chaos spawn's heart.

The Spear of Telesto entered the Malfallax's chest and sank into the writhing morass of corruption inside. Rafen pressed forward, forcing the blade through the beast's gut, up through the decayed lungs and organ matter, piercing the withered black meat of its heart. The creature screamed to the clouds, and still the Blood Angel advanced, pressing the haft of the weapon into the dying enemy until the teardrop burst from Malfallax's back, between his drooping, bloodless wings.

'I... am... undeath!' it sputtered. 'You cannot kill a child of the warp.'

'*Begone!*' Rafen bellowed, his fangs flashing. 'Your cursed realm awaits!'

'Aaaaaaaaa–' Malfallax's death rattle was deafening from its dozen mouths. 'You have not won,' spat some of them. 'Your rage will be your ending–'

'*Die!*' Rafen shouted, one final shove of the spear cutting the daemon's link to its fleshy vessel. Streaks of sizzling ecto-plasm burst out of Stele's carcass, ripping away through the blood-misted air and flashing into nothing; glistening jags of ethereal warp matter, unable to sustain permanence for even a second on the human plane of reality, banged and van-ished, taking the weave of the creature's wrecked self screaming back into the madness of the immaterium.

The mutant body turned to powdery black stone, trapping the lance inside a deformed statue. Rafen tore at the spear and it went hot in his grip, giving out a shock wave of heat that obliterated the ashen form.

'Wait,' he cried, a sudden shadow of fear passing through him; but his call came too late. Like a tornado made of nails, the black ash exploded outward in a perfect concentric ring, each tiny particle of the contaminated matter impregnated with the void-born antipathy of the Ruinous Powers. A surge of mad hate passed through Rafen and threw him into the air. The tide of rancour moved over the square, touching every single Blood Angel on the surface of Sabien, tearing the veneer of humanity from each of them, debasing the Space Marines. The noble character and high honour of the Sons of Sanguinius fled before a madness that made them all ani-mals. Malfallax's laughter echoed as his death curse exposed the insanity of the Flaw in his enemies, and to a man they fell into the horrific grip of the red thirst.

IT WAS NOT battle; it was butchery.

Among the gales of driving rain and cracks of thunder, men fell in their dozens under the frenzy of the Blood Angels.

Still-beating hearts were torn from the chests of helot troopers and crushed like ripe fruits, the nectar of heavy arterial blood drained into gaping, hungry mouths. Blood Angels nuzzled at the throats of corpses, fans of crimson covering their chins and necks, barking and growling at one another like jackals fighting over fresh carrion. Lakes of vitae poured into the square, turning the damp air sharp with the rusty, metallic tang of its scent. Blood, blood and blood; there was no end to it, torrents of the rich red fluid slicking the mud around the feet of the combatants.

The errant slave warriors were not the only ones to come to murder by the rage of the maddened Astartes; Word Bearers found themselves shocked silent from their impious revels as the Sons of Sanguinius threw all caution to the wind and fell on them in waves. The Blessed of Lorgar faced foes that were little more than a force of nature now, a living, breathing, killing storm of men without fear or compunction. The Blood Angels were berserkers, spirits of scarlet destruction that gave no quarter and asked none in return.

Warmaster Garand shot hellbolts into the bodies of the red-armoured Astartes that came in range, but the death's head shells did little to stop the crazed tide. Blood Angels with limbs missing and great fists of meat torn from them still roared on in battle frenzy, the light of humanity inside them extinguished by the Malfallax's parting gift, its ruinous hate wave. The Witch Prince of Helica had seen this sort of behaviour on the battlefield before, but never from a human opponent. In his forays into the Eye of Terror and sorties where the Word Bearers found themselves matched with other followers of the eightfold way, Garand had been cursed with the misfortune to fight alongside the World Eaters. Madmen among a culture of psychotics, the berzerker bands killed ally and foe alike in their unending lust to claim skulls for the Skull Throne of the Blood God. The Warmaster saw the same stripe of insanity here and now among the Astartes legion, a revelry in the slaughter for slaughter's sake.

'They fight like Khorne himself,' grated one of Garand's lieutenants. 'I have never seen the like...'

'I have,' spat Garand, and he snarled with anger. 'The warp take this blighted scheme. That daemon wretch has fled the field.'

Hymnals from the Unhallowed Books were turned into gurgling screams as the wild Blood Angels assault touched the Word Bearers line and necks were torn open. Garand watched in fury as a squad of his handpicked aspirants vanished under a surge of red armour, falling like cut timbers.

'Lord. Lord!' cried a voice, and he glanced down from his vantage point as a war-priest crashed toward him through the melee. 'Lord, the veil has closed to us!'

In his anger, Garand grabbed the Word Bearer and dragged him to his eye level. 'Speak plainly, fool.'

The Space Marine writhed in his grip. 'Our summonings have been ended, Lord. Every daemonform we called to be for the battle has fallen dead and inert!'

'Malfallax.' Garand released the war-priest, cursing the Lord of Change's name over and over. 'That pestilent wraith. This is his doing!'

'But how?' demanded the lieutenant.

Garand swept his hand about. 'It drew back its essence when the host-body perished, and with it all the warp-matter from the field of battle. Nothing remains. We are becalmed, lost to the empyrean here.' He shoved the war-priest aside and snatched at his lieutenant. 'Our battle here is ended. Rally. Rally!'

'Lord, you cannot mean to–'

'Retreat?' The word thundered from his lips. 'The mad ones cannot be stopped by our numbers, fool.' He tore a rod-shaped teleport beacon from the Space Marine's belt. 'We go.'

'No,' sputtered the war-priest, his ardour overwhelming his better reason. 'Ever forward, never back! That is the Word Bearers code. We do not retreat.'

Garand struck him with a brutal punch and threw him aside. 'Imbecile! Leave these freaks to themselves and what will they kill? Each other.'

'No...'

The Warmaster pressed the activation glyph and felt the warm tingle of the *Misericorde*'s teleporters reaching for him. His last action on Sabien was to shoot the war-priest in the leg and leave him there for the madmen; punishment enough for daring to speak against the Witch Prince.

MEPHISTON DID NOT notice the departure of the Word Bearers. Some, those who were injured or none too quick to run for the glowing bubbles of the teleport fields, died the moment they turned their backs on the Blood Angels, their meat and their armour joining the endless slurry of corpses littering the ruined landscape. Perhaps, in some far distant corner of his night-black soul, the part of Mephiston that was still the man who had been Brother Calistarius existed. That tiny fragment of lucidity cried and screamed for the red thirst to abate, desperately trying and failing to halt Mephiston's headlong rush into the bosom of the black rage.

On Armageddon, the Lord of Death had been transformed after seven days and seven nights of wrestling the gene-curse, but now even his iron will had snapped, caught in the maelstrom of bloodlust that filled his soul. He was not conscious of the hot weapons in his hands, only that he could kill and kill and kill with them, unstoppable and furious in the glory of it.

'Mephiston!'

The name meant nothing to him; he had no identity now, only an all-consuming hate.

'Mephiston, heed me. Reject the darkness.' A red shape moved into his blurred vision. *'Reject it!'*

With an incoherent howl, Mephiston dropped his force sword on the man-form, seeing only the pulsing flesh and hearing the beat of a warm heart inside. The mindblade Vitarus met a rod of golden light and stopped dead, the power of the impact rocking the Lord of Death back on his heels. Fangs flared, Mephiston pressed against the glittering haft and for the first time, he saw who dared to defy him.

Rafen crossed the Holy Lance, blinking away the sparks that emerged where Mephiston's sword scraped back and forth. The barbed tip of the blade was at Rafen's neck and he felt the icy cold of the crystalline blade touch his skin and open it. The Space Marine's blood pooled in the lee of his clavicle and glistened on the sword tip.

'Raaaaaaa!' There was no humanity in the Lord of Death's gaze.

'Mephiston!' It was the Spear of Telesto that had protected him, Rafen was sure of it. When Malfallax's hate had consumed all his battle-brothers, he alone kept his mind intact, the warm touch of the lance clearing his vision of the suffocating rage. It was he alone who could stem the tide of the madness, before his comrades tore each other apart. 'Step back from the abyss. In the name of Sanguinius, *release your rage!'*

Golden light gushed from the spear and struck Mephiston like a physical blow. He staggered backward, his sword falling away, the dull glitter of insanity cast from his sight. All around them, the roars of frenzy and murder subsided into the rushing murmur of the rains. The water sluiced spilt blood from the Librarian's face and chest as he looked up from his hands and into Rafen's eyes.

'You...' It was difficult for Mephiston to speak at first, the words hard and heavy in his fogged mind. 'You reclaimed me from the brink... How?'

The spear's bright colours began to fade, growing quiescent. 'I do not know,' Rafen admitted. 'I was only the instrument. My hand was guided...'

The warrior-psyker shook off the lingering taint of the thirst and shuttered it away deep within. He watched Rafen examine the silent lance, his mailed fingers tracing the shape of the carving of their primarch. The lad had, for one moment, touched the soul of the most holy weapon, and with it he had drawn his kinsmen back from the edge of a soul-killing void. Although his expression betrayed nothing, inwardly Mephiston marvelled at the potential of one who was so blessed with the touch of the Pure One.

EPILOGUE

THE SKY HAD begun to rain ruby tears when the rescue ships blasted down through the cloud cover. The grim faces of the Space Marines from the *Europae* told the tale of their inner thoughts. They saw the carnage that lay about in the city streets and did not speak of it. None of them would shame their brothers by asking after what had taken place there beneath the curtain of grey clouds, while the battle barge and the Chaos warship went back and forth with salvos of laser fire and missiles.

Rafen watched as Mephiston accepted the report of a veteran sergeant with a solemn, serious mien. A lucky hit from the *Europae's* main guns had torn open a wound in the *Misericorde* that vented directly into her weapon store, and the red-hued battleship had been hobbled. There had come a moment, the sergeant said, when something peculiar happened to the Word Bearers ship; the codicers and Librarians aboard *Europae* had cried out as one when the shock of something horrible resonated out from the shrine world below, a spillage of a black and potent evil. *Misericorde* had felt the undertow from the warp schism as well and things had died aboard the enemy ship from the pain of the passing. It was all the barge's captain had needed to press the advantage, and soon after the Word Bearers, the proud and arrogant demagogues who swore they would never fall back, disengaged from the fight and made best speed to the outer face of the debris ring. Her engines damaged, *Europae* was unfit to catch the Chaos craft and so the crew watched *Misericorde* reach free space and fall into the phantasm of a skull-formed warpgate. The snarling face hung in the dark for long seconds and then faded.

Rafen glanced at the dull sky and then to the Librarian. 'Is this victory, Lord Mephiston?'

The Lord of Death walked away toward the waiting Thunderhawks. 'For now,' he said quietly.

THEY STAYED IN orbit for another solar week while the Chapter serfs and indentured crew expedited *Europae*'s repairs. Task forces of Space Marines expert in vacuum environments were sent out into the disc of fragments that marked the site of *Bellus*'s infernal death, charged with searching the wreckage for any survivors or materials of interest to the Chapter. Those few sealed escape pods that were found contained panicked groups of Shenlongi citizens, members of Arkio's thousand who had broken when the fighting had started.

The Blood Angels treated them in the manner of all enemies of the Imperium, offering them the choice of bolter or airlock. Most chose the former, weeping on their knees in the name of Rafen's brother as they died from point-blank headshots. One of the teams located the hardened steel module from the interior of *Bellus* that housed the ship's progenoid capsules. Many of the clerics aboard *Europae* were of the opinion that the gene-seeds were tainted and fit only for the fires of the fusion furnace, but Mephiston spoke otherwise. The vital organs were placed in secure holding for the journey back to Baal; it would be Lord Commander Dante alone who would decide the fate of the pods of genetic matter.

Rafen thought on this and wondered. Did his old mentor Koris's soul still hide somewhere in his progenoid gland? And what of Bennek, Simeon and the others? Would they live again one day, or be cursed by proximity to Arkio's insurrection?

The Blood Angel knelt in a small sub-chancel off the central transept of the *Europae*'s main chapel. The vast chamber mirrored the one aboard the *Bellus* in line and form, although the decoration, the stained glass and the scripture across the walls and mosaic floor were different. Being there made Rafen feel strangely displaced: it was almost as if he were in some parallel world, an alternate version of the now where paths had been different and outcomes altered. He heard footsteps approaching behind him and raised his head, for one giddy moment expecting to see Arkio coming toward him – not the golden, winged avatar, but the strong, proud Space Marine he had met on Cybele.

Mephiston slowed to a halt and nodded to Rafen. The psyker's battle armour was absent now, and instead he wore the sacred robes of his high order. 'Brother,' he said, by way of greeting.

Rafen returned a slow nod. 'My lord.' He went to stand, but Mephiston shook his head, and bade him remain where he was. 'What do you wish of me?'

For a moment, the psyker was silent. 'We lick our wounds, Rafen, in our own ways we heal and move on. The Chaplains tell me you have not left the chapel in days.'

'No,' Rafen admitted. 'I felt it… necessary.'

'Many would agree. After the ceremonies for the fallen and the rituals of purgation, your battle-brothers have spoken to me of the need to expunge this sorry incident from our chronicles.'

'That would be a mistake,' Rafen said quietly. 'To do that would mean we have learned nothing.'

Mephiston continued. 'The ship is ready to depart, and I have ordered the astropaths to make space for Shenlong. It will be... necessary to expunge any lasting traces of the heretic Stele's plans.'

'You will destroy the forge-world.' It was not a question.

'*Exterminatus*,' breathed the Librarian. 'A sad but inevitable conclusion.' He glanced up at the altar in the main section of the chapel. Held in a magnetic field bottle was the Spear of Telesto, quiet now but still dazzling as it slowly turned about its own axis.

'Am I to share that fate as well?' Rafen asked in a level voice. 'I am no more or less tainted than the people of that wretched sphere.'

'Some would argue thus,' Mephiston admitted. 'There are voices from Baal that counsel your execution along with the loyalist survivors gathered from Sabien. They are afraid that you may take the same path as Arkio. The knowledge that you were able to wield the Holy Lance...'

'Briefly, lord. Only briefly.'

The psyker eyed him. 'Indeed. But cooler heads have prevailed. Your dedication and honour to our Chapter, however unorthodox, was unparalleled. Commander Dante will give you an audience when we make home port, but rather than hold until that day, he has given me leave to grant you a field promotion in respect of your selflessness. The leadership of a full company of men is yours. The late Captain Simeon's command, the Sixth.'

Rafen let out a breath. 'With your permission, lord, I must respectfully decline Commander Dante's great accolade.'

'You *refuse?*'

He nodded. 'If I am to earn captaincy, it will be on my terms. I do not feel I deserve such rank... not yet.'

'Then what am I to do with you, lad? This will not sit well.'

The Space Marine looked up at the Librarian. 'May I ask a favour instead, then?'

'Name it.'

'I ask for mercy, lord. Grant clemency and compassion to my battle-brothers who strayed, those who followed my sibling unwittingly.' He thought of Turcio and Corvus as they had been brought aboard *Europae* stripped of their wargear and in manacles. 'Their only error was to be blinded by their belief in Sanguinius. Their faith was turned against them and misused. They are not to blame.'

Mephiston considered his request. 'There are rites of cleansing and purification that might be employed... They are quite arduous. Many would not survive.'

'They will,' said Rafen, 'and their faith will be twice as strong for it.' He got to his feet and approached the altar. As Mephiston watched, the Space Marine reached into the mag-field and ran his bare hand over the haft of the spear. He gripped the lance and for a moment, Rafen felt the weight of it in his hands once again. He peered at the teardrop blade – the metal seemed to run and shift in the light, glistening with the blood of the dead upon it.

'What do you see?' asked the Lord of Death.

Rafen saw dark red there, and he knew that it was his brother's blood upon the blade, glittering and then gone. 'Great Angel, hear me,' he whispered. 'Take my brother Arkio to your side, bring him to the Emperor's right hand. Forgive his folly and forgive mine. This I beseech you.' He bowed his head. 'My life and my soul for the God-Emperor, for Sanguinius... For the Blood Angels.'

He closed his eyes, and there in the depths of his soul, he felt the mark of his liege lord, indelible and bright as a golden sun.

IN THE BLACKNESS, *Misericorde* limped onward, gushing gas and vital fluids into the vacuum of space, slowly bleeding to death as it crawled ever closer to the Maelstrom and the lair of the Word Bearers. Garand smacked at the chirurgeon-servitor attending to the damage on his arm and stood up. The writhing energies of the ship's teleporter had turned the War-master's limb into a distorted mess of bone and muscle. He had already killed the serf responsible for the error by feeding it to the two-headed monstrosity that had been three of his best Space Marines… At least, before the botched beam-out from Sabien.

At his feet, Garand's personal vox-servitor cowered. He had allowed the slave to keep some measure of its personality when he had taken it for his retinue. It made little sense to the Warmaster to have servants that could not be afraid of him. 'What?' he demanded of it.

'A signal from the Eye, your darkness,' it chattered. 'The burning psy-mark upon the message bears the loathsome sigil of his most foul and hateful self, the Despoiler of Worlds.'

'Abaddon,' Garand said, suddenly weary. He ignored the squealing of the servitor as he openly uttered the High War-master's name. 'Of course.' The Word Bearer laughed with harsh, brittle humour. 'And what am I to say to him? Tell me, little man-slave, how I shall phrase my words to inform the Despoiler that the allies promised him for the Thirteenth Black Crusade have been denied? With what sweet lies do I conceal the failure of the Malfallax and Stele… and myself?'

'I… I do not–'

'*Silence!*' roared Garand. 'I alone survive. I alone must take the blame!' As quickly as it had arisen, the Warmaster's anger subsided. 'Bring my death-shroud. I will have need of it.'

THE FORMLESS REALM of warp space could turn a man insane at the sight of it. The frothing mass of alien energies defied the minds of organic lifeforms. It was a raw landscape of twisted emotion, peaks and troughs cut from the stuff of nightmares. In this small pocket of the immaterium, in the churning and unknowable hell that was the nest of the dread Malfallax, screams and shrieks of anger built cages of hate from the psychoactive matter. The disembodied consciousness of the daemon, wounded by the brutal severing of its link to Stele's host-corpse, hooted and howled its pain to the endless mad vista. Its towering fury would last for uncountable ages – but then in the warp, time had no meaning and correlation to other realities.

There would come a moment when the Malfallax would calm enough to begin conceiving of revenges both subtle and gross, nursing an anger that only the most inhuman could contain. An anger directed at one man, at the single being who brought its complex schemes to ruin.

One day, there would be a reckoning for the costs of the Malfallax, and every Blood Angel would pay a thousand times over for the daemon's defeat at Rafen's hand.

APPENDIX ANGELUS

This section of the omnibus features annotations based on my original notes for the Blood Angels novels, a 'minipedia' of characters, locations and other information.

Acus Placidus
Literally, 'the Needle of Calm', a wrist-mounted ceremonial weapon often used by the sanguinary priests of the Blood Angels to deliver 'the Emperor's Peace' – a mercy kill for an Astartes too badly injured in battle to be saved. Similar in function to the reductor pistol used by Apothecaries.

Agent Magenta
A virulent bio-toxin created by the magos biologis of the Imperium of Man. Extremely lethal, it is deployed only against targets that have earned the Emperor's most serious displeasure. Among other biological and germ warfare chemicals, Agent Magenta was manufactured on the forge-world of Shenlong.

Alactus
A battle-brother of the Blood Angels Chapter, and a former comrade of Brother Rafen. Originally a member of Rafen's squad, Alactus came to the banner of Arkio the Blessed after the battles on Cybele and Shenlong convinced that Rafen's

brother was the reincarnation of the primarch Sanguinius. Rafen was reluctantly forced to kill Alactus when he attempted to prevent him from boarding the battlebarge *Bellus*.

Alchonis Campaign
A great series of battles fought by the Blood Angels. The Chapter Master Commander Dante led several companies of his Chapter through the conflict. Brother Simeon was numbered among the many officers later decorated for bravery under fire when victory was achieved.

Amareo
A warship in service to the Blood Angels Chapter, the *Amareo* was a rapid strike cruiser operating under the command of Brother-Captain Gallio. The ship's crew of helots, Chapter serfs and Gallio's contingent of Astartes were lost when the vessel was obliterated by the battle barge *Bellus*, on the direct orders of Arkio the Blessed. The *Amareo* takes it name from the **Tower of Amareo**, the sacred citadel on Baal where it is said those who fall to uncontrollable hunger of the Red Thirst are confined.

Amasec
A rich and potent alcoholic liquor popular across the Imperium. Many worlds produce a drink that goes by this name, and quality can vary widely.

Angel's Fall
A towering cliff face in the barren desert wilderness of Baal Secundus, where legend says the infant primarch Sanguinius was discovered by local scavenger tribesmen. In later years, the area became a shrine and the site of an arena where petitioners would assemble each year, in hopes of being selected to join the Adeptus Astartes.

Angel's Wings
Colloquial name for crude one-man gliders used by members of the Baalite scavenger tribes. Difficult and dangerous to fly in the harsh desert winds, the gliders test their pilot's skills to the limit.

Angels Encarmine
A successor Chapter of the Blood Angels from the Second Founding; their sigil is a red droplet of blood with black wings. They are known to be aggressive and battle-hungry.

Angels Sanguine
One of several Second Founding successor Chapters of the Blood Angels; their sigil is a winged skull. It is a peculiarity of their Chapter that they are very rarely glimpsed without their helmets, and it is rumoured they do this to conceal some form of disfigurement.

Angels Vermillion
A successor Chapter of the Blood Angels from the Second Founding; their sigil is a winged droplet of blood inset with a white skull. The Angels Vermillion are cautious in the extreme and guard their secrets carefully.

Argastes
A legendary Blood Angels Chaplain, Brother Argastes is known for his firebrand oratory and his belief in the Black Rage as a method of finding the inner strength of a battle-brother.

Ariyo
An unremarkable planet in the Dekradek system, Ariyo was home to a secret storehouse of proscribed books and apocryphal texts gathered together by the Mechlord Simbasa and his followers.

Arkio

Also known as **Arkio the Blessed**, the **Reborn Angel**. Son
of Axan and younger brother of Rafen, Arkio was born on
Baal Secundus as part of the Broken Mesa Clan; an honest
and open youth, Arkio was selected by Brother-Sergeant
Koris to become a Blood Angel initiate and in later years
became a fine example of his Chapter. Sibling rivalry
between Arkio and Rafen forced the younger brother to
strike out alone to find his own course, and he took a posting on the *Bellus* Expedition, a mission to recover the fabled
Spear of Telesto. During the mission, Arkio was promoted
to the position of honour guard for the Sanguinary Priest
Sachiel. However, Arkio was unaware that he had been chosen for manipulation by Ramius Stele, and Stele's
association with the Chaos God Tzeentch allowed him to
slowly transform the young Space Marine into an avatar of
the primarch Sanguinius. Overwhelmed by this 'miracle',
for a time Arkio truly believed he was Sanguinius Reborn,
unaware that his every move was being controlled in order
to cause a civil war within his Chapter. With only his sibling standing against him, Arkio was finally killed in single
combat with Rafen and died begging forgiveness for his
folly.

Atlas-class warhead

A heavy thruster-powered bomb of Imperial manufacture,
designed to function in an air-to-ground capacity. Typically
deployed against large ground targets like hardened
bunkers, citadels, Titans or land leviathans.

Axan

The leader of the Broken Mesa Clan, one of the larger scavenger tribes on the moon of Baal Secundus. Axan was the
father of siblings Rafen and Arkio. Axan's wife died giving
birth to Arkio, and on that day he ordered the child's elder

brother Rafen to take on the duty of protecting the boy's wellbeing.

Baal

The homeworld of the Blood Angels Chapter and location of their fortress monastery. Once a flourishing planet before the Age of the Imperium, Baal is now a radioactive desert inhabited by mutants and feral animals.

Baal Prime

Also known as **Baal Primus**. First and smallest moon of planet Baal. Home to several tribes from which the Blood Angels draw their new recruits. Baal Prime rises first in the night skies.

Baal Secundus

The second moon of Baal, largest of the two, with the larger population of indigenous scavenger tribesmen. Location of Angel's Fall, the site where the infant Sanguinius was discovered ten millennia ago.

Badelt

The airless moon of the planet Shenlong, a dull and lifeless ball of rock used as a testing range for many of the munitions constructed in Shenlong's weapons manufactoriums.

Barbarossa Hymnal

A sacred battle chant of the Blood Angels, written to commemorate the razing of Barbarossa IV in the 35th Millennia.

Bellus

A battle barge in service to the Blood Angels Chapter. Commanded by Brother Captain Ideon, the ship led an expedition into ork-held space in search of the Spear of

Telesto, an archeotech artefact missing since the time of the Horus Heresy. Ideon later gave his fealty and that of his ship to Arkio the Blessed, setting the *Bellus* on a course that would see it destroyed in orbit over the planet Sabien after a battle with its sister-ship the *Europae* and the Chaos cruiser *Misericorde*.

Bellus Expedition
A decade-long mission initiated under the orders of Chapter Master Dante in order to recover the lost Spear of Telesto, command of the *Bellus* Expedition was jointly placed in the hands of Brother-Captain Ideon, the Sanguinary High Priest Hekares and Inquisitor Ramius Stele of the Ordo Hereticus. Hekares was killed by orks early during the mission, allowing Stele to slowly consolidate his power base aboard the *Bellus* and take command of the expedition.

Bennek
A battle-brother of the Blood Angels Chapter, and a comrade of Rafen. Bennek was a member of Rafen's squad who perished on the cemetery world Cybele at the hands of the Word Bearers. When Brother Rafen's armour was destroyed in battle with the Dark Apostle Iskavan the Hated, part of the wargear given to him to replace it belonged to the late Brother Bennek.

Binder Fungus
A curious form of biological weapon created by scientists in service to the Chaos Gods. When spread on fertile ground, binder fungus grows in the shape of arcane symbols that pay homage to the daemons of the warp.

Biolume
A device for illumination, typically a clear case filled with a bioluminescent liquid stimulated by electrical charges.

Biolumes can operate for millennia, under the right conditions.

Bio-web
Gene-engineered weapons system. Bio-web resembles barbed wire, with a synthetic mechanism based on the function of lethal binding vine plants used to ensnare unwary victims into the web's clutches.

Black Rage, The
A spectre of the gene-curse that afflicts all the Blood Angels, the Black Rage is a berserker madness that grips them in the throes of battle, a moment of communion with the spirit of the primarch that pushes them beyond the point of all rational control. While some Blood Angels have the will to resist the lure of the Rage, others cannot pull themselves back from the brink. Before battles, these unlucky souls are drawn off from the main body of troops and inducted into the Death Company, there to fight until death in a blind frenzy of killing.

Blood, The
Also known as **The Folk of Pure Blood**. A term used by one of the most ancient scavenger tribes of Baal to describe themselves. The Blood discovered the infant Sanguinius, and their title later grew to become a name encompassing all the tribes of the desert moons.

Blood Angels
The IX Legiones Astartes, one of the Prime Chapters of the Space Marines created by the Emperor of Mankind to defend the Imperium and prosecute the enemies of humanity; their sigil is a winged droplet of blood. Noble and handsome in aspect, deadly and vicious in battle, they mirror the character of their great primarch, the angelic

Sanguinius – but they fight a constant battle within to deny the feral and bloodthirsty side of their nature.

Blood Crusade
A term for a planned campaign by Arkio the Blessed to take his thousand-strong Warriors of the Reborn across the galaxy. Arkio intended to unite all Blood Angels under his banner and take stewardship of the Chapter for himself.

Blood debt
A rare honour granted by the Astartes of the Blood Angels Chapter, typically given in gratitude to one who has performed a great deed or important service to the Chapter. The inquisitor Ramius Stele was granted a blood debt by Dante after he apparently saved the life of Brother Captain Tycho and single-handedly dispatched a daemon that had infested his ship.

Blood Drinkers
A successor Chapter of the Blood Angels from the Second Founding; their sigil is a droplet of blood and a grail. They are known to be strict adherents to the tenets of the *Codex Astartes*.

Book of the Fallen, The
A record of the names and deaths of warriors in the Adeptus Astartes; most Chapters have some version of this document, in which to chronicle and honour battle-brothers who have perished in combat.

Book of Lemartes, The
A collection of sermons and catechisms penned by Brother Lemartes, one of the most outspoken and inspiring priests to serve with the Blood Angels.

Book of The Lords, The
Also known **The Testaments of the Lords of Baal**. A volume of military doctrine, religious musings and philosophical thought read and venerated by many Blood Angels.

Broken Mesa Clan
One of the larger of the scavenger tribes on the moon Baal Secundus. Over the millennia, many warriors of the Broken Mesa Clan have joined the ranks of the Blood Angels, including Rafen and his sibling Arkio.

Celaeno
A warship in service to the Imperial Navy, the *Celaeno* was a Firestorm-class frigate that carried elements of the Blood Angels Fifth Company to the planet Cybele. When the Word Bearers arrived in orbit to invade the planet, the *Celaeno*'s crew resisted them long enough to send out a mayday message, but the vessel was ultimately destroyed with all hands by the Chaos warship *Dirge Eterna*.

Chalice Mountains
A series of ancient and inert volcanic calderas stretching for hundreds of kilometres across the surface of the planet Baal. The mountains are visible from the fortress-monastery of the Blood Angels.

Corvus
A battle-brother of the Blood Angels Chapter, and a member of the *Bellus* Expedition crew. Corvus was influenced to join the cult of Arkio the Blessed after the battles on Cybele and Shenlong convinced him that Rafen's brother was the reincarnation of Sanguinius; however, when Rafen forced Arkio's followers to witness the corruption in his brother's body, Corvus recanted and begged forgiveness. Corvus was

among many battle-brothers who completed a series of rigorous penitent punishments to reaffirm his loyalty to the Chapter.

Credo Vitae
A series of sacred catechisms spoken by the sanguinary priests of the Blood Angels, including the **Litany Vermillion**, the **Litergus Integritas** and the **Vermillion Catechism**.

Crucius
A Blood Angel Space Marine who died in battle on the planet Ixion; Crucius was a comrade and friend of Brother Rafen.

Cybele
An Imperial planet in the Ultima Segementum, with no indigenous population. Cybele is a cemetery world, designated **Mausoleum Valorum** by the Ecclesiarchy. Millions of war-dead from across the Imperium are interred beneath its tranquil meadows. Although it has no strategic or tactical value, it was invaded by the Word Bearers in an attempt to capture it for a propaganda victory.

Dante
Commander and Chapter Master of the Blood Angels. A very long-lived Space Marine, Dante has served his brethren for over eleven hundred years, making him one the most experienced warriors in the Imperium. Fearless and indomitable, Dante leads his men from the front and embodies the ideal of the perfect Blood Angel.

Death Company
A contingent of troops formed from Blood Angels afflicted by the madness of their gene-curse. Suffused with the dying

memories of their Chapter's primarch, these cursed warriors seek only death in battle against the enemies of the Emperor. They are distinctive by the black colouration and red saltires of their armour.

Delos

A chaplain serving aboard the *Bellus*, Delos was one of many Blood Angels who believed that Rafen's brother Arkio was the reborn avatar of the primarch Sanguinius. Delos learned the awful truth of Arkio's manipulation during the battle on the shrine world Sabien. He confronted Ramius Stele over the inquisitor's alliance with the Ruinous Powers, but was killed for his audacity.

Desert Ticks

Large, blood-sucking insects the size of a man's fist. Desert ticks attach themselves to the bodies of unwary travellers crossing the wastelands of Baal, using spiked claws and a secreted mucus-glue to adhere. Once dug in, the ticks are very difficult to remove and will feast on their victim's blood for several days.

Dirge Eterna

A Murder-class cruiser in service to the Word Bearers, and the flagship of Iskavan the Hated. While an apostle of Iskavan's rank could have taken a much larger ship for his personal command, he chose the *Dirge Eterna* for its familiarity, as Iskavan and his second Tancred had served aboard the vessel during the Harrowing.

Enigma VI

An Imperial forge world in the Ultima Segmentum that specialises in the construction and maintenance of large interstellar starships. Many of the Imperium's most impressive vessels were built in the shipyards of the Enigma system, among them the Blood Angel battle barges *Bellus* and *Europae*.

Europae

A battle-barge in service with the Blood Angels Chapter. The *Europae* was under the personal command of Chief Librarian Mephiston, and during the engagement at Sabien the vessel suffered great damage during a fight with its sister ship the *Bellus* and the Chaos vessel *Misericorde*. While the *Bellus* was destroyed and *Misericorde* escaped to the warp, the *Europae*'s crew kept the ship intact and later returned with it to Baal for refitting.

Evangelion

A planet under Imperial rule in the Ultima Segmentum. An archaeological dig in the forest regions of Evangelion's northern continent unearthed a storehouse of documents lost since the Age of Apostasy, among them records of the fate of the Spear of Telesto, thought lost in the aftermath of the Horus Heresy.

Faded Lords, The

A cadre of saints from the planet Orilan, whose piety and dedication to the Imperial Church became an example to millions. The tombs of the Faded Lords are a popular pilgrimage site.

Falkir

A captain and castellan of the Word Bearers, Falkir was part of the Ninth Host serving under the dark apostle Iskavan the Hated. Falkir led the assault to invade and capture the Ikari Fortress, the seat of governmental power on the forge-world of Shenlong. He was later killed by Iskavan when the apostle sacrificed him as part of a daemon-bonding blood ritual.

Fell Breath, The

A nerve gas created by the magos biologis of the Imperium of Man. Victims suffer an extremely painful and lingering death. It is deployed only against targets that have earned the Emperor's most serious displeasure. Among other biological and germ warfare chemicals, the Fell Breath was manufactured on the forge-world of Shenlong.

Ferrocrete

A synthetic compound mixing metallic alloys, polymers and stone. Many structures throughout the Imperium are made from ferrocrete, and once poured and set, it is extremely dense, and capable of standing for thousands of years.

Fidelis

A warship in service to the Blood Angels, the *Fidelis* was a mine-layer deployed in orbital defence missions over the planet Armageddon. Brother Ideon served aboard the ship as its executive officer during his early career.

Fire Scorpion

A large insect species native to the Baal system. Similar in form to the scorpions of Terra, Baalite Fire Scorpions are considerably larger, with a typical specimen measuring over four to eight metres in length. Fire Scorpion 'Queens' can grow even larger, with some recorded creatures being bigger than a Rhino transport vehicle. Fire Scorpions secrete a berserker pheromone when their territory is invaded by outsiders, summoning others to attack any perceived threat. The wickedly sharp barbs on their tails are laden with **Flame Venom**, a virulent bio-chemical that turns the blood of its victims into an acidic slurry.

Flesh Eaters

A successor Chapter of the Blood Angels from the Third

Founding; their sigil is a fanged mouth of teeth. Rumours of cannibalistic rites surround the rituals of the Flesh Eaters.

Flesh Tearers
A successor Chapter of the Blood Angels from the Second Founding; their sigil is a serrated circular blade inset with a droplet of blood. The smallest of the Blood Angels successor Chapters, the Flesh Tearers are extremely aggressive and exhibit a much higher incidence of the Black Rage than their kinsmen.

Fortrea Quintus
A planet in the Ultima Segmentum, Fortrea Quintus was a world that had been secretly converted to the worship of Chaos by the Word Bearers just prior to the Horus Heresy; however, the work of the Word Bearers was later undone by the Blood Angels, who swept over the planet and eradicated all taint of Chaos with ruthless skill.

Gallio
A Brother Captain of the Blood Angels, Gallio was a ranking officer whose prowess and ability had been noted by both Commander Dante and Mephiston. Under orders from Dante, Gallio took a contingent of Space Marines to the planet Shenlong to confront Arkio over his claims to be the reincarnation of Sanguinius; but when Gallio's comrade Vode attacked Arkio in a blind rage, the resulting firefight took the Blood Angel's life and that of his men.

Garand
Also known as the **Witch Prince of Helica**. A warmaster of the Word Bearers and the servant of the Ruinous Powers of Chaos, Garand was the direct commander of Iskavan the Hated. It was Garand who, in service to the daemon

Malfallax, devised the plan to sacrifice Iskavan's troops in order to facilitate the ascension of Arkio and cause a schism among the Blood Angels. However, the failure of the complex plan forced Garand to face the anger of the master of the Eye of Terror, the Great Warmaster Abbadon the Despoiler.

Ghalmek

A Chaos forge-world in the heart of the Eye of Terror, governed by the Word Bearers.

Ghona Canyon

A vast gorge on the western continent of the planet Cybele. The canyon is spanned by the **Great Penitent Bridge**, which carries a highway from Cybele's single starport to the planet's seat of governance, the Necropolita.

Ghost-metal

A psychoactive alloy, commonly used in the construction of force weapons and other psyker-based technologies.

Grand Annexe

A large, cathedral-like space in the centre of the Blood Angels fortress-monastery on Baal. It is said that the entirety of the Chapter could assemble within and still there would be room to spare.

Great Chasm Rift

A deep, steep-sided gorge on the surface of Baal. The Chasm Rift is wide enough to be visible from low orbit.

Great Sear

A desert plain on the moon Baal Secundus, visible as a broad, bone-coloured wasteland. Once the site of towering cities, the Great Sear is now a chalky wilderness of wind-eroded hills and endless sand.

Helica
A planet in the Eye of Terror from which the warmaster Garand of the Word Bearers draws much of his tithe and resources.

Hirundus
A Blood Angel Tactical Marine and a member of the Fifth Company under Brother Captain Simeon, who died during the Word Bearer assault on Cybele. Hirundus served as the company's chronicler, documenting the battles fought by Simeon and his men.

Hoek Insurgence
A battle against a xenos species of psychotic humanoid canines, fought by the battle sisters of the Adepta Sororitas.

Horin
The master astropath aboard the battle barge *Bellus*. A powerful psyker but an elderly and somewhat inward-looking man, Horin was unaware of Ramius Stele's dalliances with Chaos. Horin was murdered by Stele in order to prevent him relaying vital orders from Commander Dante to Brother-Captain Ideon.

Ideon
A brother-captain of the Blood Angels, Ideon was the long-serving commander of the battle barge *Bellus*, an excellent tactician and a key part of the *Bellus* Expedition. However, Ideon allowed himself to be swayed by the promise of Arkio the Blessed and the Reborn Angel, eventually leading to a battle with his own kinsmen in orbit over the planet Sabien. Ideon was killed when the *Bellus* was destroyed.

Ikari Fortress
A central stronghold on the forge-world of Shenlong. In design, the fortress resembled a volcanic cone, and it served as Shenlong's seat of government for the Adeptus Terra.

Iskavan the Hated

The Dark Apostle of the Ninth Host of Garand, Iskavan was a ranking Word Bearer and Champion of Chaos. Tasked by his commander, Warmaster Garand, Iskavan led his forces to attack the cemetery world of Cybele, but he was unaware that his actions were part of a larger plan to manipulate the Blood Angels and ultimately force a civil war in their Chapter. When Iskavan learned that he and his troops were to be sacrificed as part of this plan, he attempted to disrupt Garand's scheme but was killed at the hands of Arkio the Blessed.

Israfel

A Blood Angel veteran sergeant and a member of the *Bellus* Expedition, who was crushed to death by a Defiler during the Word Bearer assault on Cybele.

Ixion

A planet in the Gothic Sector, the site of a battle involving the Blood Angels. Brother Rafen's comrade and friend Crucius died during the fighting there.

Junkhunters

Colloquial name for the tribes on the moons of Baal, who survive by scavenging ancient technology from the ruins scattered across the deserts.

Kissgun

An assassination weapon, small enough to be placed in the mouth of the user. Typically, the kissgun fires needle-rounds of an extremely fine diameter.

Kolla Tallow

A form of natural fatty wax harvested from the flesh of the cave-dwelling **Kolla Bats** native to Baal Primus. Kolla

Tallow has a distinctive odour and is often used in the manufacture of candles.

Koris

A veteran sergeant Blood Angel and mentor to Brother Rafen. Koris was an uncompromising and forthright Astartes who often encouraged his subordinates to question all around them, even the core tenets of Imperial dogma. A trusted teacher and close friend of Rafen's, Koris was one of several veteran Space Marines who questioned the so-called 'ascension' of Arkio the Blessed. However, Koris died from injuries incurred in battle with a Word Bearer Chaos dreadnought after Ramius Stele induced the Black Rage in him, forcing the old warrior into the pits of madness. His last words were a warning to Rafen of Stele's duplicity.

Lemartes

A hero of the Blood Angels, Lemartes is the most senior chaplain in the legion and is held in such high esteem by his comrades that his battle armour has the honour of a skull-formed death mask.

Lestrallio

A legendary Blood Angel, now long since perished, Brother Lestrallio was a Chaplain who dared to expose himself to the dreadful power of the Black Rage. Through his sacrifice and fortitude, the sanguinary priests of the Chapter were able to gain a moment of insight into the gene-curse and the legacy of their primarch.

Litany of Armament

A rite performed by warriors of the Adeptus Astartes when donning a new suit of battle gear for the first time. Each Chapter of the Astartes has its own unique variant on the ritual.

Lords of Baal, The

The ancient name given to the warriors who became the personal guard of the primarch Sanguinius during his early life on Baal. These men were the first from the planet to become Adeptus Astartes.

Lucion

A Blood Angel Techmarine serving under the command of Brother Captain Simeon. Lucion joined Rafen and his squad on Cybele as part of a mission to take control of a missile battery and destroy the Chaos warship *Ogre Lord*. Lucion came to the banner of Arkio the Blessed after the battles on Cybele and Shenlong convinced him that Rafen's brother was the reincarnation of Sanguinius. He perished after being caught in a crossfire when Rafen attempted to overload the Ikari Fortress's fusion reactor.

Malfallax

Little is known for certain about the daemonic creature known as Malfallax. A servant beast and princeling of the great Chaos God Tzeentch, the Malfallax manipulated Inquisitor Ramius Stele over several decades to become its cat's paw, ultimately conceiving of a plan to turn the Blood Angels Chapter to the worship of the Ruinous Powers; however, the daemon's scheme was halted by the action of Brother Rafen, and in a final confrontation Malfallax was banished back to the warp. For the moment. it remains there, brooding and planning revenge.

Mandé the Amber

A Saint of the Imperial Church, formerly a Sister of Battle serving the Order of our Martyred Lady prior to her canonisation. A medical facility dedicated in her name – the Valetudinarium of Saint Mandé the Amber – was built in M35.22 on the forge-world of Shenlong.

Marain

Bodyguard and, at one point, the lover of Inquisitor Ramius Stele. Marain was Stele's trusted servant for many years, until an incident on the planet Orilan when she was finally no longer able to turn a blind eye to his experiments with the powers of the warp. Marain intended to reveal Stele's perfidy to the Ordo Hereticus, but Stele murdered her as part of a blood pact with the daemon Malfallax.

Melta mines

Combat munition, typically deployed as an area-denial weapon. Buried beneath the surface of the ground, melta mines use a one-shot microwave energy discharger triggered by vibration, odour or psi-wave sensors.

Mephiston

Also known as the **Lord of Death**. The Chief Librarian of the Blood Angels, Mephiston was once known as Brother **Calistarius**, but after becoming trapped beneath a fallen building at Hades Hive, he spent seven days and nights in the throes of the Red Thirst. Where other men's minds might have snapped, his held firm and on the final night he emerged from the rubble, having looked into the face of the Red Thirst and resisted it. He took the name Mephiston from that point onward and became the strong right arm of his chapter master, Dante. Respected and feared in equal measure by his brethren, the Lord of Death was called upon to judge the pretender Arkio's claims of 'ascension', and if not for the intervention of Rafen and the Spear of Telesto, he might have fallen to the Thirst once again.

Misericorde

The flagship of the Word Bearer Warmaster Garand. The *Misericorde* is a Desolator-class battleship some six thousand years old. It was damaged in an engagement with the Blood Angel

battle barges *Bellus* and *Europae*, but escaped to the warp
before it could be destroyed.

Mole-Mine
A complex burrowing torpedo weapon, usually deployed
against infantry targets. Fired into the ground, a mole-mine
digs through the earth beneath the feet of an enemy and surfaces among them before detonating. Swift and deadly,
mole-mines are difficult to defend against.

Molly-Knife
Colloquial name for a fractal-edged blade; the name refers to
the monomolecular cutting edge, which is capable of slicing
through all but the most resilient of materials.

Morroga
Also known as **The Slaughter-Lord**. Morroga was a notorious
Khornate Chaos Champion killed by the primarch Sanguinius
on the battlefields of Riga during the height of the Horus Heresy.
Sanguinius dispatched the daemon using the Spear of Telesto.

Moripatris
Also known as the **Mass of Doom**. The moripatris is a sacred
catechism performed by the Chaplains of the Death Company
on the eve of battle, when warriors of the Blood Angels fall
into the embrace of the Black Rage.

Mount Seraph
A towering mountain on the planet Baal. The fortress-
monastery of the Blood Angels is cut into the side of the peak's
living rock, dominating the landscape as far as the eye can see.

Necropolita
A chapel complex that serves as both a place of worship and a
centre of government on cemetery planets such as Cybele.

NeoZyklona

A bio-toxin created by the magos biologis of the Imperium of Man. Extremely lethal, it is deployed only against targets that have earned the Emperor's most serious displeasure. Among other biological and germ warfare chemicals, NeoZyklona was manufactured on the forge-world of Shenlong.

Noro

A Word Bearer Chaos Space Marine. Noro was ordered to guard a captured missile battery on Cybele, but later escaped after the facility was recaptured by the Blood Angels. Left behind by his commander, Noro attempted to assassinate Ramius Stele, but the inquisitor captured Noro and later tortured him for information. Stele eventually killed Noro, but not before draining all useful intelligence from him.

Ogre Lord

The *Ogre Lord* was a warship in service to the Ruinous Powers, under the control of the Word Bearers. A Repulsive-class grand cruiser, the ship was destroyed in orbit over Cybele after being struck by a barrage of anti-ship missiles fired from the planet below.

Omeg

A childhood friend of Rafen's and a member of the Broken Mesa Clan; Omeg joined Rafen and Arkio on their journey to Angel's Fall to seek entry to the Adeptus Astartes, but he was poisoned by the venom of shellsnake bites. Rafen was forced to kill Omeg so as not to prolong his agonizing death.

Orilan

An Imperial hive world in the Narvaji Zone. Orilan was declared untouchable by the Adeptus Terra after an apparent plague of transformation swept the planet, mutating living creatures and inorganic material alike. A force of Blood Angel warships commanded by Brother Captain Tycho enforced a cordon around Orilan and later scourged the planet with cyclonic warheads. Unknown at the time, the cause of the mutations was actually a failed attempt by Ramius Stele to cage a Tzeentchian daemon creature.

Pellis

Pellis was a magos biologis adept serving the Imperium on the forge-world of Shenlong, administrating the construction and testing of biological warfare weapons for the Imperial Guard. He was captured by the Word Bearers of Iskavan the Hated and forced to assist them to gain entry to a restricted area of the manufactory. Pellis was executed when he refused to help Iskavan release a storm of toxic bio-weapons.

Phaedra

An Imperial world, sector capital of the Phaedra Cluster. Phaedra's surface is a mix of pastoral communities and hulking industrial areas. The outer zones are dominated by mine works and smelter-cities, and the vast railways that connect them. Among the planet's exports are fine silks much in demand by moneyed Imperial aristocrats. Phaedra and the worlds in the Phaedra Cluster were the site of a bloody military campaign against the forces of Chaos, involving the Adepta Sororitas and the Adeptus Astartes. During the battle, the Blood Angels suffered massive casualties, and the nearby planet Sabien was later granted to them as a shrine world in recognition of their bravery.

Phase-iron

A rare and uncommon metal that has been psychically 'treated', making it poisonous to psykers, creatures of the warp and mind-witches. Phase-iron is sometimes used in the construction of cages for beings with high psychic ability or daemonic natures.

Predator, Baal-pattern
A tank variant favoured by the Blood Angels. The Baal Predator is armed with numerous weapons noted for their high rate of fire. It is designed to mow down enemy infantry and light vehicles with horrifying efficiency. Typical load-out includes turret-mounted twin-linked assault cannons, smoke launchers and a searchlight. Most are also fitted with a pair of sponson-mounted heavy bolters or heavy flamers.

Proteus-class warhead
A large-diameter boost-assisted missile of Imperial manufacture, designed to function in a surface-to-space capacity. Typically deployed against orbital targets like warships and sky-artillery platforms.

Puppeteers
Also known as a **Psi-Bomb** or **Eightmen**. A perverse form of Chaos weapon, binding eight bond-slave psykers together by a form of psychic imprinting. When 'detonated' by a command phrase or a trigger event, the bonded psykers release a wave of mental disruption that sends a shockwave of insanity through the minds of any living beings inside the blast radius.

Rafen
Son of Axan and elder brother of Arkio, Rafen was born on Baal Secundus as part of the Broken Mesa Clan; troubled and arrogant in his youth, Rafen petitioned to join the Blood Angels but was initially rejected by Brother Sergeant Koris. The sergeant's choice forced the young Rafen to re-evaluate his life, and finding himself in the desert and near death, the

youth saw a vision of the primarch Sanguinius. Rafen was able to redeem himself when he rescued Koris and a group of aspirants – including his sibling Arkio – after their ship crashed in a Fire Scorpion hunting ground, and Koris granted him entry into the Astartes in recognition. In later years, Rafen became a fine Space Marine, eventually serving under Koris in a tactical squad and fighting in many battles. On Cybele, Rafen was reunited with Arkio and came to witness his siblings apparent 'ascension' as the rebirth of the Blood Angels primarch; however, Rafen doubted what many of his kinsmen believed to be true and opposed Arkio. Finally, on the planet Sabien, Rafen faced his brother in single combat and killed him, granting Arkio his forgiveness; using the Spear of Telesto, Rafen banished the daemon Malfallax back to the warp and prevented a schism in his Chapter.

Razor winds
On Baal Secundus, atmospheric disturbances can create powerful windstorms that carry tons of radioactive sand into the air at incredible velocities. Unprotected humans caught in such a storm can be stripped to the bone within moments.

Recaf
A liquid stimulant popular throughout the Imperium.

Redkin
A flowering plant native to the planet Baal, extinct in the wild since the 38th Millennia, although some examples still remain in arboretums. A garden of Redkin flowers grows within the walls of the Blood Angels fortress-monastery.

Red Grail, The
The Red Grail is an artefact held in sacred trust by Brother Corbulo, apothecary senioris of the Blood Angels. The grail

was used to preserve the blood of the primarch Sanguinius after he was killed by Horus and from which the sanguinary high priests drink as part of their rituals. All sanguinary priests carry a grail of their own, fashioned in the image of the original holy icon.

Red Thirst, The

Also known as **The Scarlet Path**. A factor of the Blood Angels gene-curse like the berserker fury of the Black Rage, the Red Thirst is a terrible craving for blood that may overcome even the most steadfast of battle-brothers during combat.

While some Blood Angels have the will to resist the terrible thirst, others cannot pull themselves back from the brink. These unlucky souls are drawn off from the main body of troops and inducted into the Death Company, there to fight until they perish.

Regicide

A tabletop game, playable with a board and pieces or through a virtual display. Similar to the ancient Terran game of chess, it teaches basic tactics and shrewd thinking. Matches can be played on a 'hooded' board where only certain pieces are visible, making the game more complex and challenging.

Rocene

Formerly an Imperial world, later fallen to the forces of the Ruinous Powers. Rocene was the site of a massive battle involving millions of troops from the Imperial Guard and aviators from the Imperial Navy's flyer squadrons. A devotional garden on the cemetery world of Cybele commemorates the lives lost during the battle for Rocene.

Rot-Bane

An artificial disease created by the magos biologis of the Imperium of Man. Rot-Bane, as the name suggests, causes living flesh to disintegrate while the victim is still alive. Among other biological and germ warfare chemicals, Rot-Bane was manufactured on the forge-world of Shenlong.

Sabien

An Imperial planet in the Phaedra Cluster. Now designated as a shrine world, Sabien was a key battlefield during the brutal Phaedra Campaign, and at the time of the conflict, it saw the largest loss of life to the Blood Angels Chapter since the battles of the Horus Heresy. When the world had finally been pacified at the cost of untold expended lives, the Imperial Church had awarded custody of the planet to the Blood Angels, and the site of their desperate last stand against the forces of Chaos became a place of pilgrimage. Centuries later, Sabien was once more the site of an important battle, when Arkio the Blessed and his Warriors of the Reborn faced Mephiston and his Space Marines.

Sachiel

A sanguinary priest of the Blood Angels Chapter, and a member of the *Bellus* Expedition crew, Sachiel was a youthful rival of Rafen and the two men maintained a dislike of one another throughout their lives. Sachiel was influenced to join the cult of Arkio the Blessed after the battles on Cybele and Shenlong convinced him that Rafen's brother was the reincarnation of Sanguinius. Sachiel's vanity and ambition were his weaknesses, and Ramius Stele manipulated the priest into doing his bidding. Sachiel perished on Sabien, but not before he understood the grave errors he had made in following a false idol.

Sand Ox

Large and unruly animal native to the deserts of Baal Secundus. Often found as a domesticated beast of burden in use by the tribes of The Blood.

Sand Shark

Predatory animal native to the deserts of Baal Secundus. Sand sharks bury themselves in the thin surface sands of the moon's dune seas and lurk, using sensitive cilia to detect unwary prey passing nearby. They attack by bursting from the sands and biting down with rings of sharp, bony teeth.

Sanguinius

The primarch and lord of the Blood Angels, primogenitor of their Chapter and a son of the Emperor of Mankind. When the Emperor's sons were cast to the warp by the forces of Chaos, the infant Sanguinius was deposited on Baal Secundus, where he was discovered by the scavenger tribes of The Blood. Growing quickly to manhood, the winged warrior-lord led his adoptive tribe to supremacy, and when the Emperor found him, Sanguinius willingly joined his father in his Great Crusade across the stars. One of the most trusted and revered of the primarchs, Sanguinius fought for his father alongside his Blood Angels, and when the arch-traitor Horus turned against the Emperor, it was Sanguinius who would first face the villain at the Siege of Terra. Sanguinius died at Horus's hand, and the great psychic shock of his murder planted the seeds of the Red Thirst and the Black Rage in his Blood Angels. The blood from his corpse was recovered and held in trust by the sanguinary priests of the Chapter, while his flesh was interred in a sarcophagus of molten gold on Baal.

Sepulchre of Heroes, The

Also known as **The Hall of Heroes**. A passageway that runs the length of the fortress-monastery on Baal, filled with alcoves that feature vaults, artwork and statuary commemorating the most noble and valiant Blood Angels who have fallen in battle. Many Adeptus Astartes Chapters have similar devotional sites.

Shenlong

An Imperial forge-world, Shenlong was a manufactorum for munitions of all kinds, for use in the many ongoing wars across the Imperium of Man. The weapons shops of Shenlong are known for their functionality and practicality, and the planet's craftsmen have supplied hardware to the Imperium's armies for over ten thousand years. However, the planet was captured by the forces of the Word Bearers, forcing a contingent of the Blood Angels to liberate Shenlong in a brief and bloody ground battle, but later the world was scoured by an exterminatus order when the planet's population were judged to be too far beyond the light of the Emperor.

Shellsnake

Predatory animal native to the deserts of Baal Secundus. Shellsnakes are serpent-like creatures with a jointed, bony carapace. Fast and strong, they attack in large numbers and bring down larger prey by biting and injecting an acidic venom that prevents blood from clotting.

Silent Cloister, The

An ornate corridor on one of the higher levels of the fortress-monastery of Baal. Essentially a devotional gallery, as the name suggests no sound may be uttered by those who pass through it, as a gesture of reverence for the works that hang there. Among the most impressive pieces are the Tapestries of Riga, depicting the primarch Sanguinius in all his glory.

Simbasa Heretics

A group of Adeptus Mechanicus on the planet Ariyo under the leadership of Mechlord Raphael Simbasa, who dallied with heretical thought and gathered a storehouse of unhallowed texts in defiance of the Imperial Church. Inquisitor

Ramius Stele hunted down and exterminated all of them, leading a mission to burn the storehouse and destroy everything Simbasa had concealed.

Simeon
A Brother Captain of the Blood Angels and commander of the Fifth Company. Among the men serving under Simeon's command were Rafen and Koris. A respected and highly decorated officer, in the past Simeon had served as adjutant to Brother-Captain Tycho. Simeon was killed on Cybele by the Word Bearers.

Solus
A veteran sergeant of the Blood Angels, second-in-command aboard the battle-barge *Bellus* and aide to Brother Captain Ideon. Like many of the crew of the *Bellus* Expedition, Solus believed that Arkio the Blessed was the reincarnation of the primarch Sanguinius; but after Arkio's orders forced him to fire on allied vessels, Solus began to have serious doubts. However, before he could act on them, the *Bellus* was drawn into battle with the Chaos warship *Misericorde* and Solus was killed when a plasma conduit exploded.

Spear of Telesto, The
Also known as **The Holy Lance**, **the Spear**, the **Hasta Fatalis**. An arcane weapon of incredible power, legend says that the Spear of Telesto was one of a number of weapons forged by the Emperor of Mankind himself. The spear's blade is an elongated tear with a hollow in the centre, representing the single drop of blood that Sanguinius shed when he swore fealty to the Emperor; the blade rests atop a sculpted haft that shows Sanguinius clad in the monastic vestments of a sanguinary high priest, with a single purity seal that bares the personal mark of the Emperor himself.

Gene-sensor technology in the weapon keys the spear's use only to those who have the blood of Sanguinius in their veins. By unknown means the weapon is capable of discharging a stream of lethal energy that will leave those with the genetic marker untouched by damage. The weapon was lost in the aftermath of the Horus Heresy, only to be rediscovered millennia later in the hands of an ork warlord who was unaware of the spear's true power.

Stele, Ramius

An inquisitor lord of the Ordo Hereticus. Once a loyal servant of the Emperor, Stele became disenchanted with what he saw as a staid and decrepit Imperium. He began seeking forbidden knowledge to deepen his understanding of the nature of the warp, and after encountering a prohibited text in a clandestine collection on the planet Ariyo, Stele began to fall under the sway of Chaos. His first attempts to understand the nature of the warp caused the destruction of the hive world Orilan, and in the aftermath of that incident Stele made a pact with the Tzeentchian daemon lord Malfallax, spinning a lie that would convince the Blood Angels to honour him with a rare blood debt. That agreement led to Stele's participation in a plan to subvert the Blood Angels, but the intervention of Brother Rafen disrupted the scheme. Stele died when Malfallax used his body as a host for his monstrous form.

Tabac

A stimulant popular throughout the Imperium, commonly smoked or ingested in a powder form.

Tancred

A Chaos Space Marine in service to the Word Bearers. Tancred was the second-in-command of the Ninth Host of Garand, and chief torturer for his master Iskavan the

Hated. Tancred was gifted with the ability to read elements of the future in the entrails of his sacrificial victims. Tancred lost his arm when Iskavan bit it off after giving a prediction the dark apostle disliked; the touch of Chaos mutated him and replaced it with a nest of tentacles. Tancred was killed by Rafen during a battle inside the Ikari Fortress on Shenlong.

Tapestries of Riga, The
A holy relic of the Blood Angels, the tapestries depict the battles fought by Sanguinius and his Legion against the Slaughter-Lord Morroga and his minions at Riga, during the height of the Horus Heresy. The tapestries hang in the Silent Cloister of the fortress-monastery on Baal.

Tartarus
A world with an eccentric orbit, Tartarus is unusual in that its path veers away from its parent sun for long periods of time, forcing the world into a temporary ice age. During one of these frozen periods, Brother Rafen and the Blood Angels of the Fifth Company battled a force of Traitor Marines on the ice plains there.

Thaxted Duchy
A coalition of Imperial star systems in the Mordant Zone. The infiltration of a Chaos cult into the upper tiers of Thaxted's ruling cadre led to a brief but violent succession from Imperial Rule – the so-called Thaxted Insurrection. A contingent of Blood Angels, under the command of Brother Captain Simeon, eradicated the cult and brought the Duchy back into the Emperor's Light.

Thelio
An adept senioris of the magos biologis, Thelio served the Imperium on the forge-world, Shenlong, administrating the

construction and testing of biological warfare weapons for the Imperial Guard. He took his own life when the Word Bearers of Iskavan the Hated invaded the planet.

Thirstwater
A virulent living liquid from the Baal system that attacks the soft tissues of those who ingest it, triggering a rapid spawning action that ultimately draws all moisture from the infected victim, leaving only a dry husk of a corpse.

Toph
A young aspirant from the Junkhunter tribes of the Great Sear on Baal Secundus, who travelled to Angel's Fall in order to take part in the trials of will to become a Blood Angel initiate. Toph was selected by Brother-Sergeant Koris, but he perished before reaching the monastery on Baal, dying at the claws of a Fire Scorpion when the drop-ship he was aboard crashed in the rad-desert.

Turcio
A battle-brother of the Blood Angels Chapter, and a member of Rafen's squad. Turcio joined the loyalists of Arkio the Blessed after being convinced that Rafen's brother was the embodiment of the primarch Sanguinius; however, when Rafen forced Arkio's followers to witness the corruption in his body, Turcio disavowed Arkio and sought forgiveness. He was among many battle-brothers who completed a series of rigorous penitent punishments to re-affirm his loyalty to the Chapter.

Tusk Blade
Also known as a **Bone Dagger**. A living knife, this weapon is actually a very minor phylum of warp creature that lives by ingesting blood from its stab victims. Commonly used by Traitor Marines and other servants of the Chaos Gods.

Tycho, Erasmus

A brother-captain of the Blood Angels, formerly commander of the Third Company. Tycho was a formidable warrior;
during a battle on the planet Armageddon, Tycho was
maimed by an ork psyker and left for dead. However, he
survived his injuries and concealed his terrible disfigurement behind a half-mask, from that point on nurturing a
powerful hate for the greenskins. Tycho commanded an
interdiction force that blockaded the planet Orilan after a
plague of mutation broke out on the surface, but during
that mission his ship was infiltrated by a daemon of
Tzeentch. Tycho forced the inquisitor Ramius Stele, whom
he had rescued from certain death, to assist him in expung-
ing the creature. Tycho was rendered unconscious during
the fighting and apparently rescued by Stele – in fact, Stele
had entered into a bargain with the daemon lord Malfallax,
and the rescue was a ruse designed to ingratiate him with
the Blood Angels. Tycho was later killed at Hive Tempestora
on Armageddon.

Ulan

Personal astropath to the inquisitor lord Ramius Stele, Ulan
was the failed result of a clandestine experiment by the
Adeptus Telepathica to control the psionic potential of a
human being. Stele liberated Ulan from the laboratories
where she had spent her life and turned her to his use.
Among her abilities, Ulan could cast a zone of psionic nul-
lification that would affect all but the most powerful of
pskyers. She was killed by the daemon lord Malfallax after
the creature possessed the body of her master.

Valkyrie Towers, The

A large memorial constructed on the cemetery world Cybele
by the Adepta Sororitas, commemorating their dead. The towers featured an intricate series of channels carved through

their structure, so that winds passing over them would alter in pitch to create a mourning dirge; however, the towers were obliterated in a final scream when the Word Bearers destroyed them with a nuclear air strike.

Varon

A codicer serving with the Blood Angels under the command of Brother-Captain Tycho, Brother Varon encountered a Tzeentchian shadow-creature aboard Tycho's ship when the daemon invaded their vessel in the body of a refugee woman. Varon's attempts to raise the alarm proved futile when the creature killed him and several of his brethren before nesting in the ship's engine core.

Veho

A Blood Angel Apothecary and a member of the Fifth Company under Brother-Captain Simeon, who died during the Word Bearer assault on Cybele.

Vesta

An Imperial colony world, noted for the striking pink stone it exports to the galaxy at large. Vestan stone is often used in the construction of memorials and tombs.

Vibra-stave

A hand weapon with a long, bladed point, a favourite of torturers. A power cell in the handle of the stave oscillates the crystal-matrix blade at the frequency of organic matter, making it perfect for cutting into living flesh.

Virgon VII

A barren world in the Virgon star system, close to the edge of the Sabbat Worlds. A domed colony city on this planet was besieged by a splinter hive of xenos invaders, but the timely action of Brother-Captain Simeon of the Blood Angels saved the lives of tens of thousands of Imperial citizens. Simeon was later decorated by Chapter Master Dante for his gallantry in defence of the dome.

Virolu, Olaf

The Priest-Governor of the cemetery world of Cybele, Virolu and his staff were among the first to be killed when the Word Bearers launched an orbital bombardment of the planet prior to their invasion.

Vitarus

Also known as the **Mindblade Vitarus**. The ancient and powerful force sword used by Chief Librarian Mephiston. It is said that Vitarus was personally blessed by Sanguinius himself, with a droplet of the primarch's blood.

Vode

An epistolary serving with Blood Angels, Vode was a protégé of Mephiston and regarded as a highly talented psyker with great potential. Vode joined Brother-Captain Gallio on his mission to the planet Shenlong, to confront Arkio over his claims to be the reincarnation of Sanguinius; however, Vode was influenced by the psychic powers of Ramius Stele, who coerced him into opening fire on Arkio, sparking a firefight that claimed the lives of all of Gallio's men.

Vonorof

A civilian shuttle pilot from the planet Orilan. Vonorof's family died in the plague of mutation that swept his homeworld, and the pilot ultimately fell victim to the daemon that had created it when he too was consumed by the transformations.

Warriors of the Reborn, The

A thousand-strong helot army recruited by Arkio the Blessed from the population of the planet Shenlong. The

Warriors of the Reborn were chosen through a series of gruelling arena combats, with only the most brutal and savage surviving to the end. The army was wiped out on Sabien by the overwhelming force of the Blood Angels.

Word Bearers
A Legion of Chaos Space Marines; their sigil is the screaming face of a daemon against an eight-pointed star. The most zealous of the Legions of Chaos, the Word Bearers worship their Dark Gods by erecting horrific monuments, deconsecrating Imperial chapels and converting entire populations to the path of the Ruinous Powers.

Xanger FellEye
A veteran sergeant of the Word Bearers Chaos Space Marines, serving in the Ninth Host of Garand under the command of the Dark Apostle Iskavan the Hated. FellEye was killed on Cybele by a strike team of Blood Angels led by the sanguinary priest Sachiel.

Zaou
A contested world beyond the Gates of Varl in the Ultima Segmentum. Zaou's surface is marked by large swathes of marshy ground, making it a particularly difficult battleground. Brother Rafen fought the eldar there when he was still a Scout.

ACKNOWLEDGMENTS

With appreciation to Keith Topping, Peter J. Evans, Jon Chapman, Mike Clarke and Pete Clarke, for Games without Frontiers; and to The Tech Crew for support and friendship.

Thanks also to Lindsey Priestley, Marc Gascoigne and Christian Dunn for granting me stewardship of the Boys in Red; to all the Black Library crew for their tireless hard work; to Bill King, Dan Abnett, Ben Counter, Gav Thorpe, Nathan Long, Alex Stewart and Graham McNeill for input, advice and comradeship.

And finally, my thanks to all the readers who helped make these novels a success, all the fans who asked questions and wanted to see Rafen again, and all the guys on the frontline in the GW stores around the world, most especially Paul Reed and the lads at Bromley.

ABOUT THE AUTHOR

James Swallow's stories from the dark worlds of
Warhammer 40,000 include the Horus Heresy novel *The
Flight of the Eisenstein* and *Faith & Fire*, featuring the
Sisters of Battle, as well as short fiction for *Inferno!* and
What Price Victory. Among his other works are *Jade
Dragon*, *The Butterfly Effect*, the Sundowners series of
'steampunk' Westerns and fiction from the worlds of
Star Trek, Doctor Who, *2000AD* and Stargate. His non-
fiction features *Dark Eye: The Films of David Fincher* and
books on scriptwriting and genre television. Swallow's
other credits include writing for *Star Trek Voyager*, scripts
for videogames and audio dramas.
He lives in London.